The First Won

ONEWORLD CLASSICS

The First Women in Love

D.H. Lawrence

ONEWORLD
CLASSICS

ONEWORLD CLASSICS LTD
London House
243-253 Lower Mortlake Road
Richmond
Surrey TW9 2LL
United Kingdom
www.oneworldclassics.com

The First Women in Love first published in 1998 by Cambridge University Press
© 1998 by The Estate of Frieda Lawrence Ravagli
This edition first published by Oneworld Classics Limited in 2007
Notes and background material © Oneworld Classics Ltd, 2007

Printed in Great Britain by TJ International Ltd, Padstow, Cornwall

ISBN-13: 978-1-84749-005-6
ISBN-10: 1-84749-005-0

The Forest Stewardship Council (FSC) is an international, non-governmental organization dedicated to promoting responsible management of the world's forests. FSC operates a system of forest certification and product labelling that allows consumers to identify wood and wood-based products from well-managed forests. For more information about the FSC, please visit the website at www.fsc-uk.org.

Contents

D.H. Lawrence (1885–1930)

Lydia Lawrence,
D.H. Lawrence's mother

Ernest Lawrence,
D.H. Lawrence's brother

Jessie Chambers

Frieda Lawrence

Nottingham Road, Eastwood, *c*.1900. D.H. Lawrence was
born in Victoria Street, off this main road, on the right

D.H. Lawrence's birthplace
in Victoria Street, Eastwood

The chapel designed to house
D.H. Lawrence's ashes

Women in Love.
~~THE SISTERS.~~

by D. H. Lawrence.

Chapter I.

Ursula and Gudrun Brangwen sat one morning in the large
window-bay of their father's house in Beldover, working and talking.
Ursula was stitching a piece of brightly-coloured embroidery, and Gudrun
was drawing upon a board which she held on her knee. They were mostly
silent, talking as their thoughts strayed through their minds.

" Ursula," said Gudrun," dont you ~~dIIIIIII~~ *really want* to get married?"
Ursula laid her embroidery in her lap and looked up. Her face was calm
and considerate.   " It all depends what you mean."

" I dont know," she replied. ~~xxxxxxxxxxxxxxxxxxxxxxxxxx~~
Gudrun was slightly taken aback. She watched her sister for some moments.
~~" It always means the same thing, doesnt it?~~ *asked Gudrun lightly*
" Well," she said, huffily, " it *usually* means one thing! — *But dont you think,*
~~"Dont you think you might have a better time than you have now?"~~
anyhow, you'd be — she *frowned slightly, —* " *well, in a better position than you are in now?*"
A shadow came over Ursula's face.

" I might", she said." But I'M not sure."
Again Gudrun paused, baffled, slightly irritated. She wanted to solve her own questions by
~~"Oh well," laughed Gudrun, "are you sure of anything?"~~
putting them to her sister.
~~Yes, said Ursula, more to herself than to her sister,~~ "I'm sure a
you dont think one needs the experience of having been married ?" she asked.
~~bird in the bush is worth two in the hand."~~
" Do you think it need *be* an experience ?" replied Ursula.
~~And she gleamed with pleasure over her own witticism. Gudrun looked up~~
" Bound to be, in one way or another," said Gudrun. "Possibly undesirable, but
~~to see whether she were serious, or had merely made a slip of the tongue.~~
bound to be an experience of some sort."
~~" I think it is," laughed Gudrun;"I hate having a bird in my hand."~~
" Not really," retorted Ursula." More likely to be the end of experience."
" And while I am by myself," resumed Ursula," I am more or less a
~~bird in the bush."~~ *Gudrun sat very still, to attend to this.*
" Of course," she said, " there's *that* to consider."
~~" Now I love your romantic names for yourself," said Gudrun, pausing~~
This brought the conversation to a close. Gudrun, almost angrily, took
~~to rub out a piece of her drawing. "Dont you find when a great helpl"~~
up her rubber and began to rub out part of her drawing. Ursula stitched
absorbedly.

The First Women in Love

1

URSULA AND GUDRUN BRANGWEN sat one morning in the large window-bay of their father's house in Beldover, working and talking. Ursula was stitching a piece of brightly-coloured embroidery, and Gudrun was drawing upon a board which she held on her knee. They were mostly silent, talking as their thoughts strayed through their minds.

"Ursula," said Gudrun, "don't you *really want* to get married?"

Ursula laid her embroidery in her lap and looked up. Her face was calm and considerate.

"I don't know," she replied. "It all depends what you mean."

Gudrun was slightly taken aback. She watched her sister for some moments.

"Well," she said, huffily, "it usually means one thing!—But don't you think, anyhow, you'd be"—she frowned slightly—"well, in a better position than you are in now?"

A shadow came over Ursula's face.

"I might," she said. "But I'm not sure."

Again Gudrun paused, baffled, slightly irritated. She wanted to solve her own questions by putting them to her sister.

"You don't think one needs the *experience* of having been married?" she asked.

"Do you think it need *be* an experience?" replied Ursula.

"Bound to be, in one way or another," said Gudrun. "Possibly undesirable, but bound to be an experience of some sort."

"Not really," retorted Ursula. "More likely to be the end of experience."

Gudrun sat very still, to attend to this.

"Of course," she said, "there's *that* to consider—"

This brought the conversation to a close. Gudrun, almost angrily, took up her rubber and began to rub out part of her drawing. Ursula stitched absorbedly.

"You wouldn't even accept a good offer?" said Gudrun.

"I think I've rejected several," said Ursula.

"Really! A decent man and a decent establishment? Have you really?"

"A thousand a year, and an awfully nice man. I liked him awfully," said Ursula.

"Really! But weren't you fearfully tempted?"

"In the abstract, but not in the concrete," replied Ursula. "When it comes to the point, one isn't even tempted. Oh, if I were tempted, I'd marry like a shot.—I'm only tempted *not* to." The faces of both sisters shone with a transcendent amusement.

"Isn't it an amazing thing," cried Gudrun, "how strong the temptation is, not to marry?"

They both laughed, looking at each other. In their hearts, they were frightened.

There was a long pause, whilst Ursula stitched and Gudrun went on with her sketch. The sisters were women, Ursula twenty-six and Gudrun twenty-five. But both had the remote, virgin look of modern girls, sisters of Artemis rather than of Hebe.* Gudrun was very beautiful, passive, soft-skinned, soft-limbed. She wore a dress of dark-blue silky stuff, with ruches of blue silk lace in the neck and sleeves; and she had cherry-coloured stockings. Her look of confidence and diffidence contrasted with Ursula's sensitive expectancy. The provincial people, intimidated by Gudrun's perfect sang-froid and simple bareness of manner, said of her: "She is a smart woman." She had just come back from London, where she had spent several years, working at an art-school, as a student, and living a studio life.

"I was preparing myself to make a creditable match," she said, suddenly catching her underlip between her teeth, as if she were hurt by disappointment.

Ursula was afraid to be too serious.

"So you have come home, to find the man?" she laughed.

"Oh my dear," said Gudrun, "I wouldn't go out of my way to look for him. But if there did happen to come along a highly attractive individual of considerable means, and we caught fire like anything, you know, with each other—I might immolate myself.—" She seemed wistful. "I'm getting bored," she went on, in pathetic complaint. "Things don't seem to materialise with me, I find. There's so much that just withers in the bud."

"So much of what?" asked Ursula.

"Oh, everything—oneself—things in general."

There was a pause, whilst each sister vaguely considered her fate.

"It does frighten one," said Ursula, and again there was a pause. "But do you hope to get anywhere by just marrying?"

"It seems to be the inevitable next step," said Gudrun.

Ursula pondered this, with a little bitterness. She was a class mistress herself, in Willey Green Grammar School, as she had been for some years.

"I know," she said, "it seems like that when one thinks in the abstract. But really imagine it: a home of one's own, one's own set, oneself like a picture framed and hung up, finished!—I always feel it is selling one's soul—except for children—and I don't believe in marrying for the sake of having children."

"Certainly not," said Gudrun. "I am certainly not willing to live vicariously—which is what motherhood amounts to."

"It seems to me really cowardly," said Ursula, "to expect *children* to make a life, where one has failed oneself."

"Decidedly!" cried Gudrun. "But then I don't look to children to fulfil *my* life. I simply know they wouldn't.—But doesn't one need the experience?"

Gudrun looked at Ursula with a long, slow smile. Ursula knitted her brows.

"No," she faltered, "don't you think one *knows* it already?"

A hardness came over Gudrun's face. She did not want to admit this.

"There's such a great *quantity* of human life," said Ursula, "and it all seems to *mean* nothing."

Again Gudrun looked at her sister, almost hostile.

"Exactly," she said, to close the conversation.

The two sisters worked on in silence, Ursula having always that strange brightness of an essential flame that was caught, meshed, contravened. She lived a good deal by herself, to herself, working, passing on from day to day, and always thinking, trying to lay hold on life, to grasp it in her own understanding. Her active living was suspended, but underneath, in the darkness, something was coming to pass. If only she could break through the last integuments, to enter into a new life. She seemed to try to put her hands out, like an infant in the womb, and she could not, not yet. Still she had a strange prescience, an intimation of something beyond, yet to come.

She laid down her work and looked at her sister. She thought Gudrun so *charming*, so infinitely charming, in her softness and her fine, exquisite richness of texture and delicacy of line. There was a certain playfulness about her too, such a piquancy of ironic suggestion, an untouched reserve. Ursula admired her with all her soul.

"Why did you come home, Prune?"* she asked.

Gudrun knew she was being admired. She sat back from her drawing and looked at Ursula, from under her finely-curved lashes.

"Why did I come back, Ursula?" she repeated. "I have asked myself, a thousand times."

"And don't you know?"

"Yes, I think I do. I think my coming back home was a *reculer pour mieux sauter.*"*

And she looked with a long, slow look of knowledge at Ursula.

"I know!" cried Ursula, looking slightly dazzled and falsified, and as if she did *not* know. "But where can one jump *to*?"

"Oh, it doesn't matter," said Gudrun, somewhat superbly. "If one jumps over the edge, one is bound to land somewhere."

"But isn't it very risky?" asked Ursula.

A slow, mocking smile dawned on Gudrun's face.

"Ah!" she said, laughing. "What is it all but words!"

And so again she closed the conversation. But Ursula was still brooding.

"And how do you find home, now you have come back to it?" she asked.

Gudrun paused for some moments, coldly, before answering. Then, in a cold, truthful voice, she said:

"I find myself completely out of it."

"And father?"

Gudrun looked at Ursula, almost with resentment, as if brought to bay.

"I haven't thought about him: I've refrained," she said coldly.

"Yes" wavered Ursula; and the conversation was really at an end. The sisters found themselves confronted by a void, as if they had looked over the edge.

They worked on in silence for some time. Gudrun's cheek was flushed with repressed emotion. She resented its having been called into being.

"Shall we go out and look at that wedding?" she asked at length, in a voice that was too casual.

"Yes!" cried Ursula, too eagerly, throwing aside her sewing and leaping up, as if to escape something, thus betraying the tension of the situation, and causing a friction of dislike to go over Gudrun's nerves.

As she went upstairs, Ursula was aware of the house, of her home round about her. And she loathed it, the sordid, too-familiar place! She was afraid herself at the depth of her feeling against the home, the milieu, the whole atmosphere and condition of this ancient life. Her feeling frightened her.

The two girls were soon walking swiftly down the main road of Beldover, a wide street, part shops, part dwelling houses, utterly formless and sordid, without poverty. Gudrun, new from her life in London, shrank cruelly from this amorphous ugliness of a small colliery town in the Midlands. Yet forward she went, through the whole sordid gamut of meanness, the long, amorphous, gritty street. She was exposed to every stare, she passed on through a stretch of base torment. It was strange that she should have chosen to come back and test the full effect of this shapeless, barren ugliness upon herself. Why had she wanted to submit herself to it, did she still want to submit herself to it, the insufferable torture of these ugly, meaningless people, this defiled countryside? She felt like a beetle toiling in the dust. She was filled with repulsion.

They turned off the main road, past a black patch of common-garden, where sooty cabbage stumps stood shameless. No one thought to be ashamed. No one was ashamed of it all.

"It is like a country in an underworld," said Gudrun. "The colliers bring it above-ground with them, shovel it up. Ursula, it's marvellous, it's really marvellous—it's really wonderful, another world. The people are all ghosts, and everything is ghostly. Everything is a ghostly replica of the real world, a replica, a ghost, all soiled, everything sordid. It's like being mad, Ursula."

The two sisters were crossing a black path through a dark, soiled field. On the left was a large landscape, a valley with collieries, and opposite hills with cornfields and woods, all blackened with distance, as if seen through a veil of crape. White and black smoke rose up in steady columns, magic within the dark air. Near at hand came the long rows of dwellings, approaching curved up the hill-slope, in straight lines along the brow of the hill. They were of darkened red brick, brittle, with dark slate roofs.

The path on which the sisters walked was black, trodden in by the feet of the recurrent colliers, and bounded from the field by iron fences; the stile that led again into the road was rubbed shiny by the moleskins* of the passing miners. Now the two girls were going between some rows of dwellings, of the poorer sort. Women, their arms folded over their coarse aprons, standing gossiping at the ends of their block, stared after the Brangwen sisters with that long, unwearying stare of aborigines, children called out names.

Gudrun went on her way half dazed. If this were human life, if these were human beings, living in a complete world, then what was her own world, outside? She was aware of her rose-red stockings, her large, rose-red beaver hat, her full, soft coat, of a strong blue colour. And she felt as if she were treading in the air, quite unstable, her heart was contracted, as if at any minute she might be precipitated to the ground. She was afraid.

She clung to Ursula, who, through long usage was inured to this violation of a dark, incongruous, uncreated* world. But all the time her heart was crying, as if in the midst of some ordeal: "I want to go back, I want to go away, I want not to know it, not to know that this exists." Yet she must go forward.

Ursula could feel her suffering.

"You hate this, don't you?" she asked.

"It bewilders me," stammered Gudrun.

"You won't stay long," replied Ursula.

And Gudrun went along, grasping at release.

They drew away from the colliery region, over the curve of the hill, into the purer country of the other side, towards Willey Green. Still the faint glamour of blackness persisted over the fields and the wooded hills, and seemed to gleam in the air. It was a spring day, chill, with snatches of sunshine. Yellow celandines showed out from the hedge-bottoms, and in the cottage gardens of Willey Green, currant-bushes were breaking into leaf, and little flowers were coming white on the grey alyssum that hung over the stone walls.

Turning, they passed down the high-road, that went between high banks, towards the church. There, in the lowest bend of the road, low under the trees and the wall of the church-yard, which was above their heads, stood a little group of expectant people, waiting to see the wedding. The daughter of the chief mine-owner of the district, Thomas Crich, was getting married to a naval officer.

"Let us go back," said Gudrun, swerving away. "There are all those people."

And she hung wavering in the road.

"Never mind them," said Ursula, "they're all right. They all know me, they won't do anything."

"But must we go through them?" asked Gudrun.

"They're quite all right, really," said Ursula, going forward.

And together the two sisters approached the group of uneasy, watchful common people. They were chiefly women, colliers' wives of the more shiftless sort. They had watchful, underworld faces.

The two sisters held themselves tense, and went straight towards the gate. The women made way for them, but barely sufficient, as if grudging to yield ground. The sisters passed in silence through the stone gateway and up the steps, on the red carpet, a policeman estimating their progress.

"What price* the stockings!" said a voice at the back of Gudrun. A sudden fierce anger swept over the girl, violent and murderous. She would have liked them all to be annihilated, cleared away, so that the world was left clear for her. How she hated walking up the churchyard path, along the red carpet, continuing in motion, in their sight.

"I won't go into the church," she said suddenly, with such final decision that Ursula immediately halted, turned round, and branched off up a small side path which led to the little private gate of the Grammar School, whose grounds adjoined those of the church.

Just inside the gate of the school shrubbery, outside the churchyard, Ursula sat down for a moment on the low stone wall, under the laurel bushes, to rest. Behind her, the large red building of the school rose up peacefully, the windows all open for the holiday. Over the shrubs, before her, were the pale roofs and tower of the old church. The sisters were hidden by the foliage.

Gudrun sat down in silence. Her mouth was shut close, her face averted. She was regretting bitterly that she had ever come back. Ursula looked at her, and thought how amazingly beautiful she was, flushed with discomfiture. But she caused a constraint over Ursula's nature, a certain weariness. Ursula wished to be alone, freed from the tightness, the enclosure of Gudrun's presence.

"Are we going to stay here?" asked Gudrun.

"I was only resting a minute," said Ursula, getting up as if rebuked. "We will stand in the corner by the fives-court, we shall see everything from there."

For the moment, the sunshine fell brightly into the churchyard, there was a vague scent of sap and of spring, perhaps of violets from off the graves. Some white daisies were out, bright as angels. In the air, the unfolding leaves of a copper-beech were blood-red.

Punctually at eleven o'clock, the carriages began to arrive. There was a stir in the crowd at the gate, a concentration as a carriage drove up, wedding guests were mounting up the steps and passing along the red carpet to the church. They were all gay and excited because the sun was shining.

Gudrun watched them closely, with objective curiosity. She saw each one as a complete figure, like a character in a book, or a subject in a picture, or a marionette in a theatre, a finished creation. She loved to recognise their various characteristics, to place them in their true light, give them their own surroundings, estimate them perfectly as they passed before her along the path to the church. She knew them, they were finished, sealed and stamped and finished with, for her. There were none that had anything unknown, unresolved, until the Criches themselves began to appear. Then her interest was piqued. Here was something not quite so preconcluded.

There came the mother, Mrs Crich, with her eldest son Gerald. She was a queer unkempt figure, in spite of the attempts that had obviously been made to bring her into line for the day. Her face was pale, yellowish, with a clear, transparent skin, she leaned forward rather, her features were strongly marked, handsome, with a tense, unseeing, predative* look. Her colourless hair was untidy, wisps floating down on to her sac coat of dark blue silk, from under her blue silk hat. She looked like a woman with a monomania, furtive almost, but heavily proud.

Her son was of a fair, sun-tanned type, rather above middle height, well-made, and noticeably well-dressed. But about him also was the strange, guarded look, the unconscious reserve, as if he did not belong to the same life as the people about him. "*His* totem is the wolf," said Gudrun to herself, "a young, innocent, unconscious wolf." She wondered *how* innocent, and how far untameable. She would like to know. He looked a man of twenty eight or thirty, but young, unbroached. His gleaming, unconscious candour, his curious look of good-humour, a certain attractive handsomeness, maleness, like a young, good-humoured wolf, did not blind her to the significant stillness in his bearing, the lurking danger of his cunning, indomitable temper. "His totem is the wolf." she repeated to herself. "His mother is an old, unbroken wolf." And then she experienced a keen paroxysm, a transport, as if she had made some incredible discovery, known to nobody else on earth. A strange transport took possession of her, all her veins were in a paroxysm of violent sensation. "Good God!" she exclaimed to herself, "this is a queer go!" And then, a moment after, she was saying assuredly, "I shall know more of that man." And the next minute she was tortured with desire to see him again, only to see him again, to be sure that all this was not a mistake, that she was not deluding herself, that she really had felt this strange and overwhelming sensation, this knowledge of him in her blood, this powerful *rapport* with him. "Am I *really* connected with him in some way, is there really something that singles us out to each other?" she asked herself. And she could not believe it, she remained in a muse, scarcely conscious of what was going on around.

The bridesmaids were here, and yet the bridegroom had not come. Ursula wondered if something was amiss, and if the wedding would yet all go wrong. She felt troubled, as if it rested upon her. The chief bridesmaids had arrived. Ursula watched them come up the steps. One of them she knew, a tall, slow, reluctant woman with heavy fair hair and pale, long face. This was Hermione Roddice, a friend of the Criches. Now she came along, with her head held up, balancing an enormous flat hat of pale yellow velvet, on which were streaks of ostrich feathers, natural and grey. She drifted forward as if perfectly aimless, her long, blenched face lifted up, not to see the world. She was rich. She wore a dress of silky, frail velvet, of pale yellow colour, and she carried a lot of small rose-coloured cyclamens. Her shoes and stockings were of brownish grey, like the feathers on her hat, her hair was heavy, she drifted along with a peculiar fixity of the hips, trailing, drifting. She was impressive, in her lovely pale-yellow and brownish-rose, yet macabre, like lovely horror. People were silent when she passed, impressed, roused, wanting to jeer, yet for some reason silenced. Her long, pale face, that she carried lifted up, somewhat in the Rossetti fashion,* seemed almost drugged, as if a strange mass of thoughts coiled in the darkness within her, and she was never allowed to escape.

Ursula watched her with fascination. She knew her a little. She was the most remarkable woman in the midlands. Her father was a Derbyshire Baronet of the old school, she was a woman of the new school, full of intellectuality, and heavy, nerve-worn with consciousness. She was passionately interested in public affairs, her soul was given up to the public cause. But she was a man's woman, it was the manly world that held her.

She had various intimacies of mind and soul, with various men of capacity. Ursula knew, among these men, only Rupert Birkin, who was one of the school-inspectors for the county. But Gudrun had met others, in London. Moving with her artist friends in different kinds of society, Gudrun had already come to know a good many people of repute and standing. She had met Hermione twice, but they did not take to each other. It would be queer to meet again down here in the midlands, where their social standing was so diverse, after they had known each other on terms of equality in the houses of sundry acquaintances in town.* For Gudrun had been a social success, and had her friends among the slack aristocracy in restless London.

Hermione knew herself to be well-dressed; she knew herself to be the social equal, if not far the superior, of anyone she was likely to meet in Willey Green. She knew she was accepted in the world of culture and of intellect. She was a Kulturträger,* a medium for the culture of ideas. With all that was highest, whether in society or in thought or in public action, or even in art, she was at one, she moved among the foremost, at home with them. No one could put her down, no one could make mock of her, because she stood among the first, and those that were against her were below her, either in rank, or in wealth, or in high association of thought and progress and understanding. So, she was invulnerable. All her life, she had sought to make herself invulnerable, unassailable, beyond reach of the world's judgment.

And yet her soul was tortured, exposed. Even walking up the path to the church, confident as she was that in every respect she stood beyond all vulgar judgment, knowing perfectly that her appearance was complete and perfect, according to the first standards, yet she suffered a torture, under her confidence and her pride, feeling herself exposed to wounds and to mockery and to despite. She always felt vulnerable, vulnerable, there was always a secret chink in her armour. She did not know herself what it was. It was a lack of confidence, she had no natural sufficiency, there was a terrible void, a lack, a deficiency of being within her.

And she wanted someone to close up this deficiency, to close it up for ever. She loved Rupert Birkin. When he was there, she felt complete, she was sufficient, whole. For the rest of time she was established on the sand,* built over a chasm, and, in spite of all her pride and securities, any common maid-servant of positive, robust temper could fling her down this bottomless pit of insufficiency, by the slightest movement of jeering or contempt. And all the while the pensive, tortured woman piled up her own defences of aesthetics, and culture, and knowledge, and disinterestedness. Yet she could never stop up the terrible gap of insufficiency.

If only Birkin would form a close and abiding connection with her, she would be safe during this fretful voyage of life. He could make her sound and triumphant, triumphant over the very angels of heaven. If only he would do it! But she was tortured with fear, with misgiving. She made herself beautiful, she strove so hard to come to that degree of beauty and advantage, when he should be convinced. But always there was a deficiency.

He was perverse too. He fought her off, he always fought her off. The more she strove to bring him to her, the more he battled her back. And they had been lovers now, for years. Oh, it was so wearying, so aching; she was so tired. But still she believed in herself. She knew he was trying to leave her. She knew he was trying to break away from her finally, to be free. But still she believed in her strength to keep him, she believed in her own higher knowledge. Her own knowledge was higher, she was the first touchstone of truth. She only needed his conjunction with her.

And this, this conjunction with her, which was his highest fulfilment also, with the perverseness of a wilful child he wanted to deny. With the wilfulness of an obstinate child, he wanted to break the holy connection that was between them.

He would be at this wedding; he was to be groom's man. He would be in the church, waiting. He would know when she came. She shuddered with nervous apprehension and desire as she went through the church-door. He would be there, surely he would see how beautiful her dress was, surely he would see how she had made herself beautiful for him. He would understand, surely he would understand, he would be able to see how she was made for him, the first, how she was, for him, the highest. Surely at last he would be able to accept his highest fate, he would not deny her.

In a little convulsion of suffering yearning, she entered the church and looked slowly along her cheeks for him, her slender body convulsed with agitation. As best man, he would be standing beside the altar. She looked slowly, deferring in her certainty.

And then, he was not there. A terrible storm came over her, as if she were drowning. She was possessed by a devastating hopelessness. And she approached mechanically to the altar. Never had she known such a pang of utter and final hopelessness. It was beyond death, so utterly null, desert.

The bridegroom and the groom's man had not yet come. There was a growing consternation outside. Ursula felt almost responsible. She could not bear it, that the bride should arrive, and no groom. The wedding must not be a fiasco, it must not.

But here was the bride's carriage, adorned with ribbons and cockades. Gaily the grey horses curvetted to their destination at the church-gate, a laughter in the whole movement. Here was the quick of all laughter and pleasure. The door of the carriage was thrown open, to let out the very blossom of the day. The people on the roadway murmured faintly with distress.

The father stepped out first into the air of the morning, like a shadow. He was a tall, thin, careworn man, with a thin black beard that was touched with grey. He waited at the door of the carriage patiently, self-obliterated.

In the opening of the doorway was a shower of fine foliage and flowers, a whiteness of silk and lace, and a sound of a gay voice saying:

"How do I get out?"

A ripple of pleasure ran through the expectant people. They pressed near to receive her, looking with delight at the stooping blond head with its flower buds, and at the delicate, white, tentative foot that was reaching down to the step of the carriage. There was a sudden foaming rush, and the bride like a sudden surf-rush, floating all white beside her father in the morning shadow of trees, her veil flowing with laughter.

"There!" she said. "That's done it!"

She put her hand on the arm of her silent, dark father, and frothing her light draperies, proceeded over the eternal red carpet. Her father, sad and yellowish, his black beard making him look more careworn, mounted the steps stiffly, as if his spirit were absent; but the laughing mist of the bride went along with him undiminished.

And no bridegroom had arrived! It was intolerable for her. Ursula, her heart strained with anxiety, was watching the hill beyond; the white, descending road, that should give sight of him. There was a carriage. It was running. It had just come into sight. Yes, it was he. Ursula turned towards the bride and the people, and, from her place of vantage, gave an inarticulate cry. She wanted to warn them that he was coming. But her cry was inarticulate and inaudible, and she flushed deeply, between her desire and her wincing confusion.

The carriage rattled down the hill, and drew near. There was a shout from the people. The bride, who had just reached the top of the steps, turned round gaily to see what was the commotion. She saw a confusion among the people, a cab pulling up, and her lover dropping out of the carriage, and dodging among the horses and into the crowd.

"Tibs!* Tibs!" she cried in her sudden, mocking excitement, standing high on the path in the sunlight and waving her bouquet. He, dodging with his hat in his hand, had not heard.

"Tibs!" she cried again, looking down to him.

He glanced up, unaware, and saw the bride and her father standing on the path beyond. A queer, startled look went over his face. He hesitated for a moment. Then he gathered himself together for the leap, to overtake her.

"Ah-h-h!" came her strange, intaken cry, as, on the reflex, she started, turned, and fled, scudding with an unthinkable swift beating of her white feet and a fraying of her white garments, towards the grey church. Like a hound the young man was after her, leaping the steps and swinging past her father, his supple haunches working like those of a hound that bears down on the quarry.

"Ai-ee, Ai-ee! After her! On her, lad, on her!" cried the grooms below, carried suddenly into strange mockery.

She, her flowers shaken from her like froth, was steadying herself to turn the angle of the church. She glanced behind, and with a wild cry of laughter and terror, veered, poised, and was gone beyond the grey stone buttress. In another instant the bridegroom, bent forward as he ran, had caught the angle of the silent stone with his hand, and had swung himself out of sight, his supple, strong loins vanishing in pursuit.

Instantly cries and exclamations of excitement burst from the crowd at the gate. And then Ursula noticed again the dark, rather stooping figure of Mr Crich, waiting suspended on the path, watching with expressionless face the flight to the church. It was over, and he turned round to look behind him, at the figure of Rupert Birkin, who at once came forward and joined him.

"So we bring up the rear," said Birkin, a faint smile on his face.

"Ay!" replied the father laconically.

And the two men turned together up the path.

Birkin was as thin as Mr Crich, pale and ill-looking. His figure was narrow and finely made. He went with a slight trail of one foot, which came only from self-consciousness. Although he was dressed correctly for his part, yet there was an innate incongruity which caused a slight ridiculousness in his appearance. His nature was odd and separate, he did not fit at all in the conventional occasion.

Yet he affected to be quite ordinary, perfectly *comme-il-faut*. And he did it so well, taking so diligently the tone of his surroundings, adjusting himself so nicely to whatever man or woman he was in contact with, that he usually managed to propitiate the onlookers.

Now he spoke quite easily and pleasantly to Mr Crich, as they walked along the path; notwithstanding that he suffered from extreme self-consciousness.

"I'm sorry that we are so late," he was saying. "We couldn't find a button-hook, so it took us a long time to button our boots. But you were to the moment."

"We are usually to time," said Mr Crich.

"And I'm always late," said Birkin. "But today I was *really* punctual, only accidentally not so. I'm sorry."

The two men were gone, there was nothing more to see, for the time. Ursula was left thinking about Birkin. There was something about him that made her feel apart, wondering. He answered to something in her spirit, apart from the world she knew. Even his slight ridiculousness, something fantastic, seemed to reveal to her an other-worldliness, intangible and desirable.

She wished she could know him intimately. She had spoken with him once or twice, but only in his official capacity as inspector. She thought he seemed to acknowledge some kinship between her and him, a natural, instinctive understanding, a using of the same language. But there had been no time for the understanding to develop. And something kept her from him, as well as attracted her to him. There was a certain hostility, a hidden arrogance in him. And she hated the way he betrayed himself to everybody.

Yet she wanted to know him.

"What do you think of Rupert Birkin?" she asked, a little reluctantly, of Gudrun. She did not want to discuss him.

"What do I think of Rupert Birkin?" repeated Gudrun. "I think he's decent—a really decent man.—What I can't stand about him is his way with other people—his way of treating any little fool as if she were the greatest light.—One feels so awfully sold, oneself."

"Why does he do it?"

"Because he has no real critical faculty—of people, at all events," said Gudrun. "I tell you, he treats any little fool as he treats me or you—and it's such a lie."

"Oh, it is," said Ursula. "One must discriminate."

"One *must* discriminate," repeated Gudrun.—"But he's a wonderful chap, in other respects—a marvellous personality."

"Yes," said Ursula vaguely. She was always forced to assent to Gudrun's pronouncements, even when she was not in accord altogether.

The sisters sat silent, waiting for the wedding party to come out. Gudrun was impatient of talk. She wanted to think about Gerald Crich. She wanted to see if the strong feeling she had got from him was real. She wanted to have herself ready.

Inside the church, the wedding was going on. Hermione Roddice was thinking only of Birkin. He stood near her. She seemed to gravitate physically towards him. She wanted to stand touching him. She could hardly be sure he was near her, if she did not touch him. Yet she stood subjected through the wedding service.

She had suffered so bitterly when he did not come, that still she was dazed. Still she was gnawed as by a neuralgia, tormented by his potential absence from her. She had awaited him in a faint delirium of nervous torture. As she stood bearing herself pensively, the rapt look on her face, that seemed spiritual, like the angels, but which came from torture, gave her a certain poignancy that tore his heart with pity. He saw her bowed head, her rapt face, the face of an ecstatic. Feeling him looking, she lifted her face and sought his eyes, her own beautiful grey eyes flaring him a great signal. But he avoided her look, she sank her head in torment and shame, the gnawing at her heart going on. And he too was tortured with shame, and with acute pity for her, because he did not want to meet her eyes, he did not want to receive her flare of recognition.

The bride and bridegroom were married, the party went into the vestry. Hermione crowded involuntarily up against Birkin, to touch him. And he endured it.

Outside, Gudrun and Ursula listened for their father's playing on the organ. He would enjoy playing a wedding march. Now the married pair were coming! The bells were ringing, making the air shake. Ursula wondered if the trees and the flowers could feel the vibration, and what they thought of it, this strange motion in the air. The bride was quite demure on the arm of the bridegroom, who stared up into the sky before him, shutting and opening his eyes unconsciously, as if he were neither here nor there. He looked rather comical, blinking and trying to be in the scene, when emotionally he was violated by his exposure to a crowd. He looked a typical naval officer, manly, and up to his duty.

Birkin came with Hermione. She had a rapt, triumphant look, like the angels who have won against the devils, now she held Birkin by the arm. And he was expressionless, neutralised, possessed by her as if it were his fate, without question.

Gerald Crich came, fair, goodlooking, healthy, with a great reserve of energy. He was erect and complete, there was a strange stealth glistening through his amiable, almost happy appearance. Gudrun rose sharply and went away. She could not bear it. She wanted to be alone, to know this strange, sharp inoculation that had changed the whole temper of her blood.

The Brangwens went home to Beldover, the wedding-party gathered at Shortlands, the Criches' home. It was a long, low old house, a sort of manor farm, that spread along the top of a slope just beyond the narrow little lake of Willey Water. Shortlands looked across a sloping meadow that might be a park, because of the large, solitary trees that stood here and there, across the water of the narrow lake, at the wooded hill that successfully hid the colliery valley beyond, but did not quite hide the rising smoke. Nevertheless, the scene was rural and picturesque, very peaceful, and the house had a charm of its own.

It was crowded now with the family and the wedding guests. The father, who was not well, withdrew to rest. Gerald was host. He stood in the homely entrance hall, amiable and easy, attending to the men. He seemed to take pleasure in his social functions, he smiled, and was a very good fellow.

The women wandered about in a little confusion, brought hither and thither by the three married daughters of the house. All the while there could be heard the characteristic, imperious voice of one Crich woman or another calling, "Helen, come here a minute," "Marjory, I want you—here!" "Oh I say, Mrs Witham—." There was a great rustling of skirts, swift glimpses of smartly dressed women, a child danced through the hall and back again, a maid-servant came and went hurriedly.

Meanwhile the men stood in calm little groups, chatting, smoking, pretending to pay no heed to the rustling animation of the women's world. But they could not really talk, because of the silvery ravel of women's excited, pleased laughter and running voices. They waited, uneasy, suspended, rather bored. But Gerald remained quite genial and happy, unaware that he was waiting or unoccupied, unconscious as if he were the very pivot of being.

Suddenly Mrs Crich came noiselessly into the room, peering about with her strong, clear face. She was still wearing her hat, and her sac coat of blue silk.

"What is it, mother?" said Gerald.

"Nothing, nothing!" she answered vaguely.

And she went straight towards Birkin, who was talking to a Crich brother-in-law.

"How do you do, Mr Birkin," she said, in her low voice, that seemed to take no count of her guests. She held out her hand to him.

"Oh Mrs Crich," replied Birkin, in his readily-changing voice, "I couldn't come to you before."

"I don't know half the people here," she said, in her low voice. Her son-in-law moved uneasily away.

"And you don't like strangers, do you?" laughed Birkin. "I find it difficult to believe people are real, just because they happen to be in the room with me. Why *should* I know they are there?"

"Why indeed, why indeed!" said Mrs Crich, in her low, tense voice. "Except that they *are* there.—I don't know people whom I find in the house. The children introduce them to me—'Mother, this is Mr So-and-so.' I am no further. What has Mr So-and-so to do with his own name?—and what have I to do with either him or his name?"

She looked up at Birkin. She excited him. He was flattered too that she came to talk to him, for she took hardly any notice of anybody. He looked down at her tense clear face, with its heavy features, but he was afraid to look into her heavy-seeing blue eyes. He noticed instead how her hair looped in slack, slovenly strands over her rather beautiful ears, which were not quite clean. Neither was her neck perfectly clean. Even in that he seemed to belong to her, rather than to the rest of the company; though he was himself always well washed, at any rate at the neck and ears.

He smiled to himself, thinking these things. Yet he was uneasy, feeling that he and the elderly, estranged woman were conferring together like traitors, like spies within the camp of the other people.

"Not many people exist, actually," he said, rather unwilling to continue.

The mother looked up at him with sudden, dark interrogation, as if doubting his sincerity.

"How do you mean that?" she asked sharply.

"Most living, talking persons are just nothing but a weight and a noise," he replied, vainly giving expression to his private feelings. "They only exist in the physical-mechanical world. In the essential sense, they merely aren't there."

She watched him steadily while he spoke.

"But we don't imagine them," she said sharply.

"There's nothing to imagine, that's why they don't exist."

"Well," she said, "I would hardly go as far as that. There they are, whether they exist or no. It doesn't rest with me to decide on their existence. I only know that I can't be expected to take count of them all. You can't expect me to know them, just because they happen to be there. As far as *I* go they might as well not be there."

"Exactly," he replied.

"Mightn't they?" she asked again.

"Just as well," he repeated.

And there was a little pause.

"There are my sons-in-law," she went on, in a sort of monologue. "Now Laura's got married, there's another. And I really don't know John from James yet. They come up to me, and call me mother. I know what they will say—'How are you, mother?' I ought to say, 'I am not your mother, in any sense.' But what is the use? There they are. I have had children of my own. I suppose I know them from another woman's children."

"One would suppose so," he said.

She looked at him, somewhat surprised, forgetting perhaps that she was talking to him. And she lost her thread.

She looked round the room, vaguely. Birkin could not guess what she was looking for, nor what she was thinking. Evidently she noticed her sons.

"Do my children exist?" she asked him, abruptly.

He laughed, startled, afraid perhaps.

"I scarcely know them, except Gerald," he replied.

"Gerald!" she exclaimed. "He's a rebel, that one, a real rebel. You'd never think it, to look at him now, would you?"

"He's rebel enough," said Birkin.

The mother looked across at her eldest son, stared at him heavily for some time.

"Ay," she said, in an incomprehensible monosyllable. Birkin felt burdened, as if a weight were on him. And Mrs Crich moved away, forgetting him. But she drifted back.

"I should like him to have a friend," she said. "He has never had a friend."

Birkin looked down into her eyes, which were blue, and watching heavily. He could not understand them. "Am I my brother's keeper?" he said to himself, almost flippantly.

Then he remembered, with a slight shock, that that was Cain's cry. And Gerald was Cain, if anybody. Not that he was Cain, either, although he had slain his brother. There was such a thing as pure accident, and the consequences did not attach to one, even though one had killed one's brother in such wise. Gerald as a boy had accidentally killed his brother. What then? Why seek to draw a brand and a curse across the life that had caused the accident? A man can live by accident, and die by accident. Or can he not? Is every man's life subject to pure accident, is it only the race, the genus, the species, that has a universal reference? Or is this not true, is there no such thing as pure accident? Has *everything* that happens a universal significance? Has it? Birkin, thinking absorbedly as he stood there, had forgotten Mrs Crich, as she had forgotten him.

He did not believe that there was any such thing as accident. It all hung together, in the deepest sense.

Just as he had decided this, one of the Crich daughters came up, saying:

"Won't you come and take your hat off, mother dear? We shall be sitting down to eat in a minute, and it's a formal occasion, darling, isn't it?" She drew her arm through her mother's, and they went away. Birkin immediately went to talk with the nearest man.

The gong sounded for the luncheon. The men looked up, but no move was made to the dining room. The women of the house seemed to feel that the sound had no reference to them. Five minutes passed by. The elderly man-servant, Crowther, appeared in the doorway, pathetically. He looked with appeal at Gerald. The latter took up a large, curved horn of a mountain sheep, that lay on a shelf as a trophy, and without reference to anybody, blew a shattering blast. It was a strange, rousing noise, that made the heart beat. The summons was almost magical. Everybody came running, as if at a signal. And then the crowd in one impulse, moved to the dining room.

Gerald waited a moment, for his sister to play hostess. He knew his mother would pay no attention to her duties. But his sister merely crowded to her seat. Therefore the young man amiably directed the guests to their places.

There was a moment's lull, as everybody looked at the hors d'oeuvres that were being handed round. And out of this lull, a girl of thirteen or fourteen, with her long hair down her back, said in a calm, self-possessed voice:

"Gerald, you forget father, when you make that unearthly noise."

"Yes," he answered. And then, to the company, "Father is lying down, he is not quite well."

"How is he, really?" called one of the married daughters, peeping round the immense wedding cake, that towered up in the middle of the table, shedding its artificial flowers.

"He has no pain, but he feels tired," replied Winifred, the girl with the hair down her back.

The wine was filled, and everybody was talking boisterously. At the far end of the table sat the mother, with her loosely looped hair. She had Birkin for a partner. Sometimes she glanced fiercely down the rows of faces, bending forwards and staring unceremoniously. And she would say, in a low voice, to Birkin:

"Who is that young man?"

"I don't know," Birkin answered discreetly.

"Have I seen him before?" she asked.

"I don't think so. I haven't," he replied.

And she was satisfied. Her eyes closed wearily, a peace came over her face, she looked like a queen in repose. Then she started, a little, social smile came on her face, for a moment she looked the pleasant hostess. For a moment she bent graciously, as if everyone were welcome and delightful. And then immediately the shadow came back, a sullen, eagle look was on her face, she glanced from under her brows like a wild creature at bay, hating them all.

"Mother," called Diana, a handsome girl a little older than Winifred, "I may have wine, mayn't I?"

"Yes, you may have wine," replied the mother automatically, for she was perfectly indifferent to the question.

And Diana beckoned to the footman to fill her glass.

"Gerald shouldn't forbid me," she said calmly, to the company at large.

"All right Di," said her brother amiably.

And she was afraid of him as she drank from her glass.

There was a strange freedom, that almost amounted to anarchy, in the house. Gerald had some authority, by mere force of personality, not because of any granted position. There was a quality in his voice, amiable and purely reckless, that dominated the others, who were all younger than he.

Hermione was having a discussion with the bridegroom about the building of Dreadnoughts.*

"I cannot believe in these great armaments," she was saying. "The state forbids the individual to carry arms. That is found to be the greatest wisdom, for a whole internal nation. Then why doesn't the wisdom apply to the nation, as seen externally? Why should Britannia and John Bull go armed to the teeth, when you and I may hardly carry a pen-knife?"

"But we may," laughed the bridegroom.

"Not as a weapon," Hermione answered.

"A nation has to defend herself, whereas the state defends every individual. Who is going to forbid nations to carry arms?" put in Gerald. He loved above all things these discussions on general topics. They were almost a passion with him.

"If I may not fight my neighbour, without being hauled up by the police, how is it that I should fight my neighbouring country?" asked Hermione, emphatically.

"Because there's no police of nations," said Gerald.

"Let us make one," said Birkin. "We might agitate for an immense police force, which should arrest the government of Russia, as soon as Russia began to steal from China, or to start making a row with Turkey. And so on with all nations, exactly as with all civilians. Arrest the whole government, king, lords, deputies, of any country, immediately she starts making a disturbance. Put 'em in prison, and hold 'em over till the international sessions. 'England is arrested on a charge of breaking the peace in Africa—'"

Gerald looked blank at this suggestion.

"What an unpleasant idea!" he said. "We've got enough police."

"Too much," said Birkin. "Enrol nine-tenths of the civil police in the international corps, and leave the civilian unwatched. It isn't the individual that wants watching, it is those great uncouth Bill Sykeses,* the nations."

"I'd rather trust my nation, than the next individual I meet," said Gerald.

"Would you really! Do you mean with your life or your property,— which?" said Birkin. "Your property, I suppose—for your life isn't safe five minutes, in the hands of your nation."

"Really!" laughed Gerald.

"Not two minutes," said Birkin. "Your nation will have your life in a twinkling—but it will carefully hand on the bulk of your property to your next of kin.—Which is all you care about, I suppose. Therefore you are just like a nation yourself."

"Conundrum!" cried Laura Crich. "Why is Gerald like a nation?"

"Because he is stupid," replied Diana pertly.

"What talk for a wedding!" cried Charlotte, a married sister. "We are going to drink toasts, aren't we? Let us drink toasts, let us have some speeches. Fill the glasses—now then—"

Birkin, thinking about nations versus individuals, stared into his glass, watched the champagne bubbles, and suddenly drank up all his wine. And the company was waiting for a speech, for a toast. He looked round in confusion. A little constraint went over the assembly.

"Did I do it by accident, or did I do it out of a subconscious purpose?" he asked himself.

And he decided that he hated toasts, he hated speeches, he resented them as impertinent and boring. Then he looked round at the footman for more wine. The footman came, conspicuously. He was a hired man, and his opinion of the whole affair was not high. Instinctively he disliked Birkin, and thought it the whole of boorishness, that the latter had drunk his wine without regard to the toast.

At length it was all over. Several men strolled out into the garden. There was a lawn, then flower beds, and then a path that ran along by an iron fence separating the garden from the field or little park. The view was pleasant. The high-road ran round the end of Willey Water, under the trees; in the bright spring air, the woods opposite shone purplish, sprinkled with green. Charming Jersey cattle came up to see if there were a crust to be offered.

Birkin leaned on the fence, a cow was sniffing his hand.

"Pretty cattle, very pretty," said Marshall, one of the brothers-in-law. "They give the best milk you can have."

"Yes," said Birkin.

"Eh, my little beauty, eh, my beauty!" said Marshall, in a queer high falsetto voice, that caused the other man to have convulsions of laughter in his stomach.

"Who won the race, Lupton?" he called to the bridegroom, to hide the fact that he was laughing.

The bridegroom took his cigar from his mouth.

"The race?" he exclaimed. Then a rather thin smile came over his face. He did not want to say anything about the flight to the church door. "We got there together. At least she touched first, but I had my hand on her shoulder."

"What's this?" asked Gerald.

Birkin told him about the race of the bride and the bridegroom.

"Hm!" snorted Gerald, in disapproval. "What made you late then?"

"Lupton would talk about the immortality of the soul," said Birkin, "and then we hadn't got a button-hook."

"Oh God!" cried Marshall. "The immortality of the soul on your wedding day! Hadn't you got anything better to occupy your mind?"

"What's wrong with it?" asked the bridegroom, a clean-shaven naval man, flushing sensitively.

"Sounds as if you were going to be executed instead of married. The *immortality of the soul*!" repeated the brother-in-law, with most killing emphasis.

But he fell quite flat.

"And what did you decide?" asked Gerald, at once pricking up his ears at the thought of a metaphysical discussion.

"You don't want a soul, today, my boy," said Marshall. "It'd be in your road."*

"Christ! Marshall, go and talk to somebody else," cried Gerald, with sudden impatience.

"By God, I'm willing," said Marshall, in a temper. "Too much bloody soul, and talk altogether—"

He withdrew in a dudgeon, Gerald staring after him with angry eyes, that grew gradually calm and amiable as the stoutly built form of the other man passed into the distance.

"There's one thing, Lupton," said Gerald, turning suddenly to the bridegroom. "Laura won't have brought such a fool into the family as Lottie did."

"Comfort yourself with that," laughed Birkin.

"I take no notice of them," laughed the bridegroom.

"But it's quite in the classic tradition: flight of the bride, pursuit of the groom, and a show of rape," said Birkin, in raillery.

"I don't like it," said Gerald, phlegmatically. "What do you get yourself up in silk and lace veils for, if you're not going to carry the thing through properly!"

"*Satin* and lace veils," said Birkin.

"Satin and lace veils then," repeated Gerald.

"You think it isn't doing the satin justice?" said Birkin.

"Satin be damned! I think if you set out to do a thing, *do* it," said Gerald. "If you're out to make a formal wedding, then you should bring it off, and if you're out running with the harriers, then you should run. Do what you're doing, and don't make confusion and chaos."

"So speaks the enemy of disorder," said Birkin.

"Yes," said Gerald, "I *am* the enemy of disorder."

"But supposing, you see, that Laura *wanted* to run from Lupton. Supposing it was a natural impulse in her to bolt the moment she set eyes on him. Now the proper thing to do would be to obey that impulse, speaking in the deepest sense; otherwise she would create chaos and confusion in her own soul, her own nature."

"How do you make that out?" said Gerald. "I should say, if she controlled her impulses, she would have *more* order in her soul, not less."

"No, surely. The more she controls her natural impulses, suppresses them and diverts them, the greater chaos occurs in her *soul,* although greater regularity may be secured for her *material* life. Which do you choose? Which would you rather have, Lupton: Laura who bolts, or Laura as regular as clock-work?"

"I'd rather have her herself," said the bridegroom.

"That's all very well, but you couldn't have all life like that, everybody doing just what they want," said Gerald.

"Why not?" said Birkin. "That's the ideal. *Fay ce que vouldras** —that is the twelfth and ultimate commandment, which swallows all the others in a gulp.—If God is in me, then His voice is the still small voice* of my desire—surely?"

"What about the Devil, then?" asked Gerald, smiling.

"That is he who denies my desire. He says, 'I've decided what is and what isn't, and none of these irruptive desires are going to upset my scheme.'—The devil, Gerald, as you need to learn, is the egoistic *will* of man—your own will is the devil in you, for example."

"I should be humble, and submit my will to God?" laughed Gerald.

"Oh decidedly: decidedly! When a desire comes upon you, this is the Holy Ghost which is with you*—submit, submit. Wilde was right, profoundly, when he said temptation was given us to succumb to."*

"What a world we should have, if anybody believed you!" cried Gerald, a wicked look of mischief on his face.

"Evil is the static will," said Birkin. "That which has come to pass *wills* to remain as it is, in statu quo. And that is the root of all evil. Desire is a seed, it will bring forth the unknown. But it has against it this static entity, this accomplished I. And this is the devil, this me which has come to pass, and which wishes to crystallise for ever upon itself, unchangeable. Whereas in reality, this me which I am is only a point of equilibrium, unstable equilibrium at that, in the everlasting flux of creation."

"There is no real you?" asked Gerald, looking at his friend with smiling, cruel eyes. It seemed almost true—Birkin was so evanescent.

"No. There is no *thing* contained within a certain outline, which is absolute me. I am God, if you like; but my Self, my Ego, is only a certain basketful of knowledge, gathered from the past. And I will that this should be all, final. Which is the lie, the evil will. Because there will be more knowledge, that is not in the basket, in me. There is no absolute

I, there is only a central truth, a balancing point within the flux, a point where a pure relationship is established between all the parts. This point is my soul. But you can see that a *point* isn't anything—even in Euclid."*

"No, a point isn't anything," said Gerald. "But it is *somewhere*."

"My being is a centre of pure relationship between parts of the flux, a point of perfect equilibrium. But since the whole is a flux, ever-changing, therefore this unit dissolves again, this being disappears. That doesn't prevent the relationship from being pure and eternal. It is eternal whether it exists in Time, or whether it doesn't. Wherever the parts are, the relationship is unaltered. And that is what I am, a pure relationship, a point of pure relationship."

"It doesn't seem much," said Gerald.

"Everything, if you think about it," said Birkin. "It is perfection and immortality and everything else."

"And basta!" laughed Gerald, turning away.

"Basta!" cried Birkin in affirmation.

And the two men walked back towards the house, having come into trembling nearness of contact, in their talk. They felt tender and quivering, one towards the other. They walked in love, back to the house, there to separate in the friability of actual life, to escape each other.

2

A SCHOOL-DAY WAS DRAWING to a close. In the class-room the last lesson was in progress, peaceful and still. It was elementary botany. The desks were littered with catkins, hazel and willow, which the children had been sketching. But the sky had come over dark, as the end of the afternoon approached, there was scarcely light to draw any more. Ursula stood in front of the class, leading the children by questions to understand the structure and the meaning of the catkins.

A heavy, copper-coloured beam of light came in at the west window, gilding the outlines of the children's heads with red gold, and falling on the wall opposite in a rich, ruddy glamour. Ursula, however, was scarcely conscious of it. She was busy, the end of the day was here, the work went on as a peaceful tide that is at flood, hushed to retire.

This day had gone by like so many more, in an activity that was like a trance. At the end there was a little haste, to finish what was in hand. She was pressing the children with questions, so that they should know all they were to know, by the time the gong went. She stood in shadow in front of the class, with catkins in her hand, and she leaned towards the children, absorbed in the passion of instruction.

She heard, but did not notice the click of the door. Suddenly she started. She saw, in the shaft of ruddy, copper-coloured light near her, the face and the shoulders of a man. The face was gleaming like fire, watching her, waiting for her to be aware. It startled her terribly. She thought she was going to faint. All her suppressed, subconscious self sprang into being, with anguish.

"Did I startle you?" said Birkin, shaking hands with her. "I thought you had heard me come in."

"No," she faltered, scarcely able to speak.

He laughed, saying he was sorry. She wondered why it amused him.

"It is so dark," he said. "Shall we have the light?"

And moving aside, he switched on the strong electric lights. The classroom was distinct and hard, a strange place after the soft dim peace that filled it before he came. Birkin turned curiously to look at Ursula. Her eyes were round and wondering, bewildered, her mouth quivered slightly. She looked like one who is suddenly wakened. There was a living, tender beauty, like a tender light of dawn shining from her face. He looked at her with a new wonder, feeling gay in his heart, irresponsible.

"You are doing catkins?" he asked, picking up a piece of hazel from a scholar's desk in front of him. "Are they really as far out as this? I'd never noticed."

He looked absorbedly at the tassel of hazel in his hand.

"The red ones too!" he said to himself, looking at the flickers of crimson that came from the female bud.

Then he went in among the desks, to see the scholars' books. Ursula watched his quiet, absorbed progress. There was a stillness in his motion that hushed the activities of her heart. She seemed to be standing aside in another silence, watching him move in his own still, concentrated world. His body was so quiet, almost like a vacancy in the corporate* air.

Suddenly he lifted his face to her, and her heart quickened at the unexpected energy of his voice.

"Give them some crayons, won't you?" he said, "so that they can make the gynaecious flowers red, and the androgynous* yellow. I'd chalk them in plain, chalk in nothing else, merely the red and the yellow. Outline scarcely matters in this case. There's just the one fact to emphasise."

"I haven't any crayons," said Ursula.

"Really! Surely there are some somewhere—red and yellow, that's all you want."

Ursula sent out a boy on a quest.

"It will make the books untidy," she said to Birkin, flushing deeply.

"Oh no," he said. "You must mark in these things obviously. It's the fact you want to emphasise, not a subjective impression to record. What's the fact?—red little spiky stigmas of the female flower, dangling yellow male catkin, yellow pollen flying from one to the other. Make a pictorial record of the fact, as a child does when drawing a face—two eyes, one nose, mouth with teeth—so— !" And he drew a figure on the blackboard.

At that moment another vision was seen through the glass panels of the door. It was Hermione Roddice. Birkin went and opened to her.

"I saw your car," she said to him. "Do you mind my coming to find you? I wanted to see you when you were on duty."

She looked at him for a long time, intimate and playful, then she gave a short little laugh. And then only she turned to Ursula, who, with all the class, had been watching the little scene between the lovers.

"How do you do, Miss Brangwen," sang Hermione, in her slow, odd, singing fashion, that sounded almost as if she were poking fun. "Do you mind my coming in?"

Her grey, almost sardonic eyes rested all the while on Ursula, as if summing her up.

"Oh no," said Ursula.

"Are you *sure*?" repeated Hermione, with complete sang froid, and an odd, half bullying impulse.

"Oh no, I like it awfully," laughed Ursula, a little bit excited and bewildered, because Hermione seemed to be compelling her, coming very close to her, as if intimate with her; and yet, how could she be intimate?

This was the answer Hermione wanted. She turned satisfied to Birkin.

"What are you doing?" she sang, in her casual, inquisitive fashion.

"Catkins," he replied.

"Really!" she said. "And what do they learn about them?"

She spoke all the while in a mocking, half teasing fashion, as if making game of the whole business. She picked up a piece of the catkin, piqued by Birkin's attention to it.

She was a strange figure in the class-room, wearing a large, old cloak of greenish cloth, on which was a raised pattern of dull gold. The high collar, and the inside of the cloak, was lined with dark fur. Beneath she had a dress of fine rose-coloured cloth, trimmed with fur, and her hat was close-fitting, made of fur and the dull, green and gold figured stuff. She was tall and strange, she looked as if she had come out of some new, bizarre picture.

"Do you know the little red ovary flowers, that produce the nuts—have you ever noticed them?" he asked her. And he came close and pointed them out to her, on the sprig she held.

"No," she replied. "What are they?"

"Those are the little seed-producing flowers, and the long catkins, they only produce pollen, to fertilise them."

"Do they, do they!" repeated Hermione, looking closely.

"From those little red bits, the nuts come; if they receive pollen from the long danglers."

"Little red flames, little red flames," murmured Hermione to herself. And she remained for some moments looking only at the small buds out of which the red flickers of the stigma issued.

"Aren't they beautiful? I think they're so beautiful," she said, moving close to Birkin, and pointing to the twig with her long, white finger.

"Had you never noticed them before?" he asked.

"No, never before," she replied.

"And now you will always see them," he said.

"Now I shall always see them," she repeated. "Thank you so much for showing me. I think they're so beautiful—little red flames putting out—"

Her absorption was strange, almost rhapsodic. Both Birkin and Ursula were puzzled. The little red female flowers had some strange, almost mystic-passionate attraction for her.

The lesson was finished, the books were put away, at last the class was dismissed. And still Hermione sat at the table, with her chin in her hand, her elbow on the table, her long white face pushed up, not attending to anything. Birkin had gone to the window, and was looking from the brilliantly-lighted room on to the grey, colourless outside, where rain was noiselessly falling. Ursula put away her things in the cupboard.

At length Hermione rose and came near to her.

"Your sister has come home?" she said.

"Yes," said Ursula.

"And does she like being back in Beldover?"

"No," said Ursula.

"No. I wonder she can bear it. It takes all my strength, to bear the ugliness of this district, when I stay here.—Won't you come and see me? Won't you come with your sister to stay at Breadalby for a few days?—do—"

"Thank you very much," said Ursula.

"Then I will write to you," said Hermione. "You think your sister will come? I should be so glad. I think she is wonderful. I think some of her work is really wonderful. I have a water-wagtail, carved in wood, and painted—perhaps you have seen it?"

"No," said Ursula.

"I think it is perfectly wonderful—like a flash of instinct—"

"Her little carvings *are* lovely," said Ursula.

"Perfectly beautiful—full of instinctive passion—"

"Isn't it funny that she always likes little things?—she must always work small things, that one can put between one's hands, birds, and tiny animals."

Hermione looked down at Ursula with that long, detached, scrutinising gaze that excited the younger woman.

"Yes," said Hermione at length. "It is curious. The little things seem to be more subtle to her—"

"But they aren't, are they? A mouse isn't any more subtle than a lion, is it?"

Again Hermione looked down at Ursula with that long scrutiny, as if she were following some train of thought of her own, and barely attending to the other's speech.

"I don't know," she replied.

"Rupert, Rupert," she sang mildly, calling him to her.

He approached in silence.

"Are little things more subtle than big things?" she asked, with the odd grunt of laughter in her voice, as if she were making game of him in the question.

"Dunno," he said.

"I hate subtleties," said Ursula.

Hermione looked at her slowly.

"Do you," she said.

"I always think they are a sign of weakness," said Ursula, up in arms, as if her prestige were threatened.

Hermione took no notice. Suddenly her face puckered, her brow was knit with thought, she seemed twisted in troublesome effort for utterance.

"Do you really think, Rupert," she asked, as if Ursula were not present, "do you really think it is worth while? Do you really think the children are better for being roused to consciousness?"

A dark flash went over his face, a silent fury. He was hollow cheeked and pale, almost unearthly. And the woman, with her serious, conscience-harrowing question tortured him on the quick.

"They are not roused to consciousness," he said. "Consciousness comes to them, willy-nilly."

"But do you think they are better for having it quickened, stimulated? Isn't it better that they should remain unconscious of the hazel, isn't it better that they should see dimly, without all this distinguishing, all this knowledge?"

"Would you rather, for yourself, know or not know, that the little red flowers are there, putting out for the pollen?" he asked harshly. His voice was brutal, scornful, cruel.

Hermione remained with her face lifted up, abstracted. He hung silent in irritation.

"I don't know," she replied, balancing mildly "I don't know."

"But knowing is everything to you, it is all your life," he broke out. She slowly looked at him.

"Is it," she said.

"To know, that is your all, that is your life—you have only this, this knowledge," he cried. "There is only one tree, there is only one fruit, in your mouth."

Again she was some time silent.

"Is there," she said at last, with the same untouched calm. And then in a tone of whimsical inquisitiveness: "What fruit, Rupert?"

"The eternal apple," he replied in exasperation, hating his own metaphors.

"Yes" she said. There was a look of exhaustion about her. For some moments there was silence. Then, pulling herself together with a convulsed movement, Hermione resumed, in a sing-song, casual voice:

"But leaving me apart, Rupert; *do* you think the children are better, richer, happier, for all this knowledge, do you really think they are? Or is it better to leave them untouched, spontaneous. Hadn't they better be *animals*, simple animals, crude, violent, *anything*, rather than this self-consciousness, this incapacity to be spontaneous."

They thought she had finished. But with a queer rumbling in her throat she resumed, "Hadn't they better be anything than grow up crippled, crippled in their souls, crippled in their feelings—so thrown back—so turned back on themselves— —incapable—" Hermione clenched her fist like one in a trance—"of any spontaneous action, always deliberate, always burdened with choice, never carried away."

Again they thought she had finished. But just as he was going to reply, she resumed her queer rhapsody—"never carried away, out of themselves, always conscious, always self-conscious, always aware of themselves.— —Isn't *anything* better than this? Better be animals, mere animals with no mind at all, than this, this *nothingness*—."

"But do you think it is knowledge that makes us unliving and self-conscious?" he asked irritably.

She opened her eyes and looked at him slowly.

"Yes," she said. She paused, watching him all the while, her eyes vague. Then she wiped her fingers across her brow, with a vague weariness. It irritated him bitterly. "It is the mind," she said, "and that is death." She raised her eyes slowly to him: "Isn't the mind—" she said, with the convulsed movement of her body, "isn't it our death? Doesn't it destroy all our spontaneity, all our instincts? Are not the young people growing up today, the living dead?"

"Not because they have too much mind, but too little," he said brutally.

"Are you *sure*?" she cried. "It seems to me the reverse. They are over-conscious, burdened to death with consciousness."

"Imprisoned within a limited, false set of concepts," he cried.

But she took no notice of this, only went on with her own rhapsodic interrogation.

"When we have knowledge, don't we lose everything but knowledge?" she asked pathetically. "If I know about the flower, don't I lose the flower and have only the knowledge? Aren't we exchanging the substance for

34

the shadow, aren't we forfeiting life for this dead quantity of knowledge? And what does it mean to me, after all? What does all this knowing mean to me? It means nothing."

"You are merely making words," he said; "knowledge means everything to you. Even your animalism, you want it in your head. You don't want to be an animal, you want to be conscious of your own animal instincts, to get a thrill out of them. It is all purely secondary—and more decadent than the most hide-bound intellectualism. What is it but the worst and last form of intellectualism, this love of yours for passion and the animal instincts? Passion and the instincts—you want them hard enough, but you through your head, through your consciousness. It all takes place in your head, under that skull of yours.—Only you won't be conscious of what *actually* is: you want the lie that will match the rest of your furniture."

Hermione set hard and icy against this attack. Ursula stood covered with grief and shame. It frightened her, to see how they hated each other.

"It's all that Lady of Shallott business,"* he said, in his strong, abstract voice. He seemed to be charging her before the unseeing air. "You've got that mirror, your own fixed will, your immortal understanding, your own tight conscious world, and there is nothing beyond it. There, in the mirror, you must have everything. And because you've found all your leading ideas become stale, circumscribed as they are by your mirror-frame, you turn round, against intellectualism, against thought, against any expression of abstract truth, you want only sensationalism, which means your senses in your head. You want merely the *knowledge* of a certain set of reactions in your senses. But it is the mental, conscious experience you want, in your head. An animal—bah, you want to look at yourself in a mirror, like Shah Jehan*—you want to see your own animal actions in a mirror—your accursed Lady of Shallott mirror, which you've got in your head—and which is *you*, the beginning and the end of you—a fixed consciousness, an innumerable set of fixed conceptions, old clear and final, and bound round by your will into one perfect round mirror, in which the world takes place for you. But you would die, die rather than know that the world *doesn't* take place within your mirror, according to your universal consciousness. You'd die rather than know that your perfect consciousness doesn't stretch to the bounds and limits of the universe. You'd have to die, in the knowledge. And

35

you're tough, you're tough, you won't die. You'll take your precious mirror to the grave with you, as if it were your own immortality. And there it will lie, the tuppenny-ha'penny thing, like the combs and fibulas that come, rather tattered, out of the Saxon women's graves."

In spite of her grief and shame, Ursula was bound to laugh. It sounded so funny. And she could see the tattered combs that came out of the graves of the Saxon brides. It really seemed all a joke.

Birkin looked at her, and saw her laughing.

"It sounds so funny," she apologised to him.

A smile came on his own face. Hermione, with her long face, as a Lady of Shallott, and himself as Launcelot, that was the comic picture.

"Well," said Hermione at length, in a sighing, weary, rather indifferent tone, "you've said a great deal, Rupert. I hope it is all true."

"So do I," he said, with a grin.

But he hated her, and she made him feel ashamed. But he felt chiefly a mischievous triumph, like a boy who has broken something and is wickedly pleased.

Hermione rose at last. She turned to Ursula in a gracious manner.

"You'll come and see me, won't you? Do, I should be *so* glad."

"I should like it very much," said Ursula.

Hermione looked down at her, gratified, reflecting.

"Yes," she replied, pulling herself together. "Some time next week? And may I write to you?—Goodbye—"

Hermione held out her hand and sang her farewell in a new, gladder key. It was an unconscious relief to her, to escape from any relationship whatsoever. A curious sense of joy and freedom came over her at parting, when she was going to be left alone again.

Birkin stood aside, blanched and unreal. And now, when it was his turn to bid goodbye, he began to speak again.

"The whole difference in the world lies between spontaneous, instinctive movement, and conscious sensuality," he said, though neither of the women listened willingly. "If you've got to cover the last ground, tracing back with the consciousness the road we have come, and getting knowledge of the first steps of our sensuous experience, then let us do it. Let us be consciously sensuous till we are satisfied, till we reach a point of death. But don't deny that this is a gaining knowledge, it is a critical, analytical process. This worship of passion, of children, of parenthood is not a synthetic activity in us, it is purely analytic, a gaining of knowledge, and nothing else, science. And for us, who are going the last steps of self-consciousness, turning our primal instinct into knowledge, making our first spontaneous motions a mental property, for us to cry out upon intellectualism and the mind, that is lying. If we are out on the analytic adventure, we must penetrate the darkest continent. But we might as well know all the time what we are about, and not begin to lie to ourselves. We've got to finish the analytic venture, which we have been so proud of up to now—our great science, our great lyrical and emotional epoch has to fulfil itself in us. We've got to finish the great analytic adventure, the quest of knowledge. And if we have to push on into the darkest jungle of our own physical sensations, and discover the elements of sensuality in ourselves, we need not pretend we are being simple animals. We are the last products of the decadent movement, the analytic, lyrical, emotional, scientific movement which has had full sway since the Renaissance, and which we've been so proud of. Let us know it, and not lie. Because the adventure of knowledge is not finished for us till we have got back to the very sources, discovered satisfactorily to ourselves our own sources, in sensation, as one traces back a river. But it is knowledge, knowledge all the while, this passion, this emotionalism, this soldiering, it is a form of immediate anthropology, we study the origins of man in our own immediate experience, we push right back to the first, and last, sensations of procreation and of death."

There was silence in the room. Both women were hostile and resentful. But Hermione had withdrawn herself, his words did not touch her. She only knew they were antagonistic to her, and she withheld herself.

"But it isn't only this," said Ursula. "It isn't *only* knowledge and analysis and death."

"What isn't?" he cried.

"Life," she answered. "It isn't *all* destructive."

"Your life, my life—?" he cried. "Purely destructive and analytical, a process of reducing to their elements those combinations which the past has produced in us, unconsciously!"

"But not *all* life," Ursula persisted. "There are simple, spontaneous people."

"Behind us, following after. There's only one road, in the whole world, at the present—the way back, back to the beginnings, to the primal darkness. The decent nations follow it plainly, the indecent make spirals, and pretend that they are filled with creation. But in reality, the whole of the people in the world are going one way now, in a helpless herd, down the last slopes of sensational knowledge into the gap of darkness we came out of. It is the road to death. But if we want death, then nothing but death will do for us—like the leaves in autumn."

"Yes Rupert, nothing but death will do for us," chimed in Hermione. "But you're keeping Miss Brangwen from her tea, and I'm sure she's tired. You do find it exhausting, teaching, don't you?" she said to Ursula.

"Rather," replied Ursula.

Birkin bade goodbye. His face was as if made of fine steel, completely motionless, and white, and finely formed.

They were gone. Ursula stood looking at the door. Then swiftly, she put out the lights, and sat down in her chair, and wept bitterly.

The week passed away. On the Saturday it rained, a soft, drizzling rain that held off at times. In one of the intervals Gudrun and Ursula set out for a walk, going towards Willey Water. The atmosphere was grey and translucent, the birds sang sharply in the young twigs, the earth would be quickening and hastening in growth. The two girls walked swiftly, gladly, because of the soft, subtle rush of morning that filled the wet haze. By the road the blackthorn was in blossom, white and wet and clean, its tiny coral grains floating in the watery, tiny bowls of ivory. The purple twigs shone luminous in the grey air, the high hedges glowed like living shadows, hovering nearer, coming into creation. The morning was full of a new creation.

When the sisters came to Willey Water, the lake lay all grey and visionary, stretching into the moist, translucent vista of trees and meadow. In the woods, and in the dumbles* below the road, the birds were piping one against the other, and there was a mysterious plashing of unseen waters, issuing from the lake.

The two girls drifted swiftly along. In front of them, at the corner of the lake, near the road, was a mossy boat-house under a walnut tree, and a little landing stage where a boat was moored, wavering like a shadow on the still grey water, below the green, decayed poles. All was shadowy with coming summer.

Suddenly, from the boat-house, a white figure ran out, almost bird-like in its swift transit, across the old landing-stage. It launched in a pure white curve through the air, there was a bursting laugh of the water, and among the smooth ripples a swimmer was making out to space, in a centre of faintly heaving motion. The whole morning, wet and remote, he had to himself. He could move into the pure translucency of the grey, uncreated world.

Gudrun stood by the stone wall, watching.

"How I envy him," she said, in low, desirous tones.

"Ugh!" shivered Ursula. "How cold!"

"Yes, but how lovely, how really lovely, to swim out there!"

The sisters stood watching the swimmer move further into the grey, moist, full space of the water, pulsing with his own small, secret motion, and arched over with mist and dim woods.

"Don't you wish you could go too?" asked Gudrun, looking at Ursula.

"Very much," said Ursula. "—But I'm not sure—everywhere is so wet."

"No," said Gudrun, reluctantly.

She stood watching the man's motion on the bosom of the water, as if fascinated. He, having swum a certain distance, turned round and was swimming on his back, looking along the water at the two girls by the wall. In the faint wash of motion, they could see his ruddy face, and could feel him watching them.

"It is Gerald Crich," said Ursula.

"I know," replied Gudrun.

And she stood motionless gazing over the water at the face which washed up and down on the flood, as he swam steadily. From his separate element he saw them, and he laughed to himself because of his own superiority, his possession of a world to himself. He was immune and perfect. He loved his own vigorous, thrusting motion, and the voluptuous impulse of the very cold water against his limbs, buoying him up. He could see the girls watching him enviously, and that pleased him. He lifted his arm from the water, and waved exultantly to them.

"He is waving," said Ursula.

"Yes," replied Gudrun.

They watched him. He waved again, with a beckoning movement.

"Like a Nibelung,"* laughed Ursula.

Gudrun said nothing, only stood still looking over the water.

Gerald suddenly turned, and was swimming away swiftly, with a side stroke. He was alone now, alone and immune in the middle of the waters, which he had all to himself. He exulted in his possession of the new element, unconfined and beyond question. He was happy, free, without bond or connection anywhere, just himself within the watery world.

Gudrun envied him deeply. Even this momentary possession of pure isolation and freedom from the established world seemed to her so terribly desirable, that she felt herself hung with chains, there on the high-road.

"God, what it is to be a man!" she cried.

"What?" exclaimed Ursula, in surprise.

"The freedom, the liberty, the mobility!" cried Gudrun, strangely flushed and brilliant. "You're a man, you want to do a thing, you do it. You haven't the *thousand* obstacles a woman has in front of her."

Ursula wondered what was in Gudrun's mind, to occasion this outburst. She could not understand.

"What do you want to do?" she asked.

"Nothing," cried Gudrun, in swift refutation. "But supposing I did. Supposing I want to swim up that water. And supposing I *haven't* a bathing dress. It is impossible, it is one of the impossibilities of life, for me to take my clothes off and jump in. But isn't it *ridiculous,* doesn't it simply prevent our living!"

She was so hot, so flushed, so furious, that Ursula was astonished.

The two sisters went on, up the road. They were passing between the trees just below Shortlands. They looked up at the long, low house, dim and glamorous in the wet morning, its cedar tree slanting before the windows. Gudrun seemed to be studying it closely.

"Don't you think it's attractive, Ursula?" asked Gudrun.

"Very," said Ursula, "Very peaceful and charming."

"It has form, too—it has a period."

"What period?"

"Oh, late eighteenth century, for certain; Dorothy Wordsworth, and Jane Austen, don't you think?"

Ursula laughed.

"Don't you think so?" repeated Gudrun.

"Perhaps. But I don't think the Criches are by any means the period. I know Gerald has established a private electric plant, for lighting the house, and made all kinds of scientific improvements."

Gudrun shrugged her shoulders swiftly.

"Of course," she said, "that's quite inevitable."

"Quite," laughed Ursula. "He makes more alterations in a year than his father made in fifty. The people hate him for it, can't bear him. He seizes them all by the scruff of the neck, and fairly flings them along.

He'll have to die directly, for he'll have made every possible improvement in the pits, and in everything he's concerned with. But he's got some go."

"Certainly he's got go," said Gudrun. "In fact I've never seen a man that showed signs of so much. The unfortunate thing is, where does his go go to, what becomes of it?"

"I tell you," said Ursula. "It goes in applying the latest appliances."

"Exactly," said Gudrun.

"You know he shot his brother?" said Ursula.

"Shot his brother!" cried Gudrun, looking up aghast.

"Didn't you know? I thought you were sure to. He and his brother were playing together with a gun. He said to his brother, 'Look down the gun', and it was loaded, and blew the top of his head off.—Isn't it a horrible story?"

"How fearful!" cried Gudrun. "And how old were they?"

"Boys," said Ursula. "I think it is one of the most horrible stories I know."

"And Gerald of course did not know that the gun was loaded?"

"Oh, it was an old thing that had been lying in the stable for years. Nobody dreamed it would ever go off, and of course, no-one imagined it was loaded. But isn't it dreadful, that it should happen?"

"Frightful!" cried Gudrun. "And isn't it horrible too to think of such a thing happening to one, *by accident*. Imagine it, two boys playing together—then this overtakes them, for no reason whatever—out of the air. Ursula, it's too frightening! Oh, it's one of the things I can't bear. Murder, that is thinkable, because there's a will behind it. But a thing like that to happen to one—"

"Perhaps there was an unconscious will behind it," said Ursula. "This playing at killing has some primitive *desire* for killing in it, don't you think?"

"No," said Gudrun, wincing a little. "I can't see that they were even playing at killing. I suppose one boy said to the other, 'You look down the barrel while I pull the trigger, and see what happens.' It seems to me the purest form of accident."

"No," said Ursula. "I couldn't pull the trigger of the emptiest gun in the world, not if some-one were looking down the barrel. One instinctively refrains—one can't do it."

Gudrun was silent for some moments in displeasure.

"Of course," she said crossly, "if one is a woman, and grown up, one's instinct prevents one. But I cannot see how that applies to a couple of boys playing together."

Her voice was cold and angry.

"Yes," persisted Ursula.

At that moment they heard a woman's voice a few yards off say loudly:

"Oh damn the thing!"

They went forward and saw Laura Crich and Hermione Roddice in the field on the other side of the hedge, and Laura Crich struggling with the gate, to get out. Ursula at once hurried up and helped to lift the gate.

"Thanks so much," said Laura, looking up flushed and amazon-like, yet rather shy. "It isn't right on the hinges."

"No," said Ursula. "And fearfully heavy."

"Surprising!" cried Laura.

"How do you do," sang Hermione, from out of the field, the moment she could make her voice heard. "It's nice now. Are you going for a walk? Yes. Isn't the young green beautiful? So beautiful—quite burning. Good morning—good morning—you'll come and see me? —thank you so much—next week—yes—goodbye, go-o-o-dby-y-e."

Gudrun and Ursula moved on in some confusion, as if they had been dismissed. Laura Crich stood neutralised by Hermione's will. The four women separated.

As soon as they had gone far enough, Ursula said, her cheeks burning, "I do think she's impudent."

"Who, Hermione Roddice?" asked Gudrun. "Why?"

"The way she treats one—impudence!"

"Why Ursula, what did you notice that was so impudent?" asked Gudrun, rather coldly.

"Her whole manner—sending us off as if we were a couple of servants she had met in the road. She's an impudent woman. 'You'll come and see me,' as if we should be falling over ourselves for the privilege."

"I can't understand, Ursula, what you have to find fault with," said Gudrun, in some exasperation.

"Didn't *you* think her manner was impudent?" asked Ursula.

"No, I can*not* see it.—And if I did—pour moi, elle n'existe pas.* I don't grant her the power to be impudent to me."

"Do you think she likes you?" asked Ursula.

"Well, no, I shouldn't think she did."

"Then why does she ask you to go to Breadalby and stay with her?"

Gudrun lifted her shoulders in a slow shrug.

"After all, she's got the sense to know we're not just the ordinary run," said Gudrun. "Whatever she is, she's not a fool. And I'd rather have somebody I detested, than the ordinary amiable woman who goes round automatically in her own set."

Ursula pondered this for a time.

"I suppose we ought to be glad even that she makes us furious," she said at length.

"Exactly!" said Gudrun. "Think of the myriads of women that do not, absolutely, and cannot exist for one. She exists, if only, as you say, to make us furious—"

The two sisters were like a pair of scissors, snipping off everything that came athwart them; or like a knife and a whetstone, the one sharpened against the other.

"Of course," cried Ursula suddenly, "she ought to thank her stars if we will go and see her. You are perfectly beautiful, a thousand times more beautiful than ever she is or was, and to my thinking, a thousand times more beautifully dressed, for she never looks fresh and natural, like a flower, always like a second thought; and we *are* more intelligent than most people."

"Undoubtedly!" said Gudrun.

"And it ought to be admitted, simply," said Ursula.

"Certainly it ought," said Gudrun. "But you'll find that everything and everybody must be brought to the lowest common measure, before they can be accepted. If you are willing to be a bit of the L.C.M.,* the lowest common measure—"

"And I'm *not*," cried Ursula.

"Neither am I, finally and forever—I will not submit to be contained within the L.C.M.," declared Gudrun.

Ursula felt considerable satisfaction after this declaration. Until her class-mistress's soul began to feel uneasy about Gudrun's figure of speech.

"Though I believe," she said awkwardly, "that the Lowest Common Measure is the Least Common Multiple, and that must contain—"

Gudrun flushed deeply at finding her triumphant figure wrong.

"You know what I mean," she cried hotly. "I won't be held just like everybody else, only more so. I won't take the average of everybody, and accept that as my own measure."

"I know," said Ursula. "I'm only worried about the L.C.M. It's so awfully difficult to grasp it, really."

"Isn't it," cried Gudrun. "Isn't it one of the most difficult things in the world, to know what the L.C.M. really is."

"I'm sure it is the least common multiple," said Ursula.

But Gudrun was bored by this mathematical fact.

The sisters went home again, to read and talk and work, and wait for Monday, for school. Ursula often wondered what else she waited for, besides the beginning and end of the school week, and the beginning and end of the holidays. This was a whole life! Sometimes she had periods of abject horror, when it seemed to her that her life would pass away, and be gone, without having been more than this. But she never really believed it. Her spirit was active, her life was like a shoot that is growing steadily, but which has not yet come above ground.

One day at this time Birkin was called to London. He was not very fixed in his abode. He had rooms in Nottingham, because his work lay chiefly in that town. But often he was in London, or in Oxford. He moved about a great deal, his life seemed uncertain, without any definite rhythm, any fixed root.

On the platform of the railway station he saw Gerald Crich, reading a newspaper, and evidently waiting for the train. Birkin stood some distance off, among the people. It was against his instinct to approach anybody.

From time to time, in a manner characteristic of him, Gerald lifted his head and looked round. Even though he was reading the newspaper closely, he must keep a watchful eye on his external surroundings. There seemed to be a dual consciousness running in him. He was thinking vigorously of something he read in the newspaper, and at the same time his eye ran over the surface of the life round him, and he missed nothing. Birkin, who was watching him, was irritated by this duality. He noticed, too, that Gerald seemed always to be at bay against everybody, in spite of his queer, genial, social manner when roused.

Now Birkin started violently at seeing this genial look flash on to Gerald's face, at seeing Gerald approaching with hand outstretched.

"Hallo Rupert, where are you going?"

"London. So are you I suppose."

"Yes——"

Gerald's eyes went over Birkin's face in curiosity.

"We'll travel together if you like," he said.

"Don't you usually go first?" asked Birkin.

"I can't stand the crowd," replied Gerald. "But third'll be all right today. There's a restaurant car, we can have some tea."

The two men looked at the station clock, having nothing further to say.

"What were you reading in the paper?" Birkin asked.

Gerald looked at him quickly.

"Isn't it funny, what they *do* put in newspapers," he said. "Here are two leaders——" he held out his Daily Telegraph, "full of the ordinary newspaper cant——" he scanned the columns down——"and then there's this little—I dunno what you'd call it, essay, almost—appearing with the leaders, and saying there must arise a man who will give new values to things, give us new truths, a new attitude to life, or else we shall be a crumbling nothingness in a few years, a country full of ruin——"

"I suppose that's a bit of newspaper cant, as well," said Birkin.

"It sounds as if the man meant it, and quite genuinely," said Gerald.

"Give it me," said Birkin, holding out his hand for the paper.

The train came, and they went on board, sitting on either side a little table, by the window, in the restaurant car. Birkin glanced over his paper, then looked up at Gerald, who was waiting for him.

"I believe the man means it," he said.

"And do you think it's true? Do you think we really want a new gospel?" asked Gerald.

Birkin shrugged his shoulders.

"I think the people who say they want a new religion are the last to accept anything new. They want novelty right enough. But to stare straight at this life that we've brought upon ourselves, and reject it, and decide honestly for something better, that they'll never do. You've got very badly to want to get rid of the old, before anything new will appear."

Gerald watched him closely.

"You think we ought to break up this life, and go for something better?" he asked.

"This form of life, yes. We've got to slough it completely, or shrivel inside it, as in a tight skin. For it won't expand any more."

There was a queer little smile in Gerald's eyes, a look of amusement, calm and curious.

"And how do you propose to slough it? I suppose you mean, alter the whole form of society?" he asked.

Birkin had a slight, tense frown between the brows. He too was impatient of the conversation.

"I don't propose at all," he replied. "When we really want to go for something better, we shall do so. Until then, any sort of proposal, or making proposals, is no more than a tiresome game for self-important people."

The little smile began to die out of Gerald's eyes, and he said, looking with a cool stare at Birkin:

"So you really think things are very bad?"

"Completely bad."

The smile appeared again.

"In what way?"

"Because we are liars," said Birkin. "We are liars, and fools. Our ruling idea is sordid. The ideal is, that every Englishman should be rich and comfortable. So we cover the country with foulness, life is a sordid mass of labour, like insects scurrying in filth, so that your collier can have a pianoforte in his loathsome parlour, and you can have a butler and a motor-car in your loathsome bourgeois, barren house, and as a nation we can sport our wretched Ritz, our sordid Empire, our degraded theatre and cinema—all of it upholstered in cotton plush, and foul."

Gerald took a little time to readjust himself after this attack.

"Would you have us live without houses—return to nature?" he asked.

"I would have you do just as you please. As for nature—the craving for red plush seems universal, and therefore must be quite natural."

Again Gerald pondered. He was not going to take offence at Birkin.

"Don't you think the collier's pianoforte, as you call it, is a symbol for something very real, a real desire for something higher, in the collier's life?"

"Oh God!" cried Birkin. "Yes. It's a complete symbol of the collier's soul. The collier wants to rise in life, over a pianoforte, just as you want to rise in life over a Rolls Royce motor-car and a knighthood. And a good spiritual man is he who helps the collier to get, not only a pianoforte, but a pianola and sixty tunes to play on it. Then we are nearing heaven."

"I suppose we are," laughed Gerald,

"Can't you see," said Birkin, "that to help my neighbour* to get rich is next door to the baseness of helping myself to get rich. The idea of riches for everybody is even baser than the idea of riches for myself alone."

"You can't do without material things," said Gerald.

Which statement Birkin ignored.

"And we've got to live for *something*, we're not just cattle that can graze and have done with it," said Gerald.

"Tell me," said Birkin. "What do you live for?"

Gerald's face went hard.

"What do I live for?" he repeated. "I suppose I live to work, in so far as I am a purposive being. Apart from that, I live because I am living."

"And what's your work? Getting so many *more* thousands of tons of coal out of the earth every day. And what's the coal for—the greater part of it? Making pianofortes for colliers, and plush furniture. What does your work amount to? A great production of ugliness and uselessness. And what does our life amount to, collectively? A greater and greater acquisition of things that are worthless. A collier dies, and leaves behind him his pianoforte and his plush furniture. That is his life. There he leaves it, piled upon his young, who are striving for more pianofortes and more furniture—acquisition, endless acquisition. Humanity will disappear, and leave piles of pianos and furniture, acres of motor-cars and flying-machines and gramophones; and these, with the South Kensington Museum, and Oxford Street, and Kingsway, and the pit-hills,* and the square miles of factories, will represent the human life of the last hundred years—a huge mass of matter made hideous—that is all."

"But man *must* have something concrete to strive with. The furniture of a poor man is a symbol of his liberty," said Gerald.

"Quite. Liberty, a matter of possessions! The free soul is the soul which possesses a certain income. But it is a vicious circle. What is there inside that liberty? Nothing. Nothing. We build a wall round nothingness. We spend our days in embracing pure sterility."

"What isn't sterility then?" asked Gerald at last.

"Beauty, truth, and pure relationship.—Tell me, what is it you want in your heart of hearts? What is it *essentially* that you want?"

Gerald looked rather confused at the question. Then he raised his eyes courageously, and said:

"I want to be free."

A smile came on Birkin's face. Gerald had seemed to himself to say so much.

"Free, what for?" asked Birkin.

"I don't know," replied Gerald.

"When are you most free?" asked Birkin.

Gerald reflected.

"When I'm doing something I want to do, I suppose," he replied.

"But when are you doing something you profoundly want to do?" asked Birkin.

Gerald looked up almost furtively. He paused some moments before he answered:

"Not often."

"And what do you want to do, then, that you don't do?"

Gerald was silent for some moments. Then he answered:

"I think I want—" but he averted his face suddenly, looking out of the window, and did not finish.

"What?" asked Birkin.

But Gerald looked at him with guarded eyes, and answered:

"I couldn't say. What do you want?"

"I?" said Birkin slowly. "I want—to love a woman—first." Gerald glanced at him swiftly, as if to laugh. But the laugh did not come on the young man's face, instead, a deep gloom.

"Have you never been in love?" he asked.

"I've been in love—I've had a passion for a woman, and kissed her feet, and would let her walk on my face," Birkin replied. "But that isn't anything. It only sickens one. The real love, that grows in the soul—I've never known that."

"It may be a fiction," said Gerald.

"No. it isn't. It seems to me, if I knew such love, the real love for one woman, like a natural, new flower growing and opening in one's spirit and one's body, then my life would have been fulfilled. And without that, my life is nothing."

Gerald looked at him a long time. The evening light, flooding yellow along the fields, lit up Birkin's face with a pure, abstract steadfastness. Gerald felt a moment's peace in his own heart.

"But isn't it rather narrow, rather selfish, that?" he asked.

"I believe, if a man loved a woman, if there was creative love between them, not only passion, which is destructive, but the other, creative love, then the new life would be created of them. It isn't children I want to bring forth with a woman, but hope and truth and a new understanding."

"And it needs you and a woman?" asked Gerald.

"It can only be born of the love between a man and a woman—the living spirit, the new understanding," replied Birkin. "Then a man would be free, if he loved, and could beget hope, and understanding, if the new spirit could be born to him, in his love for a woman. There is only physical procreation in the world now—no spiritual begetting and bringing forth. Children are a stumbling block, parenthood is a pis-aller. It is the men, now, who should bring forth truth and understanding. But we are all barren, as men. We can only beget children, and suffer death."

Gerald turned and looked out of the window, at the flying, golden landscape, for some time. When he turned to Birkin again, he said:

"I can't help thinking that is rather narrow, limited, what you say."

"I am no more than myself," said Birkin. "I am limited to myself. If I love humanity, and become all humanity, I am less than myself, a barren idea. Humanity is quite sterile, this humanity which exists in our knowledge. I, in myself, have the germ of fertility—and I am limited and defined by the terms of my self,—but it is in my own, particularised self, united in love with a particular woman, that the hope lies, the germ of creation—nowhere else;—me as I am, with a woman who is with me, this is the beginning."

"But you haven't found the woman yet," said Gerald, almost sarcastically.

Birkin looked at him, but did not answer. And the two men went off into their own distant thoughts.

Gerald was held unconsciously by the other man. He wanted to be near him, he wanted to be friends with him. He wanted to say, "Birkin and I are friends." And yet he did not take any serious notice of what Birkin said. He felt that he himself, Gerald, had a more stable truth than that which might lie in utterances. He only wanted to be near the *man,* because then he felt a certain peace in his own soul.

Birkin knew this. He knew that, whatever he said, Gerald was not vitally listening. Therefore, though he was fond of the other, though there was a curious affection between them, yet he, Birkin, was apt to lose all knowledge of Gerald. It was so now. As the train ran on, Birkin sat looking at the land, and thinking, and Gerald did not exist, had lapsed out.

Birkin looked at the land, at the evening, and was thinking: "Well, if mankind is destroyed, if our race is destroyed like Sodom,* there is this beautiful evening with the luminous land and trees. That which informs it all is there, and can never be lost. After all, what is mankind but just one expression of the incomprehensible. And if mankind passes away, it will only mean that this particular expression is completed and done. That which is expressed, and that which is to be expressed, cannot be diminished. There it is, in the shining evening. Let mankind pass away— what does it matter? The creative utterances will not cease, they will only be different. If it is not the great word of humanity uttered by the incomprehensible, it will be other words. What does humanity matter, to the undiminished, whole spirit?"

Gerald interrupted him by asking,

"Where are you staying in London?"

Birkin looked up.

"With a man in Chelsea. I pay part of the rent of a flat, and stop there when I like."

"Good idea—have a place more or less your own," said Gerald.

"Yes. But I don't care for it much. I'm tired of the people I am bound to find there."

"What kind of people?"

"Art—music—London Bohemia—a poor lot, really. But I hate London lodgings so much. And this sensational crowd that Halliday mixes with, they are nihilists with regard to the conventions, even if they are ultimately bourgeois. And some of them are really, instinctively inimical to the existing world—negatively something."

"What are they?—painters, musicians?"

"Painters, musicians, writers—hangers-on, models, advanced young people, anybody who is openly at outs with the conventions, and belongs to nowhere particularly. They are often young fellows down from the university, and girls who are living their own lives, as they say."

"All loose?" said Gerald.

Birkin could see his curiosity was roused.

"In one way. Most bound, in another. For all their sensationalism, all on one note."

He looked at Gerald, and saw how his blue eyes were lit up with a little flame of desire. He saw too how good-looking he was. Gerald was attractive, his blood seemed glowing. His blue eyes burned with a fierce, yet cold light, there was a certain beauty, a beautiful passivity in all his body, his moulding, his contours had a real loveliness, complete and satisfying.

"We might see something of each other—I am in London for two or three days," said Gerald tentatively.

"Yes," said Birkin. "I don't want to go to the theatre, or the music hall,—you'd better come round to the flat, and see what you make of Halliday and his crowd. I suppose you won't be shocked."

"I wish I might," laughed Gerald. "What are you doing tonight?"

"I promised to meet Halliday at the Café Impérial. It's a bad place, but there is nowhere else."

"Where is it?" asked Gerald.

"Piccadilly Circus."

"Oh yes—well, shall I come round there?"

"By all means, if you won't loathe it too much."

The evening was falling. They had passed Bedford. Birkin watched the country, and was filled with a sort of dread. He always felt this, on approaching London. His dread of mankind, of the mass of mankind, amounted almost to horror.

> "'Where the quiet coloured end of evening smiles
>   Miles and miles—'"

he was murmuring to himself, almost like a man who is condemned to prison. Gerald, who was very keen-eyed, very keen in all his senses, leaned forward and asked, curiously:

"What were you saying?"

Birkin glanced at him, laughed, and repeated:

> "'Where the quiet coloured end of evening smiles,
>   Miles and miles,
> Over pastures where the something something sheep
>   Half asleep—'"*

Gerald also looked now at the country. And Birkin, who, for some reason was almost in tears, said to him:

"I always feel perfectly doomed when the train is running into London. I feel such a despair, so hopeless, as if it were the end of the world."

"Curious," said Gerald. "How do you account for it?"

"I don't know—unless it is my hatred or dread of man and his works—nowadays. Man, collectively, is horrifying to me."

There was a sardonic smile in Gerald's eyes.

"Really!" he said.

In a few minutes the train was running through the disgrace of out-spread London. Everybody in the carriage was on the alert, waiting to escape. At last they were under the huge arch of the station, in the tremendous shadow of the town. Birkin shuddered—he was in now.

The two men went together in a taxi-cab.

"Don't you feel like one of the damned?" asked Birkin, as they sat in the little, swiftly running enclosure, and watched the hideous great street.

"No," laughed Gerald.

"It is real death," said Birkin.

They met again in the café several hours later. Gerald went through the push doors into the large, lofty room where the faces and heads of the drinkers showed dimly through the haze of smoke, reflected more dimly, and repeated ad infinitum in the great mirrors on the walls, so that one seemed to enter a vague, dim world of shadowy drinkers humming within an atmosphere of blue tobacco smoke. There was, however, the red plush of the seats to give substance within the bubble of pleasure.

Gerald moved in his slow, observant, glad-looking motion down between the tables and the people whose shadowy faces looked up as he passed. He seemed to be floating in some strange element, drifting in a dim new liberty, among a host of licentious souls. He was pleased, and entertained. He looked over all the dim, evanescent, strangely illuminated faces that bent across the tables. Then he saw Birkin rise and signal to him.

At Birkin's table was a girl with dark, soft, fluffy hair cut short in the artist fashion, hanging level and full almost like the Egyptian princes's. She was small and delicately made, with warm colouring and large, dark, hostile eyes. There was a delicacy, almost a beauty in all her form, and at the same time a certain attractive grossness of spirit, that made a little spark leap instantly alight in Gerald's eyes.

Birkin, who looked muted, unsubstantial, his presence destroyed, introduced her as Miss Darrington. She gave her hand with a sudden, unwilling movement, looking all the while at Gerald with a dark, exposed stare. A glow came over him as he sat down.

The waiter appeared. Gerald glanced at the glasses of the other two. Birkin was drinking something green, Miss Darrington had a small liqueur glass that was empty save for a tiny drop.

"Won't you have some more—?"

"Brandy," she said, sipping her last drop and putting down the glass. The waiter disappeared.

"No," she said to Birkin. "He doesn't know I'm back. He'll be terwified when he sees me here."

She spoke her r's like w's, lisping with a slightly babyish pronunciation which was at once affected and true to her character. Her voice was dull and toneless.

"Where is he then?" asked Birkin.

"He's doing a private show at Lady Snellgrove's,"* said the girl. "Warens is there too."

There was a pause.

"Well then," said Birkin, in a fatherly, protective manner, "what do you intend to do?"

The girl paused sullenly. She hated the question.

"I don't intend to do anything," she replied. "I shall look for some sittings tomorrow."

"Who shall you go to?" asked Birkin.

"I shall go to Bentley's first. But I believe he's angwy with me for running away"

"That is from the Madonna?"

"Yes. And then if he doesn't want me, I know I can get work with Cardigan."

"Cardigan?"

"Lord Cardigan—he does photographs."

"Oh yes—chiffon and shoulders—"

"Yes. But he's awfully decent."

There was a pause.

"And what are you going to do about Julius?" he asked.

"Nothing," she said. "I shall just ignore him."

"You've done with him altogether?"

But she turned aside her face sullenly, and did not answer the question.

Another young man came hurrying up to the table.

"Hallo Birkin. *Hallo Pussum,* when did you come back?" he said eagerly.

"Today."

"Does Halliday know?"

"I don't know. I don't care either."

"Ha-ha! The wind still sits in that quarter,* does it? Do you mind if I come over to this table?"

"I'm talking to Wupert, do you mind?" she replied, coolly and yet appealingly, like a child.

"Open confession—good for the soul, eh?" said the young man, "Well,—so long."

And giving a sharp look at Birkin and at Gerald, the young man moved off, with a swing of his coat skirts.

All this time Gerald had been completely ignored. And yet he felt that the girl was physically aware of his proximity. He waited, listened, and tried to piece together the conversation.

"Are you staying at the flat?" the girl asked, of Birkin.

"For three days," replied Birkin. "And you?"

"I don't know yet. I can always go to Bertha's."

There was a silence.

Suddenly the girl turned to Gerald, and said, in a rather formal, polite voice, with the distant manner of a woman who accepts her position as an inferior, yet makes belief of equality and intimacy:

"Do you know London well?"

"I can hardly say," he laughed. "I've been up a good many times, but I was never in this place before?"

"You're not an artist, then?" she said, in a tone that placed him an outsider.

"No," he replied.

"He's a soldier, and an explorer, and a Napoleon of industry," said Birkin, giving Gerald his credentials for Bohemia.

"Are you a soldier?" asked the girl, with a cold, yet lively curiosity.

"No, I resigned my commission," said Gerald, "some years ago."

"He was in the last war," said Birkin.

"Were you really?" said the girl.

"And then he explored the Amazon," said Birkin, "and now he is ruling over coal-mines."

The girl looked at Gerald with steady, calm curiosity. He laughed, hearing himself described. He felt proud too, full of male strength. His blue, keen eyes were lit up with laughter, his ruddy face with its sharp fair hair was full of satisfaction, and glowing with life. He piqued her.

"How long are you staying?" she asked him.

"A day or two," he replied. "But there is no particular hurry."

Still she stared into his face with that slow, full gaze which was so curious and so exciting to him. He was acutely and delightfully conscious of himself, of his own attractiveness. He felt full of strength, able to give off life bountifully. And he was aware of her dark, hot-looking eyes upon him. She had beautiful eyes, dark, fully-opened, hot, naked in their looking at him. And on them there seemed to float a film of disintegration, a sort of misery and sullenness, like oil on water. She wore no hat, in the heated café, her loose, simple jumper* was strung on a string round her neck. But it was made of rich peach-coloured crème-de-chine, that hung heavily and softly from her young throat and her slender wrists. Her appearance was simple and complete, really beautiful, because of her regularity and form, her soft dark hair falling full and level on either side of her head, her straight, small, soft features, her slender neck, and the simple, rich-coloured smock hanging on her slender shoulders. She was very still, almost null, in her manner, apart and watchful, unsure.

She appealed to Gerald strongly. He felt a poignant, enjoyable pity for her, an instinctive protectiveness very near to cruelty. For she was a victim. He felt that she was in his power, and he was generous. So he was rich and potent.

They talked banalities for some time. Suddenly Birkin said:

"There's Julius!" and he half rose to his feet, motioning to the newcomer. The girl, with a curious, almost evil motion, looked round over her shoulder without moving her body. Gerald watched her dark, soft hair swing over her ears. He felt her watching intensely the man who was approaching, so he looked too. He saw a pale, full-built young man with rather long, solid fair hair hanging from under his black hat, moving cumbrously down the room, his face lit up with a smile at once naive and warm, and vapid. He approached straight towards Birkin, with a haste of welcome.

It was not till he was quite close that he perceived the girl. He recoiled, went pale, and said, in a high, squealing voice:

"Pussum, what are *you* doing here?"

The café looked up like animals when they hear a cry. Halliday hung motionless, almost imbecile. The girl only stared at him with a black look in which flared hatred and resentment, and a certain impotence.

"Why have you come back?" repeated Halliday, in the same high, hysterical voice. "I told you not to come back."

The girl did not answer, only stared in the same flaring, heavy fashion, straight at him, as he stood recoiled, as if for safety, against the next table.

"You know you wanted her to come back—come and sit down," said Birkin to him.

"No I didn't want her to come back, and I told her not to come back.— What have you come for, Pussum?"

"For nothing from *you*," she said in a heavy voice of resentment.

"Then why have you come back at *all*?" cried Halliday, his voice rising to a kind of squeal.

"She comes as she likes," said Birkin. "Are you going to sit down, or are you not?"

"No I won't sit down with Pussum," cried Halliday.

"I won't hurt you, you needn't be afraid," she said to him, very curtly, and yet with a sort of protectiveness towards him, in her voice.

Halliday came and sat at the table, putting his hand on his heart, and crying:

"Oh, it's given me such a turn. Pussum, I wish you wouldn't do these things. Why did you come back?"

"Not for anything from you," she repeated.

"You've said that before," he cried in a high voice.

She turned completely away from him, to Gerald Crich, whose eyes were shining with a subtle amusement.

"Were you ever vewy much afwaid of the savages?" she asked in her calm, dull, childish voice.

"No—never very much afraid. On the whole they're harmless—they are unformed, you can't feel really afraid of them. You know you can manage them."

"Do you weally? Aren't they very fierce?"

"Not very. There aren't many fierce things, I find. There aren't many things, neither people nor animals, that have enough spunk to be fierce."

"Aren't there really?" she said. "Oh, I thought savages were all so dangerous, they'd have your life before you could see them."

"Did you?" he laughed. "They are over-rated, savages. They're too much like other people, not exciting, after the first sight."

"Oh, it's not so very wonderfully brave then, to be an explorer?"

"No. It's more a question of hardships than of terrors."

"Oh! And weren't you *ever* afraid?"

"In my life? I don't know. Yes, I'm afraid of some things—of being shut up, locked up anywhere—or being fastened. I'm afraid of being bound hand and foot."

She looked at him steadily with her dark eyes, that rested on him and roused him pleasurably. It was rather delicious, to feel her drawing his self-revelations from him. She wanted to know. And her dark eyes seemed to be looking through into his secret being, bound upon him. He felt, she was compelled to him, she was fated to come into contact with him, must have the delight of touching him and exploring him. And this roused him vividly. Also he felt, how she wanted to relinquish herself into his hands, and be subject to him. She was so deliciously and appealingly humble, watching him, absorbed by him. It was not that she was interested in what he said; she was absorbed by his self-revelation, by *him*, she wanted the secret of him, the experience of him.

Gerald's face was lit up with an uncanny smile, full of light and rousedness, yet unconscious. He sat with his arms on the table, his sun-browned, rather blunt hands, that were animal and yet very shapely and attractive, pushed forward towards her. And they fascinated her. And she knew, she watched her own fascination.

Other men had come to the table, to talk with Birkin and Halliday. Gerald said, in a low voice, apart, to Pussum:

"Where have you come back from?"

"From the country," replied Pussum, in a very low, yet fully resonant voice. Her face closed hard. Continually she glanced at Halliday, and then a black flare came over her eyes. The heavy, fair young man ignored her completely; he was really afraid of her. For some moments she would be unaware of Gerald. He had not conquered her yet.

"And what has Halliday to do with it?" he asked, his voice still muted.

She would not answer for some seconds. Then she said, unwillingly:

"He made me go and live with him, and now he wants to throw me over. And yet he won't let me go to anybody else. He wants me to live hidden in the country. And then he says I persecute him, that he can't get rid of me."

"Doesn't know his own mind," said Gerald.

"He hasn't any mind, so he can't know it," she said. "He waits for what somebody tells him to do. He never does anything he wants to do himself—because he doesn't know what he wants. He's a perfect baby."

Gerald looked at Halliday for some moments, watching the soft, rather degenerate face of the young man. Its very softness was an attraction; it was a soft, warm, corrupt nature, into which one might plunge with gratification.

"But he has no hold over you, has he?" Gerald asked.

"You see he *made* me go and live with him, when I didn't want to," she replied. "He came and cried to me, tears, you never saw so many, saying *he couldn't* bear it unless I went back to him. And he wouldn't go away, he would have stayed for ever. He made me go back. Then every time he behaves in this fashion.—And now I'm going to have a baby, he wants to give me a hundred pounds and send me into the country, so that he would never see me nor hear of me again. But I'm not going to do it, after—"

A queer look came over Gerald's face.

"Are you going to have a child?" he asked incredulous. It seemed, to look at her, impossible, she was so young and so far in spirit from any childbearing.

She looked full into his face, and her dark, inchoate eyes had now a pleading look, and a look of a knowledge of evil, dark and indomitable. A flame ran secretly to his heart.

"Yes," she said. "Isn't it beastly?"

"Don't you want it?" he asked.

"I don't," she replied, emphatically.

"But—" he said, "how long have you known?"

"Ten weeks," she said.

All the time she kept her dark, inchoate eyes full upon him. He remained silent, thinking. Then, switching off and becoming cold, he asked, in a voice full of considerate kindness:

"Is there anything we can eat here? Is there anything you would like?"

"Yes," she said. "I should adore some oysters."

"All right," he said. "We'll have oysters."

And he beckoned to the waiter.

Halliday took no notice, until the little plate was set before her. Then suddenly he cried:

"Pussum, you can't eat oysters when you're drinking brandy."

"What has it got to do with you?" she asked.

"Nothing, nothing," he cried. "But you can't eat oysters when you're drinking brandy."

"I'm not drinking brandy," she replied, and she sprinkled the last drops of her liqueur over his face. He gave an odd squeal. She sat looking at him, as if indifferent.

"Pussum, why do you do that?" he cried in panic. He gave Gerald the impression that he was terrified of her, and that he loved his terror. He seemed to relish his own horror and hatred of her, turn it over and extract every flavour from it, in real relish. Gerald thought him a strange fool, and yet attractive.

"But Pussum," said another man, in a very small, quick, Eton voice, "you promised not to hurt him."

"I haven't hurt him," she answered.

"What will you drink?" the young man asked. He was dark, and smooth-skinned, and full of a stealthy vigour.

"I don't like porter, Maxim," she replied.

"You must ask for champagne," came the whispering, gentlemanly voice of the other.

Gerald suddenly realised that this was a hint to him.

"Shall we have champagne?" he asked, laughing.

"Yes please, dwy," she lisped, childishly.

Gerald watched her eating the oysters. She was delicate and finicking in her eating, her fingers were fine and seemed very sensitive in the tips, so she put her food apart with fine, small motions, she ate carefully, delicately. It pleased him very much to see her, and it irritated Birkin. They were all drinking champagne. Maxim, the prim young Russian with the smooth, warm-coloured face and black, oiled hair was the only one who seemed to be perfectly calm and sober. Birkin was white and abstract, unnatural, Gerald was smiling with a constant bright, amused, cold light in his eyes, leaning a little protectively towards the Pussum, who was very handsome and soft, like a velvet paw, and vainglorious now she was flushed with wine and with the excitement of men. Halliday looked foolish. One glass of wine was enough to make him drunk and giggling. Yet there was always a pleasant, warm naïveté about him, that made him attractive.

"I'm not afwaid of anything essept black-beetles," said the Pussum, looking up suddenly and staring with her black eyes, on which there seemed an unseeing film of flame, fully upon Gerald. He laughed good-naturedly. Her childish speech caressed his nerves, and her burning, filmed eyes, turned now full upon him, oblivious of all her antecedents, gave him a sort of licence.

"I'm not," she protested. "I'm not afraid of other things. But black-beetles—ugh!—" she shuddered convulsively, as if the very thought were too much to bear.

"Do you mean," said Gerald, with the punctiliousness of a slightly tipsy man, "that you are afraid of the sight of a black-beetle, or you are afraid of a black-beetle biting you, or doing you some harm?"

"Do they bite?" cried the girl.

"How perfectly loathsome," exclaimed Halliday.

"I don't know," replied Gerald, looking round the table. "Do black-beetles bite?—But that isn't the point. Are you afraid of their biting, or is it a metaphysical antipathy?"

The girl was looking full upon him all the time with inchoate eyes.

"Oh, I think they're beastly, they're horrid," she cried. "If I see one, it gives me the creeps all over. If one were to crawl on me, I'm *sure* I should die—I'm sure I should."

"I hope not," whispered the young Russian.

"I'm sure I should, Maxim," she asseverated.

"Then one won't crawl on you," said Gerald, protective and reassuring. It was evident her feeling was genuine.

"It's metaphysical, as Gerald says," Birkin stated.

There was a little pause of uneasiness. Nobody wanted Birkin to go on.

"And are you afraid of nothing else, Pussum?" asked the young Russian, in his quick, hushed, elegant manner.

"Not weally," she said. "I am afwaid of some things, but not weally the same. I'm not afwaid of *blood*."

"Not afwaid of blood!" exclaimed a young man with a thick, pale, jeering face, who had just come to the table and was drinking whisky.

The Pussum turned on him a sulky look of dislike, low and ugly.

"Aren't you really afraid of blud?" the other persisted, a sneer all over his face.

"No, I'm not," she retorted.

"Why, have you ever seen blood, except in a dentist's spittoon?" jeered the young man.

"I wasn't speaking to you," she replied rather superbly.

"You can answer me, can't you?" he said.

For reply, she suddenly jabbed a knife across his thick, pale hand. He started up with a vulgar curse,

"Shows what you are," said the Pussum in contempt.

"Curse you, you ugly bitch," said the young man, standing by the table and looking down at her with acrid malevolence.

"Stop that," said Gerald, in quick, instinctive command.

The young man stood looking down at her with sardonic contempt, a cowed, self-conscious look on his thick, pale face. The blood began to flow from his hand.

"Oh, how horrible, take it away!" squealed Halliday, turning green and averting his face.

"D'you feel ill?" asked the sardonic young man, in some concern. "Do you feel ill, Julius? G'arn, it's nothing man, don't give her the pleasure of letting her think she's performed a feat—don't give her the satisfaction, man,—it's just what she wants."

"Oh!" squealed Halliday.

"He's going to cat,* Maxim," said the Pussum warningly.

The suave young Russian rose and took Halliday by the arm, leading him away. Birkin, white and absent, looked on as if he were displeased. The wounded, sardonic young man moved away, ignoring his bleeding hand in the most conspicuous fashion.

"He's an awful coward, really," said the Pussum to Gerald. "He's got such an influence over Julius."

"Who is he?" asked Gerald.

"He's a Jew, really. I can't bear him."

"Well, he's quite unimportant. But what's wrong with Halliday?"

"Julius's the most awful coward you've ever seen, " she cried. "He always faints if I lift a knife—he's *tewwified* of me."

"Hm!" said Gerald.

"They're all afwaid of me," she said. "Only the Jew thinks he's going to show his courage. But he's the biggest coward of them all, really, because he's afwaid what people will think about him—and Julius doesn't care about that"

"They're a brave lot, altogether," said Gerald good-humouredly.

The Pussum looked at him with a slow, arch smile. She was very handsome, flushed, fine, subtle. Two little points of light glinted on Gerald's eyes.

"Why do they call you Pussum, because you're like a cat?" he asked her.

"I expect so," she said.

The smile grew more intense on his face.

"You are, rather;—or a young, female panther."

"Oh god, Gerald!" said Birkin, in some disgust.

They both looked uneasily at Birkin.

"You're silent tonight, Wupert," she said to him, with a slight insolence, being safe with the other man.

Halliday was coming back, looking forlorn and sick.

"Pussum," he said, "I wish you wouldn't do these things—Oh!" he sank in his chair with a groan.

"You'd better go home," she said to him.

"I *will* go home," he said. "But won't you all come along. Won't you come round to the flat?" he said to Gerald. "I should be so glad if you would. Do—that'll be splendid.—I say?" He looked round for a waiter. "Get me a taxi." Then he groaned again. "Oh I do feel—perfectly ghastly! Pussum, you see what you do to me."

"Then why are you such an idiot," she said with sullen calm.

"But I'm *not* an idiot! Oh, how awful! Do come, everybody, it will be *so* splendid. Pussum, you are coming.—What?—Oh but you *must* come, yes, you must. What?—Oh, my dear girl, don't make a fuss now, I feel perfectly—Oh, it's so ghastly—Hc!-er!—Oh!"

"You know you can't drink," she said to him, coldly.

"I tell you it isn't drink—it's your disgusting behaviour, Pussum, it's nothing else.—Oh, how awful! Libidnikov, *do* let us go."

"He's only drunk one glass—only one glass," came the rapid, hushed voice of the young Russian.

They all moved off to the door. The girl kept near to Gerald, and seemed to be at one in her motion with him. He was aware of this too, and filled with pride that his motion held good for two. He held her in the hollow of his will, and she was soft, secret, invisible in her nestling there.

They crowded five of them into the taxi-cab. Halliday lurched in first, and dropped into his seat against the other window. Then the Pussum took her place, and Gerald sat next to her. They heard the young

Russian giving orders to the driver, then they were all seated in the dark, crowded close together, Halliday groaning and leaning out of the window. They felt the swift, muffled motion of the car.

The Pussum sat near to Gerald, and she seemed to become soft, subtly to infuse herself into his side, as if she were passing into him in a warm, subtle flow. Her being suffused into his veins like a delirium, a lovely, intoxicating, maddening heat. Meanwhile her voice sounded out reedy and nonchalant, as she talked indifferently with Birkin and with Maxim. Between her and Gerald was this silence and this hot, thrilling transfusion in the darkness. Then she found his hand, and grasped it in her own firm, small clasp. It was so utterly secret, and yet such a naked statement, that rapid vibrations ran through his blood and over his brain, he was no longer responsible. Still her voice rang on like a bell, just tinged with a tone of mockery. And as she swung her head, her fine mane of hair just swept his face, and all his nerves were on fire, as with a subtle friction of electricity.

They arrived at a large block of buildings, went up in a lift, and presently a door was being opened for them by a Hindu. Gerald looked in surprise, wondering if he were a gentleman, one of the Hindus down from Oxford, perhaps. But no, he was the man-servant.

"Make tea, Shahid," said Halliday.

"There is a room for me?" said Birkin.

To both of which questions the man grinned, and murmured.

He made Gerald uneasy, because, being tall and slender and reticent, he looked like a gentleman.

"Who is your servant?" he asked of Halliday. "He looks very swell."

"Oh yes—that's because he's dressed in another man's clothes. He's anything but a swell, really. We found him in the road, starving. So I took him here, and another man gave him clothes. He's anything but what he seems to be—his only advantage is that he can't speak English and can't understand it, so he's perfectly safe."

"He's very dirty, " said the young Russian swiftly and silently.

Directly the man appeared in the doorway.

"What is it?" said Halliday.

The Hindu grinned, and murmured shyly:

"Want to speak to master."

Gerald watched curiously. The fellow in the doorway was good-looking and clean-limbed, his bearing was calm, he looked elegant, aristocratic. Yet he was half a savage, grinning foolishly. Halliday went out into the corridor to speak with him.

"What?" they heard his voice. "What? What do you say? Tell me again. What? Want money? Want *more* money? But what do you want money for?"

There was the confused sound of the Hindu's talking, then Halliday appeared in the room, smiling also foolishly, and saying:

"He says he wants money to buy underclothing. Can anybody lend me a shilling? Oh thanks, a shilling will do to buy all the underclothes he wants." He took the money from Gerald and went out into the passage again, where they heard him saying, "You can't want more money, you had three and six yesterday. You mustn't ask for any more. Bring the tea in quickly."

Gerald looked round the room. It was an ordinary London sitting-room in a flat, evidently taken furnished, rather common and ugly. But there were several negro statues, wood-carvings from West Africa, strange and disturbing, the carved negroes looked almost like the foetus of a human being. One was of a woman sitting naked in a strange posture, and looking tortured, her abdomen stuck out. The young Russian explained that she was sitting in childbirth, clutching the ends of the band that hung from her neck, one in each hand, so that she could bear down, and help labour. The strange, transfixed, rudimentary face of the woman again reminded Gerald of a foetus, it was also rather wonderful, conveying the suggestion of the extreme of physical sensation, beyond the limits of mental consciousness.

"Aren't they rather obscene?" he asked.

"I don't know," murmured the other rapidly. "I don't understand the obscene. I think they are very fine."

Gerald turned away. There were one or two new pictures in the room, in the Futurist manner; there was a large piano. And these, with some ordinary London lodging-house furniture of the better sort, completed the whole.

The Pussum had taken off her hat and coat, and was seated on the sofa. She was evidently quite at home in the house, but uncertain, suspended. She did not quite know her position. Her alliance for the time being was with Gerald, and she did not know how far this was understood by any of the men. She was considering how she should carry off the situation. She was determined to have her experience of Gerald. Now, at this eleventh hour, she was not to be balked. Her face was flushed as with battle, her eye was brooding but confident.

The man came in with tea and a bottle of Kümmel. He set the tray on a little table before the couch.

"Pussum," said Halliday, "pour out the tea."

She did not move.

"Won't you do it?" Halliday repeated, in a state of nervous apprehension.

"I've not come back here as it was before, " she said. "I only came because the others wanted me to, not for your sake."

"My dear Pussum, you know you are your own mistress. I don't want you to do anything but use the flat for your own convenience—you know it, I've told you ever so many times."

She did not reply, but silently, reservedly reached for the tea-pot. They all sat round and drank tea. Gerald could feel the physical connection between him and her so strongly, as she sat there quiet and withheld, that another set of conditions altogether had come to pass. Her silence and her immutability perplexed him. *How* was he going to come to her? And yet he felt it quite inevitable. He trusted to her completely. His perplexity was only superficial, new conditions reigned, the old were surpassed; here one did as one liked, no matter what it was.

Birkin rose. It was nearly one o'clock.

"I'm going to bed," he said. "Gerald, I'll ring you up in the morning at your place—or you ring me up here."

"Right," said Gerald, and Birkin went out.

When he was well gone, Halliday said in a stimulated voice, to Gerald:

"I say, won't you stay here—oh do!"

"You can't put everybody up," said Gerald.

"Oh but I can, perfectly—there are three more beds besides mine—do stay, won't you. Everything is quite ready—there is always somebody here—I always put people up—I love it above all things."

"But there are only two rooms," said the Pussum, in a cold, hostile voice.

"I know there are only two rooms," said Halliday, in his odd, high way of speaking. "But what does that matter?"

He was smiling rather foolishly, and he spoke eagerly, with an insinuating determination.

"Julius and I will share one room," said the Russian in his discreet, precise voice. Halliday and he were friends since Eton.

"It's very simple," said Gerald, rising and pressing back his arms, stretching himself. Then he went again to look at one of the pictures.

The Pussum rose. She gave a black look at Halliday, black and deadly, which brought the rather foolish, pleased smile to that young man's face. Then she went out of the room, with a cold Good-night to them all generally.

There was a brief interval, they heard a door close, then Maxim said, in his small voice:

"That's all right."

He looked significantly at Gerald, and said again, with a slight nod:

"That's all right—she's all right."

Gerald looked at his smooth, ruddy, comely face, and at his strange, significant eyes, and it seemed as if the voice of the young Russian, so small and perfect, sounded in the blood rather than in the air.

"*I'm* all right then," said Gerald.

"Yes! Yes! You're all right," said the Russian.

Halliday continued to smile, and to say nothing.

Suddenly the Pussum appeared again in the door, her small, childish face looking sullen and vindictive.

"I know you want to catch me out," came her cold, rather resonant voice. "But I don't care, I don't care how much you catch me out."

She turned and was gone again. She had been wearing a loose dressing-gown of purple silk, tied round her waist. She looked so small and childish and innocent, almost pitiful. And yet the black looks of her eyes made even Gerald feel uncomfortable, though they stimulated his nerves.

The men lit another cigarette and talked casually.

In the morning Gerald woke late. He had slept heavily. Pussum was still asleep, sleeping childishly and pathetically. There was something small and curled up and defenceless about her, that roused an unsatisfied flame of passion in the young man's blood, a devouring, avid pity. He looked at her again. But it would be too cruel to wake her. He subdued himself, and went away.

Hearing voices coming from the sitting-room, Halliday talking to Libidnikov, he went to the door and glanced in, knowing he might go about in this bachelor establishment in his trousers and shirt.

To his surprise he saw the two young men by the fire, stark naked. Halliday looked up, rather pleased.

"Good-morning," he said. "Oh—did you want towels?"

And stark naked, he went out into the hall, striding a strange, white figure between the unliving furniture. He came back with the towels, and took his former position, crouching seated before the fire on the fender.

"Don't you love to feel the fire on your skin?" he said.

"It *is* rather pleasant," said Gerald.

"How perfectly splendid it must be to be in a climate where one could do without clothing altogether," said Halliday.

"Yes," said Gerald, "if there weren't so many things that sting and bite."

"That's a disadvantage," murmured Maxim.

Gerald looked at him, and with a slight revulsion saw the human animal, golden skinned and bare, somehow trivial. Halliday was different. He had a rather heavy, slack, broken beauty, white and firm. He was like a Christ in a Pieta. The animal was not there at all, only the heavy, broken beauty. And Gerald realised how Halliday's eyes were beautiful too, so blue and warm and confused, broken also in their expression. The fireglow fell on his heavy, rather bowed shoulders, he sat slackly crouched on the fender, his face was uplifted, degenerate, perhaps slightly imbecile, and yet with a moving beauty of its own.

"Of course," said Maxim, "you've been in hot countries where the people go about naked."

"Oh really!" exclaimed Halliday. "Where?"

"South America—Amazon," said Gerald.

"Oh but how perfectly splendid! It's one of the things I want most to do—to live from day to day without *ever* putting on any sort of clothing whatever. If I could do that, I should feel I had lived."

"But why?" said Gerald. "I can't see that it makes so much difference."

"Oh, I think it would be perfectly splendid. I'm sure life would be entirely another thing—entirely different, and perfectly wonderful."

"But why?" asked Gerald. "Why should it?"

"Oh—one would *feel* things instead of merely looking at them. I should feel the air move against me, and feel the things I touched, instead of having only to look at them. I'm sure life is all wrong because it has become much too visual—we can neither hear nor feel nor understand, we can only see. I'm sure that is entirely wrong."

"Yes, that is true, that is true," said the Russian.

Gerald glanced at him, and saw him, his suave, golden coloured body with the black hair growing fine and freely, like tendrils, and his limbs made for activity. He was so healthy and well-made, why had he no beauty, why was his body so insignificant, meaningless? Why should Gerald even dislike it, why did it seem to him to detract from the dignity of the human being. A million more or less of these living bodies makes no matter, thought Gerald, it doesn't matter whether they exist or don't exist, they are merely insignificant.

It was a new thought to him. He had thought every civilised human body, every civilised life significant.

Birkin suddenly appeared in the doorway, also in a state of pure nudity, towel and sleeping suit over his arm. He was very narrow and white, like a hieroglyph.

"There's the bath-room now, if you want it," he said generally, and was going away again, when Gerald called:

"I say, Rupert!"

"What?" The long, narrow white figure appeared again, a presence in the room, unsubstantial.

"What do you think of that figure there? I want to know," Gerald asked.

Birkin, white and thin and long, went over to the carved figure of the negro woman in labour. Her nude, protuberant body, crouched in a strange, clutching posture, her hands gripping the ends of the band, above her breast.

"It's real art," said Birkin.

"Very beautiful, it's very beautiful," said the Russian.

They all drew near to look. Gerald looked at the group of naked men, the Russian golden and meaningless, Halliday tall and heavily, brokenly beautiful, Birkin very white and clear, like an abstraction even in physique, as he looked closely at the carven woman. Strangely elated, Gerald also lifted his eyes to the face of the wooden figure. And his heart contracted.

He saw vividly, with his spirit, the grey, forward-stretching face of the negro woman, African and tense, abstracted in utter physical stress. It was a terrible face, void, peaked, abstracted almost into meaninglessness by the weight of sensation beneath.

"Why is it art?" Gerald asked, shocked, resentful.

"Because it conveys a complete truth," said Birkin. "It contains the whole truth of that state, absolutely and forever."

"But you can't call it high art," said Gerald.

"Oh yes. There are centuries and hundreds of centuries of development in a straight line, behind that carving; it is an awful pitch of culture, of a definite sort."

"What culture?" Gerald asked, in opposition. He hated the gross African thing.

"Pure culture in sensation, culture in the physical consciousness, terrible, really *ultimate* physical consciousness, mindless, utterly sensual. It is so sensual as to be final, supreme."

But Gerald resented all this. To him the African figure was low and gross and to be ignored, whilst Birkin's figure, white and thin and abstract, gave it all the lie. He stood near the naked man, and the naked carven piece of wood was like dirt beside a jet of reality, to him.

"You like the wrong things, Rupert," he said.

"Oh, I want something else than all this—" Birkin replied, moving away, seeming to pass from them.

When Gerald went back to his room from the bath, he also carried his clothes. It seemed bad form in this house, not to go about naked. And after all, it was rather nice, there *was* a real simplicity.

The Pussum lay in her bed, motionless, her round, dark eyes like black, unhappy pools. He could only see the black, bottomless pools of her eyes. Perhaps she suffered. The sensation of her inchoate suffering roused the old sharp flame in him, a mordant pity, a passion almost exultant.

"You are awake now," he said to her.

"What time is it?" came her muted voice.

She seemed to flow back, almost like liquid, from his approach, to sink helplessly away from him. Her inchoate look of a violated slave, whose fulfilment lies in her further and further violation, made his nerves quiver with acutely desirable sensation. After all, his was the only will, she was the passive substance of his will. He tingled with the subtle, biting sensation. And then he knew, he must go away from her, there must be pure separation between them.

It was a quiet and ordinary breakfast, the four men all looking very clean and bathed. Gerald and the Russian were both correct and *comme il faut* in appearance and manner, Birkin was gaunt and sick, and looked a failure in his attempt to be a properly dressed man, like Gerald and Maxim. Halliday wore tweeds and a green flannel shirt, and a rag of a tie, which was just right for him. The Hindu brought in a great deal of soft toast, and looked exactly the same as he had looked the night before, statically the same.

At the end of the breakfast the Pussum appeared, in a purple silk wrap with a bright red sash. She had recovered herself somewhat, but was mute and lifeless still. It was a torment to her when anybody spoke to her. Her face was like a small, fine mask, sinister too, masked with unwilling suffering. It was almost midday. Gerald rose and went away to his business, glad to get out of it all. But he had not finished. He was coming back again at evening, they were all dining together, and he had booked seats for the party, excepting Birkin, at a music-hall.

At night they came back to the flat very late again, again rather flushed with drink. Again the man-servant—who invariably disappeared between the hours of ten and twelve at night—came in silently and inscrutably with tea, bending in a slow, strange, leopard-like fashion to put the tray softly on the table. His face was immutable, aristocratic-looking, tinged slightly with grey under the skin; he was young and good-looking. But Birkin felt a slight sickness, looking at him, and feeling the slight greyness an ash of corruption, the aristocratic inscrutability of expression a nauseating, bestial stupidity.

Again they talked cordially and rousedly together. But already a certain friability was coming over the party, Birkin was mad with irritation, Halliday was turning in an insane hatred against Gerald, the Pussum was becoming hard and cold, like a blunt knife, and Halliday was laying himself out to her. And her will, ultimately, was to capture Halliday, to have complete power over him.

In the morning they all stalked and lounged about naked again. But Gerald could feel a strange hostility to himself, in the air. It roused his obstinacy, and he stood up against it. The result was a nasty and really insane scene with Halliday in the evening. Halliday turned with hideous, imbecile animosity, upon Gerald, in the Café. There was a scene. Gerald was on the point of smashing in Halliday's face; when he was filled with sudden disgust and indifference, and he went away, leaving Halliday in a foolish state of gloating triumph, the Pussum hard and established, and Maxim standing clear. Birkin was absent, he had gone out of town again.

Gerald was piqued because he had left without giving the Pussum money. It was true, she did not care whether he gave her money or not, and he knew it. But she would have been glad of ten pounds, and he would have been *very* glad to give them to her. Now he felt in a false position. He went away chewing his lips to get at the ends of his short clipped moustache. He knew the Pussum was merely glad to be rid of him. She had got her Halliday, whom she wanted. She wanted him completely in her power. Then she would marry him. She wanted to marry him. She had set her will on marrying Halliday. She never wanted to hear of Gerald again; unless, perhaps, she were in difficulty. Because after all, Gerald was what she called a man, and these others, Halliday, Libidnikov, Birkin, the whole Bohemian set, they were only half men. But it was half men she wanted. She felt sure of herself with them. The real men, like Gerald, put her in her place too much.

Still, she liked Gerald, she really respected him. She had managed to get his address, so that she could appeal to him in time of stress. She knew he wanted to give her money. She would write to him on that inevitable rainy day.

3

B READALBY WAS A GEORGIAN HOUSE with Corinthian pillars, standing among the softer, greener hills of Derbyshire, not far from Cromford. In front, it looked over a lawn, over a few trees, down to a string of fish-ponds in the hollow of the silent park. At the back were trees, among which were to be found the stables, and the big kitchen garden, behind which was a wood.

It was a very quiet place, some miles from the high-road, back from the Derwent valley, outside the show scenery. Silent and forsaken, the golden stucco showed between the trees, the house-front looked down the park, unchanged and unchanging.

Of late, however, Hermione had lived a good deal at the house. She had turned away from London, away from Oxford, towards the silence of the country. Her father was mostly absent, abroad, she was either alone in the house, with her visitors, of whom there were always several, or there was with her brother, a bachelor, and a liberal member of Parliament. He always came down when the House was not sitting, seemed always to be present in Breadalby, although he was most conscientious in his attendance to duty.

The summer was just coming in when Ursula and Gudrun went to stay the second time with Hermione. Coming along in the car, after they had entered the park, they looked across the dip, where the fish-ponds lay in silence, at the pillared front of the house, sunny and small like an old English aquatint, on the brow of the green hill, against the trees. There were small figures on the green lawn, women in lavender and yellow moving to the shade of the enormous, beautifully balanced ilex tree.

"Isn't it complete!" said Gudrun. "It is as final as an old aquatint." She spoke with some resentment in her voice, as if she were captivated unwillingly, as if she must admire against her will.

"Do you love it?" asked Ursula.

"I don't *love* it, but in its way, I think it is perfect."

The motor car ran down the hill and up again in one breath, and they were curving up to the side door. A parlour-maid appeared, and then Hermione, coming forward with her pale face lifted, and her hands outstretched, advancing straight to the new-comers, her voice singing:

"Here you are—I'm so glad to see you—" she kissed Gudrun—"—so glad to see you—" she kissed Ursula and remained with her arm round her. "Are you very tired?"

"Not at all tired," said Ursula.

"Are you tired, Gudrun?"

"Not at all, thanks," said Gudrun.

"No—" drawled Hermione. And she stood and looked at them. The two girls were embarrassed because she would not move into the house, but must have her little scene of welcome there on the path. The servants waited.

"Come in," said Hermione at last, having fully taken in the pair of them. Gudrun was the more beautiful and attractive, she had decided again, Ursula was more physical, more womanly. She admired Gudrun's dress more. It was of green poplin, with a loose coat above it, of broad, dark-green and dark-brown stripes. The hat was of a pale, greenish straw, the colour of new hay, and it had a plaited ribbon of black and

orange, the stockings were dark green, the shoes black. It was a good
get-up, at once fashionable and completely individual. Ursula, in grey
and black, was more ordinary, though she also looked well.

Hermione herself wore a dress of prune-coloured silk, with coral
beads and coral coloured stockings. But her dress was both shabby and
soiled, even rather dirty. Ursula thought she looked sordid, her pallor
looked unclean.

"You would like to see your rooms now, wouldn't you! Come along."

Ursula was glad when she could be left alone in her room. Hermione
lingered so long, made such an intimacy. She stood so near to one, pressing
herself physically upon one, in a way that was most embarrassing and
trying. She seemed to clog one's workings.

Lunch was served on the lawn, under the great tree, whose thick,
plumy-looking foliage-masses came down close to the grass. There
were present a young Italian woman, slight and fashionable, a young,
athletic-looking Miss Bradley, a learned, dry Baronet of fifty, who was
always making witticisms and laughing at them heartily in a harsh,
horse-laugh, there was Rupert Birkin, and then two children with their
governess, a blonde slip of a Fräulein.

The food was very good, that was one thing. Gudrun, critical of
everything, gave it her full approval. Ursula loved the situation, the long
white table by the ilex tree, the scent of new sunshine, the little vision
of the leafy park, with far-off deer feeding peacefully. There seemed a
magic circle drawn about the place, shutting out the present, enclosing
the delightful, precious past, trees and deer and silence, like a dream.

But in spirit she was unhappy. The talk went on like a rattle of small
artillery, always slightly sententious, with a sententiousness that was
only emphasised by the continual crackling of a witticism, the continual
spatter of verbal jest, designed to give a tone of flippancy to a stream of
conversation that was all critical and general, a canal of conversation
rather than a stream.

The whole attitude was mental and very wearying. Only the elderly
sociologist, whose mental fibre was so tough as to be insentient, seemed
to be thoroughly happy. Birkin was down in the mouth. Hermione
seemed, with amazing persistence, to wish to ridicule him and make him
look ignominious in the eyes of everybody. And it was surprising, how
she seemed to succeed, how helpless he seemed against her. He looked
insignificant. Ursula and Gudrun, both very unused, were mostly silent,

listening to the slow, rhapsodic sing-song of Hermione, or the verbal sallies of Sir Joshua, or the prattle of Fräulein, or the responses of the other two women.

Lunch was over, coffee was brought out on to the grass, the party left the table and sat about in lounge chairs, in the shade or in the sunshine as they wished. Fräulein departed with the children, Hermione took up her embroidery, the little contessa took a book, Miss Bradley was weaving a basket out of fine grass, and there they all were on the lawn, in the early summer afternoon, working leisurely and spattering with half-intellectual, general talk.

Suddenly there was the sound of the brakes and the shutting off of a motor-car.

"There's Salsie!" sang Hermione, in her slow, amusing sing-song. And laying down her work, she rose slowly, and slowly passed over the lawn, round the bushes, out of sight.

"Who is it?" asked Gudrun.

"Mr Roddice—Miss Roddice's brother—at least, I suppose it's he," said Sir Joshua.

"Salsie, yes, it is her brother," said the little contessa, lifting her head for a moment from her book, and speaking as if to give information, in her slightly deepened, guttural English.

They all waited. And then, round the bushes came the tall form of Alexander Roddice, striding romantically like a Meredith hero who remembers Disraeli.* He was cordial with everybody, he was at once a host, with an easy, off-hand hospitality that was quite formal and mannered. He had just come down from London, from the House. At once the atmosphere of the House of Commons made itself felt over the lawn: the Home Secretary had said such and such a thing, and he, Roddice, on the other hand, thought such and such a thing, and had said so-and-so to the P. M.

Now Hermione came round the bushes with Gerald Crich. He had come along with Alexander. Gerald was presented to everybody, was kept by Hermione for a few moments in full view, then he was led away, still by Hermione. He was evidently her guest of the moment, he might be called the P.G., as Alexander Roddice called the Prime Minister the P.M.

There had been a split in the Cabinet; the minister for education had resigned owing to adverse criticism. This started a conversation on education.

"Of course," said Hermione, lifting her face like a rhapsodist, "there *can* be no reason, no *excuse* for education, except the pleasure and beauty of knowledge in itself." She seemed to rumble and ruminate with subterranean thoughts for a minute, then she proceeded: "Vocational education *isn't* education, it is the end of education."

Gerald, on the brink of a discussion, sniffed the air with delight and prepared for action.

"Not necessarily," he said. "But isn't education really like gymnastics, isn't the end of education the production of a well-trained, vigorous, energetic mind?"

"Just as athletics produce a healthy body, ready for anything," cried Miss Bradley, in hearty accord.

Gudrun looked at her in silent loathing.

"Well—" rumbled Hermione, "I don't know. To me the pleasure of knowing is *so* great, so *wonderful*—nothing has meant so much to me in all life, as certain knowledge—no, I am sure—nothing."

"What knowledge, for example, Hermione?" asked Alexander, with smart, statesmanlike interest.

Hermione lifted her face and rumbled—

"m- m- m- I don't know.— — —But one thing was the stars, when I really understood something about the stars. One feels so *uplifted*, so *unbounded*— — — — —"

Birking looked at her in a white fury.

"What do you want to feel unbounded for?" he shouted. "You are bounded tight enough."

Hermione recoiled suddenly, shocked.

"Yes, but one does have that limitless feeling," said Gerald. "It's like getting on top of the mountain and seeing the Pacific."

"Silent upon a peak in Dariayn,"* murmured the Italian, lifting her face for a moment from her book.

"Not necessarily in Darien," said Gerald, stiffly, while Ursula began to laugh.

Hermione waited for the dust to settle, and then she said, untouched:

"Yes, it is the greatest thing in life—*to know*. It is really to be happy, to be *free*."

"Knowledge is, of course, liberty," said Malleson.

"Bottled," said Birkin, looking at the dry, stiff little body of the Baronet. Immediately Gudrun saw the famous sociologist as a bottle, containing a solution of liberty. That pleased her immensely. Sir Joshua was labelled and placed forever in her mind.

"What does that mean, Rupert?" sang Hermione, in a calm snub.

"You can only have knowledge, strictly," he replied, "of things past. It's like tasting all the essence of last summer in the bottled goose-berries."

"Can one have knowledge only of the past?" asked the baronet, pointedly. "Could we call our knowledge of the laws of gravitation, for instance, knowledge of the past?"

"Yes," said Birkin.

"There is a most beautiful thing in my book," suddenly piped the little Italian woman. "It says the man came to the door and threw his eyes down the street."*

There was a general laugh in the company. Miss Bradley went and looked over the shoulder of the contessa.

"See!" said the contessa.

"Bazarov came to the door and threw his eyes hurriedly down the street," she read.

Again there was a loud laugh, the most startling of which was the Baronet's, which rattled out like a clatter of falling stones.

"What is the book?" asked Alexander, promptly.

"Fathers and Sons, by Turgenev," said the little foreigner, pronouncing every syllable distinctly. She looked at the cover, to verify herself.

"An old American edition," said Birkin.

"Ha! of course—translated from the French," said Alexander, with a fine declamatory voice. "Bazarov ouvra la porte et jeta les yeux dans la rue."

He looked brightly round the company.

"I wonder what the 'hurriedly' was," said Ursula.

They all began to guess.

And then, to the amazement of everybody, the maid came hurrying with a large tea-tray. The afternoon had passed so swiftly.

After tea, they were all gathered for a walk.

"Would you like to come for a walk?" said Hermione to each of them, one by one. And they all said yes, feeling somehow like prisoners marshalled for exercise. Birkin only refused.

"Will you come for a walk, Rupert?"

"No, Hermione."

"Are you *sure*?"

"Quite sure."

There was a second's hesitation.

"And why not?" sang Hermione's question. It made her blood run sharp, to be thwarted in even so trifling a matter. She intended them all to walk with her in the park.

"Because I don't like trooping off in a gang," he said.

Her voice rumbled in her throat for a moment. Then she said, with a curious stray calm:

"Then we'll leave a little boy behind, if he's sulky."

And she looked really gay, while she insulted him. But her impudence made him stiff with indignation.

She trailed off to the rest of the company, only turning to wave her handkerchief to him, and to chuckle with laughter, singing out:

"Goodbye, goodbye little boy."

"Goodbye impudent hag," he said to himself.

They all went through the park. Hermione wanted to show them the wild daffodils on a little slope. "This way, this way," sang her leisurely voice at intervals. And they had all to come this way. The daffodils were pretty, but who could see them? Ursula was stiff all over with resentment by this time, resentment of the whole atmosphere. Gudrun, static and objective, watched and registered everything.

They looked at the shy deer, and Hermione talked to the stag, as if he too were a boy she wanted to wheedle and fondle. They trailed home by the fish-ponds, and Hermione told them about the quarrel of two male swans, who had striven for the love of the one lady. She chuckled and laughed as she told how the ousted lover had sat with his head buried under his wing, on the gravel.

When they arrived back at the house, Hermione stood on the lawn and sang out, in a strange, small, high voice that carried very far:

"Rupert! Rupert!" The first syllable was high and slow, the second dropped down. "Roo-o-opert."

But there was no answer. A maid appeared.

"Where is Mr Birkin, Alice?" asked the mild, straying voice of Hermione. But under the straying voice, what a persistent, almost insane *will*!

"I think he's in his room, my lady."

"Is he."

Hermione went slowly up the stairs, along the corridor, singing out in her high, small call:

"Ru-oo-pert! Ru-oo-pert!"

She came to his door, and tapped, still crying; "Roo-pert."

"Yes," sounded his voice at last.

"What are you doing?"

The question was mild and curious.

There was no answer. Then he opened the door.

"We've come back," said Hermione. "The daffodils are *so* beautiful."

"Yes," he said, "I've seen them."

She looked at him with her long, slow, impassive look, along her cheeks.

"Have you," she echoed. And she remained looking at him. She was stimulated above all things by this conflict with him, when he was like a sulky boy, helpless, and she had him safe at Breadalby. But underneath she knew the split was coming, and her hatred of him was subconscious and intense.

"What were you doing?" she reiterated, in her mild, indifferent tone. He did not answer, and she made her way, almost unconsciously, into his room. He had taken a Chinese drawing of geese from the boudoir, and was copying it.

"You are copying the drawing," she said, standing near the table and looking down at his work. "Yes—How beautifully you do it! You like it very much, don't you?"

"It's a marvellous drawing," he said.

"Is it? I'm so glad you like it, because I've always been fond of it.—The Chinese ambassador gave it me."

"I know," he said.

"But what makes you copy it?" she asked, casual and sing-song.

"To know it," he replied. "You know more about China copying this, than reading books."

"And what do you know?"

He was silent, he did not want to be questioned. And yet her abiding there compelled him.

"I know the way they apprehend things," he said, "—the hot, stinging centrality of a goose in the cold flux of mud and of water—the curious stinging heat of a goose's blood, extracted from the cold corruption of mud, balanced on an unstable cold flux of water."

Hermione looked at him along her narrow, pallid cheeks. Her eyes were strange and drugged, heavy under their heavy, dropping lids. Her thin bosom shrugged convulsively. He stared back at her, hard and unchanging. With another strange, sick convulsion, she turned away, as if she were sick, could feel dissolution setting-in in her body.

"Yes," she said, as if she did not know what she were saying. "Yes." and she swallowed, and tried to regain her mind. But she could not, she was witless, decentralised. Use all her will as she might, she could not recover. She suffered the ghastliness of dissolution, broken and gone in a horrible corruption. And he stood and looked at her unmoved. She strayed out, pallid and horrible like a ghost, like one come from the grave, belonging to the wet underearth. And she was gone like a corpse, that has no presence, no connection. He remained hard and vindictive.

Hermione came down to dinner strange and sepulchral, her eyes heavy and full of sepulchral darkness, strength. She had put on a dress of stiff old greenish brocade, that fitted tight and made her look tall and rather terrible, ghastly. In the gay light of the drawing-room she was uncanny and oppressive. But seated in the half light of the dining-room, sitting stiffly before the shaded candles on the table, she seemed a power, a presence. She listened and attended with a drugged attention.

The party was gay and festive in appearance, everybody had put on evening dress except Birkin and Joshua Malleson. The little Italian contessa wore orange crape, Gudrun was in emerald green, Ursula had a thin silk the colour of red sea-weed, Miss Bradley was in a coloured silk all zig-zags, Fräulein wore pale blue. It gave Hermione a sudden convulsive sensation of pleasure, to see these brilliant colours under the candle-light. She was aware of the talk going on, ceaselessly, Joshua's voice dominating; of the ceaseless pitter-patter of women's light laughter and responses; of the brilliant colours and the white table and the shadow above and below; and she seemed in a swoon of gratification, convulsed with pleasure, and yet sick, like a *revenant*. She took very little part in the conversation, yet she heard it all, it was all hers.

They all went together into the drawing-room, as if they were one family, easily, without any attention to ceremony. Fräulein handed the coffee, everybody smoked cigarettes, or else long warden pipes* of white clay, of which a sheaf was provided.

"Wiill you smooke?—cigarettes or pipe?" asked Fräulein prettily.

There was a circle of people, Sir Joshua with his eighteenth-century appearance, Gerald the amused, handsome young Englishman, Alexander tall and of the handsome, democratic and fervent type, Hermione strange like a priestess, and the women like flowers, all dutifully smoking their long white pipes, and sitting in a half-moon in the comfortable, soft-lighted drawing-room, round the logs that flickered on the marble hearth.

The talk was very often political or sociological, and interesting, curiously anarchistic. There was an accumulation of powerful mental force in the room, powerful and destructive. Everything seemed to be thrown into the melting pot, and it seemed to Ursula they were all witches, helping the pot to bubble. There was an elation and a satisfaction in it all, but it was cruelly exhausting for the new-comers, this ruthless mental pressure, this powerful, consuming, destructive mentality that emanated from Joshua and Hermione and Birkin, and dominated the rest.

But a sickness, a fearful nausea gathered possession of Hermione. There was a lull in the talk, as it was arrested by her unconscious but all-powerful will.

"Salsie, won't you play something?" said Hermione, breaking off completely. "Won't somebody dance? Gudrun, you will dance, won't you? I wish you would. Anche tu, Palestra, ballerai?—si, per piacere.* You too, Ursula."

Hermione rose and slowly pulled the gold-embroidered band that hung by the mantel, clinging to it for a moment, then releasing it suddenly. Like a priestess she looked, unconscious, sunk in a heavy half-trance. A servant came, and soon reappeared with armfuls of silk robes and shawls and scarves, mostly oriental, things that Hermione, with her love for beautiful extravagant dress, had collected gradually.

"The three women will dance together," she said.

"What shall it be?" asked Alexander, rising briskly.

"Vergine Delle Rocche,"* said the contessa at once.

"They are so languid," said Ursula.

"The three witches from Macbeth," suggested Fräulein usefully.

It was finally decided to do Naomi and Ruth and Orpah.* Ursula was Naomi, Gudrun was Ruth, the contessa was Orpah. The idea was to make a little ballet, in the style of the Russian Ballet of Pavlova and Nijinsky.*

The contessa was ready first. Alexander went to the piano, a space was cleared, Orpah, in beautiful oriental clothes, began slowly to dance the death of her husband. Then Ruth came, and they wept together, and lamented, then Naomi came to comfort them. It was all done in dumb show, the women danced their emotion in gesture and motion. The little drama went on for a quarter of an hour.

Ursula was beautiful as Naomi. All her men were dead, it remained to her only to stand alone in sorrow, demanding nothing. Ruth, woman-loving, loved her. Orpah, a vivid, sensational, subtle widow, would go back to the former life, a repetition. The interplay between the women was real and rather frightening. It was strange to see how Gudrun clung with heavy, desperate passion to Ursula, how Ursula accepted her silently; unable to provide any more either for herself or for the other.

Hermione loved to watch. She could see the contessa's rapid, stoat-like sensationalism, Gudrun's ultimate cleaving* to the woman in her sister, Ursula's dumb helplessness, as if she were helplessly weighted, and manless.

"That was very beautiful," everybody cried with one accord. But Hermione writhed in her soul, knowing herself out of it all. She cried out for more dancing, and it was her will that set the contessa moving wickedly in Malbrouk.*

Gerald was excited by the desperate cleaving of Gudrun to Naomi. The essence of that female, subterranean recklessness penetrated his blood. He could not forget Gudrun's lifted, offered, cleaving, reckless weight. And Birkin, watching like a hermit crab from its hole, had seen the frustration and helplessness of Ursula. She was rich, full of potent love, and so single. She was like a strange unconscious bud of powerful womanhood. Why should he not gather her? She was his riches, a strange untold wealth.

Alexander played some Hungarian music, and they all danced, seized by the spirit. Gerald was marvellously exhilarated at finding himself in motion, moving towards Gudrun, dancing with feet that could not yet escape from the waltz and the two-step, but feeling his force stir along his limbs and his body, out of captivity. He did not know how to dance the free, emotional dance yet, but he knew how to begin. Birkin, when he could get free from the weight of the people present, whom he disliked, danced rapidly and with a passionate gaiety. And how Hermione hated him for this changeling gaiety.

"Now I see," cried the contessa excitedly, watching his purely gay motion, which he had all to himself "Mr Birkin, he is a changeling."

Hermione looked at her slowly, and shuddered, knowing that only a foreigner could have seen and have said this.

"Cosa vuoi dire,* Palestra?" she asked, sing-song.

"Look," said the contessa, in Italian. "He is not a man, he is bewitched."

"He is not a man, he is not a human being," sang itself over in Hermione's consciousness. And her soul writhed in the black subjugation of hatred for him, because of his power to exist other than she did, because he was non-human. She hated him in a frenzy that shattered her and broke her down, so that she suffered sheer dissolution, like a corpse, and was unconscious of everything save the horrible sickness of dissolution that was taking place within her, body and soul.

The house being full, Gerald was given the smaller room, really the dressing-room, communicating with Birkin's bedroom. When they all took their silver candles and mounted the stairs, where the lamps were burning subduedly, Hermione captured Ursula and brought her into her own bedroom, to talk to her. A sort of horror came over Ursula, in the big, strange bedroom. Hermione seemed to be bearing down on her, awful and inchoate, making some demand. They were looking at some Indian silk shirts, gorgeous and sensual in themselves, their shape, their almost corrupt gorgeousness. And Hermione came near, and her bosom writhed, and Ursula was for a moment blank with horror. And for a moment, Hermione's haggard eyes saw the horror on the face of the other, there was again a sort of crash, a crashing down. And Ursula picked up a shirt of rich red and blue silk, made for a young princess of fourteen, and was crying mechanically:

"Isn't it wonderful—who would dare to put those two strong colours together— —"

Then Hermione's maid entered silently, and Ursula, overcome with fear escaped, carried away by powerful impulse.

Birkin went straight to bed. He was feeling happy, and sleepy. Since he had danced he was happy. But Gerald would talk to him. Gerald, in evening dress, sat on Birkin's bed when the other lay down, and must talk.

"Who are those two Brangwens?" Gerald asked.

"They live in Beldover."

"In Beldover! Who are they, then?"

"Teachers in the Grammar School."

There was a pause.

"They are?" said Gerald at length. "I thought I had seen them before."

"It disappoints you?" said Birkin.

"Disappoints me? No.—But how is it Hermione invites them here?"

"She knew Gudrun in London—that's the younger one, the one with the darker hair—she's an artist—does sculpture and modelling."

"She's not a teacher in the Grammar School, then—only the other?"

"Both—Gudrun art mistress, Ursula a class mistress."

"And what's the father?"

"Handicraft instructor in the schools."

"Really!"

"You don't like it?"

Gerald was always uneasy under the slightly mocking tone of the other.

"That their father is handicraft-instructor in a school? What does it matter to me?"

Birkin laughed. Gerald looked at his face, as it lay there laughing and mocking and indifferent, on the pillow. It had a strange influence over him.

"I don't suppose you will see very much more of Gudrun, at least. She is a restless bird, she'll be gone in a week or two," said Birkin.

"Where will she go?"

"London, Paris, Rome—heaven knows. I should never be surprised to see her off to Damascus or San Francisco, now that she's had a spell of Willey Green and Beldover. It goes by contraries, like dreams."

Gerald pondered for a few moments.

"How do you know her so well?" he asked.

"Through the painting set," he replied. "Halliday and such-like. She'll know about Pussum and Libidnikov and the rest—though not from personal acquaintance, perhaps. She went about a good deal. I've known her for two years, I suppose."

"But has she got money, apart from her teaching?" asked Gerald.

"I shouldn't think so—no. But of course she can sell her models—she really *can* sell them."

"How much for?"

"A guinea—ten guineas—."

"And are they good? What are they?"

"I think sometimes they are marvellously good. That is hers, those two wagtails in Hermione's boudoir—you've seen them—they are carved in wood and painted."

"I thought it was savage carving again."

"No, hers.—That's what they are—animals and birds, sometimes odd small people in everyday dress, really rather wonderful when they come off. They have a sort of funniness that is quite unconscious and subtle."

"She might be a famous artist one day?" mused Gerald.

"She might. But I think she won't keep it up enough. She drops her art if anything else catches her. Her contrariness prevents her taking it seriously—she must never be too serious, she feels she gives herself away. And she won't give herself away to the world—she's always on the défensive. That's what I can't stand about her type.—By the way, how did things go off with Pussum after I left you? I haven't heard anything."

"Oh, rather disgusting. Halliday turned objectionable, and I only just saved myself from breaking his jaw."

Birkin was silent now, in chagrin.

"Of course," he said, "Julius is really mad. On the one hand he's a religious maniac, and on the other, he is fascinated by obscenity. Either he is a pure servant, washing the feet of Christ, or else he is making obscene drawings of Jesus—action and reaction—and between the two, nothing. He is really split mad. He worships a pure lily, a certain girl with a baby face,—the good old chaste love—and at the same time he *must* have the Pussum, just to defile himself with her."

"That's just what I can't make out," said Gerald. "Does he love her, the Pussum, or doesn't he?"

"He neither does nor doesn't. She is the harlot, the actual harlot of adultery to him.* And he's got a craving to throw himself away with her. Then he gets up and turns towards the lily of purity, the baby-faced girl, and so gets another thrill. It's the old game—action and reaction, and nothing between. He is really split to insanity now. I thought he would become unified—but he grows more and more disintegrated, two fizzing halves. It is hopeless—quite hopeless. I think it's such an insult to the Pussum—she's worth half-a-dozen of him, by now—though he was, somewhere, an extraordinarily nice and fine fellow."

"I don't know," said Gerald, after a pause, "that he does insult the Pussum so very much. She strikes me as being rather foul."

"But I thought you liked her!" exclaimed Birkin. "I always felt rather fond of her. I never had anything to do with her, personally, that's true."

"I liked her all right, for a couple of days," said Gerald. "But a week of her would have turned my stomach. There's a certain smell about the skin of those women, that in the end is sickening beyond words—even if you like it at first."

"I know," said Birkin. Then he added, rather fretfully, "But go to bed, Gerald. God knows what time it is."

Gerald looked at his watch, and at length rose off the bed, and went to his room. But he returned in a few minutes, in his shirt.

"One thing," he said, seating himself on the bed again; "we finished up rather stormily, and I never had time to give her anything."

"Money?" said Birkin. "She'll get what she wants from Halliday or from one of her acquaintances."

"But then," said Gerald, "I'd rather give her her dues, and settle the account."

"She doesn't care, really."

"No, but she needs it—and why should she give me something for nothing? I'd rather pay her."

"Well, it's not my affair," said Birkin, "so don't bother me about it. If you want a salve for your conscience, I'm not interested."

"Is it a salve for my conscience?" asked Gerald.

"What else!"

"I don't think I've got much conscience in the business—I only feel I owe her a matter of a few pounds."

"Owe them then."

"But that's what I don't want. She's a nice girl, let her have her dues—render unto Caesarina those things that are Caesarina's."*

"Go away, it wearies me—it's too late at night."

"Go to sleep then," said Gerald, putting his hand on Birkin's shoulder, affectionately, before he went away.

In the morning, when Gerald awoke and heard Birkin move, he called out:

"I still think I ought to give the Pussum ten pounds."

"Oh God," said Birkin, "don't be so materially moral. To be moral in your sinning—it's vile."

"But do you think one ought *not* to be moral?"

"Do you think one ought?" came the pertinent question in reply.

Gerald paused before he answered.

"Yes," he said. "That seems to me the proper morality of Pussums—pay them."

"And the proper morality of mistresses: keep them. And the proper morality of wives: live under the same roof with them. Integer vitae scelerisque purus—"*

"There's no need to be nasty about it," said Gerald.

"Nasty! I wish I felt nasty about it. It only bores me."

The morning was again sunny The maid had been in and brought the water* and had drawn the curtains. Birkin, sitting up in bed, looked lazily and pleasantly out on the park, that was so green and deserted, romantic, belonging to the past. He was thinking how lovely, how sure, how formed, how final all the things of the past were—the lovely accomplished past—this house, so still and golden, the park slumbering its centuries of peace. And then, what a snare and a delusion, this beauty of static things—what a horrible, dead prison Breadalby really was, what an intolerable confinement, the peace! Yet it was better than the sordid scrambling conflict of the present. If only one might create the future after one's own heart—for a little pure truth, a little unflinching application of simple truth to life, the heart cried out ceaselessly.

"I can't see why I should be any better if I didn't want to give the Pussum some money," came Gerald's voice from the lower room.

"You feel there's a spot on your soul, so you'll put a penny over it,* and it won't be there—'fly away Peter—'"*

"*Do* I feel there's a spot on my soul?" came Gerald's voice.

"There's evidently something you don't like."

In the silence Birkin could feel Gerald musing this fact.

"What don't I like?" came the inevitable question.

"I suppose," said Birkin, "one half of you *didn't* really want the Pussum. And you feel uncomfortable now in the other half—the ethical social half."

"But which half wanted her?" came the rather sarcastic question.

"Don't ask me."

"I do ask you—you needn't be afraid to tell me."

"I don't want to tell you—I'm tired of the question."

There was a pause, rather angry. Birkin got out of bed, and went to the window.

"I wanted her," said Gerald, "with my nose, but not with my stomach."

"Maybe. And will it help your digestion, to give her a ten-pound note?"

"Yes, it will.—I shall feel the affair's over, then."

"That's where you are a fool. The ten pounds makes not the slightest difference to your own inside. Ask yourself what you wanted of her, what you got, and what you didn't get, and see why you are at outs over it. Don't wrap the whole question in a ten-pound note, and throw it out of the window. You'll find it on the lawn, later on."

"But I don't want to spend any time at all, thinking about her."

"Very good. Then don't think about the money either."

Birkin and Gerald were the last to come down to breakfast. Hermione liked everybody to be early. She suffered when she felt her day was diminished, she felt she had missed her life. She seemed to grip the hours by the throat, to force her life from them. She was rather pale and ghastly, timeless and ageless, in the morning. Yet she had her power, her will was strangely pervasive. With the entrance of the two young men a sudden tension was felt.

She lifted her face, and said, in her amused sing-song:

"Good-morning! Did you sleep well?—I'm so glad."

And she turned away, ignoring them. Birkin, who knew her well, saw that she intended to discount his existence.

"Will you take what you want from the sideboard," said Alexander, in a voice slightly suggesting the disapproving schoolmaster. "I hope the things aren't cold. Oh no!—Do you mind putting out the flame under the chafing-dish, Rupert? Thank you."

Even Alexander was rather authoritative where Hermione was cool. He took his tone from her inevitably. Birkin sat down and looked at the table. He was so used to this house, to this room, to this atmosphere, through years of intimacy, and now he felt in complete opposition to it all, it had nothing to do with him. How well he knew Hermione, as she sat there, erect and silent and somewhat bemused, and yet so potent, so powerful! He knew her statically, so finally, that it was almost like a madness. It was difficult to believe one was not mad, that one was not a figure in the hall of kings in some Egyptian tomb, where the dead all sat immemorial and tremendous. How utterly he knew Joshua Malleson, who was talking in his harsh, yet rather mincing voice, endlessly, endlessly, always with a strong mentality working, always interesting, and yet always known, everything he said known beforehand, however novel it was, and clever. Alexander the pompous informal host, so stiffly free-and-easy, Fräulein so prettily chiming in just as she should, the little Italian countess taking no notice of anybody, only playing her little game, objective and cold, like a weasel watching everything, and extracting her own amusement, never giving herself in the slightest; then Miss Bradley, heavy and rather subservient, treated with cool, almost amused contempt by Hermione, and therefore slighted by every-body—how known it all was, like a game with the figures set out, the same figures, the Queen of chess, the knights, the pawns, the same now as they were hundreds of years ago, the same figures moving round in one of the innumerable permutations that make up the game. But the game is known, its going on is like a madness, it is so exhausted.

There was Gerald, an amused look on his face; the game pleased him. There was Gudrun, watching with steady, large, hostile eyes; the game fascinated her, and she loathed it. There was Ursula, with a slightly startled look on her face, as if she were hurt, and the pain were just outside her consciousness.

Suddenly Birkin got up and went out.

"That's enough," he said to himself, involuntarily.

Hermione knew his motion, though not in her consciousness. She lifted her heavy eyes and saw him lapse suddenly away, on a sudden, unknown tide, and the waves broke over her. Only her indomitable will remained static and mechanical, she sat at table making her musing, stray remarks. But the darkness had covered her, she was like a ship that has gone down. It was finished for her too, she was wrecked in the darkness. Yet the unfailing mechanism of her will worked on, she had that activity.

"Shall we bathe this morning?" she said, suddenly looking at them all.

"Splendid," said Joshua. "It is a perfect morning."

"Oh it is beautiful," said the Fräulein.

"Yes, let us bathe," said the Italian woman.

"We have no bathing suits," said Gerald.

"Have mine," said Alexander. "I must go to church and read the lessons. They expect me."

"Are you a Christian?" asked the Italian countess, with sudden interest.

"No," said Alexander. "I'm not. But I believe in keeping up the old institutions."

"They are so beautiful," said the Fräulein daintily.

"Oh they are," cried Miss Bradley.

They all trailed out on to the lawn. It was a sunny, soft morning in early summer, when life ran in the world subtly, like an idea. The church bells were ringing a little way off, not a cloud was in the sky, the swans were like lilies on the water below, the peacocks walked with long, prancing steps across the shadow and into the sunshine of the grass. One wanted to swoon into the perfection of it all.

"Goodbye," called Alexander, waving his gloves cheerily, and he disappeared behind the bushes, on his way to church.

"Now," said Hermione, "shall we all bathe?"

"I won't," said Ursula.

"You don't want to?" said Hermione, looking at her slowly.

"No, I don't want to," said Ursula.

"Nor I," said Gudrun.

"What about my suit?" asked Gerald.

"I don't know," laughed Hermione, with an odd, amused intonation. "Will a handkerchief do—a large handkerchief?"

"That will do," said Gerald.

"Come along then," sang Hermione.

The first to run across the lawn was the little Italian, small and like a cat, her white legs twinkling as she went, ducking slightly her head, that was tied in a gold silk kerchief. She tripped through the gate and down the grass, and stood, like a tiny figure of ivory and bronze at the water's edge, having dropped off her towelling, watching the swans, which came up in surprise. Then out ran Miss Bradley, like a large, soft plum in her dark-blue suit. Then Gerald came, a scarlet silk kerchief round his loins, his towels over his arms. He seemed to flaunt himself a little in the sun, lingering and laughing, strolling easily, looking warm and Bacchic. Then came Sir Joshua, in an overcoat, and lastly Hermione, striding with stiff grace from out of a great mantle of purple silk, her head tied up in purple and gold. Handsome was her stiff, long body, her straight-stepping white legs, there was a static magnificence about her as she let the cloak float loosely away from her striding. She crossed the lawn like some strange memory, and passed slowly and statelily towards the water.

There were three ponds, in three levels, descending the valley, large and smooth and beautiful, lying in the sun. The water ran over a little stone wall, over small rocks, splashing down from one pond to the level below. The swans had gone out on to the opposite bank, the reeds smelled sweet, a faint breeze touched the skin.

Gerald had dived in, after Sir Joshua, and had swum to the end of the pond. There he climbed out and sat on the wall. There was a dive, and the little countess was swimming like a rat, to join him. They both sat in the sun, laughing and crossing their arms on their breasts. Sir Joshua swam up to them, and stood near them, up to his arm-pits in the water. Then Hermione and Miss Bradley swam over, and they sat in a row on the embankment.

"Aren't they terrifying? Aren't they really terrifying?" said Gudrun. "Don't they look saurian? They are just like great lizards. Did ever you see anything like Sir Joshua? But really, Ursula, he belongs to the primeval world, when great lizards crawled about."

Gudrun looked in dismay on Sir Joshua, who stood up to the breast in the water, his long, greyish hair washed down into his eyes, his neck set into thick, crude shoulders. He was talking to Miss Bradley, who, seated on the bank above, plump and big and wet, looked as if she might roll and slither in the water almost like one of the slithering sea-lions in the zoo.

Ursula watched in silence. Gerald was laughing happily, between Hermione and the Italian. He reminded her of Dionysos, because his hair was really yellow, his figure so full and laughing. Hermione, in her large, stiff, sinister grace, leaned full near him, frightening, as if she were not responsible for what she might do. He knew a certain danger in her, a convulsive madness. But he only laughed the more, turning often to the little countess, who was flashing up her face at him.

They all dropped into the water, and were swimming together like a shoal of seals. Hermione was powerful and unconscious in the water, large and slow and powerful, Palestra was quick and silent as a water rat, Gerald wavered and flickered, a white shadow. Then, one after the other, they waded out, and went up to the house.

But Gerald lingered a moment to speak to Gudrun.

"You don't like the water?" he said.

She looked at him with a long, slow, inscrutable look, as he stood before her, naked and easy, the water standing in beads all over his skin.

"I like it very much," she replied.

He paused, expecting some sort of explanation.

"And you swim?"

"Yes, I swim."

Still he would not ask her why she would not go in. He could feel something ironic in her. He walked away, piqued for the first time.

"Why wouldn't you bathe?" he asked her again, later, when he was once more the properly-dressed, correct young Englishman.

She hesitated a moment before answering, opposing his persistence.

"Because I didn't like the crowd," she replied.

He laughed, her phrase seemed to re-echo in his consciousness. The flavour of her slang was piquant to him. Whether he would or not, she was for him the most significant person at Breadalby, he cared what *her* impression might be. He knew that she was a match for him. The others were all outsiders, instinctively, whatever they might be socially. And Gerald could not help it, he was bound to follow his instinctive self, rather than his social self.

After lunch, when all the others had withdrawn, Hermione and Gerald and Birkin lingered, finishing their talk. There had been some discussion, on the whole quite useless and cheap, about a new state, a new world of man. Supposing this old social state *were* broken and destroyed, then, out of the chaos, what then?

The great social idea, said Sir Joshua, was the *social* equality of man. No, said Gerald, the idea was, that every man was fit for some particular job, some particular status, and the business was, that every man should succeed to the job, and hence to the status, for which he was naturally fitted; the centre was the job itself.

"Oh!" cried Gudrun. "Then we shan't have names any more—we shall be like the Germans, nothing but Herr Obermeister and Herr Untermeister.* I can imagine it—Mrs Colliery-Manager Birkin—Mrs Member-of-Parliament Roddice, Miss Art-Teacher Brangwen. Very pretty that."

"Things would work very much better," said Gerald.

"What things? The relation between you and me, par exemple?"

"Yes, for example," cried the Italian. "That which is between men and women—!"

"That is non-social," said Birkin, sarcastically.

"Exactly," said Gerald. "Between me and a woman, the social question does not enter. It is my own affair."

"A ten-pound note on it," said Birkin.

"You don't admit that a woman is a social being?" asked Ursula of Gerald.

"She is both," said Gerald. "She is a social being, as far as society is concerned. But for her own private self, she is a free agent, it is her own affair, what she does."

"But won't it be rather difficult to arrange the two halves?" asked Ursula.

"Oh no," replied Gerald. "They arrange themselves naturally—we see it now, everywhere."

"Don't you laugh so pleasantly till you're out of the wood," said Birkin.

Gerald knitted his brows in momentary irritation.

"You are uncalled-for, Rupert," he said.

"*If,*" said Hermione at last, "we could only realise, that in the *spirit* we are all one, all equal in the spirit, all brothers there—the rest wouldn't matter, there would be no more of this carping and struggling which destroys, only destroys."

This speech was received in silence, and almost immediately the party rose from table. But when the others had gone, Birkin turned round in loud declamation, saying:

"It is just the opposite, just the contrary. We are all different and unequal in spirit—it is only the *social* differences that are based on accidental material conditions. We are all *materially* equal, if you like. Every man has the same hunger and thirst, two eyes, one nose and two legs. We're all the same there. But spiritually, there is every difference and every inequality. And it is upon these two bits of knowledge that you must found a state. Your democracy is an absolute lie—your brotherhood of man is a pure fiction, if you apply it further than the bread-and-butter, material considerations. We all came out of the womb, we all must eat to live, we all want to ride in motor-cars—therein lies the beginning and the end of the brotherhood of man.

"But I, myself, the potential being, what have I to do with any other man or woman? In the spirit, I am as separate as one star is from another, as different in quality and quantity. Establish a state on *that.*

One man is better than another, better, better, better, to how many degrees who knows, in essence and in spirit. Yet there *is* a common ground of equality—food and drink and substance. Every man has equal rights with every other man, to the material things of this world— *according to his desire*. Let every man *get* his share, then, let him have it, let him have his whack of all the goods in the world, so that I can be rid of his importunity, so that I can tell him: 'Now you've got what you want—you've got your fair share of the world's gear. Now, you clumsy-souled fool, now know your own inferiority. Know your own inferiority, you swine.' And when he knows that, when the herd knows its own inferiority, then it has begun to found a new state, begun to create a new society. But *that's* what you've got to found your new state upon—your *extrinsic, material* equality with me, and your intrinsic inferiority. I am a king, not by virtue of virtue, or power, or wealth, but because I can live the truth, which is creative living, whereas you can only reproduce and manufacture, at the best."

Hermione was looking at him with leering eyes, along her cheeks. He could feel violent waves of hatred and loathing of all he said, coming out of her. It was dynamic hatred and loathing, coming strong and black out of the unconsciousness. She heard his words in her unconscious self, consciously she was as if deafened, she paid no heed to them.

"It *sounds* like megalomania, Rupert," said Gerald, genially.

Hermione gave a queer, grunting sound. Birkin stood back.

"It bores me," he said suddenly, the whole tone gone out of his voice, that had been so high and strident, crying everybody down. And he went away.

But he felt, later, a little compunction. He had been violent, cruel with poor Hermione. He wanted to recompense her, to make it up. He had hurt her, he had been vindictive. He wanted to be on good terms with her again.

He went into her boudoir, a remote and very cushiony place. She was sitting at her table writing letters. She lifted her face abstractedly when he entered, watched him go to the sofa, and sit down. Then she looked down at her paper again.

He took a large volume, which he had been reading before, and became minutely attentive to his author. His back was towards Hermione. She could not go on with her writing. Her whole mind was a chaos, darkness breaking in upon it, and herself struggling to gain control with her will, as a swimmer struggles with the swirling water. But in spite of her efforts she was borne down, darkness seemed to break over her, she felt as if her heart was bursting. The terrible tension grew stronger and stronger, it was most fearful agony, like being walled up.

And then she realised that his presence was the wall, his presence was destroying her. Unless she could break out, she must die most fearfully, walled up in horror. And he was the wall. She must break down the wall—she must break him down before her, the awful obstruction of him who obstructed her life to the last. It must be done, or she must perish most horribly.

Terrible shocks ran over her body, like shocks of electricity, as if many volts of electricity suddenly struck her down. She was aware of him sitting silently there, the obscene obstruction. Only this blotted out her mind, pressed out her very breathing, his silent, stooping back, the back of his head.

A terrible voluptuous thrill ran down her arms—she was going to know her voluptuous consummation. Her arms quivered and were strong, immeasurably and irresistibly strong. What delight, what delight in strength, what delirium of pleasure! She was going to have her consummation of voluptuous ecstasy at last. It was coming! In utmost terror and agony, she knew it was upon her now, in extremity of bliss. Her hand closed on a large, beautiful ball of lapis lazuli that stood on her desk for a paper-weight. She rolled it round in her hand as she rose silently. Her heart was a pure flame in her breast, she was purely unconscious in voluptuous ecstasy. She moved towards him and stood behind him for a moment in ecstasy. He, closed within the spell, remained motionless and unconscious.

Then swiftly, in a flame that drenched down her body like fluid lightning, and gave her a perfect, unutterable consummation, unutterable satisfaction, she brought down the ball of jewel stone with all her force, crash on his head. But her fingers were in the way, and deadened the blow. Nevertheless down went his head on the table on which his book lay, the stone slid aside and over his ear, it was one convulsion of pure bliss for her. But it was not enough. She lifted her arm high to aim once more, straight down on the head that lay limp on the table. She must smash it, it must be smashed before her ecstasy was consummated, fulfilled for ever. A thousand lives, a thousand deaths mattered nothing now, only the fulfilment of this perfect ecstasy.

She was not swift, she had her time. A great warning made him lift his face and twist to look at her. Her arm was coming down again, the terrible hand clasping the ball of lapis lazuli. It was her left hand, he realised again with terror that she was left-handed.* Hurriedly, with a burrowing motion, he covered his head under the thick volume of Thucydides, and the blow came down, almost breaking his neck, and shattering his heart.

He was shattered, but he was not daunted. Twisting round to face her, he pushed the table over and got away from her. He was like a flask that is smashed to atoms, he seemed to himself that he was all fragments, smashed to bits. Yet his movements were perfectly coherent and clear, his soul was entire and unsurprised.

"No you don't, Hermione," he said in a low voice. "I don't let you."

He saw her standing tall and blank and attentive, the stone clenched tense in her hand.

"Stand away and let me go," he said.

As if drawn aside by some hand, she stood back, watching him all the time without changing, eternally confronting him.

"It is no good," he said, when he had gone past her. "It isn't I who will fail. You hear?"

He kept his face to her as he went out, lest she should strike again. While he was on his guard, she dared not strike him. And he was on his guard, she was powerless. So he had gone, and left her standing.

She remained perfectly rigid, standing as she was for a long time. Then she staggered to the couch and lay down, and went heavily to sleep. When she awoke, she remembered what she had done, but it seemed to her, she had only hit him, as any woman might do, because he tortured her. She was perfectly right. She knew that, spiritually, she was right. In her own infallible purity, she had done what must be done. She was right, she was pure. A drugged, almost sinister religious expression became permanent on her face.

Birkin, barely conscious, and yet perfectly direct in his motion, went out of the house and straight across the park, to the open country, to the moors. The brilliant day had become overcast, spots of rain were falling. He wandered on to a wild valley-side, where were thickets of hazel, many flowers, tufts of heather, and little clumps of young fir-trees, budding with soft paws. It was rather wet everywhere, there was a stream running down at the bottom of the valley, which was gloomy, or seemed gloomy.

He was aware that he could not regain his consciousness, that he was moving in a sort of darkness.

Yet he wanted something. He was happy in the wet hill-side, that was overgrown and obscure with bushes and flowers. He wanted to touch them all, to saturate himself with the touch of them all. He took off his clothes, and sat down naked among the primroses, moving his feet softly among the primroses, his legs, his knees, his arms right up to the arm-pits, then lying down and letting them touch his belly, his breasts. It was such a fine, cool, subtle touch all over him, he seemed to saturate himself with their contact.

But they were too soft. He went through the long grass to a clump of young fir-trees, that were no higher than a man. The soft sharp boughs beat upon him, as he moved deliciously against them, threw little cold showers of drops on his belly, and beat his loins with their clusters of soft-sharp needles. There was a thistle which pricked him vividly, but not too much, because all his movements were too soft and subtle. To lie down and roll in the sticky, cool young hyacinths, to lie on one's belly and cover one's back with handfuls of fine wet grass, soft as a breath, soft and more delicate and more beautiful than the touch of any woman; and then to sting one's thigh against the living dark bristles of the fir-boughs; and then to feel the light whip of the hazel on one's shoulders, stinging, and then to clasp the silvery birch-trunk against one's breast, its smoothness, its hardness, its vital knots and ridges—this was good, this was all very good, very satisfying. Nothing else would do, nothing else would satisfy, except this coolness and subtlety of vegetation travelling into one's blood. How fortunate he was, that there was this lovely, subtle, responsive vegetation, waiting for him, as he waited for it; how fulfilled he was, how happy!

As he dried himself a little with his handkerchief, he thought about Hermione and the blow. He could feel a pain on the side of his head. But after all, what did it matter? What did Hermione matter, what did people matter altogether? There was this perfect cool loneliness, so lovely and fresh and unexplored. Really, what a mistake he had made, thinking he wanted people, thinking he wanted a woman. He did not want a woman—not in the least. The leaves and the primroses and the trees, they were really lovely and cool and desirable, they really came into the blood and were added on to him. He was enrichened now immeasurably, and so glad.

It was quite right of Hermione to want to kill him. What had he to do with her? Why should he pretend to have anything to do with human beings at all? Here was his world, he wanted nobody and nothing but the lovely, subtle, responsive vegetation, and himself, his own living self.

It was necessary to go back into the world. That was true. But that did not matter, so one knew where one belonged. He knew now where he belonged. He knew where to plant himself, his seed:—along with the trees, in the folds of the delicious fresh growing leaves. This was his place, his marriage place. The world was extraneous.

He climbed out of the valley, wondering if he were mad. But if so, he preferred his own madness, to the regular sanity. He rejoiced in his own madness, he was free. He did not want that sanity of the world, which was become so repulsive. He rejoiced in the new-found world of his madness. It was so fresh and delicate and so satisfying.

As for the certain grief he felt at the same time, in his soul, that was only the remains of an old ethic, that bade a human-being adhere to humanity. But he was weary of the old ethic, of the human being, and of humanity. He loved now the soft, delicate vegetation, that was so cool and perfect. He would overlook the old grief, he would put away the old ethic, he would be free in his new state.

He was aware of the pain in his head becoming more and more difficult every minute. He was walking now along the road to the nearest station. It was raining and he had no hat. But then plenty of cranks went out nowadays without hats, in the rain.

He wondered again how much of his heaviness of heart, a certain depression, was due to fear, fear lest anybody should have seen him naked lying with the vegetation. What a dread he had of mankind, of other people! It amounted almost to horror, to a sort of dream terror—his horror of being observed by some other people. If he were on an island, like Alexander Selkirk,* with only the creatures and the trees, he would be free and glad, there would be none of this heaviness, this misgiving. He could love the vegetation and be quite happy and unquestioned, by himself.

He had better send a note to Hermione: she might trouble about him, and he did not want the onus of this. So at the station, he wrote saying:

"I will go on to town—I don't want to come back to Breadalby for the present. But it is quite all right—I don't want you to mind having biffed me, in the least. Tell the others it is just one of my moods. You were quite right, to biff me—because I know you wanted to. So there's the end of it."

In the train, however, he felt ill. Every motion was insufferable pain, and he was sick. He dragged himself from the station into a cab, quite blind, feeling his way step by step, like a blind man, and held up only by a dim will.

For a week or two he was ill, but he did not let Hermione know, and she thought he was sulking, there was a complete estrangement between them. She became nun-like in her conviction of perpetual righteousness. She lived in and by her conviction of righteousness, conviction of her own purity of spirit.

4

GOING HOME FROM SCHOOL in the afternoon, the Brangwen girls descended the hill between the picturesque cottages of Willey Green till they came to the railway crossing. There they found the gate shut, because the colliery train was rumbling nearer. They could hear the small locomotive panting hoarsely as it advanced with caution between the embankments. The one-legged man in the little signal-hut by the road stared out from his obscurity like a crab from a snail-shell.

Whilst the two girls waited, Gerald Crich trotted up on a red Arab mare. He rode well and softly, pleased with the delicate quivering of the creature between his knees. And he was very picturesque, at least in Gudrun's eyes, sitting soft and close on the slender red mare, whose long tail flowed on the air. He saluted the two girls, and drew up at the crossing to wait for the gate, looking down the railway for the approaching train. In spite of her ironic smile at his picturesqueness, Gudrun loved to look at him. He was well-set and easy, his face with its warm tan showed up his whitish, coarse moustache, and his blue eyes were full of sharp light, as he watched the distance.

The locomotive chuffed slowly between the banks, hidden. The mare did not like it. She began to wince away, as if hurt by the unknown noise. But Gerald pulled her back and held her head to the gate. The sharp blasts of the chuffing engine broke with more and more force on her. The repeated sharp blows of unknown, terrifying noise struck through her till she was rocking with chaotic terror. She recoiled like a spring let go. But an obstinate look came [into] Gerald's face. He brought her back again, unrelaxing.

The noise was released, the little red locomotive with her clanking steel connecting-rod emerged on the high-road, clanking sharply. The mare rebounded like a drop of water from hot iron. Ursula and Gudrun pressed back into the hedge, in fear. But Gerald bore down on the mare, and forced her back. It seemed as if he were physically the stronger, and could thrust her back.

"The fool," cried Ursula, loudly. "Why doesn't he ride away till it's gone by."

Gudrun was looking at him with black, lowering eyes. But he sat tense and obstinate, forcing the wheeling mare, which spun and swerved like a wind, and yet could not get out of the grasp of his will, nor escape from the mad clamour of terror that resounded through her, as the trucks thumped slowly, heavily, horrifying, one after the other, one pursuing the other, over the rails of the crossing.

The locomotive, as if wanting to see what could be done, put on the brakes, and back came the trucks rebounding on the iron buffers, striking like horrible iron cymbals, clashing nearer and nearer in frightful strident concussions. The mare opened her mouth and rose slowly, as if lifted up on a wind of terror. Then suddenly her fore feet struck out, as she convulsed herself utterly away from the horror. Back she went, and the two girls clung to each other, feeling she must fall backwards on top of him. But he leaned forward, his face stubborn with pleasant serenity, and at last he drove her down, drove her down, and was pressing her back to the mark. But as strong as the pressure of his will was the pressure of her utter terror, throwing her back away from the railway, so that she spun round and round, on two legs, as if she were in the centre of some whirlwind. It made Gudrun faint with poignant dizziness, which seemed to penetrate to her heart.

"No—! No—! Let her go! Let her go, you fool, you fool— —!" cried Ursula at the top of her voice, completely beside herself. And Gudrun hated her bitterly for being beside herself. It was unendurable that Ursula's voice was so powerful and naked.

An ugly look came on Gerald's face. He bit himself down on the mare with determination, and *forced* her round. She roared as she breathed, her nostrils were two wide, hot holes, her mouth was apart, her eyes frenzied. It was a terrible and repulsive sight. But he bore down on her vindictively, with an almost mechanical relentlessness, keen as a sword in his own inevitable conquest. Both man and horse were sweating with violence.

Meanwhile the eternal trucks were rumbling on, very slowly, threading one after the other, one after the other, like a disgusting dream that has no end. The connecting chains were grinding and squeaking as the tension varied, the mare pawed and struck away mechanically now, her terror fulfilled in her, the man was really her master; her paws were blind and pathetic as she beat the air, the man cleaved on to her, and brought her down, almost as with a blow.

"And she's bleeding!—She's bleeding!" cried Ursula, frantic now with repulsion and hatred of Gerald.

Gudrun looked and saw the trickles of blood on the sides of the mare, and she turned white. And then on the very wound the bright spurs came down, pressing relentlessly. The world reeled and passed into nothingness for Gudrun, she could not know any more.

When she recovered, her soul was calm and cold, without feeling. The trucks were still rumbling by, the man and the mare were still fighting: but she was cold and separate, she had no more feeling for them. She was quite hard and cold and indifferent.

They could see the top of the hooded guard's van approaching, the sound of the trucks was diminishing, there was hope of relief from the intolerable noise. The heavy panting of the half-stunned mare sounded automatically, the man seemed to be relaxing confidently, his will bright and unstained.

The guard's van came up, and passed slowly, the guard staring out in his transition on the spectacle in the road. And, through the man in the closed wagon Gudrun could see the whole scene spectacularly, isolated and momentary.

Lovely, grateful silence seemed to trail behind the receding train. How sweet the silence is! Ursula looked with loathing on the buffers of the diminishing wagon. The gate-keeper stood ready at the door of his hut, to proceed to open the gate. But Gudrun sprang suddenly forward, in front of the struggling horse, threw off the latch and flung the gates asunder, throwing one half to the keeper, and running with the other half, forwards. Gerald suddenly let go the horse and applied the spurs, he leaped forwards, almost on to Gudrun. She was not afraid. As he jerked aside the mare's head, Gudrun cried, in a strange, high voice, like a gull, or like a witch screaming out from the side of the road:

"I should think you're proud!"

The words were distinct and formed. The man, twisting aside on his dancing horse, looked at her in some surprise, some wondering interest. Then the mare's hoofs had danced three times on the drum-like sleepers of the crossing and man and horse were bounding springily, unequally up the road.

The two girls watched them go. The gate-keeper hobbled thudding over the logs of the crossing, with his wooden leg. He had fastened the gate. Then he also turned, and called to the girls:

"A masterful young jockey, that;—'ll have his own road,* if ever anybody would."

"Yes," cried Ursula, in her hot, overbearing voice. "Why couldn't he take the horse away, till the trucks had gone by? He's a fool, and a bully, that's what he is. But I'd be a bit more of a man than that; I wouldn't torture a poor horse."

There was a pause, then the gate keeper shook his head, and repeated:

"Masterful, that's where it is;—must be master of everything, or he'll die for it;—as different from his father as fire and water. His father, as nice a man as ever trod earth— —"

"I can't say as much for the son," cried Ursula. "I suppose he thinks it manly, to torture a horse like that."

Again there was the cautious pause. Then again the man shook his head, as if he would say nothing, but would think the more.

"I expect he's got to train the mare to stand to anything," he replied. "A pure-bred Harab—you don't often see one o' them breed round here. They say as he got her from Constantinople."

"Did he!" said Ursula. "Then he'd better have left her to the Turks, I'm sure they would never have treated her so stupidly."

The man went in to drink his can of tea, the girls went on down the lane, that was deep in soft black dust. On the left the coal-mine lifted its great mounds and its patterned head-stocks, the black railway and the trucks at rest looked like a harbour just below, a large bay of railway with anchored trucks.

Near the second level crossing, that went over many bright rails, was a farm belonging to the collieries, and a great round globe of iron, a disused boiler, huge and rusty and perfectly round, stood silently against a little wall, in a paddock by the road. The hens were pecking round it, some chickens were balanced on the drinking trough, wagtails flew away in among trucks, from the water.

On the other side of the wide crossing, by the road-side, was a heap of pale-grey stones for mending the roads, and a cart standing, and a middle-aged man with whiskers round his face was leaning on his shovel, talking to a young man in gaiters, who stood by the horse's head. Both men were facing the crossing.

They saw the two girls appear, small, brilliant figures in the near distance, in the strong light of the late afternoon. The sisters wore light, gay summer dresses, Ursula had an orange-coloured knitted coat, Gudrun a pale yellow, Ursula wore canary yellow stockings, Gudrun bright green, the figures of the two women seemed to glitter in progress over the wide bay of the railway crossing, white and orange and yellow and green glittering, in motion across a hot world silted with coal-dust.

The two men stood quite still in the heat, watching. The elder was a short, hard-faced, energetic man of middle age, the younger a labourer of twenty three or so. They stood in silence watching the advance of the sisters. They watched whilst the girls drew near, and whilst they passed, and whilst they receded down the dusty road, that had dwellings on one side, and dusty young corn on the other.

Then the elder man, with the whiskers round his face, said in a small voice to the young man:

"I'd give a week's wages for five minutes with that young woman."

"Which?" asked the young man, eagerly, with a laugh.

"Her with the green legs.—By strike,* she'd be worth it an' a'."

Again the younger man laughed.

"Your Missis ud have summat to say to you," he replied.

"My Missis; by God, she gets her dollop out o' me."

"She does?"

"Every mortal night as comes, an' won't let me go to sleep till she's had it.—But I would, I'd give a week's wages of a Friday night for a round wi' that young woman there. I would an' all, an' don't forget it. Look at her! See her?" Gudrun had turned round and looked at the two men. They were to her sinister creatures, standing watching after her, by the heap of pale grey stones. She loathed the man with whiskers round his face.

"You're first class, you are," the man said to her, and to the distance.

"What 'st say to her, Jack? What would ter part wi', to have a bit wi' her?"

"Not my week's wages," said Jack.

"You wouldn't? By God, though, I would."

The younger man looked after Gudrun and Ursula objectively, as if he wished to see what there might be, that was worth his week's wages. He shook his head with some chagrin, a slight bitterness.

"No," he said. "It non matters to me."

"It doesn't?" crowed the old man. "By God, I wish it didna to me."

And he went on shovelling his stones.

The girls descended between the houses with slate roofs and blackish brick walls. The heavy gold glamour of approaching sunset lay over all the colliery district, and the ugliness overlaid with beauty was like a narcotic to the senses. On the roads silted with black dust, the rich light fell more warmly, more heavily; over all the amorphous squalor a kind of magic was cast, from the glowing close of day.

"It has a foul kind of beauty, this place," said Gudrun, evidently suffering from the fascination. "Can't you feel, in some way, a thick, hot attraction in it? *I* can. And it quite stupifies me."

They were passing between blocks of miners' dwellings. In the back yards of several dwellings, a miner could be seen washing himself in the open on this hot evening, naked down to the loins, his great trousers of moleskin slipping almost away. Miners already cleaned were sitting on their heels, with their backs near the walls, talking and silent in pure physical well-being, tired, and taking physical rest. Their voices sounded out with rich, strong intonation, and the broad dialect was curiously caressing to the blood. It seemed to envelop Gudrun in a male caress, there was in the whole atmosphere a resonance of physical men, a glamorous thickness of virility surcharged in the air. But it was universal in the district, and therefore unnoticed by the inhabitants.

To Gudrun, however, it was potent and moving. She could never tell why Beldover was so utterly different from London and the south, why one's whole feelings were different, why one seemed to live in another sphere. Now she realised that this was the world of powerful, physical men who spent most of their time in the darkness. In their voices she could hear the voluptuous resonance of darkness, the strong, potent darkness of the senses, mindless and feline. The whole atmosphere was an atmosphere of men, one seemed to breathe the electric fluid of maleness in the air.

It was the same every evening when she came home, she seemed to move through a wave of virile fluid force, that was given off from the presence of thousands of vigorous, emotional, semi-conscious men. There was a strange glamour possessed the world at evening, at tea-time, when work was over. She sipped her tea with a curious, magic relish, everything was rich with an intangible potency.

There came over her a nostalgia for the place. She hated it, she knew how utterly cut off it was, how hideous and how sickeningly mindless. Sometimes she beat her wings like a fly stuck on a fly-paper. And yet, she was overcome by the nostalgia. She struggled to get deeper and deeper into the atmosphere of the place, she craved to get her satisfaction of it.

She felt herself drawn out at evening into the main street of the town, that was desolate and ugly, and yet full of this same potent atmosphere of emotion and virility. There were always miners about. They moved with their strange, absolved dignity, a certain beauty, a strange poignant stillness in their bearing, a look of knowledge and of resignation in their pale, often gaunt faces. They belonged to another world, they had a strange glamour, their voices were full of an intolerable deep resonance, a music more maddening than the siren's long ago.

She found herself, with the rest of the common women, drawn out on Friday evenings to the little market. Friday was pay-day for the colliers, and Friday night was market night. Every woman was abroad, every man was out, shopping with his wife, or gathering with his pals. The pavements were dark for miles around with people coming in, the little market place on the crown of the hill, and the main street of Beldover were black with thickly-crowded men and women.

It was dark, the market place was hot with kerosene flares, which threw a ruddy light on the grave faces of the purchasing wives, and on the pale abstract faces of the men. The air was full of the sound of criers and of people talking, thick streams of people moved on the pavements towards the solid crowd of the market. The shops were blazing and crowded with women, in the streets were men, mostly men, miners of all ages.

The carts that came could not pass through. They had to wait, the driver calling and shouting, till the dense crowd would make way. Everywhere, young fellows from the outlying district were making tryst with the girls, standing in the road and at the corners. The doors of the public-houses were open and full of light, men passed in and out in a continual stream. Everywhere men were calling out to one another, to know what the week's work had been, and saluting each other across the road; men who had once worked together, and who now were in different pits.

And, like any other common madam of the place, Gudrun strolled up and down, up and down the length of the brilliant two-hundred paces of the pavement nearest the market-place. She knew it was a vulgar thing to do; her father and mother could not bear it; but the nostalgia came over her, she must be among the people.

And, like any other common madam, she found her 'boy'. It was an electrician, one of the electricians introduced in Gerald's régime. He was an earnest, clever man, a scientist with a passion for sociology. He lived alone in a cottage, in lodgings, in Willey Green. He was a gentleman, and sufficiently well-to-do. His landlady spread the reports about him: he *would* have a large wooden tub in his bedroom, and every time he came in from work, he *would* have pails and pails of water brought up, to bath in, then he put on clean shirt and underclothing *every* day, and clean silk socks; fastidious and exacting he was in these respects, but in every other way, most cheerful and generous.

Gudrun knew all these things. The Brangwens' house was one to which the gossip came naturally and inevitably. Palmer was in the first place a friend of Ursula's. But in his pale, elegant, serious face there showed the same nostalgia that Gudrun felt. He too must walk up and down the street on Friday evening. So he walked with Gudrun, and a great friendship was struck up between them. But he was not in love with Gudrun; he *really* wanted to talk to Ursula, but for some strange reason, nothing could happen between her and him. He liked to have Gudrun about, as a fellow mind—but that was all. And she had no real feeling for him. He was a scientist, he had his various cold relations with women. But he never moved in any direction, save in his work. His nostalgia was for the men, for the strange glamour of the miners themselves. But of this he admitted nothing in his consciousness.

So Gudrun patrolled the streets with Palmer, till the working people came to know her and accept her. And then she had her violent revulsions, when she felt she must fly away from Beldover instantly, or she would go mad. She loathed the place in a perfect insanity of loathing. Yet she had not gone yet. Ursula, who was inured to the place, who had taken it into her blood in the years of her life she had spent there, was patient and ripe to break away from it all.

Gudrun would take sudden and passionate refuge in work. But then, the restlessness would come upon her, she *must* be in the open air. And Ursula must come with her, for she could not be alone.

One morning the sisters were sketching by the side of Willey Water, at the remote end of the lake. Gudrun had waded out to a gravelly shoal, and was seated like a Buddhist,* staring fixedly at the water-plants that rose succulent from the mud of the low shores. What she could see was mud, soft, oozy, watery mud, and from its festering chill, water-plants rose up, thick and cool and fleshy, very straight and turgid, thrusting out their leaves at right angles, and having dark poisonous colours, dark green and blotches of black-purple and bronze. But she could feel their turgid fleshy structure as in a sensuous vision, she *knew* how they rose out of the mud, she *knew* how they thrust out from themselves, how they stood stiff and succulent against the air.

Ursula was watching the butterflies, of which there were dozens near the water, little blue ones suddenly snapping out of nothingness into a jewel-life, a large black-and-red one standing upon a flower and breathing with his soft wings, intoxicatingly, breathing pure, ethereal sunshine; two white ones were wrestling in the low air; there was a halo round them; ah, when they came tumbling nearer they were orange-tips, and it was the orange that had made the halo. Ursula rose and drifted away, unconscious like the butterflies.

Gudrun, absorbed in a stupor of sensuous apprehension of the water plants, sat crouched on the shoal, drawing, not looking up for a long time, and then staring unconsciously, absorbedly at the rigid, succulent stems. Her feet were bare, her hat lay on the bank opposite.

She started out of her trance, hearing the knocking of oars. She looked round. There was a boat with a gaudy Japanese parasol, and a man in white, rowing. The woman was Hermione, and the man was Gerald. She knew it instantly. And instantly she felt the nostalgia for Gerald, almost as she felt for the streets of Beldover with the pale, physical miners. But here she would allow herself.

Beldover was concentrated in Gerald, he was the key-stone of the subterranean fabric. She saw the movement of his back, of his white, flexible loins. But it was not that; it was the shadow he bent over, the darkness towards which he stooped unconsciously.

"There's Gudrun," came Hermione's voice floating distinct over the water. "Do you mind if we go and speak to her?"

Gerald looked round and saw the girl standing by the water's edge, looking at him. He pulled the boat towards her, magnetically, without thinking of her. In his world, his conscious world, she was really an outsider. But he knew that Hermione had a curious pleasure in treading down all these differences, and he left it to her.

"How do you do, Gudrun?" sang Hermione, using the Christian name in the fashionable manner.* "What are you doing?"

"How do you do, Hermione? I *was* sketching."

"Were you." The boat drifted nearer, till the keel ground on the bank. "May we see? I should like to *so* much."

There was no resisting Hermione's cool, simple sing-song.

"Well—" said Gudrun reluctantly, for she always hated to have her unfinished work exposed—"there's nothing in the least interesting."

"Isn't there. But let me see, will you?"

Gudrun reached out the sketch-book, Gerald stretched from the boat to take it. And as he did so, he remembered Gudrun's last words to him, and her face lifted up to him as he sat on the swerving horse. A thrill of pleasure went over his nerves, because he felt, in some way she was compelled by him. The exchange of feeling between them was strong and apart from their consciousness.

And as if in a spell, Gudrun was aware of his body, stretching and surging with life, like the plants, stretching towards her, his hand coming straight forward like a stem. Her voluptuous apprehension of him made the blood faint in her veins, her mind went dim and unconscious. And he felt the life surging up in him, as if he were a great fountain of vitality, ready to give himself off in superabundance. He looked round at the boat. It was drifting off a little. He lifted the oar to bring her back. And the exquisite pleasure of grasping the oar in his balanced strength, of feeling himself the perfect fulcrum of all the swerving of the boat in the heavy, soft water, was as complete as if he had the power to fly, to poise himself the centre of the heaven and of the physical earth.

"That's what you have done," said Hermione, looking searchingly at the plants on the shore, and comparing with Gudrun's drawing. Gudrun looked round in the direction of Hermione's long, pointing finger. "That is it, isn't it?" repeated Hermione, needing confirmation.

"Yes," said Gudrun automatically, taking no real heed.

"Let me look," said Gerald, reaching forward for the book. But Hermione ignored him, he must not presume, before she had finished. But he, his will as unconscious and as unflinching as Hermione's, stretched forward till he touched the book. A little shock, a storm of revulsion against him, shook Hermione unconsciously. She released the book when he had not properly got it, and it tumbled against the side of the boat and bounced into the water.

"There!" sang Hermione, with a strange ring of malevolent joy. "I'm so sorry, so awfully sorry. Can't you get it, Gerald?"

This last was said in a note of sneering mockery that made Gerald's veins tingle with fine hate for her. He leaned far out of the boat, reaching down into the water. He could feel his position was ridiculous, his loins thrust out behind him.

"It is of no importance," came the strong, clanging voice of Gudrun. But he reached further, the boat swayed violently. Hermione, however, remained unperturbed. He grasped the book, under the water, and brought it up, dripping.

"I'm so awfully sorry—so awfully sorry," repeated Hermione. "I'm afraid it was all my fault."

"It's of no importance—really, I assure you—it doesn't matter in the least," cried Gudrun with vehemence, her face flushed scarlet. And she held out her hand impatiently for the wet book, to have done with the scene. Gerald gave it to her. He had been made to look ignominious, and he did not recover.

"I'm so dreadfully sorry," repeated Hermione, till both Gerald and Gudrun could not bear her. "Is there nothing that can be done?"

"What should be done?" asked Gudrun, with cool irony.

"Can't we save the drawings in any way?"

There was a moment's pause, wherein Gudrun made evident all her contempt of Hermione's persistence.

"I assure you," said Gudrun, with cutting distinctness, "the drawings are quite as good as ever they were, for what I want them for. They are merely for reference."

"But can't I give you a new book? I wish you'd let me do that. I feel so truly upset. I feel it was all my fault."

"As far as I saw," said Gudrun, "it wasn't your fault at all. If there was any *fault*, it was Mr Crich's. But the whole thing is *entirely* trivial, and it really is ridiculous to take any notice of it."

Gerald watched Gudrun closely, whilst she thus told off Hermione. It was so rarely anyone could do it. He watched Gudrun with an admiration that amounted to wondering respect. This was a rare reckless spirit, give and take on any field. And so complete and workmanlike too!

"I'm awfully glad if it doesn't matter," he said, "if there's no real harm done."

She looked back at him the signal with her fine blue eyes, full into his face, as she said, her voice ringing with intimacy now it was addressed to him:

"Of course it doesn't matter in the *least*."

The bond was established between them, in that look, in her tone. In her tone, she took him, she made the understanding clear—they were of the same kind, he and she, they understood each other. Henceforward, she knew, she had her power over him. Wherever they met, they would be secretly associated. And he would be helpless in the association with her. Her soul exulted.

"Goodbye! I'm so glad you forgive me. Gooood-byyye!" Hermione sang her farewell, and waved her hand. Gerald automatically took the oar and pushed off. But he was looking all the time, with a respectful admiration in his eyes, at Gudrun, who stood on the shoal shaking the wet book in her hand. She turned away and ignored the receding boat. But Gerald looked back as he rowed, watching her, forgetting what he was doing.

"Aren't we going too much to the left?" sang Hermione, as she sat forgotten under her coloured parasol.

Gerald looked round without replying, the oars balanced and glancing in the sun.

"I think it's all right," he said good-humouredly, beginning to row again without thinking of what he was doing. And Hermione loathed him for his good-humoured abstraction, she was nullified, she could not regain ascendancy.

Meanwhile Ursula had wandered on from Willey Water along the course of the bright little stream. The afternoon was full of larks' singing. On the bright hill-sides was a conflagration of yellow gorse. A few forget-me-nots flowered by the glancing water. There was a lovely dancing everywhere.

She strayed happily on, over the brooks. She wanted to go to the mill-pond above. The big mill-house was deserted, save for a laborer and his wife, who lived in the kitchen. So she passed through the empty farm-yard and through the wilderness of a garden, and mounted the bank by the sluice. When she got to the top, to see the old, velvety surface of the pond before her, she noticed a man on the bank, tinkering with a punt. It was Birkin, sawing and hammering away.

She stood at the head of the sluice, looking at him. He was perfectly unaware of anybody's presence. He looked very busy and isolated. She felt she ought to go away, he would not want anybody. He seemed to be enjoying himself by himself. But she did not want to go away. Therefore she moved along the bank till he would look up.

Which he soon did. The moment he saw her he dropped his tools and came forward, saying:

"How do you do! I'm making the punt water-tight. Come and see if you think it is right."

She went along with him.

"You are your father's daughter, so you can tell me if I have done it properly," he said.

She bent to look at the patched punt.

"I am sure I am my father's daughter," she said, fearful of having to judge. "But I don't know anything about carpentry. It *looks* right, don't you think?"

"Yes, I think it does. I hope it won't let me go to the bottom of the pond, that's all. Though even that is of no moment, I should swim up again. Would you mind helping me to get it into the water."

With combined efforts they turned over the heavy punt and set it afloat.

"Now," he said, "I'll try it, and you can watch my fate. Then if it carries I'll take you over to the island."

"Do," she cried, watching anxiously.

The pond was large, and had that perfect stillness and the dark lustre of very deep water. There were two small islands overgrown with bushes and a few trees, towards the middle. Birkin pushed himself off, and veered clumsily in the pond. Luckily the punt drifted so that he could catch hold of a willow bough, and pull in to the island.

"Rather overgrown," he said, looking inland, "but very nice. I'll come and fetch you. The boat leaks a little."

In a moment he was with her again, and she stepped into the wet punt.

"It'll float us all right," he said, and manoeuvred again to the island.

They landed under the willow tree. She shrank from the little jungle of rank plants before her, evil-smelling fig-wort and pallid hemlock. But he explored into it.

"I shall mow this down," he said, "and then it will be quite lovely—like *Paul et Virginie*."*

"And one could have lovely Watteau picnics* here," she cried with enthusiasm.

His face darkened.

"I don't want Watteau picnics here," he said.

"Only your Virginie," she laughed.

"Virginie enough," he smiled wryly. "No, I don't want her either."

Ursula looked at him closely. She had not seen him since Breadalby. He was very thin and hollow, with a set look in his face.

"You have been ill, haven't you?" she asked gently.

"Yes," he replied coldly.

They had sat down under the willow tree, and were looking at the pond, from their retreat on the island.

"Has it made you frightened?" she asked.

"What of?" he asked, turning his steady eyes to look at her. Something in him, inhuman and unmitigated, rather frightened her, and shook her out of her ordinary self.

"It *is* frightening to be very ill, isn't it?" she said. "It would terrify me out of my senses."

"It isn't pleasant," he said. "I suppose one *is* afraid of the pain and the wretchedness of it."

"And doesn't it make you feel ashamed? I think it makes one so ashamed, to be ill—illness is so terribly humiliating, don't you think?"

He considered for some minutes.

"Maybe," he said. "Though illness is only the physical manifestation of something wrong in the inner living, so I don't see why the illness itself is humiliating; I do see that the failure really to live is humiliating."

"How do you fail to live?" she asked, very much moved.

"I don't mean that I fail to exist—but I do fail in my living. My living *means* nothing—at least, not nearly enough. We are barren fig-trees."*

Ursula felt as if she were sinking to the bottom of her own unspoken dread, carried down by his words as by a heavy stone.

"But *I'm* not a barren fig-tree, am I?" she said.

"Not if you feel full of fruit," he said laconically.

She was silent for some minutes, fighting for her self-deception.

"But I'm happy—I think life is *awfully* jolly," she said.

"Good," he answered.

She reached for a bit of paper which had wrapped a small piece of chocolate he had given her, and began making a boat. He watched her without heeding her. She felt in the wrong.

"I *do* enjoy things—don't you?" she asked.

"I suppose so. But the flower is missing, off my bush at least. And it seems to me, nobody really flowers—there is no flowering of people in the world. They go on by vegetative reproduction."

"But you don't know everybody," she protested.

"Ah yes," he cried, "I know the tree, and therefore I know its fruit. You don't gather grapes of thistles."*

"But thistle flowers are *very* pretty," she insisted.

"Yes," he replied, ignoring her equivocation.

"Aren't they?" she persisted.

"Yes," he said.

And there was a silence, wherein she wanted to cry. She reached for another bit of chocolate paper, and began to fold another boat.

"And why is it," she asked at length, "that there is no flowering of human life now?"

"The whole idea is dead. Humanity itself is dry-rotten really. There are myriads of human beings hanging on the bush—and they look very nice and rosy, your healthy young men and women. But they are apples of Sodom, as a matter of fact, Dead Sea Fruit, gall-apples.* It isn't true that they have any significance—their insides are full of bitter, corrupt ash."

"But there *are* good people," protested Ursula.

"Good enough for the life of today. But mankind is a dead tree, covered with fine brilliant galls of people."

Ursula could not help stiffening herself against him, and against all he said. But neither could she help making him go on.

"And if it is so, *why* is it?" she asked, hostile. They were rousing each other to a fine passion of opposition.

"Why? Why are people all balls of bitter dust? Because they won't fall off the tree when they're ripe. They hang on to their old positions when the position is overpast, till they become infested with little worms and dry-rot."

There was a long pause. His voice had become hot and denunciatory. Ursula was trembling uncontrollably, they were both oblivious of everything but their own immersion.

"But even if everybody is wrong—where are you right?" she cried. "Where are you any better?"

"Because I don't want to lie," he cried back. "And everybody else wants to lie. They say humanity is bigger than me, when humanity is less than me. Humanity is a huge aggregate lie, and a huge lie is less than a small truth. Humanity is less, far less than the individual, because the individual may sometimes be capable of truth, and humanity is a tree of lies.— —And they say that love is the greatest thing; they persist in *saying* this, the foul liars, and just look at what they do! Look at all the millions of people who repeat every minute that love is the greatest, and charity is the greatest*—and see what they are doing all the time. By their works ye shall know them,* for dirty liars and cowards, who daren't stand by their own actions, much less by their own words."

"But," said Ursula sadly, "that doesn't alter the fact that love is the greatest, does it? What they *do* doesn't alter the truth of what they say, does it?"

"Completely. If what they say *were* true, then they couldn't help fulfilling it. But they maintain a lie, and so they run amok at last. It's a lie to say that love is the greatest. You might as well say that hate is the greatest, since the opposite of anything is its equivalent, in the absolute. Some people do try to say that hate is the greatest—and they have the popular ear, moreover, since they make it hatred of another party, for the good of their own. But love isn't the greatest—neither is hate. They are both human activities, which end in humanity. And I'm damned if humanity is anything but the barrenest of barren trees today, and there would be no *absolute* loss, if every human being perished tomorrow. The reality would be untouched. Nay, it would be better. The real tree of life would then be rid of the most ghastly heavy crop of Dead Sea Fruit, the intolerable burden of myriad simulacra of people, an infinite weight of mortal lies."

"So you'd like everybody in the world destroyed?" said Ursula.

"I should indeed."

"And the world empty of people."

"What a really beautiful thought."

The sad bitterness of his voice made Ursula pause to consider her own proposition. And really it *was* attractive: a clean, lovely, humanless world.

"But," she objected, "You'd be dead yourself, so what good would it do you?"

"I would die like a shot, to know that the earth would really be cleaned of *all* the people. It is the most beautiful and freeing thought. Then there would *never* be another foul humanity created, for a universal defilement."

"No," said Ursula, "there would be nothing."

"What! Nothing? Just because humanity was wiped out? Don't you flatter yourself. There'd be everything."

"But how, if there were no people?"

"Do you think that creation depends on *man*! Ha, the stinking conceit of human beings! Who was that impudent dirty Frenchman who said that God couldn't get on without *him*? God would get on a great deal better without him, and without all the lot of Frenchmen.* Do you think creation begins and ends with mankind? I tell you, mankind is an obstruction and a hindrance to creation. If man was swept off the face of the earth, creation would continue, perfect and marvellous and non-human. It would never create man again, as it does not create mammoths or ichthyosauri. But what lovely things, would be created, which man only obstructs now! What lovely things, what lovely things would come out of creation, save for the obstruction of man! I could howl in my soul, to know how lovely creation is prevented by man. The lovely things that would be, which I do not know, which humanity can never know, because humanity is the one condition which prevents their being! Think of bluebells and elder-blossom, and realise what non-human things can be, how lovely. Humanity is like the ichthyosauri, a creation gone wrong, become enormous instead of becoming wonderful and lovely. Even the tiger is lovely—and how long, I wonder, will it continue to exist? But man is neither lovely nor clean, he is a mere anti-creation, like the baboon."

Ursula watched him as he talked. There seemed a certain humour in him, all the while, at the same time a great fierceness. A fierce, white, destructive light was in his eyes, that made her think of the tiger he was quoting. At the same time his mouth quivered with faint humour, that seemed more sardonic. She was frightened, fear like a needle of ice in her heart. But also she exulted. She felt wonderfully liberated. Was she indeed to believe him, and be free? Yes, she hated humanity. From the bottom of her soul she hated humanity. Every human being was a millstone round her neck, every instance of mankind was a prison bar. But dare she repudiate them all? Dare she be rid of them all—everybody, father, mother, every acquaintance and every unknown person, get rid of them all out of herself, and trust to the great non-human element? She wanted to. But she felt very unsure.

"But," she said, "you believe in individual love, even if you don't believe in loving humanity—?"

"I don't believe in love at all—that is, any more than I believe in hate, or in grief. Love is one of the emotions like all the others—and so it is all right whilst you feel it. But I can't see how it becomes an absolute. It is just part of human relationships, no more. And it is only part of *any* human relationship. And why one should be required *always* to feel it, any more than one always feels sorrow or distinct joy, I cannot conceive. Love isn't a desideratum—it is an emotion you feel or you don't feel."

"Then why has it played such an important part?" she asked, obstinate now.

"We've lied about it, as usual. The love between a man and a woman, the great *mating* connection, that isn't love. It is something non-human, much deeper and greater than love. As you know, it contains everything—love, hate, affection, dislike, pity, contempt, respect, reverence—they are all contained in the chief relation between a man and a woman. But to call that relation *love* is simply to lie—using a word to make a creed cover something that it simply doesn't cover."

Ursula pondered this, with some satisfaction. Again she felt, here was something freer.

"You do think though," she urged, "that the love between a man and a woman is important?"

"The most important part of our living, the chief part. Only it isn't love. It is something non-human. It is a state wherein two human beings struggle together in the throes of non-human creation—and I don't mean procreation. It is a man and a woman thrown together to fulfil creation, the creation of sensation and emotion and idea and beauty, and the destruction of all static hindrances, a sinking of the old, barnacled ships. It is destruction of the static entities of the past, both in him and in her, and a dream-creation, the unknown coming forth in them. They are only the stem through which the blossom travels, out of the unknown creation into the known creation. But it is creation which matters, not the two human beings, and their idiotic opinions."

"Still," she persisted, "it *is* love."

He looked at her. Their eyes met. And they both broke into a laugh, without knowing why.

"I suppose so," he said. "It's the same old rose."

"And it *wouldn't* smell quite as sweet* if you rechristened it," she pleaded, her face all laughing and revealed.

"No," he said, with his sudden descent of naive seriousness. "But it is dangerous."

"Oh, you silly ass," she cried, laughing at him with sudden love and freedom.

He laughed too, laughing at himself and at her.

"I—" he began. But he bit his lip, and remained looking in her eyes. His own eyes were wide open and revealed. She saw, with terror, what he was going to say. And he, in fear and anguish like birth, wanted to say he loved her. But it was arrested on his lips. And she was glad. She could not have borne it at that moment. They both remained motionless for some seconds, knowing, and wanting to reveal to each other their knowledge. But it was too much. She sheered off. She rose and took one of her little boats and set it on the water. Her heart felt broken, quite broken, with the new revelation. As yet, she was far too much shocked and quivering to let him speak to her. But the promise that lay under all her violent trepidation was so wonderful, she knew that a new heaven and a new earth* had taken place, a new day was dawning in her.

He too went to the water's edge, and crouching, seemed gone in a busy forgetfulness. He picked a daisy and dropped it on the pond, so that the stem was a keel, the flower floated like a little water lily, staring with its open face up to the sky. It turned slowly round, in a slow, slow dervish dance, as it veered away.

That pleased him very much, he dropped several daisies into the water, and sat watching them with bright, absolved eyes, crouching near on the bank. Ursula watched also. A strange feeling possessed her, as if something were taking place. But everything was intangible. She could only watch the brilliant little discs of the daisies veering slowly in travel on the dark, lustrous water. The little flotilla was drifting into the light, a company of white specks in the distance.

"Do let us go to the shore, to follow them," she said. And they pushed off in the punt.

She was glad to be on the free land again. She went along the bank towards the sluice. The daisies were scattered broadcast on the pond, tiny glad things, like an exaltation, points of exaltation here and there. Why did they move her so strongly and poignantly?

"Look," he said, "your boat of purple paper is escorting them, and they are a convoy of ships."

Some of the daisies came slowly towards her, hesitating, making a shy bright little cotillon on the dark clear water. Their gay bright candour moved her so much as they came near, that she was almost in tears.

"Why are they so lovely?" she cried. "Why do I think them so lovely?"

"I always have a special feeling for them," he said. "I always think a daisy is like the choirs of angels that circle round the Most High, in the old system of heaven."

"Why?" she exclaimed. It seemed far-fetched and out-landish.

"The yellow ones for the Cherubim, and the white rays the Seraphim, standing round the Presence, then outside are the leaves and the grass, all the Hierarchies and the Principalities and Powers, stretching ad infinitum. It is a good figure of heaven, in the plant world."

"How very amusing!" she cried. But she mistrusted this talk of angels and Cherubim and Hierarchies.

"You know that a daisy is a company of little flowers, a concourse, not an individual. Don't the botanists put it highest in the line of development? I believe they do."

"The compositae, yes, I think so," said Ursula, who was never very sure of anything. Things she knew perfectly well, at one moment, seemed to become doubtful the next.

"Well then, there you are," he said. "The daisy is a perfect concord, circling round the Invisible, circling in rings in their proper order, the yellow ones palpitating with the Presence, absorbed in praise, the white ones transmitting the Glory, the green sepals like Hierarchies sheltering the Mystery, and the leaves and the grass around are the Multitudes and the Powers. What more do you want, for heaven?"

"Yes but," Ursula laughed, "what is the Most High, in the centre?"

"The invisible. But it is there, how would they have their wonderful centrality, otherwise? But it is purely unknowable. Only, you know it *is*."

"It's a dark horse, in fact," said Ursula, who had a grudge against mysticism in every form.

"Completely dark," he replied. "The old painters quite messed up the show by putting a man-god in the middle."

"Old and unexciting," said Ursula.

"No—not necessarily. Fra Angelico's is about forty, Raphael's even younger. I expect they all thought the Most High was a little older than themselves."

"Oh but I love Fra Angelico's angels," cried Ursula; "they are so gay and tripping."

"It is such a bore," he said, "that man must always take himself as the measure and criterion of the universe; it is such a wearying vanity. Man is one of the natural phenomena, and no more."

"Yes," said Ursula. "Men think themselves so important, they and their laws and their cocksureness, and their eternal preaching of what is and what isn't. After all, what does their precious knowledge and wisdom amount to? They are so conceited about their own tuppenny cleverness. If only they'd stop knowing, and realise that the unknown is all right, in spite of them and their damned importance. I hate men, for their centuries of jawing that they thrust down our throats."

He went pale, and set in opposition to her.

"It isn't knowing that ails them," he said, "it's not-knowing; it is that they haven't the courage to know."

"But you don't get anywhere by *knowing*," said Ursula in desperation. "You have to stop knowing, and begin to *be*."

"And how are you going to start?" he asked sarcastically. "Don't you imagine for a moment that you can *be* anything at all, merely by shutting your eyes and shouting: 'Now I can't see, and I'm *being*.' It's the wretchedest of self-deceptions. You've got to know, and know to the full, you've got to swallow the last dregs of nauseous knowledge, before you've had enough, and can start afresh."

"But I needn't know in my head," she protested. "I do know in my feel, why should I be forced to know in my head!"

"Because you'll go round and round inside what you feel, like a donkey in a pound, that doesn't know it is in a pound, but only knows it feels giddy with going round and round. What you feel *is* knowledge— sensational knowledge. And that's like a bud—it has to burst open into a flower of conscious knowledge. And *then* the seed can fall into the unknown, be delivered over to the unknown like a seed that goes into the dark underground. But you've got to know everything, before you can escape from knowing, before you can be a spontaneous spark of creation fanned up to a fire, by the unknown."

"But why, why must I know everything? It is most horrible. I am sick of knowing already. I *do* want something else."

"Somebody has to know, or we all rot in the bud. And you're not sick of knowing—you're only sick of the mechanical confinement which fixes the terms of your knowing. What you desire is *sensational* knowledge, which is called living. But sensational knowledge isn't living unless it passes on into the blossom of conscious knowledge. Have your sensational knowledge by all means—have whatsoever you want. But don't deny the finishing stage of the process. Make conscious your experience, to the very last, and then you'll find you have escaped the burden of self-consciousness, you'll fall like a ripe seed into the unknown creativity. It is horrible to know the last truths about ourselves and our sensations, because it shatters the lovely safe enclosure of our established ideas and beliefs and concepts, it is a death and destruction of our conscious self, that which we know ourselves to be. But it has got to be done, if we are not going all merely to perish in the final glistening experience of death and killing, or to rot in the bud, like the sensationalists."

Ursula was silent. She loved him for talking to her so sincerely, with so much bitter passion. Perhaps she believed him. And above all, she felt glad he was so generous, to take so much notice of her, so much trouble. But she did wish he told her something not quite so crude. She always dreamed that a man would come with a lovely revelation, so beautiful and wonderful, she would know the whole truth at once. And this was very different from her dream. This had the hard crudity of real life.

"And besides," she said, "how can one have one's sensational knowledge? You've got to find somebody to get it from, first."

"Find him then," he said.

"Yes, and where? There aren't any men who can *really* give one any new experience—anything new. One *knows* all the men, potentially. One has experienced all that the best men one has known could give; and it seems, unless one knew a negro or an animal, there isn't anything else. What is it, my experience of a man? It's merely what I knew before. The top note is missing, always missing. And if I look at a million men, I know it is missing from them all. They can't give it me. Don't I know! You tell me to get what sensational experience I want—but where? Where am I to get it? Why do you talk at me? I don't care for your philosophies. *Give* me what I want then—give it me—then I'll realise it hard enough. But don't talk to me about it."

She was drawn up before him, her throat pressed back, her eyes full of yellow beams, that seemed to dart out at him. He watched her in silence. He seemed to faint in a sudden wreath of white consuming fire. Then he came to, and found himself standing firm before her.

"All right," he said. And leaning unconsciously forward, he touched her lips with his own.

Her incandescent fury and pallor fell from her at once, she was soft and confused and beautiful, and she seemed to draw away.

"Only," he said, in a soft voice that convulsed her like a madness, "you mustn't have any reserves. It must be everything, *everything*, beyond knowledge everything—or let it be nothing. Don't have reserves."

She stood aside, looking at the water, and made no reply. As if stunned, they both stood motionless and barely conscious. The terrible naked statement that had been made between them had torn away the veils of their conscious selves, and left them like two impersonal forces, there in contact.

He became aware that he must pick up the situation, that he must say something, that he must proceed.

"You know," he said, "that I am having rooms here at the mill? We can be perfectly free."

"Oh are you?" she said, ignoring all his implication, and refusing the situation.

He saw her, and left her to her own coverings.

"If I think I can live sufficiently by myself," he continued, "I shall give up my work altogether. It has become a complete lie to me. I don't believe in the humanity I pretend to be part of, I don't believe at all in the social ideals I live by, I hate even the organic form of social mankind—so it can't be anything but a lie, to work at education. I shall drop it as soon as I am strong enough—tomorrow perhaps—and be purely on my own."

"Have you enough to live on?" asked Ursula.

"Yes—I've about two hundred a year. That makes it easy for me. I feel it's an unfair advantage. But money or no money should make no difference."

"No, it shouldn't," said Ursula.

There was a pause.

"And what about Hermione?" asked Ursula.

"That's over, finally—a pure failure, and never could be anything else."

"But you still know each other?"

"We could hardly pretend to be strangers, could we?"

There was a stubborn pause.

"But isn't that a reserve?" asked Ursula at length.

"I don't think so," he said. "You'll be able to tell me if it is."

Again there was a pause of some minutes duration. He was thinking.

"One must throw everything away, everything—let everything go, to get the one last thing one wants."

"What thing?" she asked, in challenge.

"I don't know—genuine sensual fulfilment, and conscious fulfilment."

There was heard a loud barking of the dogs below. He seemed disturbed by it. She did not notice. Only she thought he seemed uneasy.

"As a matter of fact," he said, in rather a small voice, "I believe that is Hermione come now, with Gerald Crich. She wanted to see the rooms before they are furnished."

"I know," said Ursula. "She will superintend the furnishing for you."

"Probably. Does it matter?"

"Oh no, I should think not," said Ursula. "Though remember, I can't bear her. I think she is a lie, if you like, you who are always talking about lies." Then she ruminated for a moment, when she broke out: "Yes, and I do mind if she furnishes your rooms—I do mind. I mind that you keep her hanging on at all."

He was silent now, struggling.

"All right," he said. "She shan't furnish the rooms here—and I won't keep her hanging on. Only, I needn't be churlish to her, need I?——At any rate, I shall have to go down and see them now. You'll come, won't you?"

"I don't think so," she said coldly and irresolutely.

"Won't you? Yes do. Come and see the rooms as well. Do come."

He set off down the bank, and she went unwillingly with him. Yet she would not have stayed away, either.

In the large, darkish kitchen of the mill, the laborer's wife was talking shrilly to Hermione and Gerald, who stood, he in white and she in a glistening bluish foulard, strangely luminous in the dusk of the room; whilst from the cages on the walls, a dozen or more canaries sang at the top of their voices. The cages were all placed round a small square window at the back, where the sunshine came in, a beautiful beam, filtering through green leaves of a tree. The voice of Mrs Naylor shrilled against the noise of the birds, which rose ever more wild and triumphant, and the woman's voice went up and up against them, and the birds replied with wild animation.

"Here's Rupert!" shouted Gerald in the midst of the din. He was suffering badly, being very sensitive in the ear.

"O-o-h them birds, they won't let you speak—!" shrilled the laborer's wife in disgust. "I'll cover them up."

And she darted here and there, throwing a duster, an apron, a towel, a table-cloth over the cages of the birds.

"Now will you stop it, and let a body speak for your row," she said, still in a voice that was too high.

The party watched her. Soon the cages were covered, they had a strange funereal look. But from under the towels odd defiant trills and bubblings still shook out.

"Oh, they won't go on," said Mrs Naylor reassuringly. "They'll go to sleep now."

"Really," said Hermione, politely.

"They will," said Gerald. "They will go to sleep automatically, now the impression of evening is produced."

"Are they so easily deceived?" cried Ursula.

"Oh yes," replied Gerald. "Don't you know the story of Fabre, who, when he was a boy, put a hen's head under her wing, and she straight away went to sleep?* It's quite true."

"And did that make him a naturalist?" asked Birkin.

"Probably," said Gerald.

Meanwhile Ursula was peeping under one of the cloths. There sat the canary in a corner, bunched and fluffed up for sleep.

"How ridiculous!" she cried. "It really thinks the night has come! How absurd! Really, how can one have any respect for a creature that is so easily taken in!"

"Yes," sang Hermione, coming also to look. She put a hand on Ursula's arm and chuckled a low laugh. "Yes, doesn't he look comical?" she chuckled. "Like a stupid husband."

Then, with her hand still on Ursula's arm, she drew her away, saying, in her mild sing-song:

"How did you come here? We saw Gudrun too."

"I came to look at the pond," said Ursula, "and I found Mr Birkin there."

"Did you.——This is quite a Brangwen land, isn't it!"

"I'm afraid I hoped so," said Ursula. "I ran here for refuge, when I saw you down the lake just putting off."

"Did you!—And now we've run you to earth."

Hermione's eyelids lifted with an uncanny movement, hurt and overwrought. She had always her strange, rapt look, unnatural and irresponsible.

"I was going on," said Ursula. "Mr Birkin wanted me to see the rooms. Isn't it delightful to live here? It is perfect."

"Yes," said Hermione, abstractedly. Then she turned right away from Ursula, ceased to know her existence.

"How do you feel, Rupert?" she sang in a new, affectionate tone, to Birkin.

"Very well," he replied.

"Were you quite comfortable?" The curious, sinister, rapt look was on Hermione's face, she shrugged her bosom in a convulsed movement, and seemed like one half in a trance.

"Quite comfortable," he replied.

There was a long pause, whilst Hermione looked at him for a long time, from under her heavy, drugged eyelids.

"And you think you'll be happy here," she said at last.

"I'm sure I shall."

"I'm sure I shall do anything for him as I can," said the laborer's wife. "And I'm sure my mester will; so I *hope* as he'll find himself comfortable."

Hermione turned and looked at her slowly.

"Thank you so much," she said, and then she turned completely away again. She recovered her position, and lifting her face towards him, and addressing him exclusively, she said:

"Have you measured the rooms?"

"No," he said, "I've been mending the punt."

"Shall we do it now?" she said slowly, balanced and dispassionate.

"Have you got a tape measure, Mrs Naylor?" he said, turning to the woman.

"Yes sir, I think I can find you one," replied the woman, bustling immediately to a basket. "This is the only one I've got, if it will do."

Hermione took it, though it was offered to him.

"Thank you so much," she said. "It will do very nicely. Thank you so much." Then she turned to Birkin, saving with a little gay movement: "Shall we do it now, Rupert?"

"What about the others, they'll be bored," he said reluctantly.

"Do you mind?" said Hermione, turning to Ursula and Gerald vaguely.

"Not in the least," they replied.

"Which room shall we do first?" she said, turning again to Birkin, with the same gaiety, now she was going to *do* something with him.

"We'll take them as they come," he said.

"Should I be getting your teas ready, while you do that?" said the laborer's wife, also gay because *she* had something to do.

"Would you?" said Hermione, turning to her with the curious motion of intimacy that seemed to envelop the woman, draw her almost to Hermione's breast, and which left the others standing apart. "I should be so glad? Where shall we have it?"

"Where you would like it, my lady! Shall it be in here, or out on the grass?"

"Where shall we have tea?" sang Hermione to the company at large.

"On the bank by the pond. And *we'll* carry the things up, if you'll just get them ready, Mrs Naylor," said Birkin.

"All right sir," said the pleased woman.

The party moved down the passage into the front room. It was empty, but clean and sunny. There was a window looking on to the tangled front garden.

"This is the dining room," said Hermione. "We'll measure it this way, Rupert—you go down there—"

"Can't I do it for you," said Gerald, coming to take the end of the tape.

"No thank you," cried Hermione, stooping to the ground in her bluish, brilliant foulard. It was a great joy to her to *do* things, and to have the ordering of the job, with Birkin. He obeyed her calmly. Ursula and Gerald looked on. It was a peculiarity of Hermione's, that at every moment, she had one intimate, and turned all the rest of those present into onlookers. This raised her into a state of triumph.

CHAPTER 4

They measured and discussed in the dining-room, and Hermione decided what the floor coverings must be. It sent her into a strange, convulsed anger, to be thwarted. Birkin always quietly let her have her way, for the moment.

Then they moved across, through the little hall, to the other front room, that was a little smaller than the first.

"This is the study," said Hermione. "Rupert, I have a rug that I want you to have for here. Will you let me give it you? Do—I want to give it you."

"What is it like?" he asked ungraciously.

"You haven't seen it. It is chiefly rose red, then blue, a metallic, mid-blue, and a very soft dark blue. I think you would like it. Do you think you would?"

"It sounds very nice," he replied. "What is it? Oriental?"

"Yes. It is made of camel's hair, silky. It is called Bergamos.* The length is twelve feet, and the breadth seven. Do you think it would do?"

"It would *do*," he said. "But why should you give me an expensive rug like that. I can manage perfectly well with my old Oxford Turkish."

"But may I give it you? Do let me."

"How much did it cost?"

She laughed at him, and said easily:

"I don't remember. It was quite cheap."

He looked at her, his face set.

"I don't want to take it, Hermione," he said.

"Do let me give it to the rooms," she said, going up to him and putting her hand on his arm lightly, pleadingly. "I shall be so disappointed."

"You know I don't want you to give me things," he repeated helplessly.

"I don't want to give you *things*," she laughed cheerfully. "But will you have this?"

"All right," he said coldly, and she triumphed.

They went upstairs. There were two bedrooms to correspond with the rooms downstairs. One of them was half furnished, and Birkin had evidently slept there. Hermione went round the room carefully, taking in every detail, as if absorbing the evidence of his presence, in all the inanimate things. She felt the bed and examined the coverings.

"Are you sure you were quite comfortable?" she said, pressing the pillow.

"Perfectly," he replied coldly.

"And were you warm? There is no eider-down quilt. I am sure you need one. You mustn't have a great pressure of clothes."

"I've got one," he said. "It is coming down."

They measured the rooms, and lingered over every consideration. Ursula stood at the window and watched the woman carrying the tea up the bank to the pond. She hated the palaver Hermione made, she wanted to drink tea, she wanted anything but this fuss and business.

At last they all mounted the grassy bank, to the picnic. Hermione poured out tea. She ignored now Ursula's presence. And Ursula, recovering from her ill-humour, turned to Gerald saying:

"I hated you so much the other day, Mr Crich."

"What for?" said Gerald, wincing slightly away.

"For treating your horse so badly. Oh, I hated you so much!"

"What did he do?" sang Hermione.

"He made his Arab horse stand with him at the railway-crossing whilst a horrible lot of trucks went by; and the poor thing, she was in a perfect frenzy, a perfect agony. It was the most horrible sight I have ever seen."

"Why did you do it, Gerald?" asked Hermione, calm and interrogative.

"She must learn to stand—what use is she to me, in this country, if she shies and gets into a perfect frenzy, as they call it, every time an engine whistles."

"But it was unnecessary torture," said Ursula, "to make her stand all that time at the crossing. You might just as well have ridden back up the road, and saved all that horror. Her sides were bleeding where you had spurred her. Oh, it was horrible—!"

Gerald winced and stiffened.

"I have to use her," he replied. "And if I'm going to be sure of her at *all*, she'll have to learn to stand anything."

"Why should she?" cried Ursula in a passion. "She is a living creature, why should she stand anything, just because you choose to make her? She has as much right to her own being, as you have to yours."

"There I disagree," said Gerald. "I consider that mare is there for my use. Not because I bought her, but because that is the natural order. It is more natural for a man to take a horse and use it as he likes, than for him to go down on his knees to it, begging it to do as it wishes, and to fulfil its own marvellous nature."

Ursula was just breaking out, when Hermione lifted her face and began, in her musing sing-song:

"I do think—I do really think we must have the *courage* to use the lower animal life for our needs. I do think there is something wrong, when we look on every living creature as if it were ourself. I do feel, that it is false to project our own feelings on every animate creature. It is a lack of discrimination, a lack of criticism."

"Quite," said Birkin sharply. "Nothing is so detestable as the maudlin attributing of human feelings and consciousness to animals. Better kill all the animals and have done with it."

"Or let the animals devour you," said Gerald.

"Yes," said Hermione, wearily, "we must really take a position. Either we are going to use the animals, or they will use us."

"That's a fact," said Gerald. "A horse has got a will like a man, though it has no mind to speak of. And if your will isn't master, then the horse is your master. And whatever right or wrong may be, a horse is not going to be master of me."

"If only we could learn how to use our will," said Hermione, "we could do anything. The will can cure anything, and put everything right. That I am convinced of—if we only use it intelligently."

"What do you mean, by using the will properly?" said Birkin in contempt.

"A very great doctor taught me," she said, addressing Ursula and Gerald, vaguely. "He told me, for instance, that to cure oneself of a bad habit, one should do it, force oneself to do it, against one's inclination. And then the habit would disappear."

"How do you mean?" said Gerald.

"If you bite your nails, for example. Then, when you don't want to bite your nails, bite them—make yourself bite them. And you would find the habit was broken."

"Is that so?" said Gerald.

"Yes. And in so many things, I have *made* myself well. I was a very queer and nervous girl. And by learning to use my will, simply by using my will, I *made* myself right."

Ursula looked all the while at Hermione, as she spoke in her slow, dispassionate, and yet strangely tense voice. A curious thrill went over the younger woman. Some strange, dark, convulsive power was in Hermione, fascinating and repelling.

"It is vile to use the will like that," cried Birkin harshly, "almost obscene. Such a will is an obscenity."

Hermione looked at him for a long time, with her shadowed, heavy eyes. Her face was soft and pale and thin, almost phosphorescent, her jaw was lean.

"I'm sure it isn't," she said at length. There always seemed an interval, a strange split between what she seemed to feel and experience, and what she actually said and thought. She seemed to catch her thoughts at length from off the surface of a maelstrom of chaotic black emotions and reactions, and Birkin was always filled with repulsion, she caught so infallibly, her will never failed her. Her voice was always dispassionate and tense, and perfectly confident. Yet she shuddered with a sense of nausea, a sort of sea-sickness that always threatened to overwhelm her mind. But her mind remained unbroken, her will was still perfect. It almost sent Birkin mad. But he would never, never dare to break her will, and let loose the maelstrom of her subconsciousness, and see her in her ultimate madness. Yet he was always striking at her.

"And of course," he said to Gerald, "horses *haven't* got a complete will, like human beings. A horse has *no* will. Every horse, strictly, is mad. It is only sane enough to want to put itself under the control of the human will. But every horse is potentially mad—you know that, if ever you've felt a horse bolt, while you've been driving it."

"I have felt a horse bolt while I was driving it," said Gerald, "but it didn't make me know the horse was mad. I only knew it was frightened."

Hermione had ceased to listen. She simply became oblivious when these disturbing emotions were started.

"Why is every horse mad?" asked Ursula, seized with a little horror.

"Because there is practically no relation between its subconscious impulses and emotion, and its conscious activity. That is why its conscious entity can break down at any minute, and it becomes for the time mad, purely a mad torrent of chaotic feelings, acting disconnectedly. And though horses have put themselves under the human will, yet there is somewhere a primal vicious hatred of the human principle, within them. The human principle has terrible antagonists in the life it has appropriated."

Hermione could bear no more. She rose, saying in her easy sing-song:

"Isn't the evening beautiful! I get filled sometimes with such a great sense of beauty, that I feel I can hardly bear it."

Ursula, to whom she had appealed, rose with her, moved to the last impersonal depths of pity. And Birkin seemed to her almost a monster of cruelty. She went with Hermione along the bank of the pond, talking of beautiful, soothing things, picking the gentle cowslips.

"Wouldn't you like a dress," said Ursula to Hermione, "of this yellow spotted with orange—a cotton dress?"

"Yes," said Hermione, stopping and looking at the flower, letting the thought come home to her and soothe her. "Wouldn't it be pretty? I should *love* it."

And she turned smiling to Ursula, in a feeling of real affection.

But Gerald remained with Birkin, wanting to probe him to the bottom, to know what he meant by the madness of horses. A flicker of excitement danced on Gerald's face.

Hermione and Ursula strayed on together, united in a sudden bond of deep affection and closeness.

"I really do *not* want to be forced into all this criticism and analysis of life. I really *do* want to see things in their entirety, with their beauty left to them, and their wholeness, their natural holiness.—Don't you feel it, don't you feel you *can't* be tortured into any more knowledge?" said Hermione, stopping in front of Ursula, and turning to her with clenched fists thrust downwards.

"Yes," said Ursula. "I do. I am sick of all this poking and prying."

"I'm so glad you are. Sometimes," said Hermione, again stopping arrested in her progress and turning to Ursula, "sometimes I wonder if I *ought* to submit to all this realisation, if I am not being weak in rejecting it.—But I feel I *can't*—I *can't*. It seems to destroy *everything*. All the beauty and the,—and the true holiness is destroyed,—and I feel I can't live without them."

"And it would be simply wrong to live without them," cried Ursula. "No, it is so *irreverent* to think that everything must be realised in the head. Really, something must be left to the Lord."

"Yes," said Hermione, reassured like a child, "it should, shouldn't it? And Rupert—" she lifted her face to the sky, in a muse—"he *can* only tear things to pieces. He really *is* like a boy who must pull everything to pieces to see how it is made. And I can't think it is right—it does seem so irreverent, as you say."

"Like tearing open a bud to see what the flower will be like," said Ursula.

"Yes. And that kills everything, doesn't it? It doesn't allow any possibility of flowering."

"Of course not," said Ursula. "It is purely destructive."

"It is, isn't it!"

Hermione looked long and slow at Ursula, seeming to accept confirmation from her. Then the two women were silent. As soon as they were in accord, they began mutually to mistrust each other. In spite of herself, Ursula felt herself recoiling from Hermione. It was all she could do to restrain her revulsion.

They returned to the men, like two conspirators who have withdrawn to come to an agreement. Birkin looked up at them. Ursula hated him for his cold watchfulness. But he said nothing.

"Shall we be going?" said Hermione. "Rupert, you are coming to Shortlands to dinner? Will you come at once, will you come now, with us?"

"I'm not dressed," replied Birkin. "And you know Gerald stickles for the convention."

"I don't stickle for it," said Gerald. "But if you'd got as sick as I have of clattering go-as-you-please in the house, you'd be glad if people were peaceful and conventional, at least at meals."

"All right," said Birkin.

"But can't we wait for you while you dress?" persisted Hermione.

"If you like."

He rose to go indoors. Ursula said she would take her leave.

"Only," she said, turning to Gerald, "I must say that, however man is lord of the beast and the fowl,* I still don't think he has any right to violate the feelings of the inferior creation. I still think you would have been much more sensible and natural if you'd trotted back up the road while the train went by, and spared the scene."

"I see," said Gerald, smiling, but somewhat annoyed. "I must remember another time."

"They all think I'm an interfering female," thought Ursula to herself, as she went away. But she was in arms against them.

She ran home plunged in thought. She had been very much moved by Hermione, she had really come into contact with her, so that there was a sort of league between the two women. And yet she could not bear her. But she put the thought away. "She's really good," she said to herself. "She really wants what is right." And she tried to feel at one with Hermione, and to shut off from Birkin. She was strictly hostile to him. She dared not remember how he had accepted her challenge, how he had touched her lips. She wanted to forget it, to pretend it never had been.

Only now and again, violent little shudders would come over her, out of her subconsciousness, and she knew it was the awful fact that she had stated her shocking challenge to Birkin, and he had lightly touched her on the lips. She wished he did not know; she wished he might forget, that it might be wiped out of existence, in his knowledge. What could have led her into this betrayal of herself? She shuddered, and ran away from what was ahead.

The days went by, and she received no sign. Was he going to ignore her, was he going to take no further notice of her secret? A dreary weight of anxiety and acrid bitterness settled on her. And yet she knew she was only deceiving herself, that he *would* proceed. She said no word to anybody.

Then, sure enough, there came a note from him, asking if she would come to tea, with Gudrun, to his rooms in town.

"Why does he ask Gudrun as well?" she asked herself at once. "Does he want to protect himself, or does he think I would not go alone?"

She was tormented by the shameful thought that he wanted to protect himself. She suffered very much. But at the end of all, she only said to herself:

"I don't *want* Gudrun to be there, because I want him to say something more to me. So I shan't tell Gudrun anything about it, and I shall go alone. Then I shall know."

She found herself sitting in the tram-car, mounting up the hill going out of the town, to the place where he had his lodging. She seemed to have passed into a kind of dream world, absolved from the conditions of actuality. She watched the sordid streets of the town go by beneath her, as if she were a spirit disconnected from the material universe. What had it all to do with her? She was palpitating and formless within the flux of the ghost life. She could not think any more, what anybody would say of her or think about her. People had passed out of her range, she was absolved. She had fallen strange and dim, out of the sheath of the material life, like a berry falls from the only world it has ever known, down out of the sheath on to the real unknown.

Birkin was standing in the middle of the room, when she was shown in by the landlady. He too was moved outside himself. She saw him agitated and shaken, a frail, unsubstantial body silent like the node of some violent force, that came out from him and shook her almost into unconsciousness.

"You are alone?" he said.

"Yes—Gudrun couldn't come."

He instantly divined her shame.

"Just as well," he said. "I only thought you might prefer it if she came with you."

"I thought you were thinking that," said Ursula.

And they were both seated in silence, in the terrible tension of the sitting room. She was aware that it was a pleasant room full of light and very restful in its form—aware also of a lovely fuchsia tree, with dangling scarlet and purple flowers.

"How nice the fuchsias are!" she said, to break the silence.

"Aren't they!—Did you think I had forgotten my pledge?"

A swoon went over Ursula's mind.

"I don't want you to remember it—if you don't want to," she struggled to say, through the dark mist that covered her.

There was silence for some moments.

"No," he said. "It isn't that. Only—I don't know if you want what I have to give. I *have* only certain things in me—and I don't know if they are what you want."

There was a clang of mistrust and almost anger in his voice. She did not answer. Her heart was too much contracted. She could not have spoken.

Seeing she was not going to reply, he continued, almost bitterly, giving himself away:

"I can't say it is love I have to offer—and it isn't love I want. It is something much more impersonal and harder,—and rarer."

There was a silence, out of which she said:

"You mean you don't love me?"

She suffered bitterly, saying that.

"Yes, if you like to put it like that.—Though perhaps that isn't true. I don't know. At any rate, I don't feel the emotion of love for you—no, and I don't want to. Because it gives out in the last issues."

"Love gives out in the last issues?" she asked, feeling numb to the lips.

"Yes, it does. At the very last, one is alone, beyond the influence of love. There is a great impersonal me, that is beyond love, beyond any emotional relationship. So it is with you. But we want to delude ourselves that love is the root. It isn't. It is only the branches. The root is beyond love, a naked kind of isolation, an isolated me, that does *not* meet and mingle, and never can."

She watched him with wide, troubled eyes. His face was incandescent in its abstract earnestness.

"And you mean you can't love?" she asked, in trepidation.

"Yes, if you like.—I have loved. But there is a beyond, where there is no love."

She could not submit to this death. She felt it swooning over her. But she could not submit.

"But how do you know—if you have never *really* loved?" she asked.

"It is true, what I say: there is a beyond, in you, in me, which is further than love, beyond the scope, as stars are beyond the scope of vision, some of them."

"Then there *is* no love," cried Ursula.

"Ultimately, no, there is something else. But ultimately, there *is* no love."

Ursula was given over to this statement for some moments. Then she half rose from her chair, saving, in a final, repellant voice:

"Then let me go home—what am I doing here!"

"There is the door," he said. "You are a free agent."

He was trembling finely and violently in the stress of extremity. She hung motionless for some seconds, then she sat down again.

"If there is no love, what is there?" she cried, almost jeering.

"Something," he said, looking at her, battling with her in his soul, with all his might.

"What?"

He was silent for a long time, unable to be in communication with her whilst she was in this state of opposition.

"There is," he said, in a voice of pure abstraction, "a final me which is stark and impersonal and beyond responsibility. So there is a final you. And it is there I would want to meet you—not in the emotional, loving plane—but there beyond, where there is no speech and no terms of agreement. There we are two stark, unknown beings, two utterly strange creatures, I would want to approach you, and you me.—And there could be no obligation, because there is no standard for action there, because no understanding has been reaped from that plane. It is quite inhuman,—so there can be no calling to book, in any form whatsoever—because one is outside the pale of all that is accepted, and nothing known applies. One can only follow the primal impulse, taking that which lies in front, and responsible for nothing, asked for nothing, giving nothing, only each taking according to the primal desire."

Ursula listened to this speech, her mind dumb and almost senseless, that he said was so unexpected and so untoward.

"It is just purely selfish," she said.

"If it is pure, yes. But it isn't selfish at all. Because I don't *know* what I want of you. I deliver *myself* over to the unknown, in coming to you, I am without reserves or defences, stripped entirely into the unknown. Only there needs the pledge between us, that we will both cast off everything, cast off ourselves even, and cease to be, so that that which is more than we can take place in us."

She pondered along her own line of thought.

"But it is because you love me, that you want me?" she persisted.

"No it isn't. It is because I believe in you—if I *do* believe in you."

"Aren't you sure?" she laughed, suddenly hurt.

He was looking at her steadfastly, scarcely heeding what she said.

"Yes, I must believe in you, or else I shouldn't be here saying this," he replied. "But that is all the proof I have. I don't feel any very strong belief at this particular moment."

She disliked him for his sudden relapse into weariness and faithlessness.

"But don't you think me good-looking?" she persisted, in a mocking voice.

He looked at her, to see if he felt that she was good-looking.

"I don't *feel* that you're good-looking," he said.

"Not even attractive?" she mocked, bitingly.

He knitted his brows in sudden exasperation.

"Don't you see that it's not a question of visual appreciation in the least," he cried. "I don't *want* to see you. I've seen plenty of women, I'm sick and weary of seeing them. I want a woman I don't see."

"I'm sorry I can't oblige you by being invisible," she laughed, inclined as a last resource to turn it all to a joke.

"Yes," he said, "you are invisible to me, if you don't force me to be visually aware of you. But I don't want to see you or hear you."

"What did you ask me to tea for, then?" she mocked.

But he would take no notice of her. He was talking to himself.

"I want to find you, where you don't know your own existence, the you that your glib overself denies utterly. But I don't want your good looks, and I don't want your womanly feelings, and I don't want your thoughts nor opinions nor your ideas—they are all bagatelles to me."

"You are very conceited, Monsieur," she mocked. "How do you know what my womanly feelings are, or my thoughts or my ideas? You don't even know what I think of you now."

"Nor do I care in the slightest."

"I think you are very silly. I think you want to tell me you love me, and you go all this way round to do it."

"All right," he said, looking up with sudden exasperation. "Now go away then, and leave me alone. I don't want any more of your meretricious persiflage."

"Is it really persiflage?" she mocked, her face stiffening into anger.

They were silent for many minutes, she stiff and unable to accept him, unable to give way. His concentration broke, he began to glance over the books on the shelves. The whole tension disappeared.

"Have you ever read Herman Melville's 'Moby Dick'?" he asked, in a quick, animated voice. He had relaxed altogether from his other thoughts.

"No," she said, disappointed, and rather angry.

He noticed her muted voice. But he was irritated and angry too. He wanted to have done, for the time being. He wanted to be superficial, to ignore any further realisation with her.

"It is astonishingly good," he said. "It surprises me how much older, over-ripe and withering into abstraction, this American classic literature is, than English literature of the same time. It seems as if the slip of the old tree ran more swiftly into last old age, when it was transplanted to America, than the parent tree itself did here."

"Something else will come in its place," said Ursula sullenly.

"Oh yes," he said. And he rang the bell for tea.

A young grey cat that had been sleeping on the sofa jumped down and stretched, rising on its long legs, and arching its slim back. Then it sat considering for a moment, erect and kingly. And then, like a dart, it had shot out of the room, through the open window-doors, and into the garden.

"What's he after?" said Birkin, rising.

The young cat trotted lordly down the path, waving his tail. He was an ordinary tabby with white paws, a slender young gentleman. A crouching, fluffy, brownish-grey cat was stealing up the side of the fence. The Mino walked statelily up to her, with manly nonchalance. She crouched before him and pressed herself on the ground in humility, a fluffy soft outcast, looking up at him with wild eyes that were green and lovely as great jewels. He looked casually down on her. So she crept a few inches further, proceeding on her way to the back door, crouching in a wonderful soft, self-obliterating manner, and moving like a shadow.

He, going statelily on his slim legs, walked after her, then suddenly, for pure excess, he gave her a light cuff with his paw on the side of her face. She ran off a few steps, like a blown leaf along the ground, then crouched unobtrusively, in submissive, wild patience. The Mino pretended to take no notice of her. He blinked his eyes superbly at the landscape. In a minute she drew herself together and moved softly, a fleecy brown-grey shadow, a few paces forward. She began to quicken her pace, in a moment she would be gone like a dream, when the young grey lord sprang before her, and gave her a light handsome cuff. She subsided at once, submissively.

"She is a wild cat," said Birkin. "She has come in from the woods."

The eyes of the stray cat flared round for a moment, like great green fires staring at Birkin. Then she had rushed in a soft swift rush, half way down the garden. There she paused to look round. The Mino turned his face in pure superiority to his master, and slowly closed his eyes, standing in statuesque young perfection. The wild cat's round, green, wondering eyes were staring all the while like uncanny fires. Then again, like a shadow, she slid towards the kitchen.

In a lovely springing leap, like a wind, the Mino was upon her, and had boxed her twice, very definitely, with a white, delicate fist. She sank and slid back, unquestioning. He walked after her, and cuffed her once or twice, leisurely, with sudden little blows of his magic white paws.

"Now why does he do that?" cried Ursula in indignation.

"They are on intimate terms," said Birkin.

"And is that why he hits her!" cried Ursula.

"Yes," laughed Birkin. "I think he only wants to assert his male primacy."

"Isn't it horrid of him!" she cried; and going out into the garden she called to the Mino:

"Stop it, don't bully. Stop hitting her."

The stray cat vanished like a swift, invisible shadow. The Mino glanced at Ursula, then looked from her disdainfully to his master.

"Are you a bully, Mino?" Birkin asked.

The young slim cat looked at him, and slowly narrowed its eyes.

Then it glanced away at the landscape, looking into the distance as if completely oblivious of the two human beings.

"Mino," said Ursula, "I don't like you. You are a bully like all males."

"No," said Birkin, "he is justified. He is not a bully. He is only insisting to the poor stray that he represents a higher order of understanding, and therefore she is to behave with proper respect. I am with him entirely."

"You would be!" cried Ursula.

The statuesque young cat again glanced at Birkin in disdain of the noisy woman.

"I quite agree with you, Miciotto,"* said Birkin to the cat. "Keep your male dignity of higher understanding."

Again the Mino narrowed his eyes as if he were looking at the sun. Then, suddenly affecting to have no connection at all with the two people, he went trotting off, with assumed spontaneity and gaiety, his tail erect, his white feet blithe.

"Now he will find the belle sauvage* once more, and entertain her with his superior wisdom," laughed Birkin.

Ursula looked at the man who stood in the garden with his hair blowing and his eyes smiling ironically, and she cried:

"Oh it makes me so cross, this assumption of male superiority! And it is such a lie! One wouldn't mind if there were any justification for it."

"The wild cat," said Birkin, "doesn't mind. She perceives that it is justified."

"Does she!" cried Ursula. "And tell it to the horse marines."*

"To them also."

"It is just like Gerald Crich with his horse—a lust for bullying—a real Wille zur Macht*—so base, so petty."

"I agree that the Wille zur Macht is a base and petty thing. But with the

Mino, it is the desire to subject this female cat to the higher understanding of the male—quite a different matter. It is a volonté de pouvoir,* if you like, a will to ability, taking pouvoir as a verb."

"Ah—! Sophistries! It's the old Adam."*

"Oh yes. Spiritually, Adam preceded Eve. The spirit came first, then the flesh, and out of the reunion came understanding. That is the whole of the creation myth."

"And the woman of course is the flesh?"

"Yes."

"She is not the understanding at all—that is purely male?"

"She is the understanding in the flesh. The pure, final understanding, she is *not*. That is male—when it exists at all."

Ursula dropped him a curtsey.

"Thank you," she said. "Thank you, you higher being. I must knock my head on the ground before you, mustn't I. May I speak at all in your pure presence, you higher being?"

"Yes, you say what you like. It doesn't alter things."

"May I? May I actually say what I like? May I? Thank you, your highness, thank you, your holiness, thank you, you almighty being."

"All right, I'll be thanked."

"Tea is ready, sir," said the landlady from the doorway.

They both looked at her, very much as the cats had looked at them, a little while before.

"Thank you, Mrs Daykin."

A ridiculous silence fell over the two of them, a moment of awkwardness.

"Come and have tea," he said.

"How lovely!" she replied, pulling herself together.

They sat facing each other across the tea-table.

"How hungry are you?" he asked.

"Rather hungry. I had hardly any lunch."

"Wait a minute then."

He went out, and came back with good things, at which Ursula's eyes sparkled.

"I feel so greedy," she cried.

"Good," he said.

He poured out the tea. He had everything so nice, such pretty purplish lustre china, and elegant dishes and silver and a lovely purple and grey and black table-cloth. Ursula felt almost uncouth, with the real Brangwen uncouthness.

"Your things are so lovely!" she said, almost sadly.

"*I* like them. It gives me real pleasure to see things that are lovely. And Mrs Daykin is good. She thinks they are all wonderful, for my sake."

"Really," said Ursula, "landladies are better than wives, nowadays. They certainly *care* a great deal more. It is much more beautiful and complete here now, than if you were married."

"But think of the emptiness within," he laughed.

"No," she said. "I am jealous that men have such perfect landladies and such beautiful lodgings. There is nothing left them to desire."

"In the house-keeping way, let us hope not. It is too disgusting, people marrying for a home."

"Still," said Ursula, "a man has very little need for a woman now, has he?"

"In outer things, perhaps not—except to share his bed and bear his children. But essentially, there is just the same need as ever there was. Only nobody takes the trouble to be essential."

"How essential?" she asked.

"You know I do really think that it is the man's work to produce the vision—without which the people perisheth.* I do *not* think a woman can produce it, any more than a man can produce children. And I know that no man can really produce his share of the vision, unless he is fertilised and fed all the time by the spirit of a woman. In marriage, I feed you bodily, physically, whilst you feed me spiritually. Then you give birth to the coming generation, and I give birth to the coming vision, the new truth—my share of it."

"But how can I serve you spiritually, if I see nothing to serve?" she said, with a little disgust.

"You can't. And I agree that practically all the men now are spiritually sterile, as a woman may be physically barren. They can't, the men don't seem to have it in them to produce new understanding. They can't break down the walls of the established tissue of knowledge, to give birth to new wisdom. They are futile. That is why the women abandon them, and they take to fighting and killing each other, and raking up old phrases."

"What is a woman to do?" said Ursula. "She can't make a man male. She can't *make* him spiritually something, if he is nothing."

"Quite," said Birkin.

"So we are all left in the lurch," said Ursula.

"Of course," he said, "the women also don't want to subserve anything—they want to have things off their own bat. They really want to wipe all the men out, except such as they can keep in their pockets, and then have all the world to themselves."

"Can you blame them?" said Ursula, "what is there to subserve?"

"Maybe nothing. But the women will create nothing, either, because they simply can't. A world of their creating will be merely physico-mechanical and repulsive. So there you are—a vicious circle, till somebody has a pure desire and courage enough to get out of it."

"There are the children," said Ursula.

"There usually are. All these dead and dry-rotten limbs of society were children a very little while back. What good did it do them?"

There was a long pause. Then Ursula looked at him with her eyes dark and veiled with half-subdued hostility.

"You seem so without faith," she cried in despair.

He winced, as usual, from her charge.

"Would you have me have faith in the world that is now?" he said. "I have no belief in it. It is utterly bad. I have faith in the world as it is not."

"And never will be."

"Good. I will have faith in that which never will be then. In this I have no faith, it is utterly bad."

"But you seem only to believe in yourself—always yourself, nothing but yourself," she cried bitterly. "When do you take notice of anybody else?"

"When anybody else stands in truth, I shall stand on my head with joy to be near them. But the great fact of personality and individuality bores me. I want somebody with eyes to see and courage to know—I don't care a straw about Tom's idiosyncrasies and Jack's snub nose and Violet's curious nature."

"Oh," cried Ursula, "yes, I love Jack's snub nose."

"I used to," he laughed. "But there are so many snub noses. And personality is only a sort of permutations and combinations of an infinite number of given terms. The terms are all given. It bores me."

"Yes," she said, "it bores me too."

They had talked and struggled till they were both wearied out.

"Tell me about yourself and your people," he said.

And she told him about the Brangwens, and about her mother, who was a Pole and about Skrebensky, her first love, and about her later experiences. He sat very still, watching her as she talked. And he seemed to listen with reverence. Her face was beautiful and full of baffled light as she told him all the things that had hurt her or perplexed her so deeply. He seemed to warm and comfort his soul at the beautiful light of her nature.

"If she *really* loved me," he thought to himself, with passionate yearning but hardly any hope. Yet a curious little irresponsible laughter appeared in his heart.

"We have all suffered so much," he laughed, ironically.

She looked up at him, and a flash of wild gaiety went over her face, a strange flash of yellow light coming from her eyes.

"Haven't we!" she cried, in a high, reckless cry. "It is almost absurd, isn't it?"

"It is," he said. "Suffering bores me, any more."

"So it does me."

He was almost afraid of the dazzling recklessness of her splendid face.

"Here is the virgin fire," his soul chuckled. And he was almost afraid of it. But he chuckled exultant within himself.

"You've got a sad history too, haven't you?" she cried.

"Apallingly sad," he laughed.

There was something really sardonic and wicked in him.

"It is incredible, how wrecked and near the edge of dissolution I am," he said, making a wry mouth. She felt a little shiver go over her. This was almost too much, too near the truth.

"I thought so," she said. At the same time the thought ran through her mind: "Really, nothing matters any more. We can just have our own way"

"But," he said, "I can still dance a *pas seul** on the grave of my era—or a *pas de deux*, if you please."

"We'll make it a *pas de deux*," she cried.

"Good then," he said.

5

EVERY YEAR MR CRICH GAVE a more-or-less public water-party on the lake. There was a little pleasure-launch on Willey Water, and several rowing-boats, and guests could take tea either in the marquee that was set up in the grounds of the house, or they could picnic in the shade of the great walnut-tree at the boat-house by the lake. This year the staff of the Grammar-School was invited, along with the chief officials of the firm. Gerald and the younger Criches did not care for this party, but it had become customary now, and it pleased the father, as being the only occasion when he could gather some people of the district together in festivity with him. For he loved to give pleasures to his dependents and to those poorer than himself. But his children preferred the company of their own equals in wealth. They hated their inferiors' humility or gratitude or awkwardness. Nevertheless they were willing to attend at this festival, as they had done since they were children, the more so, as they all felt a little guilty now, and unwilling to thwart their father any more, when he was so ill in health. Therefore, quite cheerfully Laura prepared to take her mother's place as hostess, and Gerald assumed responsibility for the amusements on the water.

Birkin had written to Ursula saying he expected to see her at the party, and Gudrun, although she scorned the patronage of the Criches, would nevertheless accompany her mother and father if the weather were fine.

The day came blue and full of sunshine, with little wafts of wind. The sisters both wore dresses of white cotton crape, and hats of soft grass. But Gudrun had a sash of brilliant black and pink and yellow colour wound broadly round her waist, and she had pink silk stockings, and black and pink and yellow ribbon on the brim of her hat, weighing it down a little. She carried also a yellow silk coat over her arm, so that she looked remarkable, like a painting from the Salon.* Her appearance was a sore trial to her father, who said angrily:

"Don't you think you might as well get yourself up like a Christmas cracker, an' ha' done with it?"

But Gudrun looked handsome and brilliant, and she wore her clothes in pure defiance. When people stared at her, and giggled after her, she made a point of saving loudly, to Ursula:

"Regarde, regarde ces gens-là! Ne sont-ils pas des hiboux incroyables?"* And with the words of French in her mouth, she would look over her shoulder at the giggling party.

"No, really, it's impossible!" Ursula would reply distinctly.

And so the two girls took it out of their universal enemy. But their father became more and more enraged.

Ursula was all snowy white, save that her hat was pink, and entirely without trimming, and her shoes were dark red, and she carried an orange coloured coat. And in this guise they were walking all the way to Shortlands, their father and mother going in front.

They were laughing at their mother, who, dressed in a summer material of black and purple stripes, and wearing a hat of purple straw, was setting forth with much more of the shyness and trepidation of a young girl than her daughters ever felt, walking demurely beside her husband, who, as usual, looked rather crumpled in his best suit, as if he were the father of a young family and had been holding the baby whilst his wife got dressed.

"Look at the young couple in front," said Gudrun calmly. Ursula looked at her mother and father, and was suddenly seized with uncontrollable laughter. The two girls stood in the road and laughed till the tears ran down their faces, as they caught sight again of the shy, unworldly couple of their parents going on ahead.

"We are roaring at you, mother," called Ursula, helplessly following after her parents.

Mrs Brangwen turned round with a slightly puzzled, exasperated look.

"Oh indeed!" she said. "What is there so very funny about *me*, I should like to know?"

She could not understand that there could be anything amiss with her appearance. She had a perfect calm sufficiency, an easy indifference to any criticism whatsoever, as if she were beyond it. Her clothes were always rather odd, and as a rule slip-shod, yet she wore them with ease and indifference. Whatever she had on, so long as she was barely tidy, she was right, beyond remark; such an aristocrat she was by instinct.

"You look so stately, like a country Baroness," said Ursula, laughing with a little tenderness at her mother's naive puzzled air.

"*Just* like a country Baroness!" chimed in Gudrun.

Now the mother's natural hauteur became self-conscious, and the girls shrieked again.

"Go home, you pair of idiots, great giggling idiots!" cried the father inflamed with irritation.

"Mm-m-er!" booed Ursula, pulling a face at his crossness.

The yellow lights danced in his eyes, he leaned forward in real rage.

"Don't be so silly as to take any notice of the great gabies,"* said Mrs Brangwen, turning on her way.

"I'll see if I'm going to be followed by a pair of giggling yelling jackanapes—" he cried vengefully.

The girls stood still, laughing helplessly at his fury, upon the path beside the hedge.

"Why you're as silly as they are, to take any notice," said Mrs Brangwen also becoming angry now he was really enraged.

"There are some people coming, father," cried Ursula, with mocking warning. He glanced round quickly, and went on to join his wife, walking stiff with rage. And the girls followed, weak with laughter.

When the people had passed by, Brangwen cried in a loud, stupid voice:

"I'm going back home if there's any more of this. I'm damned if I'm going to be made a fool of in this fashion, in the public road."

He was really in a rage. At the sound of his blind, vindictive voice, the laughter suddenly left the girls, and their hearts contracted with contempt. But Gudrun would conciliate him.

"But we weren't laughing to *hurt* you," she cried. "We were laughing because we're fond of you."

Explanations, however, only made one's skin bristle.

"We'll walk on in front, if they are *so* touchy," said Ursula, angry.

And in this wise they arrived at Willey Water. The lake was blue and fair, the meadows sloped down in sunshine on one side, the thick dark woods dropped steeply on the other. The little pleasure-launch was fussing out from the shore, twanging its music, crowded with people, flapping its paddles. Near the boat-house was a throng of gaily-dressed persons, small in the distance. And on the high-road, some of the common people were standing along the hedge, looking at the festivity beyond, enviously, like souls not admitted to paradise.

"My eye!" said Gudrun, sotto voce, looking at the motley of guests, "there's a pretty crowd if you like! Imagine yourself in the midst of that, my dear."

Gudrun's apprehensive horror of people in the mass unnerved Ursula.

"It looks rather awful," she said anxiously.

"And imagine what they'll be like—*imagine*!" said Gudrun, still in that unnerving, subdued voice. Still she advanced determinedly.

"I suppose we can get out of them," said Ursula anxiously.

"We're in a pretty fix if we can't," said Gudrun. Her extreme ironic loathing and apprehension was very trying to Ursula.

"We needn't stay," she said.

"I certainly shan't stay five minutes among that little lot," said Gudrun.

They advanced nearer, till they saw the policemen at the gates.

"Policemen to keep you in, too!" said Gudrun. "My word, this is a nice affair."

"We'd better look after father and mother," said Ursula anxiously.

"Mother's *perfectly* capable of settling the whole show, Criches and everybody," said Gudrun with some contempt.

But Ursula knew that her father felt uncouth and angry and unhappy, so she was far from her ease. They waited outside the gate till their parents came up. The tall, thin man in his crumpled clothes was shy and irritable as a boy, finding himself on the point of being immersed in this social function. He did not feel a gentleman, he did not feel anything except pure exasperation at his own position.

Ursula took her place at his side, they gave their tickets to the policemen, and passed in on to the grass, four abreast: the tall, hot, ruddy-dark man with his narrow boyish brow drawn with irritation, the fresh-faced, easy woman, perfectly collected though her hair was slipping on one side, then Gudrun, her eyes round and dark and staring, her full soft face impassive, almost sulky, so that she seemed to be backing away in antagonism even whilst she was advancing; and then Ursula, with the odd, brilliant, dazzled look on her face, that always came when she was in some false situation.

Birkin was the good angel. He came smiling to them with his affected social grace, that somehow was never *quite* right. But he took off his hat and smiled at them with a real smile in his eyes, so that Brangwen cried out heartily in relief:

"How do you do? You're better, are you?"

"Yes, I'm better. How do you do, Mrs Brangwen? I know Gudrun and Ursula very well."

His eyes smiled full of natural warmth. He had a soft, flattering manner with women, particularly with women who were not young.

"Yes," said Mrs Brangwen, cool but yet gratified. "I have heard speak of you often enough."

He laughed. Gudrun looked aside, feeling she was being belittled. People were standing about in groups, some women were sitting in the shade of the walnut tree, with cups of tea in their hands, a waiter in evening dress was hurrying round, some girls were simpering with parasols, some young men, who had just come in from rowing, were sitting cross-legged on the grass, coatless, their shirt-sleeves rolled up in manly fashion, their hands resting on their white flannel knees, their gaudy ties floating about, as they laughed in true virile sportfulness with the young damsels.

"Why," thought Gudrun churlishly, "don't they have the manners to put their coats on, and not to assume such cheap intimacy."

She abhorred the ordinary young man, with his hair plastered back, and his easy-going chumminess.

Hermione Roddice came up, in a handsome gown of white lace, trailing an enormous silk shawl blotched with great embroidered flowers, and balancing an enormous hat with enormous silk flowers on her head. She looked striking, astonishing, almost macabre, so tall, with the fringe of her great cream-coloured vividly-blotched shawl trailing on the ground after her, her thick hair coming low over her eyes, her face strange and long and pale, and the blotches of brilliant colour drawn round her.

"Doesn't she look *weird*!" Gudrun heard some girls titter behind her. And she could have killed them.

"How do you do!" sang Hermione, coming up very kindly; and glancing slowly over Gudrun's father and mother. It was a trying moment, exasperating for Gudrun. Hermione was really so strongly entrenched in her class, she could come up and know people out of sheer curiosity, as if they were creatures on exhibition. Gudrun would do the same herself. But she resented being in the position when somebody might do it to her.

Hermione, very stately, and distinguishing the Brangwens very much, led them along to where Laura Crich stood receiving the guests.

"This is Mrs Brangwen," sang Hermione, and Laura, who wore a stiff embroidered linen dress, shook hands and said she was glad to see her. Then Gerald came up, dressed in white, with a black-and-orange blazer, and looking very handsome. He too was introduced to the Brangwen parents, and immediately he spoke to Mrs Brangwen as if she were a lady, and to Brangwen as if he were *not* a gentleman. Gerald was so obvious in his demeanour. He had to shake hands with his left hand, because he had hurt his right, and carried it, bandaged up, in the pocket of his jacket. Gudrun was *very* thankful that none of her party asked him what was the matter with the hand.

The steam launch was fussing in, all its music jingling, people calling excitedly from on board. Gerald went to see to the debarkation, Birkin was getting tea for Mrs Brangwen, Brangwen had joined a Grammar-school group, Hermione was sitting down by their mother, the girls went to the landing stage to watch the launch come in.

She hooted and tooted gaily, then her paddles were silent, the ropes were thrown ashore, she drifted in with a little bump. Immediately the passengers crowded excitedly to come ashore.

"Wait a minute, wait a minute," shouted Gerald in sharp command.

They must wait till the boat was tight on the ropes, till the small gangway was put out. Then they streamed ashore, clamouring as if they had come from America.

"Oh it's *so* nice!" the young girls were crying. "It's quite lovely."

The waiters from on board ran out to the boat-house with baskets, the captain lounged on the little bridge. Seeing all safe, Gerald came to Gudrun and Ursula.

"You wouldn't care to go on board for the next trip, and have tea there?" he asked.

"No thanks," said Gudrun coldly.

"You don't care for the water?"

"For the water? Yes, I like it very much."

He looked at her, his eyes searching.

"You don't care for going on a launch, then?"

She was slow in answering, and then she spoke slowly.

"No," she said. "I can't say that I do."

Her colour was high, she seemed angry about something.

"Un peu trop de monde,"* said Ursula, explaining.

"Eh? *Trop de monde!*" He laughed shortly. "Yes, there's a fair number of 'em."

Gudrun turned on him brilliantly.

"Have you ever been from Westminster Bridge to Richmond on one of the Thames steamers?" she cried.

"No," he said, "I can't say I have."

"Well, it's one of the most *vile* experiences I've ever had." She spoke rapidly and excitedly, the colour high in her cheeks. "There was absolutely nowhere to sit down, not an inch of seat, a man just above sang 'Rocked in the Cradle of the Deep'* the *whole* way; he was blind and he had a small organ, one of those portable organs, and he expected money; so you can imagine what *that* was like; there came the most repulsive smell of luncheon from below, and puffs of hot oily machinery; the journey took hours and hours and hours; and for miles, literally for miles, the most repulsive boys ran with us on the shore, in that *awful* Thames mud, going in *up to the waist*—they had their trousers turned back, and down they went up to their hips in that indescribable Thames mud, their faces always turned to us, and screaming, exactly like carrion creatures, screaming "Ere y'are sir, 'ere y'are sir, 'ere y'are sir' exactly like some foul carrion birds, perfectly obscene; and paterfamilias on board, laughing when they went right down in that awful mud, and occasionally throwing them a ha'penny. And if you'd seen the intent look on the faces of those boys, and the way they darted in the filth when a coin was flung—really, no vulture or jackal could dream of approaching them, for foul horror. I *never* would go on a pleasure boat again—never."

Gerald watched her all the time she spoke, his eyes glittering with faint rousedness. It was not so much what she said: it was she herself who roused him, roused him with a small, vivid pricking.

"Of course," he said, "every civilised body is bound to have its vermin."

"Why?" cried Ursula. "*I* don't have vermin."

"And it's not that," cried Gudrun, "—it's the *quality* of the whole thing—paterfamilias laughing and thinking it sport, and throwing the ha'pennies, and materfamilias spreading her fat little knees and eating, continually eating—"

"Yes," said Ursula. "It isn't only the boys who are vermin; they're all vermin, the whole body politic, as you call it."

Gerald laughed.

"Never mind," he said. "You shan't go on the launch."

Gudrun flushed quickly at his rebuke. There were a few moments of silence. Gerald, like a sentinel, was watching the people who were going on to the boat. He was very good-looking and self-contained, it would be difficult to get at him.

"Will you have tea here then, or go across to the house, where there's a tent on the lawn?" he asked.

"Can't we have a rowing boat, and get out?" asked Ursula, who was always rushing in too fast.

"To get out?" smiled Gerald.

"You see," cried Gudrun, flushing at Ursula's outspoken rudeness, "we don't know the people, we are almost *complete* strangers here."

"Oh, I can soon set you up with a few acquaintances," he said easily.

Gudrun looked at him, to see if it were ill-meant. Then she smiled at him.

"Ah," she said, "you know what we mean. Can't we go up there, and explore that coast?" She pointed to a grove on a hillock of the meadow-side, near the shore, half way down the lake. "That looks perfectly lovely. We might even bathe. Isn't it beautiful in this light!—really, it's like one of the reaches of the Nile—as one imagines the Nile."

Gerald smiled at her factitious enthusiasm for the distant spot.

"You're sure it's far enough off?" he asked ironically, adding at once: "Yes, you might go there if we could get a boat. They seem to be all out." He looked round the lake and counted the rowing boats on its surface.

"How lovely it would be!" cried Ursula wistfully.

"And don't you want tea?" he said.

"Oh," said Gudrun, "we could just drink a cup, and be off."

He looked from one to the other, smiling. He was somewhat offended—yet sporting.

"Can you manage a boat pretty well?" he asked.

"Yes," replied Gudrun, coldly, "pretty well."

"Oh yes," cried Ursula. "We can both of us row like water-spiders."

"You can?—There's a light little canoe of mine, that I didn't take out for fear somebody should drown themselves. Do you think you'd be safe in that?"

"Oh perfectly," said Gudrun.

"What an angel!" cried Ursula.

"Don't, for my sake, have an accident—because I'm responsible for the water."

"Sure," pledged Gudrun.

"Besides we can both swim quite well," said Ursula.

"Well—then I'll get them to pack you up a tea-basket, and you can picnic all to yourselves,—that's the idea, isn't it?"

"How fearfully good! How frightfully nice if you could!" cried Gudrun warmly, her colour flushing up again. It made the blood stir in his veins, the subtle way she turned to him and infused her gratitude into his body.

"Where's Birkin?" he said, his eyes twinkling. "He might help me to get it down."

"But what about your hand? Isn't it hurt?" asked Gudrun, rather muted, as if avoiding the personal question. This was the first time the hurt had been mentioned. The curious way she skirted round the subject sent a new, subtle caress through his veins. He took his hand out of his pocket. It was bandaged. He looked at it, then put it in his pocket again. Gudrun quivered at the sight of the wrapped up paw.

"Oh, I can manage with one hand. The canoe is as light as a feather," he said. "There's Rupert!—Rupert!"

Birkin turned from his social duties and came towards them.

"What have you done to it?" asked Ursula, who had been aching to put the question for the last half hour.

"To my hand?" said Gerald. "I trapped it in some machinery."

"Ugh!" said Ursula. "And did it hurt it much?"

"Yes," he said. "It did at the time. It's getting better now. It crushed the fingers."

"Oh," cried Ursula, as if in pain, "I hate people to hurt themselves. I can *feel* it." And she shook her hand.

"What do you want?" said Birkin.

The two men carried down the slim brown cockle-boat, and set it on the water.

"You're quite sure you'll be safe in it?" Gerald asked.

"Quite sure," said Gudrun. "I wouldn't be so mean as to take it, if there was the slightest doubt. But I've had a canoe at Arundel, and I assure you I'm perfectly safe."

So saying, having given her word like a man, she and Ursula entered the frail craft, and pushed gently off. The men stood watching them. Gudrun was paddling. She knew the two men were watching her, and it made her slow and rather clumsy. The colour flew in her face like a flag.

"Thanks awfully," she called back to him, from the water, as the boat slid away. "It's lovely—like sitting in a leaf."

He laughed at the fancy. Her voice was shrill and strange, calling from the distance. He watched her as she paddled away. There was something childlike about her, trustful and deferential, like a child. He watched her all the while, as she rowed. And to Gudrun it was a real delight, in make belief, to be the childlike, fascinating woman to the man who stood there on the quay, so goodlooking and clean-lit* in his white clothes, and moreover the most important man she knew at the moment. She did not take any notice of the wavering, indistinct, lambent Birkin, who stood at his side. One figure at a time occupied the field of her attention.

The boat rustled lightly along the water. They passed the bathers whose striped tents stood between the willows of the meadow's edge, and drew along the open shore, past the meadows that sloped golden in the light of the already late afternoon. Other boats were stealing under the wooded shore opposite, they could hear people's laughter and voices. But Gudrun rowed on towards the clump of trees that balanced perfect in the distance, in the golden light.

The sisters found a little place where a tiny stream flowed into the lake, with reeds and flowery marsh of pink willow herb, and a gravelly bank to the side. Here they ran delicately ashore, with their frail boat, the two girls took off their shoes and stockings and went through the water's edge to the grass. The tiny ripples of the lake were warm and clear, they lifted their boat on to the bank, and looked round with joy. They were quite alone in a forsaken little stream-mouth, and on a knoll just behind was the clump of trees.

"We will bathe just for a moment," said Ursula, "and then we'll have tea."

They looked round. Nobody could notice them, or could come up in time to see them. In less than a minute Ursula had thrown off her clothes and had slipped naked into the water, and was swimming out. Quickly, Gudrun joined her. They swam silently and blissfully for a few minutes, circling round their little stream-mouth. Then they slipped ashore and ran into the grove again, like nymphs.

"How lovely it is to be free," said Ursula, running swiftly here and there between the tree trunks, quite naked, her hair blowing loose. The grove was of beech-trees, big and splendid, a steel-grey scaffolding of trunks and boughs, with level sprays of strong green here and there, whilst through the northern side the distance glimmered open as through a window.

When they had run and danced themselves dry, the girls quickly dressed and sat down to the fragrant tea. They sat on the northern side of the grove, in the yellow sunshine facing the slope of the grassy hill, alone in a little wild world of their own. The tea was hot and aromatic, there were delicious little sandwiches of cucumber and of caviare, and winy cakes.

"Are you happy, Prune?" cried Ursula in delight, looking at her sister.

"Ursula, I'm perfectly happy," replied Gudrun gravely, looking at the westering sun.

"So am I."

When they were together, doing the things they enjoyed, the two sisters were quite complete in a perfect world of their own. And this was one of the perfect moments of freedom and delight, such as children alone know, when all seems a perfect and blissful adventure.

When they had finished tea, the two girls sat on, silent and serene. Then Ursula, who had a beautiful strong voice, began to sing to herself, softly: "Holder klingt der Vogelsang."* Gudrun listened, as she sat beneath the trees, and the yearning came into her heart. Ursula seemed so peaceful and sufficient unto herself, sitting there unconsciously crooning her song, strong and unquestioned at the centre of her own universe. And Gudrun felt herself outside. Always this desolating, agonised feeling, that she was outside of life, an onlooker, whilst Ursula was a partaker, caused Gudrun to suffer from a sense of her own negation, and made her, that she must always demand the other to be aware of her, to be in connection with her.

"Do you mind if I do Dalcroze* to that tune, Hurtler?" she asked in a curious muted tone, scarce moving her lips.

"What did you say?" asked Ursula, looking up in peaceful surprise.

"Will you sing while I do Dalcroze?" said Gudrun, suffering at having to repeat herself.

Ursula thought a moment, gathering her straying wits together.

"While you do— —?" she asked vaguely.

"Dalcroze movements," said Gudrun, suffering tortures of self-consciousness, even because of her sister.

"Oh Dalcroze! I couldn't catch the name. *Do*—I should love to see you. You know I don't know it at all," cried Ursula, with childish surprised brightness. "What shall I sing?"

"Sing anything you like, and I'll take the rhythm from it."

But Ursula could not for her life think of anything to sing. However, she suddenly began, in a laughing, teasing voice:

"My love— —is a high-born lady—"*

Gudrun, looking as if some invisible chain weighed on her hands and feet, began slowly to dance in the eurythmic manner, pulsing and fluttering rhythmically with her feet, making slower, regular gestures with her hands and arms, now spreading her arms wide, now raising them above her head, now flinging them softly apart, and lifting her face, her feet all the time beating and running to the measure of the song, as if it were some strange incantation, her white, rapt form drifting here and there in a strange impulsive rhapsody, seeming to be lifted on a breeze of incantation, incomprehensible and mystic, shuddering with strange little runs. Ursula sat on the grass, her mouth open in her singing, her eyes laughing as if she thought it was a great joke, but a yellow light flashing up in them, as she caught some of the unconscious ritualistic suggestion of the complex shuddering and waving and drifting of her sister's white form, that was clutched in pure, mindless, tossing rhythm, and a will set powerful in a kind of hypnotic influence.

"My love is a high-born lady—My lo-o-ove— —is a high-born lady—" rang out Ursula's laughing, mocking song, and quicker, fiercer went Gudrun in the dance, stamping as if she were trying to throw off some bond, flinging her hands suddenly and stamping again, then rushing with face uplifted and throat full and beautiful, and eyes half closed, sightless. The sun was low and yellow, sinking down, and in the sky floated a thin, ineffectual moon.

Ursula was quite absorbed in her song, when suddenly Gudrun stopped and said mildly, ironically:

"Ursula!"

"Yes?" said Ursula, opening her eyes out of the trance.

Gudrun was standing still and pointing, a mocking smile on her face, towards the side.

"Ugh!" cried Ursula in sudden panic, starting to her feet.

"They're quite all right," rang out Gudrun's sardonic voice.

On the left stood a little cluster of Highland cattle, vividly coloured and fleecy in the evening light, their horns branching into the sky, pushing forward their muzzles inquisitively, to know what it was all about. Their eyes glittered through their tangle of hair, their naked nostrils were full of shadow.

"Won't they do anything?" cried Ursula in fear.

Gudrun, who was usually frightened of cattle, now shook her head in a queer, half-doubtful, half-sardonic motion, a faint smile round her mouth.

"Don't they look charming, Ursula?" cried Gudrun, in a high, strident voice, something like the scream of a sea-gull.

"Charming," cried Ursula in trepidation. "But won't they do anything to us?"

Again Gudrun looked back at her sister with an enigmatic smile, and shook her head.

"I'm sure they won't," she said, as if she had to convince herself also, and yet, as if she were confident of some secret power in herself, and had to put it to the test. "Sit down and sing again," she called in her high, strident voice.

"I'm frightened," cried Ursula, in a pathetic voice, watching the group of sturdy short cattle, that stood with their knees planted, and watched with their dark, wicked eyes, through the matted fringe of their hair. Nevertheless, she sank down again, in her former posture.

"They are quite safe," came Gudrun's high call. "Sing something, you've only to sing something."

It was evident she had a strange passion to dance before the sturdy, handsome cattle.

Ursula began to sing, in a false, quavering voice:

"It's a long long way to Tipperary———"*

She sounded purely anxious. Nevertheless, Gudrun, with her arms outspread and her face uplifted, went in a strange, palpitating dance towards the cattle, lifting her body towards them as if in a spell, her feet pulsing as if in some little frenzy of unconscious sensation, her arms, her wrists, her hands stretching and heaving and falling and reaching and reaching and falling, her breasts lifted and shaken towards the cattle, her throat exposed as in some voluptuous ecstasy towards them, whilst she drifted imperceptibly nearer, an uncanny white figure carried away in its own rapt trance, ebbing in strange fluctuations upon the cattle, that waited, and ducked their heads a little in sudden contraction from her, watching all the time as if hypnotised, their bare horns branching in the clear light, as the white figure of the woman ebbed upon them, in the slow, hypnotising convulsion of the dance. She could feel them just in front of her, it was as if she had the electric pulse from their breasts running into her hands. Soon she would touch them, actually touch them. A terrible shiver of fear and pleasure went through her. And all the while, Ursula spell-bound kept up her high-pitched thin, irrelevant song, which pierced the fading evening like an incantation.

Gudrun could hear the cattle breathing heavily with helpless fear and fascination. Oh, they were brave little beasts, these wild Scotch bullocks, wild and fleecy. Suddenly one of them snorted, ducked its head, and backed.

"Hue! Hi—eee!" came a sudden loud shout from the edge of the grove. The cattle broke and fell back quite spontaneously, went running up the hill, their fleece waving like fire to their motion. Gudrun stood suspended, out on the grass, Ursula rose to her feet.

It was Gerald and Birkin come to find them, and Gerald had cried out to frighten off the cattle.

"What do you think you're doing?" he now called, in a high, wondering, vexed tone.

"Why have you come—we were alone," came back Gudrun's strident cry of anger.

"What do you think you were doing?" Gerald repeated, automatically.

"We were doing eurythmics," laughed Ursula, in a shaken voice.

Gudrun stood aloof looking at them with large dark eyes of resentment, suspended for a few moments. Then she walked away up the hill, after the cattle, which had gathered in a little, spell-bound cluster higher up.

"Where are you going?" Gerald called after her. And he followed her up the hill-side. The sun had gone under, and shadows were clinging to the earth, the sky above was full of travelling light.

"I like your song for a dance," said Birkin to Ursula, standing before her with a sardonic, evil laugh on his face. And in another second, he was singing softly to himself, and dancing a grotesque step-dance in front of her, his limbs and body shaking loose, his face grinning and flickering palely, a constant thing, whilst his feet beat a rapid mocking tattoo, and his body seemed to hang all loose and quaking in between.

"I think we've all gone mad," she said, laughing rather frightened.

"Don't you believe it," he answered, as he kept up the incessant shaking jeering dance all the while. Then suddenly he danced up to her and kissed her lightly on the mouth, putting his face to hers and looking into her eyes with a sardonic grin. She stepped back, affronted.

"What, offended are you?" he asked ironically, suddenly going quite still and reserved again. "I thought you liked the light fantastic."

"Not like that," she said, confused and bewildered and mechanically offended. For somewhere inside her she was fascinated by the sight of his loose, vibrating, slack-waggling body, perfectly abandoned to its own dropping and swinging, and by the pallid, sardonic-smiling face above. Yet automatically she stiffened herself away, and disapproved. It seemed almost an obscenity, in a man who talked as a rule so very seriously and so morally.

"Why not like that?" he mocked. And immediately he dropped again into the incredibly rapid, slack-waggling dance, leering sardonically at her. And moving in the rapid, stationary dance, he came a little nearer, and reached forward with an incredibly mocking, evil gleam on his face, and would have kissed her again, had she not started back.

"No, don't!" she cried, really afraid.

"You're the sweet Cordelia* after all," he said satirically.

She was stung, as if this were an insult. She knew he intended it as such, and as such, involuntarily, she accepted it.

"And you," she cried in retort, "why do you always take your soul in your mouth, so frightfully full!"

"So that I can spit it out the more readily," he grinned, pleased by his own retort.

Gerald Crich, his face narrowing to an intent gleam, followed up the hill with quick strides, straight after Gudrun. The cattle stood with their noses together on the brow of a slope, watching the scene below, the men hovering about the white forms of the women, watching above all Gudrun, who was advancing slowly towards them. She stood a moment, glancing back at Gerald, and then at the cattle.

Then in a sudden motion, she lifted her arms and rushed sheer upon the long-horned bullocks, in shuddering irregular runs, pausing for a second and looking at them, then lifting her hands and running forward with a flash, till they ceased pawing the ground, and gave way, snorting with mad terror, lifting their heads from the ground and flinging themselves away, galloping off into the evening, becoming tiny in the distance, and still not stopping.

Gudrun remained staring after them, with a sullen, defiant face.

"Why do you want to drive them mad?" asked Gerald, coming up with her.

She took no notice of him, only averted her face from him.

"It's not safe, you know," he persisted. "They're nasty brutes, when they do turn."

"Turn where? Turn away?" she mocked loudly.

"No," he said, "turn against you."

"Turn against *me*?" she mocked.

He could make nothing of this.

"They gored one of the farmer's cows to death, the other day," he said.

"What do I care?" she said.

"*I* cared though," he replied, "seeing that they're my cattle."

"Yours! Yours? How yours? You haven't got them in your pocket. Give me one of them now," she said, holding out her hand.

"You know where they are," he said, pointing over the hill. "You can have one if you'd like it sent to you later on."

She looked at him in contempt.

"You think I'm afraid of you and your cattle, don't you?" she asked.

His eyes opened in surprise. He could not make out what she was getting at.

"Why should I think that?" he said.

She was watching him all the time with her dark, insolent blue eyes. She leaned forward and swung round her arm, catching him a blow on the face with the back of her hand.

"That's why," she said.

And she felt in her soul an inconquerable lust for deep brutality against him. She shut off the fear and wonder that filled her conscious mind. She wanted to do as she did, she was not going to be afraid.

He recoiled from the heavy blow across the face. He became deadly pale, and a dangerous flame darkened his eyes. For some seconds he could not speak, his lungs were so suffused with blood, his heart stretched almost to bursting with a great gush of ungovernable rage. It was as if some reservoir of black anger had burst within him, and swamped him.

"You have struck the first blow," he panted at last, forcing the words from his lungs.

"And I shall strike the last," she retorted involuntarily, with confident assurance. He was silent, he did not contradict her.

She stood negligently, staring away from him, into the distance. On the edge of her consciousness the question was asking itself, automatically,

"Why *are* you behaving in this *impossible* and ridiculous fashion?" But she was sullen, she half shoved the question out of herself. She could not get it clean away, so she felt self-conscious.

Gerald, very pale, was watching her closely. His eyes were lit up with intent lights, absorbed and gleaming. She turned suddenly on him.

"It's you who make me behave like this, you know," she said, almost suggestive.

"I? How?" he said.

But she turned away, and set off towards the lake. Below, on the water, lanterns were coming alight, faint ghosts of warm flame floating in the pallor of the first twilight. The earth was spread with darkness, like lacquer, overhead was a pale sky, all primrose, and the lake was pale as milk in one part. Away at the landing-stage, tiniest points of coloured rays were stringing themselves in the dusk. The launch was being illuminated. All round, shadow was gathering from the trees.

Gerald, white like a presence in his summer clothes, was following down the open grassy slope. Gudrun waited for him to come up. Then she put out her hand and touched him, saying softly:

"Don't be angry with me."

A flame flew over him, and he was unconscious. Yet he stammered:

"I'm not angry with you. I'm in love with you."

His mind was gone, he grasped for sufficient mechanical control, to save himself. She laughed a silvery little mockery.

"That's one way of putting it," she said.

The terrible swooning burden on his mind, the loss of all his control, was too much for him. He grasped her arm in his one hand, as if his hand were iron.

"It's all right, isn't it?" he said, holding her arrested.

She looked at the blank face with the fixed eyes, set before her, and her blood ran cold.

"Yes, it's all right," she said softly.

He walked on beside her, a striding, mindless body. But he recovered a little as he went. He suffered badly. He had killed his brother when a boy, and was set apart, like Cain.

They found Birkin and Ursula sitting together by the boats, talking and laughing. Birkin had been teasing Ursula.

"Do you smell this little marsh?" he said, sniffing the air. He was very sensitive to scents.

"It's rather nice," she said.

"No," he replied, "alarming."

"Why alarming?" she laughed.

"Everything, both physical and spiritual, is passing both upwards and downwards, as Herakleitos or somebody says," he replied, "upwards into fire, downwards into water—and that is true."

"Why is it true?" laughed Ursula.

"Because all activity is twofold, production and corruption, there is the great flux of corruption, flowing back and back and resolving down and reducing everything produced, flowing back till you reach the original homogeneous One. That is the Flux of Corruption, to which some people belong almost altogether,—all those whose great motion is the return to the origins. It has its blossoms just as fire has its blossoms. Swans and water-lilies and sea-born Aphrodite, they all belong to that stream. And it is the equal of production, because it is its opposite, therefore it is its equivalent."

"And what are you? Do you belong to the Flux of Corruption too?" laughed Ursula.

"Both. There are two fires, the slow cold fire of corruption, that returns to the origin, and the quick fire that consumes into the ultimate One, all the many things that there are now. But life is a resultant of these two— all life. The flame of the cold fire rushing germinating against the flame of the hot fire, suddenly a fusion takes place within the fiery regions, and that's a poppy—or you—or me—or a tiger. But when the hot flame darts and germinates in the cold stream of the fires of corruption, then within the flux of corruption is born a lotus flower, or a swan, or Hermione, or the nereids."*

"How very lovely!" cried Gudrun. "So I shall know now, how to place people. They are either flux of corruption—"

"Mostly that," interrupted Birkin, with equanimity.

"Oh are they? They're mostly that, are they? But *you* are the other. What is the other."

"The fiery flame," he said, smiling.

"How beautiful. So the thing to do is to say to people, "Are you Flux of Corruption, or Fiery Flame?" And then, of course, if they are Flux, you don't have anything to do with them."

"It depends," he said. "Flux is just as *good* as Flame. It all rests on what you want."

"Oh does it? Then there's a new heart-searching now. It's not, do I love God as I ought, but do I lean to Flux, or to Flame?"

"A much more pertinent question," he laughed.

"At it again," said Gerald behind them. "What's the pertinent question this time?"

"Flux of Corruption," cried Ursula joyfully. "Are you Flux of Corruption or Fiery Flame? That is the pertinent question now."

"Are you having me somewhere?" asked Gerald.

"Not at all. Tell him, Rupert. Is he Flux or Flame?"

"I don't know," said Birkin.

"We must hear more of this," said Gerald. "We'd better get off now." He fumbled with his left hand, to light a cigarette.

"Rupert, do it for me," he said.

Birkin rose and lit Gerald's cigarette.

"And give me one," said Ursula.

The match flickered in the twilight, and they were all smoking peacefully by the water-side. The lake was dim, the light dying from off it, in the midst of the dark land. The air all round was intangible, neither here nor there, and there was an unreal noise of banjoes, or suchlike music.

As the golden swim of light overhead died out, the moon gained brightness, and seemed to begin to smile forth her ascendency. The dark woods on the opposite shore melted into universal shadow. And amid this universal undershadow, there was a scattered intrusion of lights. Far down the lake were fantastic pale strings of colour, like beads of wan fire, green and red and yellow. The music came out in a little puff, as the launch, all illuminated, veered into the great shadow, stirring her outlines of half-living lights, puffing out her music in little drifts.

All were lighting up. Here and there, close against the faint water, and at the far end of the lake, where the water lay milky in the last whiteness of the sky, and there was no shadow, solitary, frail flames of lanterns floated from the unseen boats. There was a sound of oars, and a boat passed from the pallor into the darkness under the wood, where her lanterns seemed to kindle into fire, hanging in ruddy lovely globes. And again, in the lake, shadowy red gleams hovered in reflection about the boat. Everywhere were these noiseless ruddy creatures of fire drifting near the surface of the water, caught at by the rarest, scarce visible reflections.

Birkin brought the lanterns from the bigger boat, and the four shadowy white figures gathered round, to light them. Ursula held up the first, Birkin lowered the light from the rosy, glowing cup of his hands, into the depths of the lantern. It was kindled, and they all stood back to look at the great blue moon of light that hung from Ursula's hand, casting a strange gleam on her face. It flickered, and Birkin went bending over the well of light. His face shone out like an apparition, so unconscious, and again, something demoniacal. Ursula was dim and veiled, looming over him.

"That is all right," said his voice softly.

She held up the lantern. It had a flight of storks streaming through a turquoise sky of light.

"This is beautiful," she said.

"Lovely," echoed Gudrun, who wanted to hold one also, and lift it up full of beauty.

"Light one for me," she said. Gerald stood by her, incapacitated. Birkin lit the lantern she held up. Her heart beat with anxiety, to see how beautiful it would be. It was primrose yellow, with tall straight flowers growing from their green leaves, lifting their heads into the primrose day, while butterflies hovered about them, in the pure clear light.

Gudrun gave a little cry of excitement, as if pierced with delight.

"Isn't it beautiful, Oh, isn't it beautiful!"

Her soul was really pierced with beauty, she was translated beyond herself. Gerald leaned near to her, into her zone of light, as if to see. He came near to her, and stood touching her, looking with her at the primrose-shining globe. And she turned her face to his, that was faintly bright in the light of the lantern, and they stood together in one luminous spell, close together and ringed round with light, all the rest excluded.

Birkin looked away, and went to light Ursula's second lantern. It had a ruddy-gold sea-bottom, with crabs and sea-weed moving sinuously under a transparent sea, that passed into deep green above.

"You've got the heavens above, and the waters under the earth,"* said Birkin to her.

"Anything but the earth itself," she laughed, watching his hands that hovered to attend to the light.

"I'm dying to see what my second one is," cried Gudrun, in a vibrating rather strident voice, that seemed to repel the others from her.

Birkin went and kindled it. It was of a lovely deep blue colour, with a red floor, and a great white cuttle-fish flowing in white soft streams all over it. The cuttle-fish had a face that stared straight from the heart of the light, very fixed and coldly intent.

"How truly terrifying!" exclaimed Gudrun, in a voice of horror. Gerald, at her side, gave a low laugh.

"But isn't it really fearful!" she cried in dismay.

Again he laughed, and said:

"Change it with Ursula, for the crabs."

Gudrun was silent for a moment.

"Ursula," she said, "could you bear to have this fearful thing?"

"I think the colouring is *lovely*," said Ursula.

"So do I," said Gudrun. "But could you *bear* to have it swinging to your boat? Don't you want to destroy it *at once*?"

"Oh no," said Ursula. "I don't want to destroy it."

"Well—do you mind having it instead of the crabs? Are you sure you don't mind?"

Gudrun came forward to exchange lanterns.

"No," said Ursula, yielding up the crabs and receiving the cuttle-fish.

Yet she could not help feeling rather resentful at the way in which Gudrun and Gerald should assume a right over her, a precedence.

"Come then," said Birkin. "I'll put them on the boats."

He and Ursula were moving away to the big boat.

"You remember I'm a cripple, and shall have to be rowed, Rupert," said Gerald.

"Won't you go with Gudrun in the canoe?" said Birkin. "I'm sure you want to."

There was a moment's pause. Birkin and Ursula stood dimly, with their swinging lanterns, by the water's edge.

"Is that all right?" said Gudrun to him.

"It'll suit *me* very well," he said. "But what about you, and the rowing? I don't see why you should pull me."

"Why not?" she said. "I can pull you as well as I could pull Ursula." By her tone he could tell she was very pleased to have him in the boat to herself, and very glad to have him in her charge. And he wanted to be with her, in this close relationship.

She gave him the lanterns, whilst she went to fix the cane at the end of the canoe. He followed after her, and stood with the lanterns dangling against his white-flannelled thighs.

"Kiss me before we go," came his voice softly from out of the shadow above.

She stopped her work in real, momentary astonishment.

"But why?" she exclaimed, in pure surprise.

"Why?" he echoed, ironically.

And she looked at him fixedly for some moments. Then she leaned forward and kissed him, with a slow, luxurious kiss, lingering on the mouth. And then she took the lanterns from him, while he stood swooning with the perfect fire that burned in all his joints.

They lifted the canoe into the water, Gudrun took her place, and Gerald pushed off.

"Are you sure you don't hurt your hand, doing that?" she asked, solicitous. "Because I could have done it *perfectly*."

"I don't hurt myself," he said in a low, soft voice, that caressed her with inexpressible beauty.

And she watched him as he sat near her, very near to her, in the stern of the canoe, his legs coming towards hers, his feet touching hers. And she paddled softly, lingeringly, longing for him to say something meaningful to her. But he remained silent.

"You like this, do you?" she said, in a gentle, solicitous voice.

He laughed shortly.

"You are too far away," he said, in the same low, unconscious voice, as if something were speaking out of him.

She was silent, glimmering with the pleasure of this speech.

"But I'm very near," she said caressively, gaily.

"I can't feel hold of you, in this place, can I?" he asked naively. Again she was silent with pleasure, before she answered, speaking with difficulty:

"Not very well, unless you want to tip us both into the water."

A dozen or more boats on the lake swung their rosy and moon-like lanterns low on the water, that reflected as from a fire. In the distance, the steamer twanged and thrummed and washed with her faintly-splashing paddles, trailing her strings of coloured lights, and occasionally lighting up the whole scene luridly with an effusion of fireworks, Roman candles and sheafs of stars and other simple effects, illuminating the surface of the water, and showing the boats creeping round, low down. Then the lovely darkness fell again, the lanterns and the little threaded lights glimmered softly, there was a muffled knocking of oars and a waving of music.

Gudrun paddled almost imperceptibly. Gerald could see, not far ahead, the rich blue and the rose globes of Ursula's lanterns swaying softly cheek to cheek as Birkin rowed, and iridescent, evanescent gleams chasing in the wake. He was aware, too, of his own delicately coloured lights casting their softness behind him.

Gudrun rested her paddle and looked round. The canoe lifted with the lightest ebbing of the water. Gerald's shadowy knees were very near to her.

"Isn't it beautiful!" she said softly, as if reverently.

She looked at him, as he leaned back against the faint crystal of the lantern-light. She could see his face, although it was a pure shadow. But it was a piece of twilight. And her breast was keen with passion for him, he was so beautiful in his male stillness and mystery. A certain pure effluence of maleness, like an aroma from his softly, firmly moulded contours, a certain rich perfection of his presence, touched her with an ecstasy, a thrill of pure intoxication. She loved to look at him. For the present she did not even want to touch him, to handle the lovely, satisfying form of his living body. Her hands lay in her lap like slumbering birds, she only wanted to see him like a crystal shadow, to feel his essential presence.

"Yes," he said vaguely. "It is very beautiful."

He was listening to the faint near sounds, the dropping of water-drops from the oar-blades, the slight drumming of the lanterns behind him, as they rubbed against one another, the occasional rustling of Gudrun's full silk skirt, an alien land noise. His mind was almost submerged, he was almost transfused, lapsed out for the first time in his life, into the things about him. For he always kept such a keen attentiveness, was concentrated and hard in himself. Now he had let go, imperceptibly he was melting into oneness with the whole. It was like pure, perfect sleep, his first sleep of warm life. He had been so alert, on the defensive, all his life. But here was sleep, and peace, and perfect equanimity.

"Shall I row to the landing stage?" asked Gudrun wistfully.

"Anywhere," he answered. "Let it drift."

"Tell me then, if we are running into anything," she replied, in that very quiet, toneless voice of sheer intimacy, excluding all the world.

"The lights will show," he said.

So they drifted almost motionless, in silence. He wanted silence, pure and whole. But she was uneasy for some word, for some assurance.

"Nobody will miss you?" she asked, anxious for some communication.

"Miss me?" he echoed. "No! Why?"

"I wondered if anybody would be looking for you."

"Why should they look for me?" And then he remembered his manners. "But perhaps you want to get back," he said, in a changed voice.

"No, I don't want to get back," she replied. "No, I assure you."

"You're quite sure it's all right for you?"

"Perfectly all right."

And again they were still. The launch twanged and hooted, somebody was singing. Then as if the night smashed, suddenly there was a great shout, a confusion of shouting warring on the water, then the horrid noise of paddles reversed and churning violently.

Gerald sat up, and Gudrun looked at him in fear.

"Somebody in the water," he said, angrily, and desperately, looking keenly across the dusk. "Can you row up?"

"Where, to the launch?" asked Gudrun, in nervous panic.

"Yes."

"You'll tell me if I don't steer straight," she said, in nervous apprehension.

"You keep pretty level," he said, and the canoe hastened forward. The shouting and the noise continued, sounding horrid through the dusk, over the surface of the water.

"Wasn't this *bound* to happen?" said Gudrun, with heavy, hateful irony.

But he hardly heard, and she glanced over her shoulder to see her way. The half-dark waters were sprinkled with lovely bubbles of swaying lights, the launch did not look far off. She was rocking her lights in the early night. Gudrun rowed as hard as she could. But now that it was a serious matter, she seemed uncertain and clumsy in her stroke, it was difficult to paddle swiftly. She glanced at his face. He was looking fixedly into the darkness, very keen and alert and single in himself, instrumental. Her heart sank, she seemed to die a death. "Of course," she said to herself, "nobody will be drowned. Of course they won't. It would be too extravagant and sensational." But her heart was cold, because of his blank, impersonal face. It was as if he belonged naturally to dread and catastrophe, as if he were himself again.

Then there came a child's voice, a girl's high, piercing shriek:

"*Di—Di—Di—Di—Oh Di—Oh Di—Oh Di!*"

The blood ran cold in Gudrun's veins.

"It's Diana, is it," muttered Gerald. "The young monkey, she'd have to be up to some of her tricks."

And he glanced again at the paddles, the boat was not going quickly enough for him. It made Gudrun almost helpless at the rowing, this nervous stress. She kept up with all her might. Still the voices were calling and answering. "Where, Where? There you are—that's it. Which? No—No-o-o. Damn it all, here, *here*—" Boats were hurrying from all directions to the scene, coloured lanterns could be seen waving close to the surface of the lake, reflections swaying after them in uneven haste. The steamer hooted again, for some unknown reason. Gudrun's boat was travelling quickly, the lanterns were swinging behind Gerald.

And then again came the child's high, screaming voice, with a note of weeping and impatience in it now:

"*Di—Oh Di—Oh Di—Di—!*"

It was a terrible sound, coming through the obscure air of the evening.

"You'd be better if you were in bed, Winnie," Gerald muttered to himself.

He was stooping unlacing his shoes, pushing them off with the foot. Then he threw his soft hat into the bottom of the boat, and was taking off his coat.

"You can't go into the water with your hurt hand," said Gudrun, panting, in a low voice of horror.

"What?—It won't hurt."

He had struggled out of his jacket, and had dropped it between his feet. He sat bare-headed, all in white now. He felt the belt at his waist. They were nearing the launch, which stood still big above them, its myriad lamps making lovely darts, and sinuous running tongues of brilliant red and green and yellow on the lustrous dark water, under the shadow.

"*Oh get her out! Oh Di, darling! Oh get her out! Oh Daddy, Oh Daddy!*" moaned the child's voice, in distraction. Somebody was in the water, with a life-belt. Two boats paddled near, their lanterns swinging ineffectually, the boats nosing round.

"Hi there—Rockley!—hi there!"

"Mr Gerald!" came the captain's terrified voice. "Miss Diana's in the water."

"Anybody gone in for her?" came Gerald's sharp voice.

"Young Doctor Brindell, sir."

"Where?"

"Can't see no signs of them, sir. Everybody's looking, but there's nothing so far."

There was a moment's ominous pause.

"Where did she go in?"

"I think—about where that boat is," came the uncertain answer, "that one with red and green lights."

"Row there," said Gerald quietly to Gudrun.

"*Get her out, Gerald, Oh get her out*," the child's voice was crying anxiously. He took no heed.

"Lean back that way," said Gerald to Gudrun, as he stood up in the frail boat. "She won't upset."

In another moment, he had dropped clean down, soft and plumb, into the water. Gudrun was swaying violently in her boat, the agitated water shook with transient lights, she realised that it was faintly moonlight, and that he was gone. So it was possible to be gone. A terrible sense of fatality robbed her of all feeling and thought. So he was gone out of the world, there was merely the same world, and absence, his absence. The night seemed large and empty. Lanterns swayed here and there, people were talking in an undertone on the launch and in the boats. She could hear Winifred moaning: "*Oh do find her Gerald, do find her*," and someone trying to comfort the child. Gudrun paddled aimlessly here and there. The terrible, massive, cold, boundless surface of the water terrified her beyond words. Would he never come back? She felt she must jump into the water too, to know the horror also.

She started, hearing someone say: "There he is." She saw the movement of his swimming, like a water-rat. And she rowed involuntarily to him. But he was near another boat, a bigger one. Still she rowed towards him. She must be very near. She saw him—he looked like a seal. He looked like a seal as he took hold of the side of the boat. His fair hair was washed down on his round head, his moustache seemed to bristle. She could hear him panting.

Then he clambered into the boat. Oh, and the beauty of the form of his loins, white and softly luminous as he climbed over the side of the boat, made her want to die, to die. The beauty of his white and luminous loins as he climbed into the boat, his back rounded and soft—ah, this was too much for her, too final a vision! She knew it, and it was fatal. The terrible hopelessness of fate, and of beauty, such beauty!

He was not like a man to her, he was a vision, a great phase of life. She saw him press the water out of his face, and look at the bandage on his hand. And she knew it was all no good, and that she would never go beyond him, he was the final vision of life to her.

"Put the lights out, we shall see better," came his voice, sudden and human and belonging to the world. She could scarcely believe it. She could scarcely believe there was a world. She leaned round and blew out her lanterns. They were difficult to blow out. Everywhere the lights were gone, save the coloured points on the sides of the launch. The bluey-grey, early night spread level around, the moon was overhead, there were shadows of boats here and there.

Again there was a splash, and he was gone under. Gudrun sat, sick at heart, frightened of the great, level surface of the water, so heavy and deadly. She was so alone, with the level, unliving field of the water stretching beneath her. It was not a good isolation, it was a terrible, cold separation of suspense. She was suspended upon the surface of the water until such time as she also should disappear beneath it.

Then she knew, by a stirring of voices, that he had climbed out again, into a boat. She sat claiming connection with him. So strenuously she claimed her connection with him, across the invisible space of the water! But round her heart was an isolation unbearable, through which nothing would penetrate.

"Take the launch in. It's no use keeping her there. Get lines for the dragging," came the toneless, instrumental voice, that was full of the sound of the world.

The launch began gradually to beat the waters.

"*Gerald*! *Gerald*?" came the wild crying voice of Winifred. He did not answer. Slowly the launch drifted round in a pathetic, clumsy circle, and slunk away to the land, retreating into the dimness. The wash of her paddles grew duller. Gudrun rocked in her light boat, and dipped the oar automatically to steady herself.

"Gudrun?" called Ursula's voice.

"Ursula!"

The boats of the two sisters pulled together.

"Where is Gerald?" said Gudrun.

"He's dived again," said Ursula plaintively. "And I know he ought not, with his bad hand and everything."

"I'll take him home this time," said Birkin.

The boats swayed again from the wash of the steamer. Gudrun and Ursula kept a look-out for Gerald.

"There he is!" cried Ursula, who had the sharpest eyes. He had not been long under. Birkin pulled towards him, Gudrun following. He swam slowly, and caught hold of the boat with his wounded hand. It slipped, and he sank back.

"Why don't you help him?" cried Ursula sharply.

He came again, and Birkin leaned to help him in to the boat. Gudrun again watched Gerald climb out of the water, but this time slowly, heavily, with the blind clambering motions of an amphibious beast, clumsy. Again the moon shone with faint luminosity on his white, wet figure, on the stooping back and the rounded loins. But it looked defeated now, his body, it clambered and fell with slow clumsiness. He was breathing hoarsely too, like an animal that is suffering. He sat slack and motionless in the boat, his head blunt and blind like a seal's, his whole appearance inhuman, unknowing. Gudrun shuddered as she mechanically followed his boat. Birkin rowed without speaking to the landing-stage.

"Where are you going?" Gerald asked suddenly, as if just waking up.

"Home," said Birkin.

"Oh no!" said Gerald imperiously. "We can't go home while they're in the water. Turn back again, I'm going to find them."

"No," said Birkin. "You can't."

"Why can't I?"

"You're not fit to do any more."

"How do you know?"

Birkin did not answer. He rowed towards the land. And Gerald sat silent, like a dumb beast, panting, his teeth chattering, his arms inert, his head like a seal's head.

They came to the landing-stage. Wet and naked-looking, Gerald climbed up the few steps. There stood his father, in the night.

"Father!" he said.

"Yes my boy?—Go home and get those things off."

"We shan't save them, father," said Gerald.

"There's hope yet, my boy."

"Not much, father. You don't know where they are. You can't find them. And there's a current, it's as cold as hell."

"We'll let the water out," said the father. "Go home you and look to yourself. See that he's looked after, Rupert," he added in a neutral voice.

"Well father, I'm sorry. I'm sorry. But it's no good, you can't find them."

He moved away barefoot, on the planks of the platform. Then he trod on something sharp.

"Of course, you've got no shoes on," said Birkin.

"His shoes are here!" cried Gudrun from below. She was making fast her boat.

Gerald waited for them to be brought to him. Gudrun came with them. He pulled them on his feet.

"If you once die," he said, "then when it's over, it's finished. There's room under that water there for thousands to be drowned."

"Two is enough," she said, murmuring.

He dragged on his second shoe. He was shivering violently, and his jaw shook as he spoke.

"That's true," he said, "it's enough. But there's a whole universe under there, and it's as cold as hell, and you're as helpless as if your head was cut off." He could scarcely speak, he shook so violently. "There's one thing about our family, you know," he continued. "Once anything goes wrong, it can never be put right again—not with us. I've noticed it all my life—you can't put a thing right, once it has gone wrong."

They were walking across the high-road to the house.

"You should just try it down there,—cold as hell, and room for thousands to be drowned, never a one knowing the other was there— you'd wonder how it is so many are alive, why we're all up here.—Are you going? I shall see you again, shan't I? Goodnight, and thank you. Thank you very much."

The two girls waited a while, to see if there were any hope. The moon shone clearly overhead, an almost impertinent brightness, the small dark boats clustered on the water, there were voices and subdued shouts. But it was all to no purpose. Gudrun went home when Birkin returned.

He was commissioned to open the sluice that let out the water from the lake, which was pierced at one end, near the high-road, thus serving as a reservoir to supply with water the distant mines, in case of necessity. "Come with me," he said to Ursula, "And then I will walk along with you, when I've done this."

He called at the water-keeper's cottage and took the key of the sluice. They went through a little gate, from the high-road, to the head of the water, where was a great stone basin which received the overflow, and a flight of stone steps descended into the depths of the water itself. At the head of the steps was the lock of the sluice-gate.

The night was silver-grey and perfect, save for the scattered, restless sound of voices. The grey sheen of the moonlight caught the stretch of water, dark boats plashed and moved. But Ursula's mind ceased to be receptive, everything was unimportant and unreal.

Birkin fixed the iron handle of the sluice, and turned it with a wrench. The cogs began slowly to rise. He turned and turned, like a slave, his white figure become distinct. Ursula looked away. She could not bear to see him winding heavily and laboriously, bending and rising mechanically like a slave, turning the handle.

Then, a real shock to her, there came a loud splashing of water from out of the dark, tree-filled hollow beyond the road, a splashing that deepened rapidly to a harsh roar, and then became a heavy, booming noise of a great body of water falling solidly all the time. It occupied the whole of the night, this great steady booming of water, everything was drowned within it, drowned and dying. Ursula seemed to have to struggle for her life. She put her hands over her ears, and looked at the high, bland moon.

"Can't we go now?" she cried to Birkin, who was watching the water on the steps, to see if it would get any lower. It seemed to fascinate him. He looked up at her and nodded.

The little dark boats had moved nearer, people were crowding curiously along the hedge by the high-road, to see what was to be seen. Birkin and Ursula went to the cottage with the key, then turned their backs on the lake. She was very thankful. She could not bear the terrible crushing boom of the escaping water.

"Do you think they are dead?" she cried in a high voice, to make herself heard.

"Yes," he replied.

"Isn't it horrible!"

He nodded. They walked up the hill, further and further away from the noise.

"Do you mind very much?" she asked him.

"I am sorry for the living," he said. "For the dead it is all the same."

She pondered for a time.

"Yes," she said. "The *fact* that they are dead doesn't seem to matter, does it?"

"No," he said. "Lives don't matter, more or less."

"Don't they!" she said, shocked.

"No. There are millions all alike. What does quantity matter—even in human lives—or deaths? It isn't significant—the lives themselves don't signify."

"I can't believe that," she said.

"Yes. I'd rather Diana Crich were dead. Her living, somehow, was all wrong. As for the young man, poor devil—he'll escape a lot of barren bitterness. Death is all right—so clean."

"Yet *you* don't want to die," she challenged him.

He was silent for a time. Then he said, in a voice that was frightening to her in its change:

"No. I want something that isn't death. There is something else."

"I should hope so," laughed Ursula nervously.

They walked on for some way in silence, under the trees. Then he said, slowly, as if afraid:

"There is life which belongs to death, and there is life which isn't death. I am so tired of the life that belongs to death—passion and sensation and self-consciousness. I am so tired of it. I want love that is like sleep, like being born again, like being a baby that just comes into the world."

Ursula listened, half attentive, half avoiding what he said. She seemed to catch the drift of his statement, and then she drew away. She wanted to hear, but she did not want to be implicated. She was reluctant to yield there, where he wanted her to yield, as it were, her very identity.

"Why should love be like sleep?" she asked sadly.

"I don't know. So that it is like death—I *do* want to die from this life—and yet it is more than life itself. One is delivered over like a naked infant from the womb, all the old defences and the old body gone, a new air around one, that has never been breathed before."

She listened, making out what he said. She knew, as well as he knew, that words themselves do not convey meaning, that they are but a gesture we make, a dumb show like any other. And she seemed to feel his gesture through her blood, and she drew back, even though her desire sent her forward.

"But," she said gravely, "didn't you say you wanted something that was *not* love—something beyond love?"

He turned in confusion. There was always confusion in speech. Yet it must be spoken. Whichever way one moved, if one moved forwards, outwards, one must break a way through. And to know, to give utterance, was to break a way through the walls of the prison, as the infant in labour strives through the walls of the womb. There is no movement, without the breaking through of the old body, deliberately, in knowledge, in the struggle to get out.

"I don't want love," he said. "I don't want to know you. I want to be gone out of myself, and you to be lost to yourself, so we are found in one—conceived in a oneness. Then I am gone, and you, the female, are gone—there exists only the third thing, the new-created. The old two don't exist any more. So you and me."

"Like having children," she said.

He thought for a minute, then he said, sulkily:

"I don't know."

Then they walked on in silence, at outs. He was vague and lost.

"Isn't it strange," she said, suddenly putting her hand on his arm, with a loving impulse, "how we always talk like this. I suppose we do love each other, in some way."

"Oh yes," he said; "when we can get there."

She laughed almost gaily.

"You'd have to be dead certain, wouldn't you!" she teased. "You could never take it on trust."

He changed, laughed softly, and turned and took her in his arms, in the middle of the road.

"Yes," he said softly.

And he kissed her face and brow, slowly, gently, with a sort of delicate happiness which surprised her extremely, and to which she could not respond. They were soft, blind kisses, perfect in their stillness. Yet she held back from them. It was like strange moths, very soft and silent, settling on her from the darkness of her soul. She was uneasy. She drew away.

"Isn't somebody coming?" she said.

So they looked down the dark road, then set off again walking towards Beldover. Then suddenly, to show him she was no shallow prude, she stopped and held him tight, hard against her, and covered his face with hard, fierce kisses of passion. In spite of his otherness, the blood beat up in him.

"Not this, not this," he whimpered to himself, as the first perfect mood of softness and sleep-loveliness ebbed back away from the rushing of passion that came up his limbs and over his face as she drew him. And soon he was a perfect hard flame of passionate desire for her. Yet in the small core of the flame was an unyielding anguish of another love. But this also was lost; he only wanted her, with a sheer desire that seemed extreme as death, beyond question.

Afterwards, satisfied and shattered, fulfilled and destroyed, he went home away from her, drifting vaguely through the darkness, lapsed into the old fire of burning passion. Far away, far away, there seemed to be a small lament in the darkness. But what did it matter? What did it matter, what did anything matter save this ultimate and triumphant experience of physical passion, that had blazed up anew like a new spell of life. "I was becoming quite dead-alive, nothing but a word-bag,"* he said in triumph, scorning his other self. Yet somewhere far off and small, the other hovered.

The men were still dragging the lake when he got back. He stood on the bank and heard Gerald's voice. The water was still booming in the night, the moon was fair, the hills beyond were elusive. The lake was sinking. There came the raw smell of the banks, in the night air.

Up at Shortlands there were lights in the windows, as if nobody had gone to bed. On the landing-stage was the old doctor, the father of the young man who was lost. He stood quite silent, waiting. Birkin also stood and watched. Gerald came up in a boat.

"You still here, Rupert?" he said. "We can't get them. The bottom slopes, you know, very steep. The water lies between two very sharp slopes, and God knows how deep it is right in the middle. So it isn't as if it was a level bottom. You never know where you are, with the dragging."

"Is there any need for you to be working?" said Birkin. "Wouldn't it be much better to leave it to the others?"

"Leave it! What for? Do you think I should rest? We'll find 'em, before I go away from here."

"But the men would find them just the same without you—why should you waste yourself?"

Gerald looked up at him. Then he put his hand affectionately on Birkin's shoulder, saying:

"Don't you bother about me, old man. If there's anybody's health to think about, it's yours, not mine. How do you feel yourself?"

"Very well.—But you, you damage your own living—you waste your essential life."

Gerald was silent for a moment. Then he said:

"Waste it? Damn good job too!"

"Come away, won't you? You screw up all your screws up tight, and put a mill-stone of beastly memories round your neck! Come away now."

"A mill-stone of beastly memories!" Gerald repeated. Then he put his hand again affectionately on Birkin's shoulder. "God, you've got such a telling way of putting things, Rupert, you have."

Birkin's heart sank. He was irritated and weary beyond expression.

"Won't you leave it? Come over to my place—?" he urged, as one urges a drunken man.

"No," said Gerald coaxingly, his arm across the other man's shoulder. "Thanks very much, Rupert—I shall be glad to come tomorrow, if that'll do. You understand, don't you? I want to see this job through. But I'll come tomorrow, right enough. Oh, I'd rather come and have a chat with you than—than do anything else, I verily believe. Yes, I would. I don't know anything else that gives me more pleasure."

"That's very kind of you," said Birkin irritably. "You'll come when you like then. But you might just as well come now. There's no need for you to put any more into this job tonight."

"Oh, I'm doing nothing, I'm doing nothing."

"Then why not leave it? Never mind. Goodnight."

"Goodnight Rupert. Goodnight old man."

Birkin went away, saying to himself under his breath: "Curse you for a tragic fool, Gerald." But he was more miserable than angry.

The bodies of the dead were not recovered till towards dawn. Diana had her arms tight round the neck of the young man, choking him.

"That's what killed him," said Gerald.

The moon sloped down the sky and sank at last, the lake was sunk to half size, it had horrible raw banks of clay, that smelled of raw water. Dawn roused faintly behind the eastern hill. The water still boomed through the sluice.

As the birds were whistling for the first morning, and the hills at the back of the desolate lake stood radiant with new mists, there was a straggling procession up to Shortlands, men bearing the bodies on a stretcher, Gerald going beside them, the two grey-bearded fathers following in silence. Indoors the family was all sitting up, waiting.

Somebody must go to tell the mother, in her room. The doctor in secret struggled to bring back his son, till he himself was exhausted and almost dying.

Over all the outlying district was a hush of dreadful excitement on that Sunday morning. The colliery people felt as if this catastrophe had happened to them indeed, they were more shocked and frightened than if their own men had been killed. Such a tragedy at Shortlands, the high home of the district! One of the young mistresses, persisting in dancing on the cabin roof of the launch, wilful young madam, drowned in the midst of the festival, with the young doctor! Everywhere, on the Sunday morning, the colliers wandered about, discussing the calamity. At all the Sunday dinners of the people, there seemed a strange presence. It was as if the angel of death were very near, there was a sense of the supernatural in the air. The men had pale, troubled faces, the women looked solemn, some of them had been crying. The children enjoyed the excitement at first, when they got up and heard, and when they went to Sunday school feeling that something important had taken place. But later it irked them, they wanted their parents to have done with it.

Gudrun had wild ideas of rushing to comfort Gerald. She was thinking all the time of the perfect comforting, reassuring thing to say to him. And she was shocked and frightened, but she put that away, thinking of how she should deport herself with Gerald.

Ursula was deeply and passionately in love with Birkin, and she was capable of nothing. She was perfectly callous about all the talk of the accident, but her estranged air looked like trouble. She merely sat by herself, whenever she could, and longed madly, madly to see him again. She wanted him to come to the house—she would not have it otherwise, he must come at once. She was waiting for him. She stayed indoors all the day, waiting for him to knock at the door. Every minute, she glanced automatically at the window. He would be there.

6

As THE DAY WORE ON, the life-blood seemed to ebb away from Ursula, and within the emptiness a heavy despair gathered. Her passion seemed to bleed to death, and there was nothing. She sat suspended in a state of complete nullity, harder to bear than death.

"Unless something happens," she said to herself, in the perfect lucidity of suffering, "I shall die. I am at the end of my line of life."

She sat crushed and obliterated in a darkness that was the border of death. She realised how all her life she had been drawing nearer and nearer to this brink, where there was no beyond, from which one had to leap like Sappho into the unknown.* The knowledge of the imminence of death was like a drug. Darkly, without thinking at all, she knew that she was near to death. She had travelled all her life along the line of fulfilment, and it was nearly concluded. She knew all she had to know, she had experienced all she had to experience, she was fulfilled in a kind of bitter ripeness, there remained only to fall from the tree into death. And one must fulfil one's development to the end, must carry the adventure to its conclusion. And the next step was over the border into death. So it was then! There was a certain peace in the knowledge.

After all, when one was fulfilled, one was happiest in falling into death, as a bitter fruit plunges in its ripeness downwards. Death is a great consummation, a consummating experience. It is a development from life. That we know, while we are yet living. What then need we think for further? One can never see beyond the consummation. It is enough that death is a great and conclusive experience. Why should we ask what comes after the experience, when the experience is still unknown to us? Let us die, since the great experience is the one that follows now upon all the rest, death, which is the next great crisis in front of which we have arrived. If we wait, if we balk the issue, we do but hang about the gates in undignified uneasiness. There it is, in front of us, as in front of Sappho, the illimitable space. Thereinto goes the journey. Have we not the courage to go on with our journey, must we cry 'I daren't.'? On ahead we will go, into death, and whatever death may mean. If a man can see the next step to be taken, why should he fear the next but one? Why ask about the next but one? Of the next step we are certain. It is the step into death.

"I shall die—I shall quickly die," said Ursula to herself, clear as if in a trance, clear, calm, and certain beyond human certainty. But somewhere behind, in the twilight, there was a bitter weeping and a hopelessness. That must not be attended to. One must go where the unfaltering spirit goes, there must be no balking the issue, because of fear. No balking the issue, no listening to the lesser voices. If the deepest desire be now, to go on into the unknown of death, shall one forfeit the deepest desire for one more shallow?

"Then let it end," she said to herself. It was a decision. It was not a question of taking one's life—she would *never* kill herself, that was repulsive and violent. It was a question of *knowing* the next step. And the next step led into the space of death. Did it?—or was there———?

Her thoughts drifted into unconsciousness, she sat as if asleep beside the fire. And then the thought came back. The space of death! Could she give herself to it? Ah yes—it was a sleep. She had had enough. So long she had held out and resisted. Now was the time to relinquish, not to resist any more.

In a kind of spiritual trance, she yielded, she gave way, and all was dark. She could feel, within the darkness, the terrible assertion of her body, the unutterable anguish of dissolution, the only anguish that is too much, the far-off, awful nausea of dissolution set in within the body.

"Does the body correspond so immediately with the spirit?" she asked herself. And she knew, with the clarity of ultimate knowledge, that the body is only one of the manifestations of the spirit, the dissolution of the integral spirit is the dissolution of my physical body as well.—Unless I set my will, unless I absolve myself from the flux of life, fix myself and remain static, cut off from living, absolved within my own will. But better die than live mechanically a life that is a repetition of repetitions. To die is to move on with the invisible. To die is also a joy, a joy of submitting to that which is greater than the known, the pure unknown. That is a joy. But to live mechanised and cut off within the motion of the will, to live as an ego absolved from the unknown, that is shameful and ignominious. There is no ignominy in death. There is complete ignominy in a static, mechanised life. Life indeed may be ignominious, shameful to the soul. But death is never a shame. Death itself, like the illimitable space, is beyond our sullying.

Tomorrow was Monday. Monday, the beginning of another school-week! Another shameful, barren school-week, mere routine and mechanical activity. Was not the adventure of death infinitely preferable? Was not death infinitely more lovely and noble than such a life? A life of barren routine, without inner meaning, without any real significance. How sordid life was, how it was a terrible shame to the soul, to live now! How much cleaner and more dignified to be dead! One could not bear any more of this shame of sordid routine and mechanical nullity. One might come to fruit in death. She had had enough. For where was life to be found? No flowers grow upon busy machinery, there is no sky to a routine, there is no space to a rotary motion. And all life was a rotary motion, mechanised, cut off from reality. There was nothing to look for from life—it was the same in all countries and all peoples. The only window was death. One could look out on to the great dark sky of death with elation, as one had looked out of the class-room window as a child, and seen perfect freedom in the outside. Now one was not a child, and one knew that the soul was a prisoner within this sordid vast edifice of life, and there was no escape, save in death.

But what a joy! What a gladness to think that whatever humanity did, it could not seize hold of the kingdom of death, to nullify that. The sea they turned into a murderous alley and a soiled road of commerce, disputed like the dirty land of a city every inch of it. The air they claimed too, shared it up, parcelled it out to certain owners, they trespassed in the air to fight for it. Everything was gone, walled in, with spikes on top of the walls, and one must ignominiously creep between the spiky walls through a labyrinth of life.

But the great, dark, illimitable kingdom of death, there humanity was put to scorn. So much they could do upon earth, the multifarious little gods that they were. But the kingdom of death put them all to scorn, they dwindled into their true vulgar silliness in face of it.

How beautiful, how grand and perfect death was, how good to look forward to. There one would wash off all the lies and ignominy and dirt that had been put upon one here, a perfect bath of cleanness and glad refreshment, and go unknown, unquestioned, unabased. After all, one was rich, if only in the promise of perfect death. It was a gladness above all, that this remained to look forward to, the pure inhuman otherness of death. Whatever life might be, it could not take away death, the inhuman transcendent death. Oh, let us ask no question of it, what it is or is not. To know is human, and in death we do not know, we are not human. And the joy of this compensates for all the bitterness of knowledge and the sordidness of our humanity. In death we shall not be human, and we shall not know. The promise of this is our heritage, we look forward like heirs to their majority.

Ursula sat quite still and quite forgotten, alone by the fire in the drawing-room. The children were playing in the kitchen, all the others were gone to church. And she was gone into the ultimate darkness of her own soul.

She was startled by hearing the bell ring, away in the kitchen, the children came scudding along the passage in delicious alarm.

"Ursula, there's somebody."

"I know. Don't be silly," she replied. She too was startled, almost frightened. She dared hardly go to the door.

Birkin stood on the threshold, his rain-coat turned up to his ears. He had come now, now she was gone far away. She was aware of the rainy night behind him.

"Oh is it you?" she said.

"I am glad you are at home," he said in a low voice, entering the house.

"They are all gone to church."

He took off his coat and hung it up. The children were peeping at him round the corner.

"Go and get undressed now, Billy and Dora," said Ursula. "Mother will be back soon, and she'll be disappointed if you're not in bed."

The children, in a sudden angelic mood, retired without a word. Birkin and Ursula went into the drawing-room. The fire burned low. He looked at her, and wondered at the luminous delicacy of her beauty, and the wide shining of her eyes. He watched from a distance, with reverence in his heart, she seemed transfigured with light.

"What have you been doing all day?" he asked her.

"Only sitting about," she said.

He looked at her. There was a change in her. But she was separate from him. She remained apart, in a kind of brightness. They both sat silent in the soft light of the lamp. He felt he ought to go away again, he ought not to have come. Still he did not gather enough resolution to move. But he was *de trop*, her mood was absent and separate.

Then there came the voices of the two children calling shyly outside the door, softly, with self-excited timidity:

"Ursula! Ursula!"

She rose and opened the door. On the threshold stood the two children in their long nightgowns, with wide-eyed, angelic faces. They were being very good for the moment, playing the rôle perfectly of two obedient children.

"Shall you take us to bed!" said Billy, in a loud whisper.

"Why, you *are* angels tonight," she said gently. "Won't you come and say goodnight to Mr Birkin?"

The children merged shyly into the room, on bare feet. Billy's face was wide and grinning, but there was a great solemnity of being good in his round blue eyes. Dora, peeping from the floss of her fair hair, hung back like some tiny Dryad, that has no soul.

"Will you say goodnight to me?" asked Birkin, in a voice that was strangely soft and smooth. Dora drifted away at once, like a leaf lifted on a breath of wind. But Billy went softly forward, slow and willing, lifting his pinched-up mouth implicitly to be kissed. Ursula watched the full, gathered lips of the man gently touch those of the boy, so gently. Then Birkin lifted his fingers and touched the boy's round, confiding cheek, with a faint touch of love. Neither spoke. Billy seemed angelic like a cherub boy, or like an acolyte, Birkin was a tall, grave angel looking down to him.

"Are you going to be kissed?" Ursula broke in, speaking to the little girl. But Dora edged away like a tiny Dryad that will not be touched.

"Won't you say Goodnight to Mr Birkin? Go, he's waiting for you," said Ursula. But the girl-child only made a little motion away from him.

"Silly Dora, silly Dora!" said Ursula.

Birkin felt some mistrust and antagonism in the small child. He could not understand it.

"Come then," said Ursula. "Let us go before mother comes."

"Who'll hear us say our prayers?" asked Billy anxiously.

"Whom you like."

"Won't *you*?"

"Yes, I will."

"Ursula?"

"Well Billy?"

"Is it *whom* you like?"

"That's it."

"Well what is *whom*?"

"It's the accusative of who."

There was a moment's contemplative silence, then the confiding: "Is it?"

Birkin smiled to himself as he sat by the fire. When Ursula came down he sat motionless, with his arms on his knees. She saw him, how he was motionless and ageless, like some crouching grey ghost, some ageless spectre of the old world. He looked round at her, and his face, very pale and unreal, seemed to gleam with a whiteness almost phosphorescent.

"Don't you feel well?" she asked, in indefinable repulsion.

"I hadn't thought about it."

"But don't you know without thinking about it?"

He looked at her, his eyes dark and swift, and he saw her revulsion. He did not answer her question.

"Don't you know whether you are unwell or not, without thinking about it?" she persisted.

"Not always," he said coldly.

"But don't you think that's very wicked?"

"Wicked?"

"Yes. I think it's *criminal* to have so little connection with your own body that you don't even know when you are ill."

He looked at her darkly.

"Yes," he said.

"Why don't you stay in bed when you are seedy? You look perfectly ghastly."

"Offensively so?" he asked ironically.

"Yes, quite offensive. Quite repelling."

"Ah!—Well that's unfortunate."

"And it's raining, and it's a horrible night. Really, you shouldn't be forgiven for treating your body like it—you *ought* to suffer, a man who takes as little notice of his body as that."

"—takes as little notice of his body as that," he echoed mechanically.

This cut her short, and there was silence.

The others came in from church, and the two had the girls to face, then the mother and Gudrun, and then the father and the boy.

"Good-evening," said Brangwen, faintly surprised. "Came to see me, did you?"

"No," said Birkin, "not about anything in particular, that is. The day was dismal, and I thought you wouldn't mind if I called in."

"It *has* been a depressing day," said Mrs Brangwen sympathetically. At that moment the voices of the children were heard calling from upstairs: "Mother! Mother!" She lifted her face and answered mildly into the distance: "I shall come up to you in a minute Doysie." Then to Birkin: "There is nothing fresh at Shortlands, I suppose?—Ah," she sighed, "no, poor things, I should think not."

"You've been over there today, I suppose?" asked the father.

"Gerald came round to tea with me, and I walked back with him. The house is overexcited and unwholesome, I thought."

"I should think they were people without much restraint," said Gudrun.

"Too much," Birkin answered.

"Oh yes, I'm sure," said Gudrun, almost vindictively.

"They all feel they ought to behave in some unnatural fashion," said Birkin. "When people are in grief, they would do better to cover their faces and keep in retirement, as in the old days."

"Certainly!" cried Gudrun, flushed and inflammable. "What can be worse than this public grief—what is more horrible, more false! If *grief* is not private and sacred, and hidden, what is?"

"Exactly," he said. "I felt ashamed when I was there and they were all going about in a lugubrious false way, feeling they must not be natural or ordinary."

"Well—" said Mrs Brangwen, offended at this criticism, "it isn't so easy to bear a trouble like that."

And she went upstairs to the children.

He remained only a few minutes longer, then took his leave. When he was gone Ursula felt such a poignant hatred of him, that all her brain seemed turned into a sharp crystal of fine hatred. Her whole nature seemed sharpened and intensified into pure dart of hate. She could not imagine what it was. It merely took hold of her, the most poignant and ultimate hatred, pure and clear and beyond thought. She could not think of it at all, she was translated beyond herself. It was like a possession. She felt she was possessed. And for several days she went about possessed by this exquisite force of hatred against him. It surpassed anything she had ever known before, it seemed to throw her out of the world into some terrible region where nothing of her old life held good. She was quite lost and dazed, really dead to her own life.

It was so completely incomprehensible and irrational. She did not know *why* she hated him, she had no reason for hating him. She had only realised with a shock that stunned her, that she was overcome by this pure transportation of hatred. He was the enemy, fine as a diamond, and as hard and jewel-like, the quintessence of all that was inimical.

She thought of his face, white and purely wrought, and of his eyes that had such a dark, constant nonchalance, and she touched her own forehead, to feel if she were mad, she was so transfigured in white flame of essential hate.

It was not temporal, her hatred, she did not hate him for this or for that; she did not want to do anything to him, to have any connection with him. Her relation was ultimate and beyond words, the hate was pure and gem-like. It was as if he were a beam of essential enmity, a beam of light that did not only destroy her, but denied her altogether, revoked her whole world. She saw him as a clear stroke of uttermost contradiction, a strange gem-like being whose existence defined her own non-existence. When she heard he was ill again, her hatred only intensified itself a few degrees, if that were possible. It stunned her and annihilated her, but she could not escape it. She could not escape this transfiguration of hatred that had come upon her.

He lay sick and unmoved, in pure opposition to everything. He knew how near to breaking was the vessel that held his life. He knew also how strong and durable it was. And he did not yield. Better a thousand times to die than to accept a life one did not want. But best of all to persist and persist and persist for ever, till one were satisfied in life.

He knew that Ursula was referred back to him. He knew his life rested with her. But he would rather not live than accept the love she proffered. The humiliation of being loved in equality by women was too much. He wanted an absolute surrender, unconditional, only purely voluntary. He thought of Mohammed, who loved his old wife because she believed in him.* He wanted, like Mohammed, a wife who believed utterly. And to believe, a woman must, in her dark, unexpressed fashion, understand. Ursula could understand, well enough she could understand. For this reason his hope rested on her. Hermione could understand a good deal too, Hermione was a big woman. But the life in her was as if old, she was like an old woman who understands in her consciousness, but whose unconscious being is inimical, and withered. Her understanding was static, and limited just where it should begin to move into the unknown, her womb was as if dry. And, being herself arrested, she would kill him rather than let him move beyond her. If he moved beyond her she was annulled like the image of a dead religion. She was a dim abandoned statue of a bygone belief. So be it—she was abandoned with the past.

But where Hermione was old, Ursula was young. Where Hermione was old and could understand the old world, the old truths, Ursula was young, and contained the new. Only she was as yet hostile. Was she not enthroned, the female, as the first and the highest? Was not woman the creator of man, did she not bring him forth? Was not woman the highest of the human order, did not woman both in body and in understanding give birth to man, did she not produce him. Was she not the guardian and sustainer of all life, the greatest principle within humanity? The woman, the producer, she was the beginning and the end, man was her eternal offspring.

But Birkin wanted to deny this to Ursula. He wanted to pull her down, he wanted to belittle her from her high estate. He wanted to take away the supremacy from her. She, who was the mother of God, he wanted to put her down, to make her serve *him*. Ah, but she served a greater principle than he! The woman, the great producer of life, she stood against the unknown, she issued from the unknown, and to the unknown she owed her allegiance. She proceeded from the supreme unknown, and from her proceeded life, man and all his words and his deeds.

Now Birkin, in his very body, would reverse this. He would put her down, claim her vassalage. She must serve *him*, or his truth. As if she were not more than him and his truth and all the male host! She quivered with pure and exquisite hatred for him; for she was confronted by him.

And he lay in bed ill as if vampires were bleeding his life from him, feeling his life bleeding away, and hating heavily and completely the whole world, for its destroying him. He lay in the midst of destruction. But he was tough in spirit—he would not yield anything, neither would he be destroyed in the end.

For the present, there was only Gerald who had any connection. Gerald and he had a curious love for each other. It was a love that was perhaps death, a love which was complemented by the hatred for woman. It was a love that tore apart the two halves,* and brought universal death. It tore man from woman, and woman from man. The two halves divided and separated, each drawing away to itself. And the great chasm that came between the two sundered halves was death, universal death.

But if this was so, it was so. There was the love between him and Gerald and the other was denied, all other was denied. Then there must be death. Unless Ursula would yield. And he believed all the while that she would yield in the end. If not, then there was complete death. So be it. No man can create life by himself. It needs a man and a woman. And if the woman refuse, then the life is uncreated, and death triumphs. Well, no man can prevent death from triumphing, unless he can convince a woman. And if the woman will not be convinced, that is fate. No man can exceed himself.

He must convince Ursula to a belief in him, and an absolute surrender of herself, through belief. Which was a stiff task. Meanwhile he was quivering with sickness, his soul was torn, and there was nothing but to hang on, and to cover up the present with the love for Gerald, which was as much death as was Ursula's hate. But there is good death, the death of that which should pass away and be superseded by the new, and there is unlawful death of that which should not die.

For us, the imminent experience is the experience of death, the tearing asunder of the two halves. It is our desire, it is our necessity, it is our fate. There is a life which is over-dry and which must pass away. This is our universal life. We must die, we must all die, because the term of our living is over. There must be a period of death over the face of the earth, great and long.

But what does it matter if we die, seeing our term is over. It is good to die, it is a happiness to go into death, when the period of our era is ended. But somewhere, somewhere the new life must take shape and body. Either it must, or the human species ceases, and something else takes its place. The dead must bury their dead.* But somewhere the living must put off the body of the past,* shake off all connection with the past, save understanding, or we fall into one grave.

Somewhere there must be a complete departure, and a new journey. Somebody must have the courage to accept death in that which is deathly, final and accomplished death unto themselves, and yet retain the strength to be issued into a new infancy of life. Some must depart from all that has been and all that is, must depart and not look back. Otherwise the fire falls on all, the human race is an accomplished dream. And somebody must begin, or there is no beginning. And the responsibility lies on all alike.

When Birkin was ill, Gerald came to see him. The two men came together willingly. Gerald's eyes were quick and uneasy, his whole manner tense and impatient, he seemed strung up to some activity. According to his curious outward conventionality, he wore black clothes, so that he looked formal, handsome and *comme il faut*. His fair hair and his resolute, healthy face were attractive, his body seemed full of repressed energy.

Gerald really loved Birkin, though he never submitted to what he said. The other man was evanescent, clever, but too fantastic, dancing off the ground. Gerald himself represented reality, which had its feet firmly planted on the earth. And Birkin was a *Wunderkind*, wonderful, but not quite substantial enough to be taken seriously.

"Why are you seedy again?" he asked, gently, taking the sick man's hand. It was always Gerald who was protective, offering the warm shelter of his health.

"For my sins, I suppose," Birkin grinned.

"For your sins? Yes, probably that is so.—Why don't you sin less, and keep better in health?"

"You'd better teach me," said Birkin.

He looked at Gerald with mocking eyes.

"How are things with you?" asked Birkin.

"With me?" Gerald looked at Birkin, saw he was serious, and a warm light came into his eyes. "I don't know that they're any different. I don't see how they could be. There's nothing to change."

"I suppose you are conducting the business as brilliantly as ever, and ignoring everything else."

"That's it," said Gerald; "at least as far as the business is concerned. I couldn't say what I'm ignoring, I'm sure."

"No."

"Well really, could you?" laughed Gerald.

"How is your spirit progressing?"

"My spirit? I couldn't say about that. I don't know that I've got one."

"Yes you have," said Birkin, "so you might as well own up.—And what about Gudrun Brangwen?"

"What about her?" A baffled, arrested look came over Gerald. "Well," he added, "I don't know. I can only tell you, she gave me a hit over the face the last time I saw her."

"A hit over the face! What for?"

"That I couldn't tell you, either."

"Really!—But when?"

"The night of the party—when Diana was drowned. She was driving the cattle up the hill, and I went after her—you remember."

"Yes, I remember. But what made her do that? You didn't give her any occasion, I suppose?"

"I? No, not that I know of. I merely said to her, that it was dangerous to drive those Highland bullocks—as it *is*. She turned in such a way, and said—'I suppose you think I'm afraid of you and your cattle, don't you?'—So I asked her 'Why—?'—And then she flung me a back-hander across the face!"

Birkin smiled quickly, as if it pleased him. Gerald looked at him, wondering, and began to laugh as well, saying:

"I didn't laugh at the time, I assure you. I was never so taken aback in my life."

"And weren't you furious?"

"Furious? I should think I was. I'd have murdered her for a straw."

"Hm!" ejaculated Birkin. "Poor Gudrun, wouldn't she suffer afterwards for having given herself away."

"Would she suffer?" asked Gerald, pleased.

Both men smiled in malice and amusement.

"Badly, I'm sure; seeing how self-conscious she is."

"She is self-conscious is she? Then what made her do it? For I assure you it was quite uncalled for, and quite unjustified."

"I suppose it was a sudden impulse."

"Yes, but how do you account for her having such an impulse? I'd done her no hurt."

Birkin shook his head.

"The Amazon suddenly came up in her I suppose," he said.

"I tell you," replied Gerald, "I'd rather it had been the Orinoco." *

He was thinking how Gudrun had said she would strike the last blow too. But some deep reserve made him keep this back from Birkin.

"And do you resent it?" Birkin asked.

"I don't *resent* it. I don't care a tinker's curse about it." He was silent a moment, then he added, laughing, "No, I rather like her for it.—She seemed sorry herself *afterwards*."

"Did she? You've not seen her since that night?"

Gerald's face clouded.

"No," he said. "We've been—you can imagine how we've been since the accident."

"Yes. Is it calming down?"

"I don't know. It's a shock, of course. But I don't believe mother minds. I really don't believe she takes any notice. And what's so funny, she used to be all for the children—nothing mattered, nothing whatever mattered but the children. And now, she doesn't take any more notice than if it was one of the servants."

"No? Did it upset *you* very much?"

"It's a shock. But I don't feel it much now. I don't feel any different. We've all got to die, so why make any bones about it. Death's there, we know it, and we might as well just accept it—whenever or however it comes. It's just death, and there it is. It's nothing new."

"Even your own death?" asked Birkin.

Gerald looked at him with eyes blue as the purple-blue steel of a weapon. He was afraid, but undaunted. He would take death unblinking.

"Yes. I don't think death is any different for me than for anybody else. I don't want to die, but death is *there*, of course, and one doesn't pretend to get away from it.—I don't think I'm afraid."

"Except that it's a great experience," said Birkin.

"Yes," said Gerald quickly. "It's an experience, really. It must be— don't you think?—Or is it just a cancelling?"

"Perhaps—I don't know.—But is there nothing you feel you *must* have out of life, before you die?"

Gerald narrowed his eyes, his face was keen and unscrupulous as he looked at Birkin, impersonally, with a vision that did not look outwards, infinitely keen-eyed and yet blind.

"*Must* have out of life? Absolutely *must*?" he repeated, half entranced. "Yes, I want to let go somewhere, before I die. I'm going to let go somewhere."

"What?"

But the spell was broken, he could say no more. They remained silent for a time.

"No," said Gerald, continuing, "it's father who takes it to heart. It will absolutely finish him."

"Diana?"

"Yes. He's gone down under it like a felled ox. All his care is about Winnie now—that's the only thing that he notices now, Winnie. He feels her on his mind. I don't know what he wants to do with her. He says she ought to be sent away to school. And yet that's the one thing he cannot bear to think of. There's no pacifying him. And of course the child *is* in a queer state, seeing Di go like that."

"She oughtn't to be sent away to school," said Birkin.

"She oughtn't? Why?"

"She's a queer child—a special child, don't you think? And in my opinion special children should never be sent away to school. Only moderately ordinary children should be sent to school,—so it seems to me."

"I'm inclined to think just the opposite. I think it would probably make her more normal if she went away and mixed with other children."

"She wouldn't mix, you see. *You* never really mixed, did you? And she wouldn't be willing even to pretend to. She's proud, and solitary, and naturally apart. If she has a single nature, why do you want to make her gregarious?"

"Well, I don't want to make her anything. But I thought school would be good for her."

"Was it good for *you*?"

Gerald's eyes narrowed uglily. School had been torture to him. Yet he had not questioned whether one should go through this torture. He seemed to believe in education through subjection and torment.

"I might have been worse without it," he said. "No doubt I should."

"Much better," replied Birkin. "At any rate, don't force Winnie through the process. For special natures there is a special world. That should be the first maxim of education."

"Where's your special world?" asked Gerald.

"You and I are one, perhaps. Would you like us to be—well, the same as your brothers-in-law? Isn't it the special quality you value?"

Gerald looked into the eyes of the other man.

"Yes," he said, with a curious unwillingness of admission. "I believe I feel more myself with you than with anybody else."

This surprised Birkin. He turned aside, and said, laughing:

"Yet even you consider me something of a freak."

"A freak!" laughed Gerald, startled. "No—no-o—not a freak, exactly." He pondered. Then he turned to Birkin, with hot eyes and a pleading voice. "I often wonder," he said, "what you think of me—whether you care for me—well, at all—any more than you do for any man you meet in the streets."

He looked at Birkin with eyes hot with confusion and anxiety. And Birkin, whose eyes were too clear and steady and unfathomable, looked back at him.

"Yes," he admitted. "I like you more than anybody else—any other *man*."

He put out his hand from the bed, and took Gerald's brown, sinewy hand in his own. Convulsively, Gerald clasped Birkin's hand in both his, and sat with lips parted, breathing short and fast, his eyes set. Birkin looked at him, with unchanging eyes. He felt a hot pang of love for him, and a deep pity, a deep sorrow. Then finally, a cold weariness.

"We'll stand by each other, Gerald," he said slowly.

Gerald's face changed swiftly, he looked aside. He wanted the other man to put his arms round him, and hold him. He could not look at Birkin's dark, steadfast eyes any more, he turned aside, panting slightly, because he so much wanted the other man to take him in his arms and hold him close in peace and love. Yet it was so impossible.

"A Blutbrüderschaft,"* said Birkin, wearily, reassuring, as if to comfort the other.

And there was silence for a time. Then Birkin said, in a lighter tone, letting the stress of the emotion pass:

"Can't you get a good governess for Winifred?—somebody exceptional?"

"Hermione Roddice suggested we should ask Gudrun to teach her to draw and to model in clay. You know Winnie is astonishingly clever with that plasticine stuff. Hermione declares she is an artist."

"Really! I didn't know that?—Oh well then, if Gudrun *would* teach her, it would be perfect—couldn't be anything more perfect—if Winifred is an artist. Because Gudrun is one. And every true artist is the salvation of every other."

"I thought they got on so badly, as a rule."

"Perhaps. But only artists produce the world that is fit to live in. If you can arrange *that* for Winifred, it is perfect."

"But you think she wouldn't come?"

"I don't know. Gudrun is rather self-opinionated. She won't go cheap, anywhere. Or if she does, she'll pretty soon take herself back. So whether she would condescend to do private teaching, particularly here, in Beldover, I don't know. But it would be just the thing. Winifred has got a special nature. And if you can put into her way the means of her own fulfilment, that is the best thing possible.—She'll never get on with the ordinary life. You find it difficult enough yourself, and she is several skins thinner than you are. It is awful to think what her life will be like unless she does find a means of expression, some way of fulfilment. You can see what mere leaving it to fate brings. You can see how much marriage is to be trusted to—look at your own mother."

"Do you think mother is abnormal?"

"No! I think she only wanted something more, or other than the common run of life. And not getting it, she has gone wrong, perhaps."

"After producing a brood of wrong children," said Gerald gloomily.

"No more wrong than any of the rest of us. If you want to be normal, as things are, you must be a commonplace fool, or you won't fit. And if you don't fit, you're not normal."

"And if you don't fit, your life is a curse to yourself and to every body else," said Gerald, with sudden anger.

"Rubbish!" said Birkin. "Your life isn't a curse to *you*, don't flatter yourself.—And I wish it *was* a curse to everybody else—for I hate the everybody elses of this life.—Only your life's a blessing even to them."

There was silence, each thinking his own thoughts.

"She's a teacher already, isn't she?" said Gerald. "I don't see what she has to distinguish between teaching at the Grammar School, and coming to teach Win."

"The difference between a public servant and a private one. Even you might not think it derogatory to be Minister of Education. But you wouldn't be tutor to the Prince of Wales."

"I wouldn't be tutor to anybody."

"Exactly! And Gudrun will probably be the same."

Gerald thought for a few minutes. Then he said:

"At all events, father won't make her feel like a private servant. He will be fussy and grateful enough."

"So he ought to be—and so ought all of you.—Do you think you can hire a woman like Gudrun Brangwen with money?—She's the superior of most of *your* sisters, anyway."

"Is she!" said Gerald. He did not like it.

"She is. And if you haven't the guts to know it, I hope she'll leave you to your own devices."

"Nevertheless," said Gerald, "if she is my equal, I wish she weren't a teacher, because I don't think teachers as a rule are my equal."

"Nor do I, damn them. But am I a teacher because I teach, or a parson because I preach?—It bores me—."

Gerald laughed. He was always uneasy on this score. He did not want to *claim* social superiority: and he *would* not claim essential superiority, because that seemed conceited and priggish. So he fell back upon a tacit assumption of social standing. Now Birkin wanted him to accept the fact of intrinsic inequality between human beings, which he did not intend to accept. It was against his social honor, his creed. He rose to go.

"I've been neglecting my business all this while," he said, smiling.

"I admire you that you've held out so long in neglecting it," said Birkin.

"I knew you'd say that," laughed Gerald.

"So did I."

"Yes, all right, Rupert. I make the business go, because I am here on earth. When I am above the world, I shall ignore all businesses."

"Be a young Excelsior* in song."

"Ye cannot serve God and Mammon.* Mammon means money. Well, I don't care about the money, I only care about making the thing go. So I serve God, don't I, according to the reckoning?"

"Very pretty sophistry! Efficiency isn't God. Efficiency is Prime Minister to Mammon, that is all, a pure servant of Mammon. So you are a servant of a servant of Mammon."

"Am I really? And I always thought I served a pure idea, of doing a difficult thing perfectly."

"That's not an idea. That's a degree of material success."

"Is it? There goes another of my ideals," he laughed. "But," he added, "I know damn well my life is a mechanical affair; it means more coal, in the end, nothing else. And what the hell do I care about more coal?"

"You care a certain amount," said Birkin.

"I must do, I'm off to the office now, conscious of having wasted my morning. Well—"

He came near the bed, and stood looking down on the other man, whose fine throat was exposed, whose tossed hair seemed rarified round the steady darkened blue eyes, that were so strong and still in the frail face. Gerald, full-limbed and turgid with energy, stood unwilling to go, he was held by the presence of the other man.

"So," said Birkin, "goodbye." And he reached out his hand from under the bed-clothes, smiling with a glimmering look.

"Goodbye," said Gerald, taking the hot, vivid hand of his friend in his close grasp. "I shall come again. I miss you down at the mill."

"I'll be there in a few days" said Birkin.

The eyes of the two men met again. Gerald's, that were keen as a hawk's, were suffused now with warm light and with unadmitted love, Birkin looked back as out of a darkness, unsounded and unknown, yet with a kind of warmth, that seemed to flow over Gerald's brain like a fertile sleep.

"Goodbye then. There's nothing I can do for you?"

"Nothing, thanks."

Birkin watched the well-built, black-clothed form of the other man move out of the door, the bright head was gone, he turned over to sleep.

In Beldover, there was both for Ursula and for Gudrun an interval. It seemed to Ursula as if Birkin had gone out of her for the time, he had lost his significance, he scarcely mattered in her world. She had her own friends, her own activities, her own life. She turned back to the old ways with zest, away from him.

And Gudrun, after feeling every moment in all her veins conscious of Gerald Crich, connected even physically with him, was now almost indifferent to the thought of him. She was nursing new schemes for going away and trying a new form of life. All the time, there was something in her urging her to avoid the final establishing of a relationship with Gerald. She felt it would be wiser and better to have no more than a casual acquaintance with him.

She had a scheme for going to Saint Petersburg, where she had a friend who was a sculptor like herself, and who lived with a wealthy Russian whose hobby was jewel-making. The emotional, rather rootless life of the Russians appealed to her. She did not want to go to Paris. Paris was dry, and essentially boring. She would like to go to Rome, Munich, Vienna, or to St. Petersburg or Moscow. She had a friend in St Petersburg and a friend in Munich. To each of these she wrote, asking about rooms.

She had a certain amount of money. She had come home partly to save, and now she had sold several pieces of work, she had been praised in various shows. She knew she could become quite the "go,"* if she went to London. But she knew London, she wanted something else. She had seventy pounds, of which nobody knew anything. She would move soon, as soon as she heard from her friends. Her nature, in spite of her apparent placidity and calm, was profoundly restless.

The sisters happened to call in a cottage in Willey Green to buy honey. Mrs Kirk, a stout, pale, sharp-nosed woman, sly, honied, with something shrewish and dangerous beneath, asked the girls into her too-cosy, too tidy kitchen. There was a cat-like comfort and cleanliness everywhere.

"Yes, Miss Brangwen," she said, in her slightly whining, insinuating voice, "and how do you like being back in the old place then?"

Gudrun, whom she addressed, hated her at once.

"I don't care for it," she replied abruptly.

"You don't? Ay, well, I suppose you find a difference from London. You like life, and big, grand places. Some of us has to be content with Willey Green and Beldover.—And what do you think of our Grammar School, as there's so much talk about?"

"What do I think of it?" Gudrun looked round at her slowly. "Do you mean, do I think it's a good school?"

"Well, yes, if you like."

"I *do* think it's a good school."

Gudrun was very cold and repelling. She knew the common people hated the school.

"Oh, you do? I've heard some as didn't think much of it. But opinions vary, don't they? Mr Crich doesn't hold with it altogether. Ay, poor man, I'm afraid he's not long for this world. He's very poorly."

"Is he worse?" asked Ursula.

"Eh, yes—since they lost Miss Diana, he's gone off to a shadow. Poor man, he's had a world of trouble."

"Has he?" asked Gudrun, faintly ironic.

"He has, a world of trouble. And as nice and kind a gentleman as ever you could wish to meet.—His children don't take after him."

"I suppose they take after their mother?" said Ursula.

"In many ways." Mrs Kirk lowered her voice a little. "She was a proud, haughty lady when she came into these parts—my word, haughty! She mustn't be looked at, much less spoke to."

The woman made a wry, satiric face.

"Did you know her when she was first married?"

"Yes, I knew her. I nursed three of her children. And proper little terrors they were, proper ones!—Master Gerald, a little demon if ever there was one, a proper demon, at six months old."

A curious antagonistic, sleering* tone came into the woman's voice.

"Really!" said Gudrun.

"That wilful, masterful—he'd mastered one nurse at six months old. Kick, and scream, and struggle like a fiend! Many's the time I've pinched his little bottom for him, when he was a child in arms.—Ay, and he'd have been better if he'd had it pinched a bit oftener. But she wouldn't have them corrected—no-o, wouldn't hear of it. I can remember the rows she would have with the master.—When he'd got worked up, properly worked up till he could stand no more, he'd lock the study door and whip them. But she paced up and down all the while like a tiger outside, with very murder in her face. And when the door was opened, she'd go in with her hands lifted—'What have you been doing to *my* children, you coward.'—She was like one out of her mind. I believe he was frightened of her;—he had to be almost driven mad before he'd lift a finger. Didn't we used to be thankful when one of them was catching it. They were the torment of your life."

"Really!" said Gudrun.

"They *were* that. If you wouldn't let them smash their pots on the table, if you wouldn't let them drag the kitten about with a string round its neck, if you wouldn't give them whatever they asked for, every mortal thing—then there was a to-do, and their mother coming in asking—'What's the matter with him? What have you done to him? What is it, Darling?' And she'd turn on you as if she was going to trample you under her feet.—But she didn't trample on me. I was the only one that could do anything with her demons—for she wasn't going to be bothered with them herself. No, she took no notice of them. But there you are, they must just have their way, they mustn't even be spoken to. And master Gerald was pick of them. I left when he was a year and a half, I could stand no more. But I pinched his little bottom red when he was in arms, I did, sometimes when there was no holding him."

Gudrun went away in fury and loathing. The phrase, 'I pinched his little bottom red for him,' sent her into a white, stony fury. She could not bear it, she wanted to have the woman taken out at once and strangled. And yet there the phrase was lodged in her mind for ever, beyond escape. She felt, one day, she would *have* to tell him, to see him shrivel with rage and shame. And she loathed herself for the thought.

But at Shortlands the life-long struggle was coming to a close. The father was ill and was going to die. He had bad internal pains, which took away all his attentive life, and left him with only a vestige of his consciousness. More and more a silence came over him, he was less and less acutely aware of his surroundings. The pain seemed to absorb his activity. He knew it was there, he knew it would come again. It was like something lurking in the darkness within him. And he had not the power, or the will, to seek it out and to know it. There it remained in the darkness, the great pain, tearing him at times, and then lying silent. And when it tore him he crouched in silent subjection under it, and when it left him alone again, he refused to know of it. It was within the darkness, let it remain unknown. So he never admitted it, except in a secret corner of himself, where all his never-revealed shames and secrets were accumulated. For the rest, he had a pain, it went away, it made no difference.

But it gradually absorbed his life. Gradually it drew away all his potentiality, it bled him into the dark, it weaned him of life and drew him away into the darkness. And in this twilight of his life, little remained visible to him. The business, his life-work, that was gone entirely. His public interests had disappeared as if they had never been. Even his family had become extraneous to him, he could only remember, in some slight, non-essential part of himself, that such and such were his children. It was superficial fact, not vital to him. He had to make an effort to know their relation to him. Even his wife barely existed. She indeed was like the darkness, like the pain within him. By some strange association the darkness that contained the pain and the darkness that contained his wife were identical. All his thoughts and understandings became blurred and fused, and now his wife and the consuming pain were the same dark secret horror to him, that he never faced. He never drove the dread out of its lair within him. He only knew that there was a dark place, and something inhabiting this darkness which issued from time to time and rent him. But he dared not penetrate the dark place and drive the beast into the open. He had rather ignore its existence. Only, in his vague way, the dread was his wife, the destroyer, and it was the pain, the destruction, a darkness which was one and both.

He very rarely saw his wife. She kept her room. Only occasionally she came forth, with her head stretched forward, and in her low, possessed voice, she asked him how he was. And he answered her, in the habit of more than thirty years: "Well, I don't think I'm any the worse, dear." But he was frightened of her, underneath this safeguard of habit, frightened almost to the verge of death.

But all his life, he had been so constant to his lights, he had never broken down. He would die even now without breaking down, without knowing what his feelings were, towards her. All his life, he had said: "Poor Christiana, she has such a strong temper." With unbroken will, he had stood by his position with regard to her, he had substituted pity

THE FIRST WOMEN IN LOVE

for all his hostility, pity had been his shield and his safeguard, and his infallible weapon. And still, in his consciousness, he was sorry for her, her nature was so violent and so impatient.

But now his pity, with his life, was wearing thin, and the dread, almost amounting to horror, was rising into being. But before the armour of his pity really broke, he would die, as an insect when its shell is cracked. This was his final resource.

He had been so constant to his lights, so constant to charity, and to his love for his neighbour. Perhaps he had loved his neighbour even better than himself—which is going one further than the commandment.* Always, this flame had burned in his heart, sustaining him through everything, the welfare of the people. He was a large employer of labour, he was a great mine-owner. And he had never lost this from his heart, that in Christ he was one with his workmen. Nay, he had felt inferior to them, as if they, through poverty and labour, were nearer to God than he. He had always the unacknowledged belief, that it was his workmen, the miners, who held in their hands the means of salvation. To move nearer to God, he must move towards his miners, his life must gravitate towards theirs. They were, unconsciously, his idol, his God made manifest. In them he worshipped the highest.

And all the while, his wife had opposed him like one of the great demons of hell. Strange, like a bird of prey, with the fascinating beauty and abstraction of a hawk, she had beat against the bars of his philanthropy, and like a hawk in a cage, she had sunk into silence. By force of circumstance, because all the world combined to make the cage unbreakable, he had been too strong for her, he had kept her prisoner. And because she was his prisoner, his passion for her had always remained keen as death. He had always loved her, loved her with intensity. Within the cage, she was denied nothing, she was given all licence.

But she had gone almost mad. Of wild and overweening temper, she could not bear the humiliation of her husband's soft, half-appealing kindness to everybody. He was not deceived by the poor. He knew they came and sponged on him, and whined to him, the worse class among them; the majority, luckily for him, were much too proud to ask for anything, much too independent to come knocking at his door. But in Beldover, as everywhere else, there were the whining, parasitic, foul human beings who come crawling after charity, and feeding on the living body of the public like lice. A kind of fire would go over Christiana

Crich's brain, as she saw two more pale-faced, creeping women in objectionable black clothes, cringing lugubriously up the drive to the door. She wanted to set the dogs on them, "Hi Rip! Hi Ring! Ranger! At 'em boys, set 'em off." But Thomas, the butler, with all the rest of the servants, was Mr Crich's man. Nevertheless, when her husband was away, she would come down like a wolf on the crawling supplicants; "What do you people want? There is nothing for you here. You have no business on the drive at all. Simpson, drive them away, and let no more of them through the gate."

The servants had to obey her. And she would stand watching with an eye like the eagle's, whilst the groom in clumsy confusion drove the lugubrious persons down the drive, as if they were rusty fowls scuttling before him.

But they learned to know, from the lodge-keeper, when Mr Crich was away, and they timed their visits. How many times, in the first years, would Thomas knock softly at the door: "Person to see you, sir."

"What name?"

"Grocock, sir."

"What do they want?" The question was half impatient, half gratified. He liked hearing appeals to his charity.

"Something about a child, sir."

"Show them into the library, and tell them they shouldn't come after eleven o'clock in the morning."

"Why do you get up from dinner—send them off," his wife would say abruptly.

"Oh, I can't do that. It's no trouble just to hear what they have to say."

"How many more have been here today? Why don't you establish open house for them? They would soon drive us out."

"I tell you, it doesn't hurt me to hear what they have to say. And if they really are in trouble—well, it is my duty to help them out of it."

"It's your duty to invite all the rats in the world to gnaw at your bones."

"Come, Christiana, it isn't like that. Don't be uncharitable."

But she suddenly swept out of the room, and out to the study. There sat the meagre charity-seekers, looking as if they were in the doctor's outdoor dispensing room.

"Mr Crich can't see you. He can't see you at this hour. Do you think he is your club doctor,* that you can come whenever you like? You must go away, there is nothing for you here."

The poor people rose in confusion. But Mr Crich, pale and black-bearded and deprecating, came behind her, saying:

"Yes, I don't like you coming as late as this. I'll hear any of you in the morning part of the day, but I can't really do with you after.—What's amiss then, Gittins? How is your Missis?"

"Why, she's sunk very low, Mester Crich, she's almost gone, she is—"

Sometimes, it seemed to Mrs Crich as if her husband were some subtle funeral bird, feeding on the miseries of the people. It seemed to her he was never satisfied unless there was some sordid tale being poured out to him, which he drank in with a sort of mournful, sympathetic satisfaction. He would have no *raison d'être* if there were no lugubrious miseries in the world, as an undertaker would have no meaning if there were no funerals.

Mrs Crich recoiled back upon herself, she recoiled away from this world of creeping democracy. A band of tight, baleful exclusion fastened round her heart, her isolation was fierce and hard, her antagonism was passive but terribly pure, like that of a hawk in a cage. As the years went on, she lost more and more count of the world, she seemed rapt in some glittering abstraction, almost purely unconscious. She would wander about the house and about the surrounding country, staring keenly and seeing nothing. She rarely spoke, she had no connection with the world. And she did not even think. She was consumed in a fierce tension of opposition, like the negative pole of a magnet.

And she bore many children. For, as time went on, she never opposed her husband in word or deed. She took no notice of him, externally. She submitted to him, let him take what he wanted and do as he wanted with her. She was like a hawk that sullenly submits to everything. The relation between her and her husband was wordless and unknown, but it was deep, awful, a relation of utter interdestruction. And he, who triumphed in the world, he became more and more hollow in his vitality, the vitality was bled from within him, as by some hemorrhage. She was hulked like a hawk in a cage, but her heart was fierce and undiminished within her, though her mind was destroyed.

So to the last he would go to her and hold her in his arms, sometimes, before his strength was all gone. The terrible white, destructive light that burned in her eyes only excited and roused him. Till he was bled to death, and then he dreaded her more than anything. But he always said to himself, how happy he had been, how he had loved her with a pure and consuming love ever since he had known her. And he thought of her as pure, chaste, the white flame which was known to him alone, the flame of her sex, was a white flower of snow to his mind. She was a wonderful white snow-flower, which he had desired infinitely. And now he was dying with all his ideas and interpretations intact. They would only collapse when the breath left his body. Till then they would be pure truths for him. Only death would show the perfect completeness of the lie. Till death, she was his white snow-flower. He had subdued her, and her subjugation was to him an infinite chastity in her, a virginity which he could never break, and which dominated him as by a spell.

She had let go the outer world, but within herself she was unbroken and unimpaired. She only sat in her room like a moping, dishevelled hawk, motionless, mindless. Her children, for whom she had been so fierce in her youth, now meant scarcely anything to her. She had lost all that, she was quite by herself. Only Gerald, the destroyer, had some existence for her. But of late years, since he had become head of the business, he too was forgotten.

Whereas the father, now he was dying, turned for compassion to Gerald. There had always been pure opposition between the two of them. Gerald had feared and despised his father, and to a great extent had ignored him all through boyhood and young manhood. And the father had felt very often a real dislike of his eldest son, which, never wanting to give way to, he had refused to acknowledge. He had ignored Gerald as much as possible, leaving him alone.

Since, however, Gerald had come home and assumed responsibility in the firm, and had proved such a wonderful director, the father, tired and weary of all outside concerns, had put all his trust of these things in his son, implicitly, leaving everything to him, and assuming a rather touching dependence on the young enemy. This immediately roused a poignant pity and tenderness in Gerald's heart, always shadowed by contempt and by the unadmitted enmity. For Gerald was in reaction against Charity, yet he was dominated by it; it assumed supremacy in the inner life, and he could not confute it. So he was partly subject to that which his father stood for, but he was in reaction against it. Now he could not save himself. A certain pity and grief and tenderness for his father overcame him, in spite of the deeper, more sullen hostility.

The father won shelter from Gerald through compassion. But for love he had Winifred. She was his youngest child, she was the only one of his children whom he had ever hotly loved. And her he loved with all the great, overweening, sheltering love of a dying man. He wanted to shelter her infinitely, infinitely, to wrap her in warmth and love and shelter, perfectly. If he could save her she should never know one pain, one grief, one hurt. He had been so right all his life, so constant in his kindness and his goodness. And this was his last passionate righteousness, his love for the child Winifred. Some things troubled him yet. The world had passed away from him, as his strength ebbed. There were no more poor and injured and humble to protect and succour. These were all lost to him. There were no more sons and daughters to trouble him, and to weigh on him as an unnatural responsibility. These too had faded out of reality. All these things had fallen out of his hands, and left him free.

There remained the covert fear and horror of his wife, as she sat mindless and strange in her room, or as she came forth with slow, prowling step, her head bent forward. But this he put away. Even his life-long righteousness, however, would not quite deliver him from the inner horror. Still, he could keep it sufficiently at bay. It would never break forth openly. Death would come first.

Then there was Winifred! If only he could be sure about her, if only he could be sure. Since the death of Diana, and the development of his illness, his craving for surety with regard to Winifred amounted almost to obsession. It was as if, even dying, he must have some anxiety, some responsibility of love, of Charity, upon his heart.

She was an odd, sensitive, inflammable child, having her father's dark hair and quiet bearing, but being quite detached, momentaneous. She was like a changeling indeed, as if her feelings did not matter to her, really. She often seemed to be talking and playing like the gayest and most childish of children, she was full of the warmest, most delightful affection for a few things—for her father, and for her animals in particular. But if she heard that her beloved kitten Leo had been run over by the motor-car, she put her head on one side, and replied, with a faint contraction like resentment on her face: "Has he?" Then she took no more notice. She only disliked the servant who would force bad news on her, and want her to be sorry. She wanted not to know, and that seemed her chief motive. She avoided her mother, and most of the members of her family She *loved* her Daddy, because he wanted her always to be happy, and because he seemed to become young again, and irresponsible in her presence. She liked Gerald, because he was so self-contained. She loved people who would make life a game. She had an amazing instinctive critical faculty, and was a pure anarchist, a pure aristocrat at once. For she accepted her equals wherever she found them, and she ignored with blithe indifference her inferiors, whether they were her brothers and sisters, or whether they were wealthy guests of the house, or whether they were the common people or the servants. She was quite single and by herself, deriving from nobody. It was as if she were cut off from all purpose or continuity, and existed simply moment by moment.

The father, as by some strange final illusion, felt as if all his fate depended on his ensuring to Winifred her happiness. She who could never suffer, because she never formed vital connections, she who could lose the dearest things of her life and be just the same the next day, the whole memory dropped out, as if deliberately, she whose will was so strangely and easily free, anarchistic, almost nihilistic, who like a soulless bird flits on its own will, without attachment or responsibility beyond the moment, who in her every motion snapped the threads of serious relationship, with blithe, free hands, really nihilistic, because never troubled, she must be the object of her father's final passionate solicitude.

When Mr Crich heard that Gudrun Brangwen might come to help Winifred with her drawing and modelling he saw a road to salvation for his child. He believed that Winifred had talent, he had seen Gudrun, he knew that she was an exceptional person. He could give Winifred into her hands as into the hands of a right being. Here was a direction and a positive force to be lent to his child, he need not leave her directionless and defenceless. If he could but graft the girl on to some tree of life before he died, he would have fulfilled his responsibility. And here it could be done. He did not hesitate to appeal to Gudrun.

Meanwhile, as the father drifted more and more out of life, Gerald experienced more and more a sense of exposure. His father after all had stood for the living world to him. Whilst his father lived, Gerald was not responsible for the world. But now his father was passing away, Gerald found himself left exposed and unsheltered before the storm of living, like the captain of a ship that has lost its course, and who sees only a terrible chaos in front of him. He did not inherit an established order and a living idea. The whole unifying idea of mankind seemed to be dying with his father, the centralising force that had held the whole together seemed to collapse with his father, the parts were ready to go asunder in terrible disintegration. Gerald was as if left on board of a ship that was going asunder beneath his feet, he was in charge of a vessel whose timbers were all coming apart.

He knew that all his life he had been wrenching at the frame of life to break it apart. And now, with something of the terror of a destructive child, he saw himself on the point of inheriting his own destruction. And during the last months, under the influence of death, and of Birkin's talk, and of Gudrun's penetrating being, he had lost entirely that mechanical certainty that had been his triumph. Sometimes spasms of hatred came over him, against Birkin and Gudrun and that whole set. He wanted to go back to the dullest conservatism, to the most stupid of conventional people. He wanted to revert to the strictest Toryism. But the desire did not last long enough to carry him into action.

During his childhood and his boyhood he had wanted a sort of savage freedom. The days of Homer were his ideal, when a man was chief of an army of heroes, and spent his ten years encamped before the beleaguered city. He hated bitterly and violently the circumstances of his own life, so much so that he never really saw Beldover and the colliery valley. He turned his face entirely away from the blackened mining region that stretched away on the right hand of Shortlands, he turned entirely to the country and the woods beyond Willey Water. It was true that the panting and rattling of the coal mines could always be heard at Shortlands. But from his earliest childhood, Gerald had paid no heed to this. He had ignored the whole of the industrial sea which surged in coal-blackened tides against the grounds of the house. The world was really a wilderness where one hunted and swam and rode. He rebelled against all authority. Life was a condition of savage freedom.

Then he had been sent away to school, which was so much death to him. He refused to go to Oxford, choosing a German university. He had spent a certain time at Bonn, at Berlin, and at Frankfurt. There, a curiosity had been aroused in his mind. He wanted to see and to know, in a curious objective fashion, as if it were an amusement to him. Then he must try war. Then he must travel into the savage regions that had so attracted him.

The result was, he found that humanity is very much alike everywhere, and that, to a mind like his, curious and cold, the savage was duller, less exciting than the European. So he took hold of all kinds of sociological ideas, and ideas of reform. But they never went more than skin-deep, they were never more than a mental amusement.

He discovered at last a real adventure in the coal-mines. His father asked him to help in the firm. Gerald had been educated in the science of mining, and it had never interested him. Now, suddenly, with a sort of exultation, he laid hold of the world.

There was impressed photographically on his consciousness the great industry. Suddenly, it was real, he was part of it. Down the valley ran the colliery railway, linking mine with mine. Down the railway ran the trains, short trains of heavily-laden trucks, long trains of empty wagons, each one bearing in big white letters the initials:

"C. B. & Co."

These white letters on all the wagons he had seen since his first childhood, and it was as if he had never seen them, they were so familiar, and so ignored. Now at last he saw his own name written on the wall. Now he had a vision of power.

So many wagons, bearing his initial, running all over the country. He saw them as he entered London in the train, he saw them at Dover. So far his power ramified. He looked at Beldover, at Selby, at Whatmore, at Lethley Bank, the great colliery villages which depended entirely on his mines. They were hideous and sordid, during his childhood he had been as if blind to them. And now he saw them with pride. Four great villages, and many ugly industrial hamlets were crowded under his dependence. He saw the stream of miners flowing along the causeways from the mines at the end of the afternoon, thousands of blackened, slightly distorted human beings with red mouths, all moving subjugate to his will. He pushed slowly in his motor car through the little market-top on Friday nights in Beldover, through a solid mass of human beings that were making their purchases and doing their weekly spending. They all depended on him. They were ugly and uncouth, but they were his dependents. He was a feudal lord, and better. They made way for his motor-car grudgingly, slowly.

He did not care whether they made way with alacrity, or grudgingly. He did not care what they thought of him. His vision had suddenly crystallised. Suddenly he had conceived the pure instrumentality of mankind. There had been so much humanitarianism, so much talking of sufferings and feelings, It was ridiculous. The sufferings and feelings of individuals did not matter in the least. They were mere conditions, like the weather. What mattered was the pure instrumentality of the individual. As a man as of a knife: does it cut well? Nothing else mattered.

Everything in the world has its function, and is good or not good in so far as it fulfils this function more or less perfectly.* Was a miner a good miner? Then he was complete. Was a manager a good manager? That was enough. Gerald himself, who was responsible for all this industry, was he a good director? If he were, he had fulfilled his life.

The mines were there, they were old. They were giving out, it did not pay to work the seams. There was talk of closing down two of them. It was at this point that Gerald arrived on the scene.

He looked around. There lay the mines. They were old, obsolete. They were like old lions, no more good. He looked again. Pah, the mines were nothing but the clumsy efforts of impure minds. There they lay, abortions of a half-trained mind. Let the idea of them be swept away. He cleared his brain of them, and thought only of the coal in the under earth. How much was there?

There was plenty of coal. The old workings could not get at it, that was all. Then break the neck of the old workings. The coal lay there in its seams, even though the seams were thin. There it lay, inert matter, as it had always lain, since the beginning of time, subject to the will of man. The will of man was the determining factor. Man was the arch-god of earth. His mind was obedient to serve his will. Man's will was the absolute, the only absolute.

And it was his will to subjugate Matter to his own ends. The subjugation itself was the point, the fight was the be-all, the fruits of victory were mere results. It was not for the sake of money that Gerald took over the mines. He did not care about money, fundamentally. He was neither ostentatious nor luxurious, neither did he care about social position, not greatly. What he wanted was the pure fulfilment of his own will in a struggle with the natural conditions. His will was now, to take the coal out of the earth, profitably. The profit was merely the condition of victory, but the victory itself lay in the work achieved. He quivered with joy before the challenge. Every day he was in the mines, examining, testing, he consulted experts, he gradually gathered the whole situation into his mind, as a general grasps the obstacles to his campaign.

Then there was need for a complete break. The mines were run on an old system, an obsolete idea. The initial idea had been, to obtain as much money from the earth as would make the owners comfortably rich, would allow the workmen sufficient wages and good conditions, and would increase the wealth of the country altogether. Gerald's father, following in the second generation, having a sufficient fortune, had thought only of the men. The mines, for him, were primarily great fields to produce bread and plenty for all the hundreds of human beings gathered about them. He had lived and striven with his fellow owners to benefit the men every time. And the men had been benefited in their fashion. There were no poor, and no needy. All was plenty, because the mines were good and easy to work. And the miners, in those days, finding themselves richer than they might have expected, felt glad and triumphant. They thought themselves well-off, they congratulated themselves on their good-fortune, they remembered how their fathers had starved and suffered, and they felt that better times had come. They were grateful to those others, the pioneers, the new owners, who had opened out the pits and let forth this stream of plenty.

But man is never satisfied, and soon the miners, from gratitude to their owners, passed on to murmuring. Their sufficiency decreased with knowledge, they wanted more. Why should the masters be so out of all proportion rich?

There was a crisis when Gerald was a boy, when the Masters' Federation closed down the mines because the men would not accept a reduction. This lock-out had forced home the new conditions to Thomas Crich. Belonging to the Federation, he had been compelled by his honour to close the pits against his men. He, the father, the patriarch, was forced to deny the means of life to his sons, his people. He, the rich man who would hardly enter heaven because of his possessions,* must now turn upon the poor, upon those who were nearer Christ than himself, those who were humble and despised and closer to perfection, those who were manly and noble in their labours, and must say to them: "Ye shall neither labour nor eat bread."*

It was this recognition of the state of war which really broke his heart. He wanted his industry to be run on love, Oh, he wanted love to be the directing power even of the mines. And now, from under the cloak of love, the sword was cynically drawn, the sword of grudging cupidity.

This really broke his heart, He must have the illusion—and now the illusion was destroyed.—The men were not against *him*, but they were against the masters. It was war, and willy nilly he found himself on the wrong side, in his own conscience. Seething masses of miners met daily, carried away by a new religious impulse. The idea flew through them: "All men are equal on earth," and they would carry the idea to its material fulfilment. After all, is it not the teaching of Christ? And what is an idea, if not the germ of action in the material world. "All men are equal in spirit, they are all sons of God. Whence then this disquality?"* It was a religious creed pushed to its material conclusion. Thomas Crich at least had no answer. He could but admit, according to his sincere tenets, that the disquality was wrong. But he could not give up his goods, which were the stuff of disquality. So the men would fight for their rights. A religious passion, the only religious passion left on earth, the passion for equality, inspired them.

Seething mobs of men marched about, their faces lighted up as for holy war, with a smoke of base cupidity. How disentangle the passion for equality from the passion of cupidity, when we begin to fight for equality of possessions? It is possession that darkens us all, and gives us over to confusion and despair. It is the passion for possession which outlasts every other, and brings on the ultimate death.

Riots broke out, Whatmore pit-head was in flames. This was the pit furthest in the country, near the woods. Soldiers came. From the windows of Shortlands, on that fatal day, could be seen the flare of fire in the sky not far off, and now the little colliery train, with the workmen's carriages which were used to convey the miners to the distant Whatmore, was crossing the valley full of soldiers, full of red-coats. Then there was the far-off sound of firing, then the later news that the mob was dispersed, one man was shot dead, the fire was put out.

Gerald, who was a boy, was filled with the wildest excitement and delight. He longed to go with the soldiers to shoot the men. But he was not allowed to go out of the lodge gates. At the gates were stationed sentries with guns. Gerald stood near them in delight, whilst gangs of derisive miners strolled up and down the lanes, calling and jeering:

"Now then, three ha'porth o' coppers,* let's see thee shoot thy gun." Insults were chalked on the walls and the fences, the servants left.

And all this while Thomas Crich was breaking his heart, and giving away hundreds of pounds in charity. Everywhere there was free food, a surfeit of free food. Anybody could have bread for asking, and a loaf cost only three ha'pence. Every day there was a free tea somewhere, the children had never had so many treats in their lives. On Friday afternoon great basketfuls of buns and cakes were taken into the schools, and great pitchers of milk, the school-children had what they wanted. They were sick with eating too much cake and milk.

And then it came to an end, and the men went back to work. But it was never the same as before. There was a breach between masters and men that would never be closed up as long as owners were owners, and employees were employees. Gerald longed to be a man, to fight the men. His father, however, was broken. He knew his position as a Christian was anomalous, false. Yet what could he do? It seemed to him he could not give away all he had.* He wanted to consider himself a father, a purely benevolent father to the men. But for them, they refused to see the father in him, though they always spoke well of him, and sadly. They were enemies by force of circumstance.

As Gerald grew up, however, when he had knocked about the world, he no longer wanted to fight the men. They did not interest him. The whole question of equality was *vieux jeu*. He *had* position and authority, and he did not care a rap about abstract rights. He would just do as he liked. There had been so much talk about rights—rights bored him. Humanity altogether bored him. As for Man, he felt perfectly cynical with regard to him. When he read the laments of the sweated,* he said: "What the hell of difference does it make whether you sweat or don't sweat? What the hell does it matter what you are and what you do and what you feel? You're nothing, you're precisely nothing. You don't matter either way. I'd give you as much as you wanted, in reason, to make you work well and look more sightly. But I don't care one small damn for the whole lot of your rights and wrongs, nor for you, nor for anything that appertains to you. You're an addled egg, you are, you working classes. If you spent half the time learning to do your job properly, that you spend crying for more, you bloody little Oliver Twists, the world would be all right."

So he set himself to work, to put the great industry in order. In his travels, and in his accompanying readings, he had come to the conclusion that the essential secret of life was harmony. He did not define to himself at all clearly what harmony was. The word pleased him, he felt he had come to his own conclusions. And he proceeded to put his philosophy into practice by forcing order into the established world, translating the mystic word harmony into the practical word order.

Immediately he *saw* the firm, he realised what he could do. He had a fight to fight with Matter, with the earth and the coal it enclosed. This was the sole idea, to turn upon the inanimate matter of the underground, and reduce it to his will. And for this fight with matter, one must have perfect instruments in perfect organisation, a mechanism so subtle and harmonious in its workings that it represents the single mind of man, and by its relentless repetition of given movement, will accomplish a purpose irresistibly, inhumanly. It was this inhuman principle in the mechanism he wanted to construct that inspired Gerald with an almost religious exaltation. He, the God, could interpose a perfect, changeless, godlike medium between himself and the Matter he had to subjugate. There were two opposites, his will and the resistant Matter of the earth. And between these he could establish the very expression of his will, the incarnation of his power, a great and perfect system, an activity of pure order, pure transcendent harmony.

He had his life-work now, to extend over the earth a great and perfect system in which the will of man ran smooth and unthwarted, timeless, almost a miracle. He had to begin with the mines. The terms were given: first the resistant Matter of the underground; then the instruments of its subjugation, instruments human and metallic; and finally his own pure will, his own mind. It would need a marvellous adjustment of myriad instruments, human, animal, metallic, kinetic, dynamic, a marvellous casting of myriad tiny wholes in to one great perfect entirety. And then, in this case there was perfection attained, the will of the highest was perfectly fulfilled, the will of mankind was perfectly fulfilled; for was not mankind almost solely engaged in this struggle with inanimate Matter, was not the history of mankind just the history of this struggle?

The miners were overreached. While they were still in the toils of divine equality of man, Gerald had passed on, granted essentially their case, and proceeded in his quality of human being to fulfil the will of mankind as a whole. He merely represented the miners in another sense when he perceived that the only way to fulfil perfectly the will of man was to establish the perfect, inhuman machine. But he represented them very essentially, they were far behind, out of date, squabbling for their material equality. The desire had already transmuted into this new and greater desire, for a perfect intervening mechanism between man and Matter, the desire to translate the Godhead into pure mechanism.

As soon as Gerald entered the firm, the convulsion of death ran through the old system. He had all his life been tortured by a furious and destructive demon, which possessed him sometimes like an insanity. This temper now entered like a virus into the firm, and there were cruel eruptions. Terrible and inhuman were his examinations into every detail; there was no privacy he would spare, no old sentiment but he would turn it over. The old grey managers, the old grey clerks, the doddering old pensioners, he looked at them, and removed them as so much lumber. The whole concern seemed like a hospital of invalid employees. He had no emotional qualms. He arranged what pensions were necessary, he looked for efficient substitutes, and when these were found, he substituted them for the old hands.

"I've a pitiful letter here from Letherinton," his father would say, in a tone of deprecation and appeal. "Don't you think the poor fellow might keep on a little longer. I always fancied he did very well."

"I've got a man in his place now, father. He'll be happier out of it, believe me. You think his allowance is plenty, don't you?"

"It is not the allowance that he wants, poor man. He feels it very much, that he is superannuated. Says he thought he had twenty more years of work in him yet."

"Not of this kind of work I want. He doesn't understand."

The father sighed. He wanted not to know any more. He believed the pits would have to be overhauled if they were to go on working. And after all, it would be worst in the long run for everybody, if they must close down. So he could make no answer to the appeals of his old and trusty servants, he could only repeat "Gerald says."

So the father withdrew more and more out of the light. The whole frame of the real life was broken for him. He had been right according to his lights. And his lights had been those of the great religion. Yet they seemed to have become obsolete, to be superseded in the world. He could not understand. He only withdrew with his lights into an inner room, into the silence. The beautiful candles of belief, that would not do to light the world any more, they would still burn sweetly and sufficiently in the inner room of his soul, and in the silence of his retirement.

Gerald rushed into the reform of the firm, beginning with the office. It was needful to economise severely, to make possible the great alterations he must introduce.

"What are these widows' coals?" he asked.

"We have always allowed all widows of men who worked for the firm a load of coals every three months."

"They must pay cost price henceforward. The firm is not a charity institution, as everybody seems to think."

Widows, these stock figures of sentimental humanitarianism, he felt a dislike at the thought of them. They were almost repulsive. Why were they not immolated on the pyre of the husband, like the sati in India? At any rate, let them pay the cost of their coals.

In a thousand ways he cut down the expenditure, in ways so fine as to be hardly noticeable to the men. The miners must pay for the cartage of their coals, ample cartage too; they must pay for their tools, for the sharpening, for the care of lamps, for many trifling things that made the bill of charges against every man mount up to a shilling or so in the week. It was not grasped very definitely by the miners, though they were sore enough. But it saved hundreds of pounds every week for the firm.

Gradually Gerald got hold of everything. And then began the great reform. Expert engineers were introduced in every department. An enormous electric plant was installed, both for lighting and for haulage underground, and for power. The electricity was carried to every mine. New machinery was brought from America, such as the miners had never seen before, great iron men, as the cutting machines were called, and other unusual appliances. The working of the pits was thoroughly changed, all the control was taken out of the hands of the miners, the butty system* was abolished. Everything was run on the most accurate and delicate scientific method, educated and expert men were in control everywhere, the miners were reduced to mere mechanical instruments. They had to work hard, much harder than before, the work was terrible and heart-breaking in its mindlessness.

But they submitted to it all. The joy went out of their lives, the hope seemed to perish as they became more and more mechanised. And yet they accepted the new conditions. They even got a further satisfaction out of them. At first they hated Gerald Crich, they swore to do something to him, to murder him. But as time went on, they accepted everything with some fatal satisfaction. Gerald was their high priest, he represented the religion they really felt. His father was forgotten already. There was a new world, a new order, strict, terrible, inhuman, but satisfying in its very destructiveness. The men were satisfied to belong to the great and wonderful machine, even whilst it destroyed them. It was what they wanted, it was the highest that man had produced, the most wonderful and superhuman. They were exalted by belonging to this great and superhuman system which was beyond feeling or reason, something really godlike. Their hearts died within them, but their souls were satisfied. It was what they wanted. Otherwise Gerald could never have done what he did. He was just ahead of them in giving them what they wanted, this participation in a great and perfect system that subjected life to pure mathematical principles. This was a sort of freedom, the sort they really wanted.

Gerald too was satisfied. He knew the colliers said they hated him. But he had long ceased to hate them. When they streamed past him at evening, their heavy boots slurring on the pavement wearily, their shoulders slightly distorted, they took no notice of him, they gave him no greeting whatever, they passed in a grey-black stream of sullen acceptance. But they were not important to him, save as instruments. As miners they were necessary and admirable. He admired their qualities. But as men, personalities, they were just negligible, as were the horses and the ponies of the mines.

And Gerald had succeeded. He had converted the industry into a new and terrible life. There was a greater output of coal than ever, the wonderful and delicate system ran almost perfectly. He had a set of expert engineers, both mining and electrical, and they did not cost much. A highly educated man did not cost much more than a workman. His managers, who were all rare men, cost no more than the old bungling fools of his father's day, who were merely colliers promoted. His chief manager, who had twelve hundred a year, saved the firm at least ten thousand. The whole system was now so perfect that Gerald was hardly necessary any more.

It was so perfect, that sometimes, a strange fear came over him, and he did not know what to do. He went on for some years in a sort of trance of activity. What he was doing seemed supreme, he was almost like God. He was a pure and exalted activity.

But now he had succeeded—he had finally succeeded. And once or twice lately, when he was alone in the evening and had nothing to do, he had suddenly stood up in terror, not knowing what he was. And he went to the mirror and looked long and closely at his own face, at his own eyes, seeking for something. He was afraid, and he knew not what of. He looked at his own face. There it was, shapely and healthy and the same as ever, yet somehow, it was not real, it was a ghost. He dared not touch it, for fear it should prove to be only ghostly. His eyes were blue and keen as ever, and as firm in their look. Yet he was not sure that they were not blue small bubbles that would burst in a moment and leave clear annihilation. He could see the darkness in them, as if they were only bubbles of darkness. He was afraid that the darkness would break right from him, and he would be annihilated, a pure annihilation.

But his will yet held good, he was able to go away and read, and think about things. He liked to read books about the primitive man, books of anthropology, and also works of speculative philosophy. His mind was very active. But it was like a bubble floating in the darkness. At any moment it might burst and the darkness would be upon him. In a strangely calm and cold way, he was frightened. But the fear was all in the darkness outside him. It was as if fear were all around the house, outside, but within he was quite unmoved and calculative, quite free and deliberate.

Yet it was a strain. He knew there was no equilibrium. He would have to go in some direction, shortly, to find relief. Only Birkin could ease the fear in him, and make him free and released into life. But then he must always come away from Birkin, as from a church service, back to the real hard world of work and life. There it was, it did not alter, and words were futilities. He had to keep himself adjusted to the world of work and material life. And it became more and more difficult, such a strange pressure was upon him, as if the very middle of him were a vacuum, and outside were an awful tension.

He had found his most satisfactory relief in women. After a really wild time with some woman, he went on quite easy and forgetful. The devil of it was, it was so hard to find a woman now, who would mean anything to him. Little Pussums were all right in their way, but they were such a trivial event.

Gudrun knew that it was a critical thing for her to go to Shortlands. She knew it was equivalent to her accepting Gerald Crich as a lover. And though she hung back, though she wanted not to know him any further, yet she wanted still more to go on. She equivocated. She said, remembering with some confusion the blow and the kiss on the night of the party: "After all, what is it? What is a blow, what is a kiss? Life is momentaneous. I can go to Shortlands just for a time, before I go away, if only to see what it is like." For she had an insatiable curiosity to see and to know everything.

She also wanted to know what Winifred was really like. Having heard the child calling from the steamer in the night, she felt some mysterious connection with her.

Gudrun talked with the father in the library. Then he sent for his daughter. She came accompanied by Mademoiselle.

"Winnie, this is Miss Brangwen, who will be so kind as to help you with your drawing and making models of your animals," said the father.

The child looked at Gudrun for a moment with interest, before she came forward and with face averted offered her hand. There was a complete *sang froid* and indifference under Winifred's childish reserve, a certain irresponsible lightness.

"How do you do?" said the child, not lifting her face.

"How do you do," said Gudrun.

Then Winifred stood aside, and Gudrun was introduced to Mademoiselle.

"You have a fine day for your walk," said Mademoiselle, in a bright manner.

"*Quite* fine," said Gudrun.

Winifred was watching from her distance. She was as if amused, but rather unsure as yet what this new person was like. She saw so many new persons, and so few became real to her. Mademoiselle was of no count whatever, the child merely put up with her, calmly and easily, accepting her little authority with faint scorn, compliant out of childish indifference.

"Well Winifred," said the father, "aren't you glad Miss Brangwen has come? She makes animals and birds in wood and in clay, that the people in London write about in the papers, praising them to the skies."

Winifred smiled slightly.

"Who told you, Daddie?" she asked.

"Who told me? Hermione told me, and Rupert Birkin."

"Do you know them?" Winifred asked, of Gudrun, turning to her with faint challenge.

"Yes," said Gudrun.

Winifred readjusted herself a little. She had been ready to accept Gudrun as a sort of servant. Now she saw it was on terms of friendship they were intended to meet. She was rather glad. She had so many half inferiors, whom she tolerated with perfect good-humour.

Gudrun was very calm. She also did not take these things very seriously. A new occasion was mostly spectacular to her. However, Winifred was a detached, ironic child, she would never attach herself. Gudrun liked her and respected her. The first meetings went off with a certain humiliating clumsiness. Neither Winifred nor her instructress had any social grace.

Soon however, they met in a kind of make-belief world. Winifred did not notice human beings unless they were like herself, playful and slightly mocking. She would accept nothing but the world of play, and the serious people of her life were the animals she had for pets. On those she lavished, almost ironically, her affection and her companionship. To the rest of the human scheme she submitted with a faint bored indifference.

She had a pekinese dog called Looloo, which she loved.

"Let us draw Looloo," said Gudrun, "and see if we can get his Looliness in the drawing, shall we?"

"Darling!" cried Winifred, rushing to the dog, that sat with contemplative sadness on the hearth, and kissing its bulging brow. "Darling one, will you be drawn? Shall its mummy draw its portrait?" Then she chuckled gleefully, and turning to Gudrun, said: "Oh let's!"

They proceeded to get pencils and paper, and were ready.

"Beautifullest," cried Winifred, hugging the dog, "sit still while its Mummy draws its beautiful portrait." The dog looked up at her with grievous resignation in its large, prominent eyes. She kissed it fervently, and said: "I wonder what my portrait will be like. It's sure to be awful."

As she sketched she chuckled to herself, and cried out at times:

"Oh darling, you're so beautiful!"

And again chuckling, and rushing to embrace the dog, in penitence, as if she were doing him some subtle injury. He sat all the time with the resignation and fretfulness of ages on his dark velvety face. She drew slowly, with a wicked concentration in her eyes, her head on one side, an intense stillness over her. She was as if working the spell of some enchantment. Suddenly she had finished. She looked at the dog, and then at her drawing, and then cried, with real grief for the dog, and at the same time a wicked exultation:

"My beautiful, why did they?"

She took her paper to the dog, and held it under his nose. He turned his head aside as in chagrin and mortification, and she impulsively kissed his velvety bulging forehead.

"'s a Loolie, 's a little Loozie! Look at his portrait, darling, look at his portrait, that his mother has done of him." She looked at her paper and chuckled. Then, kissing the dog once more, she rose and came gravely to Gudrun, offering her the paper.

It was a grotesque little drawing of a grotesque little dog, so wicked and so comical, a slow smile came over Gudrun's face, unconsciously. And at her side Winifred chuckled with glee, and said:

"It isn't like him, is it? He's much lovelier than that. He's *so* beautiful— mmm, Looloo, my sweet darling." And she flew off to embrace the chagrined little dog. He looked up at her with reproachful, saturnine eyes, vanquished in his extreme agedness of being. Then she flew back to her drawing, and chuckled with satisfaction.

"It isn't like him, is it?" she said to Gudrun.

"Yes, it's very like him," Gudrun replied.

The child treasured her drawing, carried it about with her, and showed it, with a silent embarrassment, to everybody.

"Look," she said, thrusting the paper into her father's hand.

"Why that's Looloo!" he exclaimed. And he looked down in surprise, hearing the almost inhuman chuckle of the child at his side.

Gerald was away from home when Gudrun first came to Shortlands. But the first morning he came back he watched for her. It was a sunny, soft morning, and he lingered in the garden paths, looking at the flowers that had come out during his absence. He was clean and fit as ever, shaven, his fair hair scrupulously parted at the side, bright in the sunshine, his short, fair moustache closely clipped, his eyes with their humorous kind twinkle, which was so deceptive. He was dressed in black, his clothes sat well on his well-nourished body, he was keen and bright and full of energy. Yet as he lingered before the flower-beds in the morning sunshine, there was a certain isolation, a pathos about him, as of something wanting.

Gudrun came up quickly, unseen. She was dressed in blue, with woollen yellow stockings and a yellow hat. He glanced up in surprise. Her stockings always disconcerted him, the pale-yellow stockings and the rather heavy black shoes. Winifred, who had been playing about the garden with Mademoiselle and the dogs, came flitting towards Gudrun. The child wore a dress of black and white stripes. Her hair was rather short, cut round and hanging level in her neck.

"We're going to do Bismarck, aren't we?" she said, linking her hand through Gudrun's arm.

"Yes, we're going to do Bismarck. Do you want to?"

"Oh yes—Oh I do! I want most awfully to do Bismarck. He looks *so* splendid this morning, so *fierce*. He's almost as big as a lion." And the child chuckled sardonically at her own hyperbole. "He's a real king, he really is."

"Bonjour mademoiselle," said the little French governess, wavering up with a slight bow, a bow of the sort that Gudrun loathed, insolent.

"Combien Winifred veut faire le portrait de Bismarck—! Oh, mais tout le matin, c'est—'We will do Bismarck this morning!'— Bismarck, Bismarck, toujours Bismarck! C'est un lapin, n'est-ce pas, mademoiselle?"

"Oui, c'est un grand lapin blanc et noir. Vous ne l'avez pas vu?" said Gudrun in her good, but rather heavy French.

"Non, mademoiselle, Winifred n'a jamais voulu me le faire voir. Tant de fois je le lui ai demandé, 'Qu'est-ce donc que ce Bismarck, Winifred?' Mais elle n'a pas voulu me le dire. Son Bismarck, c'était un mystère."

"Oui, c'est un mystère, vraiment un mystère! Miss Brangwen, say that Bismarck is a mystery," cried Winifred.

"Bismarck is a mystery, Bismarck, c'est un mystère, der Bismarck, er ist ein Wunder," said Gudrun, in mocking incantation.

"Ja, er ist ein Wunder," repeated Winifred, with odd seriousness, under which lay a wicked chuckle.

"Ist er auch ein Wunder?" came the slightly mocking voice of Mademoiselle.

"Doch!" said Winifred briefly, indifferent.

"Doch ist er nicht ein König. Beesmarck, he was not a king, Winifred, as you have said. He was only—il n'était que chancelier."

"Qu'est-ce qu'un chancelier?"* said Winifred, with slightly contemptuous indifference.

"A chancelier is a chancellor, and a chancellor is I believe a sort of judge," said Gerald coming up and shaking hands with Gudrun. "You will make a song out of Bismarck soon," said he.

Mademoiselle waited, and discreetly made her inclination, and her greeting.

"So they wouldn't let you see Bismarck, Mademoiselle?" he said.

"No monsieur."

"Ah, very mean of them. What are you going to do to him, Miss Brangwen? I want him to be sent to the kitchen and cooked."

"Oh no," cried Winifred.

"We're going to draw him," said Gudrun.

"Skin him and draw him* and cook him!" he said, being purposely fatuous.

"Oh *no*!" cried Winifred with emphasis, chuckling.

Gudrun detected the tang of mockery in him, and she looked up and smiled into his face. He felt his blood stir. Their eyes met in knowledge.

"How do you like Shortlands?" he asked.

"Oh, very much," she said, with nonchalance.

"Glad you do. Have you noticed these flowers?"

He led her along the path. She followed intently. Winifred came, and the governess lingered in the rear. They stopped before some veined salpiglossis flowers.

"Aren't they wonderful!" she cried, looking at them absorbedly. Strange how her reverential, almost ecstatic admiration of the flowers caressed his blood. She stooped down, and touched the trumpets, with infinitely fine and delicate-touching finger-tips. It filled him with satisfaction to see her. When she rose, her eyes, hot with the beauty of the flowers, looked into his.

"What are they?" she asked.

"Sort of petunia, I suppose," he answered. "I don't really know them."

"They are quite strangers to me," she said.

They stood together in a close intimacy, a close contact. And he was in love with her, he wanted her.

She was aware of Mademoiselle standing near, like a little French beetle, observant and calculative. She moved away with Winifred, saying they would go to find Bismarck.

Gerald watched them go, looking all the while at the soft, full, still body of Gudrun, in its silky cashmere. How silky and rich and soft her body must be. An access of worship came over his mind, she was the all-desirable, the all-beautiful. He wanted only to come to her, nothing more. He was only this, this being that should come to her, and be given to her.

At the same time he was finely and acutely aware of Mademoiselle's neat, brittle finality of form. She was like some elegant beetle with thin ankles, perched on her high heels, her glossy black dress perfectly correct, her dark hair done high and admirably. How repulsive her completeness and her finality was! He loathed her.

Yet he did admire her. She was perfectly correct. And it did rather annoy him, that Gudrun came dressed in startling colours, like a macaw, when the family was in mourning. Like a macaw she was! He watched the lingering way she took her feet from the ground. And her ankles were pale yellow, and her dress a deep blue. Yet it pleased him. It pleased him very much. He felt the challenge in her very attire—she challenged the whole world. And he thrilled as to the note of a trumpet.

Gudrun and Winifred went through the house to the back, where were the stables and the out-buildings. Everywhere was still and deserted. Mr Crich had gone out for a short drive, the stable-man had just led round Gerald's horse. The two girls went to the hutch that stood in a corner, and looked at the great black and white rabbit.

"Isn't he beautiful! Oh, do look at him listening! Doesn't he look a jewel-darling! Oh, I must do him listening, he listens with so much of himself, don't you darling Bismarck?"

"Can we take him out?" said Gudrun.

"He's terribly strong. He really is, he is as strong as a lion."

"But we'll try, shall we?"

"Yes, do let's. But he kicks most terribly if he is angry.—Don't kick this time dear one, your mother won't hurt you."

They took the key to unlock the door. The rabbit exploded in a wild rush round the hutch.

"He does scratch most awfully, too," cried Winifred in excitement. "Oh do look at him, isn't he the wonderfullest! Sweet, darling Bismarck. But he really scratches dreadfully, don't you, swweetest?—The mystery—" The child chuckled at the word. "Is he a mystery, Bismarck dearest?" and she chuckled again. "Come, my mystery one! Come, dear, sweet one, come to its own mother." She chuckled again at the words. "Isn't he really a mystery? He really is one," she said, turning round to look at Gudrun, rather wondering.

They unlocked the door of the hutch. Gudrun thrust in her arm and seized the great, lusty rabbit as it crouched still, grasping its long ears. It set its four feet flat, and thrust back. There was a long scraping sound as it was hauled forward, and in another instant it was in mid-air, lunging wildly, its body flying like a spring coiled and released, as it lashed out, suspended from the ears. Gudrun held the black-and-white tempest at arms length, averting her face. But the rabbit was immensely strong, it was all she could do to keep her grasp. She almost lost her presence of mind.

"Bismarck, Bismarck, you *are* a terrible mystery," said Winifred in a dangerous voice, "Oh do put him down, he's beastly."

Gudrun stood for a moment astounded by the thunder-storm that had sprung into being in her grip. Then her colour came up, a heavy anger grew in her eyes. She stood shaken like a house in a storm, and did not know how to get out of her predicament. Her heart grew black with fury at the meaninglessness and the utter stupidity of this struggle. Besides, her wrists were badly scored by the claws of the beast.

Gerald came round as she was trying to capture the flying rabbit under her arm. He saw, almost with dread, her sullen ferocity.

"You should let one of the men do that for you," he said, hurrying up.

"Oh he's *so* beastly!" cried Winifred, almost frantic.

He held out his nervous, sinewy hand and took the rabbit by the ears, from Gudrun.

"It's most *fearfully* strong," she cried, in a high voice, like the crying of a seagull, strange and vindictive.

The rabbit made itself into a ball in the air, and lashed out, flinging itself into a bow. It really seemed demoniac. Gudrun saw Gerald's body tighten, saw a sharp blindness come into his eyes.

"I know this beggar of old," he said.

The long, demon-like beast lashed out again, spread on the air as if it were flying, looking something like a dragon, then closing up again, inconceivably powerful and explosive. The man's body, strung to its efforts, vibrated strongly. Then a sudden deep, congenital anger came up in him. Swift as lightning he drew back and brought his free hand down like a hawk on the neck of the rabbit. Simultaneously, there came the unearthly, abhorrent scream of a rabbit in the fear of death. It made one immense writhe, tore his wrists and his sleeves in a final convulsion, all its belly flashed white in a whirlwind of paws, and then he had slung it round and had it under his arm, fast. It cowered and skulked. His face was smiling with anger.

"You wouldn't think there was all that force in a rabbit," he said, looking at Gudrun. And he saw her eyes black as night in her pallid face, she looked almost unearthly. The scream of the rabbit, after the violent tussle, seemed to have torn the veil of her consciousness. He looked at her in wonder, and subterranean fear.

"Oh, but he's *not* a good rabbit, he's *not* good. He's a horrid mystery, I think he's a *horrid* one," Winifred was crooning in dislike and in resentment.

A smile twisted Gudrun's face, as she recovered. She hated to be revealed.

"Don't they make the most fearful noise when they scream?" she cried, the high note in her voice, like a sea-gull's cry.

"Abominable," he said.

"You shouldn't be so naughty, when your mother wants to take you out," Winifred was crooning wickedly, putting out her hand and touching the rabbit most delicately, as it skulked under his arm, motionless as if it were dead.

"He's not dead, is he Gerald?" she asked.

"No, more's the pity," he said.

"Oh no," cried the child. And she touched the rabbit with more confidence. "His heart is beating *so* fast. Isn't he terrible! He really is."

"Where do you want him?" asked Gerald.

"In the little green court," she said.

Gudrun looked at Gerald with strange, darkened eyes, almost supplicating, like those of a creature which is at his mercy. He did not know what to say to her. He felt he ought to say something, that she was waiting for him to come to her.

"He didn't hurt you, did he?" he asked.

"No," she said.

"The little beast, I'd break his neck if he did."

They came to the little court, which was shut in by old red walls, in whose crevices wall-flowers were growing. The grass was soft and fine and old, a level floor carpeting the old court, the sky was blue overhead. Gerald tossed the rabbit down. It crouched still and would not move. Gudrun watched it with faint horror.

"Why doesn't it move?" she cried.

"It's skulking," he said.

She looked up at him, and a slight sinister smile contracted her white face.

"Isn't it a *fool*!" she cried. "Isn't it a sickening *fool*?"

The vindictive mockery in her voice made his veins quiver. Glancing up at him, into his eyes, she revealed the mocking, blood-cruel recognition of him. There was a bond between them. He saw, with secret recognition, how utterly she loathed the rabbit, how she would wish it and all its kind annihilated. And they were mutually related, he and she, in this secret cruelty. He quailed for a moment. Then he laughed.

"How many scratches have you?" he asked, showing his forearm, white and hard and torn in red gashes.

"How really vile!" she cried, flushing with indignation. "Mine is nothing."

She lifted her arm and showed a deep red score down the silken white flesh.

"It's bad enough!" he exclaimed. "What a devil!"

He wanted to touch the exquisite, silken soft skin of her arm. But he had not the courage at this moment. They looked at each other with half-smiling eyes of unconfessed knowledge, as if recognising a blood-brotherhood.

"It doesn't hurt you very much, does it?" he asked, solicitous.

"Not at all," she cried.

And suddenly the rabbit, which had been crouching as if it were a flower, so still and soft, suddenly burst into life. Round and round the court it went, as if shot from a gun, round and round like a furry meteorite, in a tense hard circle that seemed to bind their brains. They all stood in amazement, smiling uncannily, as if the rabbit were obeying some unknown incantation. Round and round it flew, on the grass under the old red walls, like a storm.

And then quite suddenly it settled down, hobbled among the grass, and sat considering, its nose twitching like a bit of fluff in the wind. After having considered for a few minutes, a soft bunch with a black, open eye, which perhaps was looking at them, perhaps was not, it hobbled calmly forward and began to nibble the grass with that mean motion of a rabbit's quick eating.

"It's mad," said Gudrun. "It is most decidedly mad."

He laughed.

"The question is," he said, "what is madness? I don't suppose it is rabbit-mad."

"Don't you think it is?" she asked.

"No, I don't. I think it is perfectly rabbit-normal. It only isn't human. You've got to get over the anthropomorphic habit."

"But how very terrifying the beasts of the field become, if you think they are like that!" she said, after a pause.

"They *are* like that. You don't know anything about them, what they are, because you always look at them as if they were human beings. They're tricky things, the animals."

"I should think so," she said, in some fearsome awe. She looked up at him curiously. How had he got his inkling of the otherness of the beasts?

"Eat, eat my darling!" Winifred was softly conjuring the rabbit, and creeping forward to touch it. It hobbled away from her. "Let its mother stroke its fur then, darling, because it is so mysterious— —"

7

AFTER HIS ILLNESS BIRKIN WENT to the south of France for a time. He did not write, nobody heard anything of him. Ursula, left alone, felt as if she had died. There seemed to be no hope in the world. One was on a tiny little rock with the tide of destruction and nothingness rising higher and higher. The world was in flood again, and there was no Noah, and no Noah's ark this time. Soon the waters of destruction would cover the whole face of the earth, and hope would be gone. For life was destructive, purely destructive, and every day the tide of destruction seemed to creep higher. There was no resistance anywhere, all humanity seemed to unite in one destructive flood. She felt herself cut off on her tiny scrap of foothold. And soon this would be lost too. For the world desired this flood, it desired this universality of destruction. Even those who cried out in lamentation, exulted unconsciously. The flood of death was what they wanted, even those who wept over the wrongness of the world. The fulfilment of mankind was now in this ruinous tide of death, which covered all. And they must be fulfilled. That which is desired comes to pass, and when death is desired, then death takes place for us. There is no room for life any more, there is only room for death.

Cut off, isolated, ringed round with the forces of death, she kept the last resistance alive in her. But soon she must succumb also. Her heart was already almost dead. She did not know where to turn. Only blindly she went down to the mill, to sit by the lake, as if she had a little peace there. Helplessly, in her pure isolation, she went to the mill to talk with the laborer's wife, and to be in the one place where her heart had some peace.

It was as if the pressure of the ruinous atmosphere grew stronger every day, till it stunned and dazed her. Soon she would become quite unconscious and mechanical. Or the strings of her heart would break. For it was more than one could bear, this great universal pressure of violent and active death, death triumphant in every soul. In what-ever eyes she looked, she could see death, in all the voices she could hear the paean of death, the paean of triumphant victory over life.

She went out one evening, numbed by this constant spiritual suffering. Those that are ripe for death must die, it is their honour. It is not the body, it is the soul which seeks death. And those souls that seek death must find it, it is their glorification. But the souls that seek also life and a new hope, what are they to do?

Ursula set off to Willey Green, towards the mill. She came to Willey Water. It was almost full again, after its period of emptiness. Then she turned off through the woods. The night had fallen, it was dark. But she forgot to be afraid. Among the trees, far from any human beings, there was a sort of peace. The more one could find a pure loneliness, the better one felt.

She started, noticing something on her right hand, between the tree trunks. It was like a great presence, watching her, dodging her. She started violently. It was only the moon, risen through the thin trees. But it seemed so sinister, with its white and deathly smile. And there was no avoiding it. Night or day, one could not escape the face of death, triumphant and radiant like this moon, with a high smile. She hurried on, cowering from the white planet. She would just see the pond at the mill before she went home.

Not wanting to go through the yard, because of the dogs, she turned off along the hill-side to descend on the pond from above. The moon was transcendent over the bare, open space, she suffered from being exposed to it. There was a glimmer of nightly rabbits across the ground. The night was as clear as crystal, and very still. She could hear a distant coughing of a sheep.

THE FIRST WOMEN IN LOVE

So she swerved down to the steep, tree-hidden bank above the pond, where the alder trees twisted their roots. She was glad to pass into the shade out of the moon. There she stood, at the top of the fallen-away bank, her hand on the rough trunk of a tree, looking at the water, that was perfect in its stillness, floating the moon upon it. But for some reason she was disappointed. It did not give her anything. She listened hungrily to the hoarse rustle of the sluice. And she wished for something else out of the night, she wanted another night, not this moon-brilliant hardness. She could feel her soul crying out in her, lamenting desolately.

She saw a shadow moving by the water. It would be Birkin. He had come back then, unawares. She accepted it without remark, nothing mattered to her. She sat down among the roots of the alder tree, dim and veiled, hearing the sound of the sluice like dew distilling audibly into the night. The islands were dark and half revealed, the reeds were dark also, only some of them had a little frail fire of reflection. A fish leaped secretly, revealing the light in the pond. This fire of the chill night breaking constantly on to the pure darkness, troubled her. She wished it were perfectly dark, perfectly, and noiseless and without motion. Birkin, small and dark also, his hair tinged with moonlight, wandered nearer. He was quite near, and yet he did not exist in her. He did not know she was there. Supposing he did something he would not wish to be seen doing, thinking he was quite private? But there, what did it matter? What did the small privacies matter? How could it matter, what he did? How can there be any secrets, we are all the same organisms? How can there be any secrecy, when everything is known to all of us.

He was touching unconsciously the dead husks of flowers as he passed by, and talking disconnectedly to himself.

"You can't go away," he was saying. "There *is* no away. You only withdraw upon yourself."

He threw a dead flower-husk on to the water.

"An antiphony—they lie, and you sing back at them.—There wouldn't have to be any truth, if there weren't any lies——then one needn't assert anything—"

He stood still, looking at the water, and throwing upon it the husks of the flowers.

"Cybele—curse her! The accursed Syria Dea!*—Does one begrudge it her?—Something else as well.—The other half—what about that?—"

He stood staring at the water. Then he stooped and picked up a stone, which he threw, sharply, at the pond. Ursula was aware of the bright moon leaping and swaying, all distorted, in her eyes. It seemed to shoot out arms of fire like a cuttle-fish, like a luminous polyp, palpitating strongly before her.

And he, a shadow on the border of the pond, was watching for a few moments, then he stooped and groped on the ground. Then again there was a burst of sound, and a burst of brilliant light, the moon had exploded on the water, and was flying asunder in flakes of white and dangerous fire. Rapidly, like white birds, the fires all broken rose across the pond, fleeing in clamorous confusion, battling with the flock of dark waves that were forcing their way in. The furthest waves of light, fleeing out, seemed to be clamouring against the shore for escape, the waves of darkness came in stealthily, running under towards the centre. But at the centre, the heart of all, was still a vivid, anguished quivering of a white moon not quite destroyed, a white sheaf of fire writhing and striving and not even now broken open, not yet violated. It seemed to be drawing itself together with strange, violent pangs, in blind effort. It was getting stronger, it was re-asserting itself, the inviolable moon. And the rays were hastening in in thin lines of light, to return to the strengthened moon, that shook upon the water in triumphant reassumption.

Birkin stood and watched, motionless, till the pond was almost calm, the moon was almost serene. Then, satisfied of so much, he looked for more stones. She felt his invisible tenacity. And in a moment again, the broken lights scattered in explosion over her face, dazzling her; and then, almost immediately, came the second shot. The moon leapt up white and burst through the air. Darts of bright light shot asunder, darkness swept over the centre. There was no moon, only a battlefield of broken lights and shadows, running close together. Shadows, dark and heavy, struck again and again across the place where the heart of the moon had been, obliterating it altogether. The white fragments pulsed up and down, and could not find where to go, apart and brilliant on the water like the petals of a rose that a wind has blown far and wide.

Yet again, they were flickering their way to the centre, finding the path blindly, enviously. And again, all was still, as Birkin and Ursula watched. The waters were loud on the shore. He saw the moon regathering itself insidiously, saw the heart of the rose intertwining vigorously and blindly, calling back the scattered fragments, winning home the petals, in a pulse and an effort of return.

And he was not satisfied. Like a madness, he must go on. He got large stones, and threw them, one after the other, at the white-burning centre of the moon, till there was nothing but a rocking of hollow noise, and a pond surged up, no moon any more, only a few broken flakes tangled and glittering broadcast in the darkness, without aim or meaning, a darkened confusion, like a black and white kaleidoscope tossed at random. The hollow night was rocking and crashing with noise, and from the sluice came sharp, regular flashes of sound. Flakes of light appeared here and there, glittering tormented among the shadows, far off, in strange places, among the dripping shadow of the willow on the island. Birkin stood and listened, and was satisfied.

Ursula was dazed, her mind was all gone. She felt she had fallen to the ground and was spilled out, like water on the earth. Motionless and spent, she sat lost in the gloom. Though even now she was aware, unseeing, that in the darkness was a little tumult of ebbing flakes of light, a cluster dancing secretly in a round, twining and coming stealthily together. They were gathering a heart again, they were coming once more into being. Gradually the fragments caught together, re-united, heaving, rocking, dancing, falling back as in panic, but working their way home again persistently, making semblance of fleeing away when they had advanced, but always flickering nearer, a little closer to the mark, the cluster growing mysteriously larger and brighter, as gleam after gleam fell in with the whole, until a ragged rose, a distorted, frayed moon was shaking upon the waters again, re-asserted, renewed, trying to recover from its convulsion, to get over the disfigurement and the agitation, to be whole and composed, at peace.

Birkin lingered vaguely by the water. Ursula was afraid that he would stone the moon again. She slipped from her seat and went down to him, saying:

"You won't throw stones at it any more, will you?"

"Were you there all the time?" he asked.

"Yes. You won't throw any more stones at it, will you?"

"I wanted to see if I could make it be quite gone off the pond," he said.

"Yes, it was terrible, really. Why should you hate the moon? It hasn't done you any harm, has it?"

"I didn't know I hated it," he said.

And they were silent for a few minutes.

"When did you come back?" she said.

"Today."

"Why did you never write?"

"I felt there was nothing to say."

"Why was there nothing to say?"

"I don't know. One can't manage those things."

"No."

Again there was a space of silence. Ursula looked at the moon. It had gathered itself together, and was quivering slightly.

"Was it good for you, to be alone?" she asked.

"Very, I think. I looked at the sea, and felt dumb. Did you do anything important?"

"No. I looked at England, and thought I'd done with it."

"Why England?" he asked in surprise.

"I don't know, it came like that."

"It isn't a question of nations," he said. "France is far worse."

"Yes, I know. I felt I'd done with it all."

They went and sat down on the roots of the trees, in the shadow. And being silent, he remembered the beauty of her eyes, which were sometimes filled with light, like spring, suffused with wonderful promise. So he said to her, slowly:

"There is a golden light in you, which I wish you would give me."

She was startled, she seemed to leap clear of him. Yet also she was pleased.

"What kind of a light?" she asked.

But he was shy, and did not say any more. So the moment passed for this time. And gradually a feeling of sorrow came over her.

"My life is so unfulfilled," she said.

"Yes," he answered briefly, not wanting to hear this.

"And you don't really love me," she said.

But he did not answer.

"You think, don't you," she said slowly, "that I only want physical things? It isn't true. I want you to serve my spirit."

"I know you do. I know you don't want physical things by themselves.— But, I want you to give me—to give your spirit to me—that golden light which is you—which you don't know—give it me—"

After a moment's silence she replied:

"But how can I, you don't love me! You only want your own ends. You don't want to serve *me*, and yet you want me to serve you. It is so one-sided."

It was a great pain to him to maintain this conversation, and to press for the thing he wanted from her, the surrender of her spirit.

"It is so different" he said. "The two kinds of service are so different. I serve you in another way—not your *knowledge*, something else. It isn't the apple I want to share with you—not the tree of knowledge. It is the paradisal Eve."

"But I don't *want* to share any knowledge with you. What you say seems so stupid to me. What do you mean by a paradisal Eve?—I hate those old things. Can't you say something *new*!"

But this only made him shut off from her.

"Ah well," he said, "words make no matter, any way. The thing *is* between us, or it isn't."

"You don't even love me," she cried.

"I do," he said angrily. "But I want—" His mind saw again the lovely golden light transfused through her eyes, as through some wonderful window. And he wanted her to surrender to him the transcendence of her spirit. But it was shameful to say so any more. It must happen beyond the sound of words. And it was shameful to take her in the toil of words. This was not a bird to be netted, it must fly of itself into the nest. And he was ashamed to put himself forward. He felt ashamed.

"I always think you love me—and then you don't, really. You *don't* love me, you know. You don't want to serve me. You only want yourself."

A shiver of rage went over his veins, at this repeated: "You don't want to serve me."

"No," he said in anger, "I don't want to serve you, because there is nothing there to serve. What you want me to serve, is nothing, mere nothing. It isn't even you, it is your conscious ego. And I wouldn't give a straw for your conscious ego—it's a rag doll."

"Ha!" she laughed in mockery. "That's all you think of me, is it? And then you have the impudence to say you love me!"

She rose in anger, to go home.

"You want the paradisal Eve," she said, turning round on him as he still sat half-visible in the shadow. "I know what that means, thank you.

You want me to be your thing, never to criticise you or to have anything to say for myself. You want me to be a mere *thing* for you! No thank you! *If* you want that, there are plenty of women who will give it you. There are plenty of women who will lie down for you to walk over them—go to them then, if that's what you want—go to them."

"No," he said, outspoken with anger. "I want your *understanding* surrender. You can criticise as much as you like. But I want you to accept me, both in reason and in spirit, as a husband. I don't want to be a master—not of anybody. Why should I be a master? Let everybody be master of himself. But I want *you*, at least, to take me for a leader, to give me unquestioned allegiance—at least in the main things—"

"But why?" she cried, with satire. "Why should I give you unquestioned allegiance? Why?—you only suffer from megalomania. You suffer from megalomania, and so I must give you unquestioned allegiance!——And how do you know that I *don't* give you unquestioned allegiance, on the main points? How do you know that I don't?"

"Because you reserve complete independence of judgment—complete independence."

"And why shouldn't I? Am I to give up my independence of judgment? It has cost enough to get it, I am not going to throw it away on the first little man that likes to ask me for it."

"Ultimately—ultimately, I know better than you—that's why you should pledge your allegiance," he said. "I may be wrong a thousand times, and you may tell me so. But ultimately, I *know*, and you do *not know*—at least in your consciousness. Therefore you should serve with unquestioning allegiance and be glad you can serve."

"Ha!" she laughed. "If I *could* serve you, I would be glad. But I don't believe in your ultimate wisdom, thank you. As soon as you begin to talk about ultimates, I am wary of you, my fine friend, I mistrust you completely. Let me hear a little humility from you, and I'll believe in you a little more readily."

"And now," he said in a fury, "will you please go away, and rid me of your presence."

"I'm going," she said, hurt in spite of her hotness against him.

They went down the bank in silence. Already he had taken the silence and the space to himself again, she was not there for him. He wrapped himself round with a grateful and rich solitude, of which he had at last the gift.

"You won't want me to go along with you?" he asked, in a cold voice of mere politeness.

"I should be glad if you went just through the wood," she said, rather humbly.

He walked straight along without answering. He was thinking about things, he had the world to himself again, she was obliterated. They went quickly, in silence, through the moon-brindled wood. She was softened now, she hoped he would say something. But he was far away, and quite cold.

"Are you cross with me now?" she asked, gently touching him with her hand.

"Leave me alone," he said.

"Yes," she said sadly, but purely obstinate, almost derisive in spirit. They came out on the high-road.

"You'll be all right now," he said.

"Yes thank you."

So they parted. He was glad to be free of her, out in the open night. She shut off his freedom of living, he liked to be alone with the open sky. Yet in his innermost heart he was acutely unhappy at having failed with her again. And she went on her way, piqued and defiant, saying with chagrin to herself, that he did not love her, and despising him for the fact. She merely despised a man that could not love her. But it hurt too.

The next day, however, he felt wistful and yearning. He thought he had been unnecessarily disagreeable. If he had insisted only on his love, and ignored the rest, all might have been well. It might. He did not quite convince himself. He believed that she loved him. But he did not quite believe that she would give him the surrender he wanted. Still, perhaps he was wrong to insist. Perhaps he ought to win her with love. One should not *demand* on these occasions. One should give love.

As the day wore on, a greater and greater yearning and tenderness came over him. He felt sorry for his ugly behaviour. She was really so sensitive; her skin was so delicate and even over-fine. And he was so crude. He had been wrong. He was sorry for her too, with tenderness. He was so rare and so sensitive. He hid away from him the fact that she was as obstinate and indomitable as she was rare and sensitive, he insisted only on the gentle qualities.

So he must go to her. In spite of his subconscious knowledge, that she was as unyielding and unchanged as ever, he said she was tender and

232

hurt, she would be glad if he came to her with love. So at last, towards evening, he must set out. He could not wait any longer. It was his nature to be too insistent and hasty for his own way.

He drifted on swiftly to Beldover, half unconscious of his own movement. He saw the town on the slope of the hill, like Jerusalem to his fancy. The world was all strange and transcendent.

Rosalind opened the door to him. She started slightly, as a young girl will, and said:

"Oh, I'll tell father."

With which she disappeared, leaving Birkin in the hall, looking at some reproductions from Pisarro,* lately introduced by Gudrun. He was admiring the almost wizard, sensuous apprehension of the earth, when Will Brangwen appeared, rolling down his shirt sleeves.

"Well," said Brangwen, "I'll get a coat." And he too disappeared for a moment. Then he returned, and opened the door of the drawing room, saying:

"You must excuse me, I was just doing a bit of work in the shed. Come inside, will you."

Birkin entered and sat down. He looked at the bright, reddish face of the other man, at the narrow brow and the very bright eyes, and at the rather sensual lips that unrolled wide and expansive under the black cropped moustache. How curious it was that this was a human being! What Brangwen thought himself to be, how meaningless it was, confronted with the real stuff of him. Birkin could see only a strange, inexplicable, almost patternless collection of passions and desires and suppressions and traditions and mechanical ideas, all cast unfused and disunited into this slender, bright-faced man of nearly fifty, who was as unlived now as he was at twenty, and as uncreated. How could he be the parent of Ursula, when he was not created himself? He was not a parent. A slip of living flesh had been transmitted through him, but the spirit had not come from him. The spirit had not come from any ancestor, it had come out of the unknown. What a darkening of counsel is all this heredity idea. A child is the child of God, or it is uncreated. What is a human parent? A mere vessel, not in any wise a creator. And parenthood is the last of the vanities!

"The weather's not so bad as it has been," said Brangwen, after waiting a moment. There was hostility between the two men.

"No," said Birkin. "It was full moon two days ago."

233

"Oh! You believe in the moon then, changing the weather?"

"No, I don't think I do. I don't really know anything about it."

"You know what they say?—The moon and the weather may change together, but the change of the moon won't change the weather."

"Is that it?" said Birkin. "No, I hadn't heard it."

There was a pause. Then Birkin said:

"Am I hindering you? I called to see Ursula, really. Is she at home?"

"I don't believe she is. I believe she's gone to the library. I'll just see."

Birkin could hear him enquiring in the dining room.

"No," he said, coming back. "But she won't be long. You wanted to speak to her?"

Birkin looked across at the other man with curious calm, clear eyes.

"As a matter of fact," he said, "I wanted to ask her to marry me."

A point of light came on the golden-brown eyes of the elder man.

"O-oh?" he said, looking at Birkin, then dropping his eyes before the calm, slightly mocking look of the other. "I'd heard nothing of it."

"No," said Birkin.

"I didn't know anything of this sort was intending."

Birkin looked back at him, and said to himself: "I wonder if he means *impending*." Aloud he said:

"No, it's quite sudden." At which, thinking of the traditional "Oh Mr So-and-so, this is *so* sudden," his eyes flickered with amusement.

"Oh, it's quite sudden?" said Brangwen, rather baffled and irritated.

"Quite," replied Birkin.

There was a moment's pause, after which Brangwen said:

"Well, she pleases herself—"

"Yes," said Birkin.

A vibration came into Brangwen's strong voice, as he replied:

"Though I should be sorry for her to be in too big a hurry, either. I don't want her to look round her when it's too late."

"Oh, it's never too late," said Birkin, "as far as that goes."

"How do you mean?" asked the father.

"If one repents being married, the marriage is at an end," said Birkin.

"You think so?"

"Certainly."

"Ay, well that may be your way of looking at it."

Birkin, in silence, thought to himself: "So it may. As for *your* way of looking at it, William Brangwen, it needs no explaining."

"I suppose," said Brangwen, "you know what sort of a girl she's like—what sort of a bringing-up she's had?"

"'*She*'," thought Birkin to himself, censorious, "is the cat's mother."

"*Do* I know what sort of a bringing-up she's had?" he asked simply. That seemed to nettle Brangwen.

"Well," he said, "she's had everything that's right for a girl to have—as far as was possible."

"I'm sure she has," said Birkin.

Which caused a most perilous full-stop. The father was becoming irritated. There was something naturally irritant to him in Birkin's mere presence.

"And I don't want to see her going away from that," he said, in a clanging voice.

"Why?" said Birkin.

This monosyllable exploded in Brangwen's brain like a madness.

"Why!" he repeated. "Why don't I? Because I don't believe in your new-fangled ways and your new-fangled ideas—off and on as if it was a penny ride on a tram. It won't do, that won't."

Birkin watched him with steady, sardonic eyes. The radical antagonism in the two men was roused.

"Yes, but what *are* my new-fangled ways and ideas?" asked Birkin.

"What they are—?" Brangwen caught himself up. "I'm not speaking of you in particular," he said. "What I mean is that my children have been brought up to think and do according to the religion I was brought up in myself, and I don't want to see them going away from that."

There was a dangerous pause.

"And how does this apply to me?" asked Birkin.

The father hesitated. He was in a nasty position.

"How does it apply to you?" he repeated. "I don't know as it applies to you. All I mean is that my daughters—" he tailed off into silence, overcome by futility. There was a distinct unfinished suspense in the air.

"Well," said Birkin, "I don't want to divert anybody away from their own true beliefs."

There was a complete silence, because of the futility. Birkin felt merely weary. Her father was not a coherent human being, he was a roomful of old echoes. The eyes of the younger man rested on the face of the elder. Brangwen looked up, and saw Birkin looking at him. His face was covered with inarticulate anger and humiliation and hopelessness.

"And as for beliefs, that's one thing," he said. "But I'd rather see my daughters dead tomorrow than that they should be at the beck and call of the first man that likes to come and whistle after them."

A queer, painful light came into Birkin's eyes.

"As to that," he said, "I only know that it is Ursula who torments *me* and puts me off on every occasion, that *I* am at *her* beck and call, not she at mine."

Again there was a pause. The father was somewhat mollified.

"I know," he said, "she'll please herself—she always has done. I've done my best for them—but that doesn't matter. They care for nothing and nobody when it comes to, but themselves."

Brangwen was thinking his own thoughts.

"Ay, and I'd rather bury 'em, than see them mixed up with a lot of wickedness and looseness as becomes nobody.—It becomes nobody, that kind of life—."

Birkin was irritated.

"You see," he cried, "neither you nor I have the option of burying anybody, till they die in the natural course—"

Brangwen looked at him in a sudden gleam of mad anger.

"Look here, young man," he said, "don't try your bullyragging on me, not in *my* house. Go out of it, if that's all you can do."

Birkin's brows knitted suddenly, his eyes concentrated in fury. But he remained perfectly stiff and still. There was a pause.

"I've nothing against you marrying Ursula," Brangwen began again at length. "It's got nothing to do wi' me. She'll do as she likes, me or no me."

Birkin turned away in silence, looking out of the window and letting go his consciousness of the other man. After all, what good was all this? It was purely meaningless. He would sit on till Ursula came home, then speak to her, then go away. He would not even accept trouble at the hands of her father. It was all a meaningless rattle, this dissension.

The two men sat in complete silence, Birkin almost unconscious of his own whereabouts. He had come to ask her to marry him—well then, he would ask her, though the skies fell. As for what she said, whether she accepted or not, he did not care. He would say what he had come to say, and that was all he cared about. He was aware of the complete alienation of this household from him. But everything now was as if fatal, limited to one step ahead. He could see one stroke ahead, and no further. For the rest, it had to be left to fate and development to disclose all the issues.

At length they heard the gate. They saw her coming up the steps with a bundle of books under her arm. Her face was bright and abstracted as usual, with the abstraction, that look of being not quite *there*, not quite present to the facts of reality, that galled her father so much. She had a maddening faculty of assuming a light of her own, which excluded the reality, and within which she looked radiant as if in sunshine.

They heard her go into the dining room, and drop her armful of books on the table.

"Did you bring me that Girl's Own?"* cried Rosalind.

"Yes, I brought it. But I forgot which one it was you wanted."

"You would," cried Rosalind angrily.—"It's right, for a wonder."

Then they heard her say something in a lowered tone.

"Where?" cried Ursula.

Again her sister's voice was muffled.

Brangwen opened the door, and called, in his strong, brazen voice: "Ursula."

She appeared in a moment, wearing her hat.

"Oh how do you do!" she cried, seeing Birkin, and all dazzled as if taken by surprise. He wondered at her, knowing she was aware of his presence. She had her queer, radiant, breathless manner, as if dazzled by the actual world, unreal to it.

"Have I interrupted a conversation?" she asked.

"No, only a complete silence," said Birkin.

"Oh," said Ursula, vaguely, absent. She was withheld, she did not take them in. It was a subtle insult that never failed to exasperate her father.

"Mr Birkin came to speak to *you*, not to me," said her father.

"Oh, did he!" she exclaimed vaguely, as if it did not concern her. Then, recollecting herself, she turned to him rather radiantly, but still quite abstractedly, and said: "Was it anything special?"

"I hope so," he said, ironically.

"—To propose to you, according to all accounts," said her father.

"Oh," said Ursula.

"Oh," mocked her father, imitating her. "Have you nothing more to say?"

She winced as if violated.

"Did you really come to propose to me?" she asked of Birkin.

"Yes," he said, as if it were doubtful. "I suppose I came to 'propose.'"
He seemed to fight shy of the last word.

"Did you!" she cried, with her vague radiance. He might have been
saying anything whatsoever.

"Yes," he answered. "I wanted to—I wanted you to agree to marry
me."

She looked at him. His eyes were flickering with shy hope, wanting
something of her. She shrank a little, as if she were exposed to his eyes,
and as if it were a violation. She darkened, her soul clouded over, she
turned aside. She had been driven out of her own radiant, single world.
She dreaded contact, it was almost unnatural to her at these times.

"Yes," she said vaguely, in a doubting, absent voice.

Birkin's heart contracted swiftly, in a sudden fire of bitterness. It all
meant nothing to her. He had been mistaken again. She was as if in
some dream-world of her own. The outside realities were accidentals,
violations to her. It drove her father to a pitch of mad exasperation. He
had had to put up with this all his life, from her.

"Well, what do you say?" he cried.

She winced. Then she glanced down at her father, half-frightened,
and she said:

"I didn't speak, did I?" as if she were afraid she might have committed
herself.

"No," said her father, exasperated. "But you needn't look like an idiot.
You've got your wits, haven't you?"

She ebbed away in silent hostility.

"I've got my wits, what does that mean?" she repeated, in a sullen
voice of antagonism.

"You heard what was asked you, didn't you?" cried her father in
anger.

"Of course I heard."

"Well then, can't you answer?" thundered her father.

"Why should I?"

At the impertinence of this retort, he went stiff. But he said nothing.

"No," said Birkin, to help out the occasion, "there's no need to answer
at once. You can say when you like."

Her eyes flashed with a powerful yellow light.

"Why should I say anything?" she cried. "You do this off your *own*
bat, it has nothing to do with me. Why do you both want to bully me!"

"Bully you! Bully you!" cried her father, in bitter, rancorous anger. "Bully you! Why, it's a pity you can't be bullied into some sense and decency. Bully you! You'll see to that, you self-willed bargust."*

She stood suspended in the middle of the room, her face glimmering and dangerous. She was set in satisfied defiance. Birkin looked up at her. He too was angry.

"But no-one is bullying you," he said, in a very soft, dangerous voice also.

"Oh yes," she cried. "You both want to force me into something."

"That is an illusion of yours," he said ironically.

"Illusion!" cried her father. "A self-opinionated fool, that's what she is."

Birkin rose, saying:

"However, we'll leave it for the time being."

And without another word, he walked out of the house.

"You fool!—You fool!" her father cried to her, with extreme bitterness. She left the room, and went upstairs, singing to herself. But she was terribly fluttered, as after some dreadful fight. From her window, she could see Birkin going up the road. He went in such a blithe drift of rage, that her mind wondered over him. There was the unknown quantity in him. Still, she was as if escaped from some danger.

Her father sat below, motionless with hatred and black anger. It was as if he were possessed with all the devils, after one of these unaccountable conflicts with Ursula. He hated her as if his only reality were in hating her, to the last degree. He had murder in his heart. But he went away, to escape himself.

Ursula's face closed, she completed herself against them all. Recoiling upon herself, she became hard and self-completed, like a jewel. She was bright and invulnerable, quite free and happy, perfectly liberated in her self-possession. Her father had to learn not to see her blithe obliviousness, or it would have sent him mad. She was so radiant with all things, in her possession of perfect hostility.

She would go on now for days like this, in this bright frank state of seemingly pure spontaneity, so essentially oblivious of the existence of anything but herself, but so ready and facile in her interest. Ah it was a bitter thing for a man to be near her, and her father cursed his fatherhood. But he must learn not to see her, not to know.

She was perfectly stable in resistance when she was in this state: so bright and radiant and attractive in her pure opposition, so very pure, and yet mistrusted by everybody, finally disliked. Only Gudrun was in accord with her. It was at these times that the intimacy between the two sisters was most complete, as if their intelligence were one. They felt a strong, bright bond of understanding between them, surpassing everything else. And during all these days of blind bright nonchalance and intimacy of his two daughters, the father seemed to breathe an air of death, as if he were destroyed in his very being. He was irritable to madness, he could not rest, his daughters seemed to be destroying him. But he was inarticulate and helpless against them. He was forced to breathe the air of his own death. He cursed them in his soul, and only wanted, that they should be removed from him.

They continued radiant in their easy female transcendency, beautiful to look at. They exchanged confidences, they were intimate in their revelations to the last degree, giving each other at last every secret. They withheld nothing, they told everything, till they seemed to border on evil. And they armed each other with knowledge, they extracted the subtlest flavours from the apple of knowledge. It was curious how their knowledge was complementary, that of each to that of the other.

Ursula saw her men as sons, pitied their yearning and admired their courage, and wondered over them as a mother wonders over her child, with a certain delight in their novelty. But to Gudrun, they were the opposite camp. She feared them and despised them, and respected their activities even overmuch.

"Of course," she said easily, "there is a quality of life in Birkin which is quite remarkable. There is an extraordinary rich spring of life in him, really amazing, the way he can give himself to things. But there are so many things in life that he simply discounts. Either he is not aware of their existence at all, or he dismisses them as merely negligible—things which are vital to the other person. In a way, he is not clever enough, he is too all of a piece."

"Yes," cried Ursula, "a fanatic. He is really a fanatic."

"Exactly! He can't hear what anybody else has to say—he simply cannot hear. His own voice is so loud."

"Yes. He cries you down."

"He cries you down," repeated Gudrun. "And by mere force of violence. And of course it is hopeless. Nobody is convinced by violence. It makes talking to him impossible—and living with him I should think would be more than impossible."

"You don't think one could live with him?" asked Ursula.

"I think it would be too wearing, too exhausting. One would not be allowed to have a thought of one's own, nor to make a single independent movement. He would want to control you entirely. He cannot allow that there is any other mind than his own. And then the real clumsiness of his mind, its lack of self-criticism—. No, I think it would be perfectly intolerable."

"Yes," assented Ursula vaguely. She did agree with Gudrun. "It's such a nuisance, that one would find almost any man intolerable after a fortnight."

"It's perfectly ghastly," said Gudrun. "But Birkin—he really doesn't allow you to call your soul your own. Of him that is strictly true."

"Yes," said Ursula. "You must have *his* soul."

"Exactly! And what can you conceive more deadly?"

This was all so true, that Ursula felt jarred to the bottom of her soul, with ugly distaste. She went on, with the discord jarring and jolting through her, in the most barren of misery.

Then there started a revulsion from Gudrun. She finished life off so thoroughly, she made things so ugly and so final. As a matter of fact, even if it were as Gudrun said, about Birkin, other things were true as well. But Gudrun would draw two lines under him and cross him out like an account that is settled. There he was, summed up, paid for, settled, done with. And it was such a lie. This finality of Gudrun's, this dispatching of people and things in a sentence, it was all such a lie. Ursula began to revolt from her sister.

One day as they were walking along the lane, they saw two robins sitting on the top twigs of two bushes, singing shrilly. The sisters stood to look at them. An ironical smile flickered on Gudrun's face.

"Don't they look important?" laughed Ursula.

"*Don't* they!" exclaimed Gudrun, with a little ironical grimace. "Aren't they a pair of little Lloyd-George's of the air."

"Aren't they! That's just what they are," cried Ursula in delight. And for days, she saw the strident, voicey birds as stout, short politicians making themselves heard, little men who must inflict themselves whole-sale on life.

But even from this there came the revulsion. Some yellow-ammers suddenly went along the road in front of her. And they looked to her so uncanny and inhuman, like hot barbs shooting through the air on some weird, inconceivable errand, that she said to herself: "After all, it is impudence to call them little Lloyd-Georges. They are really unknown to us, they are the unknown forces. It is impudence to look at them as if they were the same as human beings. They are of another world. What stupid arrogance the anthropomorphic habit is, so undeveloped! Gudrun is really impudent, uneducated, making herself the measure of everything, making everything come down to human standards. Rupert is quite right, human beings are arrogant fools, painting the universe with their own image. The universe is non-human, thank God." It seemed to her such irreverence, so destructive of all true life, to make little Lloyd-Georges of the birds. It was such a lie towards the robins, and such a defamation.

So she withdrew away from Gudrun and from that which she stood for, she turned in spirit towards Birkin again. She had not seen him since the fiasco of his proposal. She did not want to, because she did not want the question of her acceptance thrust upon her. She knew what Birkin meant when he asked her to marry him; vaguely, without putting it into speech, she knew. She knew what kind of love, what kind of surrender he wanted. And she was not at all sure that this was the kind of love that she herself wanted. She was not at all sure that it was a spouse she wanted, in a man. She did not want to become an espoused wife. At least, she wanted to want it. She wished she could give herself up to a man. But she mistrusted herself. She did not believe that really, in the complete and old sense in which he meant marriage, she wanted to marry. In another sense, she could marry him. But in this sense, of abandoning herself to his making,—no, this she could not want, even though she wished it. She must remain spiritually inviolate, a virgin in spirit, though she could give her body joyfully, she could accept motherhood with certainty. She was made for motherhood, but for this ultimate espousal, this yielding up of the essential spirit of her womanhood to a man,—no, she could not trust herself to this. She could not actually *want* to do it. And yet somewhere in her, dimly, she wanted nothing else but this. Everything might go, if but she could give herself up in marriage and be gone in a oneness with the man. But the greater part of her emphatically did *not* want it.

After the fiasco of the proposal, Birkin had hurried blindly away from Beldover, in a whirl of fury with her. He felt he had been a complete fool, that the whole scene had been a farce of the first water. But that did not trouble him at all. He was deeply furious that Ursula persisted always in this old cry: "Why do you want to bully me?" That made his blood boil.

He went straight to Shortlands. There he found Gerald standing with his back to the fire, in the library, as motionless as a man is, who is completely and emptily restless, utterly hollow. He had done all the work he wanted to do—and now there was nothing. He could go out in the car, he could run to town. But he did not want to go out in the car, he did not want to run to town, he did not want to call on the Thirlbys. He was suspended motionless, in an agony of inertia, like a machine that is without power.

This was very bitter to Gerald, who had never known what boredom was, who had gone from activity to activity, never at a loss. Now, suddenly, everything seemed to have stopped in him. He did not want any more to do the things that offered. Something dead within him just refused to respond to any suggestion. He cast over in his mind, what it would be possible to do, to save himself from this misery of nothingness, relieve the stress of this hollowness. And there were only two things that would fill him, make him live. One was to make love to somebody, the other was to be soothed by Birkin. And there was nobody for the moment to make love to—he had Gudrun at the back of his mind. And he knew Birkin was out. So there was nothing to do but to bear the stress of his own emptiness.

When he saw Birkin his face lit up in a sudden, wonderful smile:

"By God, Rupert," he said, "I'd just come to the conclusion that nothing in the world mattered to one, but the right people."

The smile in his eyes was very beautiful, as he looked at the other man.

"And there aren't any right people," said Birkin.

"What? There aren't any? Well, very few."

He laughed as he said it. Birkin sat down near the fire.

"What were you doing?" he asked.

"I? Nothing. I don't know what's come over me, I can settle to nothing, neither work nor play. I don't know whether it's a sign of old age, I'm sure."

"You mean you're bored?"

"Bored! I don't know.—I can't apply myself. I feel I don't know what to do with myself."

Birkin glanced up and looked in his eyes.

"Would you like something to *hit*?" he asked grimly.

Gerald smiled.

"Well, I shouldn't mind what I did, so long as I did it."

"Quite!" said Birkin, in his soft voice.

There was a long pause, during which each man could feel the presence of the other.

"One has to wait for an opportunity," said Birkin.

"Wait? I'm willing to wait, till Doomsday. But it's the damned waiting that I complain of. It's nothing but waiting, this blasted life—either waiting, or messing about doing things that you know right well don't matter a hang—don't matter a hang, they don't, the things we spend our lives for."

"I know that. The only thing is to turn round like a bull on its driver, and full tilt go slap at the whole show. Turn round on it."

"Ah yes; I know that." He took his hands out of his trousers pockets, and reached for a cigarette. He was tense and nervous. He lit the cigarette over a lamp, reaching forward and drawing steadily. He was dressed for dinner, as usual in the evening, although he was alone.

"Did you," he said to Birkin, "ever do any boxing, or anything of that sort?"

"No, I don't think I did," said Birkin.

"Ay—" Gerald lifted his head and blew the smoke slowly into the air.

"Why?" said Birkin.

"Nothing.—I thought we might have a round. It might take this devil out of me.—I really, sometimes, could beat my brains out against the wall."

"Upset are you?"

"No, I'm not upset. No—I wish I was. I wish there was something to be upset about. No, I'm not upset. I tell you, I believe I'm done for at times. I do, I assure you."

He looked down at Birkin, and his eyes flashed with a sort of terror, like the eyes of a stallion, that are bloodshot and overwrought, turned glancing backwards in a stiff terror.

"I feel that if I don't watch myself, I shall find myself doing something silly. I do, it's no joke."

"No," said Birkin, "it's no joke."

Gerald listened with quick impatience. He kept glancing down at Birkin, as if looking for something from the other man.

"I used to do some Japanese wrestling," said Birkin. "A Jap lived in the same house with me in Heidelberg, and he taught me a little. But I was never much good at it."

"You did!" exclaimed Gerald. "Now that's one of the things I've never even seen done. You mean jiu-jitsu, I suppose?"

"Yes. But I am no good at those things—they don't interest me."

"They don't? No, I suppose not. But I should like to see some done, nevertheless."

"I'll do my best for you, if you like," said Birkin.

"You will?" A queer, smiling look tightened Gerald's face for a moment, as he said, "Well, I'd like it very much."

"Then we'll try jiu-jitsu. Only you can't do much in a starched shirt."

"Then let us strip, and do it properly.—Half a minute—" He rang the bell, and waited for the butler.

"Bring a couple of sandwiches and a syphon," he said to the man, "and then don't trouble me any more tonight—or let anybody else."

The man went. Gerald turned to Birkin with his eyes lighted.

"And you used to wrestle with a Jap?" he said. "Did you strip?"

"Sometimes."

"You did! What was he like then, as a wrestler?"

"Good, I believe. I am no judge. He was very quick and slippery and full of electric fire. It is a remarkable thing, what a curious sort of fluid force they seem to have in them, those people—really like electricity."

Gerald nodded.

"I should imagine so," he said, "to look at them. They repel me, rather."

"Repel and attract, both. They are very repulsive when they are cold, and they look grey. But when they are hot and roused, there is a definite attraction—a curious kind of electric fluid fire."

"Well—, yes—, probably."

The man brought in the tray and set it down.

"Don't come in any more, Thomas," said Gerald.

The door was closed.

"Well then," said Gerald; "shall we strip and begin? Will you have a drink first?"

"No, I don't want one."

"Neither do I."

Gerald fastened the door and pushed the furniture aside. The room was large, there was plenty of space, it was thickly carpeted. Then he quickly threw off his clothes, and waited for Birkin. The latter, white and thin, came over to him.

"Now," he said, "I will show you what I learned, and what I remember. You let me take you so—" And his hands closed on the naked body of the other man. In another moment, he had Gerald swung over lightly and balanced against his knee, head downwards. Relaxed, Gerald sprang to his feet with eyes glittering.

"That's quite smart," he said. "Now try again."

So the two men began to struggle together. They were very dissimilar. Birkin was narrow, his bones were very thin and fine. Gerald was much heavier and more plastic. His bones were strong and round, his limbs were rounded, all his contours were beautifully and fully moulded. He seemed to stand with a proper, rich weight on the face of the earth, whilst Birkin was unsubstantial almost as an idea, as a piece of script. And Gerald had a good, heavy kind of strength, rather slow, but rhythmic and invincible, whereas Birkin was quick as to be almost intangible. He moved quickly round the body of the other man, scarcely seeming to touch him, like a garment, and then suddenly clinching in a tense fine grip that seemed to penetrate into the very inside of Gerald's being.

They stopped, they discussed methods, they practised grips and throws, they became more accustomed to each other, to each other's rhythm, they got a kind of mutual physical understanding. And then again they had a real struggle. They seemed to drive their white flesh deeper and deeper against each other, as if they would fuse it into a oneness. Birkin had a latent energy, that would suddenly urge upon the other man with an uncanny force, overcome him like a sudden spell put upon him. Then it would pass, and Gerald would heave free.

So the two men entwined and wrestled with each other, working nearer and nearer. Both were white and clear, but Gerald flushed ruddy where he was touched, and Birkin remained white and glistening. He seemed to penetrate into Gerald's heavier, riper bulk, to interfuse his body through the body of the other, as if to bring it subtly into his influence, always seizing with some rapid sensuous foreknowledge every motion of the other body, converting and counteracting it, playing upon the limbs and frame of Gerald like some strong wind. It was as if Birkin's whole physical intelligence flickered over Gerald's body, as if his fine, sublimated energy penetrated into the flesh of the heavier man like some spell, casting a fine net, a web, through the muscles into the very depths of Gerald's physical being.

So they wrestled swiftly, astonishingly, intent and mindless at last, two naked white figures ever working into a tighter, closer oneness of struggle, with a strange, octopus-like knotting and flashing of limbs in the subdued light of the room; a tense white knot of flesh gripped in silence between the walls of old brown books. Now and again came a sharp gasp of breath, or a sound like a sigh, then the rapid thudding of movement on the thickly-carpeted floor, then the strange sound of flesh escaping under flesh. Often in the white, interlaced knot of violent living flesh that swayed silently, there was no head to be seen, only the swift, tight limbs, the solid white torsos, the physical unity of the two bodies clinched like malleable metal into oneness. Then would appear the bright, ruffled head of Gerald, as the struggle changed, then for a moment the dun-coloured, strange head of the other man would lift up from the conflict, the eyes wide and brilliant and sightless.

At length Gerald lay back inert on the carpet, his breast rising in great slow panting, whilst Birkin kneeled over him, almost unconscious. Birkin was much more exhausted. He caught little, short breaths, he could scarcely breathe any more. The earth seemed to tilt and sway, and a complete darkness was coming over his mind. He did not know what happened. He slid forward quite unconscious, over Gerald, and Gerald did not notice. Then he was half-conscious again, aware only of the strange tilting and sliding of the world. The world was sliding, everything was sliding off into the darkness. And he was sliding endlessly, endlessly away.

He came to consciousness again, hearing an immense knocking outside. What could be happening, what was it, the great hammer-strokes resounding through the house? He did not know. And then it came to him that it was his own heart beating. But that seemed impossible, the noise was outside. No, it was inside himself, it was his own heart. And the beating was painful, so strained, surcharged. He wondered if Gerald heard it. He did not know whether he were standing or lying or falling.

When he realised that he was fallen prostrate upon Gerald's body he wondered, he was surprised. But he sat up, steadying himself with his hand and waiting for his heart to become stiller and less painful. It hurt very much, and took away his consciousness.

"Of course—" panted Gerald, "I didn't have to be rough—with you—I had to keep back—my force—"

Birkin heard the sound as if his own spirit stood behind him, outside him, and listened to it. His body was in a trance of exhaustion, his spirit heard thinly. His body could not answer. Only he knew his heart was getting quieter. He was divided entirely between his spirit, which stood outside, and knew, and his body, that was a plunging, unconscious stroke of blood.

"I could have thrown you—using violence—" panted Gerald. "But you beat me right enough."

"But," said Birkin, hardening his throat and producing the words in the tension there, "you're much stronger than I—you could beat me—easily."

Then he relaxed again to the terrible plunging of his heart and his blood.

"It surprised me," panted Gerald, "what strength you've got. Almost—supernatural."

"For a moment," said Birkin.

He still heard as if it were his own disembodied spirit hearing, standing at some distance behind him. It drew nearer however, his spirit. And the violent striking of blood in his chest was sinking quieter, allowing his mind to come back. He realised that he was leaning with all his weight on the soft body of the other man. It startled him because he thought he had withdrawn. He recovered himself, and sat up. But he was still vague and unestablished. He put out his hand to steady himself. It touched the hand of Gerald, that was lying out on the floor. And Gerald's hand closed warm and close over Birkin's, they remained exhausted and breathless, their hands clasped closely.

The normal consciousness however was returning, ebbing back. Birkin could breathe almost naturally again. Gerald's hand slowly relaxed its hold, Birkin slowly, dazedly rose to his feet and went towards the table. He poured out a whiskey and soda. Gerald also came for a drink.

"It was good though, wasn't it?" said Birkin, looking at Gerald with darkened eyes.

"It did me good," said Gerald. He looked at the frail body of the other man, and added: "It wasn't too much for you, was it?"

"No. It was a satisfaction. One ought to wrestle and strive and be physically close. It makes one sane."

"You do think so?"

"I do. Don't you?"

"Yes," said Gerald, "it's life for me—"

There were long spaces of silence between their words.

"We are mentally, spiritually intimate, therefore we should be more or less physically intimate too—it is more whole."

"Certainly it is," said Gerald. Then he laughed happily, adding: "I know I'm all the better."

"And so am I," said Birkin. "—I don't know why one should have to justify oneself."

"No."

The two men began to dress.

"I think also that you are beautiful," said Birkin to Gerald, "and that is something too. One should take what is given."

"You think I am beautiful—how do you mean, physically?" asked Gerald, his eyes glistening.

"Yes. You have a northern kind of beauty, still like snow—and a beautiful plastic form. Yes, that too is there to enjoy. We should enjoy everything."

Gerald laughed in his throat, and said:

"That's certainly one way of looking at it.—I can say this much, this has done me more good than anything else I can think of would have done."

"And the things that make one feel freer and better, those are the good things to do," said Birkin. "There's no other criterion. And that's the whole of morality, as long as time lasts."

"Certainly," said Gerald.

They drew to the fire, with the decanters and the glasses and the food.

"I always eat a little before I go to bed," said Gerald. "I sleep better."

"I should not sleep so well," said Birkin.

"No? There you are, we are not alike.—I'll put a dressing-gown on." Birkin remained alone, looking at the fire. His mind had reverted to Ursula. She seemed to fill again the field of his consciousness. Gerald came down wearing a gown of thick black-and-green silk, brilliant and striking.

"You are very fine," said Birkin, looking at the emerald silk with its broad black bars.

"It was a caftan in Bokhara," said Gerald. "I like it."

"I like it too."

Birkin was silent, thinking how scrupulous Gerald was in his attire, how expensive too. He wore thick silk socks, and studs of fine workmanship, and silk underclothing, and silk braces. Curious! This was another of the differences between them. Birkin was careless and unimaginative about his own appearance.

"Of course you," said Gerald, as if he had been thinking; "there's something curious about you. You're as sharp as lightning—something very curious—"

Birkin laughed. He was looking at the handsome figure of the other man, blond and attractive in the rich robe, and he was half thinking of the difference between it and himself—so different; as far, perhaps, apart as man from woman, yet in another direction. But really it was Ursula, it was the woman who was gaining ascendance over Birkin's being, at this moment. He did not vitally heed Gerald.

"Do you know," he said suddenly, "I went and proposed to Ursula Brangwen tonight, that she should marry me."

He saw the blank wonder come over Gerald's face.

"You did?"

"Yes. Almost formally—speaking first to her father, as it should be, in the world—though that was accident—or mischief."

Gerald only stared in wonder, as if he did not grasp.

"You don't mean to say that you seriously went and asked her family to let you marry her?"

"Yes," said Birkin, "I did."

"What, had you spoken to her before about it, then?"

"No, not a word. I suddenly thought I would go there and ask her—and her father happened to come instead of her—so I asked him first."

"If you could have her?" concluded Gerald.

"Ye-es, that."

"And you didn't speak to her?"

"Yes. She came in afterwards. So it was put to her as well."

"It was!—And what did she say then?—You're an engaged man?"

"No,—she only said she didn't want to be bullied into answering."

"She what?"

"Said she didn't want to be bullied into answering."

"'Said she didn't want to be bullied into answering!' Why what did she mean by that?"

"I dunno. Didn't want to be bothered just then, I suppose."

"But is this really so?—And what did you do then?"

"I walked out of the house and came here."

"You came straight here?"

"Yes."

Gerald stared in amazement and amusement. He could not take it in.

"But is this really true, as you say it now?"

"Word for word."

"It *is*?"

He leaned back in his chair, filled with delight and amusement.

"Well that's good," he said. "And so you came here to wrestle with your good angel,* did you?"

"Did I?" said Birkin.

"Well it looks like it. Isn't that what you did?"

Now Birkin could not follow Gerald's meaning.

"And what's going to happen?" said Gerald. "You're going to keep open the proposition, so to speak?"

"I suppose so. I vowed to myself I would see them all to the devil. But I suppose I shall ask her again, in a little while."

Gerald watched him steadily.

"So you're fond of her then?" he asked.

"I think—I love her," said Birkin, his face going very still and fixed.

Gerald glistened for a moment with pleasure, as if it were something done specially to please him. Then his face assumed a fitting gravity, and he nodded his head slowly.

"You know," he said, "I always believed in love—*true* love.—But where does one find it, nowadays?"

"I don't know," said Birkin.

"Very rarely," said Gerald. Then, after a pause, "I've never felt it myself—not what I should call love. I've gone after women—and been keen enough over some of them. But I've never felt love. I don't believe I've ever felt as much *love* for a woman as I have for you—not *love*.—You understand what I mean?"

"Yes. I'm sure you've never loved a woman."

"You feel that, do you?—And do you think I ever shall? You understand what I mean?" He put his hand to his breast, closing his fist there, as if

251

he would draw something out. "I mean that—that— —I can't express what it is, but I know it."

"What is it, then?" asked Birkin.

"You see, I can't put it into words. I mean, at any rate, something abiding, something that can't change— —"

His eyes were bright and puzzled.

"Now do you think I shall ever feel that for a woman?" he asked anxiously.

Birkin looked at him and shook his head.

"I don't know," he said. "I could not say."

Gerald had been on the *qui vive*, as if awaiting his fate. Now he drew back in his chair.

"No," he said, "and neither do I, and neither do I."

"We are different, you and I," said Birkin. "I can't tell your life."

"No," said Gerald, "no more can I. But I tell you—I begin to doubt it."

"That you will ever love a woman?"

"Well—yes—what you would truly call *love*—"

"You doubt it?"

"Well—I begin to."

There was a long pause.

"Life has all kinds of things," said Birkin. "There isn't only one road."

"Yes, I believe that too. I believe it.—And mind you, I don't care how it is with me—I don't care how it is—so long as I don't feel—" he paused, and a blank, barren look passed over his face, to express his feeling—"so long as I feel I've *lived*, somehow—and I don't care how it is—but I want to feel that—"

"Fulfilled," said Birkin.

"We-ell, perhaps it is, fulfilled;—I don't use the same words as you."

"It is the same. We want to be fulfilled—each in our own road."

8

GUDRUN WAS AWAY IN LONDON, having a little show of her work, with a friend, and looking round, preparing for flight from Beldover. Come what might, she would be on the wing in a very short time. She received a letter from Winifred Crich, ornamented with drawings.

"Father also has been to London, to be examined by the doctors. It made him very tired. They say he must rest a very great deal, so he is mostly in bed. He brought me a lovely tropical parrot in faience, of Dresden ware, also a man ploughing, and two mice climbing up a stalk, also in faience. The mice are Copenhagen ware.* They are the best, but mice don't shine so much, otherwise they are very good, their tails are slim and long. They all shine nearly like glass. Of course it is the glaze, but I don't like it. Gerald likes the man ploughing the best, his trousers are torn, he is ploughing with an ox, being I suppose a German peasant. It is all grey and white, white shirt and grey trousers, but very shiny and clean. Mr Birkin likes the girl best, under the hawthorn blossom, with a lamb, and with daffodils painted on her skirts, in the drawing room. But that is silly, because the lamb is not a real lamb, and she is silly too.

"Dear Miss Brangwen are you coming back soon, you are very much missed here. I enclose a drawing of father sitting up in bed. He says he hopes you are not going to forsake us. Oh dear Miss Brangwen, I am sure you won't. Do come back and draw the ferrets, they are the most lovely noble darlings in the world. We might carve them in holly wood, playing against a background of green leaves. Oh do let us, for they are most beautiful.

"Father says we might have a studio. Gerald says we could easily have a beautiful one over the stables, it would only need windows to be put in the slant of the roof, which is a simple matter. Then you could stay here all day and work, and we could live in the studio, like two real artists, like the man in the picture in the hall, with the frying-pan and the walls all covered with drawings. I long to be free, to live the free life of an artist. Even Gerald told father that only an artist is free, because he lives in a creative world of his own.————"

Gudrun caught the drift of the family intentions, in this letter. Gerald wanted her to be attached to the household at Shortlands, he was using Winifred as his stalking-horse. The father thought only of his child, he saw a rock of salvation in Gudrun. And Gudrun admired him for his perspicacity. The child, moreover, was really exceptional. Gudrun was quite content. She was quite willing, given a studio, to spend her days at Shortlands. She disliked the Grammar School already thoroughly, she wanted to be free. If a studio were provided, she would be free to go on with her work, she would await the turn of events with complete serenity. And she was really interested in Winifred, she would be quite glad to understand the girl.

So there was quite a little festivity on Winifred's account, the day Gudrun returned to Shortlands.

"You should make a bunch of flowers to give to Miss Brangwen when she arrives," Gerald said smiling to his sister.

"Oh no," cried Winifred, "it's silly."

"Not at all. It is a very charming and ordinary attention."

"Oh, it *is* silly," protested Winifred, with all the extreme *mauvaise honte** of her years. Nevertheless, the idea appealed to her. She wanted very much to carry it out. She flitted round the green-houses and the conservatory looking wistfully at the flowers on their stems. And the more she looked, the more she *longed* to have a bunch of the blossoms she saw, the more fascinated she became with her little vision of ceremony, and the more consumedly shy and self-conscious she grew, till she was almost beside herself. She could not get the idea out of her mind. It was as if some haunting challenge prompted her, and she had not enough courage to take it up. So again she drifted into the green-houses, looking at the lovely roses in their pots, and at the virginal cyclamens, and at the mystic white clusters of a creeper. The beauty, oh the beauty of them, and oh the paradisal bliss, if she should have a perfect bouquet and could give it to Gudrun the next day. Her passion and her complete indecision almost made her ill.

At last she slid to her father's side.

"Daddy—" she said.

"What my precious?"

But she hung back, the tears almost coming to her eyes, in her extreme sensitive confusion. Her father looked at her, and his heart ran hot with tenderness, an anguish of poignant love.

"What do you want to say to me, my love?"

"Daddy—!" her lips quivered—"isn't it silly if I give Miss Brangwen some flowers when she comes?"

The sick man looked at the bright, wonderful eyes of his child, and his heart burned with love.

"No, darling, that's not silly. It's what they do to queens."

This was not very reassuring to Winifred. She half suspected that queens in themselves were a silliness. Yet she so wanted her little romantic occasion.

"Shall I then?" she asked.

"Give Miss Brangwen some flowers? Do, Birdie. Tell Wilson I say you are to have what you want."

The child smiled a small, subtle, unconscious smile to herself, in anticipation of her way.

"But I won't get them till tomorrow," she said.

"Not till tomorrow, Birdie.—Give me a kiss then—"

Winifred silently kissed the sick man, and drifted out of the room. She again went the round of the green-houses and the conservatory, informing the gardener, in her high, peremptory, simple fashion, of what she wanted, telling him all the blooms she had selected.

"What do you want these for?" Wilson asked her.

"I want them," she said. She wished servants did not ask questions.

"Ay, you've said as much. But what do you want them for, for decoration, or to send away, or what?"

"I want them for a presentation bouquet."

"A presentation bouquet! Who's coming then?—the Duchess of Portland?"

"No."

"Oh, not her—Well you'll have a rare poppy-show* if you put all the things you've mentioned into your bouquet."

"Yes, I want a rare poppy-show."

"You do! Then there's no more to be said."

The next day Winifred, in a dress of silvery velvet, and holding a gaudy bunch of flowers in her hand, waited with keen impatience in the schoolroom, looking down the drive for Gudrun's arrival. It was a wet morning. Under her nose was the strange fragrance of hot-house flowers, the bunch was like a little fire to her, she seemed to have a strange new fire in her heart. This slight sense of romance stirred her like an intoxicant.

At last she saw Gudrun coming, and she ran downstairs to warn her father and Gerald. They, laughing at her anxiety and gravity, came with her into the hall. The manservant came hastening to the door, and there he was, relieving Gudrun of her umbrella, and then of her raincoat. The welcoming party hung back till their visitor entered the hall.

Gudrun was flushed with the rain, her hair was blown in loose little curls, she was like a flower just opened in the rain, the heart of the blossom just newly visible, seeming to emit a warmth of retained sunshine. Gerald groaned in spirit, seeing her so beautiful and unknown. She was wearing a soft blue dress, and her stockings were of dark red.

Winifred advanced with odd, stately formality.

"We are so glad you've come back," she said. "These are your flowers." She presented the bouquet.

"Mine!" cried Gudrun. She was suspended for a moment, then a vivid flame went over her, she was as if blinded for a moment with a flame of pleasure. Then her eyes, strange and flaming, lifted and looked at the father, and at Gerald. And again Gerald groaned in spirit, as if it would be more than he could bear, as her hot, exposed eyes rested on him. There was something so revealed, she was revealed beyond bearing, to his eyes. He turned his face aside. And he felt he would not be able to avert her. And he writhed under the imprisonment.

Gudrun put her face into the flowers.

"But how beautiful they are!" she said, in a muffled voice. Then, with a strange, suddenly revealed passion, she stooped and kissed Winifred.

Mr Crich went forward with his hand held out to her.

"I was afraid you were going to run away from us," he said, playfully.

Gudrun looked up at him with a luminous, roguish, unknown face.

"Really!" she replied. "No, I didn't want to stay in London."

Her voice seemed to imply that she had wanted so much to get back to Shortlands; her tone was warm and subtly caressing.

"That is a good fortune," smiled the father. "You see you are very welcome here among us."

Gudrun only looked into his face with dark-blue, warm, shy eyes. She was unconsciously carried away by her own power.

"And you look as if you came home in every possible triumph," Mr Crich continued, holding her hand.

"No," she said, glowing strangely. "I haven't had any triumph till I came here."

"Ah come come! We're not going to hear any of those things. Haven't we read notices in the paper, Gerald?"

"You came off pretty well this time," said Gerald to her, shaking hands. "Did you sell anything?"

"No," she said, "not much."

"Just as well," he said.

She wondered what he meant. But she was all aglow with her reception, carried away by this little flattering ceremonial on her behalf.

"Winifred," said the father, "have you a pair of shoes for Miss Brangwen? You had better change at once——"

Gudrun went out with her bouquet in her hand.

"Quite a remarkable young woman," said the father to Gerald, when she had gone.

"Yes," replied Gerald briefly, as if he did not like the observation.

Mr Crich liked Gudrun to sit with him for half an hour. Usually he was ashy and wretched, with all the life gnawed out of him. But as soon as he rallied, he liked to make belief that he was just as before, quite well and in the midst of life—not of the outer world, but in the midst of a strong essential life. And to this belief, Gudrun contributed perfectly. With her, he could get those precious half-hours of strength and exaltation and pure freedom, when he seemed to live more than he had ever lived.

She came to him as he lay propped up in the library. His face was like yellow wax, his eyes darkened, as it were sightless. His black beard, now streaked with grey, seemed to spring out of the waxy flesh of a corpse. Yet the atmosphere about him was energetic and playful. Gudrun subscribed to this, perfectly. To her fancy, he was just an ordinary man. Only his rather terrible appearance was photographed upon her soul, away beneath her consciousness. She knew that, in spite of his playfulness, his eyes could not change from their darkened vacancy, they were the eyes of a man who is dead.

"Ah, this is Miss Brangwen," he said, suddenly rousing as she entered, announced by the man-servant. "Thomas, put Miss Brangwen a chair here—that's right." He looked at her soft, fresh face with pleasure. It gave him the illusion of life. "Now, you will have a glass of sherry and a little piece of cake.—Thomas——"

"No thank you," said Gudrun. And as soon as she had said it, her heart sank horribly. The sick man seemed to fall into a gap of death, at her contradiction. She ought to play up to him, not to contravene him. In an instant she was smiling her rather roguish smile.

"I don't like sherry very much," she said. "But I like almost anything else."

The sick man caught at this straw instantly.

"Not sherry! No! Something else! What then? What is there Thomas?"

"Port wine—curaçao——"

"I would love some curaçao—" said Gudrun, looking at the sick man confidingly.

"You would. Well then Thomas, Curaçao—and a little cake, or a biscuit?"

"A biscuit," said Gudrun. She did not want anything, but she was wise.

"Yes."

He waited till she was settled with her little glass and her biscuit. Then he was satisfied.

"You have not heard the plan," he said with some excitement, "of a studio for Winifred, over the stables?"

"No," exclaimed Gudrun, in mock wonder.

"Ah! There is a fine room under the roof, above the stables. We had thought of converting it into a studio."

"How *very* nice that would be!" cried Gudrun with mock warmth.

"You think it would? Well, it can be done."

"But how perfectly splendid for Winifred! Of course, it is just what is needed, if she is to work at all seriously. One must have one's workshop, otherwise one never ceases to feel an amateur."

"Is that so? Yes.—Of course.—Of course, I should like you to share it with Winifred."

"Thank you so much."

Gudrun knew all these things already, but she must look shy and very grateful, as if overcome.

"Of course, what I should like best, would be if you could give up your work at the Grammar School, and just avail yourself of the studio, and work there—well, as much or as little as you like—"

He looked at Gudrun with dark, vacant eyes. She looked back at him as if full of gratitude. These phrases of a dying man were so complete and natural, coming like echoes through his dead mouth.

"And as to your earnings—you don't mind taking from me what you have taken from the Education Committee, do you? I don't want you to be a loser."

"Oh," said Gudrun, "if I can have the studio and work there, I can earn money enough, really I can."

"Well," he said, pleased to be the benefactor, "we can see about all that.—You wouldn't mind spending your days here?"

"If there were a studio to work in," said Gudrun, "I could ask for nothing better."

"Is that so?"

He was really very pleased. But already he was getting tired. She could see the grey, awful semi-consciousness of mere pain and dissolution coming over him again, the torture coming into the vacancy of his darkened eyes. It was not over yet, this process of death. She rose softly, saying:

"Perhaps you will sleep. I must look for Winifred."

She went out, telling the nurse that she had left him. Day by day the tissue of the sick man was further and further reduced, nearer and nearer the process came, towards the last knot which held the human being in its unity. But this knot was hard and unrelaxed, the will of the dying man never gave way. He might be dead in nine-tenths, yet the remaining tenth remained unchanged, till it too was torn apart. With his will he held the unit of himself firm, but the circle of his power was ever and ever reduced, it would be reduced to a point at last, then swept away.

To adhere to life, he must adhere to human relationships, and he caught at every straw. Winifred, the butler, the nurse, Gudrun, these were the people who meant all to him, in these last resources. Gerald, in his father's presence, stiffened with fear and repulsion. It was so, to a less degree with all the other children except Winifred. They could not see anything but the death, when they looked at their father. It was as [if] some subterranean horror overcame them. They could not see the familiar face, hear the familiar voice. They were overwhelmed by the horror of visible and audible death. Gerald could not breathe in his father's presence. He must get out at once. And so, in the same way, the father could not bear the presence of his son. It sent a final irritation through the soul of the dying man.

The studio was made ready, Gudrun and Winifred moved in. They enjoyed so much the ordering and the appointing of it. And now they need hardly be in the house at all. They had their meals in the studio, they lived there safely. For the house was becoming dreadful. There were two nurses in white, flitting silently about, like heralds of death. The father was confined to his bed, there was a come and go of lugubrious sisters and brothers and children.

Winifred was her father's constant visitor. Every morning, after breakfast, she went into his room when he was washed and propped up in bed, to spend half an hour with him.

"Are you better, Daddy?" she asked him invariably.

And invariably he answered:

"Yes, I think I'm a little better, pet."

She held his hand in both her own, lovingly and protectively. And this was very dear to him.

She ran in again as a rule at lunchtime, to tell him the course of events, and every evening, when the curtains were drawn, and his room was cosy, she spent a long time with him. Gudrun was gone home, Winifred was alone in the house, she liked best to be with her father. They talked and prattled at random, he always as if he were well, just the same as when he was going about. So that Winifred, with a child's wonderful faculty for not seeing the painful things, never realised that there was anything serious the matter. Instinctively, she withheld her attention, and was happy.

Then, when she was gone, he gave himself up to the misery of his pain and his dissolution. But there were still these bright hours, though as his strength waned, his faculty for attention grew weaker, and the nurse had to send Winifred away, to save him from exhaustion.

He never admitted to anybody that he was going to die. He knew it was so, he knew it was the end. Yet even to himself he would not admit it. His will was rigid. This death was one of the things one put away and did not acknowledge. And yet, at times, he felt a great need to cry out and to wail and complain. He would have liked to cry aloud to Gerald, so that his son should comfort him. Gerald was instinctively aware of this, and he recoiled in horror, to avoid any such thing. This ignominy and uncleanness of death repelled him too much. One should die quickly, like the Romans, one should be master of one's fate in dying as in living. He was convulsed in the clasp of this death of his father's, as in the coils of the great serpent of Laocoon.* The great serpent had got the father, and the son was dragged into the embrace of horrifying death along with him. He resisted like a madness.

The last time the dying man asked to see Gudrun he was grey with slow death. Yet he must see someone, he must, in the intervals of consciousness, catch into connection with the living world, lest he should have to face the knowledge of his own situation. Fortunately he was most of his time dazed and half gone. But there were times even to the end when he was capable of realising what was happening to him. And these were the times when he called in outside help, no matter whose. For to realise this death that he was dying was a death beyond death, never to be borne.

Gudrun was shocked by his appearance, and by the darkened, almost sightless eyes, that still sought for the outer life.

"Well," he said in his weakened voice, "and how are you and Winifred getting on?"

"Oh, very well indeed," replied Gudrun.

There were slight dead gaps in the conversation, as if the ideas called up were only elusive straws floating on the dark chaos of the sick man's dying.

"The studio answers all right?" he said.

"Splendid. It couldn't be more beautiful and perfect," said Gudrun.

She waited for what he would say next.

"And you think Winifred has the makings of a sculptor?"

It was strange how hollow the words were, meaningless.

"I'm sure she has. She will do good things one day."

"Ah! Then her life won't be altogether wasted, you think?"

Gudrun was rather surprised.

"Sure it won't!" she exclaimed.

"That's right."

Again Gudrun waited for what he would say.

"You find it easy to get along in life, don't you?" he asked, with a pitiful faint smile that was almost too much for Gudrun.

"Yes," she smiled—she would lie at random—"I get a pretty good time I believe."

"That's right. A happy nature is a great asset."

Again Gudrun smiled, though her soul was dry with repulsion. Did one have to die like this, having the life extracted forcibly from one, whilst one smiled and made conversation to the end? Was there no other way? Must one go through all the horror of this victory over death, the triumph of the integral will, that would not be broken till it disappeared utterly? One must, it was the only way. She admired the self-possession and the control of the dying man exceedingly. But she loathed the death itself. She was glad the everyday world held good, and she need not recognise anything beyond.

"You are quite contented with everything here—nothing you find wrong in your position?"

"Except that you are too good to me," said Gudrun.

"Ah, well, the fault of that lies with yourself," he said, and he felt a little exultation, that he had made this speech. He was still so strong and living! But the nausea of death began to creep back on him, in reaction.

Gudrun went away, back to Winifred. Mademoiselle had left, Gudrun stayed a good deal at Shortlands, and a tutor came in to carry on Winifred's education. But he did not live in the house, he was connected with the Grammar School.

One day, Gudrun was to drive with Winifred and Gerald and Birkin to town, in the car. It was a dark, showery day. Winifred and Gudrun were ready and waiting at the door. Winifred was very quiet, but Gudrun had not noticed. Suddenly the child asked, in a voice of unconcern:

"Do you think my father's going to die, Miss Brangwen?"

Gudrun started.

"I don't know," she replied.

"Don't you truly?"

"Nobody knows for certain. He *may* die, of course."

The child pondered a few moments, then she asked:

"But do you *think* he will die?"

It was put almost like a question in geography or science.

"Do I think he will die?" repeated Gudrun. "Yes, I do."

But Winifred's large eyes were fixed on her, and the girl did not move.

"He is very ill," said Gudrun.

A small smile came over Winifred's face, subtle and sceptical.

"*I* don't believe he will," the child asserted, and she moved away into the drive. Gudrun watched the isolated figure, and her heart stood still. Winifred was playing with a little rivulet of water, absorbedly, as if nothing had been said.

"I've made a proper dam," she cried, out of the moist distance.

Gerald came to the door from out of the hall behind.

"It is just as well she doesn't care to believe it," he said.

Gudrun looked at him. Their eyes met; and they exchanged a sardonic understanding.

"Just as well," said Gudrun.

He looked at her again, and a fire flickered up in his eyes.

"I would dance while Rome burned, wouldn't you?" he said.

She was rather taken aback. But, gathering herself together, she replied:

"Oh—better dance than wail, certainly."

"So I think."

And they both felt the subterranean desire to let go, to fling away everything, and lapse into a sheer licentious revelry, brutal and callous. A strange black passion surged up pure in Gudrun. She felt strong. She felt her hands so strong, as if she could tear the world asunder with them. She remembered the fearful revels of the Romans, and her heart grew hot. She knew she wanted this herself also—or something, something else. Ah, if that which was unknown and suppressed in her were once let loose, what a violent and satisfying orgy it would be. And she wanted it, she trembled slightly from the proximity of the man, who stood just behind her, suggestive of the same black licentiousness that rose in herself. She wanted it with him, this unacknowledged black frenzy. For a moment the clear perception of this preoccupied her, distinct and perfect in its final reality. Then she shut it off completely, saying:

"We might as well go down to the lodge after Winifred—we can get in the car there."

"So we can," he answered, going with her.

They found Winifred at the lodge admiring the litter of pure-bred white puppies. The girl looked up, and there was a rather ugly, unseeing cast in her eyes as she turned to Gerald and Gudrun. She did not want to see them.

"Look!" she cried. "Three new puppies! Holliday says this one seems perfect. Isn't it a sweetling? But it isn't so nice as its mother." She turned to caress the fine white bull-terrier bitch who stood uneasily near her.

"My dearest Lady Crich," she said, "you are beautiful as an angel on earth. Angel—angel—*don't* you think she's good enough and beautiful enough to go to heaven, Gudrun?—archangel! They will go with *me* to heaven, won't they— —and *especially* my darling Lady Crich.—Mrs Holliday, I say!"

"Yes Miss Winifred?" said the woman, appearing at the door.

"Oh do call this one Lady Winifred, if she turns out perfect, will you? Do tell Holliday to call it Lady Winifred."

"I'll tell him—but I'm afraid that's a gentleman puppy, Miss Winifred."

"Oh *no*!" There was the sound of a car. "There's Rupert!" cried the child, and she ran to the gate.

Birkin, driving his car, pulled up outside the lodge gate.

"We're ready!" cried Winifred. "I want to sit in front with you, Rupert. May I?"

"I'm afraid you'll fidget about and tumble," he said.

"No I won't. I do want to sit in front next to you. It makes my feet so lovely and warm, from the engines."

Birkin helped her up, amused at sending Gerald to sit by Gudrun in the body of the car.

"Have you any news, Rupert?" Gerald called, as they rushed along the lanes.

"News?" exclaimed Birkin.

"Yes." Gerald looked at Gudrun, who sat by his side, and he said, his eyes laughing, "I want to know whether I ought to congratulate him, but I can't get anything definite out of him."

Gudrun flushed deeply.

"Congratulate him on what?" she asked.

"There was some mention of an engagement—at least, he said something to me about it."

Gudrun flushed darkly.

"You mean with Ursula?" she said, in challenge.

"Yes. That's right, isn't it?"

"I don't think there's any engagement," said Gudrun coldly.

"That so?—Still no developments, Rupert?" he called.

"Where? Matrimonial? No."

"How's that?" called Gerald.

Birkin looked round. There was irritation in his eyes also.

"It's beyond me," he replied. "What do you think of it, Gudrun?"

"Oh," she cried, determined to fling her stone also into the pool, since they had begun, "I don't think she wants an engagement. She says a bird in the bush is worth two in the hand." Gudrun's voice was clear and gong-like. It reminded Rupert of her father's, so strong and vibrant.

"And I," said Birkin, his face set like a shield, "want marriage—I don't want love."

They were both startled. *Why* this public avowal? Gerald seemed suspended a moment, in amusement.

"Does the one exclude the other?" he called.

"Seems so," said Birkin.

"Ha, well that's being *too* cynical," said Gerald, and the car ran on through the mud.

"What is it, really?" said Gerald, turning to Gudrun.

This was an assumption of a sort of intimacy that exasperated Gudrun beyond words. It seemed to her that Gerald was purposely insulting her, and infringing on the decent privacy of them all.

"What is it?" she said, in her rough, callous voice. "Birkin wants a faithful submissive wife, and Ursula isn't moved that way at *all*."

"Is that it? One of Rupert's bees he's got in his bonnet, I suppose?"

"Exactly! That is the trouble, as it seems to me. Instead of wanting love from a woman, he wants his *ideas* fulfilled. Which, when it comes to actual life, is not good enough."

"Certainly not. The bee's stung him and sent him a bit askew this time." Then he seemed to glimmer in himself. "—You think love is enough, do you?" he asked.

"I think it is as much as you can expect," came Gudrun's voice, strident above the noise.

"And marriage is just thrown in, or not thrown in, as you please?"

"Marriage is a social arrangement you take advantage of when you are sufficiently in love," she said.

She could speak like a book, when the occasion came. His eyes were dancing on her all the time. She felt as if he were kissing her freely and mockingly. It made the colour burn in her cheeks, but her heart was quite firm and unfailing.

"You think Rupert is off the mark altogether, then?" Gerald asked.

Her eyes flashed with anger.

"Yes," she said, "I do. There is such a thing as two people being in love for the whole of their lives—and marrying. But the marriage is like the house they live in, an outward thing. The love is the all. And they are *both* lovers, equally."

"Yes," said Gerald. "That's how it strikes me. And what does Rupert say?"

"He says, in that case, a woman is a mistress, and not a wife, and the man is a lover, and not a husband. And he doesn't want a mistress, and he won't be a lover."

"He won't? Not safe enough?"

"I don't think it is a matter of safety. I'm sure a mistress is more likely to be faithful than a wife—just because she is her own mistress. No—he says he believes that a man and wife are one flesh, one body—of which the man is the head, and the woman is the bowels of compassion and love—or something to that effect."

Gerald laughed. Birkin sat motionless, driving the car. He could not hear what they were saying. And Gudrun, sitting immediately behind him, felt a sort of ironic pleasure in thus uncovering him.

"He says," she added, with a grimace of irony, "that you can't have two heads on one body."

"Neither can you," said Gerald. "Unless you are like the little boy in the story—'Mein Bruder er ist im Spiritus—er hat zwei Köpf!'"*

"Exactly," said Gudrun, with a little frown at the story.

"But it is a retrogressive position to take up," said Gerald.

"Oh, retrogressive! It is too obsolete."

Birkin, as he drove, felt a queer creeping of the spine, as if somebody was threatening his neck with a dagger. It began to rain. He was glad. He stopped the car and got down to put up the hood.

They came to the town, and left Gerald at the railway station. Gudrun and Winifred were to come to tea with Birkin, who expected Ursula also. In the afternoon, however, the first person to turn up was Hermione. Birkin was out, so she went in the drawing-room, looking at his books and papers, and playing the piano. Then Ursula arrived. She was surprised, unpleasantly so, to see Hermione, of whom she had heard nothing for some time.

"It is a surprise to see you," she said.

"Yes," said Hermione—"I've been away at Aix—"

"Oh, for your health?"

"Yes."

The two women looked at each other. Ursula resented Hermione's long, grave, downward-looking face. There was something of the stupidity and the unenlightened self-esteem of a horse in it. "She's got a horse-face," Ursula said to herself, "she runs between blinkers." It did seem as if Hermione, like the moon, had only one side to her penny. There was no obverse. She stared out all the time on the narrow, but to her complete world of the achieved consciousness. In the darkness, she did not exist. Like the moon, one half of her was lost to life. Her self was all in her head, she did not know what it was, spontaneously to run or move, like a fish in the water, or a weasel on the grass. She must always *know*.

But Ursula only suffered from Hermione's one sidedness. She only felt Hermione's cool confidence, which seemed to put her down as nothing. Hermione, who brooded and brooded till she was exhausted with the ache of her effort at consciousness, spent and ashen in her body, who gained so slowly and with such effort her hard and dead conclusions of knowledge, was apt, in the presence of other women, whom she thought simply female, to wear the conclusions of her bitter meditations like jewels which conferred on her an unquestionable distinction, established her in a higher order of life. She was apt, mentally, to condescend to women such as Ursula, whom she regarded as purely emotional. Poor Hermione, it was her one possession, this aching knowledge of hers, it was her only justification. She must be confident here, for God knows, she felt humble and deficient enough elsewhere. In the life of thought, of the spirit, she was one of the elect. And she wanted to be universal. But there was a devastating cynicism at the bottom of her. She did not believe in her own universals—they were sham. She did not believe in the inner life—it was a trick, not a reality. She did not believe in the spiritual world—it was an affectation. In the last resort, she believed in Mammon, the flesh, and the devil*—these at least were not sham. She was a priestess without belief, without conviction, suckled in a creed outworn,* and condemned to the reiteration of mysteries that were not real to her. Yet there was no escape for her. She was a leaf upon a dying tree. What help was there then, but to fight still for the old, withered truths, to die for the old, outworn belief, to be a sacred and inviolate priestess of desecrated mysteries? The old great truths *had* been true. And she was a leaf of the old great tree of knowledge, that was withering now. To the old and last truth then she must be faithful, even though cynicism and mockery took place at the bottom of her soul.

"I am so glad to see you," she said to Ursula, in her slow voice, that was like an incantation. "—You and Rupert have become quite friends?"

"Oh yes," said Ursula. "He is always somewhere in the background."

Hermione paused before she answered. She saw perfectly well the other woman's vaunt.

"Is he!" she said slowly, and with perfect equanimity. "And do you think you will marry?"

The question was so calm and mild, so simple and bare and dispassionate that Ursula was somewhat taken aback, rather attracted. It pleased her almost like a wickedness. It was like some delightful naked irony in Hermione.

"Well," replied Ursula, "*He* wants to badly enough, but I'm not so sure."

Hermione watched her with slow calm eyes. She noted this new expression of vaunting. How she envied Ursula a certain unconscious positivity!

"Why aren't you sure?" she asked, in her easy sing-song. She was perfectly at her ease, perhaps even rather happy in this conversation. "You don't really love him?"

Ursula flushed a little at the mild impertinence of this question. And yet she could not definitely take offence. Hermione seemed so calmly and sanely candid. After all, it was rather great to be able to be so sane.

"He says it isn't love he wants," she replied.

"What is it then?" Hermione was slow and level.

"He wants me really to submit to him in marriage."

Hermione was silent for some time, watching Ursula with slow, pensive eyes.

"Does he," she said at length, without expression. Then, rousing, "And what is it you don't want then? You don't want to marry?"

"It isn't that. I don't want to give the sort of *submission* he insists on having. He wants me to give myself up to him—and I simply don't feel that I *can*."

Again there was a long pause, before Hermione replied:

"Not if you don't want to." Then again there was silence. Hermione shuddered with a strange desire. Ah, if only he had asked *her* to subserve him, to be his slave! She shuddered with desire.

"You see I can't—"

"But exactly in what does—"

They had both begun at once, they both stopped. Then Hermione, assuming priority of speech, resumed as if wearily:

"To what does he want you to submit?"

"He says he wants me to take him on faith—to take it on faith that he is right, and to serve him in faith.—But I can't do that if I don't think he *is* right, can I?—and if he won't serve *me*, if he won't admit *my* being, my understanding? He says I *have* no understanding. Well—"

"No," said Hermione slowly. "You can't have faith at will."

And immediately Ursula doubted herself.

"Not only what he says," she resumed. "He wants me to accept *him* as—as an absolute—he wants to be both my life and his own—he wants to live for both of us—he doesn't want me to think, at all—"

There was a long pause, bitter for Hermione. Ah, if only he would have made this demand of her! Her he *drove* into thought, drove inexorably into knowledge—and then execrated her for it.

"He wants me to sink myself in him," Ursula resumed, "not to have any being of my own— —"

"Then why doesn't he marry an odalisk?" said Hermione in her mild sing-song, "if it is that he wants." Her long face looked sardonic and amused.

"Yes," said Ursula vaguely.—After all, to do him justice, he did *not* want an odalisk, he did not want a slave. Hermione would have been his slave—there was in her a passionate desire to prostrate herself before a man—the same desire that was so plain and so horrible in Charlotte Bronte.—Ursula shuddered, and realised that she was belying Birkin. He did not want her to prostrate herself, he wanted her to give herself to him, as she would give herself in the end, she knew.—But she felt so unsure. Would he acknowledge her? Would he acknowledge that their life was made of the two of them? or would he go on with his own private concerns, and use her for his own private satisfactions? That was what the other men had done. They had not wanted to combine with her, to produce a third thing, a true life, the product of both of them. They had wanted their old dead show, and they would not admit her, they turned all she was into nothingness. Just as Hermione now betrayed herself. As a woman Hermione was like a man, she believed only in men's things.

"Yes," said Hermione, as each woman came out of her own separate reverie. "It would be a mistake—I think it would be a mistake—"

"To marry him?" asked Ursula.

"Yes," said Hermione slowly—"I think you need a man—active, strong willed— —" Hermione held out her hand and clenched it with rhapsodic intensity. "You want a man like the Gothic heroes—to stand behind him as he rushes into battle, and see his strength, and hear his shout— —You need a man physically strong, and *virile* in his will, *not* a sensitive man— —" there was a break, as if the pythoness had uttered the oracle, and now the woman went on, in a rhapsody-wearied voice: "And you see, Rupert isn't this, he isn't. He is frail in health and body, he needs great, great care. Then he is so changeable and unsure of himself—it requires the greatest patience and understanding to help him. And I don't think you are patient. You would have to be prepared to suffer—dreadfully. I can't *tell* you how much suffering it would take to make him happy. He lives an *intensely* spiritual life, at times—too, too wonderful. And then come the reactions.—I can't speak of what I have been through with him.— —We have been together so long, I really do know him, I *do* know what he is.— —And I feel I must say it. I feel it would be perfectly disastrous for you to marry him—for you even more than for him."—Hermione lapsed into bitter reverie.—"He is so uncertain, so unstable—he wearies, and then reacts. I couldn't *tell* you what his reactions are. I couldn't tell you the agony of them.— — That which he affirms and loves one day—a little later he turns on it in a fury of destruction.— —He is never constant, always this awful, dreadful reaction.— —Always the quick change from good to bad, bad to good.—And nothing is so devastating, nothing— —"

"Yes," said Ursula humbly, "you must have suffered."

An unearthly light came on Hermione's face. She clenched her hand like one inspired.

"And one must be willing to suffer—willing to suffer for him hourly, daily—if you are going to help him, if he is to keep true to anything at all— —"

"And I don't *want* to suffer hourly and daily," said Ursula. "I don't, I should be ashamed. I think it is degrading not to be happy."

Hermione stopped and looked at her a long time.

"Do you," she said at last. And this utterance seemed to her a mark of Ursula's far distance from herself. For to Hermione suffering was the greatest reality, come what might.

"Yes," said Hermione, listlessly now, "I can only feel that it would be disastrous, disastrous— —at least, to marry in a hurry. Can't you be together without marriage? Can't you go away and live somewhere without marriage?—I do feel that marriage would be fatal, for both of you. I think for you even more than for him—and I think of his health— —"

"Of course," said Ursula, "*I* don't care about marriage—it isn't really important to me—it's he who wants it."

"It is his idea for the moment," said Hermione, with that weary finality, and a sort of *si jeunesse savait** infallibility.

There was a pause. Then Ursula broke into faltering challenge.

"You think I'm merely a physical woman, don't you?"

"No indeed," said Hermione. "No indeed. But I think you are vital and *young*—it isn't a question of years, or even of experience—it is almost a question of race. Rupert is race-old, he comes of an old race—and you are young, you come of a young, untutored race."

"Do I!" said Ursula.—"But I think he is awfully young, on one side."

"Yes, perhaps—childish in many respects. Nevertheless— —"

They both lapsed into silence. Ursula was filled with deep resentment of Hermione. "It isn't true," she said, silently addressing her adversary. "It isn't true. And it is *you* who want a physically strong, bullying man, not I. It is you who want an unsensitive man, not I. You *don't* know anything about Rupert, not really, in spite of the years you have had him. You don't give him a woman's love, you give him a man's love, and that is why he reacts away from you. You *don't* know. You only know the dead things. Any kitchen maid would know something about him, you don't know. What do you think your knowledge is but dead understanding, that doesn't mean a thing. You are so false, and untrue, how could you know anything? What is the good of your talking about love—you untrue spectre of a woman! How can you know anything, when you don't believe? You don't believe in yourself, and your own womanhood—so what good is your conceited, shallow cleverness—?"

The two women sat on in antagonistic silence. Hermione felt injured, that all her good intention, all her offering of her soul, only left the other woman in vulgar antagonism. But then, Ursula could not understand, never would understand, could never be more than the usual jealous and unreasonable female, with a good deal of powerful female emotion, female attraction, and a fair amount of female understanding, but no mind. Hermione had decided long ago that where there was no mind, it was useless to appeal for reason—one had merely to ignore the ignorant. And Rupert—he had now reacted towards the strongly female, healthy, selfish woman—it was his reaction for the time being—there was no helping it all. It was all a foolish backward and forward, a violent oscillation that would at length be too violent for his coherency, and he would smash and be dead. There was no saving him. This violent and directionless reaction between animalism and spiritual truth would go on in him till he tore himself in two between the opposite directions, and disappeared meaninglessly out of life. It was no good— —he too was without unity, without *mind*, in the ultimate stages of living; not quite man enough to make a destiny for a woman.

They sat on till Birkin came in and found them together. He felt at once the antagonism in the atmosphere, something radical and insuperable, and he bit his lip. But he affected a bluff manner.

"Hello, Hermione, are you back again? How do you feel?"

"Oh, better. And how are you—you don't look well—"

"No.—I believe Gudrun and Winnie Crich are coming in to tea. At least they said they were. We shall be a tea-party. What train did you come by, Ursula?"

It was rather pathetic to see him trying to placate both women at once. Both women watched him, Hermione with deep resentment and pity for him, Ursula very impatient. He was nervous and apparently in quite good spirits, chattering the conventional commonplaces. Ursula was amazed and indignant at the way he made small-talk; he was adept as any *fat** in Christendom. She became quite stiff, she could not answer. It all seemed to her so false and so belittling. And still Gudrun did not appear.

"I think I shall go to Florence for the winter," said Hermione at length.

"Will you?" he answered. "But it is so cold there."

"Yes, but I shall stay with Palestra. It is quite comfortable."

"What takes you to Florence?"

"I don't know," said Hermione slowly. Then she looked at him with her slow, heavy gaze. "Barnes is starting his school of aesthetics, and Olandese is going to give a set of discourses on the Italian national policy—"

"Both rubbish," he said.

"No, I don't think so," said Hermione. "I don't agree."

"Which do you admire, then?"

"I admire both. Barnes is a pioneer.—And then I am interested in Italy, in her coming to national consciousness."

"I wish she'd come to something better than national consciousness, then," said Birkin; "especially as it is bound to be a sort of commercial industrial consciousness. I hate Italy and her national rant.—And I think Barnes is an amateur."

Hermione was silent for some moments, in a state of hostility. But yet, she had got Birkin back again into her world! How subtle her influence was, she seemed to start his irritable attention into her direction exclusively, in one minute. He was her creature.

"No," she said, "you are wrong." Then a sort of tension came over her, she raised her face like the pythoness inspired with oracles, and went on, in rhapsodic manner: "il Sandro mi scrive che ha accolto il più grande entusiasmo, tutti i giovani, e fanciulle e ragazzi, sono appassionati, appassionati per l'Italia, e vogliono assolutamente imparare tutto—— "* She went on in Italian, as if, in thinking of the Italians she thought in their language.

He listened with a shade of distaste to her rhapsody, then he said:

"For all that, I don't like it. Their nationalism is just a vulgar emulation—that loathsome emulation I detest so much."

"I think you are wrong—I think you are wrong—" said Hermione. "It seems to me purely spontaneous and beautiful, the modern Italian's *passion*, for it is a passion, for Italy, L'Italia—"

"Do you know Italy well?" Ursula asked of Hermione. Hermione hated to be broken in upon in this manner. Yet she answered mildly:

"Yes, pretty well.——I spent several years of my girlhood there, with my mother.——My mother died in Florence."

"Oh."

There was a pause, painful to Ursula and to Birkin. Hermione however seemed abstracted and calm. Birkin was white, his eye glowed as if he were in a fever, he was far too overwrought. How Ursula suffered in this tense atmosphere of strained wills! Her head seemed bound round by iron bands.

Birkin rang the bell for tea. They would not wait for Gudrun any longer. When the door was opened, the cat walked in.

"Micio! Micio!" called Hermione, in her slow, deliberate sing-song. The young cat turned to look at her, then, with his slow and stately walk he advanced to her side.

"Vieni—vieni qua," Hermione was saying, in her strange caressive, protective voice, as if she were always the elder, the mother superior. "Vieni dire Buon Giorno alla zia. Mi ricorde, mi ricorde bene—non è vero, piccolo? È vero che mi ricordi? È vero?"* And slowly she rubbed his head, slowly and with ironic indifference.

"Does he understand Italian?" said Ursula, who knew nothing of the language.

"Yes," said Hermione at length. "His mother was Italian. She was born in my waste-paper basket, in Florence, on the morning of Rupert's birthday. She was his birthday present."

Tea was brought in. Birkin poured out for them. It was strange how inviolable was the intimacy which existed between him and Hermione.

Ursula felt that she was an outsider. The very tea-cups and the old silver was a bond between Hermione and Birkin. It seemed to belong to an old, past world which they inhabited together, and in which Ursula was a foreigner. She was almost a parvenue in their old conventional world. Her convention was not their convention, their standards were not her standards. But theirs were established, they had the sanction and the grace of age. He and she together, Hermione and Birkin, were people of the same old tradition, the same withered, deadening culture. And she, Ursula, was an intruder. So they always made her feel.

Hermione poured a little cream into a saucer. The simple way she assumed her rights in Birkin's room maddened and discouraged Ursula. There was a fatality about it, as if it were bound to be. Hermione lifted the cat and put the cream before him. He planted his two paws on the edge of the table and bent his graceful young head to drink.

"Siccuro che capisce italiano," sang Hermione, "non l'avrà dimenticato, la lingua della Mamma."

She lifted the cat's head with her long, slow white fingers, not letting him drink, holding him in her power. It was always the same, this joy in power she manifested, peculiarly in power over any male being. He blinked forbearingly, with a male, bored expression, licking his whiskers. Hermione laughed in her short, grunting fashion.

"Ecco, il bravo ragazzo, come è superbo, questo!"*

She made a vivid picture, so calm and strange with the cat. She had a true static impressiveness, she was a social artist in some ways.

The cat refused to look at her, indifferently avoided her fingers, and began to drink again, his nose down to the cream, perfectly balanced, as he lapped with his odd little click.

"It's a bad business, teaching him to eat at table," said Birkin.

"Yes," said Hermione, easily assenting.

Then, looking down at the cat, she resumed in her old, mocking, humorous sing-song:

"Ti imparano fare brutte cose, brutte cose——"

She lifted the Mino's white chin on her fore-finger, slowly. The young cat looked round with a supremely forbearing air, avoided seeing anything, withdrew his chin, and began to wash his face with his paw. Hermione grunted her laughter, pleased.

"Bel giovanotto——"* she said.

The cat reached forward again and put his fine white paw on the edge of the saucer. Hermione lifted it down with delicate slowness. This deliberate, delicate carefulness of movement reminded Ursula of Gudrun.

"No. Non è permesso di mettere il zampino nel tondinetto. Non piace al babbo. Un signor gatto così selvatico dispiace molto a lui."*

And she kept her finger on the softly planted paw of the cat, and her voice had the same whimsical, humorous note of bullying.

Ursula was miserable. She wanted to go away now. It all seemed no good. Hermione was established for ever, she herself was ephemeral and had not yet even arrived.

"I will go now," she said suddenly.

Birkin looked at her in fear—he so dreaded her anger.

"But there is no need for such hurry," he said.

"Yes," she answered. "I will go." And turning to Hermione, before there was time to say any more, she held out her hand and said: "Goodbye."

"Goodbye—" sang Hermione, detaining the hand. "Must you really go now?"

"Yes, I think I'll go," said Ursula, her face set, and averted from Hermione's eyes.

"You think you will— —"

But Ursula had got her hand free. She turned to Birkin with a quick, almost jeering: "Goodbye," and she was opening the door before he had time to do it for her.

When she got outside the house she ran down the road in fury and agitation. It was strange, the unreasoning rage and violence Hermione roused in her, by her very presence. Ursula knew she gave herself away to the other woman, she knew she looked ill-bred, uncouth, exaggerated. But she did not care. She only ran up the road, lest she should go back and jeer in the faces of the two she had left behind. For they outraged her.

It was only the next day when Birkin sought Ursula out. It happened to be the half-day at the Grammar-School. He appeared towards the end of the morning, and asked her, would she drive with him in the afternoon. She consented. But her face was closed and unresponsing, and his heart sank.

The afternoon was fine and dim. He was driving the motor-car, and she sat beside him. But still her face was closed against him, unresponsing. When she became like this, like a wall against him, his heart contracted with dread.

His life seemed so shorn away, there was little left that attached him to his fellow men, little that connected him with life at all. He felt on the brink of failure, hopelessness, and dissolution, his health gone, and his vitality, which, in spite of his frail physique, had always been so abundant, now wasted and almost spent. One step further, and he was finished. The hope that still held him integral would break, and he would be finished.

Abstract, almost inhuman in his extremity, his blind instinct led him to placate her, to try to win her. But everything in him was so darkened, he had barely a normal consciousness left, he could scarcely say the ordinary things.

"Look," he said, "what I bought."

And he gave her a little bit of screwed-up paper. She took it and opened it.

"How lovely!" she cried.

She examined the gift.

"How perfectly lovely!" she cried again. "But why do you give them me?"

He caught his underlip between his teeth, his face was white and obsessed.

"I wanted to," he said.

"But why? Why should you?"

"I wanted to," he repeated.

There was a silence, whilst she examined the rings that had been screwed up in the paper.

"I think they are *beautiful*," she said, "especially this. This is wonderful—"

It was a large round opal, red and fiery, set in a circle of tiny rubies.

"You like that best?" he said.

"I think I do."

"I like the sapphire," he said.

"This?"

It was a rose-shaped, beautiful sapphire, with small brilliants.

"Yes," she said, "it *is* lovely." She held it in the light. "Yes, perhaps it *is* the best—"

"The blue—" he said.

"Yes, wonderful—"

He suddenly swung the car out of the way of a farm-cart. It tilted on the bank. He was a careless driver, yet very accurate. But Ursula was frightened. There was always that diabolic streak in him which terrified her. She suddenly felt he might kill her, by making some dreadful accident with the motor-car. For a moment she was stony with fear.

"Isn't it rather dangerous, the way you drive?" she asked him.

"No, it isn't dangerous," he said. And then, after a pause: "Don't you like the yellow ring at all?"

It was a squarish topaz set in a frame of steel, or some other similar mineral, finely wrought.

"Yes," she said, "I do like it. But why did you buy three rings?"

"I wanted them. They are second-hand."

"You bought them for yourself?"

"No. Rings look wrong on my hands."

"Why did you buy them then?"

"I bought them to give to you."

"But why? Surely you ought to give them to Hermione! You belong to her."

He did not answer. She remained with the jewels shut in her hand. She wanted to try them on her finger, but something in her would not let her. And moreover, she was afraid her hands were too large, she shrank from the mortification of a failure to put them on any but her little finger. They travelled in silence through the empty lanes.

Driving in a motor-car excited her, she forgot his presence even.

"Where are we?" she asked suddenly.

"Not far from Worksop."

"And where are we going?"

"Anywhere."

It was the answer she liked.

She opened her hand to look at the rings. They gave her *such* pleasure, as they lay, the *three* circles, with their knotted jewels, entangled in her palm. She would have to try them on. She did so secretly, trying not to let him see, so that he should not know her finger was too large for them. But he saw nevertheless, and was glad.

Only the opal, with its thin wire loop, would go on her ring finger. And she was superstitious. No, there was ill-portent enough, she would not accept this ring from him in pledge.

"Look," she said, putting forward her hand, that was half-closed and shrinking. "The others don't fit me."

He looked at the red-glinting, soft stone, on her over-sensitive skin.

"Yes," he said.

"But opals are unlucky, aren't they?" she said wistfully.

"No. Nothing is unlucky. There's no such thing as luck. What one likes, is lucky—what one doesn't like, is unlucky."

"But why?" she laughed.

And, consumed with desire to see how the other rings would look on her hand, she put them on her little finger.

"They can be made a little bigger," he said.

"Yes," she replied, doubtfully. And she sighed. She knew that, in accepting the rings, she was accepting a pledge. Yet fate seemed more than herself. She looked again at the jewels. They were very beautiful to her eyes—not as ornament, or wealth, but as tiny fragments of loveliness.

"I'm glad you bought them," she said, putting her hand, half unwilling, gently on his arm.

He smiled, abstractedly. He was very much afraid of her, lest she should refuse to join with him. If she refused the union with him, he had failed in life, he had only known the terrible process of death, in which he was fulfilled. Her reluctant, over-sensitive, tentative movements towards him were so precious, and he was so terrified that she would withdraw again—for she was like some shrinking, unrealised creature that had never yet come forth, and of which he had even no living knowledge—that he could not answer, he could only wait in an agony of suspense.

She now became very happy. The motor-car ran slowly and easily, the afternoon was soft and dim, she chattered happily about people, about Gudrun, about Gerald. He answered vaguely. He was not very much interested any more in personalities and in people—people were all different, but they were all enclosed in a definite limitation, he said; the permutations and combinations of the given possibilities were numberless, but the terms given were limited, and known: you never knew what the next pattern in the kaleidoscope would be, but you knew the kaleidoscope and every fragment it contained only too well. And every human being was contained within the kaleidoscope. Therefore people were not vitally interesting—they were really all known beforehand. None of them transcended the given terms.

Ursula did not agree—people were still an adventure to her—but—perhaps not as much as she tried to persuade herself. Perhaps too she was merely going on mechanically, superficially, in her interest. There was an under-space in her where she did not care for people and their idiosyncrasies. She seemed to touch for a moment this undersilence in herself, she became still, and she cleaved for a moment to Birkin.

"Won't it be lovely to go home in the dark?" she said. "We might have tea rather late—shall we?—and have high tea?—wouldn't that be rather nice?"

"I promised to be at Shortlands for dinner," he said.

"But—it doesn't matter—you can go tomorrow—."

"Hermione is there," he said, in rather an uneasy voice. "She is going away in two days. I suppose I ought to say goodbye to her—"

Ursula drew away, closed in a violent silence. He knitted his brows, and his eyes began to stare again in tortured conflict.

"You don't mind, do you?" he asked irritably.

"No, I don't care—why should I?—Why should I mind?"

Her tone was jeering and terrible.

"That's what I ask myself," he said; "why *should* you mind! But you seem to." His brows were tense with unbearable irritation.

"I *assure* you I don't, I don't mind in the least. Go where you belong—it's what I want you to do."

"Ah you fool!" he cried, "with your 'go where you belong.' It's finished between Hermione and me. She means much more to *you*, if it comes to that, than she does to me. For you can only revolt in pure reaction from her—and to be her opposite is to be her counterpart."

"Ah, opposite!" cried Ursula. "I know your dodges. I am not taken in by your word-twisting. You belong to Hermione and her dead show.—Well, if you do, you do. I don't blame you. But then you've nothing to do with me."

In his inflamed, overwrought exasperation, he stopped the car, and they sat there, in the middle of the country lane, to have it out. It was a war to the death between them, so they did not see the ridiculousness of their situation.

"If you weren't a fool, if only you weren't a fool," he cried in bitter despair, "you'd see that one could be decent, even where one has been wrong. I *was* wrong to go on all those years with Hermione—it was a deathly process. But after all, one can have a little human decency.—But no, you would tear my soul out with your jealousy, at the very mention of Hermione's name."

"I jealous! *I*—jealous! You *are* mistaken if you think that. I'm not jealous in the least of Hermione, she is nothing to me, not *that*!" And Ursula snapped her fingers. "No, it's you who are a liar. It's you who must return, like a dog to his vomit.* It is what Hermione *stands for* that I *hate*, I *hate* it, it is lies, it is false, it is death.—But you want it, you can't help it, you can't help yourself. You belong to that old, deathly way of living—then go back to it.—But don't come to me, for I've nothing to do with it."

And in the stress of her violent emotion, she got down from the car and went to the hedgerow, picking unconsciously some flesh-pink spindle berries, some of which were burst, showing their orange seeds.

"Ah, you are a fool," he cried, blindly.

"Yes, I am. I *am* a fool. And thank God for it. I'm too big a fool to swallow your clevernesses, God be praised. You go to your clever women—go to them—they are your sort. You've always had a string of them trailing after you—and you always will. Go to your spiritual brides—but don't come to me for your common needs, because I'm not having any, thank you.—You're not satisfied, aren't you? Your spiritual brides can't give you what you want, they aren't common and fleshly enough for you, aren't they? So you come to me, and keep them in the background! You will marry me, for daily use. But you'll keep yourself well provided with spiritual brides, in the background.—I know your dirty little game." Suddenly a flame ran over her, and she stamped her foot madly on the road, and he winced, afraid she would strike him. "And *I*, *I'm* not spiritual enough, *I'm* not as spiritual as that Hermione—!" Her brows knitted, her eyes blazed like a tiger's. "Then go to her, that's all I say, go to her, go.—Ha, she spiritual—*spiritual*, she! A dirty materialist as she is. *She* spiritual?—What does she care for, what *is* her spirituality? What *is* it?" Her fury seemed to blaze out and burn his face. He shrank a little. "I tell you it's *dirt*, *dirt*, and nothing *but* dirt.—And it's dirt you want, you crave for it.—Spiritual! Is *that* spiritual, her bullying, her conceit, her sordid materialism? She's a fishwife, a fishwife, she is such a materialist. And all so sordid. What does she work out to, in the end, with all her social passion, as you call it. Social passion—what social passion has she?—show it me!—where is it? She wants petty, immediate *power*, she wants the illusion that she is a great woman, that is all.—In her soul she's a common unbeliever, common as dirt. That's what she is at the bottom. And all the rest is *pretence*—but you love it. You love the sham spirituality, it's your food. Then have it."

She turned away, spasmodically tearing the twigs of spindle berry from the hedge, and fastening them, with vibrating fingers, in the bosom of her coat.

"Really," he said at length, half stunned, "this is merely degrading."

"Yes, it's merely degrading," she said. "But more to me than to you."

"Since you choose to degrade yourself," he said. Again the flash came over her face, the yellow lights concentrated in her eyes.

"*You!*" she cried. "You! You truth-lover! you purity-monger! It *stinks*, your truth and your purity. It stinks of the offal you feed on, you scavenger dog, you eater of corpses.—You are foul, *foul*—and you must know it. Your purity, your candour, your goodness—yes thank you, we've had some. What you are is a foul, deathly thing, obscene, that's what you are, obscene and perverse.—You, and love! You may well say you don't want love. No, you want *yourself*, and dirt, and death—that's what you want. And then—"

"There's a bicycle coming," he said, in torture under her loud denunciation.

She glanced down the road.

"I don't care," she cried.

Nevertheless she was silent. The cyclist, having heard the voices raised in altercation, glanced curiously at the man, and the woman, and at the standing motor car, as he passed.

"—Afternoon," he said, cheerfully.

"Good-afternoon," replied Birkin coldly.

They were silent as the man passed into the distance.

A grey look, expressionless and dead, had come over Birkin's face.

"And all this," he said, in his satirical, dreary way, "because I am going to dinner with Hermione Roddice at Shortlands tonight."

"No, not at all, not in the least," she replied. "I don't care in the least where you go.—But," and her voice sprang into flame, "I say it because it is *true*, do you see, because you are *you*, a foul and false liar, a whited sepulchre. That's why I say it. And you, hear it."

"And be grateful," he added, with a satirical grimace.

"Yes," she cried, "and if you have a spark of decency in you, be grateful."

"Not having a spark of decency, however—" he retorted.

"No," she cried, "you haven't a *spark*. And so you can go your way, and I'll go mine. It's no good, not the slightest.—So you can leave me now, I don't want to go any further with you—leave me—."

"You don't even know where you are," he said.

"Oh, don't bother, I assure you I shall be all right. I've got ten shillings in my purse, and that will take me back from anywhere *you* have brought me to." She hesitated. The rings were still on her fingers, two on her little finger, one on her ring finger. Still she hesitated.

"Very good," he said. "The only hopeless thing is a fool."

"You are quite right," she said.

Still she hesitated. Then an ugly, malevolent look came over her face, she pulled the rings from her fingers, and tossed them at him. One hit his face, the others hit his coat, and they scattered into the mud.

"And take your rings," she said, "and go and buy yourself a female elsewhere—there are plenty to be had, who will be quite glad to be rid of your spiritual mess, to leave it to a Hermione."

With which she walked away, desultorily, up the road. He stood motionless, watching her sullen, rather ugly walk. She was sullenly picking and pulling at the twigs of the hedge as she passed. She grew smaller, she seemed to pass out of his life. A darkness came over his mind. Only a small, mechanical speck of consciousness hovered near him.

He felt tired and weak. He went and sat on the bank. She would come back. It was true, perhaps, what she said. Perhaps it was all true. But what did it matter! Granted it was all true—it did not alter the other truths. She would have to come back. There was a surviving truth. His heart, everything, had died in a moment of complete extinction. Now he felt still surviving the tension between him and her. She would come back. She was life, and all the rest was death. There was this thread of life, that connected him and her. All the rest was death.

He could not bear to see the rings lying in the pale mud of the road. He picked them up, and wiped them unconsciously on his hands. They were the little tokens of the connection between him and her.—But he had made his hands all dirty and gritty.

There was a darkness over his mind. The terrible knot of consciousness that had persisted there like an obsession was broken, gone, his life was dissolved in darkness over his limbs and his body. But the knot of anxiety was in his heart now. Perhaps she had gone for ever. He breathed lightly and regularly like an infant, that breathes innocently, beyond the touch of responsibility.

She was coming back. He saw her drifting desultorily under the high hedge, advancing towards him slowly. He did not move, he did not look again. He was as if asleep, at peace, slumbering and utterly relaxed.

She came up and stood before him, hanging her head.

"See what a flower I found you," she said, wistfully, holding a piece of purple-red bell-heather under his face. He saw the clump of coloured bells, and the tree-like, tiny branch: also her hands, with their over-fine, over sensitive skin.

"A pretty one," he said, vacantly, taking the flower. He sat looking at it unseeing.

Then a hot impulse of submission and strength filled into his heart. He stood up and looked into her face. It was new and oh, so delicate in its luminous wonder and fear. He put his arms round her, and she hid her face on his shoulder.

It was peace, peace at last, as he stood folding her to his heart there on the open lane. It was peace at last. His empty, barren cup was filled full at last, his soul was strong and at rest.

She looked up at him. The wonderful yellow light in her eyes now was soft and yielded, they were at peace with each other. He kissed her, softly, many, many times. A laugh came into her eyes.

"Did I schimpf* you?" she asked, using the German word for "scold."

He smiled too, and took her hand, that was so soft and given.

"Never mind," she said, "it is all for the good."

He kissed her again, softly, many times.

"Isn't it?" she said.

"All for the good," he repeated, docile.

She laughed suddenly, with a wild catch in her voice, and flung her arms round him.

"You are mine, my love, aren't you?" she cried, straining him close.

"Yes," he said, softly. "And you're mine."

His voice was so soft and final, she went very still, as if under a fate which had taken her. She did not acquiesce—but it was accomplished without her acquiescence. He was kissing her quietly, repeatedly, with a soft, still happiness she almost envied him.

"My love!" she cried, lifting her face and looking into his with eyes all a dazzle of yellow, excitable light. But his eyes were beautiful and soft and immune from passion or excitement, sure and impersonal like a dark, changeless sky. She hid her face on his shoulder, hiding before him, because he could see her so completely. She knew he loved her, and she was afraid, she was in a strange element, a new heaven round about her. She wished he were passionate, because in passion she was at home. But this was so big and frightening, as space is more frightening than force.

Again, quickly, she lifted her head.

"Do you love me?" she said, quickly, impulsively.

"Yes," he replied, not heeding her motion, only her stillness.

She knew it was true. She broke away.

"So you ought," she said, turning round to look at the road. "Did you pick up the rings?"

"Yes."

"Where are they?"

"In my pocket."

She was restless.

"Shall we go," she said.

"Yes," he answered. And they mounted the car once more, and left behind them this memorable battle-field.

They drifted through the mild, late afternoon, in a beautiful motion that was all peace and fulfilment. His mind was relaxed, the life flowed through him like a creative sleep, a sleep of life along all his limbs and body.

"Are you happy?" she asked him suddenly.

"Yes," he said.

"So am I," she cried in sudden ecstasy, putting her arm round him and clutching him violently against her, as he steered the motor-car.

"Don't drive much more," she said. "I know it isn't good for you."

"It isn't," he said. "But we'll finish this little journey, and then we'll be free."

"We will, my love, we will," she cried in delight, kissing him as he turned to her.

He drove on in a loose, warm, living sleep, all his muscles soft and given to the swinging of the road. It was a pleasure also to guide the car like this, not from his mind, but from his blood, as a bird flies, all his physical being adjusting itself to all the variations of the physical world.

They dropped down a long hill in the dusk, and suddenly Ursula recognised on her right hand, below in the hollow, the form of Southwell Minster.

"Are we here!" she cried with pleasure.

The rigid, sombre, ugly cathedral was settling under the gloom of the coming night, as they entered the narrow town, the golden lights showed like slabs of revelation, in the shop-windows.

"Father came here with mother," she said, "when they first knew each other. He loves it—he loves the minster. Do you?"

"Yes. It looks like quartz crystals sticking up out of the dark hollow. We'll have our high tea at the Saracen's Head."

As they descended, they heard the Minster bells playing a hymn, when the hour had struck six.

> "Glory to thee my God this night
> For all the blessings of the light— —"*

So, to Ursula's ear, the tune fell out, drop by drop, from the unseen sky on to the dusky town. It was like dim, bygone centuries sounding. The past was so far off. She stood in the old yard of the inn, smelling of straw and stables and petrol. Above, she could see the first stars. Where was she? This was no actual world, it was the dream-world of one's expectation—rather frightening also.

They sat together in a little parlour by the fire.

"Is it true?" she said, doubtfully.

"What?"

"Everything—I can't believe you love me even now."

"What a Thomasine!*—Do believe it then. I know you love me," he said.

"Do you? Do I love you? Are you sure?" she asked, for she was mortally frightened. It seemed to haunt her like a dark nightmare, that she would wake up to find she did not love, that she was not beloved, that it was all hallucination. Her eyes, so wide with fear and wonder and strained with years of tension, looked up at him like frightening flowers. She was so beautiful, and so like a flower that for years has not been able to open, but has shrunk back in bud, away from the bitter air, and which now unfolds with anguish of fear and timidity, delivered up out of its own safe-keeping. She felt she was being delivered out of her own safe, enclosed keeping. And she could not, she could not allow it, she must draw back.

Seeing her flower-like, frightened face dilated and upturned to him in cruel doubt, he remembered all the torture of the way here, the years of coming to this yielding-up. But it all seemed behind now, he seemed to have a new, star-like being, that was beyond suffering, so strange and steadfast and absolved.

"Yes," he said, kissing her fresh cheeks. "*I* know you love me."

"*Do* I?" she asked, looking up at him with a brow tortured by misgiving, a sort of hopelessness.

"Yes," he said, indifferently, hardly heeding her fears, though she knew, by the glance of his eyes over her face, that he saw it. But the other truth, the certainty, was so present, this anguish of doubt in her left him unmoved, only gentle towards her. His finger-tips went delicately, finely over her face. They seemed to take away her fear, almost like removing a veil.

"And do you love me?" she asked, her heart bounding with joy.

"I do."

"Sure?"

Her face was now one dazzle of released, golden light, as she looked up at him, and clutched her arms round his legs as he stood near her. He bent down and kissed her softly on her wide, happy mouth. She was so happy, so released, she could hardly bear it. Ah, the awful prison of her life! Could it be true that she was liberated?

It was true. She knew he was sure. She knew by his eyes, that were so steady and infinite. They seemed to envelop her as the sky envelops a bird. She knew it was true. Her heart leaped in her breast, as if it would burst with magnificence, as a rocket, high up in the night, bursts with a great cloud of beautiful gold flakes of light.

"My love," she cried, lifting her face to him, her eyes, her mouth open in transport.

"My love," he whispered, bending and kissing her, always kissing her, rather frightened and unsure in this new land.

She knew he was frightened. She recovered herself, and sat still, saying:

"I'm so happy—are you?"

"Yes, I am happy," he said.

"Quite?"

He nodded to her. And he knew that it was the first time in his life he had ever been happy, as flowers are happy, as the heedless things of the earth are happy. He had known ecstasy and delight before, but now, for the first time, he knew the grace of happiness, the strange, immortal serenity.

"Where are the rings?" she cried suddenly. "Give them to me."

He rose and got them. She cleaned them assiduously with her handkerchief and a hair-pin, to remove all the grains of sand and the traces of mud.

"I like them all," she said. "I shan't have any special one for *the* ring— you know—"

The last two words she said with bright significance, as if to say "You understand what I mean by *the* ring."

"Three rings for one man," he said.

"Oh more—there's still another."

"Yes—four," he said.

"Four rings for one man! It ought to be enough!" she cried in delight. "Better than four men to one ring, any way.—Isn't it, my love?—Give me a kiss."

He kissed her, wondering over her last speech, and they sat down to the collation provided. There was cold chicken, and ham, and water-cress, and beet-root, and cheese, and butter, and cream, and little apple tarts, and a silver tea-pot with tea.

"What *good* things!" she cried with pleasure. "Give me some, quick, quick!—Shall I pour out the tea?—I *do* hope I shan't make a mess on the beautiful cloth. I'm so bad at these things.—The angel, it pours beautifully! I like these tea-pots with proud thin spouts—they look so proud, don't they?—I'm so happy, my love—"

The golden lights danced like wine in her eyes. He smiled at her across the table.

"We'll write our resignations here—chuck up our jobs here, shall we?" he said.

She was startled, and wondering.

"What? Write out our resignations here? You mean give up school?— And you your inspecting? Do you want to?"

"I do. I've done with the world. I'm going into another life now, leave the world and begin the life of happiness."

She looked at him doubtfully across the table.

"*Are* you?" she said, slowly. "Are you going to make me be an anchorite and a hermitess, and you an ascetic? Don't—I don't want to. Promise you won't be an ascetic. You are so terribly extreme."

"Not an ascetic—only happy," he said. His voice could be so soft and happy-go-lucky, it seemed to touch her veins as if she were a harp.

"Only happy—*my love*!" she echoed in delight, thrusting her hand across the table to him. He kissed her fingers.

"But we must leave the world," he persisted.

"Must we?" she said, wrinkling her brows.

"The world is big and wrong," he said. "One must make one's way out of it."

She meditated.

"But where can one go?" she asked, anxiously. "After all, there *is* only the world, so long as we are human beings."

"Ah no," he said. "There is the world of humanity, and the world of space and truth and living reality. One need renounce nothing but humanity. The human world is a lie from beginning to end. I don't want any more to acquiesce in the lie. There is a world I do want."

Still she meditated.

"You see, my love," she said, "I'm so afraid that while we are only people, we've got to take the world that's given—because there isn't any other."

"Yes there is," he said. "There are kingdoms inside you and me—a new heaven and a new earth.—But don't be frightened—I only want to go some distance off, and turn my back on the world, and my face to the open space, and take the new heaven and the new earth that lies in front— put up a flagstaff in it, so to speak.—You see, though you do scoff at my saying it, I believe that desire is holy, and the deepest desire is the holiest, but the little desire is holy too.—I want you to think, that *whatever* you really want, whatever it is, it is yours by rights, and you are to take it if you can get it.—Only do believe me, that one doesn't want the world any more—one has had enough, more than enough. One wants another, truer world, freedom to live from the bottom-most desire of one's heart, and freedom not to lie. In the world, one must lie—one *is* a lie—"

The last sentence was a cry of anguish, a lament. Ursula did not see, specifically, what he meant, but her soul understood.

"Yes," she said, "it *is* a lie. They all live for outside things they don't even believe in—and it is true, one has to be the same."

"One has. If I talk to a man, God knows how many falsities I have to utter and acquiesce in. Because the whole thing is dead. No man has anything to say to me, really. He won't allow himself to admit that the world is worthless—and there is nothing to say till you've said that."

But Ursula was thinking by herself.

"How lovely!" she said. "We will have a little house near the sea—Where? In England?"

"I don't care. No, not England. Not my native land. That is above all the old dead world one must leave.—We'll wander till we find a place."

"How lovely!—And begin today."

A slight shade crossed his face.

"Begin today, if you like," he said.

"How lovely!—And I can have a nice little house, and have the curtains *just* as I like—?"

"Just!"

"How perfect!—You know, my love, I don't care about the world. J'en ai soupé*—and a nasty mouthful it's been.—But I may go to London sometimes to the music-hall, mayn't I? I love it so."

"It bores me. But you do as you like."

"Sure?—I'm so frightened of you! I know what a Mogul you are by nature—aren't you? I believe you only say 'desire is all', because you are naturally the most awful tyrant, and you want to avoid the pitfall of your own inclination—Isn't that so, my love?"

"Perhaps," he said. "But that doesn't alter the fact that desire *is* holy."

"No, it wouldn't," she teased, "since it is your dictum."

"But the deepest desire is for perfect truth in our lives—the free inner life, and a pure, truthful relation with all things and all men."

"Yes, my love!—" she mocked. "Have you finished your high tea? Shall we write our resignations?"

"Yes," he said.

He rang the bell, and ordered note-paper without a printed address. The waiter cleared the table.

"Now then," he said, "yours first. Put your home address, and the date—then 'Director of Education, Town Hall—Sir—' Now then!—I don't know how one really stands—I suppose one could get out of it in less than a month—Anyhow 'Sir—I beg to resign my post as class-mistress in the Willey Green Grammar School. As I wish to go abroad immediately, I should be very grateful if you would liberate me from my duties as soon as possible, without waiting for the expiration of my month's notice.'—That'll do. Have you got it? Let me look. 'Ursula Brangwen.' Good! Now I'll write mine. I ought to give them three months, but I can plead health. I can arrange it all right."

He sat and wrote out his formal resignation.

"Now," he said, when the envelopes were sealed and addressed, "shall we post them here, both together?—I know Jackie will say 'Here's a coincidence!', when he receives them in all their identity. Never mind— let him."

"Isn't it rather horrid, if everybody knows?" she said.

"How do you feel?"

"I feel I don't want them to. It isn't their affair."

"Neither is it," he said. "We'll post yours, and I'll take mine in tomorrow myself to Jackie. Then there will be no coincidence. I don't want anybody to speak to me about you. It's got nothing to do with them."

"It hasn't, has it?" she said.

She lifted her face to him, all shining and open. It was as if he might enter straight in to the source of her radiance. His face contracted a little, and he looked aside.

"Shall we go?" he said.

"As you like," she replied.

But there was a torment in him now. Seeing her all radiant and open to him, the old, destructive passion began to seethe in his veins again. It was the salt, delicious foam of Aphrodite that filled his nostrils, and again he began to swoon in the ecstasy of poignant desire. But underneath, he cried out like a prisoner, like one who feels himself relapsing into a vicious habit. It was not this, not this he wanted with her—not the poignant ecstasies of sex passion. Yet he did want them also, with an old craving of habit. And the desire seemed like death to him. For beyond this was the small, yearning hope of a new sort of love, a new sort of intercourse, that was gentle and still and so happy, it was chastity and innocence of itself. This, this new, gentle possession, should be the true consummation of their marriage. Yet, seeing the lovely open flower of her face, shaking with exquisite lights like an offering, and nothing debarred to him, he felt the old madness of lust coming up again, the old sensual fire leaped in his veins, it would be the old, fierce, destroying embrace.

He had better tell her—better have everything open, and accept the inevitable.

"I am so afraid of passion any more," he said to her, baffled.

Her face went still with wonder.

"Afraid of it,—why?" She asked.

"It has been so much—one has had so much passion—I have had enough."

Her brows knitted, it seemed to him, with a little disappointment.

"Why have you had enough—with whom?" she asked. Then, with a touch of malice. "With Hermione?"

"Hermione? With her also.—Ah, you don't know the women, what is the good of my talking about them—just as I don't know your men—"

"But you do, all of them," she said.

"Yes, their names. You know as much of my women.—It doesn't interest me. It bores me. It is the past. I am tired of it, tired of l'amour, l'amour. J'en ai soupé, as you are so fond of saying. I want something else."

"So do I," she said, in contradiction. "I want something different—but it is always *love*—unless you want—heaven knows what you want—"

"I am frightened of passion, of that sort of love," he cried in distress. "It is a friction, a breaking down, a destruction. There is enough of breaking down and destruction—let it be something else—"

She looked at him, at his drawn, tormented face, in wonder.

"But yes—I don't make it anything, do I? I don't ask you for passion, do I, if you don't want it!"

Her face was all wondering and dismayed. He pulled himself up. He was so terrified of himself, that he was accusing *her* of being a temptress. He recovered from his panic.

"You are tired of passion, too, aren't you?" he asked wistfully.

"You mean—what do you mean?"

"I only mean of that *way* of having a man—the sensual excitement—the violent passion."

"But can it be passionless?" She asked, in some mocking opposition.

"Different—different," he cried in lamentation. He had broken down now, and was like an infant crying in the night.* "It only hurts one, that old way.—One should be soft, and all gentle, and so near, so near—."

His brow was twisted, his eyes full of torment. Like a dram-drinker who smells alcohol, he felt the madness of violent desire going over his brain, and his soul was in anguish. She watched him in wonder. She had not been prepared for this. She felt as if he accused her, accused her of some harlotry.

"But I know," she said, in remonstrance. "I don't *want* you to be violent. What makes you imagine it?—I thought you loved me—"

He recovered, and looked straight at her.

"I do love you," he said. "That's why I don't want to take you as a mistress—never—not even once."

"But I don't want you to," she protested.

"Nay, are you sure?" he replied. "*Don't* you want passion?—the extremities of passion? Have you had them?—because I've had mine.— But still—" he stiffened, and looked aside—"if you haven't, if you're not satisfied in that way—you have a perfect right to me in any way you want. You have a perfect right to what you want of me—whatever it is."

There leaped up in his heart the subtle hope, that she would accept him, demand of him this satisfaction. The old demon-like desire for sensual ecstasy overcame him with violence. Still, the choice should be with her—the responsibility should again be with Eve.

She looked at him almost aghast. She too knew what he meant, what he offered—that terrible intoxication of sensual extremity. Over her, too, as over him, it exerted the ultimate fascination, the spell. To be gone with him in that violent conflict of sensual ecstasy—ah, her nerves quivered with keen desirous bliss at the suggestion. But having seen his face, the torment, the twisting of evil: having seen so plainly the sinister and marvellous serpent glide from his mouth, she was shocked, startled into reflection. She would have to choose now, and choose deliberately. She waited for the beating of her heart to tell what she chose.

"But one can't decide these things in this fashion," she said, rather indignant. "One can't be so deliberate. It is indecent. We must take what comes."

"Ah no," he said, "one chooses. At length, one must choose. I know one must. The leaving one way for another must be an act of choice, an act of volition."

"Oh no," she said. "It happens."

"Yes—the very choice 'happens'—when one has had enough—more than enough—unless one chooses death—"

"And what have you had enough of?" she asked.

"Of physical passion—you know—the top note of joy in— voluptuousness, animal ecstasy—call it what you like.—At least I *think* I have had enough." He would leave himself this loophole. Then he tried to retract. "I only know this, that I *do* want something else—the other—the pure coming together, flowing together. That I have never had, and it is my heart's desire. Whereas I *have* had the top note of physical passion—which is a process of ecstasy by friction, a reaction, a reduction one against the other. I *know* that—whether I have finished with it—heaven help us, I don't know—"

"And I don't know," she murmured, helplessly.

He stood before the fire lost in pale, dim thought. She sat only waiting.

At last he made a move to her.

"At any rate," he said, looking down at her and touching her cheek with the tips of his fingers. "I know I love you—I love your face." The knowledge was a great comfort to him, a rock. "And if we go wrong—I shall know—ich habe es nicht gewollt.* But things go wrong often in coming right—don't they? We won't be afraid. I am always so frightened of falling back, that I can hardly go on.—But one never falls *right* back, does one?—Only part way. I won't be frightened.—Never mind me.—I love you—it's a new thing that's happened to me—and I've been in love hard enough before—but not this—always desire, always passion.— And now, it isn't that.—This is peace, peace of soul—only peace. And the peace is the greatest reality, even if we make war—isn't it?"

But her eyes were full of sad tears, and she did not answer.

9

THOMAS CRICH DIED SLOWLY, terribly slowly. It seemed impossible to everybody, that the thread of life could be drawn out so thin, and yet not break. The sick man lay unutterably weak and spent, kept alive by morphia and by drinks, which he sipped slowly. He was only half conscious—a thin strand of consciousness linking the darkness of death with the light of day. Yet his will was unbroken, he was integral, complete. Only he must have perfect stillness about him.

Any presence but that of the nurses, was a strain and an effort to him now. Every morning, Gerald went into the room, hoping to find his father passed away at last. Yet always he saw the same transparent face, the same weary dark hair on the waxen forehead, and the awful, inchoate dark eyes, which seemed to be decomposing into formless darkness, having only a tiny grain of vision within them.

And always, as the dark, inchoate eyes turned to him, there passed through Gerald's bowels a burning stroke of horror, that seemed to resound through his whole being, threatening to drown out his mind with its clangour, and make him mad.

Every morning, the son stood there, erect and taut with life, gleaming in his blondness like a sword. The gleaming blondness of his keen, watchful son put the father into a fever of fretful irritation. He could not bear to meet the penetrating, downward look of Gerald's blue eyes. But it was only for a moment. Each on the brink of breaking, the father and son looked at each other, then parted.

For a long time Gerald preserved a perfect sang froid, he remained quite collected. But at last, horror undermined him. He was afraid of some horrible collapse in himself He had to stay and see this thing through. Some perverse will made him watch his father drawn over the borders of life. And yet, now, every day, the great red-hot stroke of horror through the bowels of the son struck a further inflammation, Gerald went about all day with a tendency to cringe, as if there were the point of a sword of Damocles pricking the nape of his neck.

There was no escape—he was bound to his father, he had to see him through. And the father's will never bowed or yielded to death. It would have to snap when death at last snapped it,—if it did not persist after physical death. In the same way, the will of the son never yielded. He stood firm and immune, he was beyond this death and this dying.

It was a trial by ordeal. Could he stand and see his father slowly dissolve and disappear in death, without once yielding his will, without once admitting the omnipotence of death. Like a Red Indian undergoing torture, Gerald would experience the whole process of slow death without wincing or flinching. "I am the master of my fate. I am the Captain of my Soul."

But in the stress of this ordeal, Gerald too lost his hold on the outer, daily life. That which was much to him, came to mean nothing. Work, pleasure—it was all left behind. He went on more or less mechanically with his business, but this activity was all extraneous. The real activity was this ghastly wrestling with death, in his own soul. And his own will should triumph. Come what might, he would not bow down or submit or acknowledge he had a master. He had no master in death. He craved to make good this assertion.

But as the fight went on, and all that he had been and was continued to be destroyed, so that life was a hollow shell all round him, roaring and clattering like the sound of the sea, a noise in which he participated

CHAPTER 9

externally, and inside this hollow shell was all the darkness and fearful space of death, he knew he would have to find reinforcements, otherwise he would collapse inwards upon the great dark void of death which circled at the centre of his soul. His will held his outer life, his outer mind, his outer being unbroken and unchanged. But the pressure was too great. He would have to find something to make good the equilibrium. Something must come with him into the hollow void of death in his soul, fill it up, and so equalise the pressure within to the pressure without. For day by day he felt more and more like a bubble filled with darkness, round which whirled the iridescence of his consciousness, and upon which the pressure of the outer world, the outer life, roared vastly.

In this extremity his instinct led him to Gudrun. He threw away everything now—he only wanted the relation established with her. He would follow her to the studio, to be near her, to talk to her. He would stand about the room, aimlessly picking up the implements, the lumps of clay, the little figures she had cast—they were whimsical and grotesque—looking at them without perceiving them. And she felt him following her, dogging her heels like a doom. She held away from him, and yet she knew he drew always a little nearer, a little nearer.

"I say," he said to her one evening, in an odd, unthinking, uncertain way, "won't you stay to dinner tonight?—I wish you would."

She started slightly. He spoke to her like a man making a request to another man.

"They'll be expecting me at home," she said.

"Oh, they won't mind, will they?" he said. "I should be awfully glad if you'd stay."

Her long silence gave consent at last.

"I'll tell Thomas, shall I?" he said.

"I must go almost immediately after dinner," she said.

It was a dark, cold evening. There was no fire in the drawing-room, they sat in the library. He was mostly silent, absent, and Winifred talked little. But when Gerald did rouse himself, he smiled and was pleasant and ordinary with her. Then there came over him again the long blanks, of which he was not aware.

She was very much attracted by him. He looked so good-looking, and his strange, blank silences, which she could not read, moved her and made her wonder over him, made her feel reverential towards him.

But he was very kind. He gave her the best things at the table, he had a bottle of slightly sweet, delicious golden wine brought out for dinner, knowing she would prefer it to the burgundy. She felt herself esteemed, needed almost.

As they took coffee in the library, there was a soft, very soft knocking at the door. He started, and called "Come in." The timbre of his voice, like something vibrating at high pitch, unnerved Gudrun. A nurse in white entered, half hovering in the doorway like a shadow. She was very good-looking, but strangely enough, shy and self-mistrusting.

"The doctor would like to speak to you, Mr Crich," she said, in her low, discreet voice.

"The doctor!" he said, starting up. "Where is he?"

"He is in the dining room."

"Tell him I'm coming."

He drank up his coffee, and followed the nurse, who had dissolved like a shadow.

"Which nurse was that?" asked Gudrun.

"Miss Inglis—I like her best," replied Winifred.

After a while Gerald came back, looking absorbed by his own thoughts, and having some of that gravity and importance which is seen in a slightly drunken man. He did not say what the doctor had wanted him for, but stood before the fire, with his hands behind his back, and his face determined and as if thoughtful. Not that he was really thinking— he was only coiled up in suspense inside himself, and thoughts streamed through his mind without order.

"I must go now and see Mama," said Winifred, "and see Dadda before he goes to sleep."

She bade them both goodnight.

Gudrun also rose to take her leave.

"You needn't go yet, need you?" said Gerald, glancing quickly at the clock. "It is early yet. I'll walk down with you when you go. Sit down, don't hurry away."

Gudrun sat down, as if, absent as he was, his will had power over her. She felt helpless. He was strange to her, something unknown. What was he thinking, what was he feeling, as he stood there so absorbed, saying nothing. He needed her—she could feel that. He would not let her go. She watched him in humble submissiveness.

"Had the doctor anything new to tell you?" she asked softly, at length, with that gentle, timid sympathy which touched a keen fibre in his heart.

He lifted his eyebrows with a negligent, indifferent expression.

"No—nothing new," he replied, as if the question were quite casual, trivial. "He says the pulse is very weak indeed—but that doesn't necessarily mean much, you know."

He looked down at her. Her eyes were dark and soft and unfolded, with a stricken look that roused him.

"No," she murmured at length. "—I don't know anything about these things."

"Just as well not," he said.—"I say, won't you have a cigarette?—do!" He quickly fetched the box, and held her a light. Then he stood before her on the hearth again.

"No," he said, "we've never had much illness in the house, either—not till father." He seemed to meditate a while. Then, looking down at her, he added, "I tell you what, I wouldn't mind being shot tomorrow—*or* hanged.—But this lingering death business is absolutely too much for me—absolutely."

He moved his feet uneasily on the marble hearth, and put his cigarette to his mouth, looking up at the ceiling.

"I know," murmured Gudrun; "it is dreadful."

He smoked without knowing. Then he took the cigarette from his lips, bared his teeth, and putting the tip of his tongue between his teeth, spat off a grain of tobacco, turning slightly aside, like a man who is alone, or who is lost in thought.

"I don't know what it does to me, I'm sure," he said, and again he looked down at her. Her eyes were dark and stricken, looking into his. He saw that she was with him, and he turned aside his face. "But I absolutely need somebody to talk to—I do, really. Do you mind if I talk to *you*? Does it seem horribly feeble?"

"No, why should it?" she murmured, a flood of heavy pleasure filling her heart.

He turned, and flipped the ash from his cigarette on to the great marble hearth-stone, that lay bare to the room, without fender or bar.

"I dunno, I'm sure," he replied. "But I do think a man should bear his own burdens, and not try to force them on to anybody else—" He paused a moment. "But, do you know—it would mean an awful lot to me if I felt that you were—if I felt that I could just speak to you. Do you understand what I mean?—There is some sort of correspondence between us, don't you think? I think we understand each other—or we *might*—"

He shifted spasmodically on the hearth, crunching a cinder under his heel. He looked down at it. Gudrun was aware of the beautiful marble panels of the fireplace, swelling softly carved, round him and above him. She felt as if she were taken in a snare, and very glad, glad in great trepidation, to be caught by him in the toils.

"I don't know," she murmured humbly, "whether I could help you at all—whether I should be of any use—really—"

He looked down at her critically.

"I don't want you to *help*," he said, slightly *de haut en bas*. "So long as I just know you are *there*, that you admit, don't you see, that there *is* a natural correspondence between us—"

She was rather puzzled. She looked down at her hands.

Then there was the sound of the door softly opening. Gerald started. It was his starting that really startled Gudrun. Then he went forward, with quick, graceful, kindly courtesy.

"Oh, mother!" he said. "How nice of you to come down. How are you?"

The elderly woman, loosely and bulkily wrapped in a purple gown, came forward silently, slightly hulked, as usual. Her son was at her side. He pushed her up a chair, saying:

"You know Miss Brangwen, don't you?"

The mother glanced at Gudrun indifferently.

"Yes," she said. Then she turned her wonderful, forget-me-not blue eyes up to her son, as she slowly sat down in the chair he had brought her.

"I came to ask you about your father," she said, in her rapid, scarcely-audible voice. "I didn't know you had company."

"No? Didn't Winifred tell you?—Miss Brangwen stayed to dinner, to make us a little more lively—"

Mrs Crich turned slowly round to Gudrun, and looked at her, but with unseeing eyes.

"I'm afraid it would be no treat to her." Then she turned again to her son. "Winifred tells me the doctor had something to say about your father. What is it?"

"Only that the pulse is very weak—misses altogether a good many times—so that he might not last the night out," Gerald replied.

Mrs Crich sat perfectly impassive, as if she had not heard. Her bulk seemed hunched in the chair, her fair hair hung slack over her ears. But her skin was clear and fine, her hands, as she sat with them forgotten and folded, were quite beautiful, full of potential energy. A great mass of energy seemed decaying in that silent, hulking form.

She looked up at her son, as he stood, keen and soldierly near to her. Her eyes were most wonderfully blue, bluer than forget-me-nots. She seemed to have a certain confidence in Gerald, and to feel a certain motherly anxiety.

"How *are* you?" she muttered, in her strangely quiet voice, as if nobody should hear but him. "You're not getting into a state, are you? You're not letting it bear you down?"

The curious challenge in the last words startled Gudrun.

"I don't think so, mother," he answered cheerfully. "Somebody's got to feel it, you know."

"Why? Why?" answered his mother rapidly. "Why should you let it drag *you* down? What have *you* to do, going through it all? You can do no *good*!"

"No, I don't suppose I can do any good," he answered. "It's just how it affects us, you see."

"Then don't be affected—don't. It's quite unnecessary. You have no need to stop at home. Why don't you go away?"

These sentences, evidently the result of many hours of thought, took Gerald by surprise.

"I don't think I'll go away now, mother, at the last minute," he said.

"You take care of yourself," replied his mother. "You mind *yourself*, that's your business. You've got nothing to do with all this—you mind yourself."

"I'm all right, mother," he said. "There's no need to worry about *me*, I assure you."

"Let the dead bury their dead—leave it alone—that's what I tell you. I know you well enough."

He did not answer this, not knowing what to say. The mother sat bunched up in silence, her beautiful white hands, that had no rings whatsoever, clasping the pommels of her arm-chair.

"You can't do it," she said, almost bitterly. "You haven't the nerve. You're as nervous as a cat, really—always were.—Is this young woman staying here?"

"No," said Gerald. "She is going home tonight."

"Then she'd better have the carriage. Does she go far?"

"Only to Beldover."

"Ah." The elderly woman never looked at Gudrun, yet she seemed to take knowledge of her presence.

"Your business is to mind yourself, Gerald," said the mother, pulling herself to her feet, with a little difficulty.

"Will you go, mother?" he said.

"Yes, I'll go up again," she replied. Turning to Gudrun, she bade her "Goodnight." Then she went slowly to the door, as if she were unaccustomed to walking. At the door she lifted her face to him, implicitly. He kissed her.

"Don't come any farther with me," she said, in her barely audible voice. "I don't want you any farther."

He bade her goodnight, watched her cross to the stairs and mount slowly. Then he closed the door and came back to Gudrun. Gudrun rose also, to go.

"A queer being, my mother," he said.

"Yes," replied Gudrun.

"She has her own thoughts."

"Yes," said Gudrun.

Then they were silent.

"You want to go?" he asked. "Half a minute, I'll just have a horse put in—"

"No," said Gudrun, "I want to walk."

He had promised to walk with her down the long, lonely mile of drive, and she coveted this.

"You might *just* as well drive," he said.

"I'd *much rather* walk," she asserted, with emphasis.

"You would?—Then I will come along with you.—You know where your things are?—I'll put boots on."

He put on a cap, and an overcoat over his evening dress. They went out into the night.

"Let us light a cigarette," he said, stopping in a sheltered angle of the porch. "You have one too."

So, with the scent of tobacco on the night air, they set off down the dark drive, that ran between close-cut hedges through sloping meadows.

He wanted to put his arm round her. If he could put his arm round her, and draw her against him as they walked, he would equilibrate himself. For now he felt like a pair of scales, the half of which tips down and down into an infinite void. He must recover some sort of balance. And here was the hope and the perfect recovery.

Blind to her, in his need and desire, he slipped his arm softly round her waist, and drew her to him. Her heart fainted, feeling herself taken. But then, his arm was so strong, she quailed under its powerful close grasp. She died a little death, and was drawn against him as they walked down the stormy darkness. He seemed to balance her perfectly in opposition to himself, in their dual motion of walking. So, suddenly, he was liberated and perfect, strong, heroic.

He put his hand to his mouth and threw his cigarette away, a gleaming point, into the unseen hedge. Then he was quite free to balance her.

"That's better," he said, with true exultancy.

The exultation in his voice was sweet to her. Did she then mean so much to him?

"Are you happier?" she asked, wistfully.

"I'm happy," he said, in the same exultant voice, "and I *was* miserable."

She nestled against him. He felt her all soft and warm, she was the rich, lovely substance of his being. The warmth and motion of her walk suffused through him wonderfully.

"I'm *so* glad if I help you," she said.

"So am I," he answered. "There's nobody else could do it, if you wouldn't."

"He loves me," she said to herself, with a thrill of elation.

As they walked, he seemed to lift her nearer and nearer to himself, till she moved upon the firm vehicle of his body. He was so strong, like steel, and he could not be opposed. She drifted along in a wonderful interfusion of physical motion, down the dark, blowy hill-side. Across, shone the little yellow lights of Beldover, many of them, spread in a thick patch on another dark hill. But he and she were walking in perfect, isolated darkness, outside the world.

"But how much do you care for me?" came her voice, almost querulous. "You see, I don't know, I don't understand."

"How much!" His voice rang with a painful elation. "I don't know either—but I care for nothing else." He exulted in this declaration. So, he stripped himself of every other desire, of every other relation in life. He lived only in so far as he was connected with her. He exulted in the statement.

"But I can't believe it," said her low voice, amazed, dismayed. She was trembling with fear and wonder. This was the thing she wanted to hear, only this. Yet now she heard it, heard the strange clapping vibration of truth in his voice as he said it, she could not believe. She could not believe—she did not believe.

"Why not?" he said. "Why don't you believe it?—It's true. It is true, as I stand at this moment—" he stood still with her in the wind; "I care for nothing on earth, or in heaven, outside you and me, at this moment. And of the two of us, it's you I care for. I'd rather be cut to pieces on this road, than lose you altogether—rather die any death, than forfeit *this*."

He drew her closer to him, with definite movement.

"No," she murmured, afraid. Yet this was what she wanted. Why did she so lose courage?

They resumed their strange walk. They were such strangers—and yet they were so frightfully, unthinkably near. It was like a madness. Yet it was what she wanted, it was what she wanted.

They had descended the hill, and now they were coming to the square arch where the road passed under the colliery railway. The arch, Gudrun knew, had walls of squared stone, mossy on one side with water that trickled down, dry on the other side. She had stood under it to hear the train rumble thundering over the logs overhead. And she knew that under this dark and lonely bridge the young colliers stood in the darkness with their sweethearts, in rainy weather. And so she wanted to stand under the bridge with *her* sweetheart, and be kissed under the bridge in the invisible darkness. Her steps dragged as she drew near.

So, under the bridge, they came to a standstill, and he lifted her upon his breast. His body vibrated taut and powerful as he closed upon her and crushed her, breathless and dazed and destroyed, crushed her upon his breast. Ah, it was terrible, and perfect. Under this bridge, the colliers pressed their lovers to their breast. And now, under the bridge, the master of them all pressed her to himself! And how much more powerful and terrible was his embrace, than theirs, how much more concentrated and supreme his love was, than theirs, in the same sort. She felt she would swoon, die, under the vibrating, inhuman tension of his arms and his body—she would pass away. Then the unthinkable, high vibration slackened and become more undulating, he slackened and drew her with him to stand with his back to the wall.

She was almost unconscious. So, the colliers' lovers would stand with their backs to the walls, holding their sweet-hearts and kissing them as she was being kissed.—Ah, but would their kisses be fine and powerful as the kisses of the firm-mouthed master? Even the keen, short-cut moustache—the colliers would not have that.

And the colliers' sweethearts would, like herself, hang their heads back limp over their shoulder, and look out from the dark archway, at the close patch of yellow lights on the unseen hill in the distance, or at the vague form of trees, and at the buildings of the colliery wood-yard, in the other direction.

His arms were fast round her, he seemed to be gathering her into himself, her warmth, her softness, her adorable weight, drinking in the suffusion of her physical being, avidly. He lifted her, and seemed to pour her into himself, like wine into a cup.

"This is worth everything," he said, in a strange, thick voice.

So she relaxed, and seemed to melt, to flow into him, as if she were some infinitely warm and precious suffusion filling into his veins, like an intoxicant. Her arms were round his neck, he kissed her and held her perfectly suspended, she was all slack and flowing in to him, and he was the firm, strong cup that receives the wine of her life. So she lay drifted, stranded, lifted up against him, melting and melting under his kisses, melting into his limbs and bones, as if he were soft iron becoming surcharged with her electric life.

Till she seemed to swoon, gradually her mind went, and she passed away, everything in her was melted down and fluid, and she lay still, become contained by him, sleeping in him as lightning sleeps in a heavy, soft stone. So she was passed away and gone in him, and he was perfected.

When she opened her eyes again, and saw the patch of lights in the distance, it seemed to her strange that the world still existed, that she was standing under the bridge resting her head on Gerald's breast. Gerald—who was he? He was the exquisite adventure, the desirable unknown to her.

She looked up, and in the darkness saw his face above her, his shapely, male face. And a thrill of pleasure passed through her soul. She reached up, like Eve reaching to the apples on the tree of knowledge, and she kissed him, touching his face with her infinitely delicate, discerning, desirous fingers. Her fingers went over the mould of his face, over his features.

How perfect and *other* he was—but how perfect! Her soul thrilled with complete knowledge. This was the precious, forbidden apple, this face of a man. She kissed him, putting her fingers over his face, his eyes, his nostrils, over his brows and his ears, to his neck, to know him, to gather him in by touch. He was so firm and shapely, with such satisfying, inconceivable shapeliness, strange yet unutterably clear. She wanted to touch him and touch him and touch him, till she had him all in her hands, till she had strained him into her knowledge. Ah, if she could have the precious *knowledge* of him, she would be filled, and nothing could deprive her of this.

"You are so beautiful," she murmured in her throat.

He wondered, and was afraid. But she felt him quiver, and come down involuntarily nearer upon her. He could not help himself. Her fingers had him under their power. The fathomless, fathomless desire they could evoke in him was deep as death, where he had no choice.

But she knew now, and it was enough. For the time, it was enough. She knew. And this knowledge she must first store up in her heart. How much more of him was there to know. Ah much, much, many days harvesting for her large, yet perfectly subtle and intelligent hands, upon the field of his living, plastic beauty. Ah, her hands were eager, greedy for knowledge. But for the present it was enough, enough, as much as her soul could bear. Too much, and she would shatter herself, she would fill the fine vial of her soul too quickly, and it would break. Enough now—enough for the time being. There were all the afterdays when her hands, like birds, could feed upon the fields of his lovely plastic form. Till then enough.

And even he was glad to be checked, rebuked, held back. For to desire is better than to possess, the joy of the long, eager flight is more perfect than the sudden settling, and the satisfaction, and the spent grief.

They walked on towards the town, towards where the lamps threaded singly, at long intervals down the dark high-road of the valley. They came at length to the gate of the drive.

"Don't come any further," she said.

"You'd rather I didn't?" he asked, relieved. He did not want to go up the public streets with her, his soul all naked with passion as it was.

"Much rather—good-night." She held out her hand. He grasped it, then touched the perilous, potent fingers with his lips.

"Good-night," he said. "Tomorrow."

And they parted. He went home full of the strength and the power of living desire.

But the next day, she did not come, she sent a note, that she was kept indoors by a cold. Here was a torment! But he possessed his soul in some sort of patience, writing a brief answer, telling her how sorry he was not to see her.

The day after this, he stayed at home—it seemed so futile to go down to the offices. His father could not live the week out. And he wanted to be at home, to know.

Gerald sat on a chair by the window in his father's room. The landscape outside was black and winter-sodden. His father lay grey and ashen on the bed, a nurse moved silently in her white dress, neat and elegant, even beautiful. There was a faint scent of eau-de-cologne in the room. The nurse went out of the room, Gerald was alone with death, facing the winter-black landscape.

"Is there much more water in Denley?" came the faint voice, determined and querulous, from the bed. The dying man was asking about a leakage from Willey Water into one of the pits.

"Some more—we shall have to run off the lake," said Gerald.

"Will you—?" The faint voice filtered to extinction.

There was dead stillness. The grey-faced, sick man lay with eyes closed, more dead than death. Gerald looked away. He felt his heart was seared, it would burst if this went on much longer.

Suddenly he heard a strange noise. Turning round, he saw his father's eyes wide open, strained and rolling in a frenzy of inhuman struggling. Gerald started to his feet, and stood transfixed in horror.

"Wha—a—ah-h-h—" came a horrible choking rattle from his father's throat, the fearful, frenzied eye, rolling awfully in its wild fruitless search for help, passed blindly over Gerald, then up came the dark blood and mess pumping over the face of the agonised man, the tense body relaxed, the head fell aside, down the pillow.

Gerald stood transfixed, his soul echoing in horror: "Ah God—Ah God!" He would move, but he could not. He could not move his limbs. "Ah God—Ah God!" His brain seemed to re-echo, like a pulse.

The nurse in white softly entered. She glanced at Gerald, then at the bed.

"Ah!" came her soft, whimpering cry, and she hurried forward to the dead man. "Ah—h!" came the slight sound of her agitated distress, as she stood bending over the bedside. Then she recovered, turned, and came for towel and sponge. She was wiping the dead face carefully, and murmuring, almost whimpering, very softly: "Poor Mr Crich!—Poor Mr Crich!—Oh poor Mr Crich!"

"Is he dead?" clanged Gerald's sharp voice.

"Oh yes, he's gone," replied the soft, moaning voice of the nurse, as she looked up at Gerald's face. She was young and beautiful and quivering. A strange sort of grin went over Gerald's face, over the horror. And he walked out of the room.

He was going to tell his mother. On the landing he met his brother Basil.

"He's gone, Basil," he said, scarcely able to subdue his voice, not to let an unconscious, frightening exultation sound through.

"What?" cried Basil, going pale.

Gerald nodded. Then he went on to his mother's room.

She was sitting in her purple gown, sewing, very slowly sewing, putting in a stitch, then another stitch. She looked up at Gerald with her blue, undaunted eyes.

"Father's gone," he said.

"He's dead? How do you know?"

"Oh, you know, mother, if you see him."

She put her sewing down, and slowly rose.

"Are you going to see him?" he asked.

"Yes," she said.

By the bedside the children already stood in a weeping group.

"Oh mother—!" cried the daughters, almost in hysterics, weeping loudly.

But the mother went forward. The dead man lay in repose, as if gently asleep, so gently, so peacefully, like a young man sleeping in purity.

"Ay," she said bitterly, speaking as if to the presence of all her children. "He's dead." She stood for some minutes in silence, looking down. "Beautiful," she asserted, "beautiful as if life had never touched him—never touched him.—But when a man is dead, he should look different.—He's no business to have his young looks about him like this. He didn't die a youth—yet look what a youth he lies there! Where is his manhood then?—where is it?—But it's not my fault—" She turned on her group of children, and the colour was flushed bright and rosy in her cheek, she was vividly beautiful—"it's not *my* fault, is it, that he lies like that—as if he'd never known any of us, never been altered by anything?—It's not my fault, is it?" Her voice was strong and possessed.

"No mother," came the strange, clarion voice of Gerald from the background, "it isn't."

She turned her face aside from her children, and went out. Gerald went away also—he wanted to be by himself. He took the motor-car, and drove away into the country. He could not bear to meet his brothers and sisters.

When Gudrun heard that Mr Crich was dead, she felt rebuked. She had stayed away lest Gerald should think her too easy of winning. And now, he was in the midst of trouble, whilst she was cold.

The following day she went up as usual to Winifred, who was glad to see her, glad to get away into the studio. The girl had wept, and then, too frightened, had turned aside to avoid any more tragic realisation. She and Gudrun resumed work as usual, in the isolation of the studio, and this seemed an immeasurable happiness, a pure world of freedom, after the aimlessness and misery of the house—Gudrun stayed on till evening. She and Winifred had dinner brought up to the studio, where they ate in freedom, away from all the people in the house.

After dinner Gerald came up. The great high studio was full of shadow and a fragrance of coffee, Gudrun and Winifred had a little table near the fire at the far end, with a white lamp whose light did not travel far. They were a tiny world to themselves, the two girls, surrounded by lovely shadows, the beams and rafters shadowy overhead, the benches and implements shadowy down the studio.

"You are cosy enough here," said Gerald, going up to them.

There was a low brick fireplace full of fire, an old blue turkish rug, the little oak table with the lamp and the white cloth and the dessert, and Gudrun making coffee in an odd brass and glass coffee-maker, and Winifred scalding a little milk in a tiny saucepan.

"Have you had coffee?" said Gudrun.

"I have—but I'll have some more with you," he replied.

"Then you must have it in a glass—there are only two cups," said Winifred.

"It is the same to me," he said, taking a chair and coming into the charmed circle of the girls. How happy they were, how cosy and glamorous it was with them, in a world of lofty shadows! The outside world, in which he had been transacting funeral business all the day, was completely wiped out. In an instant he snuffed happiness and magic.

They had all their things very dainty, two odd and lovely little cups, scarlet and solid gilt, and a little jug with scarlet discs, and the curious coffee-machine, whose spirit-flame flowed steadily, almost invisible. There was the effect of rather exquisite oddness, in which Gerald at once escaped himself.

They all sat down, and Gudrun carefully poured out the coffee.

"Will you have milk?" she asked, calmly, yet nervously poising the little black jug with its big red dots. She was always so completely controlled, yet so nervous.

"No, I won't," he replied.

So, with a curious humility, she placed him the little cup of coffee, and herself took the awkward tumbler. She seemed to want to serve him.

"Why don't you give me the glass—it is so clumsy for you," he said. He would much rather have had it, and seen her daintily served. But she was silent, pleased with the disparity, with her self-abasement.

"You are quite en ménage,"* he said.

"Yes. We aren't really at home to visitors," said Winifred.

"You're not? Then I'm an intruder."

For once he felt his evening dress was out of place, he was an outsider.

Gudrun was very quiet. She did not feel drawn to talk to him. At this stage, silence was best—or mere light words. It was best to leave serious things aside. So they talked gaily and cosily, till they heard the man below lead out the horse, and call it to "back—back!" into the dog-cart that was to take Gudrun home. So she put on her things, and shook hands with Gerald, without once meeting his eyes. And she was gone.

The funeral was loathsome. Afterwards, at the tea-table, the daughters kept saying—"He was a good father to us—the best father in the world"—or else "We shan't easily find another man as good as father was."

Gerald acquiesced in all this. It was the right conventional attitude, and, as far as the world went, he believed in the conventions. He took it as a matter of course. But Winifred hated it, and hid in the studio, and cried her heart out, and wished Gudrun would come.

Luckily everybody was going away. The Criches never stayed long at home. By dinner-time, Gerald was left quite alone. Even Winifred was carried off to London for a few days, with her sister Laura.

But when Gerald was really left alone, he could not bear it. One day passed by, and another. And all the time he was like a man hung in chains over the edge of an abyss. Struggle as he might, he could not turn himself to the solid earth, he could not get footing. He was suspended on the edge of a void, writhing. Whatever he thought of, was the abyss—whether it were friends or strangers, or work or play, it all showed him only the same bottomless void, in which his heart swung perishing. There was no escape, there was nothing to grasp hold of. He must writhe on the edge of the chasm, suspended in chains of mere physical life.

At first he was quiet, he kept still, expecting the extremity to pass away, expecting to find himself released into the world of the living, after this extremity of penance. But it did not pass, and terror gained way over him.

As the evening of the third day came on, his heart rang with fear. He could not bear another night. Another night was coming on, for another night he was to be suspended in chains of physical life, over the bottomless pit of nothingness! And he could not bear it. He could not bear it. He was frightened deeply, and coldly, frightened in his soul. He did not believe in his own strength any more. He could not fall into this infinite void, and rise again. If he fell, he would be all gone. He must withdraw, he must seek adherents. He did not believe in his own single self, any further than this.

After dinner, faced with the ultimate experience of his own nothingness, he turned aside. He pulled on his boots, put on his coat, and set out to walk in the night.

It was dark and misty. He went through the wood, stumbling and feeling his way, to the Mill. Birkin was out. Good—he was half glad. He turned up the hill, and stumbled blindly over the wild slopes, having lost the path in the complete darkness. It was tiring. Where was he going? No matter. He stumbled on till he came to a path again. Then he went on through another wood. No matter where he went—no matter where. His mind became dark, he went on blindly, being tired, and forgetting where he was. Without thought or sensation, he stumbled unevenly on, out into the open again, fumbling for stiles, losing the path, and going along the hedges of the fields till he came to the outlet.

And at last he came to a high-road. It had satisfied him to struggle blindly through the maze of darkness. But now, he must take a direction. And he did not even know where he was. But he must take a direction now.

He stood still on the road, that was high in the utterly dark night, and he did not know where he was. It was a strange sensation: his heart beating, and ringed round with the utterly unknown darkness. So he stood for some time. He was tired.

Then he heard footsteps, and saw a small, swinging light. He immediately went towards this. It was a miner.

"Can you tell me," he said, "where this road goes?"

"Road?—Why, it goos ter Whatmore."

"Whatmore! Oh thank you, that's right. I thought I was wrong. Goodnight."

"Goodnight," replied the broad voice of the miner.

Gerald guessed where he was. At least, when he came to Whatmore, he would know. He was glad to be on a highroad. He walked forward as in a sleep.

That was Whatmore village—? Yes, the Kings Head—and there the hall gates. He descended the steep hill almost running. Winding through the hollow, he passed the Grammar School, and came to Willey Green Church. The churchyard! He halted.

Then in another moment he had clambered up the wall and was going among the graves. Even in this darkness he could see the heaped pallor of old white flowers at his feet. This then was the grave. He stooped down. The flowers were cold and clammy: there was a raw scent of chrysanthemums and tube-roses, deadened. He felt the clay beneath, and shrank, it was so horribly cold and sticky. He stood away in revulsion.

Here was one centre then, here in the complete darkness beside the unseen, raw grave. But there was nothing for him here. No, he had nothing to stay here for. He felt as if some of the clay were sticking cold and unclean, on his heart. No, enough of this.

Where then?—home? Never! It was no use going there. That was less than no use. It could not be done. There was somewhere else to go. Where?

A dangerous resolve formed in his heart, like a daring smile. There was Gudrun.—She would be safe in her home.—But he could get at her—he *would* get at her. He would not go back tonight till he had come to her, if it cost him his life. In his heart, he staked his whole manhood against the performance of this deed, this coming into unhindered touch with her.

Tired as he was, he set off walking straight across the fields towards Beldover. It was so dark, nobody would ever see him. His feet were wet and cold, heavy with clay. But he went on persistently, like a wind, straight forward, as if to his fate. There were great gaps in his consciousness. He was conscious that he was at Winthorpe hamlet, but quite unconscious how he had got there. And then, as in a dream, he was in the long street of Beldover, with its street-lamps.

There was a noise of voices, and of a door shutting loudly, and being barred, and of men talking in the night. The "Lord Nelson" had just closed, and the drinkers were going home. He had better ask one of these where she lived—for he did not know the side streets at all.

"Can you tell me where Somerset Drive is?" he asked of one of the uneven men.

"Where's that?" replied the tipsy miner's voice.

"Somerset Drive."

"Somerset Drive!—I've heerd o' such a place, but I couldn't for my life say wheer it is.—Who might you be wanting?"

"Mr Brangwen—William Brangwen."

"William Brangwen—?—?"

"Who teaches at the Grammar School, at Willey Green—his daughter teaches there too."

"OO—O—O—Oh, Brangwen! *Now* I've got you. Of *course*, William Brangwen! Yes, Yes, he teaches 'em drawin' an' such like?—Ay, that's him!—that's him!—Why certainly I know where he lives, back your life* I do! Yi——what place do they ca' it?"

"Somerset Drive," repeated Gerald patiently. He knew his own colliers fairly well, so he was not put out.

"Somerset Drive, for certain!" said the collier, swinging his arm as if catching something up. "Somerset Drive—yi!—I couldn't for my life lay hold o' the lercality o' the place. Yis, I know the place, to be sure I do—"

He turned unsteadily on his feet, and pointed up the dark, nigh deserted road.

"You go up theer—an' you ta'e th' first—yi, th' first turnin' on your left—o' that side—past Withamses pot-shop—"

"*I* know," said Gerald.

"Ay! You go down a bit, past wheer th' Wesleyan parson lives—and then the Somerset Drive, as they ca' it, branches off on 't right-hand side—an' there's nowt but three houses in it, no more than three, there isn't—an' I'm a'most certain as theirs is th' last—ay, th' last."

"Thank you very much," said Gerald. "Goodnight."

And he started off, leaving the tipsy man there standing rooted.

Gerald went past the dark shops and houses, most of them sleeping now, and twisted round to the little blind road that ended on a field of darkness. He slowed down, as he neared his goal, not knowing how he should proceed. What if the house were closed in darkness?

But it was not. He saw a big lighted window, and heard voices, then a gate banged. His quick ears caught the sound of Birkin's voice, his keen eyes made out Birkin, with Ursula standing in a white blouse on the step of the garden path. Then Ursula stepped down, and came along the road, holding Birkin's arm.

Gerald went across into the darkness and they dawdled past him, talking happily, Birkin's voice low, Ursula's high and distinct. Gerald went quickly to the house.

The blinds were drawn before the big, lighted window of the dining-room. Looking up the path at the side, he could see the door left open, shedding a soft coloured light from the hall lamp. He went quickly and silently up the path, and looked up into the hall. There were pictures on the walls, and the antlers of a stag—and the stairs going up on one side—and just near the foot of the stairs the half-opened door of the dining-room.

With heart drawn tense, Gerald stepped into the hall, whose floor was of coloured mosaic, went quickly and looked into the large, pleasant room. In a chair by the fire, the father sat asleep, his head tilted back against the side of the big oak chimney piece, his ruddy face seen foreshortened, the nostrils open, the mouth fallen a little. It would take the merest sound to wake him.

Gerald stood a second suspended. He glanced down the passage behind him. It was all dark. Again he was suspended. Then he went swiftly upstairs. His senses were so finely, almost supernaturally keen, that he seemed to maintain a perfect equilibrium in the midst of the precarious house.

He came to the first landing. There he stood, scarcely breathing. Again, corresponding to the door below, there was a door ajar. That would be the mother's room. He could hear her moving about in the candle-light. She would be expecting her husband to come up. He looked along the dark landing.

Then silently, on infinitely careful feet, he went along the passage, feeling the wall with the extreme tips of his fingers. There was a door. He stood and listened. He could hear two people's breathing. It was not that. He went stealthily forward. There was another door, slightly open. The room was in darkness. Empty. Then there was the bathroom, he could smell the soap and the heat. Then at the end was another bedroom—one soft breathing. This was she.

With an anguish of carefulness he turned the door handle, and opened the door an inch. It creaked slightly. Then he opened it another inch—then another. His heart did not beat, he seemed to create a silence about himself, an obliviousness.

He was in the room. Still the sleeper breathed softly. It was very dark. He felt his way forward inch by inch, with his feet and hands. He touched the bed, he could hear the sleeper. He drew nearer, bending close as if his eyes would disclose whatever there was. And then, very near his face, to his fear, he saw the round, dark head of a boy.

He recovered, turned round, saw the door ajar, a faint light revealed. And he retreated swiftly, drew the door to without fastening it, and passed rapidly down the passage. At the head of the stairs he hesitated. There was still time to flee.

But it was a matter of life or death. And he would maintain his will. He melted past the door of the parental bedroom like a shadow, and was climbing the second flight of stairs. They creaked under his weight—it was torture. Ah what agony, if the mother's door opened just beneath him, and she saw him! It would have to be, if it were so. He held the control still.

He was not quite up these stairs when he heard a quick running of feet below, the outer door was closed and locked, he heard Ursula's voice, then the father's sleepy exclamation. He pressed on swiftly to the upper landing.

Again a door was ajar, a room was empty. Feeling his way forward, with the tips of his fingers, travelling rapidly, like a blind man, anxious lest Ursula should come upstairs, he found another door. There, with his preternaturally fine senses alert, he listened. He heard someone moving in bed. This would be she.

Softly now, like one who has only one sense, the tactile sense, he turned the latch. It clicked. He held still. The bed-clothes rustled. His heart did not beat. Then again he drew the latch back, and very gently pushed the door. It made a sticking noise as it gave.

"Ursula?" said Gudrun's voice, frightened. He quickly opened the door and pushed it behind him.

"Is it you, Ursula?" came Gudrun's frightened voice. He heard her sitting up in bed. In another moment she would scream.

"No, it's me," he said, feeling his way to the bed. "It's only me."

She sat motionless in her bed in sheer astonishment. She was too astonished, too much taken by surprise, even to be afraid.

"Gerald!" she echoed, in blank amazement.

He had found his way to the bed, and his outstretched hand touched her warm breast, blindly. She shrank away.

"Let me make a light" she said, springing out of bed.

He stood perfectly motionless. He heard her touch the match-box, he heard her fingers in their movement. Then he saw her in the light of a match, which she held to the candle. The light rose in the room, then sank to a small dimness, as the flame sank down on the candle, before it rose again.

She looked at him, as he stood near the other side of the bed. His cap was pulled low over his brow, his black overcoat was buttoned close up to his chin. His face was strange and fixed, there was no getting away from him. When she had seen him, she knew. She knew there was something ultimate in the situation, and she must accept it. Yet she must challenge him.

"How did you come up?" she asked.

"I walked up the stairs—the door was open." She looked at him.

"I haven't closed this door, either," he said. She walked swiftly across the room, and closed her door, softly, and locked it. Then she came back.

She was very beautiful, with startled eyes and flushed cheeks, and her plait of hair rather short and thick down her back, and her long, fine white night-dress falling to her feet.

She saw that his boots were all clayey, even half way up his trousers, solid clay. And she wondered if he had made footprints all the way up. He was a very strange figure, standing in her bedroom, near the tossed bed.

"But what made you come like this?" she asked, almost querulous.

"I couldn't do anything else," he replied.

And this she could see, from his face. It was fate.

"You are so muddy," she said.

He looked down at his feet.

"I was walking in the dark," he replied, ashamed. But he felt triumphant. There was a pause. He stood on one side of the tumbled bed, she on the other. He did not even take his cap from his brows.

"And what do you want of me," she challenged.

He looked aside, and did not answer. Save for the extreme beauty and irresistible attractiveness of his distinct, strange face, she would have sent him away. But his face was too wonderful and beautiful to her.

"What do you want of me?" she repeated, in a softened voice.

He pulled off his cap, in a sort of movement of liberation, and went across to her. But he could not touch her, because she stood barefoot in her night-dress, and he was muddy and damp. Her eyes, wide and large and wondering, watched him, and asked him the question.

"I came—because there was nothing else to be done," he said. "I believe I should have been dead by morning if I hadn't come."

She looked at him in doubt and wonder.

"Why?" she said.

He shook his head slightly.

"Couldn't say," he replied.

There was a curious, and becoming air of triumph, almost childish, about him.

"But why did you come to me?" she persisted.

"Because—what else was I to do? If there hadn't been you in the world, then I shouldn't have been in the world, either."

She stood looking at him, with large, wide, wondering, stricken eyes. His eyes were looking steadily into hers all the time, and he seemed fixed in an odd steadfastness. She sighed. She was caught now. She had no choice.

"Won't you take off your boots," she said. "They must be wet."

He dropped his cap on a chair, unbuttoned his overcoat, lifting up his chin to unfasten the throat buttons. His short, fair hair was ruffled. He was so beautifully fair, like wheat. He pulled off his overcoat. He was in evening dress, as usual.

Quickly he pulled off his jacket, pulled loose his black tie, and was unfastening his studs, which were headed each with a pearl. She listened, watching, hoping no-one would hear the starched linen crackle. It seemed to snap like pistol-shots.

It was his vindication. She let him hold her in his arms, clasp her close against him. He found in her an infinite relief. Into her he poured all his pent-up darkness and corrosive death, and he was whole again. It was wonderful, marvellous, it was a miracle. This was the ever-recurrent miracle of his life, at the thought of which he was lost in an ecstasy of relief and wonder. And she, subject, received him, was a vessel filled with his bitter potion of death. She had no power at this crisis to resist. The terrible corrosive violence of death filled her, and she received it in an ecstasy of subjection, in throes of acute, violent sensation.

As he drew nearer to her, he plunged deeper into her enveloping soft warmth, a wonderful creative heat that penetrated his veins and gave him life again. He felt himself dissolving and sinking to rest in the bath of her living strength. It seemed as if her heart in her breast were a second inconquerable sun, into the glow and creative strength of which he penetrated further and further. All his veins, that were murdered and lacerated, healed softly as life came pulsing in, stealing invisibly in to him as if it were the all-powerful effluence of the sun. His blood, which seemed to have been drawn back into death, came ebbing on the return, surely, beautifully, powerfully.

He felt his limbs growing fuller and flexible with life, his body gained an unknown strength. He was a man again, strong and rounded. And he was a child, so soothed and restored and full of gratitude.

And she, she was the great origin of life, he worshipped her. Mother and fountain of all life she was. And he, child and worshipper, received of her and was made whole. The miraculous, soft effluence of her breast suffused over him, over his seared, hurt brain, like a healing lymph, like a soft, soothing flow of life itself, perfect as if he were bathed in the womb again.

His brain was hurt, seared, the tissue was as if destroyed. He had not known how hurt he was, how his tissue, the very tissue of his brain was damaged by the corrosive flood of death. Now, as the healing lymph of her body flowed through him, he knew how destroyed he was, like a plant whose tissue is burst from inwards by a frost.

He buried his small, hard head between her breasts, and pressed her breasts against him with his hands. And she with quivering hands pressed his head against her, as he lay suffused out, and she lay fully conscious. The lovely, creative warmth flooded through him like a sleep of fecundity within the womb. Ah if only she would grant him the flow of this living effluence, he would be restored, he would be complete again. He was afraid she would deny him before it was finished. Like a child at the breast, he cleaved intensely to her, and she could not put him away. And his seared, ruined membrane relaxed, softened, that which was seared and stiff and withered yielded again, became soft and flexible, palpitating with new life. He was infinitely grateful, as to God, or as an infant is at its mother's breast. He was glad and grateful like a delirium, as he felt his own wholeness come over him again, as he felt the full, unutterable sleep coming over him, the sleep of complete exhaustion and restoration.

But Gudrun lay wide awake, destroyed into perfect consciousness. She lay motionless, with wide eyes staring motionless into the darkness, whilst he was sunk away in sleep, his arms round her.

She seemed to lie hearing waves break on a hidden shore, long, slow, gloomy waves breaking with the rhythm of fate, so monotonously that it seemed eternal. This endless breaking of slow, sullen waves of fate held her like a possession, whilst she lay with dark, wide eyes looking into the darkness. She could see so far, as far as eternity—yet she saw nothing. She was suspended in perfect consciousness—and of what was she conscious?

This mood of extremity, when she lay staring into eternity, utterly suspended, and conscious of everything, to the last limits, passed, and left her uneasy. She had lain so long motionless. She moved, she became self-conscious. She wanted to look at him, to see him.

But she dared not make a light, because she knew he would wake, and she did not want to break his perfect sleep, that she knew he had got of her.

She disengaged herself, softly, and rose up a little to look at him. There was a faint light, it seemed to her, in the room. She could just distinguish his features, as he slept the perfect sleep. In this darkness, she seemed to see him so distinctly. But he was far off, in another world. Ah, she could shriek with torment, he was so far off, and perfected, in another world. She seemed to look at him as at a pebble far away under clear, dark water. And here was she, left with all the anguish of consciousness, whilst he was sunk deep into the other element of living, mindless sleep. He was beautiful, far-off, and perfected. They would never be together. Ah, this awful, inhuman distance which would always be interposed between her and the other being!

There was nothing to do but to lie still and endure. She felt an overwhelming tenderness for him, and a dark understirring of jealous hatred, that he should lie so perfect and immune, whilst she was tormented with violent wakefulness, cast out in the outer darkness.

She lay in intense and vivid consciousness, an exhausting super-consciousness. The church clock struck the hours, it seemed to her, in quick succession. She heard them distinctly in the tension of her vivid consciousness. And he slept as if time were one moment, unchanging and unmoving.

She was exhausted, wearied. Yet she must continue in this state of violent active superconsciousness. She was conscious of everything—her childhood, her girlhood, all the forgotten incidents, all the unrealised influences and all the happenings she had not understood, pertaining to herself, to her family, to her friends, her lovers, her acquaintances, everybody. It was as if she drew a glittering rope of knowledge out of the sea of darkness, drew and drew and drew it out of the fathomless depths of the past, and still it did not come to an end, there was no end to it, she must haul and haul at the rope of glittering conscious, pull it out phosphorescent from the endless depths of the unconsciousness, till she was weary, aching, exhausted, and fit to break, and yet she had not done.

Ah, if only she might wake him! She turned uneasily. When could she rouse him and send him away? When could she disturb him? And she relapsed into her activity of automatic consciousness, that would never end.

But the time was drawing near when she could wake him. It was like a release. The clock had struck four, outside in the night. Thank God the night had passed almost away. At five he must go, and she would be released. Then she could relax and fill her own place. Now she was driven up against him like a knife white-hot on a grindstone.

The last hour was the longest. And yet, at last, it passed. Her heart leapt with relief—yes, there was the slow, strong stroke of the church clock—at last, after this night of eternity. She waited to catch each slow, fatal reverberation—"Three— — —four— — —*five*!" There, it was finished. A weight rolled off her.

She raised herself, leaned over him tenderly, and kissed him. She was sad to wake him. After a few moments, she kissed him again. But he did not stir. The darling, he was so deep in sleep! What a shame to take him out of it. She let him lie a little longer. But he must go—he must really go.

With full over-tenderness she took his face between her hands, and kissed his eyes. The eyes opened, he remained motionless, looking at her. Her heart stood still. To hide her face from his dark-opened eyes, in the darkness, she bent down and kissed him, whispering:

"You must go, my love."

He put his arms round her. Her heart sank.

"But you must go, my love. It's late."

"What time is it?" he said.

Strange, his man's voice. She quivered.

"Past five o'clock," she said.

But he only closed his arms round her again. Her heart cried within her in distress. She disengaged herself firmly.

"You really must go," she said.

"Not for a minute," he said.

She lay still, nestling against him, but unyielding.

"Not for a minute," he repeated, clasping her closer.

"Yes," she said, unyielding. "I'm afraid if you stay any longer."

There was a certain coldness in her voice that made him release her, and she rose and lit the candle. That then was the end.

He got up. He was warm and full of life and desire. Yet he felt a little bit ashamed, humiliated, putting on his clothes before her, in the candle-light. For he felt revealed, exposed to her, at a time when she was in some way against him. It was all very difficult to understand. He dressed himself quickly, without collar or tie. Still he felt full and complete, perfected.

"It is like a workman getting up to go to work," thought Gudrun, thrilled. "And I am like a workman's wife."

He pushed his collar and tie into his overcoat pocket. Then he sat down and pulled on his boots. They were sodden, as were his socks and trouser-bottoms. But he himself was quick and warm.

"Perhaps you ought to have put your boots on downstairs," she said.

At once, without answering, he pulled them off again, and stood holding them in his hand. She had thrust her feet into slippers, and flung

319

a loose robe round her. She was ready. She looked at him as he stood waiting, his black coat buttoned to the chin, his cap pulled down, his boots in his hand. And her passionate tenderness revived for a second. His face was so warm-looking, wide-eyed and full of newness, so young. She felt old, old. She went to him heavily, to be kissed. He kissed her quickly. She wished his warm, expressionless beauty did not still attract her so much. It was a burden upon her, that she could not escape. Yet when she looked at his straight, man's brows, and at his rather small, well-shapen nose, and at his open blue eyes, the passion contracted her heart again, she could not yet escape it.

They went downstairs quickly. It seemed they made a prodigious noise. He followed her, as, wrapped in her vivid green wrap, she preceded him with the light. She suffered badly with fear, lest her people should be roused. He hardly cared, only this secrecy was tiresome to him now.

She led the way to the kitchen. It was neat and tidy, as the woman had left it. He looked up at the clock—twenty minutes past five! Then he sat down on a chair to put on his boots. She waited, watching his every movement. She wanted it to be over now.

He stood up—she unbolted the back door, and looked out. A cold, raw night, not yet dawn, with a piece of a moon in the vague sky. She was glad she need not go out.

"Goodbye then," he murmured.

"I'll come to the gate," she said.

And again she hurried on in front, to warn him of the steps. And at the gate, once more she stood on the step whilst he stood below her.

"Goodbye," she whispered.

He kissed her, dutifully, and turned away. She suffered torments hearing his firm tread going so distinctly down the road.

She closed the gate, and crept quickly and noiselessly back to bed. When she was in her room, and the door closed, and all safe, she breathed freely, and a great weight fell off her. She nestled down in bed, in the groove his body had made, in the warmth he had left. And, excited, tired, happy, she fell soon into a deep, refreshing sleep.

Gerald walked quickly through the raw darkness of the coming dawn. He met nobody. His mind was beautifully still and thoughtless, like a still pool, and his body full and warm and rich. He went quickly along towards Shortlands, in a grateful well-being of soul.

10

THE BRANGWEN FAMILY was going to move from Beldover. It was necessary now for the father to be in town.

Birkin had taken out a marriage licence, yet Ursula deferred from day to day. She would not fix any definite time—she still wavered. Her month's notice to leave the Grammar School was in its third week. Christmas was not far off.

Gerald waited for the Ursula-Birkin marriage. It was something crucial to him.

"Shall we make it a double-barrelled affair?" he said to Birkin one day.

"Who for the second shot?" asked Birkin.

"Gudrun and me," said Gerald, the venturesome twinkle in his eyes.

Birkin looked at him steadily, as if somewhat taken aback.

"Serious—or joking?" he asked.

"Oh, serious.—Shall I? Shall Gudrun and I rush in along with you?"

"Do by all means," said Birkin.—"I didn't know you'd got that length."

"Much further," said Gerald. And he told Birkin the last adventure.

"Very good," said Birkin. "You outflanked her in a masterly fashion, I hope you will manoeuvre a marriage as brilliantly."

"You think she'll make objections?" said Gerald, rather pleased.

"I don't know, I'm sure," said Birkin. "But I expect she will."

"I'll ask her, to keep you company," said Gerald.

"Right—though I hope that's not your only object."

Gerald laughed.

"It is," he said. "I know I should *live* with her, anyway—somehow and somewhere. But as for marriage—I tell you, I'll do it to keep you company, so that you shan't appear at too great a disadvantage. For I don't think much of the institution—in fact I hate it."

"Really!" exclaimed Birkin, in astonishment. "Then why on earth enter it?"

"Oh," said Gerald, "I've always calculated on taking the step, some time—when the day came to nip the top off my sprouts and give up—when the show was over, and you had to go somewhere to spend the remainder of the weary night—" he smiled at his own euphuisms.

"Really!" said Birkin laughing. "What funny things you say, Gerald! You sound quite clever and cynical.—But what do you hope for *now*, then—now that you *will* marry."

"I? I don't know. I tell you, I do it because you do—and because, of course, I *want* to live with her. But, leaving you out, I'd rather live with her unmarried than married—it is freer and a cleaner sweep, it seems to me—"

"You don't feel that marriage is freedom?" asked Birkin.

"Do I? Does it look like freedom, when you remember your own father and mother, and when you look at the rest of people? Freedom—!—"

"I tell you what, Gerald," said Birkin, "Death itself is the only real giver of freedom. When you know that you will die—then you are free.—It is the pagan 'Memento Mori.'—That is all the religion one needs."

Gerald looked blank astonishment.

"Death—freedom?" he exclaimed. "By Gad, if you'd seen my father die, you wouldn't say so."

"Because he wouldn't give in," said Birkin. "He wanted to conquer death with his own will.—But when at last one has realised in one's soul, that one will die—I tell you it is a peace and a happiness beyond any other. It is like having a great window where you can stand and look into the beyond, where there is pure reality, and the making of lies does not happen."

A tightness came over Gerald's face.

"It's a bad business if our only happiness lies in death," he replied. "Hang it, that is the very worst side of religion—you who hate religion so much."

"I don't run after—death—and I didn't say happiness—I said peace and liberation."

"You said happiness—"

"Well, I mean liberation.—Now I'll tell you, Gerald. When I want to move, I remember death, how it is ultimate and inevitable, and pure. Then I am free to move properly in life. It is like a man who wants to think, going and standing in front of a window. The space purifies one's soul.—And death is a window to me, with the darkness outside. And when I stand there, looking out, then the world and its active life seems only like a roomful of light and racket behind me, where I am taking part for a time, but not staying for long. It does not contain me and confine me. When I stand peacefully looking out on death, what is true in my soul disengages itself and is free and clear and untrammelled, I know what to do, I am sure, and free, and glad. Then I can turn into the world again.

"And so, in the face of death I know that my true desire in life is, for a living marriage with Ursula—and in that marriage, in some way, to come into a new world of man.

"When one stands in front of the darkness, and knows that one's own life will pass away there also, into the darkness—then, in the peace that accompanies this knowledge, one can declare simply that the existing world of man is base and wrong, and must go, we know that our lives contain the inception of a new earth.

"Because life is here on earth—we shall never know what death is.— And it is our business to live.—But, remembering death, I know that the life of the world as it is now is not living, it is a bad process of dying. And what we must live for is a new world of life. It doesn't matter when we die, so long as we live fulfilling the deepest desire that is in us. And a life which is a denial of the deepest desire is much worse than any death, it is a sheer lie.

"If one accepts death, and knows that nothing can take us away from that, one has the freedom and strength to live in truth, putting down the lies that pretend they own our living. But one must have the pure knowledge of death behind one, before one has really faith to tackle life and falsity. Being sure in death I am strong in life. And so, in life, and in all the world of man, I have no master, save the deepest desire of my own soul, in which death and life are at one."

Gerald sat strained and uncomfortable under this dissertation of Birkin's. He was fond of Birkin and had given him a certain allegiance which he would never take back. But this discourse was uncalled for, and too much. Gerald felt constrained, irritated, as if he were being forced in some direction.

There was a jumble market every Monday afternoon in the old market-place in town. Ursula and Birkin strayed down there one afternoon. They had been talking of furniture, and they wanted to see if there was any fragment they would like to buy, amid the heaps of rubbish collected on the cobble-stones.

The old market square was not very large, a mere bare patch of granite setts, usually, with a few fruit-stalls under a wall. It was in a poor quarter of the town. Meagre houses stood down one side, there was a hosiery factory, a great blank with myriad oblong windows, at the end, a street of little shops with flagstone pavement down the other side, and, for a crowning monument, the public baths, of new red brick, with a clock-tower. The people who moved about seemed stumpy and sordid, the air seemed to smell rather dirty, there was a sense of many mean streets ramifying off into warrens of meanness. Now and again a great chocolate and yellow tram-car ground round a difficult bend under the hosiery factory.

Ursula was superficially thrilled when she found herself out among the common people, in the jumbled place piled with old bedding, heaps of old iron, shabby crockery in pale lots, muffled lots of unthinkable clothing. She and Birkin went unwillingly down the narrow aisles between the rusty wares. He was looking at the goods, she at the people.

She excitedly watched a young woman, who was going to have a baby, and who was turning over a mattress and making a young man, down-at-heel and dejected, feel it also. So secretive and active and anxious the young woman seemed, so reluctant, slinking, the young man. He was going to marry her because she was having a child.

When they had felt the mattress, the young woman asked the old man seated on a stool among his wares, how much it was. He told her, and she turned to the young man. The latter was ashamed and self conscious, he turned his face away, though he left his body standing there and muttered aside. And again the young woman anxiously and actively fingered the mattress and added up in her mind and bargained with the old, unclean man. All the while, the young man stood by, shamefaced and down-at-heel, submitting.

"Look," said Birkin, "there is a pretty chair."

"Charming!" cried Ursula. "Oh charming."

It was an arm-chair of simple wood, probably birch, but of such fine delicacy of grace, standing there on the sordid stones, it almost brought tears to the eyes. It was square in shape, of the purest, slender lines, and four short lines of wood in the back, that reminded Ursula of harp-strings.

"It was once," said Birkin, "gilded—and it had a cane seat. Somebody has nailed this wooden seat in.—Look, here is a trifle of the red that underlay the gilt. The rest is all black, except where the wood is worn pure and glossy.—It is the fine unity of the lines that is so attractive—look, how they run and meet and counteract.—But of course the wooden seat is wrong—it destroys the perfect lightness and unity in tension the cane gave.—I like it though—"

"Ah yes," said Ursula, "so do I."

"How much is it?" Birkin asked the man.

"Ten shillings."

"And you will send it—?"

It was bought.

"So beautiful, so pure!" Birkin said. "It almost breaks my heart." They walked along between the heaps of rubbish. "My beloved country—it had something to express even when it made that chair."

"And hasn't it now?" asked Ursula. She was always angry when he took this tone.

"No, it hasn't.—When I see that clear, beautiful chair, and I think of England, even Jane Austen's England—it had living thoughts to unfold even then, and pure happiness in unfolding them. And now, we can only fish among the rubbish heaps for the remnants of their old flowering. There is no production in us now, only sordid and foul decay."

"It isn't true," cried Ursula. "Why must you always praise the past, at the expense of the present?—*Really*, I don't think so much of Jane Austen's England. It was materialistic enough, if you like—"

"It could afford to be materialistic," said Birkin, "because it had the power to be something other—which we haven't. We are materialistic because we haven't the power to be anything else—try as we may, we can't bring off anything but materialism."

Ursula was subdued into angry silence. She did not heed what he said. She was rebelling against something else.

"And I hate your past—I'm sick of it," she cried. "I believe I even hate that old chair, though it *is* beautiful.—It isn't *my* sort of beauty.—I wish it had been smashed up when its day was over, not left to preach the beloved past at us—I'm sick of the beloved past."

"Not so sick as I am of the accursed present," he said.

"Yes—just the same. I hate the present—but I don't want the past to take its place—I don't want that old chair."

He was rather angry for a moment. Then he looked at the sky shining beyond the tower of the public baths, and he seemed to get a new heart. He laughed.

"All right," he said, "then let us not have it. I'm sick of it all, too. At any rate one can't go on living on the old bones of beauty."

"One can't," she cried. "I *don't* want old things."

"The truth is, we won't want things at all," he replied. "The thought of houses and furniture in England is hideous to me."

This startled her, for a moment. Then she replied:

"So it is to me.—But one must live somewhere."

"You know I think," he said, "that one should go into the wilderness and live the life of contemplation—pure thought, and not submit to this show. No, *I* don't want that chair. It is a beautiful chair, I could weep over it.—But one must stop weeping and looking backward, one must *get out*."

She clung to his arm as they walked away from the market.

"But there *is* no wilderness," she said. "And the life of contemplation isn't enough, is it? One must *act* as well—one must *live*."

"There will be you and me, that will be living enough.—As for action, taking part in the world's activity, *now*,—that is the very reverse of living, it is null, simple nullity. If one wants to be null and void, one becomes part of the world's activity. Come, we'll go away somewhere, and live in a lonely cottage, and lead the contemplative life. Come on, let's us go—"

She stood in the street, laughing at him. He was laughing also, in his eyes. But he meant it.

"All right," she said. "Which way?"

He looked down the various barren streets, then at the market.

"We'll tell the man first, that we don't want the chair," he said.

"But we've *bought* it," she cried.

"Then we'll give it him back."

They retraced their steps.

There, in front of some furniture, stood the young couple, the woman who was going to have a baby, and the narrow-faced youth.

"Let us give it to *them*," whispered Ursula. "Look, they are getting a home together."

"*I* won't aid and abet them in it," he said petulantly, instantly sympathising with the reluctant, humiliated youth, against the active, procreant female.

"Oh yes," cried Ursula. "It's right for them—there's nothing else, for them."

"Very well," said Birkin, "you offer it them—I'll watch."

Ursula went rather nervously to the young couple, who were discussing an iron washstand—or rather, the man was glancing furtively and reluctantly at the abominable article, whilst the woman was arguing.

"We bought a chair," said Ursula, "and we don't want it. Would you have it? We should be glad if you would."

The young couple faced round on her, not believing that she could be addressing them.

"Would you care for it?" repeated Ursula. "It's really *very* pretty—but—but—" she smiled rather dazzlingly.

The young couple only stared at her, and looked furtively at each other, to know what to do.

"We wanted to *give* it you," explained Ursula, now overcome with confusion and dread of them. She rather liked the look of the young fellow—a narrow-faced neer-do-well with something distinct and individual about him. But the couple remained stubbornly silent, as if they had not been addressed at all.

"Won't you have it?" Ursula faltered.

Birkin, who had been grinning in the background now came to the rescue.

"They don't care for your chair?" he asked her, smiling with mischief to see her so unhappy and frightened.

"Was you speaking to us?" asked the young woman who was going to have a baby. She roused up now a man was there.

"Yes," said Birkin, "offering you a chair we have just bought—there it is, do you see it?—the little wooden arm-chair, with the label on it—"

"Oh yes," said the young woman, non committal.

"Don't you want it yourselves?" muttered the young man, in a quick, low voice, a half-smile twisting his suspicious, sneering mouth, his eyes, which were fine and which *looked* thoughtful, though perhaps it was only a touch of vice, glancing rapidly over Birkin's face.

Birkin looked back at him with smiling, half-contemptuous glance, and said:

"Because we decided we didn't want any furniture at all—"

A slow, cunning smile came over the face of the youth, because he did not understand. He was thin and handsome, with a wisp of black hair on his forehead, and a thin line of black moustache over his twisting mouth, and a downcast look in his dark blue eye. He twisted his face in a cunning smile of non-apprehension and lowered his long black lashes over his eyes. The woman looked tough and acquisitive.

"Well, thank you, if you've bought it and don't want it—" she began, in an uncertain voice. "What do *you* say, Fred?" She turned to the young man. A sickly grin came on his face.

"You see," interposed Ursula, "we suddenly decided to go to Italy, so we shouldn't want any furniture at all. And we bought the chair because we liked it so much—so—so I thought I'd give it you instead of giving it back to the man.—It's not *worth* much, it only cost ten shillings—but it's really beautiful in shape—"

"I assure you," said Birkin, in his mocking way, "it has real beauty, real form."

The young woman still stood unsure that she was not being "had."

"Why don't you take it," said the young man to the woman, with the acquisitive cunning grin of the street arab.

"Why don't *you* take it, it's offered you as much as me. Why must *I* always have the say?" retorted the young woman.

He turned his face away, with a slight mocking sneer of discomfort and street-arab embarrassment, and did not answer.

"Anybody 'ud think you was out of it, altogether—" persisted the woman.

Still, with cunning, rat-like evasion, he didn't answer.

"Well now," said Birkin, "shall we go and tell the dealer it's yours—or shall we leave it?"

"If you *mean* us to have it—" said the woman, very awkwardly. She had a snub nose. She tried to put a little gratitude into her tone.

"I assure you I do," said Birkin.

They trailed off to the dealer, the beautiful, weedy youth slouching behind.

"There's the chair!" said Birkin. "Will you take it with you, or have the address altered?"

"Oh, I think we can carry it, thank you."

It was handed across to her.

"Don't you think it *is* a pretty chair?" Ursula asked, laughing, of the young fellow.

He grinned with cunning evasion, and did not answer.

"Good afternoon," said Birkin.

"Good afternoon—an' thank yer," said the woman, who stood holding the chair. Immediately they had turned, they heard the woman break into deep abuse of the lout of a youth. The chair had only tipped the fat into the fire.

Glancing back, Ursula saw the young woman, active and excited, extremely excited by the gift, extremely angry with her partner for the ungraciousness of both of them, leading the way, followed by the young man, whose trousers sank over his heels, and who, mortified with the self-conscious shame of his conspicuousness, was carrying the slim old arm-chair under one arm, his arm over the back, his hand grasping the slim lower bar, while the fine, square, tapering legs swayed perilously near the granite setts.

"Now how can a man look so beautiful, such a perfect *aristocrat*, and yet be such—such a lout, worse than a lout?" demanded Ursula.

"He isn't a lout," said Birkin. "He's a rat—a city rat."

"But a rat isn't so goodlooking! He was perfectly beautiful, with his long, narrow face and well-cut features—and those soft, strange eyes—"

"Yes, a rat is an aristocrat in its way," said Birkin.

They waited for the tram-car. Ursula sat on top and looked out on the town. The dusk was just dimming the hollows of crowded houses.

"And are we really going away—are we really going to lead the contemplative life?" she cried, clinging to his arm, and laughing.

"I am. We'll both go back into Paradise, and listen to creation, while we sleep," he replied.

"I've always wanted it," she said. "I've always wanted to get away into—into something that was free—"

He was rather surprised. *Had* she always wanted the anchorite's atmosphere of ultimate reality.

"I suppose you have," he said.

"Oh, I have," she cried. "And really, the world can't go on *without* somebody leaving it.—But back to Paradise—how lovely, my dear!—But do you think they'll let us in?"

"Sure. Glad to have somebody to look after the garden," he said.

"And it isn't shirking life—we *know* life, don't we?—One has to go on, beyond this life. It is the only adventure, isn't it?"

"The only adventure," he repeated.

"The Columbuses!" she cried, suddenly catching at his arm. "My love, it makes me so happy!"

"So it does me," he smiled. "Adam and Eve making a new start."

There was a long silence. Her face was radiant like gold.

"And we'll be married," she whispered.

He closed his hand over hers.

"We'll be married tomorrow, shall we?" she whispered happily. "Can we?"

"Yes," he said.

"Then let us—shall we?"

"Yes."

"And how soon can we go away?"

"We'll go at Christmas—only three weeks."

"Yes," she whispered happily.

As they sat at tea in his rooms, she was saying:

"I'm already thinking what things we shall take with us."

"All the *small* nice things," he said. "No furniture—at least, nothing much."

"No—but the china, and the rugs, and the pictures, and the books—and I've got two lovely statuettes, and some beautiful stuff for curtains—and—"

They broke off with a laugh.

"And where shall we go?" she asked.

"We'll see—somewhere among the mountains of Italy—in the Carrara region—or near Siena—or to California—which?"

"California—near the Pacific Ocean!—how wonderful!—But perhaps Italy first.—Shall we?"

"Yes, Italy first—and then further—and never come back."

"Never come back," she said solemnly, rather afraid.

There was a pause. He was sitting looking at her. She smiled with wonderful, delighted eyes.

"And what shall we *do*?" she cried.

"Meditate—and write—and teach about truth, if anybody comes;—be *really* happy."

"*Really* happy," she echoed, with glad solemnity. "And not be miserable *any* more."

"Never *really* miserable, whatever troubles there are—only really happy," he said. "And quite safe in a Paradise of truth."

"How lovely! How lovely!" she cried, kissing him, lest she should cry.

"One has known death," he said. "Now there is the life to come. Now there is to start again, like Adam and Eve in a real Paradise Regained."*

"*Our* life to come," she cried in joy.

"Yes," he said; "the happy, creative, contemplative life."

"Paradisal," she said.

At which he laughed with joy.

That evening, Ursula returned home very bright-eyed and wondrous—which irritated her people. Her father came home at supper-time, tired after the evening class, and the long journey home. Gudrun was reading, the mother sat in silence.

Suddenly Ursula said, to the company at large, in a bright voice:

"Rupert and I are going to be married tomorrow."

Her father turned round, stiffly.

"You what?" he said.

"Tomorrow!" echoed Gudrun.

"Indeed!" said the mother.

But Ursula only smiled wonderfully, and did not reply.

"Married tomorrow!" cried her father harshly. "What are you talking about!"

"Yes," said Ursula. "Why not?" Those two words, from her, always drove him mad. "Everything is all right—we shall go to the registrar's office—"

There was a second's hush in the room, after Ursula's blithe vagueness.

"*Really*, Ursula!" said Gudrun.

"Might we ask why there has been all this secrecy?" demanded the mother, rather superbly.

"But there hasn't," said Ursula. "You knew."

"Who knew?" now cried her father. "Who knew? What do you mean, by your '*you knew*'?" He was in one of his stupid rages, she instantly closed against him.

"Of course you knew," she said coolly. "You knew we were going to get married."

There was a dangerous pause.

"We knew you were going to get married, did we? Knew! Why when does anybody know anything about *you*, you shifty bitch!"

"Father!" cried Gudrun, flushing deep in violent remonstrance. Then, in a cold, but gentle voice, as if to win her sister to be tractable. "But isn't it a *fearfully* sudden decision, Ursula?" she asked.

"No, not really," replied Ursula, with the same maddening cheerfulness. "He's been *wanting* me to say yes, for weeks—he's had the licence ready. Only I—I wasn't ready in myself. Now I am ready—is there anything to be disagreeable about?"

"Certainly not," said Gudrun, but in a tone of cold reproof. "You are perfectly free to do as you like."

"'Ready in yourself'—*yourself*, that's all that matters, isn't it. 'I wasn't ready in myself,'" he mimicked her phrase offensively. "You and *yourself*, you're of some importance, aren't you?"

She drew herself up and set back her throat, her eyes shining yellow and dangerous.

"I am to myself," she said, wounded and mortified. "I know I am not to anybody else. You only wanted to *bully* me—you never cared for my happiness."

He was leaning forward watching her, his face intense like a spark.

"Ursula, what are you saying? Keep your tongue still," cried her mother. Ursula swung round, and the lights in her eyes flashed.

"No I won't," she cried. "I won't hold my tongue and be bullied.— What does it matter which day I get married—what does it *matter*! It doesn't affect anybody but myself."

Her father was tense and gathered together like a cat about to spring.

"Doesn't it?" he cried, coming nearer to her. She shrank away.

"No, how can it?" she replied, shrinking but stubborn.

"It doesn't matter to *me* then, what you do—what becomes of you—?" he cried, in a strange voice like a cry.

The mother and Gudrun stood back as if hypnotised.

"No," stammered Ursula. Her father was very near to her. "You only want to— —"

She knew it was dangerous, and she stopped. He was gathered together, every muscle ready.

"What—?" he challenged.

"Bully me," she muttered, and even as her lips were moving, his hand had caught her smack at the side of the head and she was sent banging up against the door.

"Father!" cried Gudrun in a high voice—"It is *impossible*!"

He stood unmoving. Ursula recovered, her hand was on the door-handle. She slowly drew herself up. He seemed doubtful now.

"It's true," she declared, with brilliant tears in her eyes, her head lifted up in defiance. "What has your love meant—what did it ever mean?— bullying, and repression—it did—"

He was advancing again with strange, tense movements, and clenched fist, and the face of a murderer. But swift as lightning she had flashed out of the door, and they heard her running upstairs.

He stood for a moment looking at the door. Then, like a defeated animal, he turned and went back to his seat by the fire.

Gudrun was very white. Out of the intense silence, the mother's voice was heard saying, cold and angry:

"Well, you shouldn't take so much notice of her."

Again the silence fell, each followed a separate set of emotions and thoughts.

Suddenly the door opened again: Ursula, dressed in hat and furs, with a small valise in her hand:

"Goodbye!" she said, in her maddening, bright, almost mocking tone. "I'm going."

And in the next instant the door was closed, they heard the outer door, then her quick steps down the garden path, then the gate banged, and her light footfall was gone. There was a silence like death in the house.

Ursula went straight to the station, hastening heedlessly, on winged feet. There was no train, she must walk on to the junction. As she went through the darkness, she began to cry, and she wept bitterly, with a dumb, heart-broken, child's anguish, all the way on the road, and in the train. Time passed unheeded and unknown, she did not know where she was, nor what was taking place. Only she wept from fathomless depths of hopeless, hopeless grief, the terrible grief of a child, that knows no extenuation.

Yet her voice had the same defensive brightness as she spoke to Birkin's landlady at the door.

"Good evening! Is Mr Birkin in? Can I see him?"

"Yes, he's in. He's in his study."

Ursula stepped past the woman. His door opened. He had heard her voice.

"Hello!" he exclaimed in surprise, seeing her standing there with the valise in her hand, and marks of tears on her face. She was one who wept without showing many traces, like a child.

"Do I look a sight?" she said, shrinking.

"No—why? Come in," he took the bag from her hand and they went into the study.

There, immediately, her lips began to tremble like those of a child that remembers again, and the tears came rushing up.

"What's the matter?" he asked, taking her in his arms. She sobbed violently on his shoulder, whilst he held her very still, waiting.

"What's the matter?" he said again, when she was quieter. But she only pressed her face further into his shoulder, shyly, and in pain, like a child that cannot tell.

"What is it, then?" he asked.

Suddenly she broke away, wiped her eyes, regained her composure, and went and sat in a chair.

"Father hit me," she announced, sitting bunched up, rather like a ruffled bird, her eyes very bright.

"What for?" he said.

She looked away, and would not answer. There was a pitiful redness about her sensitive nostrils, and her quivering lips.

"Why?" he repeated, in his strange, soft, penetrating voice.

She looked round at him, rather defiantly.

"Because I said I was going to be married tomorrow, and he bullied me."

"Why did he bully you?"

Her mouth dropped again, she remembered the scene once more, the tears came up.

"Because I said he didn't care—and he doesn't, it's only his domineer-ingness that's hurt—" she said, her mouth pulled awry by her weeping, all the time she spoke, so that he almost smiled, it seemed so childish. Yet it was not childish, it was a deep conflict, a deep wound.

"It isn't quite true," he said. "And even so, you shouldn't *say* it."

"It *is* true—it *is* true," she wept. "And I won't be bullied by his pretending it's love—when it *isn't*—he doesn't care, how can he—no, he can't—."

He sat in silence. She moved him beyond himself.

"Then you shouldn't rouse him, if he can't," replied Birkin quietly.

"And I *have* loved him, I have," she wept, "I've loved him always, and he's always done this to me, he has—."

"It's been a love of opposition, then," he said. "Never mind—it will be all right. It's nothing desperate."

"Yes," she wept, "it is, it is."

"Why?"

"I shall never see him again——"

"Not immediately—Don't cry, you had to break with him, it had to be—don't cry."

334

He went over to her and kissed her fine, fragile hair, touching her wet cheeks gently.

"Don't cry," he repeated, "don't cry any more."

He held her head close against him, very close and quiet.

At last she was still. Then she looked up, her eyes wide and frightened.

"Don't you want me?" she asked.

"Want you?" His darkened, steady eyes shamed the question in her.

"Do you wish I hadn't come?" she asked, anxious now again, for fear she might be out of place.

"No," he said. "I wish there hadn't been the violence—so much breaking—but perhaps it was inevitable."

She watched him in silence. He seemed saddened.

"But where shall I stay?" she asked, feeling humiliated.

He thought for a moment.

"Here, with me," he said. "We're married as much today as we shall be tomorrow."

"But—"

"I'll tell Mrs Varley," he said. "Never mind now."

He sat looking at her. She could feel his darkened, steady eyes looking at her all the time. It made her a little bit frightened. She pushed her hair off her forehead nervously.

"Do I look ugly?" she said.

And she blew her nose again.

A small smile came round his eyes.

"No," he said, "fortunately."

And he went across to her, and gathered her like a belonging in his arms. She was so tenderly beautiful, he could not bear to see her, he could only bear to hide her against himself. Now, washed all clear by her tears, she was new and frail like a flower just unfolded, a flower so new, so tender, so made up of perfect inner light, that he could not bear to look on her, he must hide her against himself, cover his eyes against her. She had the perfect candour of a child, something translucent and simple, like a radiant, silken flower that moment unfolded in primal blessedness. She was so new, so wonder-clear, so undimmed. And he was so old, so steeped in heavy memories. Her soul was like a child's, undefined and glimmering with the unseen. And his soul was dark and gloomy, it had only one grain of living hope, like a grain of mustard seed.* But this one living grain in him matched the perfect youth in her.

335

"I love you," he whispered as he kissed her, and trembled with pure hope, like a man who is born again to a wonderful, lovely hope far exceeding the bounds of death.

She could not know how much it meant to him, how much he meant by the few words. Almost childish, she wanted proof, and statement, even overstatement. For everything seemed still uncertain, unfixed to her.

But the passion of gratitude with which he received her into his soul, the extreme, unthinkable gladness of knowing himself living and fit to unite with her, he, who was so nearly dead, who was so near to being gone with the rest of his race down the slope of mechanical death, could never be understood by her. He worshipped her as age worships youth, he gloried in her because, in his one grain of faith, he was young as she, he was her proper mate. This marriage with her was his resurrection and his life.*

All this she could not know. She wanted to be made much of, to be adored. There were infinite distances of silence between them. How could he tell her of the immanence of her beauty, that was not form or weight or colour, but something like a strange golden light! How could he know himself what her beauty lay in, for him. He said "Your nose is beautiful, your chin is adorable." But it sounded like lies, and she was disappointed, hurt. Even when he said, whispering with truth, "I love you, I love you," it was not the real truth. It was something beyond love, such a gladness of being beyond oneself, of having transcended oneself. How could he say 'I', when he was something new and unknown, not himself at all? This I, this old formula of the ego, was a bondage.

In the new, golden bliss, a paradise superseding knowledge, there was no I and you, there was only the third, unrealised wonder, the wonder of existing not as oneself, but as an absolute consummation of his being and of her being in a new One, a new, paradisal oneness regained from the duality. How can I say "I love you", when I have ceased to be, and you have ceased to be, we are both caught up and transcended into a new oneness where everything is silent, because there is nothing to answer, all is perfect and at one. Speech travels between the separate parts. But in the perfect One there is perfect silence of bliss.

They were married by law on the next day, and she did as he bade her, she wrote to her father and mother. Her mother replied, not her father.

She did not go back to school. She stayed with Birkin in his rooms, or at the Mill, moving with him as he moved. But she did not see anybody, save Gudrun and Gerald. She was all strange and wondering as yet, but happy as the dawn.

Gerald sat talking to her one afternoon, in the warm study down at the Mill. Rupert had not yet come home.

"You are happy?" Gerald asked her, with a smile.

"Very happy!" she cried, shrinking a little in her brightness.

"Yes, one can see it."

"Can one?" cried Ursula, in surprise.

He looked up at her with a benevolent smile.

"Oh yes, very plainly."

She was pleased. She meditated a moment.

"And can you see that Rupert is happy as well?"

He lowered his eyelids, and looked aside.

"Oh yes," he said.

"Really?"

"Oh yes."

He was very quiet, as if it were something not to be talked about by him. He seemed sad.

She was very sensitive to suggestion. She asked the question he wanted her to ask.

"Why don't you be happy as well?" she said. "You could be just the same."

He paused a moment.

"With Gudrun?" he asked.

"Yes!" she cried, her eyes glowing. But there was a strange tension, an emphasis, as if they were asserting their wishes, against the truth.

"You think Gudrun would have me, and we should be happy?" he said.

"Yes, I'm *sure*," she cried.

Her eyes were round with delight. Yet underneath she was constrained, she felt she was false.

"Oh, I'm *so* glad," she added.

He smiled.

"What makes you glad?" he said.

"For *her* sake," she replied. "I'm sure you'd—you're the right man for her."

It was rather an unconvincing attempt. Still he smiled.

"You do?" he said. "And do you think she would agree with you?"

"Oh yes!" she exclaimed hastily. Then, upon reconsideration, very uneasy: "Though Gudrun isn't very simple, is she? One doesn't know her in five minutes, does one? She's not like me in that."

She laughed at him with her strange, open, dazzled face.

"You think she's not much like you?" Gerald asked.

She knitted her brows.

"Oh, in many ways she is.—But I never know what she will do when anything new comes."

"You don't?" said Gerald. He was silent for some moments. Then he moved tentatively. "I was going to ask her, in any case, to go away with me at Christmas," he said, in a very small, cautious voice.

"Go away with you? For a time, you mean?"

"As long as she likes," he said, with a deprecating movement.

They were both silent for some minutes.

"Of course," said Ursula at last, "she *might* just be willing to rush into marriage. You can see."

"Yes," smiled Gerald, "I can see.—But in case she won't—would you ask her to go abroad with me for a few days—or a fortnight if you were me?"

"Oh yes," said Ursula. "I'd ask her."

"Do you think we might all go together?"

"All of us?" Again Ursula's face lighted up. "It would be rather fun, don't you think?"

"Great fun," he said.

"And then you could see," said Ursula.

"What?"

"How things went.—I think it is best to take the honeymoon before the wedding—don't you?"

She was pleased with this 'mot.' He laughed.

"Occasionally," he said. "I'd rather it were so in my own case."

"Would you!" exclaimed Ursula. Then doubtingly, "Yes, perhaps you're right.—One should please oneself."

Birkin came in a little later, and Ursula told him what had been said.

"Gudrun!" exclaimed Birkin. "She's a born mistress, just as Gerald is a born lover—*amant en titre.** If as somebody says all women are either wives or mistresses, then Gudrun is a mistress."

"And all men either lovers or husbands?" cried Ursula. "But why not both?"

"The one excludes the other," he laughed.

"Then I want a lover," cried Ursula.

"No you don't," he said.

"But I do," she wailed.

He kissed her, and laughed.

It was two days after this that Ursula was to go to fetch her things from the house in Beldover. The removal had taken place, the family had gone. Gudrun had rooms in Willey Green.

Ursula had not seen her parents since her marriage. She wept over the rupture, yet what was the good making it up! Good or not good, she could not go to them. So her things had been left behind, and she and Gudrun were to walk over for them, in the afternoon.

It was a wintry afternoon, with red in the sky, when they arrived at the house. The windows were dark and blank, already the place was frightening. A bare, void, dim entrance hall struck a chill to the hearts of the girls.

"I don't believe I dare have come in alone," said Ursula. "The walls frighten me."

"Ursula!" cried Gudrun. "Isn't it amazing? Can you believe you went about this place and never knew? How I lived here a day without dying of the most complete terror, I cannot conceive!"

They looked in the big dining room. It was a good room, but now, a cell would have been lovelier. The large bay windows were naked, the floor was naked, and a border of dark polish went round the tract of pale boarding. In the faded wall-paper were dark shapes where furniture had stood, where pictures had hung. The sense of walls, dry, thin, brittle, flimsy-seeming walls, and a flimsy flooring, pale with its artificial black edges, was sterilising to the mind. The substance somehow was all wrong, there was a sense of enclosure within an unreal structure, for the walls gave no sense of weight. Where were they standing, on earth, or suspended in some box of sterile nullity? In the hearth was burnt paper, and scraps of half-burnt paper.

"To think that we lived here!" said Ursula.

"I know," cried Gudrun. "It is too frightening. What *must* human beings be like, if this is the outward shape of their daily life!"

"Horrible!" said Ursula. "It really is."

And she recognised half burnt covers of the "Fashions for All"*—half-burnt representations of women in coloured gowns—lying under the grate.

They went to the drawing room. Another piece of shut-in air, without weight or substance, only a sense of the most intolerable, frightening imprisonment by nothingness. The kitchen did look as if it had been inhabited by human beings, because of the red-tiled floor and the cupboards.

The two girls tramped hollowly up the bare stairs. Every sound re-echoed in their hearts. They tramped down the bare corridor. Against the wall of Ursula's bedroom were her things—a trunk, a work-basket, some books, loose coats, a hat-box, standing desolate in the universal bareness of the frightening dusk.

"A cheerful sight, aren't they?" said Ursula, looking down at her forsaken possessions.

"Very cheerful," said Gudrun.

The two girls set to, carrying everything down to the front door. Again and again they made the hollow, reechoing transit. The whole place seemed to resound about them with a noise of hollow, mocking laughter. In the distance the empty, invisible rooms sent forth a diabolic laughter. They almost fled with the last articles, into the out-of-doors.

But it was cold. They were waiting for Birkin, who was coming with the car. They went indoors again, and upstairs to their parents' front bedroom, whose windows looked down on the road, and across the country at the black-barred sunset, black and red barred, without light.

They say down in the window-seat, to wait. Both girls were looking over the room. It was void, with that unmeaning timeless atmosphere that was almost dreadful.

"Really," said Ursula, "this room isn't sacred—is it?"

Gudrun looked over it with slow eyes.

"It is not," she replied.

"When I think of their lives—father's and mother's—their love, and their marriage, and all us children, and our bringing up—would you have such a life, Prune?"

"I wouldn't Ursula."

"It all seems so nothing—their two lives—there's no *meaning* in it.— Really, if they had *not* met, and *not* married, and *not* lived together—it wouldn't have mattered, would it?"

"Of course—you can't tell," said Gudrun.

"No.—But if I thought my life was going to be like it—Prune," she caught Gudrun's arm, "I should run."

Gudrun was silent for a few moments.

"As a matter of fact, one cannot contemplate the ordinary married life—one cannot contemplate it," replied Gudrun. "With you, Ursula, it is quite different. You will be out of it all, with Birkin. He's a special case.—But with the ordinary man, who has his life fixed in one place, marriage is just impossible.—There may be, and there *are*, thousands of women who want it, and could conceive of nothing else. But the very thought of it sends me *mad*.—One must be free, above all, one must be free. One may forfeit everything else, but one must be free—one must not become 7 Pinchbeck Street—or Somerset Drive—or Shortlands.— No man will be sufficient to make that good—no man!—To marry, one must have a free lance, or nothing, a comrade in arms, a Glücksritter.* A man with a position in the social world—well, it is just impossible, impossible!"

"What a lovely word—a Glücksritter!" said Ursula. "So much nicer than a soldier of fortune."

"Yes, isn't it!" said Gudrun. "I'd ride over the world with a Glücksritter. But a home, an establishment—Ursula, what would it mean?—*think*!"

"I know," said Ursula. "We've had one home—that's enough for me."

"Quite enough," said Gudrun.

"The little grey home in the west,"* quoted Ursula ironically.

"*Doesn't* it sound grey, too!" said Gudrun grimly.

They were interrupted by the sound of the car. There was Birkin— Ursula was surprised that she felt so glad, that she became suddenly so indifferent to the problems of grey homes in the west.

They heard his heels click on the hall pavement below.

"Hello!" he called, his voice echoing alive through the house. Ursula smiled to herself. *He* was frightened of the place too.

"Hello! Here we are," she called downstairs.

And they heard him quickly running up.

"This is a ghostly situation," he said.

"These houses don't have ghosts—they've never had any personality, and only a place with personality can have a ghost," said Gudrun.

"I suppose so. Are you both weeping over the past?"

"We are," said Gudrun grimly.

Ursula laughed.

"Not weeping that it's gone—but weeping that it ever *was*," she said.

"Oh," he replied, relieved.

He sat down for a moment. There was something in his presence, Ursula thought, so strong and alive. It made even the impertinent structure of this null house give way to life.

"Gudrun says she could not bear to be married and put into a house," said Ursula, meaningful—they knew this referred to Gerald.

He was silent for some moments.

"Well," he said, "if you know beforehand you couldn't stand it, you're safe."

"Quite!" said Gudrun.

"Why *does* every woman think her aim in life is to have a hubby and a little grey home in the west? Why is this the goal of life? Why should it be?" asked Ursula.

"Il faut avoir le respect de ses bêtises," said Birkin.

"But you needn't have the respect for the bêtise before you've committed it," laughed Ursula.

"Ah then: 'il faut avoir le respect des bêtises du papa'."

"Et de la maman," added Gudrun satirically.

"Et des voisins,"* said Ursula.

They all laughed, and rose. It was getting dark. They carried the things to the car. Gudrun locked the door of the empty house. Birkin had lighted the lamps. It all seemed very happy.

"Do you mind stopping at Coulsons. I have to leave the key there," said Gudrun.

"Right," said Birkin, and they moved off.

They stopped in the main street. The shops were just lighted, the miners were passing home along the causeways, half visible shadows in their grey pit-dirt, moving through the blue air. But their feet rang harshly, in manifold sound, along the pavement.

How pleased Gudrun was to come, out of the shop, and enter the car, and be borne swiftly away into the down-hill of palpable dusk, with Ursula and Birkin! What an adventure life seemed at this moment! How deeply, how suddenly she envied Ursula! Life for her was so quick and reckless and full—so reckless, as if not only this world, but the world that was gone and the world to come were nothing to her. Ah, if she could be *just like that*, it would be perfect.

For always, except in her moments of excitement, she felt a want within herself, she was unsure. She had felt that now, at last, in Gerald's strong and violent love, she was living fully and finally. But when she compared herself with Ursula, already her soul was jealous, unsatisfied. She was not satisfied—she was never to be satisfied.

What was she short of now? It was marriage—it was the wonderful stability of marriage. She did want it, let her say what she might. She had been lying. The old idea of marriage was right even now—marriage and the home. Yet her mouth gave a little grimace at the words. She thought of Gerald and Shortlands—marriage and the home! Ah well, let it rest! He meant a great deal to her—but—! Perhaps it was not in her to marry. She was one of life's outcasts, one of the drifting lives that have no root. No, no—it could not be so. She suddenly conjured up a rosy room, with herself in a beautiful gown, and a handsome man in evening dress who held her in his arms in the firelight, and kissed her. This picture she entitled "Home." It would have done for the Royal Academy.

"Come with us to tea—*do*," said Ursula, as they ran nearer to the cottages of Willey Green.

"Thanks awfully—but I *must* go in—" said Gudrun. She wanted very much to go on with Ursula and Birkin. That seemed like life indeed to her. Yet a certain perversity would not let her.

"Do come—yes, it would be so nice," pleaded Ursula.

"I'm awfully sorry—I should love to—but I can't—really—"

She descended from the car in trembling haste.

"Can't you really!" came Ursula's regretful voice.

"No, really I can't," responded Gudrun's pathetic, chagrined words out of the dusk.

"All right, are you?" called Birkin.

"Quite!" said Gudrun. "Goodnight!"

"Goodnight," they called.

"Come whenever you like, we shall be glad," called Birkin.

"Thank you very much," called Gudrun, in the strange, twanging voice of lonely chagrin that was very puzzling to him. She turned away to her cottage gate, and they drove on. But immediately she stood to watch them, as the car ran vague into the distance. And as she went up the path to her strange house, her heart was full of incomprehensible bitterness.

In her parlour was a long-case clock, and inserted into its dial was a ruddy, round, slant-eyed, joyous-painted face, that wagged over with the most ridiculous ogle when the clock ticked, and back again with the same absurd glad-eye at the next tick. All the time the absurd smooth, brown-ruddy face gave her an obtrusive "glad eye." She stood for minutes, watching it, till a sort of maddened disgust overcame her, and she laughed at herself, hollowly And still it rocked, and gave her the glad eye from one side, then from the other, from one side, then from the other. Ah, how unhappy she was! In the midst of her most active happiness, ah, how unhappy she was! She glanced at the table. Gooseberry jam, and the same home-made cake with too much soda in it. Still, gooseberry jam was good, and one so rarely got it.

All the evening she wanted to go to the Mill. But she coldly refused to allow herself. She went the next afternoon instead. She was happy to find Ursula alone. It was a lovely, intimate, secluded atmosphere. They talked endlessly and delightedly. "I am *fearfully* happy here!" said Gudrun to herself, glancing at her own bright eyes in the mirror.

"How really beautifully this room is done," she said aloud. "This hard plaited matting—what a lovely colour it is, the colour of cool light!"

And it seemed to her perfect.

"Ursula," she said at length, in a voice of question and detachment: "Did you know that Gerald Crich had suggested our going away all together at Christmas?"

"Yes, he's spoken to Rupert."

A deep flush dyed Gudrun's cheek. She was silent a moment, as if taken aback, and not knowing what to say.

"But don't you think," she said at last, "it is *amazingly cool*!"

Ursula laughed.

"I liked him for it," she said.

Gudrun was silent. It was evident that, whilst she was almost mortified by Gerald's taking the liberty of making such a suggestion to Birkin, yet the idea itself attracted her strongly.

"There's a rather lovely simplicity about Gerald, I think," said Ursula. "So defiant, somehow!—Oh, I think he's *very* lovable."

Gudrun did not reply for some moments. She had still to get over the feeling of insult at the liberty taken with her freedom.

"What did Rupert say—do you know?" she asked.

"He said it would be most awfully jolly," said Ursula.

Again Gudrun looked down, and was silent.

"Don't you think it would?" said Ursula, tentatively. She was never quite sure how many defences Gudrun was having round herself.

Gudrun raised her face with difficulty, and held it averted.

"I think it *might* be awfully jolly, as you say," she replied. "But don't you think it was an unpardonable liberty to take—to talk of such a thing to Rupert—who after all—You see what I mean, Ursula—they might have been two men arranging an outing with some little *type** they'd picked up. Oh, I think it's unforgivable, quite!" She used the French word 'type.'

Her eye flashed, her soft face was flushed and sullen. Ursula looked on, rather frightened, frightened most of all because she thought Gudrun seemed rather common, really like a little *type*. But she had not the courage quite to think this—not right out—

"Oh no," she cried, stammering. "Oh no—not at all like that—oh no!—No, I think it's rather beautiful, the friendship between Rupert and Gerald. They just are quite simple—they say anything to each other, like brothers."

Gudrun flushed deeper. She could not *bear* it that Gerald gave her away—even to Birkin.

"But do you think even brothers have any right to exchange confidences of that sort?" she asked, with deep anger.

"Oh yes," said Ursula. "There's never anything said that isn't perfectly direct and simple.—No, the thing that's amazed me most in Gerald—how perfectly simple and direct he can be!—And you know, it takes rather a big man. Most of them *must* be indirect, they are such cowards."

But Gudrun was still silent with anger. She wanted the absolutest secrecy kept, with regard to her movements.

"Won't you go?" said Ursula. "Do, we might all be so happy!—There is something I *love* about Gerald—he's *much* more lovable than I thought him. He's free, Gudrun, he really is."

Gudrun's mouth was still closed sullen and ugly. She opened it at length.

"Do you know where he proposes to go?" she asked.

"Yes—to the Tyrol, where he used to go when he was in Germany—a lovely place where students go, small and rough and lovely, for winter sport!"

Through Gudrun's mind went the angry thought—"they know everything."

"Yes," she said aloud, "about forty miles from Innsbruck, isn't it?"

"I don't know exactly where—but it would be lovely, don't you think, high in the perfect snow—?"

"Very lovely!" said Gudrun, sarcastically.

Ursula was put out.

"Of course," she said, "I think Gerald spoke to Rupert so that it *shouldn't* seem like a little outing with a *type*—"

"I know, of course," said Gudrun, "that he quite commonly does take up with that sort."

"Does he!" said Ursula, pained. "Why how do you know?"

"I know of a model in Chelsea," said Gudrun coldly.

Now Ursula was silent.

"Well," she said at last, with a painful laugh, "I hope he has a good time with her." At which Gudrun only looked more glum.

Christmas drew near, all four prepared for flight. Birkin and Ursula were busy packing their best loved things, making them ready to be sent off, to whatever country and whatever place they might choose on at last. Gudrun was very much excited. She loved to be on the wing.

She and Gerald, being ready first, set off via London and Paris to Innsbruck, where they would meet Ursula and Birkin. In London they stayed one night. They went to a music-hall, and afterwards to the Café Impérial.

Gudrun hated the Café, yet she always went back to it, as did most of the artists of her acquaintance. She loathed its atmosphere of petty vice and petty jealousy and petty art. Yet she always went again, when she was in town. It was as if she *had* to return to this small, slow, central whirlpool of disintegration and dissolution. Here the living body of England was slowly disintegrating, with an inward disease.

She sat with Gerald drinking some esoteric liqueur, and staring with black, sullen looks at the various groups of people at the tables. She would greet nobody, but young men nodded to her frequently, with a kind of sneering familiarity. She cut them all. And it gave her pleasure to sit there, cheeks flushed, eyes black and sullen, seeing them all objectively, as put away from her, like creatures in some menagerie of apish, degraded souls. God, what a foul crew they were! Her blood beat black and thick in her veins with rage and loathing. Yet she must sit and watch, watch. One or two people came to speak to her. From every side of the Café, eyes turned half furtively, half jeeringly at her, men looking over their shoulders, women under their hats.

The old crowd was there, Thomas in his corner with his pupils and his girl, Halliday and Libidnikov and the Pussum—they were all there. Gudrun watched Gerald. She watched his eyes linger a moment on Halliday, on Halliday's party. These last were on the look-out—they nodded to him, he nodded again. They giggled and whispered among themselves. Gerald watched them with the steady twinkle in his eyes. They were urging the Pussum to something.

She at last rose. She was wearing a curious dress of dark silk splashed and spattered with zigzags of all colours, a curious motley effect. She was thinner, her eyes were perhaps hotter, more disintegrated. Otherwise she was just the same. Gerald watched her with the same steady twinkle in his eyes as she came across.

She held out her thin brown hand to him.

"How are you?" she said.

He shook hands with her, but remained seated, and let her stand near him, against the table. She nodded blackly to Gudrun, whom she did not know to speak to, but well enough by sight and reputation.

"I am very well," said Gerald. "And you—?"

"Oh I'm all wight.—What about Wupert?"

"Rupert?—He's very well too."

"Yes, I don't mean that. What about him being married?"

"Oh—yes, he is married."

The Pussum's eyes had a hot flash.

"Oh, he's weally bwought it off then, has he? When was he married?"

"A week or two ago."

"Weally! He's never written."

"No."

"No.—Don't you think it's too bad?"

This last was in a tone of challenge. The Pussum let it be known, by her tone, that she was aware of Gudrun's listening.

"I suppose he didn't feel like it," replied Gerald.

"But why didn't he?" pursued the Pussum.

This was received in silence. There was an ugly mocking persistence in the small, beautiful figure of the depraved girl, as she stood near Gerald.

"Are you staying in town long?" she asked.

"Tonight only."

"Oh, only tonight.—Are you coming over to speak to Julius?"

"Not tonight."

"Oh very well. I'll tell him then." Then came her touch of diablerie. "You're looking awf'lly fit."

"Yes—I feel it." Gerald was quite calm and easy, a spark of satiric amusement in his eye.

"I suppose you're having a good time."

This was a direct blow for Gudrun, spoken in a level, toneless voice of callous ease.

"Yes," he replied, quite colourlessly.

"I'm awf'lly sorry you aren't coming round to the flat.—You aren't very faithful to your fwiends."

"Not very," he said.

She nodded them both 'Goodnight', and went back slowly to her own set. Gudrun watched her curious walk, stiff and wagging at the loins. They heard her level, toneless voice distinctly.

"He won't come across just now," it said.

There was more laughter and lowered voices and mockery at the table.

"Is she a friend of yours?" said Gudrun, looking calmly at Gerald.

"I've stayed at Halliday's flat with Birkin," he said, meeting her slow, calm eyes. And she knew that the Pussum was one of his mistresses— and he knew she knew.

She looked round, and called for the waiter. She wanted an iced cocktail, of all things. This amused Gerald—he wondered what was up.

The Halliday party was tipsy, and malicious. They were talking out loudly about Birkin, ridiculing him on every point, particularly on his marriage.

"Oh, *don't* make me think of Birkin," Halliday was squealing. "He makes me perfectly sick. He is as bad as Jesus. 'Lord, *what* must I do to be saved'."*

He giggled to himself tipsily.

"Do you remember," came the quick voice of the Russian, "the letters he used to send. "'Desire is holy—'"

"Oh yes!" cried Halliday. "Oh, how perfectly splendid! Why, I've got one in my pocket. I'm sure I have."

He took out various papers from his pocket book.

"I'm sure I've—*hic!*—*Oh dear!*—got one."

Gerald and Gudrun were watching absorbedly.

"Oh yes, how perfectly—*hic!*—splendid!—Don't make me laugh, Pussum, it gives me the hiccup. Hic!—" They all giggled.

"What did he say in that one?" the Pussum asked, leaning forward, her dark, soft hair falling and swinging against her face. There was something curiously indecent, obscene, about her small, longish, dark skull; the strange obscenity of the ancient Egyptians.

"Wait—oh do wait! *No—o*, I won't give it you, I'll read it aloud. I'll read you the choice bits—*hic!* Oh dear! Do you think if I drank water it would take off this hiccup? Hic! Oh, I feel perfectly helpless."

"Isn't that the letter about uniting the dark and the light—and the Flux of Corruption?" asked Maxim, in his precise, quick voice.

"I believe so," said the Pussum.

"Oh is it? I'd forgotten—*hic!*—it was that one," Halliday said, opening the letter. "*Hic!*—Oh yes. How perfectly splendid! This is one of the best.—'There is a phase in every race—'" he read in the sing-song, slow, distinct voice of a clergyman reading the Scriptures, "'when the desire for destruction overcomes every other desire. In the individual, this desire is ultimately a desire for destruction in the self'—*hic!*—" he paused and looked up.

"I hope he's going ahead with the destruction of himself," said the quick voice of the Russian. Halliday giggled, and lolled his head back vaguely.

"There's not much to destroy in Birkin," said the Pussum. "He's not *weally* alive."

"Oh, isn't it beautiful! I love reading it! I believe it has cured my hiccup!" squealed Halliday. "Do let me go on.—'It is a desire for the reduction process in oneself, a reducing back to the origins, a return along the Flux of Corruption, to the original rudimentary conditions of being—' Oh, but I *do* think it is wonderful. It *almost* supersedes the Bible—"

"Yes—Flux of Corruption," said the Russian. "I remember that phrase."

"Oh, he was always talking about Corwuption," said the Pussum. "He must be corwupt himself, to have it so much on his mind."

"Exactly!" said the Russian.

"Do let me go on! Oh, this is a perfectly wonderful piece! But do listen to this. 'And in the great retrogression, the reducing back of the

349

created body of life, we get knowledge, and beyond knowledge, the phosphorescent ecstasy of acute sensation.'—Oh, I do think those phrases are too absurdly wonderful. Oh but don't you think they are—they're nearly as good as Jesus.—'—and if, Julius you want this ecstasy of reduction with the Pussum, you must go on till it is fulfilled. But surely there is in you also, somewhere, the living desire for new creation, new creation in yourself, when all this process of active corruption, with all its flowers of mud, is more or less finished—'—I do wonder what the flowers of mud are. Pussum, you are a flower of mud."

"Thank you—and what are you?"

"Oh, I'm another, surely, according to this letter! We're all flowers of mud.—Oh, do save me from myself, dear Jesus!" Halliday giggled.

"Go on—go on," said Maxim. "What comes next. It's really very interesting."

"I think it's awful cheek to write like that," said the Pussum.

"Yes—yes, so do I," said the Russian. "He is a megalomaniac, of course—the ravings of a megalomaniac. But go on, Julius—go on reading."

"Surely," Halliday intoned, "Surely goodness and mercy hath followed me all the days of my life—"* he broke off, and giggled. Then he began again, intoning like a clergyman. "Surely there will come an end in us to this desire—for the constant going apart,—this passion for putting asunder—everything—ourselves, reducing ourselves part from part,—reacting in intimacy only for reduction,—using sex as a great reducing agent, reducing the two great elements of male and female from their highly complex unity,— reducing the old ideas, reducing the Godhead to its anthropomorphic elements—reducing the body politic to a nothingness, a dead level of homogeneous null units—reducing the social law to a dead letter—reducing—"

"I want to go," said Gudrun to Gerald, as she signalled the waiter. Her eyes were flashing, her cheeks were flushed. The strange effect of Birkin's letter read aloud in a perfect clerical sing-song, clear and resonant, phrase by phrase, made the blood mount into her head as if she were mad.

She rose, whilst Gerald was paying the bill, and walked over to Halliday's table. They all glanced up at her.

"Excuse me," she said. "Is that a genuine letter you are reading?"

"Oh yes," said Halliday. "Quite!"

"May I see?"

In silence he handed it to her, as if hypnotised.

"Thank you," she said.

And she turned and walked out of the Café, all down the brilliant room, between the tables, in her measured fashion.

From Halliday's table came half articulate cries, then somebody booed, then all the far end of the place began booing after Gudrun's retreating form. She was fashionably dressed in a wide-brimmed, slanting hat of emerald velvet, trimmed with a stiff film of silver, an emerald velvet coat with a high collar of chinchilla fur, and a band of chinchilla fur round the bottom, that swung almost hoop-like as she walked, whilst her skirt was dark-green, her stockings also dark green. She moved with slow, fashionable indifference out of the café. The porter at the door opened obsequiously for her, and, at her nod, hurried to the edge of the pavement and whistled for a taxi. The two lights of a vehicle almost immediately curved round towards her, like two eyes.

Gerald had followed in wonder, amid all the booing, not having caught her misdeed. He heard the Pussum's voice saying:

"Go and get it back from her! I never heard of such a thing! Go and get it back from her.—Tell Gerald Crich—there he goes—go and make him give it up."

Gudrun stood at the door of the taxi, which the man held open for her.

"To the hôtel?" she asked, as Gerald came out, hurriedly.

"Where you like," he answered.

"Right!" she said. Then, to the driver: "Wallenhof—Kingsway."

The driver bowed his head, and put down the flag.

Gudrun entered the taxi, with the deliberate, cold movement of a woman who is well-dressed and contemptuous in her soul. Yet she was frozen with overwrought feeling. Gerald followed her.

"You've forgotten the man," she said coolly, with a slight motion of her hat. Gerald gave the porter a shilling. The man saluted. They were in motion.

"What was all the row about?" asked Gerald, in wondering excitement.

"I walked away with Birkin's letter," she said, and he saw the crushed paper in her hand.

His eyes glittered with satisfaction.

"Ah!" he said. "Splendid!—A set of dirty dogs!"

"I could have *killed* them!" she cried in passion. "*Dogs*!—they *are* dogs!—Why is Rupert such a *fool* as to write such letters to them? *Why* does he give himself away to such canaille? It's a thing that *cannot be borne*—"

Gerald wondered over her strange passion.

And she could not rest any longer in London. They must go by the morning train from Charing Cross. As they drew over the bridge, in the train, having glimpses of the river between the great iron girders, she cried:

"I feel I could *never* see this *foul* town again—. I couldn't *bear* to come back to it."

11

URSULA WENT ON IN AN UNREAL suspense, the last weeks before going away. She was not herself—she was not anything. She was something that is going to be—soon—soon—very soon. But as yet, she was only imminent.

She went to see her parents. It was a rather stiff, sad meeting, more like a verification of separateness than a reunion. But they were all gentle and indefinite with one another, submitting to the fate that moved them apart.

She did not really come to, until she was on the ship crossing from Dover to Ostend. Dimly she had come down to London with Birkin, London had been a vagueness, so had the train-journey to Dover. It was all like a sleep.

And now, at last, as she stood in the stern of the ship, in a pitch-dark, rather blowy night, feeling the motion of the sea, and watching the small, rather desolate, little lights that twinkled on the shores of England, as on the shores of nowhere, watched them sinking smaller and smaller on the profound and living darkness, she felt her soul stirring to awake from its anaesthetic sleep.

"Let us go forward, shall we?" said Birkin. He wanted to be at the tip of their projection. So they left off looking at the faint sparks that glimmered out of nowhere, in the far distance, in an uneven line, and turned their faces to the unfathomed night in front.

They went right to the bows of the softly plunging vessel. In the complete obscurity, Birkin found a somewhat sheltered nook, where a great rope was coiled up. It was quite near the very point of the ship, near the black, unpierced space ahead. Here they sat down, folded together, folded round with the same rug, creeping in nearer and ever nearer to one another, till it seemed they had crept right in to each other, and become one substance. It was very cold, and the darkness was palpable.

One of the ship's crew came along the deck, dark as the darkness, not really visible. They then made out the faintest pallor of his face. He felt their presence, and stopped, unsure—then bent forward.

When his face was near them, he saw the faint pallor of their faces. Then he withdrew, like a phantom. And they watched him without making any sound.

They seemed to fall away into the profound darkness. There was no sky, no earth, only one unbroken darkness, into which, with a soft, sleeping motion, they seemed to fall, like one closed ball of life falling through dark, fathomless space.

They had forgotten where they were, forgotten all that was and all that had been, conscious only in their heart, and there conscious only of this pure trajectory through the surpassing darkness. The ship's prow cleaved on, with a faint noise of cleavage, into the complete night, without knowing, without seeing, only surging on.

In Ursula the sense of the unrealised world ahead triumphed over everything. In the midst of this profound darkness, there seemed to glow on her heart the effulgence of a paradise unknown and unrealised, a virgin paradise which she, Eve, happy and fulfilled, was to enter. Her heart was full of the most wonderful light, golden like honey of darkness, sweet like the warmth of day, a light which was not shed on the world, only on the unknown paradise towards which she was going, a sweetness of habitation, a delight of living quite unknown, but hers infallibly.

In her transport she lifted her face suddenly to him, and he touched it with his lips. So cold, so fresh, so sea-clear her face was, it was like kissing a flower that grows near the surf.

But he did not know the ecstasy of bliss in foreknowledge, that she knew. To him, the wonder of this transit was overwhelming. He was falling through a gulf of infinite darkness, like a meteorite plunging across the chasm between the worlds. The world was torn in two, and he was plunging like an unlit star through the ineffable rift. What was beyond was not yet for him. He was overcome by the stupendous trajectory.

In a trance he lay enfolding Ursula round about. His face was against her fine, fragile hair, he breathed its fragrance with the sea and the profound night. And his soul was at peace; yielded, as he fell into the unknown. This was the first time that an utter and absolute peace had entered his heart, now, in this final transit out of life.

When there came some stir on the deck, they roused. They stood up. How stiff and cramped they were, in the night-time! And yet the paradisal glow on her heart, and the unutterable peace of darkness in his, this was the all-in-all.

They stood up and looked ahead. Low lights were seen down the darkness. This was the world again. It was not the bliss of her heart, nor the peace of his. It was the old world. Yet not quite the old world. For the peace and the bliss in their hearts was everlasting.

Strange, and desolate above all things, like disembarking from the Styx into the desolated underworld, was this landing at night. There was the raw, half-lighted, covered-in vastness of the dark place, boarded and hollow underfoot, with only desolation everywhere. Ursula had caught sight of a dim sign, with the word "Ostend," standing in the darkness. Everybody was hurrying with a blind, insect-like intentness through the dark grey air, porters were calling in unEnglish English, then trotting with heavy bags, their colourless blouses looking ghostly as they disappeared; Ursula stood at a long, low, zinc-covered barrier, along with hundreds of other spectral people, and all the way down the vast, raw darkness was this low stretch of open bags and spectral people, whilst, on the other side of the barrier, pallid officials in peaked caps and moustaches were turning the underclothing in the bags, then scrawling a chalk-mark.

It was done. Birkin snapped the hand bags, off they went, the porter coming behind. They were through a great doorway and in the open night again—ah, a railway platform! Voices were still calling in inhuman agitation through the dark-grey air, spectres were running along the darkness between the trains.

"Köln—Berlin—" Ursula made out on the boards hung on the high train on one side.

"Here we are," said Birkin. And on her side she saw:

"ELSASS—LOTHRINGEN—Luxembourg, Metz—BASEL."*

That was it, Basle!

The porter came up:

"A Basle—deuxième classe?—Voilà."*

And he clambered into the high train. They followed. The compartments were already some of them taken. But many were dim and empty. The luggage was stowed, the porter was tipped.

"Nous avons encore—?" said Birkin, looking at his watch and at the porter.

"Encore une demi-heure."* With which, in his blue blouse, he disappeared. He was ugly and insolent.

"Come," said Birkin. "It is cold. Let us eat."

There was a coffee-wagon on the platform. They drank hot, watery coffee, and ate the long rolls, split, with ham between, which were such a wide bite that it almost dislocated Ursula's jaw, and they walked under the high trains. It was all so strange, so extremely desolate, like the underworld, grey, grey, dirt-grey, desolate, forlorn, nowhere—grey, dreary nowhere.

At last they were moving through the night. In the darkness Ursula made out the flat fields, the wet flat dreary darkness of the continent. They pulled up surprisingly soon—Bruges! Then on through the level darkness, with glimpses of sleeping farms and thin poplar trees and deserted high-roads. She sat dismayed, hand in hand with Birkin. He, pale, immobile, like a *revenant* himself, looked sometimes out of the window, sometimes closed his eyes. Then his eyes opened again, dark as the darkness outside.

A flash of a few lights on the darkness—Ghent station! A few more spectres moving outside on the platform—then the bell—then motion again through the level darkness.

Ursula saw a man with a lantern come out of a farm by the railway, and cross to the dark farm-buildings. She thought of the Marsh, the old, intimate farm-life at Cossethay. My God, how far was she projected from her childhood, how far was she still to go! In one life-time one travelled through aeons. The great chasm of memory, from her childhood in the intimate country surroundings of Cossethay and the Marsh Farm—she remembered the servant Tilly, who used to give her bread and butter sprinkled with brown sugar, in the old living-room where the grandfather clock had two pink roses in a basket painted above the figures on the face—and now, when she was travelling into the unknown with Birkin,

355

an utter stranger—was so great, that it seemed she had no identity, that the child she had been, playing in Cossethay churchyard, was a little creature of imagination, not really herself.

They were at Brussels—half an hour for breakfast. They got down. On the great station clock it said six o'clock. They had coffee and rolls and honey in the vast, desert refreshment room, so dreary, always so dreary, dirty, so spacious, such desolation of space. But she washed her face and hands in hot water, and combed her hair—that was a blessing.

Soon they were in the train again and moving on. The greyness of dawn began. There were several people in the compartment, large, florid Belgian business-men with long brown beards, talking incessantly in an ugly French she was too tired to follow.

It seemed the train ran by degrees out of the darkness into a faint light, then beat after beat into the day. Ah, how weary it was! Faintly, the trees showed, like shadows. Then a house, white, had a curious distinctness. How was it? Then she saw a village—there were always houses passing.

This was the old world she was still journeying through, winter-heavy and dreary. There was plough-land and pasture, and copses of bare trees, copses of bushes, and homesteads naked and work-bare. No new earth had come to pass.

She looked at Birkin's face. It was white and still and eternal, too eternal. She linked her fingers imploringly in his, under the cover of her rug. His fingers responded, his eyes looked back at her. How dark, like a night, his eyes were, like another world beyond! Oh, if he were the world as well, if only the world were he! If only he could call a world into being, that should be their own world!

The Belgians left, the train ran on, through Luxembourg, through Alsace-Lorraine, through Metz. But she was blind, she could see no more. Her soul did not look out.

They came at last to Basle, to the hotel. It was all a drifting trance, from which she never came to. They went out in the morning, before the train departed. She saw the streets, the river, she stood on the bridge. But it all meant nothing. She remembered some shops—one full of pictures, one with orange velvet and ermine. But what did these signify?—nothing.

She was not at ease till they were in the train again. Then she was relieved. So long as they were moving onwards, she was satisfied. They

356

came to Zurich, then, before very long, ran under the mountains, that were deep in snow. At last she was drawing near. This was the other world, now.

Innsbruck was wonderful, deep in snow, and evening. They drove in an open sledge over the snow: the train had been so hot and stifling. And the hotel, with the golden light glowing under the porch, seemed like a home.

They laughed with pleasure when they were in the hall. The place seemed full and busy.

"Do you know if Mr and Mrs Crich—English—from Paris, have arrived?" Birkin asked in German.

The waiter reflected a moment, and was just going to answer, when Ursula caught sight of Gudrun sauntering down the stairs, wearing her emerald velvet coat.

"Gudrun! Gudrun!" she called, waving up the well of the staircase: "Yu-hu!"

Gudrun looked over the rail, and immediately lost her sauntering, diffident air. Her eyes flashed.

"Really—Ursula!" she cried.

And she began to move downstairs as Ursula ran up. They met at a turn and kissed with laughter and exclamations inarticulate and stirring.

"But!" cried Gudrun, mortified. "We thought it was *tomorrow* you were coming! I wanted to come to the station."

"No, we've come today!" cried Ursula. "Isn't it lovely here!"

"Adorable!" said Gudrun. "Gerald's just gone out to get skis or something.—Ursula, aren't you *fearfully* tired?"

"No, not so very. But I look a filthy sight, don't I?"

"No, you don't. You look almost perfectly fresh.—I like that fur cap *immensely*!"

She glanced over Ursula, who wore a big soft coat with a collar of deep, soft, grey fur, and a soft grey cap of fur.

"And you!" cried Ursula. "What do you think *you* look like!"

Gudrun assumed an unconcerned, expressionless face.

"Do you like it?" she said.

"It's *very beautiful*!" cried Ursula.

"Go up—or come down," said Birkin.

For there the sisters stood, Gudrun with her hand on Ursula's arm, on the turn of the stairs half way to the first landing, blocking the way, and affording full entertainment to the whole of the hall below, from the door porter to the plump Jew in black clothes.

The two young women slowly mounted, followed by Birkin and the waiter.

"First floor?" asked Gudrun, looking back over her shoulder.

"Second madam—the lift—!" the waiter replied, and he darted to the elevator, to forestall the two women. But they ignored him, as, chattering without heed, they set to mount the second flight. Rather chagrined, the waiter followed.

It was curious, the delight of the sisters in each other, at this meeting. It was as if they met in exile, and united their solitary forces against all the world. Birkin looked on with some mistrust and wonder.

When they had bathed and changed, Gerald came in. He looked shining and handsome.

"Go with Gerald and smoke," said Ursula to Birkin. "Gudrun and I want to talk."

Then the sisters sat in Gudrun's bedroom, and talked clothes, and experiences. Gudrun told Ursula the experience of the Birkin letter in the Café Impérial, Ursula was shocked and frightened.

"Where is the letter?" she asked.

"I kept it," said Gudrun.

"You'll give it me, won't you?" she said. But Gudrun was silent for some moments, before she replied:

"Do you really want it, Ursula?"

"I want to read it," said Ursula.

"Certainly," said Gudrun.

Even now, she could not admit, to Ursula, that she wanted to keep it, as a memento, or a symbol. But Ursula knew, and was not pleased. So the subject was switched off.

"What did you do in Paris?" asked Ursula.

"Oh," said Gudrun laconically—"the usual things. We had a fine party one night in Fanny Rath's studio."

"Did you? And you and Gerald were there! Who else? Tell me about it."

"Well," said Gudrun. "There's nothing particular to tell. You know Fanny is *frightfully* in love with that painter, Billy Macfarlane. *He* was there—so Fanny warmed everything up steaming.*—It was really fun! Of course, everybody got fearfully drunk—but in a decent way, not like that filthy London crowd. The fact is, these were all people that matter, which makes all the difference. There was a Roumanian, a fine chap. He got completely drunk, and climbed to the top of a high studio ladder, and gave the most marvellous address—really, Ursula, it was wonderful! He began in French—La vie, c'est une affaire d'âmes impériales*—in a most beautiful voice—he was a fine-looking chap—but he had got into Roumanian before he had finished, and not a soul understood. But Sholto Bannerman was worked to a frenzy. He dashed his glass to the ground, and declared, by God, he was glad he had been born, by God, it was a miracle to be alive.—And do you know, Ursula, so it was, to be alive among people like that—"

"But how was Gerald among them all?" asked Ursula.

"Gerald! Oh, my word, he came out like a dandelion in the sun! He's a whole Saturnalia in himself, once he is roused. I shouldn't like to say whose waist his arm did not go round.—Really, Ursula, he seems to reap the women like a harvest: there wasn't one that would have resisted him. It was too amazing! Can you understand it?"

Ursula reflected, and a dancing light came into her eyes.

"Yes," she said, "I can. He is such a whole-hogger."

"Whole-hogger!—I should think so!" exclaimed Gudrun. "But really, Ursula, every woman in the room was ready to surrender to him—Chanticler* isn't in it—even Fanny Rath, who is *really* in love with Billy Macfarlane! I never was more amazed in my life!—And you know, afterwards—I felt I was a whole *roomful* of women! I was no more myself to him, than I was Queen Victoria. I was a whole roomful of women at once. It was most astounding!—But my eye, I'd caught a Sultan* that time—"

Gudrun's eyes were flashing, her cheek was hot, she looked some wonderful, exotic flower. Ursula was fascinated at once—and yet uneasy.

They had to get ready for dinner. Gudrun came down in a daring gown of broad stripes of vivid green and scarlet with fur trimming, and having bunches of red berries and green leaves, in her hair. She was really brilliantly beautiful, and everybody noticed her. Gerald was in that full-blooded, gleaming state when he was most handsome. Birkin watched them with quick, laughing, half-frightened eyes, Ursula quite lost her head. There seemed a spell, almost a blinding spell, cast round their table, as if they were lighted up more strongly than the rest of the dining-room.

359

"Don't you love to be in this place?" cried Gudrun. "Isn't the snow wonderful! Do you notice how it exalts everything? It is simply marvellous. One really does feel übermenschlich*—more than human."

"One does," cried Ursula. "But isn't that partly the being out of England?"

"Oh, of course," cried Gudrun. "One could never feel like this in England, for the simple reason that the damper is *never* lifted off one, there. It is quite impossible to really let go, in England, of that I am assured."

And she turned again to the caviare she was eating. She was fluttering with vivid intensity and beauty.

"It's quite true," said Gerald, "it never is *quite* the same in England.— But perhaps we don't want it to be—perhaps it's like bringing the light a little too near the powder-magazine, to let go altogether, in England. One is afraid what might happen, if *everybody else* let go."

"My God!" cried Gudrun. "But wouldn't it be wonderful, if all England *did* suddenly go off like a display of fireworks."

"It couldn't," said Ursula. "They are all too damp, the powder is damp in them."

"I'm not so sure of that," said Gerald.

"Nor I," said Birkin. "When the English really begin to go off, *en masse*, it'll be time to shut your ears, and run."

"They never will," said Ursula.

"We'll see," he replied.

"Isn't it marvellous," said Gudrun, "how thankful one can be, to be out of one's country. I cannot believe myself, I am so transported, the moment I set foot on a foreign shore. I say to myself 'Here steps a new creature into life.'"

"Don't be too hard on poor old England," said Gerald. "Though we curse it, we love it really."

To Ursula, there seemed a fund of cynicism in these words.

"We do," said Birkin. "But it's a damnably uncomfortable love: like a love for an aged parent who suffers horribly from a complication of diseases, for which there is no hope."

Gudrun looked at him with dilated dark eyes.

"You think there is no hope for England?" she asked, in her pertinent fashion.

But Birkin backed away. He would not answer such a question.

"Any hope of England's becoming a living, sound, free people?" he said. "—I don't know. She'll have to die and be born again."

"And you don't think she ever *will* be born again?" persisted Gudrun. It was strange, her tense interest in his answer. Was this one of her problems too? Her dark, dilated eyes rested on Birkin, as if she could conjure the truth of the future out of him, as out of some instrument of divination.

He went pale. Then, reluctantly, he answered:

"Yes—when she has died."

Gudrun watched him as if in a hypnotic state, her eyes wide and fixed on him.

"When England has died, she will be born again?" she persisted.

He stirred like one held down by the point of a spear.

"Yes," he said. "At least the English *people*. As for nations—" he made a strange wave of dismissal with his hand.

Gudrun continued to watch him.

"But when will England die?" she asked.

He spread his hands in a motion of hopeless impotence.

"How do I know? In the time to come. I only want to get out, now, and leave the dying England to her death—since it must be so.—I want the Hesperides."*

Gudrun watched him still for a few seconds. Then she turned away. It was finished, her spell of divination in him. She felt already purely cynical. She looked at Gerald. He looked like a fruit made to eat. He was her apple of knowledge. She felt she could set her teeth in him and eat him to the core. She smiled to herself at her fancy. And what was the core then, the part she would throw away? Something worthless to her, perhaps.

He was looking dim and abstracted, puzzled, for the moment. She stretched out her beautiful arm, with its fluff of green tulle, and touched his chin with her subtle, artist's fingers.

"What are they then?" she asked, with a strange, knowing smile.

"What?" he replied, his eyes suddenly dilating with wonder.

"Your thoughts."

Gerald looked like a man coming awake.

"I think I had none," he said.

"Really!" she said, with grave laughter in her voice.

And to Birkin, it was as if she killed Gerald, with that touch.

361

"Ah but," cried Gudrun, "let us drink to Britannia—let us drink to Britannia."

It seemed there was regret and despair in her voice. Gerald laughed, and filled the glasses.

The next day, they descended at the tiny railway station of Hohenhausen, at the end of the tiny valley railway. It was snow everywhere, a white, perfect cradle of snow, new and frozen, sweeping up up on either side, black crags and white sweeps of silver towards the blue pale heavens.

As they stepped out on to the naked platform, with only snow around and above, Gudrun shrank as if it chilled her heart.

"My God, Jerry," she said, turning to Gerald with sudden intimacy, "you've done it now."

"What?"

She made a faint gesture, indicating the world on either hand.

"Look at it!"

She seemed afraid to go on. He laughed.

They were in the heart of the mountains. From high above, on either side, swept down the white fold of snow, so that one seemed small and tiny in a valley of pure heaven, all strangely radiant and changeless and silent.

"It makes one so bright and alone," said Ursula, turning to Birkin and laving her hand on his arm.

"You're not sorry you've come, are you?" said Gerald to Gudrun.

She looked doubtful. They went out of the station between banks of snow.

"Ah," said Gerald, sniffing the air in elation, "this is perfect.—There's our sledge.—We'll walk a bit—we'll run up the road."

Gudrun, always doubtful, dropped her heavy coat on the sledge, as he did his, and they set off. Suddenly she threw up her head and set off scudding along the road of snow, pulling her cap down over her ears. Her blue, bright dress fluttered in the wind, her thick scarlet stockings were brilliant above the whiteness. Gerald watched her: she seemed to be fleeing from her fate, in vain. He let her get some distance, then, loosening his limbs, he went after her.

Everywhere was deep and silent snow. Great snow-eaves weighed down the broad-roofed Tyrolese houses, that were sunk to the window-sashes in snow. Peasant women, full-skirted, wearing each a cross-over shawl and thick snowboots, turned in the way to look at the soft, rhapsodic girl running with such strange fleetness from the man, who was overtaking her inevitably.

They passed the inn with its painted shutters and balcony, a few cottages half buried in the snow; then the silent saw-mill by the snow-buried bridge, which crossed the hidden stream, over which they ran into the very depth of the untouched sheets of snow. It was a silence and a sheer whiteness exhilarating to madness. But the perfect silence was most terrifying, isolating the soul, surrounding the heart with frozen air.

"It's a marvellous place, for all that," said Gudrun, looking into his eyes with a strange, meaning look. His soul leapt with an almost satanic bound.

"Good!" he said.

A fierce, electric energy seemed to flow over all his limbs, his muscles were surcharged, his hands felt hard with strength. They walked along rapidly up the snow-road, that was marked by withered branches of trees stuck in at intervals. He and she were separate, like opposite poles of one fierce energy. But they felt powerful enough to leap over the confines of life into the forbidden places, and back again.

Birkin and Ursula were running along also, over the snow. He had disposed of the luggage, and they had a little start of the sledges. Ursula was excited and happy, but she kept turning suddenly to catch hold of Birkin's arm, to make sure of him.

"This is something I never expected," she said. "I am beyond myself, here."

They went on into a snow meadow. There they were overtaken by the sledge, that came tinkling through the silence. It was another mile before they came upon Gudrun and Gerald, on the steep up-climb, beside the pink, half-buried shrine.

Then they passed into a gulley, where were walls of black rock, and a river filled with snow, and a still blue sky above. Over a covered bridge they went, drumming roughly over the boards, crossing the snow-bed once more, then slowly up and up, the horses walking swiftly, the driver cracking his long whip as he walked beside, and calling his strange wild heu-heu, the walls of rock passing slowly by, till they emerged again between slopes and masses of snow. Up and up, gradually, they went, through the cold shadow-radiance of the afternoon, silenced by the imminence of the mountains, the heavy, dazing sides of snow that rose above them and fell away beneath.

They came forth at last in a little high table-land of snow, where stood the last peaks of snow like the petals of an open rose. In the midst of the last deserted valleys of heaven stood a lonely building with brown wooden walls and white-heavy roof, deep and deserted in the waste of snow, like a dream. It stood like a rock that had rolled down from the last steep slopes, a rock that had taken the form of a house and was now half buried. It was unbelievable that one could live there uncrushed by all this terrible waste of whiteness and silence and clear, upper, ringing cold.

Yet the sledges ran up in fine style, people came to the door laughing and excited, the floor of the hostel rang hollow, the passage was wet with snow, it was a real, warm interior.

The new-comers tramped up the bare wooden stairs, following the serving woman. Gudrun and Gerald took the first bedroom. In a moment they found themselves alone in a bare, smallish, close-shut bedroom that was all of golden-coloured wood, floor, walls, ceiling, door, all of the same warm-gold panelling of oiled pine. There was a window opposite the door, but low down, because the roof sloped. Under the slope of the ceiling were the table with wash-hand bowl and jug, and across, another table with mirror. On either side the door were two beds piled high with an enormous blue-checked overbolster,* enormous.

This was all—no cupboard, none of the amenities of life. Here they were shut up together in this cell of golden-coloured wood, with two blue-checked beds. They looked at each other and laughed, frightened by this naked nearness of isolation.

A man knocked and came in with the luggage. He was a sturdy fellow with flattish cheek-bones, rather pale, and with coarse fair moustache. Gudrun watched him put down the bags, in silence, then tramp heavily out.

"It isn't too rough, is it?" Gerald asked.

The bedroom was not very warm, and she shivered slightly.

"It is wonderful," she equivocated. "Look at the colour of this panelling—it's wonderful, like being inside a nut."

He was standing watching her, feeling his short-cut moustache, leaning back slightly and watching her with his keen, unwilling eyes, dominated by the constant passion, that was like a doom upon him.

She went and crouched down in front of the window, curious.

"Oh, but this—!" she cried involuntarily, almost in pain.

In front was a valley shut in under the sky, the last huge slopes of snow and black rock, and at the end, like the navel of the earth, a white-folded wall, and two peaks glimmering in the late light. Straight in front ran the cradle of silent snow, between the great slopes, that were fringed with a little roughness of pine-trees, like shadow, round the base. But the cradle of snow ran on to the eternal closing-in, where the walls of snow and rock rose impenetrable, and the mountain peaks above were in heaven near at hand. This was the centre, the knot, the navel of the world, where the earth belonged to the skies, pure, unapproachable, impassable.

It filled Gudrun with a strange rapture. She crouched in front of the window, clenching her face in her hands, in a sort of trance. At last she had arrived, she had reached her place. Here at last she folded her wings and settled down like a crystal in the navel of snow, and was gone.

Gerald bent above her and was looking out over her shoulder. Already he felt he was alone. She was gone. She was completely gone, and there was icy vapour round his heart. He saw the blind valley, the great cul de sac of snow and mountain peaks, under the heaven. And there was no way out. The terrible silence and cold and the glamorous whiteness of the dusk wrapped him round, and she remained crouching before the window, as at a shrine, a shadow.

"Do you like it?" he asked, in a voice that sounded far off and unfamiliar. At least she might be grateful to him for having brought her. But she only averted her soft, mute face a little from his gaze. And he knew that there were tears in her eyes, her own tears, tears of her strange religion, that had nothing to do with him.

Quite suddenly, he put his hand under her chin and lifted up her face to him. Her dark-blue eyes, in their wetness of tears, dilated as if she was startled in her very soul. They looked at him through their tears in terror and a little horror. His light-blue eyes were keen, small-pupilled and brilliant. Her lips parted, as she breathed with difficulty.

The passion came up in him, stroke after stroke, like the ringing of a bronze bell, so strong and unflawed and indomitable. His knees tightened to bronze, as he hung above her soft face, whose lips parted and whose eyes dilated in a strange violation. In the grasp of his hand her chin was unutterably soft and silken. He felt strong as a weapon of living metal, invincible and not to be turned aside. His heart rang proud within him.

He lifted her up in his arms. She was soft and inert, motionless. All the while her eyes, in which the tears had not yet dried, were dilated as if in a kind of swoon of fear and helplessness. He had her in his power.

He lifted her close and folded her against him. Her softness, her inert, relaxed weight lay against his own hard, bronze-like limbs in a heaviness of desirability that would break his heart, if he were not fulfilled. She moved convulsively, recoiling away from him. His heart went up like a flame, he closed over her like steel. He would die if she denied him.

But the steel trap of his body was too much for her. She relaxed again, and lay loose and soft, panting in a little delirium. And to him, she was so sweet, she was such delight, that he would have suffered a whole eternity of torture rather than forego one second of this pang of unsurpassable bliss.

"My God," he said to her, his face drawn and strange, transfigured, "that was something!"

She lay perfectly still, with a still, child-like face and dark eyes, looking at him. She was lost, fallen right away.

"I shall always love you," he said, looking at her.

But she did not hear. She lay looking at him as at something she could never understand, never: as a child looks at a grown-up person, without hope of understanding, only submitting.

He kissed her, kissed her eyes shut, so that she should not look any more. He wanted something now, some recognition, some sign, some admission. But she only lay silent and child-like and remote, like a child that is overcome and cannot understand, only feels lost. He kissed her again, giving up.

"Shall we go down and have coffee and Kuchen?"* he asked.

The twilight was falling slate-blue at the window. She closed her eyes, closed away the monotonous level of dead wonder, and opened them again to the everyday world.

"Yes," she said briefly, regaining her will with a click.

She went again to the window. Blue evening had fallen over the cradle of snow and over the great pallid slopes. But in the heaven the peaks of snow were rosy, glistening like transcendent, radiant spikes of blossom in the heavenly upper-world, so lovely and beyond.

Gudrun saw all their loveliness, she *knew* how immortally beautiful they were, great pistils of rose-coloured, cold fire in the blue twilight of the heaven. She could *see* it, she knew it, but she was not of it. She was divorced, debarred, a soul shut out.

With a last look of remorse, she turned away, and was doing her hair. He had unstrapped the luggage, and was waiting, watching her. She knew he was watching her. It made her a little hasty and feverish in her precipitation.

They went downstairs, both with a strange, other-world look on their faces, and with a glow in their eyes. They saw Birkin and Ursula sitting at the long table in a corner, waiting for them.

"How good and simple they look together," Gudrun thought, jealously. She envied them some simplicity, an intimacy to which she herself could never approach.

"Such *good* Kranzkuchen!" cried Ursula greedily. "So *good*!"

"Right," said Gudrun. "Can we have Kaffee mit Kranzkuchen?"* she added, to the waiter.

And she seated herself on the bench, beside Gerald. Birkin, looking at them, felt a pain of tenderness for them.

"I think the place is really wonderful, Gerald," he said, "prachtvoll and wunderbar and wunderschön and unbeschreiblich* and all the other German adjectives."

Gerald broke into a slight smile.

"*I* like it," he said.

The tables, of white scrubbed wood, were placed round three sides of the room, as in a Gasthaus.* Birkin and Ursula sat with their backs to the wall, which was of golden-coloured wood, and Gerald and Gudrun sat in the corner next them, near the stove. It was a fairly large place, with a tiny bar, just like a country inn, but quite simple and bare, and all of oiled wood, ceilings and walls and floor, the only furniture being the tables and benches going round three sides, the great green stove, and the bar and the doors on the fourth side. The windows were double, and quite uncurtained. It was early evening.

The coffee came—hot and good—and a whole ring of cake.

"A whole Kuchen!" cried Ursula. "They give you more than us! I want some of yours."

There were other people in the place, ten altogether, so Birkin had found out: two artists, three students, a man and wife, and a Professor and two daughters,—all Germans. The four English people, being newcomers, sat in their coign of vantage to watch. The Germans peeped

367

in at the door, called a word to the waiter, and went away again. It was not meal-time, so they did not come into this dining room, but betook themselves, when their boots were changed, to the Reunionsaal.*

The English visitors could hear the occasional twanging of a zither, the strumming of a piano, snatches of laughter and shouting and singing, a faint vibration of voices. The whole building being of wood, it seemed to carry every sound, like a drum, but instead of increasing each particular noise, it decreased it, so that the sound of the zither seemed tiny, as if a diminutive zither were playing somewhere, and it seemed the piano must be a small one, like a little spinet.

The host came when the coffee was finished. He was a Tyrolese, broad, rather flat-cheeked, with a pale, pock-marked skin and flourishing moustaches.

"Would you like to go to the Reunionsaal and be introduced to the other ladies and gentlemen?" he asked, bending forward and smiling, showing his large, strong teeth. His blue eyes went quickly from one to the other—he was not quite sure of his ground with these aloof English people. He was unhappy too because he spoke no English, and he was not sure whether to try his French.

"Shall we go to the Reunionsaal and be introduced to the other people?" repeated Birkin, laughing.

There was a moment's hesitation.

"I suppose we'd better—better break the ice," said Gerald.

The women rose, rather flushed. And the Wirt's* black, beetle-like, broad-shouldered figure went on ignominiously in front, towards the noise. He opened the door and ushered the four strangers into the play-room.

Instantly a silence fell, a slight embarrassment came over the company. The newcomers had a sense of many blond faces looking their way. Then the host was bowing to a short, energetic-looking man with large moustaches, and saying in a low voice:

"Herr Professor, darf ich Sie vorstellen—"*

The Herr Professor was prompt and energetic. He bowed low to the English people, smiling, and began to be a comrade at once.

"Nehmen die Herrschaften teil an unserer Unterhaltung?"* he said, with a little obsequious suavity, his voice curling up in the question.

The four English people smiled, lounging with an attentive uneasiness in the middle of the room. Birkin, who was spokesman, said that they would willingly take part in the entertainment. Gudrun and Ursula, laughing, excited, felt the eyes of all the men upon them, and they lifted their heads and looked nowhere, and felt royal.

The Professor announced the names of those present, sans cérémonie, there was a bowing to the wrong people and to the right people. Everybody was there, except the man and wife. The two tall, clear-skinned, athletic daughters of the professor, with their plain-cut, dark blue blouses and loden skirts, their rather long, strong necks, their clear blue eyes and carefully banded hair, and their blushes, bowed and stood back; the three students bowed very low, in the humble hope of making an impression of extreme good-breeding; then there was a small, dark-skinned man with full eyes, an odd creature, like a child, and like a troll, quick, detached: he bowed slightly; his companion, a large fair young man, stylishly dressed, blushed to the eyes and bowed very low.

It was over.

"Herr Loerke was giving us a recitation in the Cologne dialect," said the Professor.

"He must forgive us for interrupting him," said Birkin, "we should like very much to hear it."

There was instantly a bowing and an offering of seats. Gudrun and Ursula, Gerald and Birkin sat in the deep sofas against the wall. The room was of glowing panelling, like the rest of the house. It had a piano, sofas and chairs, and a couple of tables with books and magazines. In its complete absence of decoration, save for the big blue stove, it was cosy and lovely.

Herr Loerke was the little man with the boyish figure, and the round, full, sensitive-looking head, and the quick, full eyes, like a mouse's. He glanced swiftly from one to the other of the strangers, and held himself aloof.

"Please, go on with the recitation," said the Professor, suavely, with his slight authority. Loerke, who was sitting hunched on the piano stool, blinked and did not answer.

"It would be a great pleasure," said Ursula, who had been getting the sentence ready, in German, for some minutes.

Then suddenly, the small, unresponding man swung aside, towards his previous audience, and broke forth, exactly as he had broken off, in a controlled, mocking voice, giving an imitation of a quarrel between an old Cologne woman and a railway guard.

His body was slight and unformed, like a boy's, and his voice was mature, sardonic, its movement had the flexibility of essential energy, and of a mocking, penetrating understanding. Gudrun could not understand a word of his monologue, but she was spell-bound watching him. He must be an artist: nobody else could have such fine adjustment and singleness. The Germans were doubled up with laughter, hearing his strange, droll words, his droll phrases of dialect. And in the midst of their paroxysms, they glanced with deference at the four English strangers, the elect. Gudrun and Ursula were forced to laugh. Then the room rang with shouts of laughter, the blue eyes of the Professor's daughters were swimming over with laughter-tears, their clear cheeks were flushed crimson with mirth, their father broke out in the most astonishing peals of laughter, the students bowed their heads on their knees in excess of joy. Ursula looked round amazed, the laughter was bubbling out of her involuntarily. She looked at Gudrun, Gudrun looked at her: and the two sisters burst out to astonished peals, carried away. Loerke glanced at them swiftly, with his full eyes. Birkin was sniggering involuntarily, Gerald Crich sat erect, with a glistening look of amusement on his face. And the laughter crashed out again, in wild paroxysms, the Professor's daughters were reduced to shaking helplessness, the veins in the Professor's neck were swollen, his face was purple, he was strangled in ultimate silent spasms of laughter, the students were shouting half articulated words that tailed off in helpless explosions. Then suddenly the rapid patter of the artist ceased, there were little whoops of subsiding mirth, Ursula and Gudrun were wiping their eyes, and the Professor was crying loudly:

"Ja, das war merkwürdig, das war famos—"

"Wirklich famos!" echoed his exhausted daughters, faintly.

"And we couldn't understand it," cried Ursula.

"Oh leider, leider," cried the Professor.

"You couldn't understand it?" cried the students, let loose at last in speech with the new-comers. "Ja, das ist wirklich Schade, das ist Schade, gnädige Frau. Wissen Sie———"*

The mixture was made, the new-comers were stirred into the party, like new ingredients, the whole room was alive. Gerald said nothing, but his face glistened with a strange amusement. Perhaps even he, in the end, would break forth. He was erect and keen, full of attention.

Ursula was prevailed upon to sing "Annie Lowrie,"* as the Professor called it. There was a hush of *extreme* deference. She had never been so flattered in her life. Gudrun accompanied her on the piano, playing from memory.

Ursula had a beautiful ringing voice, but usually no confidence, she spoiled everything. This evening she felt queenly and untrammelled. Birkin was a background of strength, she was so happy with him, the Germans made her feel so immeasurably superior and infallible, that she was liberated into free self-revelation. She felt like a bird flying in the air, as her voice soared out, enjoying extremely the balance and flight of the song, like the motion of a bird's wings that is up in the wind, sliding and playing on the air, sustained by such rapturous attention. She was very happy, singing that song by herself, full of a sense of freedom and power and a joy in motion, like a bird moving gladly in the air, exerting itself with gratification, giving immeasurable gratification to the warm, sentimental Germans.

At the end, the Germans were all touched with admiring, humble melancholy, they praised her in soft, reverent voices, they could not say too much.

"Wie schön, wie rührend! Ach, die Schottischen Lieder, sie haben so viel Stimmung! Aber die gnädige Frau hat eine *wunderbare* Stimme; die gnädige Frau ist wirklich eine Künstlerin, aber wirklich!"*

She was dilated and beautiful, like a flower in the morning sun. She felt Birkin looking at her, so unbelievably near to her, and her breasts thrilled, her veins were all golden. She was as happy as a flower that has just opened out of bud. And everybody seemed so gentle and radiant, it was perfect.

After dinner she wanted to go out for a minute, to look at the world. The company tried to dissuade her—it was so terribly cold. But just to look, she said.

They all four wrapped up warmly, and found themselves in a vague, unsubstantial outdoors of dim snow and ghosts of an upper-world, that made strange shadows before the stars. It was indeed cold, bruisingly, frighteningly, unnaturally cold. Ursula could not believe the air in her nostrils. It seemed conscious, malevolent, purposive in its intense, murderous coldness.

Yet it was wonderful, an intoxication, a silence of dim, unrealised snow, of the Invisible intervening between her and the visible, between her and the flashing stars. She could see Orion sloping up. How wonderful he was, wonderful enough to make one cry aloud.

And all around was this cradle of snow, and there was firm snow underfoot, that struck with heavy cold through her boot-soles. It was night, and silence. She imagined she could hear the stars. She imagined distinctly she could hear the celestial, musical motion of the stars, quite near at hand. She seemed like a bird flying amongst their harmonious motion.

And she clung close to Birkin. Suddenly, she realised she did not know what he was thinking. She did not know where he was ranging.

"My love!" she said, stopping to look at him.

His face was pale, his eyes dark, there was a faint spark of starlight on them. And he saw her face soft and upturned to him, very near. He kissed her softly.

"What then?" he asked.

"Do you love me?" she asked.

"Too much," he answered, quietly.

She clung a little closer.

"Not too much," she pleaded.

"Even too much—all in all," he said, almost sadly.

"And does it make you sad, that I am everything to you?" she asked, wistful.

He held her close to him, kissing her, and saying, scarcely audible:

"No, but I feel like a beggar—I feel you might refuse me."

She was silent, looking at the stars now. Then she kissed him.

"Don't be a beggar," she pleaded, wistfully. "It isn't ignominious, that you love me."

"That I depend on you so utterly is ignominious," he said, "isn't it?"

"Why?—why should it be?" she asked. He only stood still, in the terribly cold air that moved invisibly over the mountain tops, folding her round with his arms.

"I couldn't bear this white, eternal place without you," he said. "I couldn't bear it, it would kill the quick of my life."

She kissed him again, suddenly.

"Do you hate it?" she asked, puzzled, wondering.

"If I couldn't come near to you, if you weren't here, I should hate it, I couldn't bear it," he answered.

"But the people are nice," she said.

"I mean the snow, the stillness, the cold, the frozen eternality," he said.

She wondered. Then her spirit came home to him, nestling unconscious in him.

"Yes, it is good we are warm and living," she said.

And they turned home again. They saw the golden lights of the hotel glouring* out in the night of snow-silence, small in the hollow, like a cluster of yellow berries. It seemed like a bunch of sun-sparks, tiny and orange in the midst of the snow-darkness. Behind, was a high shadow of a peak, blotting out the stars, like a ghost.

They drew near to their home. They saw a man come from the dark building, with a lighted lantern which swung golden, and made that his dark feet walked in a halo of snow. He was a small, dark figure in the darkened snow. He unlatched the door of an outhouse. A smell of cows, hot, animal, almost like beef, came out on the heavily cold air. There was a glimpse of two cattle in their dark stalls, then the door was shut again, and not a chink of light showed. It had reminded Ursula again of home, of the Marsh, of her childhood, and of the journey to Brussels, and, strangely enough, of Anton Skrebensky.

Oh God, could one bear it, this past which was gone down the abyss? Could she bear, that it ever had been! She looked round this silent, upper world of snow and stars and powerful cold. There was another world, like views on a magic lantern: the Marsh, Cossethay, Ilkeston, lit up with a common, unreal light. There was a shadowy, unreal Ursula, a whole shadow-play of an unreal life. It was as unreal, and circumscribed, as a magic-lantern show. She wished the slides could all be broken. She wished it could be gone for ever, like a lantern-slide which is broken. She wanted to have no past. She wanted to have come down from the slopes of heaven to this place, with Birkin, not to have toiled out of the murk of her childhood and her upbringing, slowly, all soiled. She felt that memory was a dirty trick played upon her. What was this decree, that she should 'remember'! Why not a bath of pure oblivion, a new birth, without any recollections or blemish of a past life. She was with Birkin, she had just come into life, here in the high snow, against the stars. What had she to do with parents and antecedents? She knew herself new and unbegotten, she had no father, no mother, no anterior connections, she was herself, pure and silvery, she belonged only to the oneness with Birkin, a oneness that struck deeper notes, sounding into the heart of the universe, the heart of reality, where she had never existed before.

Even Gudrun was a separate unit, separate, separate, having nothing to do with this self, this Ursula, in her new world of reality. That old shadow-world, the actuality of the past—ah, let it go! She rose free on the wings of her new being.

Gudrun and Gerald had not come in. They had walked up the valley straight in front of the house, not like Ursula and Birkin, on to the little hill at the right. Gudrun was driven by a strange desire. She wanted to plunge on and on, till she came to the end of the valley of snow. Then she wanted to climb the wall of white finality, climb over, into the peaks that sprang up like sharp petals in the heart of the frozen, mysterious navel of the world. She felt that there, over the strange, blind, terrible wall of rocky snow, there in the navel of the mystic world, among the final cluster of peaks, there, in the infolded navel of it all, was her consummation. If she could but come there, alone, and pass into the infolded navel of eternal snow and of uprising, immortal peaks of snow and rock, she would be a oneness with all, she would be herself the eternal, infinite silence, the sleeping, timeless, frozen centre of the All.

They went back to the house, to the Reunionsaal. She was curious to see what was going on. The men there made her alert, roused her curiosity. It was a new taste of life for her, they were so warm and deferential.

The party was boisterous; they were dancing all together, dancing the Schuhplatteln, the Tyrolese dance of the clapping hands and tossing the partner in the air, at the crisis. The Germans were all proficient—they were from Munich chiefly. There were three zithers twanging away in a corner. It was a scene of great animation and confusion. The professor was initiating Ursula into the dance, stamping, clapping, and swinging her high, with amazing force and zest, when the crisis came. Birkin was behaving manfully with one of the professor's fresh, strong daughters, who was exceedingly happy. Everybody was dancing, there was the most boisterous turmoil.

Gudrun looked on with delight. The solid wooden floor resounded to the knocking heels of the men, the air quivered with the clapping hands and the zither music, there was a golden dust about the hanging lamps.

Suddenly the dance finished, Loerke and the students rushed out to bring in drinks. There was an excited clamour of voices, a chinking of mug-lids, a great crying of "Prosit—Prosit."* Loerke was everywhere at once, like a gnome—suggesting drinks for the women, making an obscure, slightly risky joke with the men, confusing and mystifying the waiter.

He wanted very much to dance with Gudrun. From the first moment he had seen her, he wanted to make a connection with her. Instinctively she felt this, and she waited for him to come up. But a kind of sulkiness kept him away from her, so she thought he disliked her.

"Will you schuhplattern, gnädige Frau?" said the large, fair youth, Loerke's instrument. He was too soft, too humble for Gudrun's taste. But she wanted to dance, and the fair youth, who was called Leitner, was handsome enough, in his uneasy, slightly abject fashion, a humility that covered a certain degradation.

The zithers sounded out again, the dance began. Gerald looked on, laughing. Ursula danced with one of the students, Birkin with the other daughter of the Professor, the Professor with Frau Kramer, and the rest of the men danced together, with quite as much zest as if they had had women partners.

Because Gudrun had danced with the well-built, soft youth, his pleasure-companion, Loerke was more pettish and exasperated than ever, and would not even notice her existence in the room. This piqued her, but she made up to herself by dancing with the professor, who was strong as a mature, well-seasoned bull, and as full of coarse energy. She could not bear him, critically, and yet she enjoyed being rushed through the dance, and tossed up into the air, on his coarse, powerful impetus. The professor enjoyed it too, he eyed her with strange, large blue eyes, full of galvanic fire. She hated him for the seasoned, semi-paternal animalism with which he regarded her, but she admired his weight of strength.

The room was charged with excitement and strong, animal emotion. Loerke was kept away from Gudrun, to whom he wanted to speak, as by a hedge of thorns, and he felt a sardonic, ruthless hatred for his young love-companion, Leitner, who was his penniless dependent. He mocked the youth, with an acid ridicule, that made Leitner red in the face and impotent with resentment.

Gerald, who had learned the dance, was dancing with the younger of the Professor's daughters, who was almost dying of virgin excitement, because she thought Gerald so handsome, so superb. He had her in his power, as if she were a palpitating bird, a fluttering, flushing, bewildered creature. And it made him smile, as she shrank convulsively between his hands, violently, when he must throw her into the air. At the end, she was so overcome with prostrate love for him, that she could scarcely speak sensibly at all.

Birkin was dancing with Ursula. There were odd little fires playing in his eyes, he seemed to have turned into something licentious and flickering, mocking, suggestive, quite impossible. Ursula was frightened of him, and fascinated. Clear, before her eyes, as in a vision, she could see the sly, licentious freedom of his eyes, he moved towards her with subtle, animal, indecent approach. The strangeness of his hands, which came sly and cunning, inevitably to the vital place beneath her breasts, and, lifting with mocking, suggestive impulse, carried her through the air as if without strength, through black-magic, made her swoon with fear. For a moment she revolted, it was horrible, he was obscene, a devil. She would break the spell. But before the resolution had formed she had submitted again, yielded to her fear. He knew all the time what he was doing. She could see it in his smiling, concentrated eyes. It was his responsibility, she would leave it to him.

When they were alone in the darkness, she felt the strange licentiousness of him hovering upon her. She was troubled and repelled. Why should he turn like this?

"What is it?" she asked in dread.

But his face only glistened on her, unknown, leering, horrible. And yet she was fascinated. Her impulse was to repel him violently, break from this spell of mocking brutishness. But she was too fascinated, she wanted to submit, she wanted to know. What would he do to her?

He was so attractive, and so repulsive at once. The leering, mocking, lambent suggestivity that flickered over his face and looked from his narrowed eyes, made her want to hide, to hide herself away from him, and watch him from somewhere unseen.

"Why are you like this?" she demanded again, rousing against him with sudden force and animosity.

The flickering fires in his eyes concentrated as he looked into her eyes. Then the lids drooped with a faint motion of satiric contempt. Then they rose again to the same remorseless flickering sport. And she gave way, he might do as he would. His licentiousness was her licentiousness. He was self-responsible, she would trust him.

They might do as they liked, and not be ashamed—this she realised as she went to sleep. How could anything that gave one satisfaction be shameful? What was degrading?—nothing, if one wanted to do it. And he was so flickering and unrestrained. Wasn't it rather horrible, a man who could be so soulful and spiritual, now to be so—she balked at her own thoughts and memories: then she added:—so bestial? So bestial, they two!—so degraded! She winced. But after all, why not? After all, it was his principle. She went to sleep, relieved and liberated.

Gudrun, who had been watching Gerald in the Reunionsaal, suddenly thought:

"He should have all the women he likes—it is his nature. It is absurd to call him monogamous—he is naturally promiscuous. That is his nature."

The thought came to her involuntarily. It shocked her somewhat. It was as if she had seen some new Mene! Mene! upon the wall.* Yet it was merely true. A voice seemed to have spoken it to her so clearly, that for the moment she believed in inspiration.

"It is really true," she said to herself again.

She knew quite well she had believed it all along. She knew it implicitly. But she must keep it dark—almost from herself. She must keep it completely secret. It was knowledge for her alone, and scarcely to be admitted even to herself.

The deep resolve formed in her, to combat him. One of them must triumph over the other. Which should it be? Her soul steeled itself with strength. Almost she laughed within herself, at her confidence. It woke a certain keen, half-contemptuous pity, tenderness for him: she was so ruthless.

Everybody retired early. The professor and Loerke went into a small lounge to drink. They both watched Gudrun go along the landing, by the railing, upstairs.

"Ein schönes Frauenzimmer," said the Professor.

"Ja!"* assented Loerke, shortly.

Gerald walked with his queer, long wolf-steps across the bedroom to the window, stooped and looked out, then rose again, and turned to Gudrun, his eyes sharp with an abstract smile. He seemed very tall to her, she saw the glisten of his whitish eyebrows, that met between his brows.

"How do you like it?" he said.

He seemed to be laughing inside himself, quite unconsciously. She looked at him. He was a phenomenon to her, not a man.

"I like it very much," she replied.

"Who do you like best downstairs?" he asked, standing tall and glistening above her, with his glistening stiff hair erect.

"Who do I like best?" she repeated wanting to answer his question, and finding it difficult to collect herself. "Why I don't know, I don't know enough about them yet, to be able to say. Whom do *you* like best?"

"Oh I don't care—I don't like or dislike any of them. It doesn't matter about me. I wanted to know about you."

"But why?" she asked, going rather pale.

The abstract, unconscious smile in his eyes was intensified.

"I wanted to know," he said.

She turned aside, breaking the spell. In some strange way, she felt he was getting power over her.

"Well I can't tell you already," she said.

She went to the mirror to take out the hairpins from her hair. She stood before the mirror every night for some minutes, brushing her fine dark hair. It was part of the inevitable ritual of her life.

He followed her, and stood behind her. She was busy, with bent head, taking out the pins and shaking her warm hair loose. When she looked up, she saw him in the glass, standing behind her, watching unconsciously, not consciously seeing her, and yet watching, with fine-pupilled eyes that *seemed* to smile, and which were not really smiling.

She started. It took all her courage for her to continue brushing her hair, as usual, for her to pretend she was at her ease. She was far, far from being at her ease with him. She beat her brains wildly for something to say to him.

"What are your plans for tomorrow?" she asked, nonchalant, whilst her heart was beating so furiously, her eyes were so bright with strange nervousness, she felt he could not but observe. But she knew also that he was completely blind, blind as a wolf looking at her. It was a strange battle between her consciousness and his unconsciousness.

"I don't know," he replied; "what would you like to do?"

He spoke emptily, his mind was sunk away.

"Oh," she said, with easy protestation, "I'm ready for anything—anything will be fine for *me*, I'm sure."

And to herself she was saying:

"God, why am I so nervous,—why are you so *nervous*, you fool. If he sees it I'm done for for ever—you *know* you're done for for ever, if he sees the absurd state you're in."

And she smiled to herself as if it were all child's play. Meanwhile her heart was plunging, she was almost fainting. She could see him, in the mirror, as he stood there behind her, tall and keen—blond and terribly frightening. She glanced at his reflection with furtive eyes, willing to give anything to save him from knowing she could see him. He did not know she could see his reflection. He was looking steadily, unblinking down at her head, from which the hair fell loose, as she brushed it with wild, nervous hand. She held her head aside and brushed and brushed her hair madly. For her life, she could not turn round and face him. For her life, *she could not*. And the knowledge made her almost sink to the ground in a faint, helpless, spent. She was aware of his erect, tall figure standing imminent close behind her, she was aware of his hard, strong, unyielding chest. And she felt she could not bear it any more, in a few minutes she would fall down at his feet, grovelling at his feet, kissing his feet in prostration.

The thought pricked up all her sharp intelligence and presence of mind. She dared not turn round to him—and there he stood motionless, unbroken. Summoning all her strength, she said in a full, resonant, nonchalant voice, that was forced out with all her remaining self-control:

"Oh would you mind looking in that bag behind there and giving me my———"

Here her power fell inert. "My what—my what—?" she screamed in silence to herself.

But he had turned round, surprised and startled that she should ask him to look in her bag, which she always kept so *very* private to herself. She turned now, her face white, her dark eyes blazing with uncanny, overwrought excitement. She saw him stooping to the bag, undoing the loosely buckled strap. She had conquered him, he was stooping down, servile.

"Your what?" he asked.

"Oh, a little enamel box—yellow—with a design of a cormorant plucking her breast—"

She went towards him, stooping her beautiful, bare arm, and deftly turned some of her things, disclosing the box, which was exquisitely painted.

"That is it, see," she said, taking it from under his eyes.

And he was baffled now. He was left to fasten up the bag, whilst she swiftly did up her hair for the night, and sat down to unfasten her shoes. She would not turn her back to him any more.

He was baffled, frustrated, but unconscious. She had the whip hand over him now. She knew he had not realised her terrible panic. Her heart was beating heavily still. Fool, fool that she was, to get into such a state! How she thanked God for Gerald's obtuse blindness. Thank God he could see nothing.

She sat slowly unlacing her shoes, and he too commenced to undress. Thank God that crisis was over. She felt almost fond of him now, almost in love with him.

"Ah Gerald," she laughed, caressively, teasingly, "Ah, what a fine game you played with the Professor's daughter—didn't you now?"

"What game?" he asked, looking round.

"*Isn't* she in love with you—oh *dear*, isn't she in love with you!" said Gudrun, smiling in her gayest, most attractive mood.

"I shouldn't think so," he said.

"'Shouldn't think so!'" she teased. "Why the poor girl is lying at this moment overwhelmed, dying with love for you. She thinks you're *wonderful*—oh marvellous, beyond what man has ever been.—*Really*, isn't it funny?"

"Why funny, what is funny?" he asked.

"Why to see you working it on her," she said, with a half reproach that confused the male conceit in him. "Really Gerald, the poor girl——!"

"I did nothing to her," he said.

"Oh, it was too shameful, the way you simply swept her off her feet."

"That was Schuhplatteln," he replied, with an odd grin.

"Ha—ha—ha!" laughed Gudrun.

Even her mockery quivered through his muscles with gratification. When he slept he seemed to crouch down in the bed, lapped up in his own strength, that yet was hollow.

And Gudrun slept profoundly, a victorious sleep. Then suddenly she was almost fiercely awake. The small timber room glowed with the dawn, that came upwards from the low window. She could see down the valley when she lifted her head: the snow with a pinkish, half-revealed magic, the fringe of pine-trees at the bottom of the slope. And one tiny figure moved over the vaguely-illumined space.

She glanced at his watch: it was seven o'clock. He was still completely asleep. And she was so hard awake, it was almost frightening—a hard, metallic wakefulness. She lay looking at him.

He slept in the subjection of his own health and defeat. She was overcome by a sincere respect for him. Till now she was afraid before him. She lay and thought about him, what he was, what he represented in the world. A fine, independent will, he had. She thought of the revolution he had worked in the mines, in so short a time. She knew that, if he were confronted with any problem, any hard actual difficulty, he would overcome it. If he laid hold of the idea of political reform, he would be an unthwarted reformer. He had the faculty of making order out of confusion. Only let him grip hold of a situation, and he would bring to pass an inevitable conclusion.

For a few moments she was carried away on the wild wings of ambition. Gerald, with his force of will and his power for comprehending the actual world, should be set to solve the problems of the day, the problems of industrialism in the modern world. She knew he would, in the course of time, effect the changes he desired, he could re-organise the industrial system. She knew he could do it. As an instrument, in these things, he was marvellous, she had never seen any man with his potentiality. He was unaware of it, but she knew.

He only needed to be hitched on, he needed that his hand should be set to the task, because he was so unconscious. And this she could do. She would marry him, he would go into Parliament in the Conservative interest, he would clear up the great muddle of labour and industry. He was so superbly confident, dauntless, he never doubted that every problem could be worked out, in life as in geometry. And he would care neither about himself nor about anything but the pure working out of the problem. He was very pure, really.

Her heart beat fast, she flew away on wings of elation, imagining a future. He would be a Napoleon of peace, or a Bismarck—and she the woman behind him. She had read Bismarck's letters,* and had been deeply moved by them. And Gerald would be freer, more dauntless than Bismarck.

But even as she lay in glorious transport, bathed in the strange, rich sunshine of hope in constructive life, something seemed to snap in her, and a terrible cynicism began to gain upon her, blowing in like a little wind. Everything turned to irony with her: the last flavour of everything, was ironical. When she felt her pang of undeniable reality, this was when she knew the hard irony of hopes and ideas.

She lay and looked at him, as he slept. He was beautiful, he was a perfect instrument. To her mind, he was a pure, perfectly-made instrument. His instrumentality appealed so strongly to her, she wished she were God, to use him as a tool.

And at the same instant, came the ironical question: "What for?" She thought of the colliers' wives, with their linoleum and their lace curtains and their little girls in high-laced boots. She thought of the wives and daughters of the pit-managers, their tennis-parties, and their terrible struggles to be superior each to the other, in the social scale. There was Shortlands with its meaningless distinction, the meaningless crowd of the Criches. There was London, the House of Commons, the extant social reformers. My God!

Young as she was, Gudrun had touched the whole pulse of social England, she had no ideals of rising in the world. She knew, with the perfect cynicism of cruel youth, that to rise in the world meant to have one outside show instead of another, the advance was like having a spurious half-crown instead of a spurious penny. The whole coinage of valuation was spurious. Yet of course her cynicism knew well enough that, in a world where spurious coin was current, a bad sovereign was better than a bad penny. She intended to be rich, not poor.

Already she laughed at herself for her wild dreams. They could be fulfilled easily enough. But she recognised too well, in her spirit, the mockery of her own impulses. What did she care, that Gerald had created a richly-paying industry out of an old worn-out concern? What did she care? The worn-out concern, and the rapid, splendidly-organised industry, they were alike indifferent to her, they were bad money. Yet of course, she cared a great deal outwardly—and outwardly was all that mattered, for inwardly was a bad joke.

Everything was intrinsically a piece of irony to her. She leaned over Gerald and said in her heart, with breaking compassion:

"Oh, my dear, my dear, you are a sword too good to unsheath. You are as fine a tool as God ever forged,—why should you be used on such dirt!"

Her heart was breaking with passionate pity and grief for him. And at the same moment, a grimace came over her mouth, of mocking irony at her own unspoken tirade. Ah, what a farce it was! She thought of Parnell and Katherine O'Shea.* Poor Parnell! Because, after all, who can take the nationalisation of Ireland* seriously? Who can take political Ireland really seriously, whatever it does? And who can take political England seriously? Who can? Who can care a straw, really, how the old, patched-up Constitution is tinkered at any more? Who cares a button for our national ideals, any more than for our national bowler hat? Aha, it is all old hat, it is all old bowler hat?

That's all it is, Gerald, my young reformer. At any rate we'll spare ourselves the ignominy of stirring the old broth any more. You be beautiful, my Gerald, and reckless. There *are* perfect moments. Wake up, Gerald, wake up, convince me of the perfect moments, oh convince me, I need it.

He opened his eyes, and looked at her. She greeted him with a mocking, enigmatic smile in which was a poignant gaiety. Over his face went the reflection of the smile, he smiled too, purely unconsciously.

That filled her with extraordinary delight, to see the smile cross his face, reflected from her face. She remembered, that was how a baby smiled. It filled her with extraordinary radiant delight.

"You've done it," she said.

"What?" he asked, dazed.

"Convinced me."

And she bent down, kissing him passionately, passionately, so that he was bewildered. He did not ask her of what he had convinced her, though he meant to. He was glad she was kissing him. She seemed to be feeling for his very heart, to touch the quick of him. And he wanted her to touch the quick of his being, he wanted that most of all.

Outside, somebody was singing, in a manly, reckless, handsome voice:

> "Ich hab' die Nacht gemahlen
> Mit zwei so wunderschönen Knaben
> Vom Abend bis zum Tag
> Dass ich nicht aufsteh'n mag."*

Gudrun knew, that that song would sound through her eternity, sung in a manly, reckless, mocking voice. It marked one of her supreme moments, the supreme pangs of her nervous gratification. There it was, fixed in eternity for her.

The day came fine and bluish. There was a light wind blowing among the mountain-tops, keen as a rapier where it touched, carrying with it a fine dust of snow-powder. Gerald went out with the fine, blind face of a man who is in his state of fulfilment. Gudrun and he were in perfect static unity this morning, both unseeing and unwitting. They went out with a toboggan, leaving Ursula and Birkin to follow.

Gudrun was all scarlet and royal blue—a scarlet jersey, and a royal blue skirt and cap. She went gaily over the white snow, with Gerald beside her, in white and grey, pulling the little toboggan. They grew small in the distance of snow, climbing the steep slope.

For Gudrun herself, she seemed to pass altogether into the whiteness of the snow, she became a pure, thoughtless crystal. When she reached the top of the slope, in the wind, she looked round, and saw peak beyond peak of rock and snow, bluish, transcendent in heaven. And it seemed to her like a garden, with the peaks for pure flowers, and her heart gathering them. She had no separate consciousness for Gerald.

She held on to him as they went sheering down over the keen slope. She felt as if her spirit were being whetted on some fine grindstone, that was keen as flame. The snow sprinted* on either side, like sparks from a blade that is being sharpened, the whiteness round about ran swifter, swifter, in pure flame the white slope flew against her, and she and Gerald fused like one molten, dancing globule, rushed through a white intensity. Then there was a great swerve at the bottom, when they swung as it were in a fall to earth, in the diminishing motion.

They came to rest. But when she rose to her feet, she could not stand. She gave a strange cry, turned and clung to him, sinking her face on his breast, fainting in him. Utter oblivion came over her, as she lay for a few moments abandoned against him.

"What is it?" he was saying. "Was it too much for you?"

But she heard nothing.

When she came to, she stood up and looked round, astonished. Her face was white, her eyes brilliant and large.

"What is it?" he repeated. "Did it upset you?"

She looked at him with her brilliant eyes, that seemed to have undergone some transfiguration, and she laughed, with a terrible merriment.

"No," she cried, with triumphant joy. "It was the complete moment of my life."

And she looked at him with her dazzling, overweening laughter, like one possessed. A fine blade seemed to enter his heart.

But they climbed up the slope again, and they flew down through the white flame again, splendidly, splendidly. Gudrun was laughing and flashing, powdered with snow-crystals, Gerald worked perfectly. He felt hc could guide the toboggan to a hair's-breadth, almost he could make it pierce into the air and right into the very heart of the sky. It seemed to him the flying sledge was but his wings spread out, he had but to move his arms, the motion was his own. They explored the great slopes, to find another slide. He felt there must be something better than the ordained Rodelbahn.* And he found what he desired, a perfect long, fierce sweep, sheering past the foot of a rock and into the trees at the base. It was dangerous, he knew. But then he knew also he could direct the sledge as if it were a pencil between his fingers.

The first days passed in an ecstasy of physical motion, sleighing, ski-ing, skating, moving in an intensity of speed and white light that surpassed life itself, and carried the souls of the human beings beyond into an inhuman abstraction of velocity and weight and eternal, frozen snow.

Gerald's eyes became hard and strange, and as he went by on his skis he was more like some powerful, fateful bird than a man, his muscles elastic in a perfect, soaring trajectory, his body projected in pure flight, mindless, soulless, whirling along one perfect line of will.

Luckily there came a day of snow, when they must all stay indoors: otherwise, Birkin said, they would all lose their faculties, and begin to utter themselves in cries and shrieks, like some strange, unknown species of snow-birds.

It happened in the afternoon that Ursula sat in the Reunionsaal talking to Loerke. The latter had seemed unhappy lately. He was lively and full of mischievous humour, as usual. But Ursula had thought he was sulky about something. His partner, too, the big, fair, good-looking youth, was ill at ease, going about as if he belonged to nowhere, and was kept in some sort of subjection, against which he was rebelling.

Loerke had hardly talked to Gudrun. His associate, on the other hand, had paid her constantly a soft, over-deferential attention. Gudrun wanted to talk to Loerke. He was a sculptor, and she wanted to hear his view of his art. And his figure attracted her. There was the look of a little wastrel about him, that intrigued her, and an old man's look, that interested her, and then, beside this, an uncanny singleness, a quality of being by himself, not in contact with anybody else, that marked out an artist to her. He was a chatterer, a mag-pie, a maker of mischievous word-jokes, that were sometimes very clever, but which often were not—And she could see in his brown, gnome's eyes, the black look of disintegration, which lay behind all his small buffoonery.

His figure interested her—the figure of a boy, almost of a street arab. He made no attempt to conceal it. He always wore a simple loden suit, with knee breeches. His legs were thin, and he made no attempt to disguise the fact: which was a rare thing in a German. And he never ingratiated himself anywhere, not in the slightest, but kept to himself, for all his apparent playfulness.

Leitner, his companion, was a great sportsman, very handsome with his big limbs and his blue eyes. Loerke would go tobogganing, or ski-ing, or skating, in little snatches, but he was indifferent. And his fine, thin nostrils, the nostrils of a pure-bred street arab, would quiver with contempt at Leitner's splothering* gymnastic displays. It was evident that the two men, who had travelled and lived together in the last degree of intimacy, had now reached the stage of loathing. Leitner hated Loerke with an injured, soft, impotent hatred, and Loerke treated Leitner with a fine-quivering contempt and sarcasm. Soon the two would have to go apart.

Already they were rarely together. Leitner ran attaching himself to somebody or other, always deferring to them, Loerke was a good deal alone. Out of doors he wore a Westphalian cap, a close brown-velvet head with big brown-velvet flaps over his ears, so that he looked like a rabbit, or a troll. His face was brown-red, with a dry, bright skin, that seemed to crinkle with his mobile expressions. His eyes were arresting—brown, full, like a rabbit's, or like a troll's, or like the eyes of a lost being, having a strange, dumb, depraved look of knowledge, and a quick spark of uncanny fire. Whenever Gudrun had tried to talk to him he had shied away unresponsive, looking at her with his watchful dark eyes, but entering into no relation with her. He had made her feel that her slow French, and her slower German, were hateful to him. As for his own inadequate English, he was much too awkward to try it at all. But he understood a good deal of what was said, nevertheless. And Gudrun, piqued, left him alone.

This afternoon, however, she came into the lounge as he was talking to Ursula. His fine, black hair was thin on his full, sensitive-looking head, it was worn at the temples, he sat hunched up, as if his spirit were old. And Gudrun could see he was making some slow confidence to Ursula, unwilling, a slow, grudging, scanty self-revelation. She went and sat by her sister.

He looked at her, then looked away again, as if he took no notice of her. But as a matter of fact, she troubled him deeply.

"Isn't it interesting, Prune," said Ursula, turning to her sister, "Herr Loerke is doing a great frieze for a factory in Cologne, for the outside, the street."

She looked at him, at his thin, brown, nervous hands, that were blunt, and somehow like talons, like 'griffes,'* inhuman.

"What in?" she asked.

"Aus was?" repeated Ursula.

"Granit,"* he replied.

It had become immediately a laconic series of question and answer between fellow craftsmen.

"What is the relief?" asked Gudrun.

"Alto rilievo."*

"And at what height?"

It was very interesting to Gudrun, to think of his making the great granite frieze for a great granite factory in Cologne. She got from him some notion of the design. It was a representation of a fair, with peasants and artizans in an orgy of enjoyment, drunk and absurd in their modern dress, whirling ridiculously in roundabouts, gaping at shows, kissing and staggering and rolling in knots, swinging in swing-boats, and firing down shooting-galleries, a frenzy of chaotic motion.

There was a swift discussion of technicalities. Gudrun was very much impressed.

"But how wonderful, to have such a factory!" cried Ursula. "Is the whole building fine?"

"Oh yes," he replied. "The frieze is part of the whole architecture. Yes, it is a colossal thing."

Then he seemed to redden, shrugged his shoulders, and went on:

"Sculpture and architecture must go together. The epic sculpture is always part of an architectural conception. And since churches are all museum stuff, since industry is our business, now, then let us make our places of industry our art—our factory-area our Parthenon—ecco!"*

Ursula pondered.

"I suppose," she said, "there is no *need* for our great works to be so hideous."

Instantly he broke into motion.

"There you are!" he cried, "there you are! There is not only *no need* for our places of work to be ugly, but their ugliness ruins the work, in the end. Men will not go on submitting to such intolerable ugliness. In the end it will hurt too much, and they will make an end of it. And they will make an end of the *work* as well. They will think the work itself is ugly: the machines, the very act of labour. Whereas machinery and the acts of labour are extremely, maddeningly beautiful. But this will be the end of our civilisation, when people will not work because work has become so intolerably ugly to their sense, it nauseates them too much, they would rather starve. *Then* we shall see the hammer used only for smashing, then we shall see it.—Yet here we are—we have the opportunity to make beautiful factories, beautiful machine-houses— we have the opportunity—"

Gudrun could only partly understand. She could have cried with vexation.

"What does he say?" she asked Ursula. And Ursula translated, stammering and brief. Loerke watched Gudrun's face, to see her judgment.

"And do you think then," said Gudrun, "that art should serve industry?"

"Art should *interpret* industry, as art once interpreted religion," he said.

"But does your fair interpret industry?" she asked him.

"Certainly. What is man doing, when he is at a fair like this? He is fulfilling the counterpart of labour—the machine works him, instead of he the machine. He enjoys the mechanical motion in his own body."

"But is there nothing but work—mechanical work?" said Gudrun.

"Nothing but work?" he repeated, leaning forward, his eyes two flames. "No, it is nothing but this—serving a machine, or enjoying the motion of a machine—motion, that is all.—You have never worked for hunger, or you would know what God controls us."

Gudrun quivered and flushed. For some reason she was almost in tears.

"No, I have not worked for hunger," she replied. "But I have worked?"

"Travaillé—lavorato?" he cried. "E che lavoro—che lavoro? Quel travail est-ce que vous avez fait?"*

He broke into a mixture of Italian and French, instinctively using a foreign language when he spoke to her.

"You have never worked as the world works," he said to her, with sarcasm.

"Yes," she said, "I have. And I do—I work now for my daily bread."

He paused, looked at her steadily, then dropped the subject entirely. She seemed to him to be trifling.

"But have *you* ever worked as the world works?" Ursula asked him gently.

He looked at her untrustful.

"Yes," he replied, with a surly bark. "I have known what it was to lie in bed for three days, because I had nothing to eat."

Gudrun was looking at him with large, grave eyes, that seemed to draw the confession from him as the marrow from his bones. All his nature held him back from confessing. And yet her large, grave eyes upon him seemed to open some valve in his veins, and involuntarily he was telling.

"My father was a man who did not like work, and we had no mother. We lived in Austria, Polish Austria. How did we live? Ha!—somehow! Mostly in a room with three other families—one set in each corner—and the W.C. in the middle of the room—a pan with a plank on it—ha! I had two brothers and a sister—and there was a woman who lived with my father. He was a free being, in his way—would fight with any man in the town—a garrison town—and was a little man too. But he wouldn't work for anybody—set his heart against it, and wouldn't."

"And how did you live then?" asked Ursula.

He looked at her—then, suddenly, at Gudrun.

"Do you understand?" he asked.

"Enough," she replied.

Their eyes met for a moment. Then he looked away. He would say no more.

"And how did you become a sculptor?" asked Ursula.

"How did I become a sculptor—" he paused. "Dunque—"* he resumed, in a changed manner, and beginning to speak French—"I became old enough—I used to steal from the market-place. Later, I went to work—I imprinted the stamp on clay bottles, before they were baked. It was an earthenware-bottle factory. There I began making models. One day, I had had enough. I lay in the sun and did not go to work. Then I walked to Munich—then I walked to Italy—begging, begging everything.

"The Italians were very good to me—they were good and honorable to me. From Bozen to Rome, almost every night, I had a meal and a bed, perhaps of straw, with some peasant. I love the Italian people, with all my heart.

"Dunque, adesso—maintenant*—I earn a thousand pounds in a year, or I earn two thousand—."

He looked down at the ground, his voice tailing off into silence.

Gudrun looked at his fine, thin, shiny skin, reddish-brown from the sun, drawn tight over his full temples; and at his thin hair—he was going bald; and at the thick, coarse, brush-like moustache, cut short above his mobile, rather shapeless mouth.

"How old are you?" she asked.

He looked up at her with his full, elvin* eyes, startled.

"Wie alt?"* he repeated. And he hesitated. It was evidently one of his reticencies.

"How old are *you*?" he replied, without answering.

"I am twenty six," she answered.

"Twenty six," he repeated, looking into her eyes. He paused. Then he said:

"Und Ihr Herr Gemahl, wie alt ist er?"*

"Who?" asked Gudrun.

"Your husband," said Ursula, with a certain irony.

"I haven't got a husband," said Gudrun in English. In German she answered.

"He is thirty one."

But Loerke was watching closely, with his uncanny, fiery, suspicious eyes. Something in Gudrun seemed to accord with him. He was really like one of the "little people"* who have no soul, and has found his mate in a human being. But he suffered in his discovery. She too was fascinated by him, fascinated, as if some strange creature, a weasel or a rat, had begun to talk to her. But also, she knew what he was unconscious of, his tremendous power of understanding, of apprehending her living motion. He did not know his own power. He did not know how, with his full, submerged, watchful eyes, he could look into her and see her, what she was, see her secrets. He would only want her to be herself.— He knew her verily, with a subconscious, sinister knowledge, devoid of illusions and hopes.

To Gudrun, there was in Loerke the rock-bottom of all life. Everybody else had their illusion, must have their illusion, their before and after. But he, with a perfect stoicism, did without any before and after, dispensed with all illusion. He did not deceive himself, in the last issue. In the last issue he cared about nothing, he was troubled about nothing, he made not the slightest attempt to be at one with anything. He existed a pure, unconnected will, stoical and momentaneous. There was only his work.

It was curious too how his poverty, the degradation of his earlier life, attracted her. There was something insipid and tasteless to her, in the idea of a gentleman, a man who had gone the usual course through school and university. A certain violent sympathy, however, came up in her for this street arab. He seemed to be on the bed-rock of life, planted. There was no going beyond him. He was a real *ne plus ultra*.

Ursula too was attracted by Loerke. In both sisters he commanded a certain homage. But there were moments when to Ursula he seemed indescribably inferior, false, a vulgarism.

Both Birkin and Gerald disliked him, Gerald ignoring him with some contempt, Birkin exasperated.

"What do the women find so impressive in that little German sculptor?" Gerald asked.

"God above knows," replied Birkin; "unless it's the sort of appeal he makes to them, which has such a power over them."

Gerald looked up in surprise.

"*Does* he make an appeal to them?" he asked.

"Unconsciously," replied Birkin. "He is the perfectly isolated being, existing in a state of real isolation. And the women rush towards that, like a current of air towards a vacuum."

"It's a pity one can't rush towards something a little more positive," said Gerald.

"It's a pity one can't crack the vacuum," said Birkin.

Gerald stood still, suspended in thought.

"Do you think he ought to be cracked?" he asked, pensive.

"Sure," said Birkin. "There's nothing to do with that glassy envelope of a will but smash it. Except one doesn't want to know the horrors that are inside it."

Gerald looked out into the mist of fine snow that was blowing by. Everywhere was blind today, horribly blind.

"Why?" he asked.

"A fixed will?" replied Birkin. "Because it's timeless and absolved and obscene, in the midst of life.—Look at him, Loerke. He keeps himself perfectly intact, perfectly unchanged, he makes no connection with anything whatsoever, only he uses other life to feed his life, like a parasitic insect. He uses other living beings to send a sensation and a warmth and a satisfaction through his glassy shell, into the horrible mess inside him—really like an insect on the living body of man."

"But why does anybody submit their living body to him?" asked Gerald.

"Because they want to—they want to be devoured in that way—it's a form of sensationalism—it satisfies them."

Still Gerald stood and stared at the blind haze of snow outside.

"I don't understand your terms, really," he said, in a flat, doomed voice. "But it sounds a rum sort of satisfaction."

Meanwhile Gudrun and Ursula waited for the next opportunity to talk to Loerke. It was no use beginning when the men were there. They could get into no touch with the isolated little sculptor. He had to be alone with them. And he preferred Ursula to be there, as a sort of transmitter to Gudrun.

"Do you do nothing but architectural sculpture?" Gudrun asked him one evening.

"Not now," he replied. "I have done all sorts—except portraits—I never did portraits. But other things—"

"What kind of thing?" asked Gudrun.

He paused a moment, then rose, and went out of the room. He returned almost immediately with a little roll of paper, which he handed to her. She unrolled it. It was a photogravure reproduction of a statuette, signed F. Loerke.

"That is quite an early thing—*not* mechanical," he said, "more popular."

The statuette was of a naked girl, small, finely made, sitting on a great naked horse. The girl was young and tender, a mere bud. She was sitting sideways on the horse, her face in her hands, as if in shame and grief, in a little abandon. Her hair, which was short and must be flaxen, fell forward, divided, half covering her hands.

Her limbs were young and tender. Her legs, scarcely formed yet, the legs of a maiden just passing towards cruel womanhood, dangled childishly over the side of the powerful horse, pathetically, the small feet folded one over the other, as if to hide. But there was no hiding. There she was exposed naked on the naked flank of the horse.

The horse stood stock still, stretched in a kind of start. It was a massive, magnificent stallion, rigid with pent up power. Its neck was arched and terrible, like a sickle, its flanks were pressed back, rigid with power.

Gudrun went pale, and a darkness came over her eyes, like shame, she looked up with a certain supplication, almost slave-like. He glanced at her, and jerked his head a little.

"How big is it?" she asked, in a toneless voice, persisting in appearing casual and unaffected.

"How big?" he replied, glancing again at her. "Without pedestal—so high—" he measured with his hand—"with pedestal, so—"

He looked at her steadily. There was a little brusque, turgid contempt for her in his swift gesture, and she seemed to cringe a little.

"And what is it done in?" she asked, throwing back her head and looking at him with affected coldness.

He still gazed at her steadily, and his dominance was not shaken.

"Bronze—green bronze."

"Green bronze!" repeated Gudrun, coldly accepting his challenge. She was thinking of the slender, immature, tender limbs of the girl, smooth and cold in green bronze.

"Yes, beautiful," she murmured, looking up at him with a certain dark homage.

He closed his eyes and looked aside, triumphant.

"Why," said Ursula, "did you make the horse so stiff? It is as stiff as a block."

"Stiff!" he repeated, in arms at once.

"Yes. *Look* how stock and stupid and brutal it is. Horses are sensitive, quite delicate and sensitive, really."

He raised his shoulders, spread his hands in a shrug of slow indifference, as much as to inform her she was an amateur and an impertinent nobody.

"Wissen Sie,"* he said, with an insulting patience and condescension in his voice, "that horse is a certain *form*, part of a whole form. It is part of a work of art, a piece of form. It is not a picture of a friendly horse to which you give a lump of sugar, do you see—it is part of a work of art, it has no relation to anything outside that work of art."

Ursula, angry at being treated quite so insultingly de haut en bas,* from the height of esoteric art to the depth of general exoteric amateurism, replied hotly, flushing and lifting her face:

"But it *is* a picture of a horse, nevertheless."

He lifted his shoulders in another shrug.

"As you like—it is not the picture of a cow, certainly."

Here Gudrun broke in, flushed and brilliant, anxious to avoid any more of this, any more of Ursula's foolish persistence in giving herself away.

"What do you mean by 'it is a picture of a horse'?" she cried at her sister. "What do you mean by a horse? You mean an idea you have in *your* head, and which you want to see represented. This is another idea altogether, quite another idea. Call it a horse if you like, or say it is not a horse. I have just as much right to say that *your* horse isn't a horse, that it is a falsity of your own make-up."

Ursula wavered, baffled. Then her words came.

"But why does he have this idea of a horse?" she said. "I know it is his idea. I know it is a picture of himself, really—"

Loerke snorted with rage.

"A picture of myself!" he repeated, in derision. "Wissen Sie, gnädige Frau,* that is a Kunstwerk, a work of art. It is a work of art, it is a picture of nothing, of absolutely nothing. It has nothing to do with anything but itself, it has no relation with the every day world of this and the other, there is no connection between them, absolutely none, they are two different and distinct planes of existence, and to translate one into the other is worse than foolish, it is a darkening of all counsel, a making confusion everywhere. Do you see, you *must not* confuse the relative world of action, with the absolute world of art. That you *must not do*."

"That is quite true," cried Gudrun, let loose in a sort of rhapsody. "The two things are quite and permanently apart, they have nothing to do with one another. *I* and my art, they have *nothing* to do with each other. My art stands in another world, I am in this world."

Her face was flushed and transfigured. Loerke, who was sitting with his head ducked, like some creature at bay, looked up at her swiftly, almost furtively, and murmured:

"Ja—so ist es, so ist es."*

Ursula was silent after this outburst. She was furious. She wanted to poke a hole into them both.

"It isn't a word of it true, of all this harangue you have made me," she replied flatly. "The horse is a picture of your own stock stupid brutality, and the girl was a girl you loved and tortured and then ignored."

He looked up at her with a small smile of contempt in his eyes. He would not trouble to answer this last charge. Gudrun too was silent in exasperated contempt. Ursula *was* such an insufferable outsider, rushing in where angels would fear to tread.* But there—fools must be suffered, if not gladly.*

But Ursula was persistent too.

"As for your world of art and your world of reality," she replied; "you have to separate the two, because you can't bear to know what you are. You can't bear to realise what a stock, stiff, hide-bound brutality you *are* really, so you say 'it's the world of art.' The world of art is only the truth about the real world, that's all—but you are too far gone to see it."

She was white and trembling, intent. Gudrun and Loerke sat in stiff dislike of her. Gerald too, who had come up in the beginning of the speech, stood looking at her in complete disapproval and opposition. He felt she was undignified, she put a sort of vulgarity over life. He joined his forces with the other two. They all three wanted her to go away. But she sat on in silence, her soul weeping, sobbing violently, her fingers twisting her handkerchief.

The others maintained a dead silence, letting the display of Ursula's obtrusiveness pass by. Then Gudrun asked, in a voice that was quite cool and casual, as if resuming a casual conversation:

"Was the girl a model?"

"Nein, sie war kein Modell. Sie war eine kleine Malschülerin."*

"An art student!" replied Gudrun.

And how the situation revealed itself to her! She saw the girl art-student, unformed and of pernicious recklessness, too young, her straight flaxen hair cut short, hanging just into her neck, curving inwards slightly, because it was rather thick; and Loerke, the well-known master-sculptor, and the girl, probably well-brought-up and of good family, thinking herself so great to be his mistress. Oh how well she knew the common callousness of it all. Dresden, Paris, or London, what did it matter? She knew it.

"Where is she now?" Ursula asked.

Loerke raised his shoulders, to convey his complete ignorance and indifference.

"That is already six years ago," he said; "she will be twenty-three years old, no more good."

Gerald had picked up the picture and was looking at it. It attracted him also. He saw on the pedestal, that the piece was called "Lady Godiva."*

"But this isn't Lady Godiva," he said, smiling good-humouredly. "She was the middle-aged wife of some Earl or other, who covered herself with her long hair."

"So Maud Allan* makes it appear," said Gudrun lightly, with a mocking grimace.

"Why Maud Allan?" he replied. "Isn't it so?—I always thought the legend was that."

"Yes, Gerald dear, I'm quite *sure* you've got the legend perfectly."

She was laughing at him, with a little, caressive, intimate contempt.

"To be sure, I'd rather see the woman than the hair," he laughed in return.

"Wouldn't you just!" mocked Gudrun.

Ursula rose and went away, leaving the three together.

Gudrun took the picture again from Gerald, and sat looking at it closely.

"Of course," she said, turning to tease Loerke now, "You *were* fond of your little Malschülerin."

He raised his eyebrows and his shoulders in a complacent shrug.

"Of this little girl?" asked Gerald, pointing to the figure. Gudrun was sitting with the picture in her lap. She looked up at Gerald, full into his eyes, so that he seemed to be blinded.

"*Wasn't* he fond of her!" she said to Gerald, in a slightly mocking, humourous playfulness. "You've only to look at the feet—*aren't* they darling, so pretty and tender—oh, they're really wonderful, they are really—"

She lifted her eyes slowly, with a hot, flaming look into Loerke's eyes. His soul was filled with her burning recognition, he seemed to grow stronger and keener.

Gerald looked at the small, sculptured feet. They were turned together, half covering each other in pathetic shyness and fear. He looked at them a long time, fascinated. Then, in some pain, he put the picture away from him. He felt full of barrenness.

"What was her name?" Gudrun asked Loerke.

"Annette von Weck," Loerke replied, reminiscent. "Ja, sie war hübsch.* She was pretty—but she was tiresome. She was a nuisance—not for a minute would she keep still—not until I'd slapped her hard and made her cry—then she'd sit for five minutes."

He was thinking over the work, his work, the all-important to him.

"Did you really slap her?" asked Gudrun, coolly. He glanced back at her, reading her challenge.

"Yes, I did," he said, nonchalant, "harder than I have ever smacked anybody in my life.—I had to, I had to.—It was the only way I got the work done."

Gudrun watched him with large, dark-filled eyes, for some moments. She seemed to be considering his very soul. Then she looked down, in silence.

"Why did you have such a young Godiva then?" asked Gerald. "She is so small, besides, on the horse—not big enough for it—such a child."

A queer spasm went over Loerke's face.

"Yes," he said, "I don't like them any bigger, any older. Then they are beautiful, at sixteen, seventeen, eighteen—after that, they are no use to me."

There was a moment's pause.

"Why not?" asked Gerald.

Loerke shrugged his shoulders.

"I don't find them interesting—or beautiful—they are no good to me, for my work."

"Do you mean to say a woman isn't beautiful after she is twenty?" asked Gerald.

"For me, no. Before twenty, she is small and fresh and tender and slight. After that—let her be what she likes, she has nothing for me. The Venus of Milo is a bourgeoise—so are they all."

"And you don't care for women at all after twenty?" asked Gerald.

"They are no good to me, they are of no use in my art," Loerke repeated impatiently. "I don't find them beautiful."

"You are an epicure," said Gerald, with a slight sarcastic laugh.

"And what about men?" asked Gudrun suddenly.

"Yes, they are good at all ages," replied Loerke. "A man should be big and powerful—whether he is old or young is of no account, so he has the size, something of massiveness and form."

Ursula went out alone into the world of pure, new snow. But the dazzling whiteness seemed to beat upon her till it hurt her, she felt the cold was slowly strangling her soul. Her head felt dazed and numb.

Suddenly, she wanted to go away. It occurred to her, like a miracle, that she might go away into another world. She had felt so doomed up here in the eternal snow, as if there were no beyond.

Now suddenly, as by a miracle, she remembered that away beyond, below her, lay the dark fruitful earth, that towards the south there were stretches of land dark with orange trees and cypress, grey with olives, that palm trees waved their long, frayed boughs in shadow against a blue sky. Miracle of miracles!—this utterly silent, frozen world of the mountain-tops was not universal! One might leave it and have done with it. One might go away.

She wanted to realise the miracle at once. She wanted at this instant to have done with the snow-world, the terrible static, ice-built mountain tops. She wanted to see the dark earth, to smell its earthy fecundity, to see the patient wintry vegetation, to feel the sunshine touch a response in the buds.

She went back gladly to the house, full of hope. Birkin was reading, lying in bed.

"Rupert," she said, bursting in on him, "I want to go away."

He looked up at her slowly.

"Do you?" he replied mildly.

She sat by him and put her arms round his neck. It surprised her that he was so little surprised.

"Don't *you*?" she asked, troubled.

"I hadn't thought about it," he said. "But I believe I do."

She sat up, suddenly erect.

"I hate it," she said. "I hate this barren snow, and the unnaturalness of it, the unnatural light it throws on everybody, the unnatural feelings it makes everybody have."

He lay still, and laughed, meditating.

"Well," he said, "we can *go* away—we can go tomorrow. We'll go tomorrow to Verona, and be Romeo and Juliet, and sit in the amphitheatre—shall we?"

Suddenly she hid her face against his shoulder with joy and shyness. He lay so untrammelled.

"Yes," she said softly, filled with joy. She felt her soul had new wings, now he was so simple in fulfilling her needs. "I shall love to be Romeo and Juliet," she said.—"My love!"

"Though a fearfully cold wind blows in Verona," he said, "from out of the Alps. We shall have the smell of the snow in our noses."

She sat up and looked at him.

"Are you glad to go?" she asked, troubled. His eyes were soft and laughing. She hid her face against his neck, clinging close to him, pleading:

"Don't laugh at me—don't laugh at me."

"Why—how's that?" he laughed, putting his arms round her.

"Because I don't want to be laughed at," she whispered.

He laughed more, as he kissed her delicate, finely perfumed hair.

"Do you love me?" she whispered, in wild seriousness.

"Yes," he answered, laughing.

Suddenly she lifted her mouth to be kissed. Her lips were taut and quivering and strenuous, his were soft, deep and delicate. He waited a few moments in the kiss. Then a shade of sadness went over his soul.

"Your mouth is so hard," he said, in faint reproach.

"And yours is so soft and nice," she said gladly.

"But why do you always grip your lips?" he asked, regretful.

"Never mind," she said swiftly. "It is my way."

She knew he loved her; she was sure of him. Yet she could not let go a certain hold over herself, she could not bear him to question her. She gave herself up in delight to being loved by him. She knew that, in spite of his joy when she abandoned herself, he was a little bit saddened too. She could give herself up to *love*. But she could not yield herself to *him*, to his being—not yet. He must wait—he must wait for her. Meanwhile she abandoned herself to her pleasure, took her joy of him. And she enjoyed his giving, fully. But she turned aside from the slight reproach of his face. She felt glorious and free, full of life and liberty. And he was still and soft and peaceful, slumbrous, like a plant in the sunshine.

They made their preparations to leave the next day. First they went to Gudrun's room, where she and Gerald were just dressed ready for the evening indoors.

"Prune," said Ursula. "I think we shall go away tomorrow. I can't stand the snow any more. It hurts my skin and my soul."

"Does it really hurt your soul, Ursula?" asked Gudrun in some surprise. "I can quite believe it hurts your skin—it is *terrible*. But I thought it was *admirable* for the soul."

"No, not for mine. It just injures it," said Ursula.

"Really!" cried Gudrun.

There was a silence in the room. And Ursula and Birkin could feel that Gudrun and Gerald were relieved by their going.

"You will go south?" said Gerald, a little ring of satisfaction in his voice.

"Yes," said Birkin, turning away.

There was a queer, indefinable hostility between the two men, lately. Birkin was so soft and indifferent, drifting along in a dim, easy flow, unnoticing and peaceful, since he came abroad, whilst Gerald, on the other hand, was intense and gripped upon himself, like a young victor. The two men annulled one another.

Gerald and Gudrun were very kind to the two who were departing, solicitous for their welfare as if they were two children. Gudrun came to Ursula's bedroom with three pairs of the coloured stockings for which she was notorious, and she threw them on the bed. But these were thick silk stockings, vermilion, cornflower blue, and dark grey, bought in Paris. Ursula was in raptures. She knew Gudrun must be feeling *very* loving, to give away such treasures.

"I can't take them from you Prune," she cried. "I can't possibly deprive you of them—the jewels."

"*Aren't* they jewels!" cried Gudrun, eying her gifts with an envious eye. "*Aren't* they real lambs!"

"Yes, you *must* keep them," said Ursula.

"I don't *want* them, I've got three more pairs. I *want* you to keep them—I want you to have them—they're yours, there—."

And with trembling, excited hands she put the coveted stockings under Ursula's pillow.

"One gets the greatest joy of all out of really lovely stockings," said Ursula.

"One does," replied Gudrun; "the greatest joy of all."

And she sat down in the chair. It was evident she had come for a last talk. Ursula not knowing what she wanted, waited in silence.

"Do you feel, Ursula," Gudrun began, "that 'you are going away for ever, never to return—' sort of thing?"

"Oh, we shall come back," said Ursula.

"Yes, I know. But spiritually, so to speak, you are going out of life?"

Ursula quivered.

"I don't know a bit what is going to happen," she said. "I only know we are going."

Gudrun waited.

"And you are glad?" she asked.

Ursula meditated for a moment.

"I believe I am *very* glad," she replied.

But Gudrun read the unconscious brightness on her sister's face, rather than the uncertain tones of her speech.

"But don't you think you'll *want* the old connection with the world—Father and the rest of us, and all that it means, England and the world of thought—don't you think you'll *need* that, really to make a world?"

Ursula was silent, trying to imagine.

"I think," she said at length, involuntarily, "that Rupert is right—one wants a new space to be in, and one must turn one's face away from the old."

Gudrun watched her sister with impassive face and steady eyes.

"One wants a new space to be in, I quite agree," she said. "But *I* think that a new world is a development from this world, and that to isolate oneself with one other person, isn't to find a new world at all, but only to secure oneself in one's illusions."

Ursula looked out of the window. In her soul she began to wrestle, and she was frightened. She was always frightened of words, because she knew that mere word-force could always make her believe what she did not believe.

"Perhaps," she said, full of mistrust, of Birkin and everybody. "But," she added, "I do think that one can't have anything new whilst one belongs to the old—do you know what I mean?—even fighting the old is belonging to it.—I know, one is tempted to stop with the world, just to fight it.—But then one loses oneself with it."

Gudrun considered herself.

"Yes," she said. "In a way, one is of the world if one lives in it. But isn't it really an illusion, to think you can get out of it? After all, a cottage in the Abruzzi, or wherever it may be, isn't a new world.—No, the only thing to do with the world, is to see it through."

Ursula looked away. She was so frightened of argument.

"But there *can* be something else, can't there?" she said. "One can see it through in one's soul, long before it sees itself through in actuality. And then, when one has seen in one's soul, one can try for something else."

"*Can* one see it through in one's soul?" asked Gudrun. "If you mean that you can see to the end of what will happen, I don't agree—I really can't agree.—And anyhow you can't suddenly fly off on to a new planet, because you think you can see to the end of *this*."

Ursula suddenly straightened herself.

"Yes," she said, "yes—one knows. You *can't* do any more here—you've *got* to get away to a new planet—There's no going any further with this show. You've got to hop away into space."

Gudrun reflected for a few moments. Then a smile of opposition, almost of contempt, came over her face.

"And what will happen when you find yourself in space?" she cried in derision. "After all, the great ideas of the world are the same there. You above everybody can't get away from the fact that love, for instance, is the supreme thing, in space as well as on earth."

"No," said Ursula, "it isn't. Love is too human and little. I believe in something inhuman, of which love is only a little part. I believe what we must fulfil comes out of the Unknown to us, and it is something infinitely more than love. It isn't so merely *human*."

Gudrun looked at Ursula with steady, balancing eyes. She admired and despised her sister so much, both. Then suddenly she averted her face, saying coldly, uglily:

"Well, I've got no further than love, yet."

Over Ursula's mind flashed the thought: "Because you never *have* loved, you can't get beyond it."

Gudrun rose, came over to Ursula and put her arm round her neck.

"Go and find your new world, dear," she said, her voice clanging with false benignity. "After all, the happiest voyage is the quest of Rupert's Blessed Isles."*

Her arm rested round Ursula's neck, her fingers on Ursula's cheek, for a few moments. Ursula was supremely uncomfortable meanwhile. There was an insult in Gudrun's protective patronage that was really too hurting. Feeling her sister's resistance, Gudrun drew awkwardly away, turned over the pillow and disclosed the stockings again.

"Ha—ha!" she laughed to herself "How we do talk indeed—new worlds and old—!"

And they passed to the familiar, worldly subjects.

Gerald and Birkin had walked on ahead, waiting for the sledge to overtake them, conveying the departing guests.

"How much longer will you stay here?" asked Birkin, glancing up at Gerald's very red, keen face.

"Oh I dunno," Gerald replied. "Till we get tired of it."

"You're not afraid of the snow melting first?" asked Birkin.

Gerald laughed.

"Does it melt?" he said.

"You are so very happy?" said Birkin.

Gerald screwed up his eyes a little.

"Happy?" he said. "I never know what those common words mean. I'm having the time of my life."

"What about when you get back?" asked Birkin.

"Oh, I don't know. We may never get back. I don't look before and after,"* said Gerald lightly.

"Become Snow King and Snow Queen," said Birkin.

"Perhaps. There's something final about this. And Gudrun seems so soft, her skin is like silk, her limbs and her muscles. It goes to your brain. But it's more like swallowing vitriol than milk—it burns your inside out." He went on a few paces, staring ahead, his eyes fixed, looking like a werewolf. "Yet I couldn't do without her—I'd rather be killed by inches—"

He was talking grudgingly, almost sullenly. Then suddenly he braced himself up with a kind of rhapsody and looked at Birkin with vindictive, wolf-like eyes, saying:

"Do you know what it is to die when you are with a woman? She's so beautiful, so perfect, you find her *so good*, her flesh like a silk, and every stroke and bit perfect—ha, that perfection, when you go beyond yourself, you lose yourself!—And then—" he stopped on the snow and suddenly opened his clenched hands—"it's nothing—your heart might have burst inside you—and"—he looked round into the air with a queer histrionic movement—"it's nothing—you understand what I mean—it was a great experience, something final—and then—nothingness."

He walked on in silence. It seemed like bragging, but like a man bragging.

"Of course," he resumed, "I wouldn't *not* have felt it: it's a final experience. And she's a wonderful woman. But—I think she's deadly, I do really."

Birkin looked at him, at his strange, scarcely conscious face. Gerald seemed to wonder at his own words.

"Surely you've had enough now?" said Birkin. "Surely you can stop now?"

"Oh," said Gerald, "it's not finished yet."

And the two walked on. But Birkin wanted to hear the sound of the sledge bells. He felt under an unbearable oppression, walking with Gerald, as if he were in a vice.

The sledge came. Gudrun dismounted and they all made their farewells. They wanted to go apart, all of them. Birkin took his place, and the sledge drove away leaving Gudrun and Gerald standing on the snow, waving. Something froze Birkin's heart, seeing them standing there in the isolation of the snow, growing smaller and more isolated.

12

WHEN URSULA AND BIRKIN WERE GONE, Gudrun felt herself free in her contest with Gerald. As they grew more used to each other, he seemed to press upon her more and more. At first she could manage him, so that her own will was always left free. But very soon, he began to ignore her female tactics, he dropped his respect for her whims and her privacies, he began to exert his own will, blindly, without submitting to hers.

Already a vital contest had set in, which frightened them both. But he was alone, whilst already she had begun to cast round for external resource.

When Ursula had gone, Gudrun felt her own existence had become stark and elemental. She went and crouched alone in her bedroom, looking out of the window at the big, flashing stars. In front was the faint shadow of the mountain-knot. That was the pivot. She felt strange and inevitable, as if she were centred upon the pivot of all existence, there was no further reality.

Presently Gerald opened the door. She knew he would not be long before he came. She was rarely alone now, he pressed upon her like a frost, wearying her.

"Are you alone in the dark?" he said. And she could tell by his tone he resented it, he resented the isolation she had drawn round herself. Yet, feeling static and inevitable, she was kind towards him.

"Would you like to light the candle?" she asked.

He did not answer, but came and stood behind her, in the darkness.

"Look," she said, "at that lovely star up there. Do you know its name?"

He crouched beside her, to look through the low window.

"No," he said. "It is very fine."

"*Isn't* it beautiful? Do you notice how it darts different coloured fires—it flashes really superbly—"

They remained in silence. With a mute, heavy gesture she put her hand on his knee, and took his hand.

"Are you regretting Ursula?" he asked.

"No, not at all," she said. Then, in a slow mood, she asked:

"Do you love me?"

He stiffened himself further against her.

"Do you think I do, or do you think I don't?" he asked.

"I don't know," she replied.

"But what is your opinion," he asked.

There was a pause. At length, in the darkness, came her voice, hard and cruel:

"I think you don't," she said coldly His heart went black at the sound of her voice.

"Why don't I love you?" he asked, as if admitting the truth of her accusation, yet hating her for it.

"I don't know why you don't—I've been good to you. You were in a fearful state, really—almost mad."

Her heart was beating to suffocate her, yet she was stony and unrelenting.

"When was I almost mad?" he asked.

"When you first came to me. I *had* to take pity on you.—But you can't love."

It was that reiterated accusation 'But you can't love,' which did nearly drive him mad.

"Why must you repeat it so often, that I can't love?" he said in a voice strangled with rage.

"Well you *don't*, do you?" she asked.

He was silent with cold passion of anger.

"You can't say you *do* love me, can you?" she repeated, almost with a sneer.

"No," he said.

"And you never *have* loved me, have you?"

"I don't know what you mean by the word 'love'," he replied.

"Yes you do.—You have never loved me, really, have you?"

"No," he said, prompted by some barren spirit of truthfulness and obstinacy.

"And you never will love me," she said finally. "Will you?"

"No," he said.

"Good," she replied. "What are you doing here then, with me?"

He was silent in black, insane rage and despair. "If only I could kill her," his heart was whispering repeatedly "If only I could kill her—I should be free." It seemed to him that death was the only severing of this Gordian knot.

"Why do you torture me?" he said.

She flung her arms round his neck.

"Ah, I don't want to torture you," she said pityingly, as if she were comforting a child. The impertinence made his veins go cold, he was insensible. She held her arms round his neck, in a triumph of pity. And her pity for him was as cold as stone, its deepest motive was fear of him, fear of his power over her, which she must always counter-foil.*

"Say you love me," she pleaded. "Say you will love me for ever—won't you—won't you?"

But it was her voice only that coaxed him. Her senses were entirely apart from him, cold.

"Won't you say you'll love me always?" she coaxed. "Say it, even if it isn't true—say it Gerald, do."

"I will love you always," he repeated, in real agony, forcing the words out.

She gave him a quick kiss.

"Fancy your actually having said it," she said, with a touch of raillery.

He stood as if he had been beaten.

"Try to love me a little more, and to want me a little less," she said, in a half sullen, half fretful tone.

The darkness seemed to be swaying in waves across his mind, great waves of darkness plunging across his mind. It seemed to him he was degraded at the very quick, made of no account.

"You mean you don't want me?" he said.

"You are so insistent, and there is so little grace in you, so little fineness. You are so blind and crude. You break me—you only waste me—it is horrible to me."

"Horrible to you?" he repeated.

"Yes. Don't you think I might have a room to myself, now Ursula has gone? You can say you want a dressing room."

"You do as you like—you can leave altogether if you like," he managed to articulate.

"Yes I know that," she replied. "So can you. You can leave me whenever you like—without notice even."

The great tides of darkness were swinging across his mind, he could hardly stand upright. A terrible weariness overcame him, he felt he must lie on the floor. Dropping off his clothes, he got into bed, and lay like a man suddenly overcome by drunkenness, the darkness lifting and plunging as if he were lying upon a black, giddy sea. He lay still in this strange, horrific reeling for some time, purely unconscious.

At length she slipped from her own bed and came over to him. He remained rigid, his back to her. He was all but unconscious.

She put her arms round his terrifying, rigid body, and laid her cheek against his hard shoulder.

"Gerald," she whispered. "Gerald."

There was no change in him. She caught him against her. She pressed her breasts against his shoulders, she kissed his shoulder, through the sleeping-jacket. Her mind wondered, over his rigid, unliving body. She was bewildered and wretched, only her heart was hot for him to speak to her.

"Gerald, my dear!" she whispered, bending over him, kissing his ear.

Her warm breath playing, flying rhythmically over his ear, seemed to relax the tension. She could feel his body gradually relaxing a little, losing its terrifying, unnatural rigidity. Her hands clutched his limbs, his muscles, going over him spasmodically.

The hot blood began to flow again through his veins, his limbs relaxed.

"Turn round to me," she whispered, forlorn with insistence and terror.

So at last he was given again, warm and flexible. He turned and gathered her in his arms. And feeling her soft against him, so perfectly and wondrously soft and recipient, his arms tightened on her, she was as if crushed powerless in him. His brain seemed hard and invincible now like a jewel, there was no resisting him.

His passion was awful to her, tense and awful and impersonal, like a destructive tension. She felt it would kill her, she was being killed.

"My God, my God!" she cried in anguish, in his embrace, feeling her life being killed within her. And when he was kissing her, soothing her, her breath came slowly, as if she were really spent, dying.

"Shall I die, shall I die?" she repeated to herself.

And in the night, and in him, there was no answer to the question.

And yet, next day, it all seemed exaggerated, overdone, she did not go away, she remained to finish the holiday, admitting nothing. He scarcely ever left her alone, but followed her like a shadow, he was like a doom upon her, a continual 'thou shalt', 'thou shalt not.' Sometimes it was he who was filled with strength and handsomeness, whilst she crept about near the earth, like the lowest and most nonvital of beings, sometimes it was the reverse. But always it was this eternal see-saw, they were never strong and happy together, one was always cast down when the other was lifted up.

"In the end," she said to herself, "I shall go away from him."

"I can be free of her," he said to himself in his paroxysms of suffering.

And he set himself to be free. He even prepared to go away, to leave her in the lurch. But for the first time there was a flaw in his will.

"Where shall I go?" he asked himself.

"Can't you be self-sufficient?" he replied to himself, putting himself upon his pride.

"Self-sufficient?" he repeated.

He knew that Gudrun was virtually sufficient unto herself, closed round and completed, like a seed closed in its envelope. In the calm, static reason of his soul, he recognised this, and admitted it was her right, to be closed round upon herself, self-complete, without desire. He realised it, he admitted it, it only needed one last effort on his own part, to win for himself the same completeness. He knew that it only needed one convulsion of his will for him to be able to turn upon himself also, to close upon himself as a stone shuts upon itself, and is impervious, self-completed, a thing to itself.

This knowledge threw him into a terrible chaos. Because, however much he might *will* to be immune and self-complete, the desire for this state was lacking, and he could not create it. He could see that, to succeed at all, he must be perfectly free of Gudrun, leave her if she wanted to be left, demand nothing of her, have no claim upon her.

But then, to have no claim upon her, he must stand by himself, be complete in himself. He knew what this meant: he *had* been complete in himself these thirty years of his life though never before conscious of it. And what was it?—a static state of instrumentality.

A strange rent had been torn in him; like a victim that is torn open and given to the heavens, so he had been torn apart and given to Gudrun. Why should he close again? This wound, this strange, infinitely sensitive opening of his soul, where he was exposed, like an open flower, to all the universe, and in which he was given to his complement, the other, the unknown, this wound, this disclosure, this unfolding of his own covering, leaving him incomplete, limited, unfinished, leaving [him] like an open flower under the sky, this was his cruellest joy. Why then should he forego it. Why should he close up and become impervious, immune, like a partial thing in its sheath, when he had broken forth, like a seed that has germinated, to issue forth in being, embracing the unrealised heavens.

He would keep the unfinished bliss of his own yearning even through the torture she inflicted upon him. A strange obstinacy possessed him. He would not go away from her whatever she said or did. A strange, deathly yearning carried him along with her. She was the determinating influence of his very being. Though she treated him with contempt, repeated rebuffs and denials, still he would never be gone, since in being near her even he felt the quickening, the going forth in him, the release, the knowledge of his own limitation and the magic of the promise.

She tortured the open heart of him even as he turned to her. And she was tortured herself. It may have been her will was stronger. She felt, with horror, as if he tore at the bud of her heart, tore it open, like an irreverent, persistent being. Like a boy who pulls off a fly's wings, or tears open a bud to see what is in the flower, he tore at her privacy, at her very life, he would destroy her as an immature bud, torn open, is destroyed.

She might open towards him, a long while hence, in her dreams, when she was a pure spirit. But now she was not to be violated and ruined. She closed against him fiercely.

They climbed together, at evening, up the high slope, to see the sun set. In the finely breathing, keen wind they stood and watched the yellow sun sink in crimson and disappear. Then in the east the peaks and ridges glowed with living rose, incandescent like immortal flowers against a brown-purple sky, a miracle, whilst down below the world was a bluish shadow, and above, like an annunciation, hovered a rosy transport in mid air.

409

To her it was so beautiful, it was a delirium, she wanted to gather the glowing, eternal peaks to her breast, and die. He saw them, saw they were beautiful. But there arose no clamour in his breast, only a bitterness that she had departed. He wished the peaks were grey and unbeautiful, so that she should not be transported to them. Why did she betray him so terribly, for the sake of the glow of evening? Why did she leave him standing there, with the ice-wind blowing through his heart, like death, to soar herself among the rosy snow-tips?

"What does the twilight matter?" he said. "Why do you get into such a state about it? Is it so important to you?"

She winced in violation and in fury.

"Go away," she cried, "and leave me to it. It is beautiful, beautiful," she sang, in strange, rhapsodic tones. "It is the most beautiful thing I have ever seen in my life. Don't try and come between it and me. Take yourself away, you are out of place—"

He stood back a little, and left her standing there, statue-like, transported into the mystic glowing east. Already the rose was fading, large white stars were flashing out. He waited, in his nonentity. He would forego everything but the yearning.

"That was the most perfect thing I have ever seen," she said in cold, brutal tones, when at last she turned round to him. "It amazes me that you should want to destroy it. If you can't see it yourself, why try to debar me?"

"One day," he said, softly, looking up at her, "I shall murder you, as you stand looking at a sunset. Then *I* shall have something to look at."

There was a soft, voluptuous promise to himself in the words. She was chilled, but arrogant.

"Ha!" she said. "I am not afraid of your melodramatic conceit."

She denied herself to him, she kept her room rigidly private to herself. But he waited on, in a curious patience, belonging to his yearning for her.

"In the end," he said to himself, with real voluptuous promise, "when it reaches that point, I shall murder her." And he trembled delicately in every limb, in terrible anticipation, as he trembled in his most violent accesses of passionate approach to her, trembling with too-much desire.

She had a curious sort of allegiance with Loerke, all the while, now, something traitorous. Gerald knew of it. But in the unnatural state of patience, and the unwillingness to harden himself against her, in which he found himself, he took no notice, although her soft kindliness to the other man, whom he hated as a noxious insect, made him shiver again with an access of the strange shuddering that came over him repeatedly.

He left her alone only when he went ski-ing, a sport he loved, and which she did not practise. Then he seemed to sweep out of life, to be a projectile into the beyond. And often, when he went away, she talked to the little German sculptor. They had an invariable topic, in their art.

They were almost of the same beliefs. He hated Mestrovic,* he was not satisfied with the Futurists, he liked the West African wooden figures, the grotesque-obscene. He was all for ridicule, conflict, and mechanical motion.

They had a curious game with each other, Gudrun and Loerke, persuading themselves that they had some rare esoteric understanding of life, that they alone were initiated into the central secrets, all the rest were outsiders. They might have been sharers in some religious mystery, some black and symbolist knowledge belonging to Bel,* or an obscene African deity, or the Syria Dea.

The temple of Art was their refuge, and the inner mysteries of sensation their sanctuary. Art and Life were to them the Reality and the Unreality.

"Of course," said Gudrun, "life doesn't *really* matter—it is one's art which is central. What one does in one's life has peu de rapport,* it doesn't signify much."

"Yes, that is so, exactly," replied the sculptor. "What one does in one's art, that is the breath of one's being. What one does in one's life, that is a bagatelle for the outsiders to fuss about."

It was curious what a sense of elation and freedom Gudrun found in this communication. She felt established for ever. Of course Gerald was bagatelle—love was one of the temporal things in her life, except in so far as she was an artist. She thought of Cleopatra—Cleopatra must have been an artist; she reaped the essential from a man, she harvested the ultimate sensation, and threw away the husk; and Mary Stuart, and Eleonora Duse, panting with her lovers* after the theatre, these were the mystic priestesses of love. After all, what was the lover but fuel for the transport of art, for a female art, the art of pure, perfect knowledge in sensuous understanding.

One evening Gerald was arguing with Loerke about Italy and Tripoli.* The Englishman was in a strange, inflammable state, the German was excited. It was a contest of words, but it meant a conflict in spirit between the two men. And all the while Gudrun could see in Gerald an arrogant, English contempt for a foreigner. Although Gerald was quivering, his eyes flashing, his face flushed, in his argument, there was a brusqueness, a savage contempt in his manner, that made Gudrun's blood flare up, and made Loerke keen and mortified. For Gerald came down like a sledge-hammer with his assertions, anything the little German said was merely contemptible rubbish.

At last Loerke turned to Gudrun, raising his hands in helpless irony, a shrug of ironical dismissal, something appealing and child-like:

"Sehen Sie, Gnädige Frau—" he began.

"Bitte sagen Sie nicht immer gnädige Frau,"* cried Gudrun, her eyes flashing, her cheeks burning. She looked like a vivid Medusa. Her voice was loud and clamorous, the other people in the room were startled.

"Please don't call me Mrs Crich," she cried aloud.

The name, in Loerke's mouth particularly, had been an intolerable chain and stigma upon her, these many days.

The two men looked at her in amazement. Gerald went white at the cheek-bones.

"What shall I say, then?" asked Loerke, with soft, mocking insinuation.

"Sagen Sie nur nicht das,"* she muttered, her cheeks flushed crimson.

She saw, by the dawning look on Loerke's face, that he had understood. She was *not* Mrs Crich! So-o-o, that explained a great deal.

"Soll ich Fräulein sagen?"* he asked, mischievously.

She looked at him with some aversion.

"I am not married," she said, with some hauteur.

Her heart was fluttering now, crying like a bewildered bird. She knew she had dealt a cruel wound, and she could not bear it.

Gerald sat erect, perfectly still, his face pale and calm, like the face of a statue. He was unaware of her, or of Loerke, or anybody. He sat perfectly still, in an unalterable calm. Loerke, meanwhile, was crouching and ill at ease.

Gudrun was tortured for something to say, to relieve the suspense. She twisted her face in a smile, and glanced knowingly at Loerke.

"It had to come out sooner or later," she said to him.

But all the while, she was under the domination of Gerald, now, because she had dealt him a wound, and she did not know how he had taken it. She watched him. He was interesting to her. She had lost her interest in Loerke.

Gerald rose at length, and went over, in a leisurely, beautiful movement, to the professor. The two began a conversation on Goethe.

She was rather piqued by the simplicity of Gerald's demeanour this evening. He did not seem angry or disgusted, only he looked curiously innocent and pure, really beautiful. Sometimes it came upon him, this look of clear innocence, and it always fascinated her.

She waited, troubled, throughout the evening. She thought he would avoid her, or give some sign. But he spoke to her simply and kindly, as he would to anyone else in the room. A certain peace, an abstraction possessed his soul.

She went to his room, hotly, violently in love with him. He was so beautiful and inaccessible. He kissed her, he was a lover to her. And she had extreme pleasure of him. But he did not come to, he remained remote and candid, unconscious. She wanted to speak to him. But this innocent beautiful state of unconsciousness that had come upon him prevented her. She felt tormented and dark.

In the morning, however, he looked at her with a little aversion, some horror and some hatred darkening into his eyes. She withdrew on to her old ground. But still he would not gather himself together, against her.

Loerke was waiting for her now. The little artist, isolated in his own complete envelope, felt that here at last was a woman from whom he could get something. He was uneasy all the while, waiting to talk with her, subtly contriving to be near her. Her presence filled him with keenness and inspiration, he gravitated cunningly towards her, as if she had some unseen force of attraction.

He was not in the least doubtful of himself, as regards Gerald. Gerald was one of the outsiders. Loerke only hated him for being rich and proud and of fine appearance. All these things, however, riches, pride of social standing, handsome physique, were externals. When it came to the relation with a woman such as Gudrun, he, Loerke, had a force and a power that Gerald never dreamed of.

How should Gerald hope to satisfy a woman of Gudrun's calibre? Did he think that pride or masterful will or physical strength would help him? Loerke knew a secret beyond these things. The greatest power is the one that is subtle and adjusts itself, not the one which blindly attacks. And he, Loerke, had understanding where Gerald was a calf. He, Loerke, could penetrate into depths far out of Gerald's knowledge, Gerald was left behind like a postulant in the ante-room of this temple of mysteries, this woman. But he, Loerke, could he not penetrate into the inner darkness, find the spirit of the woman in its inner recess, and wrestle with it there.

What was it, after all, that a woman wanted? Was it mere social effect, fulfilment of ambition in the social world, in the community of mankind? Who but a fool would accept this of Gudrun? This was but the street-view of her wants. Cross the threshold, and you found her completely, completely cynical about the social world and its advantages. Once inside the house of her soul, and there was a pungent atmosphere of corrosion, an inflamed darkness of sensation, and a vivid, subtle, serpent consciousness, not of the mind.

What then, what next? Was it sheer blind force of passion that would satisfy her now? Not this, but the subtle thrills of extreme sensation. It was an unbroken will reacting against her unbroken will in a myriad subtle thrills of reduction, the last subtle activities of reduction, carried out in the darkness of her, whilst the outside form, the individual ego, was utterly unchanged.

But between two people, any two people on earth, the range of pure sensational experience is limited. The climax of sensual ecstasy, once reached in any direction, is reached finally, there is no going on. There is only repetition possible, or the going apart of the two protagonists, or the subjugating of the one will to the other, or death.

Gerald had penetrated all the outer places of Gudrun's soul. He was to her the most crucial instance of the existing world, the ne plus ultra of the world of man as it existed for her. In him she knew the world, and had done with it. Knowing him finally she was Alexander seeking new worlds.—But there *were* no new worlds, there were only new isolated individuals now, tense, dark fragments like Loerke. The world was finished now, for her. There was only the inner, individual darkness of sensation within the ego, the obscene religious mystery, the outer world gone.

All this Gudrun knew in her subconsciousness, not in her mind. She knew her next step, she knew what she would move on to, when she left Gerald. She was afraid of Gerald, that he might kill her. But she did not intend to be killed. A fine thread still united her to him. It should not be *her* death which broke it. She had further to go, a further, slow, exquisite experience to reap, unthinkable subtleties of sensation to know, before she was finished.

Of the last series of ecstasy Gerald was not capable. He could not touch the quick of her. But where his ruder blows could not penetrate, the fine, insinuating blade of Loerke's will could. At least, it was time for her now to pass over to the other man, the master-craftsman. She knew that Loerke, in his innermost soul, was detached from everything, for him there was neither heaven nor earth nor hell. He admitted no allegiance, he gave no adherence anywhere. He was single and, by abstraction from the rest, absolute in himself.

Whereas in Gerald's soul there still lingered some attachment to the rest, to the whole. And this was his limitation. He was limited, borné,* subject to his necessity, in the last issue, for goodness, for righteousness, for oneness with the ultimate purpose. That the ultimate purpose might be the perfect and subtle experiencing of the process of death, that was not allowed in him. And this was his limitation.

There was a hovering triumph in Loerke, since Gudrun had denied her marriage with Gerald. The artist seemed to hover like a creature on the wing, waiting to settle. He did not approach Gudrun violently, he was never ill-timed. But, carried on by a sure instinct in the complete darkness of his soul, he corresponded mystically with her, imperceptibly, but palpably.

For two days, he talked to her, continued the discussions of art, of life, in which they both found such pleasure. They praised the by-gone things, they took a sentimental, fine delight in the achieved perfection of the past. Particularly they liked the late eighteenth century, the period of Goethe and of Shelley.

The delight in this past acquired its most poignant frisson because it implied a subtle, almost diabolic negation of the future. They never mentioned the future, except Gudrun laughed out some mocking dream of the destruction of the world by a ridiculous catastrophe of man's invention: a man invented such a perfect explosive that it blew the earth in bits among the stars, or that the world became so perfect that by unanimous consent it committed suicide, because it had come to pass that any step taken by any man was an infringement of the rights of some other man.

Apart from these stories, they never talked of the future. They delighted most either in mocking imaginations of destruction, or in sentimental, fine appreciations of the past. It was a sentimental delight to reconstruct the world of Goethe at Weimar, or of Schiller and poverty and faithful love, or to see again Hazlitt receiving Coleridge, or Shelley's first glance at Mary Godwin.

They talked together for hours, of literature and sculpture and painting, laughing about Flaxman and Blake and Fuseli, with tenderness, and about Feuerbach and Böcklin.* It would take them a life-time, they felt, to live again the lives of the great artists. But they loved best to stay in the eighteenth and the nineteenth centuries.

They talked in a mixture of languages. The groundwork was French, in either case. But he ended most of his sentences in a stumble of English and a conclusion of German, she skilfully wove herself to her end in whatever phrase came to her. She took a peculiar delight in this conversation. It was full of odd, whimsical expression, of double meanings, of evasions, of suggestive vagueness. It was a real physical pleasure to her to make this thread of conversation out of the different-coloured strands of three languages.

And all the while they two were hovering, hesitating round the flame of some declaration. He wanted it, but was held back by some invisible bond. She wanted it also, but she wanted to put it off, to put it off indefinitely. She still had some pity for Gerald, some connection with him. And the most fatal of all, she had the reminiscent sentimental compassion for him. Because of what *had* been, she felt herself held to him by immortal, invisible threads—because of what *had* been, because of his coming to her that first night, into her own house, in his extremity, because——.

Gerald was gradually overcome with a revulsion of loathing for Loerke. He did not take the man seriously, he despised him merely, except as he felt in Gudrun's veins the influence of the little creature. It was this that drove Gerald wild, the feeling in Gudrun's veins of Loerke's presence, Loerke's being, flowing dominant through her.

"What makes you so smitten with that little vermin?" he asked, really puzzled. For he, man-like, could not see anything attractive or important *at all* in Loerke. Gerald expected to find some handsomeness or nobleness, to account for a woman's subjection. But he saw none here, only an insect-like repulsiveness.

Gudrun flushed deeply. It was these attacks she would never forgive.

"What do you mean?" she replied. "I have to thank my stars I am not married to you, or I can see what it would be."

Her voice of flouting and contempt scotched him. He was brought up short. But he recovered himself.

"Tell me, only tell me," he reiterated, in a dangerous, narrowed voice—"tell me what it is that fascinates you in him."

"I am not fascinated," she said, with cold, repelling innocence.

"Yes you are. You are fascinated by that little dry worm, like a bird gaping ready to fall down its throat—"

She looked at him with black fury.

"I don't choose to be discussed by you," she said.

"It doesn't matter whether you choose or not," he replied, "that doesn't alter the fact that you are ready to fall down and kiss the feet of that little insect. And I don't want to prevent you—do it, fall down and kiss his feet. But I want to know, what it is that fascinates you—what is it?"

She was silent, suffused with black rage.

"How *dare* you come brow-beating me," she cried, "how dare you, you little squire, you bully. What right have you over me, do you think?"

His face was white and gleaming, she knew by the light in his eyes that she was in his power—the wolf. And because she was in his power, she hated him with a power that she wondered did not kill him. In her will she killed him as he stood, effaced him.

"It's not a question of right," said Gerald, sitting down on a chair. She watched the change in his body: she saw his clenched, mechanical body moving there like a machine. Her hatred of him was complete. "It's not a question of my right over you—though I *have* some right, remember. I want to know, I only want to know what it is that subjugates you to that little toad of a sculptor downstairs, what it is that brings you down like a pack of cards, in worship of him. I want to know what you worship."

She stood over against the window, listening. Then she turned round.

"Do you?" she said, in her most easy, most cutting voice. "Do you want to know what it is in him? It's because he has some understanding of a woman, because he is not stupid, that's why it is."

A queer, sinister, animal-like smile came over Gerald's face.

"But what understanding is it?" he said. "The understanding of a flea, a hopping flea. Why should you fall down all of a heap before the understanding of a flea?"

There passed through Gudrun's mind Blake's representation of the soul of a flea.* She wanted to fit it to Loerke. That was interesting. But it was necessary to answer Gerald.

"Don't you think the understanding of a flea is more interesting than the understanding of a fool—?" she asked.

"A fool?" he repeated—

"A fool, a conceited fool—a Dummkopf," she replied, adding the German word.

"Do you call me a fool?" he replied. "Well, wouldn't I rather be the fool I am, than that toad downstairs?"

She looked at him. A certain blunt, blind stupidity in him palled on her soul.

"You give yourself away by that last," she said.

He sat and wondered.

"I shall go away soon," he said.

She turned on him.

"Remember," she said, "I am completely independent of you— completely. You make your arrangements, I make mine."

He pondered this.

"You mean we are strangers from this minute?" he asked.

She halted and flushed. He was putting her in a trap, forcing her hand. She turned round on him.

"Strangers," she said, "we can never be. But if you *want* to make any movement apart from me, then I wish you to know you are perfectly free to do so. Do not consider me in the slightest."

Even so slight an implication that she needed him and was depending on him still was sufficient to rouse his passion. As he sat, a change came over his body, the hot, molten stream mounted involuntarily through his veins. He groaned inwardly, under its bondage, but he loved it. He looked at her with clear eyes, waiting for her.

She knew at once, and was shaken with cold revulsion. *How* could he look at her with those clear, warm, waiting eyes, waiting for her, even now? What had been said between them, was it not enough to put them worlds asunder, to freeze them forever apart? And yet he was all transfused and roused, waiting for her.

It confused her. Turning her head aside, she said:

"I shall always *tell* you, whenever I am going to make any change—"

And with this she moved out of the room.

He sat suspended in a fine recoil of disappointment, that seemed gradually to be destroying his understanding. But the unconscious state of patience persisted in him. He remained motionless, without thought or knowledge, for a long time. Then he rose, and went downstairs, to play at chess with one of the students. His face was open and clear, with a certain innocent laisser-aller that troubled Gudrun most, made her almost afraid of him, whilst she disliked him deeply for it.

It was after this that Loerke, who had never yet spoken to her personally, began to ask her of her state.

"You are not married at all, are you?" he asked.

She looked full at him.

"Not in the least," she replied, in her measured way.

Loerke laughed, wrinkling up his face oddly. There was a thin wisp of his hair straying on his forehead, she noticed that his skin was of a clear brown colour, his hands, his wrists. And his hands seemed closely prehensile.

"Good," he said.

Still it needed some courage for him to go on.

"Was Mrs Birkin your sister?" he asked.

"Yes."

"And was *she* married?"

"She was married."

"Have you parents, then?"

"Yes," said Gudrun, "we have parents."

And she told him, briefly, laconically, her position. He watched her closely, curiously all the while.

"So!" he exclaimed with some surprise. "And the Herr Crich, is he rich."

"Yes, he is rich, a coal-owner."

"How long has your friendship with him lasted?"

"Some months."

There was a pause.

"Yes, I am surprised," he said at length. "The English, I thought they were so cold.—And what do you think to do when you leave here?"

"What do I think to do?" she repeated.

"Yes. You cannot go back to the teaching. No—" he shrugged his shoulders—"that is impossible. Leave that to the canaille who can do nothing else. You, for your part—well, you are a remarkable woman,

419

eine seltsame Frau.* Why deny it—why make any question of it. You are an extraordinary woman, why should you follow the ordinary course, the ordinary life?"

Gudrun sat looking at her hands, flushed. She was pleased that he said, so simply, that she was a remarkable woman. He would not say that to flatter her—he was far too isolated and objective by nature. He said it as he would say, a piece of sculpture was remarkable, because he knew it was so.

And it gratified her to hear it from him. Other people had such a passion to make everything of one degree, of one pattern. In England it was chic to be perfectly ordinary. And it was a relief to her to be acknowledged extraordinary. Then she need not fret about the common standards.

"You see," she said, "I have no money whatsoever."

"Ach, money!" he cried, lifting his shoulders. "When one is grown up, money is lying about at one's service. It is only when one is young that it is rare. Take no thought for money—that always lies to hand."

"Does it?" she said, laughing.

"Always. Der Gerald* will give you a sum, if you ask him for it—"
She flushed deeply.

"I will ask anybody else," she said, with some difficulty—"but not him."

Loerke looked closely at her.

"Good," he said. "Then let it be somebody else. Only don't go back to that England, that school. No, that is stupid waste."

Again there was a pause. He was afraid to ask her outright to go with him, she was afraid to be asked.

"The only other place I know is Paris," she said, "and I can't stand that."

She looked with her wide, steady eyes full at Loerke. He lowered his head and averted his face.

"Paris, no!" he said. "Between the *religion d'amour*,* and the latest 'ism', and the new turning to Jesus, one had better ride on a carrousel all day. But come to Dresden. I have a studio there—I can give you work—Oh, that would be easy enough. I haven't seen any of your things, but I believe in you. Come to Dresden—that is a fine town to be in, a good life—some reality. You have everything there, without the frippery of Paris or the grossness of Munich."

He sat and looked at her, quizzically. What she liked about him was that he spoke to her simple and flat, as to himself. He was a fellow craftsman, a fellow being to her, first.

"No—Paris," he resumed, "it makes me sick. Pah—l'amour. I detest it. L'amour, l'amore, die Liebe—I detest it in every language. Women and love, there is no greater tedium," he cried.

She was slightly offended. And yet, this was her own basic feeling. Men, and love—there was no greater tedium.

"I think the same," she said.

"A bore," he repeated. "What does it matter, whether I wear this hat or another. So love! I needn't wear a hat at all, only for convenience. Neither need I love, except for convenience.—I tell you what, gnädige Frau—" and he leaned towards her—then he made a quick, odd gesture, as of striking something aside—"gnädiges Fräulein, never mind.—I tell you what, I would give everything, everything, all your love, for a little communion in intelligence—" his eyes flickered darkly, evilly at her.—"You understand?" he asked, with a faint smile. "It wouldn't matter if she was a hundred years old, a thousand—it would be all the same to me, so that she can understand." He shut his eyes with a little snap.

Again Gudrun was rather offended. Did he not think her pretty, then? Suddenly she laughed.

"I shall have to wait for age then," she said. "I am ugly enough, aren't I?"

He looked at her with an artist's sudden, critical, estimating eye.

"You are beautiful," he said, "and I am glad of it. But it isn't that—it isn't that," he cried, with emphasis that flattered her. "It is that you are sympathetic, it is force of understanding. For me, I am little, chétif,* insignificant in appearance. Good! Do not ask me to be strong and handsome, then. But it is the *me*—" he put his fingers to his mouth, oddly—"it is the *me* that is looking for a mistress, and my *me* is waiting for the *you* of the mistress, for the courtship and the unexpressed marriage. You understand—"

"Yes," she said. "I understand."

"As for the other, this amour—" he made a gesture, dashing his hand aside, as if to dash away something troublesome—"it is unimportant, unimportant. Does it matter, whether I drink white wine this evening, or whether I drink nothing? It *does not matter*, it does not matter.

So this love, this amour, this *baiser*. Yes or no, soit ou soit pas,* today, tomorrow, or never, it is all the same, it does not matter—no more than the white wine."

He ended with an odd dropping of the head in a desperate negation. Gudrun watched him steadily. She had gone pale.

Suddenly she stretched over and seized his hand in her own.

"That is true," she said, in rather a high, vehement voice, "that is true for me too. It is the understanding that matters."

He looked up at her almost frightened, furtive. Then he nodded, a little sullenly She let go his hand: he had made not the slightest response. And they sat in silence.

"Do you know," he said, suddenly looking at her with dark, lowering, prophetic eyes, "your fate and mine, they will run together, till—" and he broke off in a little grimace.

"Till when?" she asked, blenched, her lips going white. She was terribly susceptible to these evil prognostications. But he only shook his head.

"I don't know," he said, "I don't know."

Gerald did not come in from his ski-ing until night-fall, he missed the coffee and cake that she took at four o'clock. The snow was in perfect condition, he had travelled a long way, by himself, among the snow ridges, on his skis. He had climbed high, so high that he could see over the top of the pass, five miles distant, could see the Marienhütte, the hostel on the crest of the pass, half buried in snow, and over into the deep valley beyond, to the dark of the pine trees. One could go that way home—one could travel on skis down there, and come to the old imperial road, below the pass. He had been happy by himself, high up there alone, travelling swiftly on skis, taking far flights, and skimming past the dark rocks veined with brilliant snow.

But he felt something icy gathering at his heart. This strange mood of patience and innocence which had persisted in him for some days, was passing away, he would be left again a prey to the horrible passions and tortures.

So he came down reluctantly, snow-burned, snow-estranged, to the house in the hollow, between the knuckles of the mountain tops. He saw its lights shining yellow, and he held back, wishing he need not go in, to confront all those people, to hear the turmoil of voices and to feel the confusion of other presences.

The moment he saw Gudrun, something jolted in his soul. She was looking rather lofty and superb, smiling slowly and graciously to the Germans. A sudden desire leapt in his heart, to kill her. He thought, what a perfect voluptuous fulfilment it would be, to kill her. His mind was absent all the evening, estranged by the snow and his passion. But he kept the idea constant within him, what a perfect voluptuous consummation it would be to strangle her, to strangle every spark of life out of her, till she lay completely inert, soft, relaxed for ever, a soft heap lying between his hands. Then he would have had her finally and for ever, there would be such a perfect voluptuous finality.

Gudrun was unaware of what he was feeling, he seemed so quiet and amiable, as usual. His amiability even made her feel brutal towards him.

She went into his room where he was partially undressed. She did not notice the curious, glad gleam of pure hatred, with which he looked at her. She stood near the door, with her hand behind her.

"I have been thinking, Gerald," she said, with an insulting nonchalance, "that I shall not go back to England."

"Oh," he said. "Where will you go then?"

But she ignored his question. She had her own logical statement to make, and it must be made as she had thought it.

"I can't see the use of going back," she continued. "It is over between me and you—"

She paused for him to speak. But he said nothing. He was only talking to himself, saying 'Over, is it? I believe it is over. But it isn't finished. Remember, it isn't finished. We must put some sort of a finish on it. There must be a conclusion, there must be a conclusion.'

So he talked to himself, but aloud, he said nothing whatever.

"What has been has been," she continued. "There is nothing that I regret. I hope you regret nothing—"

She waited for him to speak.

"Oh, I regret nothing," he said, accommodatingly.

"Good then," she answered, "good then. Then we neither of us cherishes any regrets, which is as it should be."

She spoke with heavy sarcasm.

"Quite as it should be," he said aimlessly.

She paused, to gather up her thread again.

"Our attempt has been a failure," she said. "But we can try again."

A little flicker of rage ran through his blood. It was as if she were rousing him, goading him.

"Attempt at what?" he asked.

"At being lovers, I suppose," she said, a little baffled.

"Our attempt at being lovers has been a failure?" he repeated aloud.

To himself, he was saying: 'I ought to kill her here. There is only this left, for me to kill her.' A heavy, overcharged desire, to bring about her death, possessed him.

She was unaware.

"Hasn't it?" she asked. "Do you think it has been a success?"

Again the insult of the question ran through his blood like a current of fire.

"It had some of the elements of success, our relationship," he replied. "It—might have come off."

But he paused before concluding the last phrase. Even as he began the sentence, he did not believe in what he was going to say. He knew it never could have been a success.

"No," she replied. "You cannot love."

"And you?" he asked.

Her wide, dark-filled eyes were fixed on him, like two moons of darkness.

"I couldn't love you," she said.

A blinding flash went over his brain, his body jolted. His heart had burst into flame. His consciousness was gone into his wrists, into his hands. He was one blind, incontinent desire, to kill her. His wrists were bursting, there would be no satisfaction, till his hands had closed on her.

But even before his body swerved forward on her, a sudden, cunning comprehension was expressed on her face, and in a flash she was out of the door. She ran in one flash to her room and locked herself in. She was afraid, but confident. She knew her life trembled on the edge of an abyss. But she was curiously sure of her footing. She knew her cunning could outwit him.

She trembled, as she stood in her room, with excitement and exhilaration. She knew she could beat him. She could depend on her presence of mind, and on her wits. But it was a fight to the death, she knew it now.

"I will go away the day after tomorrow," she said.

She only did not want Gerald to think that she was afraid of him, that she was running away because she was afraid of him. She was not afraid of him, fundamentally. She knew it was her wisest plan to avoid his physical brutality. But even physically she was not afraid of him. She wanted to prove it to him. When she had proved it, that, whatever he was, she was not afraid of him; when she had proved that she could leave him forever. But meanwhile the fight between them, terrible as she knew it to be, was inconclusive. And she wanted to be confident in herself. However many terrors she might have, she would be unafraid, uncowed by him. He could never cow her, nor dominate her, nor have any right over her; this she would maintain until she had proved it. Once it was proved, she was free of him for ever.

But she had not proved it yet, neither to him nor to herself. And this was what still bound her to him. She was bound to him, she could not live beyond him. She sat up in bed, closely wrapped up, for many hours, thinking endlessly to herself. It was as if she would never have done weaving the great provision of her thoughts.

"It isn't as if he really loved me," she said to herself. "He doesn't. Every woman he comes across, he wants to make her in love with him. He doesn't even know that he is doing it. But there he is, before every woman he unfurls his male attractiveness, displays his great desirability, he tries to make every woman think how wonderful it would be to have him for a lover. His very ignoring of the women is part of the game: he is never *unconscious* of them. He should have been a cockerel, so he could strut before fifty females, all his subjects. But really, his Don Juan does *not* hold me enthralled. If he is Don Juan, then I am Dona Juanita, and I'll see if I'm not more than a match for him—with his bullying conceit. Really, the fathomless conceit of these men, it is disgusting.

"They are all alike. Look at Birkin. Built out of solid conceit they are, and nothing else. Really, it is time they were taken down.

"As for Loerke, there is a thousand times more in him than in a Gerald. Gerald is so wooden, somewhere. He would grind on at the old mills forever. And really, there is no corn between the mill-stones any more. They grind on and on, when there is nothing to grind—saying the same things, believing the same things, acting the same things—Oh my God, it would wear out the patience of a stone.

"I don't expect much of Loerke, but at any rate, he is a free individual. He is not grinding dutifully at the old mills. Oh God, when I think of Gerald, and his work—those offices at Beldover, and the mines—it makes my heart sick. What *have* I to do with it—the horrible old mills that grind on, without a grain of ideas between their rollers; only Gerald's, like little animated power-accumulators, like batteries, keeping them going. It is too horribly and unutterably wearying, one cannot contemplate it.

"At least, in Dresden, one will have one's back to it all. And there will be amusing things to do. It will be amusing to go to these eurythmic displays, and the German opera, the German theatre. It *will* be amusing to take part in German Bohemian life. And Loerke *is* an artist, he is a free individual. One will escape from so much—that is the chief thing—escape so much hideous boring repetition of dead actions, dead phrases, dead postures. I don't delude myself that I shall find an elixir of life in Dresden. I know I shan't. But I shall get away from people who have their own homes and their own children and their own acquaintances and their own this and their own that. I shall be among people who *don't* own things and who *haven't* got a home and a domestic servant in the back-ground, who *haven't* got a standing and a status and a degree and a circle of friends of the same. Oh God, the wheels within wheels of society—it makes one's head tick like a clock, with a very madness of dead mechanical monotony and meaninglessness. How I *hate* life, how I hate it. How I hate the Geralds that they can offer one nothing else.

"Shortlands!—Heavens! Think of living there, one week, then the next, and *then the third*— —

"No, I won't think of it—it is too much— —"

And she broke off, really terrified, really unable to bear any more. The thought of the mechanical succession of day following day, day following day, ad infinitum, was one of the things that made her heart palpitate with a real approach of madness. The terrible bondage of this tick-tack of time, this twitching of the hands of the clock, this eternal repetition of hours and days,—Oh God, it was too awful to contemplate. And there was no escape from it, no escape.

She almost wished Gerald were with her, to save her from the terror of her own thoughts. Oh, how she suffered, lying there alone, confronted by the terrible clock, with its eternal tick-tack. All life, all life resolved itself into this: tick-tack, tick-tack, tick-tack; then the striking of the hour; then the tick-tack, tick-tack, and the twitching of the clock-fingers.

Gerald could not save her from it. He, his body, his motion, his life—it was the same ticking, the same twitching across the dial, a horrible, mechanical twitching forward over the face of the hours. What were his kisses, his embraces. She could hear their tick-tack, tick-tack.

Ha—ha—she laughed to herself, so frightened that she was trying to laugh it off—ha—ha, how maddening it was, to be sure, to be sure!

Then, with a fleeting self-conscious motion, she wondered if she would be very much surprised, on rising in the morning, to realise that her hair *had* turned white. She had *felt* it turning white so often, under the intolerable burden of her thoughts and her sensations. Yet there it remained, brown as ever, and there she was herself, looking a picture of health.

Perhaps she was healthy. Perhaps it was only her unabateable health that left her so exposed to the truth. If she were sickly she would have illusions, imaginations. As it was, there was no escape. She must always see and know and never escape. She could never escape. There she was, placed before the clock-face of life. And if she turned round, as in a railway station, to look at the book-stall, still she could see, with her very spine she could see the clock, always the great white clock-face. In vain she fluttered the leaves of books, or made statuettes in clay. She knew she was not *really* reading, she was not *really* working. She was watching the fingers twitch across the eternal, mechanical, monotonous clock-face of time. She never really lived, she only watched. Indeed, she was like a little, twelve-hour clock, vis-à-vis with the enormous clock of eternity—there she was, like Dignity and Impudence,* or Impudence and Dignity.

The picture pleased her. Didn't her face really look like a clock dial—rather roundish, and often pale, and impassive. She would have got up to look, in the mirror, but the thought of the sight of her own face, that was like a twelve-hour clock-dial, filled her with such deep terror, that she hastened to think of something else.

Oh, why wasn't somebody kind to her? Why wasn't there somebody who would take her in their arms, and hold her to their breast, and give her rest, pure, deep, healing rest. Oh why wasn't there somebody to take her in their arms and fold her safe and perfect, for sleep. She wanted so much this perfect enfolded sleep. She lay always so unsheathed in sleep. She would lie always unsheathed in sleep, unrelieved, unsaved. Oh how could she bear it, this endless unrelief, this eternal unrelief.

Gerald! Could *he* fold her in his arms and sheathe her in sleep? Ha! He needed putting to sleep himself—poor Gerald. That was all he needed. What did he do, he made the burden for her greater, the burden of her sleep was the more intolerable, when he was there. He was an added weariness upon her unripening nights, her unfruitful slumbers. Perhaps he got some repose from her. Perhaps he did. Perhaps this was what he was always dogging her for, like a child that is famished crying for the breast. Perhaps this was the secret of his passion, his forever unquenched desire for her—that he needed her to put him to sleep, to give him repose.

What then! Was she his mother? Had she asked for a child, whom she must nurse through the nights, for her lover. She despised him, she despised him, she hardened her heart. An infant crying in the night, this Don Juan.

Yes, but how she hated the infant crying in the night. She would murder it gladly. She would stifle it and bury it, like Hetty Sorrell did. No doubt Hetty Sorrell's infant cried in the night—no doubt Arthur Donnithorne's infant* would. Ha—the Arthur Donnithornes, the Geralds of this world. So manly by day, yet all the while, such a crying of infants in the night. Let them turn into mechanisms, let them. Let them become instruments, pure machines, pure wills that work like clock-work, in perpetual repetition. Let them be this, let them be taken up entirely in their work, let them be perfect parts of a great machine, having a slumber of constant repetition. Let Gerald manage his firm. There he would be satisfied, as satisfied as a wheel-barrow that goes backwards and forwards along a plank all day—she had seen it.

The wheel-barrow—the one humble wheel—the unit of the firm. Then the cart, with two wheels; then the truck, with four; then the donkey-engine, with eight; then the winding-engine, with sixteen, and so on, till it came to the miner, with a thousand wheels, and then the electrician, with three thousand, and the underground manager, with twenty thousand, and the general manager, with a hundred thousand little wheels working away to complete his make-up, and then Gerald, with a million wheels and cogs and axles.

Poor Gerald, such a lot of little wheels to his make-up! He was more intricate than a chronometer-watch, But oh heavens, what weariness! What weariness, God above. A chronometer-watch—a beetle—her soul fainted with utter ennui, from the thought. So many wheels to count and consider and calculate! Enough, enough—there was an end to man's capacity for complications, even. Or perhaps there was no end.

Meanwhile Gerald sat in his room, reading. When Gudrun was gone, he was left stupefied with arrested desire. He sat on the side of the bed for an hour, stupefied, little strands of consciousness appearing and reappearing. But he did not move, for a long time he remained inert, his head dropped on his breast.

Then he looked up and realised that he was going to bed. He was cold. Soon he was lying down in the dark.

But what he could not bear, was the darkness. The solid darkness confronting him drove him mad. So he rose, and made a light. He remained seated for a while, staring in front. He did not think of Gudrun, he did not think of anything.

Then suddenly he went downstairs for a book. He had all his life been in terror of the nights that should come, when he could not sleep. He knew that this would be too much for him, to have to face nights of sleeplessness and of inert watching the hours.

So he sat for hours in bed, like a statue, reading. His mind, hard and acute, read on rapidly, his body understood nothing. In a state of rigid unconsciousness, he read on through the night, till morning, when, weary and disgusted in spirit, disgusted most of all with himself, he slept for two hours.

Then he got up, hard and full of energy. Gudrun scarcely spoke to him, except at coffee she said:

"I shall be leaving tomorrow."

"We will go together as far as Innsbruck, for appearances sake?" he asked.

"Perhaps," she said.

She said 'Perhaps' between the sips of her coffee. And the sound of her taking her breath in the word, was detestable to him. He rose quickly, to be away from her.

He went and made arrangements for the departure on the morrow. Then, taking some food, he set out for the day on the skis. Perhaps, he said to the Wirt, he would go up to the Marienhütte, perhaps to the village below.

To Gudrun, this day was full of a promise like spring. She felt an approaching release, a new fountain of life rising up in her. It gave her pleasure to dawdle through her packing, it gave her pleasure to dip into books, to try on her different garments, to look at herself in the glass. She felt a new lease of life was come upon her, and she was happy like a child, very attractive and beautiful to everybody, with her soft, luxuriant figure and her happiness. Yet underneath was death itself.

In the afternoon she had to go out with Loerke. Her tomorrow was perfectly vague before her. This was what gave her pleasure. She might be going to England with Gerald, she might be going to Dresden with Loerke, she might be going to Munich, to a girl-friend she had there. Anything might come to pass on the morrow. And today was the white, snowy, iridescent threshold of all possibility. All possibility—that was the charm to her, the lovely, iridescent, indefinite charm—pure illusion.

She did not want things to materialise out, to take any definite plan. She wanted, suddenly, at one moment of the journey tomorrow, to be wafted into an utterly new course, by some utterly unforeseen event, or motion. So that, although she wanted to go out with Loerke for the last time into the snow, she did not want to be serious or business-like.

And Loerke was not a serious figure. In his brown velvet cap, that made his head as round as a chestnut, with the brown-velvet flaps loose and wild over his ears, and a wisp of elf-like, thin black hair blowing above his full, elf-like dark eyes, the shiny, transparent brown skin crinkling up into odd grimaces on his small-featured face, he looked an odd little boy-man, a gnome. But in his figure, in the greeny loden suit, he looked chétif and puny, though still strangely vital.

He had taken a little toboggan, for the two of them, and they trudged between the blinding slopes of snow, that burned their now hardening faces, laughing in an endless sequence of quips and jests and polyglot fancies. The fancies were the reality to both of them, they were both so happy, tossing about the little coloured balls of verbal humour and whimsicality. Their natures seemed to sparkle in full interplay, they were enjoying a pure game. And they wanted to keep it on the level of a game, their relationship: *such* a fine game.

Loerke did not take the tobogganing very seriously. He put no fire and intensity into it, as Gerald did. Which pleased Gudrun. She was weary, oh so weary of Gerald's gripped intensity of physical motion. Loerke let the sledge go wildly and gaily, like a flying leaf, and when, at a bend, he pitched both her and him out into the snow, he only waited for them both to pick themselves up unhurt off the keen white ground, to be laughing and pert as a robin. She knew he would be making ironical, playful remarks as he wandered in hell—if he were in the humour. And that pleased her immensely. It seemed like a rising above the dreariness of actuality, the monotony of contingencies.

They played till the sun went down, in pure amusement, careless and timeless. Then, as the little sledge twirled riskily to rest at the bottom of the slope,

"Wait!" he said suddenly, and he produced from somewhere a large thermos flask, a packet of Kekse,* and a bottle of Schnapps.

"Oh Loerke," she cried, "what an inspiration! What a comble de joie* indeed! What is the Schnapps?"

He looked at it, and laughed.

"Heidelbeer!"* he said.

"No! From the bilberries under the snow. Doesn't it look as if it were distilled from snow. Can you—" she sniffed, and sniffed at the bottle— "Can you smell bilberries? Isn't it wonderful! It is exactly as if one could smell them through the snow."

She stamped her foot lightly on the ground. He kneeled down and whistled, and put his ear to the snow. As he did so his black eyes twinkled up at her merrily, mockingly.

"Ha! Ha!" she laughed, warmed by the whimsical way in which he mocked at her verbal extravagances. He was always teasing her, mocking her ways. But as he in his mockery was even more absurd than she in her extravaganzas, what could one do but laugh and feel liberated.

She could feel their voices, hers and his, ringing silvery like bells in the frozen, motionless air of the first twilight. How perfect it was, how *very* perfect it was, this silvery isolation and interplay.

She sipped the hot coffee, whose fragrance flew around them like bees murmuring around flowers, in the snowy air, she drank tiny sips of the Heidelbeerwasser, she ate the cold, sweet, creamy wafers. How good everything was! How perfect everything tasted and smelled and sounded, here in this utter stillness of snow and falling twilight.

"You are going away tomorrow?" his voice came at last.

"Yes."

There was a pause, when the evening seemed to rise in its silent, ringing pallor infinitely high, to the infinite which was near at hand.

"Wohin?"

That was the question—wohin? where to? wohin? What a lovely word! She *never* wanted it answered. Let it chime for ever.

"I don't know," she said, smiling at him.

He caught the smile from her.

"One never does," he said.

"One never does," she repeated.

There was a silence, wherein he ate biscuits rapidly, as a rabbit eats leaves.

"But," he laughed, "where will you take a ticket to?"

"Oh heaven!" she cried. "One must take a ticket!"

Here was a blow. She saw herself at the wicket, at the railway station. Then a relieving thought came to her. She breathed freely.

"But one needn't go," she said.

"Certainly not," he said.

"I mean one needn't go where one's ticket says."

That struck him. One might take a ticket, and never travel to the destination it indicated. One might break off, and leave the ticket unfulfilled. That had never occurred to him.

"Then take a ticket to London," he said. "One should never go there."

"Right," she answered.

He poured a little coffee into a tin can.

"You won't tell me where you will go?" he asked.

"Really and truly," she said, "I don't know. It depends which way the wind blows."

He looked at her quizzically, then he pursed up his lips, like Zephyrus,* blowing across the snow.

"It goes towards Germany," he said.

"I believe so," she laughed.

Suddenly, they were aware of a vague white figure near them. It was Gerald. Gudrun's heart leapt in sudden terror, profound terror. She rose to her feet.

"*They* told me where you were," came Gerald's voice, like a judgment in the whitish air of twilight.

"Maria!—you come like a ghost," exclaimed Loerke.

Gerald did not answer. His presence was unnatural and ghostly to them.

Loerke shook the flask—then he held it inverted over the snow. Only a few brown drops trickled out.

"'s ist aus."*

To Gerald, the smallish, odd figure of the German was distinct and objective, as if seen through field glasses. And he disliked the small figure exceedingly, he wanted it removed.

Then Loerke rattled the box which held the biscuits.

"Biscuits there are still," he said.

And reaching, from his seated posture in the sledge, he handed them to Gudrun. She fumbled, and took one. He would have held them to Gerald, but Gerald so definitely did not want to be offered a biscuit, that Loerke, rather vaguely, put the box aside. Then he took up the small bottle, and held it to the light.

"Also there is some Schnapps," he said to himself.

Then suddenly, he elevated the bottle gallantly in the air, a strange grotesque figure leaning towards Gudrun, and said:

"Gnädiges Fräulein," he said, "wohl—."*

There was a crack, the bottle was flying, Loerke had started back, the three stood quivering in violent emotion.

Loerke turned to Gerald, a devilish leer on his bright-skinned face.

"Well done!" he said, in a satirical, demoniac frenzy. "C'est le sport, sans doute."*

The next instant he was sitting ludicrously in the snow, Gerald's fist having rung against the side of his head. But Loerke pulled himself together, rose, quivering, looking full at Gerald, his body weak and furtive, but his eyes demoniacal with satire.

"Vive le héros, vive—"*

But he flinched, as, in a black flash Gerald's fist came upon him, crashed into the side of his head, and sent him blown aside like a broken straw.

But Gudrun had moved forward. She raised her clenched hand high, and brought it down, with a great downward stroke, over the face and on to the breast of Gerald.

A great astonishment burst upon him, as if the air had broken. Wide, wide his soul opened, in wonder, feeling the pain. Then it laughed, turning, with strong hands outstretched, at last to take the apple of his desire. At last he could finish his desire.

He took the throat of Gudrun between his hands, that were hard and indomitably powerful. And her throat was beautifully, so beautifully soft. Save that, within, he could feel the hard frame of her life. And this he crushed, this he could crush. What bliss! Oh what bliss, at last, what satisfaction, at last. The pure bliss of satisfaction filled his soul. He was watching the unconsciousness come into her swollen face, watching her eyes roll back. How ugly she was! What a fulfilment, what a satisfaction! How good this was, oh how good it was, what a god-given gratification, at last! He was unconscious of her fighting and struggling. That struggling was her reciprocal lustful passion in this embrace, the more violent it became, the greater the frenzy of delight, till the zenith was reached, the crisis, the struggle was overborne, her movement became softer, appeased.

Loerke roused himself on the snow, too dazed and hurt to get up. Only his eyes were conscious.

"That also," he said, in his thin, bitter voice: "*that's* the sport." He was acridly sarcastic.

A revulsion of contempt and disgust came over Gerald's soul. The disgust went to the very bottom of him, a nausea. Ah, what was he doing, to what depths was he letting himself go?—As if he cared about her enough to kill her, to have her life on his hands?

A weakness ran over his body, a terrible relaxing, a thaw, a decay of strength. Without knowing, he had let go his grip, and Gudrun had fallen to her knees. Must he see, must he know?

A fearful weakness possessed him, his joints were turned to water. He drifted, as on a wind, veered, and went drifting away.

"I didn't want really," was the last confession of disgust in his soul, as he drifted up the slope, weak, finished, only sheering off unconsciously from any further contact. "I've had enough—I want to go to sleep. I've had enough." He was sunk under a sense of nausea.

He was weak, but he did not want to rest, he wanted to go on and on, to the end. Never again to stay, till he came to the end, that was all the desire that remained to him. So he drifted on and on, unconscious and weak, not thinking of anything, so long as he could keep in action.

The twilight spread a weird, unearthly light overhead, bluish-rose in colour, the cold blue night sank on the snow In the valley below, behind, in the great bed of snow, were two small figures, Gudrun dropped on her knees, like one executed, and Loerke sitting propped up near her. That was all.

Gerald stumbled on up the slope of snow, in the bluish darkness, always climbing, always unconsciously climbing, weary though he was. On his left was a steep slope with black rocks and fallen masses of rock and veins of snow slashing in and about the blackness of rock, veins of snow slashing vaguely in and about the blackness of rock. Yet there was no sound, all this made no noise.

To add to his difficulty, a small bright moon shone brilliantly just ahead, on the right, a painful brilliant thing that was always there, unremitting, from which there was no escape. He wanted so to come to the end—he had had enough. Yet he could not sleep yet.

He surged painfully up, sometimes having to cross a slope of black rock, that was blown bare of snow. Here he was afraid of falling, very much afraid of falling. And high up here, on the crest, moved a wind that almost overpowered him with a sleep-heavy iciness. Only it was not here, the end, he must still go on. His nausea would not let him stay.

Having gained one ridge, he saw the vague shadow of something higher, in front. Always higher, always higher. He knew he was going the track towards the summit of the slopes, where was the Marienhütte, and the descent on the other side. But he was not really conscious. He only wanted to go on, to go on whilst he could, to move, to keep going, that was all, to keep going, until it was finished. He had lost all his sense of place. And yet, in the remaining instinct of life, his feet sought the track where the skis had gone.

He slithered down a sheer snow-slope. That frightened him. He had no alpenstock, nothing. But having come safely to rest, he began to walk on, in the illuminated darkness. It was as cold as sleep. He was between two ridges, in a hollow. So he swerved. Should he climb the other ridge, or wander along the hollow. How frail the thread of his being was stretched!

He would perhaps climb the ridge. The snow was firm and simple. He went along. There was something standing out of the snow. He approached, with dimmest curiosity.

It was a half buried crucifix, a little Christ under a little sloping hood, at the top of a pole. He sheered away. Somebody was going to murder him. He had a great dread of being murdered.

Yet why be afraid. It was bound to happen. To be murdered! He looked round in terror at the snow, the rocking, pale-shadowy slopes of the upper world. He was bound to be murdered, he could see it. This was the moment when the death was uplifted, and there was no escape.

Lord Jesus, was it then bound to be—Lord Jesus? He could feel the blow descending, he knew he was murdered. Vaguely wandering forward, his hands lifted as if to feel what would happen, he was waiting for the moment when he would stop, when it would cease. It was not over yet.

He had come to the hollow basin of snow, surrounded by sheer slopes and precipices, out of which rose a track that brought one to the top of the mount. But he wandered on unconsciously, till he slipped and fell down, and immediately went to sleep for ever.

13

WHEN THEY BROUGHT THE BODY HOME, the next morning, Gudrun was shut up in her room. From her window she saw men coming along with a burden, over the snow. She sat still and let the minutes go by.

There came a tap at her door. She opened. There stood a woman, saying softly, oh, far too reverently:

"They have found him, madame?"

"Il est mort!"*

"Yes—some hours ago."

Gudrun did not know what to say. What should she say? What should she feel? What should she do? What did they expect of her? She was coldly at a loss.

"Thank you," she said, and she shut the door of her room. The woman went away mortified. Not a word, not a tear—ha, Gudrun was cold, a cold woman.

Gudrun sat on in her room, her face pale and impassive. What was she to do? She could not weep and make a scene. She could not alter herself. She sat motionless, hiding from people. Her one motive was to avoid actual contact with events. She only wrote out a long telegram to Ursula and Birkin.

In the afternoon, however, she rose suddenly, to look for Loerke. She glanced with apprehension at the door of the room that had been Gerald's. Not for worlds would she enter there.

She found Loerke sitting alone in the lounge. She went straight up to him.

"It isn't true, is it?" she said.

He looked up at her. A small smile of misery twisted his face.

"No, one can't believe it," he said.

"We haven't killed him?" she asked. He hated her coming to him like this. He raised his shoulders wearily.

"No," he said. "It has happened."

She looked at him. He sat crushed and frustrated for the time being, quite as emotionless and barren as herself. My God, this was a barren tragedy, barren, barren.

She returned to her room to wait for Ursula and Birkin. She wanted to get away, only to get away. She could not think or feel until she had got away, till she was loosed from this position.

The day passed, the next day came. She heard the sledge, saw Ursula and Birkin alight. And she shrank from these also.

Ursula came straight up to her.

"Gudrun!" she cried, the tears running down her cheeks. And she took her sister in her arms. Gudrun hid her face on Ursula's shoulder, but still she could not escape the cold devil of irony that froze her soul.

"Ha—ha!" she thought, "this is the right behaviour."

But she could not weep, and the sight of her cold, pale, impassive face soon stopped the fountain of Ursula's tears. In a few moments, the sisters had nothing to say to each other.

"Was it very vile to be dragged back here again?" Gudrun asked at length.

Ursula looked up in some bewilderment.

"I never thought of it," she said.

"I felt a beast, fetching you," said Gudrun. "But I simply couldn't see people. That is too much for me."

"Yes," said Ursula, chilled.

Birkin tapped and entered. His face was grave and heavy, full of judgment. She knew he judged her. He gave her his hand, saying:

"This is final enough, at any rate." Gudrun glanced at him, afraid.

There was silence between the three of them, nothing to be said. At length Ursula asked, in a small voice:

"Have you seen him?"

He looked back at Ursula with a hard, cold look, and did not trouble to answer.

"Have you seen him?" she repeated.

"I have," he said coolly.

Then he looked at Gudrun.

"Have you done anything?" he said.

"Nothing," she replied, "nothing."

She shrank in cold disgust from making any statement.

"Loerke says that Gerald came to you when you were sitting on the

437

sledge at the bottom of the Rudelbahn, that you had words, and Gerald walked away.—What were the words about?—I had better know so that I can satisfy the authorities, if necessary."

Gudrun looked up at him, white, child-like, mute with trouble.

"There weren't even any words," she said. "He knocked Loerke down and stunned him, he half strangled me, then he went away."

To herself she was saying: "*Here's* an example of the eternal triangle!" And she turned ironically away, because she knew that the fight had been between Gerald and herself, and that the presence of the third party was a mere contingency—an inevitable contingency perhaps, but a contingency none the less. But let them have it as an example of the eternal triangle, the trinity of hate. It would be simpler for them.

Birkin went away, his manner cold and damning. But she knew he would do things for her, nevertheless, he would see her through. She smiled slightly to herself, with contempt. Let him do the work, since he was so extremely *good* at looking after other people.

Birkin went again to Gerald. He had loved him. And yet he felt chiefly disgust at the inert body lying there. It was so inert, so disgustingly dead, a carcase, like the carcase of an animal. It was a great pity that it should ever have been recovered. Why hadn't it melted with the snow.

It was the carcase of a dead male. Birkin remembered a stallion, which had been killed and which he had seen lying prostrate. That too had sickened him. Alive, it was bursting with power and splendour. But it was a sickening weight on the earth, dead.

"That human stallion!" He remembered Dostoevsky's word about Vronsky.* Well, why not a human stallion? Why not—until the carcase of the stallion lies dead, and then the ignominy! Oh God, what ignominy, Gerald's body lying there, a slack dead thing. The majesty of death? The complete ignominy of such death. A live dog is better than a dead lion?—Ah yes, in the kingdom of the lower animals! But was a dead dog any better than a dead lion? And Trelawney, living, was he better than a dead Shelley?* No, Shelley lay dead in beautiful immortality of being, Trelawney lived and died like the animals, mortal.

There needed something else, something that was neither of life or death. There needed some quality that was not subject either to life or death.

Birkin's grief was chiefly misery. He could not bear that the beautiful, virile Gerald was a heap of inert matter, a transient heap, rubbish on the face of the earth, really.

He went over the snow-slopes, climbing up, to see where the death had been. At last he came to the great shallow among the precipices and slopes, near the summit of the pass. It was all white snow, icy, silent, horrible with black rock in the distance, and a slope sheering down from a frozen peak.

It is well to die, for the soul to pass into this eternal whiteness. But the warm, handsome, virile body? Better be Gerald, than be the man who picks up the body. What a burden, what a burden for a man to carry all his life, this ignominious cold corpse of a dead male. Why cannot one utterly do away with it, utterly.

To climb up the wall of snow, out of this shallow pot, on to the very summit of the pass, the guides in the Marienhütte had driven iron stakes deep into the snow, and carried a rope along. So that by digging one's toes into the snow, one could haul oneself up the great, massive whiteness, to come out on the open, round crest of the top. But Gerald had not found the rope.

Man must achieve his immortality in life or, dead, he was no more than a heap of matter, transient, pitiful, abject, like a dead animal. A dead animal—a dead body! Poor Gerald. Yet he had tried. But had he? or had he only wriggled? He had refused to accept death, and know his own deathlessness, in life. He had kept death at bay, during his lifetime, instead of accepting, submitting, and rising again in living indestructibility. Poor Gerald! Birkin's heart was frozen as he went back. How can one judge—we are *not* masters of our fate—we die as we were born, uncreated or created.

He looked again at the dead, at the dead, comely features, that were mute and expressionless and material as the snow outside. And still Birkin's heart was frozen in his breast. This, then, was the end. He had loved Gerald, he loved him still. But the love was frozen in his breast, frozen by the death that possessed himself, as well as Gerald.

He went about the business of the day silent, and frozen, doing what need be done. And at night he sat utterly weary and overcome in his bedroom. Suddenly the grief broke out of his heart with a strange cry, he broke into tears, crying,

"I didn't want it to be like this—I wanted him to be happy—I wanted him to be happy."

He sat in the chair, his head dropped, his body shaken by bitter sobbing, and the tears, the burning tears of his life-time suddenly breaking down his face. Ursula looked at him aghast, at the broken, shaken body, and the sunken head, she heard aghast the heart-tearing sound of his sobbing. And, in fear, she slipped out of the room.

He cried till he became quiet. Then he wiped his face, and went back to Gerald.

"Never mind," he whispered to his dead friend. "Never mind, perhaps it had to be this way—But I had hoped—" the hot tears of anguish surged up from his heart again—"I had hoped we might all be happy together, Gerald."

Birkin cried in a paroxysm of pain, beside the dead body.

"And it's failed," he murmured, in a poignancy of pain, "you're dead."

Then gradually the wound in his breast seemed to get quiet again.

"Never mind, Gerald," he murmured, "never mind. Perhaps it had to be like this.—It needn't destroy that which *does* live—why should it?" The tears rose again. "I *did* want it to come right for us all, I did want you to be happy, I *didn't* want you to be alone, and die."—The tears ran freely down Birkin's face.—"But we couldn't help it—there was no helping it.—I wish it needn't have been—" The acute pain convulsed his features again. "But perhaps this was the only way—this nothingness—perhaps it was. Perhaps something *must* be a living nothingness—perhaps it must.—We won't feel bitter and frozen—perhaps your death is the same as your life—Only it seems so *empty*, so nothing—it all seems *nothing*—"

His heart tore with anguish. It was not the death he could not bear, but the nothingness of the life and death put together. It killed the quick of one's life.

"At any rate, you sleep," he said, through his tears and pain. "At any rate you sleep now: we needn't grieve for you any more. We will cover you over, and leave you—and you will be warm in death. We will love you—you won't be cold—."

Then again his face broke with tears.

"But it was horrible for you," he cried. "And then—nothing—nothing—never to struggle clear—never to struggle clear—Gerald—"

He could not bear it. His heart seemed to be torn in his chest.

"But even then," he strove to say, "we needn't all be like that. All is not lost, because many are lost.—I am not afraid or ashamed to die and be dead."

Note on the Text and Illustrations

The text in the present volume is that of the 1998 Cambridge University Press edition, edited by John Worthen and Lindeth Vasey, with minor corrections based on D.H. Lawrence's manuscripts. The author's spelling mistakes, punctuation, inconsistencies and his drawing on p. 30 have been preserved.

The photograph of the *First Women in Love* typescript is reproduced courtesy of the Harry Ransom Humanities Research Center, The University of Texas at Austin. The photographs of D.H. Lawrence, Lydia Lawrence, Jessie Chambers and Frieda Lawrence are reproduced with kind permission from John Worthen. The photograph of D.H. Lawrence's chapel is reproduced with kind permission from Keith Sagar.

Notes

p. 4, *Hebe*: Ancient Greek goddess of youth and cup-bearer to the gods.

p. 6, *Prune*: A now antiquated term of endearment.

p. 6, *reculer pour mieux sauter*: "Draw back in order to jump better" (French), a French adage which can be found in Michel de Montaigne's essay 'On Solitude'.

p. 8, *moleskins*: Protective durable work trousers made from moleskin.

p. 8, *uncreated*: In this context the word seems to mean "amorphous" or "indistinct".

p. 9, *What price*: This expression, originally stemming from betting terminology, could here be substituted by "how about".

p. 10, *predative*: This barbarism presumably means "predatory".

p. 11, *the Rossetti fashion*: I.e. as found in the pre-Raphaelite paintings of Dante Gabriel Rossetti (1828–82)

p. 12, *in town*: I.e. in London.

p. 12, *Kulturträger*: "Culture-bearer" (German).

p. 13, *established on the sand*: See Matthew 7:26–7.

p. 15, *Tibs*: A diminutive form of Theobald.

p. 23, *the building of Dreadnoughts*: Dreadnoughts were advanced steam-powered battleships produced by the Royal Navy, which entered service in 1906 and triggered a worldwide arms race.

p. 24, *Bill Sykeses*: Bill Sykes is a memorable villain in Charles Dickens's *Oliver Twist* (1832).

p. 26, *in your road*: In your way.

p. 27, *Fay ce que vouldras*: "Do what you will" (French). This was the motto of François Rabelais's fictitious utopian order of the Abbey of Thélème, as described at the end of *Gargantua* (1534).

p. 27, *His voice is the still small voice*: See 1 Kings 24:11.

p. 27, *Holy Ghost which is with you*: See John 16:7–15.

p. 27, *Wilde was right...succumb to*: A reference to Oscar Wilde's famous epigram, "I can resist everything except temptation", actually pronounced by his character Lord Darlington in his 1891 play *Lady Windermere's Fan*.

p. 28, *even in Euclid*: Euclid defined a point as having a position but no magnitude.

p. 29, *corporate*: Here used in its obsolete sense of "corporeal", "physical".

p. 29, *gynaecious... androgynous*: Birkin erroneously uses the adjective "androgynous", but is referring to the botanical distinction between the gynoecium and the androecium.

p. 35, *that Lady of Shallott business*: A reference to an 1833 poem by Lord Alfred Tennyson, 'The Lady of Shalott', which retells the Arthurian tale of the Lady of Shallott, who, due to a curse, is forced to look at the world through a mirror. However, when she glimpses Lancelot through her mirror, she turns around to look at him directly, which precipitates her demise.

p. 35, *in a mirror, like Shah Jehan*: Shah Jahan, as his name is more commonly spelt, (1592–1666) was the fifth emperor of the Mughal Empire – which spanned a large section of the Indian subcontinent – and was famous for building the Taj Mahal. The reference to the mirror is unclear, but could allude to Shah Jahan's perceived vanity.

p. 38, *dumbles*: Hollow with a stream running through it.

p. 39, *a Nibelung*: According to Norse mythology, a member of the underworld race of dwarfs who guarded a fabled treasure.

p. 42, *pour moi, elle n'existe pas*: "For me, she doesn't exist" (French).

p. 43, *the L.C.M.*: LCM in fact means "lowest common multiple".

p. 47, *to help my neighbour*: See Luke 10:25–37.

p. 47, *the pit-hills*: Slag heaps generated by collieries.

p. 50, *destroyed like Sodom*: Genesis 19:24–25.

p. 51, *Half asleep*: Birkin misquotes the first four lines of Robert Browning's 1852 poem 'Love Among the Ruins'.

p. 53, *Lady Snellgrove's*: Marshall and Snelgrove (misspelt by Lawrence) was a well-known London department store.

p. 54, *The wind still sits in that quarter*: A reminiscence of *Much Ado About Nothing*, Act II, Sc. 2, l. 108.

p. 55, *her loose, simple jumper:* "Jumper" in this context refers to a loose jacket.

p. 61, *to cat:* To vomit.

p. 74, *a Meredith hero who remembers Disraeli*: The Cambridge University Press edition points out that this may be a reference to George Meredith's 1892 novel *The Tragic Comedians* and its protagonist Alvan.

p. 75, *Silent upon a peak in Dariayn*: This is the final line of John Keats's famous 1817 sonnet 'On First Looking into Chapman's Homer'.

p. 76, *threw his eyes down the street*: As the Cambridge University Press edition points out, this sentence does not seem to stem from any known edition or translation *Fathers and Sons* (1862). It is suggested that Lawrence may have been remembering a translation of another Russian novel.

p. 79, *long warden pipes*: A type of long clay pipe.

p. 80, *Anche tu, Palestra, ballerai?—si, per piacere*: "You too, Palestra, will you dance? Yes, please" (Italian).

p. 80, *Vergine Delle Rocche*: A misspelling of *Le vergini delle rocce* (*The Virgins of the Rocks*), an 1895 novel by Italian poet, novelist, playwright and patriot Gabriele D'Annunzio (1863–1938).

p. 80, *Naomi and Ruth and Orpah*: As recounted in the Book of Ruth, Ruth and Orpah were the daughters-in-law of the widow Naomi.

p. 80, *the Russian Ballet of Pavlova and Nijinsky*: Anna Pavlova (1882–1931) and Vaslav Nijinsky (1890–1950) were famous Paris-based Russian ballet dancers at the beginning of the twentieth century.

p. 81, *cleaving*: See Ruth 1:15.

p. 81, *Malbrouk*: A reference to the traditional French song 'Malbrough s'en va-t-en guerre'.

p. 82, *Cosa vuoi dire*: "What do you mean" (Italian).

p. 84, *the harlot… of adultery to him*: See Revelation 17:1–6.

p. 85, *render unto… are Caesarina's*: See Matthew 22:21.

p. 86, *Integer vitae scelerisque purus*: "Of unblemished life and spotless reputation" (Latin). This is a quotation from Horace, *Odes* I, 22, l.1.

p. 86, *brought the water*: Because the house has no heated indoor plumbing.

p. 86, *put a penny over it*: A reference to the superstition that placing a penny over a spot would remove it.

p. 86, *fly away Peter*: A quotation from the children's nursery rhyme 'Two Little Dicky Birds'.

p. 91, *Herr Obermeister and Herr Untermeister*: "Mr Over-foreman and Mr Under-foreman" (German).

p. 95, *he realised again with terror that she was left-handed*: He subscribes to traditional superstitions about left-handedness.

p. 97, *Alexander Selkirk*: Alexander Selkirk (1676–1721) was famously stranded on an uninhabited island in the South Pacific, a tale which inspired Daniel Defoe's *Robinson Crusoe*.

p. 101, *have his own road*: Have his own way.

p. 102, *By strike*: A euphemism for "by Christ".

p. 106, *seated like a Buddhist*: Lawrence is presumably referring to some form of the lotus position.

p. 107, *using the Christian name in the fashionable manner*: Instead of using more formal, conventional forms of address.

p. 111, *Paul et Virginie*: A famous French 1787 novel by Jacques-Henri Bernardin de Saint-Pierre (1737–1814), notable for its vivid depiction of nature and innocence.

p. 111, *Watteau picnics*: Jean-Antoine Watteau (1684–1721) was a famous French painter specializing in festive bucolic scenes.

p. 111, *barren fig-trees*: See Matthew 21:19–20.

p. 112, *know its fruit. You don't gather grapes of thistles*: See Matthew 7:16

p. 112, *apples of Sodom... Dead Sea Fruit, gall-apples*: Apples of Sodom, also known as Dead Sea Fruit, are proverbial for being pleasant on the outside, but turning to ashes and dust once picked. A "gall-apple" is an abnormal swelling on an oak tree caused by insects or fungi.

p. 113, *love is the greatest, and charity is the greatest*: See 1 Corinthians 13:13.

p. 113, *By their works ye shall know them*: See Matthew 7:20.

p. 114, *impudent dirty Frenchman... the lot of Frenchmen*: This is probably a reference to eighteenth-century French Enlightenment sceptics. The individual referred to may be the freethinking Huguenot Pierre Bayle (1647–1706), as suggested in the Cambridge University Press edition.

p. 116, *same old rose... smell quite as sweet*: See Shakespeare, *Romeo and Juliet*, Act II, Sc. 2, l. 13.

p. 116, *a new heaven and a new earth*: See Isaiah 65:17, 2 Peter 3:13 and Revelation 21:1.

p. 122, *the story of Fabre... went to sleep*: A reference to an episode recounted in *Souvenirs entomologiques* (1879–1907), by the renowned French entomologist Jean Henri Fabre (1823–1915).

p. 125, *Bergamos*: This is a reference to a famous type of fabric actually produced in the Italian town of Bergamo.

p. 130, *lord of the beast and the fowl*: See Genesis 9:2.

p. 137, *Miciotto*: "Pussycat" (Italian).

p. 137, *belle sauvage*: "Beautiful savage woman" (French).

p. 137, *tell it to the horse marines*: An expression of disbelief.

p. 137, *Wille zur Macht*: "Will to power" (German), a reference to Nietzsche's central concept of *Der Wille zur Macht*.

p. 138, *volonté de pouvoir*: "Will to power" (French). See note above.

p. 138, *old Adam*: This seems to refer to unredeemed humanity bearing the burden of original sin. This phrase can be found in The Ministration of Public Baptism of Infants in the *Book of Common Prayer* and in Freudian psychoanalysis.

p. 139, *the vision... the people perisheth*: Lawrence adapts Proverbs 29:18: "Where there is no prophetic vision the people cast off restraint, but blessed is he who keeps the law."

p. 141, *pas seul*: A solo dance, as opposed to the pas de deux.

p. 142, *the Salon*: The annual major art exhibition of the Académie des Beaux-Arts in Paris, which in Lawrence's time would have been the most important one in the world.

p. 143, *Regarde... hiboux incroyables?*: "Look, look at the people there! Are they not unbelievable owls?" (French).

p. 144, *gabies*: Simpleton.

p. 147, *Un peu trop de monde*: "A few too many people" (French).

p. 148, *Rocked in the Cradle of the Deep*: An 1832 song by Emma Hart Willard (1787–1870) and Joseph P. Knight (1812–87).

p. 151, *clean-lit*: This is an obscure expression; it has been suggested that Lawrence has combined "clean-limbed" and "sun-lit".

p. 152, *Holder klingt der Vogelsang*: "The birdsong sounds lovelier" (German), the opening line of the song 'Minnelied' by Ludwig Hölty (1748–76), which was set to music by Franz Schubert (1797–1828) in 1816.

p. 152, *Dalcroze*: This is a reference to the Swiss music teacher and composer Émile Jacques-Dalcroze (1865–1950) and his Dalcroze or "eurhythmic" method, which involved the teaching of musical concepts through movements of the body, with a view to transforming musical activity into an organic mode of self-expression.

p. 153, *My love— —is a high-born lady*: This is the chorus to the 1896 song 'My Gal is a High Born Lady' by Barney Fagan (1850–1937).

p. 154, *It's a long long way to Tipperary*: 'It's a Long Way to Tipperary' was a 1912 song by Harry J. Williams (1874–1924) and Jack Judge (1878–1938), which gained huge success as a First World War marching song and remains famous to this day.

p. 156, *the sweet Cordelia*: A reference to King Lear's youngest daughter and her refusal to flatter her father.

p. 159, *the nereids*: The daughters of the sea god Nereus in Greek mythology.

p. 161, *the heavens above, and the waters under the earth*: See Exodus 20:4.

p. 174, *word-bag*: A variation, perhaps, on "windbag".

p. 177, *to leap like Sappho into the unknown*: According to myth, the classical poet Sappho committed suicide by throwing herself off the Leucadian cliffs out of love for the ferryman Phaon.

p. 184, *who loved his old wife because she believed in him*: According to some sources, Khadijah, Muhammad's first wife, was forty when she married the twenty-five-year-old, and was also one of the first to recognize him as the prophet of Islam.

p. 185, *the two halves*: This is probably an allusion to Aristophanes' theory, in Plato's *Symposium*, that all humans used to be spherical single-gendered beings, which were then divided into men and women by Zeus in order to diminish their power, and that consequently love and sexual appetite are in fact the instinct to reunite into this primeval state of wholeness.

p. 186, *The dead must bury their dead*: See Matthew 8:22.

p. 186, *the living must put off the body of the past*: See Ephesians 4:22 and Colossians 3:9.

p. 188, *it had been the Orinoco*: The Orinoco is a major South American river: Gerald somewhat feebly puns on the word "Amazon", as it refers to both a female warrior and a river.

p. 191, *Blutbrüderschaft*: "Blood-brotherhood" (German). The correct spelling is *Blutsbruderschaft*.

p. 193, *Excelsior*: "Higher" (Latin). 'Excelsior' is also the title of an 1841 poem by Henry Wadsworth Longfellow (1807–82).

p. 193, *Ye cannot serve God and Mammon*: See Matthew 6:24 and Luke 16:13.

p. 194, *quite the "go,"*: "The flavour of the month".

p. 195, *sleering*: Contemptuous, mocking.

p. 198, *one further than the commandment*: See Matthew 22:39.

p. 200, *club doctor*: A "club" was a private insurance scheme to which miners contributed a part of their wages, a "club doctor" being a doctor working under such a scheme.

p. 206, *What mattered... less perfectly*: This echoes the debate on the concept of "function" in Plato's *Republic*, 353a–c.

p. 207, *the rich man... his possessions*: See Matthew 19:23.

p. 207, *Ye shall neither labour nor eat bread*: Lawrence seems to adapt Leviticus 23:14: "And you shall eat neither bread nor grain parched or fresh until this same day..."

p. 208, *disquality*: Presumably this means inequality.

p. 208, *three ha'porth o' coppers*: Literally, "three halfpennies", used to deride the boy's insignificance.

p. 209, *he could not give away all he had*: See Matthew 19:21.

p. 209, *the sweated*: The exploited and underpaid.

p. 212, *the butty system*: The system of having a middleman between the mine owners and the workmen, who guaranteed a certain amount of extracted coal at a predetermined price.

p. 218, *Bonjour mademoiselle... Quest-ce qu'un chancelier?*: "Hello, miss"... "Winifred wants to do Bismarck's portrait so much—! Oh, but all morning it's... Bismarck, Bismarck, always Bismarck! It's a rabbit, isn't it, miss?"; "Yes, it's a big black-and-white rabbit. Have you not seen him?"... "No, miss, Winifred has never wanted to show it to me. Many times I've asked her, 'What is this Bismarck, Winifred?' But she wouldn't tell me. Her Bismarck, it was a mystery."; "Yes, it's a mystery, really a mystery!..."; "Bismarck... it's a mystery, Bismarck, he is a marvel,"... "Yes, he is a marvel,"... "Is he really a marvel?"... "Certainly!"... "However he isn't a king... he was only chancellor."; "What's a chancellor?" (French and German).

p. 219, *draw him*: Remove the insides (a pun on the dual meaning of the verb "to draw").

p. 226, *Cybele... Syria Dea*: Cybele, known as the Great Mother of the Gods, was the ancient Phrygian goddess of fertility. "Syria Dea" refers to Astarte, the great ancient Middle-Eastern goddess of war and sexual love.

p. 233, *Pisarro*: A (misspelt) reference either to the French Impressionist painter Camille Pissarro (1830–1903) or his son Lucien Pissarro (1863–1944), who was part of the so-called Camden Town Group of post-Impressionist painters.

p. 237, *Girl's Own*: *Girl's Own Paper* was a popular magazine for young women, which included stories, educational articles and fashion advice.

p. 239, *bargust*: Nottinghamshire dialect, usually referring to an ill-behaved or loud child.

p. 251, *to wrestle with your good angel*: This is an allusion to the popular Biblical motif of Jacob wrestling with an angel, although Genesis 32:24–30 never explicitly states that the mysterious man Jacob wrestles is in fact an angel.

p. 253, *Dresden ware... Copenhagen ware*: Meissen, near Dresden, and Copenhagen were both famous for producing superior painted porcelain figurines.

p. 254, *mauvaise honte*: "Bashfulness" (French), literally "bad shame".

p. 255, *poppy-show*: Dialect for puppet show, in this context meaning a general display or spectacle.

p. 260, *the great serpent of Laocoon*: According to Greek myth, Laocoon (more correctly spelt Laocoön), a priest and seer of Apollo, was crushed to death, along with his two sons, by two giant serpents, after incurring the wrath of Apollo.

p. 266, *Mein Bruder... zwei Köpf!*: "My brother he is in spirits – he has two heads" (German). This possibly refers to the practice of preserving human bodies with abnormalities in spirits, as a medical reference or fairground curiosity.

p. 267, *Mammon, the flesh, and the devil*: A reference to the following petition in the Litany contained in the *Book of Common Prayer*: "from all the deceits of the world, the flesh, and the devil, spare us, good Lord".

p. 267, *suckled in a creed outworn*: A quotation from line 10 of Wordsworth's 1807 poem 'The world is too much with us'.

p. 270, *si jeunesse savait*: From the saying *si jeunesse savait, si vieillesse pouvait*: "If youth only knew, if only old age could" (French).

p. 272, *fat*: "Conceited person" (French).

p. 273, *il Sandro… imparare tutto*: "Sandro writes to me that he has been greeted with the greatest enthusiasm, all the youngsters, both girls and boys, are passionate, passionate for Italy, and they absolutely want to learn everything" (Italian).

p. 273, *Vieni—vieni… È vero?*: "Come—come here"… "Come and say good morning to Auntie. You remember me, you remember me well—isn't it true, little one? Is it true that you remember me? Is it true?" (Italian).

p. 274, *Siccuro che… superbo, questo!*: "Of course he understands Italian… he won't have forgotten it, the mother tongue"… "Look, the nice boy, how proud he is, this one!" (Italian).

p. 274, *Ti imparano… Bel giovanotto*: "They are teaching you to do bad things, bad things"… "Nice lad" (Italian).

p. 275, *No. Non… molto a lui*: "No. It is not permitted to put one's little paw in the saucer. Daddy doesn't like it. Mr Wild Cat is most displeasing to him" (Italian).

p. 280, *return, like a dog to his vomit*: See Proverbs 26:11.

p. 283, *schimpf*: "Scold" (German), normally not used transitively.

p. 285, *Glory to thee… the light*: The first opening lines of a 1692 hymn by Thomas Ken (1637–1711).

p. 285, *a Thomasine*: A female doubting Thomas.

p. 289, *J'en ai soupé*: "I'm sick of it" (French).

p. 291, *an infant crying in the night*: Lawrence quotes LIV, l. 18 of Tennyson's long 1850 poem *In Memoriam A.H.H.*

p. 293, *ich habe es nicht gewollt*: "I didn't want it" (German).

p. 308, *en ménage*: "In a state of domesticity" (French).

p. 311, *back your life*: Of course.

p. 330, *a real Paradise Regained*: A reference to John Milton's *Paradise Regained* (1671).

p. 335, *like a grain of mustard seed*: See Matthew 13:31–2 and 17:20.

p. 336, *his resurrection and his life*: See John 11:25.

p. 338, *amant en titre*: "Official lover" (French).

p. 339, *covers of the "Fashions for All"*: A monthly magazine about dressmaking.

p. 341, *Glücksritter*: "Fortune-hunter" (German).

p. 341, *The little grey home in the west*: A popular 1911 song by D. Eardley-Wilmot and Hermann Löhr.

p. 342, *Il faut avoir le respect... des voisins*: "One must have respect for one's follies"... "one must have respect for daddy's follies"... "And mummy's"... "And the neighbours" (French).

p. 345, *type*: Unlike here, the colloquial French term *type* ("bloke") usually applies to a male.

p. 348, *Lord, what must I do to be saved*: See Acts 16:30.

p. 350, *Surely goodness... days of my life*: See Psalm 23:6.

p. 354, *ELSASS—LOTHRINGEN... BASEL*: Elsass-Lothringen and Basel are the German names for Alsace-Lorraine and Basle

p. 355, *A Basle—deuxième classe?—Voilà*: "To Basle—second class? —Here you are" (French).

p. 355, *Nous avons encore—?... Encore une demi-heure*: "We still have—?"... "Half an hour left" (French).

p. 358, *warmed everything up steaming*: This presumably means something along the lines of "livened up the festivities".

p. 359, *La vie, c'est une affaire d'âmes impériales*: "Life, it's a matter of majestic souls" (French).

p. 359, *Chanticler*: An old-fashioned word for a rooster, more correctly spelt "chanticleer".

p. 359, *caught a Sultan*: The phrase is more commonly known as "caught a Tartar", which means "to seek for someone who, when caught, proves difficult to handle".

p. 360, *übermenschlich*: "Superhuman" (German), a well-known Nietzschean concept.

p. 361, *Hesperides*: A reference to the Garden of the Hesperides in Greek mythology, an orchard of immortality-bestowing apples guarded by the daughters of Hesperus and the dragon Ladon.

p. 364, *overbolster*: A thick bed cover.

p. 366, *Kuchen*: "Cake" (German).

p. 367, *Kaffee mit Kranzkuchen*: "Coffee with ring cake" (German).

p. 367, *prachtvoll... wunderbar... wunderschön... unbeschreiblich*:

"Magnificent... wonderful... utterly beautiful... indescribable" (German).

p. 367, *Gasthaus*: "Guest house" (German).

p. 368, *Reunionsaal*: "Function room" (Austrian German).

p. 368, *Wirt*: "Landlord" (German).

p. 368, *Herr Professor, darf ich Sie vorstellen*: "Professor, may I introduce you" (German).

p. 368, *Nehmen die... unserer Unterhaltung?*: "Would the ladies and gentlemen like to partake in our entertainment?" (German).

p. 370, *Ja, das war... Wissen Sie*: "Yes, that was remarkable, that was excellent"... "Really excellent!"... "What a pity, what a pity"... "Yes, that really is a shame, that's a shame, Madam. You know" (German).

p. 370, *Annie Lowrie*: 'Annie Laurie' was a well-known nineteenth-century Scottish song based on a poem by William Douglas (1672–1748), adapted by Lady Alicia Scott (1810–1900).

p. 371, *Wie schön... aber wirklich!*: "How beautiful, how moving! Ah, Scottish songs, they have such spirit! But Madam has a *wonderful* voice; Madam really is an artist, no really!" (German).

p. 373, *glouring*: "Glowing" in local dialect.

p. 374, *Prosit—Prosit*: "Cheers—Cheers" (German).

p. 377, *Mene! Mene! upon the wall*: See Daniel 5:5–25 – a reference to the mysterious writing on a wall which prophesied the downfall of Belshazzar, the King of Babylon.

p. 377, *Ein schönes Frauenzimmer... Ja!*: "A beautiful lady"... "Yes!" (German).

p. 381, *Bismarck's letters*: The letters of Otto von Bismarck (1815–98) to his wife were compiled in various editions and widely read after his death.

p. 382, *Parnell and Katherine O'Shea*: The discovery of an affair with the married Katherine O'Shea (1845–1921) paved the way for the political downfall of the leader of the pro-independence Irish Party, Charles Stewart Parnell (1846–91).

p. 382, *the nationalisation of Ireland*: Irish independence from English administration, a topical issue at the time.

p. 383, *Ich hab'... aufsteh'n mag:* "I've spent the night on the grind / With two such beautiful lads / From evening till day / That I don't want to get up" (German), a quotation from 'Die lustige Müllerin', an old German folk song.

p. 384, *sprinted*: Leapt.

p. 385, *Rodelbahn*: "Toboggan run" (German).

p. 386, *splothering*: Clumsy.

p. 387, *griffes*: "Claws" (French).

p. 387, *Auswas?... Granit*: "Made out of what?"... "Granite" (German).

p. 387, *Alto rilievo*: "High relief" (Italian).

p. 387, *ecco!*: "That's it!" (Italian).

p. 388, *Travaillé—lavorato... avez fait?*: "Worked—worked?... And what work—what work? What work have you done?" (French and Italian).

p. 389, *Dunque*: "So" (Italian).

p. 390, *adesso—maintenant*: "Now—now" (Italian and French).

p. 390, *elvin*: This word is obscure: Lawrence probably means "elfin" here, or perhaps he is thinking of "elvan", a dialectical term for various types of dark-coloured rock.

p. 390, *Wie alt?*: "How old?" (German).

p. 390, *Und Ihr Herr Gemahl, wie alt ist er?*: "And your consort, how old is he?" (German).

p. 390, *little people*: Fairies.

p. 393, *Wissen Sie*: "Let me tell you" (German).

p. 393, *de haut en bas*: "Disdainfully" (French).

p. 394, *Wissen Sie, gnädige Frau*: "Let me tell you, Madam" (German).

p. 394, *Ja—so ist es, so ist es*: "Yes—it is so, it is so" (German).

p. 395, *rushing in... fear to tread*: A reference to the famous phrase (line 625) in Alexander Pope's 'An Essay on Criticism' (1711): "For fools rush in where angels fear to tread."

p. 395, *fools must be suffered, if not gladly*: See 2 Corinthians 11:19.

p. 395, *Nein, sie war... eine kleine Malschülerin*: "No, she wasn't a model. She was a little art-student" (German).

p. 395, *Lady Godiva*: According to legend, the eleventh-century noblewoman Lady Godiva rode naked on horseback through Coventry to persuade her husband to alleviate the taxes he had imposed on the townspeople.

p. 396, *Maud Allan*: The Canadian Maud Allan (1883–1956) was a famous interpretative dancer.

p. 396, *Ja, sie war hübsch*: "Yes, she was pretty" (German).

p. 402, *Blessed Isles*: According to classical myth, these were islands where the souls of a select few were transported after death.

p. 403, *don't look before and after*: A possible reference to Percy Bysshe Shelley's 'The Skylark', ll. 86–7 (1820).

p. 406, *counterfoil*: This usage is erroneous; Lawrence presumably means "counter", "oppose".

p. 411, *Mestrovic*: Ivan Meštrović (1883–1962) was a Croatian sculptor, famous for his religious works.

p. 411, *Bel*: Bel (or Ba'al), meaning "lord", can refer to various gods in Assyrian and Babylonian mythology.

p. 411, *peu de rapport*: "Very little connection" (French), i.e. "very little connection with art".

p. 411, *Mary Stuart... Eleonora Duse... lovers*: Mary Stuart, Queen of Scots (1542–87) famously married three times. Eleonora Duse (1858–1924) was a well-known glamorous Italian actress of the time.

p. 412, *Italy and Tripoli*: Italy had occupied the Lybian capital Tripoli in 1911 and remained in control of the city until 1943.

p. 412, *Sehen Sie... nicht immer gnädige Frau*: "You see, Madam" ... "Please don't keep saying Madam" (German).

p. 412, *Sagen Sie nur nicht das*: "Of all things, don't say that" (German).

p. 412, *Soll ich Fräulein sagen?*: "Shall I say Miss?" (German).

p. 415, *borné*: "Limited" (French).

p. 416, *Flaxman... Böcklin*: Lawrence is referring to the draughtsman and sculptor John Flaxman (1755–1826), the artist and poet William Blake (1757–1827), the painter Henry Fuseli (1741–1825), the German painter Anselm Feuerbach (1828–80) and the Swiss painter Arnold Böcklin (1827–1901).

p. 418, *Blake's representation of the soul of a flea*: A reference to William Blake's painting *The Ghost of a Flea* (*c*.1819–20).

p. 420, *eine seltsame Frau*: "A peculiar woman" (German). Perhaps Lawrence had meant to convey the more positive sense of "extraordinary".

p. 420, *Der Gerald*: "The Gerald" (German, colloquial).

p. 420, *religion d'amour*: "Religion of love" (French).

p. 421, *chétif*: "Puny" (French).

p. 422, *baiser... soit ou soit pas*: "Kiss... whether it is or whether it isn't" (French).

p. 427, *Dignity and Impudence*: A reference to a famous 1839 painting, depicting two dogs, by Sir Edwin Landseer (1803–73).

p. 428, *Hetty Sorrell... Arthur Donnithorne's infant*: In George Eliot's

1859 novel *Adam Bede*, Captain Arthur Donnithorne walks out on Hetty Sorrell, his beautiful lover, who proceeds to abandon their illegitimate child to die in a field.

p. 431, *Kekse*: "Biscuits" (German).

p. 431, *comble de joie*: "Absolute bliss" (French).

p. 431, *Heidelbeer*: "Bilberry" (German). "Heidelbeerwasser" on the next page refers to schnapps made from bilberries.

p. 432, *Zephyrus:* In Ancient Greek mythology, the god of the west wind.

p. 432, *'s ist aus*: "It's over" (German).

p. 433, *wohl*: The German term *wohl* is difficult to translate in this context without the rest of the sentence. It could mean "well" or "maybe".

p. 433, *C'est le sport, sans doute*: "That's sport, no doubt" (French), i.e. "I suppose you think that's fun".

p. 433, *Vive le héros, vive*: "Long live the hero, long live" (French).

p. 436, *Il est mort!*: "He is dead!" (French).

p. 438, *That human stallion... Dostoevsky's word about Vronsky*: Count Alexei Kirillovich Vronsky is a character in Tolstoy's *Anna Karenina* (1875–77), who falls in love with the married eponymous heroine, but Dostoevsky's description of him as a "human stallion" about him is undentified.

p. 438, *Trelawney, living... a dead Shelley?*: Edward John Trelawny (1792–1881) was the friend and biographer of Percy Bysshe Shelley (1792–1822).

Extra Material

on

D.H. Lawrence's

The First Women in Love

D.H. Lawrence's Life

David Herbert Lawrence was born on 11th September 1885 in *Birth and Early Life*
Eastwood, a small colliery town just outside Nottingham. He
was the fourth of five children – three brothers and two sisters. His father, and most of his other relatives, were involved
in some capacity with work at one of the collieries, including
labour at the coalface.

His mother Lydia had once had ambitions to be a teacher,
but the poverty of her parents had thwarted her earlier aspi-
rations. However, she still took an interest in reading and in
intellectual matters. She tried to contribute to the Lawrence
family income by running a small clothes shop from the
ground floor of the family house – a financial venture which
was never very successful. Lydia tried to encourage all of her
children to save money and study, but Arthur, her husband,
would go out drinking most evenings, leading to arguments
and tension.

The boys in the local school were almost all destined to finish up down the mine, while the girls also would work in the
colliery canteens and laundries. However, from an early age
the Lawrence children seemed to aim for higher things, and
took their school studies extremely seriously. Furthermore,
they regularly attended the local Nonconformist Christian
chapel, and all took the pledge early in their lives not to touch
alcohol.

A major dramatic occurrence in D.H. Lawrence's early life *Bereavement and Illness*
was the death in 1901 of his elder brother Ernest from ery-
sipelas. After this traumatic experience, Lawrence developed
severe pneumonia and nearly died. This may have been a con-
tributing factor to the tuberculosis and general ill health which
dogged his later years, and which finally caused his death.

Teaching Career   Lawrence was at the time reading omnivorously in the local municipal library and at school. In 1902 he became a pupil teacher at a senior school in Eastwood – a common arrangement at the time. Some of the more promising older pupils were given lessons by the headmaster early in the mornings, and then they proceeded to teach the other pupils, usually for nothing or a nominal sum, since the personal tuition they received was meant to constitute their reward. Lawrence's token recompense was £12 per year. He took the opportunity of spending some time each week at what would now be called "teachers' centres" in Nottingham and at Ilkeston in Derbyshire, which ran training courses for other people in his situation living in the area; this led to a huge expansion of his social and intellectual horizons.

After two years as a pupil teacher, Lawrence successfully sat the King's Scholarship Examination in 1904, which gave him entry to a teacher-training college, or even, if he so wished, the opportunity to study for a degree at a university – almost unheard of at the time for anybody from a lower-class background. Interviews with this "working-class boy made good" were subsequently published in the local press and in the national teachers' magazines *The Schoolmaster* and *The Teacher*.

Although success in the examination conferred access to higher education, it gave little financial assistance, and so Lawrence and his family now had to decide whether he should do the degree full-time, supported by his family, or part-time, working to finance himself, as there were no student grants at the time.

It was finally decided he should spend a further year as a pupil teacher at a salary of £50 per year before going to university to do his teacher training. He entered the teacher-training department of Nottingham University in September 1906, but between the scholarship examination and entry to higher education he had started to write. He experimented with poetry, and in 1906 began writing *Laetitia*, the earliest version of his first published novel, *The White Peacock*.

Jessie Chambers   Lawrence was by now spending a considerable amount of time in the company of a young woman he had met some five years earlier, Jessie Chambers. They read together and discussed literature, philosophy and other intellectual subjects. His sisters and mother were worried that this blossoming relationship would be a distraction to "Bert"; they wanted him and Jessie either to get engaged, or meet less frequently. Lawrence took all this to heart, and told Jessie they must cut down the number of their meetings drastically for the time being. She was deeply hurt, and this was the first of numerous occasions on which he treated Jessie, and other women, with seeming insensitivity and selfishness.

At teacher-training college, Lawrence met socialists and *Early Writing* freethinkers, and his whole universe expanded. He spent a great deal of time writing and revising his novel. He found the course boring, but ploughed ahead with it and finally gained his teaching certificate in 1908. He also wrote more poetry and experimented with short-story writing. He submitted three stories to a competition in the biggest Nottingham newspaper, and one of these – 'The Prelude' – submitted for him by Jessie Chambers under her own name – won the prize for best story in its category and was printed in the paper. Lawrence also apparently sent some work – possibly one or more essays or sketches – to G.K. Chesterton, then literary editor at the *Daily News* in London, but these were returned with such negative comments that he nearly decided to give up writing altogether.

Lawrence was still living at home but, under the influence of the new ideas he was encountering at college, he began to react against his narrow upbringing, particularly the world of the Nonconformist chapel his parents attended, and religion in general. Unlike his fellow graduates, Lawrence was prepared to bide his time waiting for a good job to turn up – which might, besides providing him with a reasonable salary, enable him to escape from home. In the meantime he did jobs including farm work and clerking until he obtained a position as a teacher at a boys' school in Croydon, a working-class area of South London, just after his twenty-third birthday.

He started work in London in October 1908 and moved *London* into rooms in a family-run private house nearby. This was the first time he had lived away from home for any extended period, and working at the school proved extremely demanding, as he found it difficult to enforce discipline. However, in his leisure time he went up to central London to attend concerts and plays, and visited art galleries and bookshops. He continued his reading and writing, including further revisions to *Laetitia*.

459

Literary Breakthrough

Lawrence's breakthrough into the literary world came with some of his poems, which he sent initially to Jessie Chambers – still in Nottingham – for comment. Without his knowledge, she submitted them in September 1909 to Ford Madox Hueffer (later known as Ford Madox Ford), the illustrious critic and editor of the recently established radical journal *The English Review*. Hueffer decided to print a few of them and encouraged Lawrence to send him any further work of his, whatever the genre. Hueffer knew all the major London literati, and invited Lawrence to artistic gatherings, where he met, among others, Wells, Yeats and Pound.

Because his journal pursued a radical line, Hueffer was especially interested in promoting Lawrence as an "author from the collieries", and suggested that Lawrence should write about the life of the people he was familiar with. Accordingly, Lawrence's first two plays, written around this period (*A Collier's Friday Night* and *The Widowing of Mrs Holroyd*), were concerned with the life of mining families and partly written in the Nottinghamshire dialect. In December 1910 he sent the manuscript of *Laetitia* to the London publisher Heinemann, accompanied by a letter of recommendation from Hueffer. Heinemann asked for some cuts and alterations – which Lawrence made, including renaming it *The White Peacock* – and accepted it for publication.

Love Life

Despite his efforts, Lawrence had failed to forge a physical relationship with any of his various female acquaintances. Around this time, he suggested to his long-time intellectual companion, Jessie Chambers – still living in Nottinghamshire – that they should become lovers. Jessie agreed, but Lawrence did not wish to be tied down by one woman, and the affair was extremely unhappy and bitter. In August 1911 the sexual side of the relationship ended, and two months later Lawrence's mother became seriously unwell, possibly with the first signs of the cancer that would ultimately kill her.

All the following year his mother was in increasingly severe pain, and he was now without Jessie. In this sense of isolation and sadness he embarked on the composition of a new novel, largely drawn from his own experiences at the time. He was at this period re-establishing contact with a friend from his adolescence, Louie Burrows, then living in Leicester. She was apparently not as intellectual as Jessie Chambers, but very loving and fond of Lawrence. Possibly on the rebound from Jessie Chambers, Lawrence proposed marriage to Louie.

Just at this time *The White Peacock* appeared in print, and Lawrence personally put the first copy of it into his mother's hands – possibly to signify that he was now moving on to a different path from that which she had planned for him, and that he was slipping free of her influence. His mother would die later that year, on 9th December.

Lawrence's second novel, entitled at this point *The Saga of Siegmund*, was rejected by Heinemann; they suggested numerous revisions and a change of title. Accordingly, Lawrence reworked the novel, which would appear as *The Trespasser* in 1912. At the same time as composing the later stages of *The Saga of Siegmund*, he had started on a third novel, which he planned to entitle *Paul Morel*. By now he had begun to realize his engagement to Louie had been a mistake – since she could not provide the lifelong intellectual companionship he desired – and agonized over ending their relationship. He became very depressed, and in November 1911 developed a severe, near-fatal case of pneumonia – possibly an early symptom of the lung problems which would plague Lawrence throughout his entire life. He spent a month convalescing at a hotel in Bournemouth, making the final revisions to his second novel and progressing with *Paul Morel*. He gave up teaching on the advice of his doctors and returned to Eastwood in February 1912. There he completely rewrote *Paul Morel* – Jessie Chambers reading all his drafts and making suggestions – while living in his childhood home with his father and two sisters.

It was at this time that one of the major events of Lawrence's *Frieda* life occurred: he met the woman with whom he was to spend most of his life – Frieda Weekley. Née von Richthofen, she was the daughter of minor German aristocrats from the Metz region. She was the wife of the Professor of Modern Languages at Nottingham University, Ernest Weekley, whom she had met and married at the age of nineteen. The couple lived in a respectable suburb of Nottingham with their three children. Lawrence first met her when in March 1912 he came to their house to enquire about the possibility of finding teaching work in Germany. He immediately fell passionately in love with her, even though she was eight years his senior. Since she reciprocated his feelings, he convinced her that she

461

was wasting her best years in her current, comfortable way of life and persuaded her to start a relationship with him.

Travels and Writing   In May 1912 *The Trespasser* was published, to reasonably favourable reviews, and on the 12th of the same month Frieda left her husband and travelled with Lawrence to Metz. Ernest Weekley immediately asked for a divorce, stipulating that she should never see the children again. While in Germany staying with her relations, Lawrence made his final revision of *Paul Morel* and sent it off to Heinemann. The publisher rejected it as being poorly written and too sexually explicit. However, Edward Garnett, the reader for Duckworth publishers, assured Lawrence that if, under his guidance, he made a large number of alterations, he would recommend the novel for publication. Lawrence and Frieda undertook a walking tour of Germany, Austria and finally Italy, where they intended to stay for some months as it was much cheaper than Germany and they were short of money.

In Italy, in rooms near Gargnano, on the Lake Garda, Lawrence made the requisite alterations to *Paul Morel*, renaming it *Sons and Lovers* in the process. He sent the novel off to Duckworth and, after further negotiations, the novel was accepted for publication. Lawrence now worked intensively on poems, plays and ideas for possible future novels, finally settling down to a project he provisionally entitled *The Sisters*, which would ultimately, over the next seven years, become *The Rainbow* and *Women in Love*. In June 1913, the couple finally returned to England, since Frieda desperately wanted to see her children again before consenting to a divorce which would forbid her access to them. *Sons and Lovers* had by this time been published to mixed but generally favourable reviews.

Frieda did not succeed in seeing her children, and was threatened with legal action if she attempted to do so again. The couple returned to Italy, this time to Lerici, near La Spezia. There Lawrence produced the first section of a completely revised version of *The Sisters* – which detailed the sexual relationships and emotional development of two sisters, Ella (later Ursula) and Gudrun Brangwen. Having sent this draft to Garnett – who lambasted it as very badly written – Lawrence set about a further revision. However, following the success of *Sons and Lovers*, other publishers were now making overtures to Lawrence, some offering him lucrative contracts for the novel – which by this time had been renamed

The Wedding Ring. Garnett once again criticized the new version heavily, and in March Lawrence returned to London to negotiate a possible deal with another publisher: Methuen outbid Duckworth and were promised the novel. Finally, in April 1914, Frieda gained her divorce, and Lawrence married her in July of that year. Things seemed to be looking up on all fronts for Lawrence.

Then war broke out and the couple faced enormous problems in returning abroad. The war also hindered the possibility of getting further novels published, since there was a paper shortage, and the entire economy was now geared towards providing for the military effort. Furthermore, Frieda was regarded with suspicion because of her German origin. Lawrence – profoundly disillusioned with the war – felt that the conflict was barbaric and that the entire British national and racial consciousness had been polluted. *War and Rejection*

Suddenly Methuen returned the manuscript of *The Wedding Ring*, claiming the subject matter was too risqué, and that publishers' lists were being cut back drastically because of the war. Lawrence and Frieda were once again without money, so they moved to a small cottage in Chesham, Buckinghamshire. He rewrote *The Wedding Ring* between November 1914 and March 1915, splitting the novel into *The Rainbow* and what was ultimately to become *Women in Love*. However, *The Rainbow* became even more sexually explicit than the previously rejected drafts.

During these years, Lawrence had begun to enter new literary circles. Among others he had become acquainted with Lady Ottoline Morrell, the aristocratic society and artistic hostess. At her receptions he met famous intellectuals, such as E.M. Forster and Bertrand Russell. Lawrence's letters from 1914 and 1915 – principally to Russell – show the evolution of his ideas on the best way to live one's life and to develop one's real inner self. At first, Russell was highly impressed by Lawrence, but then became deeply disturbed by what he saw as the authoritarian character of his personality and beliefs, which he later characterized as "leading straight to Auschwitz".

The Rainbow was published in September 1915 and received vicious reviews. Bookstalls and libraries refused to stock it, because of what was perceived to be the pornographic nature of its material. Finally, in November 1915, the police seized *The Rainbow Controversy* all unsold copies and the book was prosecuted in the law courts for obscenity, the magistrates ordering all copies to be destroyed. Although some of Lawrence's artistic entourage protested against this censorship, it was generally the idea of censorship itself they were criticizing: most in fact detested the book as an aesthetic creation.

Move to Cornwall Lawrence now seriously thought of emigrating permanently to America with Frieda to set up an artists-and-writers' commune in Florida, encouraging their various acquaintances to come and join them. However, Lawrence could only acquire a passport if he declared himself ready to be summoned for military service at any time, which he could not bring himself to do. If they could not leave Britain, they decided to move as far from the centre of war activities in London as they could. Accordingly they hired a cottage in Cornwall, where they lived by growing their own vegetables, settling there in December 1915. In this cottage, Lawrence produced books of poetry and reminiscences of his time in Italy, as well as reviews and other pieces of writing that procured them a very meagre income. Although Lawrence was often ill with colds and pulmonary complaints – perhaps because of the winds from the sea and the moors – both he and Frieda enjoyed the open countryside and often entertained guests from London in their cottage.

Lawrence now began to recast the material left over from *The Wedding Ring*, using that work's original title, *The Sisters*, for the first draft of this reworking. After several revisions the manuscript went through the usual round of publishers, who all rejected it – one even asked if it was really finished. In addition to their reservations about the content, they were probably frightened off by Lawrence's reputation and the police prosecution of *The Rainbow*. Lady Ottoline Morrell had caught a glimpse of the manuscript, thought herself slandered in the person of the novel's society hostess Hermione, and consequently severed all ties with Lawrence.

Because of his weak lungs, Lawrence was rejected for conscription on medical grounds in June 1916, and the locals in Cornwall became suspicious and irritated at this non-combatant writer living with a German wife, and spread rumours that they were spies. They would sometimes be stopped by the coastguard while out on their walks, and return to their cottage to find it had been broken into and searched.

In September 1917 they were finally served with a legal order excluding them from Cornwall altogether, so they moved back to London, staying in a series of cheap lodgings. In London Lawrence attempted to settle down to writing his next novel, *Aaron's Rod*, but progress was slow due to their precarious living conditions and the fact that he was at the same time trying to eke out a living by writing poetry, reviews and essays. In May 1918, they moved back to the Midlands – to a cottage in Middleton-by-Wirksworth in Derbyshire – because it was so much cheaper to live there than in the south. Although he was now closer to his family, Lawrence felt himself to be "lost and exiled", sinking into severe depression and growing extremely pessimistic as to his future prospects.

Return to London and Derbyshire

In September 1918 Lawrence was compulsorily examined for military service: by this time the British Army was so desperate for manpower for the war effort that it was willing to conscript almost anybody. He was enlisted for "light non-military duties", a decision which drove him into a fury: "I've done with society and humanity. Labour and military can alike go to hell. Henceforth it is for myself, my own life, I live." He was never actually called up, since war ended in November 1918. In February 1919 he went down with a serious bout of influenza, and nearly died – the disease was then killing millions of people worldwide.

The armistice meant that Lawrence and Frieda could finally obtain passports, and they decided to abandon England for good. In December 1919 they moved to Capri, and then to Taormina in Sicily. Lawrence now concentrated on his work, *Psychoanalysis and the Unconscious*, followed by his next two novels, *The Lost Girl* and *Mr Noon*. *The Lost Girl* was published in Britain in November 1920 but, because of his reputation, many bookshops again refused to stock it. His publisher demanded both major revisions to this novel and further alterations to *Women in Love*, since the composer Philip Heseltine (better known by his pen name of Peter Warlock) had perceived himself as portrayed and libelled in the novel's character of Julian Halliday.

Leaving England

As a result of all this, the Lawrences grew utterly fed up with Europe, and decided to renew their attempt at moving to the US, as Lawrence had been invited at this time to set up residence in Taos, a colony of writers and artists in New Mexico. Disillusioned with society, humanity and the artistic life, he

Australia and New Mexico

465

and Frieda set off to the States. En route to New Mexico, they spent short periods in Ceylon and New Zealand, and six weeks in Australia, where Lawrence met the Australian writer Mollie Skinner, and collaborated with her in producing *The Boy in the Bush* – probably the least didactic of his novels and the one most similar to an ordinary adventure story. He also began to draft his next novel, *Kangaroo*, also based on Australian life. The couple finally arrived in San Francisco in August 1922, then making their way down to Taos, establishing themselves on a ranch on Lobo Mountain. Lawrence was overwhelmed by the primeval beauty of the landscape opening up around him. At Taos he completed *Kangaroo* and earned a slender living by journalism, reviews and a book of essays on American literature.

Mexico and Return to Europe

In March 1923, Lawrence and Frieda visited Mexico and, by the lake near the settlement of Chapala in the south-west, Lawrence began work on his next novel, *The Plumed Serpent*, which dealt with pagan Mexican religion and political insurrection. Before taking up residence permanently in America, they decided to pay a brief visit to Europe, as Frieda in particular desperately wanted to see both her German and English families again. However, just before they were due to sail, the Lawrences had a huge row, the causes of which are unclear. Frieda sailed to Europe alone, and Lawrence returned to Mexico. It's possible that Frieda may have wanted to return to Europe permanently, whereas Lawrence detested the old Continent so wholeheartedly that he was determined this was going to be his last visit – the shorter the better.

Frieda did not return and, at the end of 1923, he finally wrote to her offering a separation, with the provision of a regular income. She begged him to return to Europe, and other old friends also expressed their desire to see him. Finally in November of that year he set off with the greatest reluctance. He wrote: "I don't want much to go to England – but I suppose it is the next move in the battle which never ends and which I never win." As soon as he reached England, he was confined to bed with a severe cold and, although he visited friends and relations, he declared openly that he now loathed London and the entire country. He once again appealed to friends to come back to America with him and set up an artists-and-writers' commune, but only the artist Dorothy Brett would commit to doing so. At a farewell party, Lawrence drank too much and vomited over the meal table – this traumatic final event in England symbolizing all his loathing for European culture.

Lawrence, Frieda and Dorothy sailed back to the States in March 1924, and they all moved to a ranch just two miles away from their previous residence on Lobo Mountain. Unfortunately, his American publisher now went bankrupt, depriving him of a great deal of expected royalties. However, Lawrence at last seemed to have found some slight measure of happiness there, writing and living the simple life away from the civilization he so detested. The only major drawback was that he suffered from serious chest ailments, and began spitting blood – possibly as a result of the altitude of 2,600 metres. In Autumn 1924 came news that his father had died at the age of seventy-eight, but he did not return to Europe to attend the funeral. *Return to America*

In order to complete *The Plumed Serpent*, Lawrence felt he needed to spend more time in Mexico to imbibe the atmosphere, so in October he, Frieda and Dorothy travelled down to Oaxaca, which seemed a warm paradise conducive to the subject matter of the book and to sustained writing. However, tensions were now surfacing between Frieda and Dorothy, and Dorothy returned to America after just ten days. Lawrence finally finished the book in late January 1925, and immediately went down with a combination of influenza, typhoid and malaria which nearly cost him his life. Although he survived, his lungs were fatally damaged by these illnesses, and he was finally diagnosed with tuberculosis. He was given at most two years to live, and decided to return with Frieda to his ranch in the US. The doctor at the border initially refused Lawrence re-entry, as he now showed obvious signs of tuberculosis, a dangerous and contagious disease, but they were eventually granted a six-month residency. *Tuberculosis*

Once back at the ranch, he recovered somewhat, and began writing again. In September 1925 – the six months having expired – the now forty-year-old Lawrence sailed back to Europe. The couple once again visited Lawrence's family, Frieda taking the opportunity to see her now adult children, before moving on through Germany and down to Italy, to a villa in Spotorno, a Ligurian town on the coast. Lawrence took up writing again, and started work in 1926 on his final novel, *Lady Chatterley's Lover*. Although Lawrence's health was generally stable, he still had bouts of blood-spitting, and felt his general condition slowly deteriorating. They then moved to a villa in Tuscany; Lawrence thought briefly of returning to America, but realized that in his sick state he almost certainly would not be allowed entry, and that the strain of the long journey would exhaust his body still further.

Lady Chatterley's Lover   Lawrence was occupied with completing *Lady Chatterley's Lover* from October 1926 to summer 1928. The manuscript underwent countless radical alterations throughout these months, and during the final stages of revision, Lawrence was writing up to four thousand words a day. Although he had few hopes of its publication, because of its sexually explicit subject matter, he had discovered that it would be possible to publish the novel at his own expense on the Continent. 1,200 copies of the book, which he had arranged to be printed privately in Florence, finally appeared in June 1928. *Lady Chatterley's Lover* was an instant commercial success, and Lawrence for the first time in his life was relatively free from financial worries. After the publication of this novel, he decided to get away from the baking heat of Italy and live for a few months in the Swiss Alps, to see whether the mountain air would improve his condition. Although this change of environment benefited him somewhat, his coughing became more frequent, and he suffered increasingly severe haemorrhages. He tried not to let his illness defeat him, writing in a letter: "I feel so strongly as if my illness weren't really me – I feel perfectly well and all right, in myself. Yet there is this beastly torturing chest superimposed on me, and it's as if there was a demon lived there, triumphing, and extraneous to me." Frieda would later remark that she had never heard him complain about his health.

Last Days   With the money from *Lady Chatterley*, Lawrence and Frieda had some choice about where to live, and they selected a pleasant hotel in Bandol, on the French coast near Toulon. Lawrence tried to write newspaper articles and poems, but he could not undertake any further major projects, as his health was now deteriorating rapidly. He began to compose what would be his final work, *Apocalypse*: its purpose was to offer modern man a kind of psychic recovery of his connections with the old world, by providing a fresh view of humanity's "old, pagan vision" and the "pre-Christian heavens". But his physical condition by now was very poor, and he finally agreed to enter the Ad Astra sanatorium in Vence, near Nice.

There he grew very despondent, and decided to discharge himself, as he wanted to die on his own terms. He and Frieda rented a villa in Vence, and hired nurses to look after him. On Sunday 2nd March 1930 his condition worsened considerably; he admitted he needed morphine, and a doctor administered the drug. Lawrence died that evening. Frieda wrote that he was buried "in the little cemetery of Vence which looks over the Mediterranean that he cared so much about". In 1935 his body was exhumed and cremated, and a chapel was erected near his second ranch in the mountains overlooking Taos to house his ashes.

D.H. Lawrence's Works

D.H. Lawrence wrote his first novel, *The White Peacock*, under various working titles, between 1906 and 1910. As mentioned above, the London publisher William Heinemann accepted it for publication, and the book came out in 1911. The novel follows a first-person narrator, Cyril Beardsall, who is continually questioning his identity and his place in the world – even at this stage of Lawrence's career, his writing probes the question of the alienation of modern humanity from its natural roots and instincts. The setting is the countryside around Nottingham (Beardsall, incidentally, was the maiden name of Lawrence's mother).

The White Peacock

Cyril and his sister Lettie have had a conventional middle-class upbringing: they are cultured and artistic, but they are dissatisfied with their life, and the novel deals with their failure to find genuine love. Cyril courts Emily Saxton, a farmer's daughter, who ends up marrying somebody else, while Lettie, although deeply in love with Emily's brother George, makes a conventional marriage to a narrow-minded man of a much higher social rank. Following this rejection, George marries a pub landlord's daughter, which leaves him unfulfilled, and he becomes an apathetic alcoholic.

There is one further major character, who represents the rejection of modern culture and civilization and embodies the return to nature and the instincts. This is Frank Annable, who had been a student at Cambridge University, before becoming a vicar and marrying a local aristocrat, Lady Crystabel. He has rejected his former life and is now a gamekeeper on a large estate, living in the woods with a second wife and a large family. He is generally disliked by the local men, apparently because, with his animal vitality, he has a great deal of success with their wives. Cyril is attracted by his superb physique and personality, but Annable is found dead at the bottom of a quarry – it is not certain whether he has slipped or been pushed over by a gang of locals. It is interesting to note that, in his very last novel, *Lady Chatterley's Lover*, written around twenty years later, earthiness and return to one's natural instincts are also represented by a gamekeeper who has rejected his middle-class educated background.

George and Lettie therefore are left at the end of the novel feeling that they have not managed to unite their alienated artistic nature with the innate animal instinctive level of their own humanity; neither have they succeeded in bonding at any meaningful level with the members of the human race who are much more attuned with these instincts than they are.

The Trespasser   The follow-up to *The White Peacock*, *The Trespasser*, was composed between March 1910 and February 1912. It was originally to be titled *The Saga of Siegmund*, but was finally published in 1912 as *The Trespasser*. Mainly set on the Isle of Wight, with other scenes in north and south London and Cornwall, the novel centres on Siegmund Macnair, an orchestral musician and music teacher, who is married, with five children, to Beatrice. Despite his domestic comforts, he is restless and gets involved in a relationship with one of his pupils, Helena Verden. The bulk of the novel deals with the week they spend together on the Isle of Wight. The relationship does not work on a physical level: he is passionately attracted to her, but she is very withdrawn. Siegmund, in despair at all the conflicts and tensions in his life, hangs himself, and his wife, for the children's sake, deliberately suppresses all memory of him. But something has died within Helena Verden after this tragedy: she has entered a deep period of emotional stasis, and the novel ends with her new friend and possible future lover, Cecil, trying desperately to arouse her from this state.

Sons and Lovers   Around the same time *The Trespasser* was written, Lawrence was working on another manuscript, provisionally entitled *Paul Morel*, which was completed in 1912 and published as *Sons and Lovers* in 1913. It incorporates numerous elements of Lawrence's life. The "Bestwood" of the novel is the author's home village of Eastwood, and the Morel family bears many resemblances to his own. The novel charts the protagonist

Paul Morel's sexual, emotional and intellectual development from his childhood up to the age of twenty-five. The first part of the novel is devoted to a recreation of the early married life and environment of Paul's parents. Like Lawrence's own family, the father is a miner who drinks, while the mother is intellectual, artistic and well informed; this leads to inevitable arguments. Paul shares his mother's artistic nature and becomes strongly attached to her. Following the early death of his brother from illness, Paul too nearly dies at the age of sixteen and, from then on, the novel concerns Paul's developing emotional and sexual relationships, and his attempt to become independent in all ways from his mother. He has done exceptionally well at school, and wishes to become an artist, but, during the period covered by the novel, works as a clerk at a local factory. At the age of sixteen, he meets his first love, Miriam, who bears many resemblances to Jessie Chambers. They are both passionate about art and ideas, and very much in love, but the sexual side of their relationship is fraught with difficulties. Paul feels he is betraying his mother, while Miriam at first does not want to involve herself in sex outside marriage. Paul constantly tries to force the issue, and Miriam finally acquiesces unwillingly, feeling she is making a great sacrifice for him. This turns out to be a disastrous experience, and Paul ends their relationship. He then enters on a brief and much more fulfilling relationship with an older married woman, but she finally decides to remain faithful to her husband. Near the end of the novel, Paul's mother dies, and he is left on the threshold of his maturity alone, but having become much more aware of his own identity.

The extremely convoluted gestation of Lawrence's next novel, *The Rainbow*, should be studied with that of the following work, *Women in Love*, since they are both developments of what was originally planned as one novel. *The Rainbow* was published just two years after the commencement of the first draft, in 1913, but the reworking of the later material as a second volume, *Women in Love*, took until 1920. The preliminary drafts were written between March 1913 and August 1915. The first draft, under the provisional title *The Sisters*, was written between March and June 1913. A complete revision, still with the same provisional title, took place between August 1913 and January 1914. This was then substantially revised again, under the new title *The Wedding*

The Rainbow

471

Ring, from February to May 1914, and Lawrence finally took the decision to split the material into two books. The first, now known as *The Rainbow*, was forged between November 1914 and March 1915, and published in September 1915. The book portrays the earlier generations of the Nottinghamshire family whose modern members are treated at length in *Women in Love*. The setting is mainly the industrial counties of Nottinghamshire and its neighbour Derbyshire. Tom Brangwen, a young Midlands farmer, marries a Polish exile, Lydia Lensky, in 1867, when he is twenty-eight and she is thirty-four. Lydia is more cultured and intellectual than Tom, and the novel explores firstly the tensions in their marriage, and the way their relationship gradually evolves into a harmonious loving partnership. The couple live with Lydia's daughter, Anna, by her first marriage to a Polish revolutionary. We are shown Anna's development to maturity, until she finally marries Will Brangwen, the son of Tom's brother Alfred. Their stormy marriage is depicted in detail and, although they ultimately achieve some sort of harmony, this is not to the same degree of happiness as Anna's parents, but represents more of a compromise. One of the major differences is in religion: Anna is a "pagan", in that she worships nature and the instinctive physical life, whereas Will is a Christian mystic, hankering after experiences of the eternal and absolute.

The major part of the novel is taken up with the third generation of this family, and mainly describes the life of Will and Anna's daughter, Ursula Brangwen. She is profoundly conscious of her responsibility to form her own personality, and to gain independence from her early upbringing and family; she questions her father's Christianity, and has various relationships, including a lesbian affair. She trains as a student teacher, later becoming a passionate critic of contemporary industrial society and of the alienation of the natural instincts from everyday life. She becomes engaged to a young soldier, Anton Skrebensky, but she gradually opens her eyes to his conventionality and adherence to social norms. She breaks off their relationship and he, unbeknown to her, marries another woman and is posted on military service to India. Ursula discovers she is pregnant by him, and writes to him asking for marriage after all. However, before receiving an answer, she is involved in a traumatic incident while out walking, becomes dangerously ill and suffers a miscarriage. This leads her to a period of epiphany, self-discovery and rebirth; she is delighted when she learns that Skrebensky is already married, realizing that she must wait for the right man "created by God" to come along. She glimpses a rainbow, and has a vision of a new reality for the whole of society, which will enable it to grow once more from its organic roots, and throw off the shackles of industrialization.

When Lawrence had reworked *The Rainbow* to his satisfaction and sent it off to the publisher, he comprehensively recast the remaining material, between April and June 1916, into a new narrative, and resurrected for it the former title *The Sisters* (normally entitled *Sisters III* in a scholarly context). Between July 1916 and January 1917 this was once again rewritten drastically, and given the new title *Women in Love* (it is this first version of the novel, now known as *The First Women in Love*, that is contained within the present volume). Unfortunately, by this time *The Rainbow* had been prosecuted for obscenity and all unsold copies withdrawn and destroyed by legal order. Lawrence submitted the manuscript of his new novel to various publishers, including Duckworth, Constable and Secker, and they all rejected it, commenting that, in the present climate of public opinion, and due to Lawrence's reputation, it would be unpublishable without drastic revision. Furthermore, several of Lawrence's acquaintances who had seen the manuscript claimed to perceive themselves satirized in its text. Accordingly, Lawrence, fearing presumably not only another prosecution for obscenity, but libel suits into the bargain, rethought the entire project, and radically reworked *Women in Love* over the two years between March 1917 and September 1919. The novel was first published in June 1921, and then further significant changes were made to the second edition, to produce *Women in Love* as it is now generally known, following threats of a lawsuit from the composer Peter Warlock, who thought that the portrait of the composer Halliday in the novel was a scurrilous portrayal of him.

The setting of the first part of the novel is the English Midlands around "Beldover", which bears strong resemblances to Lawrence's home village of Eastwood. The estate of "Breadalby" seems to be modelled on Ottoline Morrell's Garsington Manor in Oxfordshire, which Lawrence had started visiting in mid-1915. Further scenes are set in London and on the Continent, principally in the Austrian Tyrol. Part of the

Women in Love and The First Women in Love

story takes place during the First World War, and Lawrence says in his foreword to the novel that "the bitterness of the war may be taken for granted in the characters".

Women in Love traces the adventures of the Ursula Brangwen of *The Rainbow*, now aged twenty-six, and a teacher at a grammar school. She is the lover of Rupert Birkin, an articulate school inspector who has sufficient private means to be able to retire if he so wishes. Ursula's sister Gudrun is twenty-five, has completed a course at art college and teaches at the same school; she is extremely self-confident and dresses in a bright and bohemian fashion. Gudrun's lover is Gerald Crich, who is around thirty, and the son of a wealthy colliery owner. He is handsome, blond, physically active, and he runs the colliery. However, he lacks a sense of any deep meaning in his life, and his relationship with Gudrun runs into the sands because, rather than striving to achieve a mutual unity of their two personalities, he needs constant reassurances of her affections.

The novel may be said to explore love and sexual relationships in both their creative and destructive aspects. Rupert Birkin contains both of these opposites within him. He despairs of the modern industrial world and of the human race; however, he refuses to surrender to cynicism and apathy, but persists in his belief in personal fulfilment and integration through interpersonal relationships. These relationships will form the bedrock of a new, organic society, not distorted by over-intellectualism or industrialization. Birkin is, in fact, largely a self-portrait of Lawrence, or Lawrence as he liked to view himself at this period. Like Lawrence, he believes that throughout history the human race has either experienced periods of creative progress, or of disintegration. With industrialization and the war, the world is currently, according to him, in a "destructive" cycle. Most of the characters throughout the novel display various degrees of over-intellectualism and alienation from the natural world and from their instincts. Birkin is at the beginning of the novel involved in a relationship with the wealthy aristocrat Hermione Roddice, who is described as "a medium for the culture of ideas" – that is, entirely locked up inside her own head, and cut off from her instincts. Not surprisingly, the relationship collapses. However, the liaison between Gerald and Gudrun is purely sensual, and is ultimately just as unfulfilling. In the end, Ursula and Birkin both resign from their jobs, marry and retire to the Continent – presumably having enough money to do so from Rupert's private income. Their relationship appears to be developing into an integrated and harmonious success. However, Gerald and Gudrun's sensual affair has gone off the rails; she has despairingly taken another lover and, in the Austrian Tyrol, he attempts to strangle her and then flees into the snows in a deliberate suicide attempt.

The First Women in Love, the earlier, more explicit version of the published book, shows significant differences in the psychology of some of the main characters and their relationships. Many key scenes, and notably the ending, are also radically different.

Eight months before *Women in Love* came off the press, *The Lost Girl* D.H. Lawrence completed *The Lost Girl*, a novel he had begun composing as early as December 1912, and which had also undergone several rewrites and title changes. It was eventually published in November 1920.

The novel follows the events of the main protagonist, Alvina Houghton, the "lost girl" of the title, from the age of twenty-three to thirty-two. She is the daughter of well-to-do tradespeople in Woodhouse, a fictional mining town based on Eastwood. Initially, she is "lost" because she seems destined to end up as an old maid, but subsequently she becomes "lost" to those around her because of her rebellion against her conventional upbringing: she plans to move to Australia with her lover, and then, on being talked out of this, moves to north London to train as a maternity nurse – where she gains first-hand experience of the poverty of the capital's slums. On her return to Woodhouse, she finds that no one can afford to hire her services as a nurse on a private basis, and so abandons the idea of earning a living in this manner for the time being. She toys with the idea of marrying various rich men, but decides they are all too cold and inhuman. At the age of thirty, after her father's death, she joins a travelling theatre group, which contains a number of dark passionate foreigners, whom she feels drawn to but ultimately rejects. Leaving the itinerant actors, she takes up her former occupation as a maternity nurse again and becomes engaged to an older wealthy doctor. However, she breaks off this engagement, marries the Italian Ciccio – who was part of her former theatre group – and moves to the mountains of Italy with him. Ciccio is called

475

up for military service, and the novel ends with Alvina, now pregnant, having to bear and bring up a child alone. She is once more lost in an alien environment from which she feels cut off.

Aaron's Rod

Aaron's Rod, a novel which Lawrence had written between October 1917 and November 1921, was published in England in 1922. Aaron Sisson is a mine worker and secretary of the local miners' union in Beldover – again modelled on Eastwood – and also a talented musician, principally on the flute and piccolo. He had originally trained to be a teacher, but he ultimately decided he preferred manual labour. At the age of thirty-three, having inherited a substantial amount of money from his recently deceased mother, he leaves his wife and three children well provided for, and sets off to London in a journey of self-discovery. There he becomes an orchestral musician and frequents intellectual and artistic circles. He is seduced by a scheming female acquaintance, but decides that this is not the type of relationship he left his family for. He falls into depression and succumbs to severe physical illness. The writer Rawdon Lilly, a "freak" and "outsider" by his own description, nurses him back to health, and reinforces Aaron's sense of revulsion at modern marriage, and his fear of being entrapped therein. Aaron goes back to see his wife, who not surprisingly is extremely bitter, so he leaves for Italy at an invitation from Rawdon. There he has a passionate relationship with a noble Italian woman, but Aaron once again distances himself from the relationship, because he wants to withdraw still deeper into himself and avoid being tied down. The novel ends with Rawdon helping Aaron to accept his intuition that the "love urge" has been exhausted by civilization, and that the new creative urge now is that of a power surging from the deepest reaches of the soul, which must be used to renew civilization.

Kangaroo

As mentioned, from June to July 1922, while he was in Australia, Lawrence wrote the bulk of a novel, *Kangaroo*, set around Sydney, which was later published in 1923.

The novel is about Richard Somers and his wife Harriett, who have come to Australia to start a new life, after becoming disillusioned with Europe. Their neighbours, Jack and Victoria Callcott, turn out to be members of a clandestine paramilitary organization planning to seize political power by force. Jack offers Somers the chance to become a member, and takes him to see the leader of the movement, Benjamin Cooley, usually referred to as "Kangaroo". Cooley advocates love and brotherhood, but sees this all within a strictly hierarchical model of society controlled by one all-powerful leader. Somers, although in essence sympathetic to his cause, is sceptical and will not commit himself, while Harriett is resentful of her husband's attraction to Kangaroo and the organization. Somers then becomes interested in socialism, but is equally sceptical: Kangaroo's organization is based on love organized through power, whereas the socialists' ideals are based on love for humanity as a generalized and abstract concept, without taking the individual into account. Neither system is what Somers believes he, or humanity in general, needs on a personal level. He is present when the socialists and the right-wingers fight at a rally and numerous men are killed. Kangaroo is wounded, and Somers goes to visit him. Kangaroo asks him once and for all to dedicate himself to the movement, but Somers cannot bring himself to do this. Kangaroo dies, and Somers and his wife start to consider moving to America. Before he leaves, Somers declares that he can only commit himself to nature, to "non-human gods, non-human human being".

Having met the author Mollie Skinner in Australia, *The Boy in the Bush* Lawrence collaborated on a novel with her, *The Boy and the Bush*, which was published in 1924. Although both names appear on the title page, the precise degree of participation of either author is unclear. It relates the story of Jack Grant, who arrives in Australia from England in 1882 at the age of eighteen, after having been expelled from school and agricultural college, and having been involved in various other dubious doings. The novel depicts how he becomes a successful sheep farmer and gold miner by his early twenties. There is little of the didacticism and pretentiousness of Lawrence's other novels, and it is in essence an uncomplicated adventure story.

Lawrence turned to Mexico for the setting of his next novel, *The Plumed Serpent* *The Plumed Serpent*, which he wrote on location in order to immerse himself fully in the country's atmosphere and accustom himself to the mores of the indigenous population. He completed the novel in 1925 and it was published in England the following year. In *The Plumed Serpent* a revolutionary movement in Mexico intends to overthrow Christianity and re-establish worship of the old gods, such as Quetzalcoatl

477

– the "plumed serpent" of the title. The leaders of this movement even assume the names of these old gods. Kate Leslie, an Irish widow of around forty who is visiting Mexico, is at first impressed by the animal pagan vigour of the organization, but then becomes suspicious of its mysticism and barbarity. The novel simultaneously charts the progress of the movement and Kate's fluctuating sympathies towards it. The movement comes to control large swathes of the country, but Kate grows increasingly alienated by its inhumanity. However, she cannot resist the pagan "soul power" of one of the revolutionary leaders who has named himself Quetzalcoatl, and she agrees to participate in a ritual marriage with him. But even after the ceremony she is profoundly dubious, and at the end of the novel we are left wondering whether the movement will be crushed and whether she will become utterly disillusioned and try to withdraw from it.

Lady Chatterley's Lover was Lawrence's final and most successful major novel. It was written between 1926 and 1928: during this time he completed three separate versions, each of which was subsequently published. The first version, and the only one to appear in Lawrence's lifetime, was privately printed first in Florence in 1928 and then in Paris the following year. In Britain, due to the book's controversial content, it was only published by Secker in a radically expurgated version in February 1932. The first British unexpurgated printing, by Penguin in August 1960, was prosecuted for obscenity; following the collapse of the case, it went on general sale in November of that year, becoming an instant best-seller. A second version of the tale, under the title of *John Thomas and Lady Jane* – which corresponds to the version Lawrence was working on between late 1926 and early 1927 – was first published by Heinemann in 1972. The third version, referred to as *The Second Lady Chatterley's Lover*, uses the text written between December 1927 and January 1928 and was first published by Cambridge University Press in 1993.

The novel is set in Eastwood and other Nottinghamshire towns, as well as Sheffield and Chesterfield – with brief scenes in Venice and London. Its protagonist is Connie Reid, who has had a wealthy, artistic and unconventional upbringing. She and her elder sister Hilda are allowed a great deal of freedom, and both have had sexual affairs by the time they are eighteen. At the beginning of the First World War they settle

Lady Chatterley's Lover

briefly in London and become part of a coterie of university intellectuals. Hilda marries and Connie forms an attachment with Clifford Chatterley – a shy and nervous young aristocrat, who had been studying at Cambridge at the outbreak of war, but then joined the army – marrying him in 1917 when he is home on leave. Clifford is seriously wounded in battle, and becomes sexually impotent. Following the deaths of relatives, he becomes heir to the family title and estate. Clifford is not only impotent, but seriously depressed, and takes up writing as a therapy, eventually becoming a successful author. He plays host to gatherings of literati and other intellectuals, and Connie begins to feel more and more empty, frustrated and peripheral. In 1924, when she is twenty-seven, she sees the gamekeeper Mellors washing his naked body in the woods and feels herself flaming back into life. She and Mellors become lovers, and they both rediscover their deep inner selves and connection with nature. Mellors is in fact an educated man who has rejected his middle-class upbringing to revert to a more meaningful working life. Therefore, though he can discourse on intellectual subjects, and can speak with a refined accent, he prefers to talk in broad dialect, and to project a working-class persona. He too, before he met Connie, had become sad and isolated, disillusioned by the war and the destruction of nature by industrialization. He has previously had various loveless affairs with women, including a now estranged wife. However, his liaison with Connie removes all his encrusted bitterness. Connie becomes pregnant, and at the end of the novel they are both waiting for divorces so that they can marry, live on a farm and start a new life together, sheltered from the artificiality they see around them.

Mr Noon is an unfinished novel in two parts, which Lawrence wrote between 1920 and 1922. Secker posthumously published the first part in 1934, at the end of a collection of Lawrence's short stories, and fifty years later the Cambridge University Press edition appeared, including the very incomplete second part. The novel relates the past life of Gilbert Noon, a science teacher at a school in Nottinghamshire. It is revealed that he came from a working-class background, but proved to be so brilliant at maths, science and music that he gained a scholarship to go to Cambridge University, becoming one of the most outstanding mathematicians of the age. However, due to his somewhat dissipated lifestyle, he

Mr Noon

479

did not manage to progress up the academic ladder, and so returned home and became a teacher. He is caught in the act of having sex with Emmie Bostock, a twenty-three-year-old schoolteacher and, upon her apparently becoming pregnant, he is forced to resign his teaching post. In the second part of the novel Gilbert roams around Germany and elopes with a married woman over the Alps into Italy, where he feels himself to be "reborn" – at which point the fragment ends.

Other Works   During the course of his life, Lawrence issued twelve volumes of poetry and had scores of poems published in journals. He produced three collections of short stories and six novellas, as well as a large number of stories published in magazines which were not collected during his lifetime. He also wrote seven plays, and his prolific non-fiction includes volumes on psychoanalysis and philosophy, travel sketches and hundreds of reviews and articles for the press.

Screen Adaptations

Most of Lawrence's novels – including such lesser-known ones as *The Boy in the Bush* and *Kangaroo* – plus a number of his short stories, have been filmed either for television or cinema. Although the earliest of these date from the late 1940s, they were all extremely expurgated until the late 1960s, when a more liberal social climate began to allow more explicit imagery and language in films and stage plays. By this time, D.H. Lawrence's outlook chimed with that of the new generation, as attested by the 1969 cult classic *Easy Rider*, in which an alcoholic failed lawyer played by Jack Nicholson immediately opens a bottle on his release from prison for drunk and disorderly behaviour with the words: "To ol' D.H. Lawrence". The two protagonists, played by Peter Fonda and Dennis Hopper, on their way across America visit a commune reminiscent of Taos, where Lawrence spent some time, and the film implies that Lawrence was in some way a forerunner of the permissive and sexually liberated Sixties.

The first feature-film adaptation of any major Lawrence novel seems to have been the 1960 version of *Sons and Lovers*, with Trevor Howard as Paul Morel. The first and only film version of *Women in Love* appeared in the UK in 1969, directed by Ken Russell and with a screenplay by Larry Kramer. The film became notorious because it showed for the first time full-frontal male nudity in a wrestling scene between Alan Bates and Oliver Reed. It was highly acclaimed, although Russell appears to have come to doubt the wisdom of incorporating so much music and dance into the film. Alan Bates played the role of Rupert Birkin, while Oliver Reed was Gerald Crich; Glenda Jackson was Gudrun Brangwen, Jennie Linden played Ursula Brangwen, while Eleanor Bron played Hermione Roddice. Glenda Jackson won the Academy Award for best actress, and Russell for best director, while Kramer was nominated for the best adapted screenplay.

In 1988, Ken Russell also adapted – in collaboration with his wife Vivien – and directed *Women in Love*'s predecessor, *The Rainbow*. Ursula Brangwen was played by Sammi Davis, while Paul McGann played Anton Skrebensky, and Glenda Jackson was Anna Brangwen. In the same year *The Rainbow* appeared on BBC TV in three fifty-five minute episodes, directed by Stuart Burge and with a screenplay by Anne Devlin. In 1989, Ken Russell wrote *A British Picture*, detailing at length his filming of both *The Rainbow* and *Women in Love*. Nine years earlier, a 125-minute biographical film of Lawrence appeared, entitled *The Priest of Love*. The screenplay was by Alan Plater, Ian McKellen played Lawrence, and Janet Suzman was Frieda. In 1986, also with a screenplay by Plater, ITV produced an eighty-minute-long biography of Lawrence entitled *Coming Through*, with Kenneth Branagh as Lawrence and Helen Mirren as Frieda.

Select Bibliography

Standard Edition
The authoritative edition of *The First Women in Love* is the Cambridge University Press edition, edited by John Worthen and Lindeth Vasey (Cambridge: Cambridge University Press, 1998), which includes extensive annotations.

Biographies:
Aldington, Richard, *Portrait of a Genius, but…: A Biography of D.H. Lawrence* (London: Heinemann, 1950)
Meyers, Jeffrey, *D.H. Lawrence: A Biography* (London: Macmillan, 1990)
Moore, Harry Thornton, *The Priest of Love: A Life of D.H. Lawrence*, 2nd ed. (London: Heinemann, 1974)

Nehls, Edward, ed., *D.H. Lawrence: A Composite Biography* (Madison, WI: University of Wisconsin Press, 1959)

Sagar, Keith, *The Life of D.H. Lawrence: An Illustrated Biography* (London: Eyre Methuen: 1980)

Squires, Michael and Talbot, Lynn K., *Living at the Edge: A Biography of D.H. Lawrence and Frieda von Richthofen* (London: Robert Hale, 2002)

Worthen, John, *D.H. Lawrence: The Early Years 1885–1912* (Cambridge: Cambridge University Press, 1991)

Worthen, John, *D.H. Lawrence: The Life of an Outsider* (London: Allen Lane, 2005)

Additional Background Material:

Boulton, James T., ed., *The Selected Letters of D.H. Lawrence* (Cambridge: Cambridge University Press, 1997)

Miller, Henry, *The World of Lawrence: A Passionate Appreciation* (London: Calder, 1985)

Poplawski, Paul, *D.H. Lawrence: A Reference Companion* (Westport, CT & London: Greenwood Press, 1996)

On the Web:
www.nottingham.ac.uk/mss/online/dhlawrence

Acknowledgements

The Publisher wishes to thank Brian Reeve for writing the apparatus and for his excellent editorial advice, Lindeth Vasey for her editorial work and Keith Sagar and John Worthen for their support and for providing visual material.

ONEWORLD CLASSICS

ONEWORLD CLASSICS aims to publish mainstream and lesser-known European classics in an innovative and striking way, while employing the highest editorial and production standards. By way of a unique approach the range offers much more, both visually and textually, than readers have come to expect from contemporary classics publishing.

CHARLOTTE BRONTË: *Jane Eyre*

EMILY BRONTË: *Wuthering Heights*

ANTON CHEKHOV: *Sakhalin Island*
Translated by Brian Reeve

CHARLES DICKENS: *Great Expectations*

JANE AUSTEN: *Pride and Prejudice*

JAMES HANLEY: *Boy*

JACK KEROUAC: *Beat Generation*

JANE AUSTEN: *Emma*

WILKIE COLLINS: *The Moonstone*

DESIDERIUS ERASMUS: *Praise of Folly* and
Pope Julius Barred from Heaven
Translated by Roger Clarke

BRAM STOKER: *Dracula*

GIOVANNI BOCCACCIO: *Decameron*
Translated by J.G. Nichols

DANTE ALIGHIERI: *Poems*
Translated by J.G. Nichols

PETRONIUS ARBITER: *Satyricon*
Translated by Andrew Brown

ALEXANDER PUSHKIN: *Eugene Onegin*
Translated by Roger Clarke

FYODOR DOSTOEVSKY: *The Insulted and Injured*
Translated by Ignat Avsey

CONNOISSEUR

The CONNOISSEUR list will bring together unjustly neglected works, making them available again to the English-reading public. All titles are printed on high-quality, wood-free paper and bound in black cloth with gold foil-blocking, end papers, head and tail bands and ribbons. Each title will make a perfect gift for the discerning bibliophile and will combine to make a wonderful and enduring collection.

∽

CECCO ANGIOLIERI: *Sonnets*
Translated by C.H. Scott

BOILEAU: *The Art of Poetry* and *Lutrin*
Translated by William Soames and John Ozell

ANONYMOUS: *The Song of Igor's Campaign*
Translated by Brian Reeve

AMBROSE BIERCE: *The Monk and the Hangman's Daughter*

SAMUEL GARTH: *The Dispensary*

JOHN ARBUTHNOT: *The History of John Bull*

TOBIAS SMOLLETT: *The History and Adventures of an Atom*

ALESSANDRO TASSONI: *The Rape of the Bucket*
Translated by James Atkinson and John Ozell

UGO FOSCOLO: *Poems*
Translated by J.G. Nichols

JOHANN WOLFGANG GOETHE: *Urfaust*
Translated by J.G. Nichols

GIUSEPPE PARINI: *A Fashionable Day*
Translated by Herbert Bower

GIAMBATTISTA VICO: *Autobiography*
Translated by Stephen Parkin

To order any of our titles and for up-to-date information about our current and forthcoming publications, please visit our website on:

www.oneworldclassics.com